THE ELEMENT ENCYCLOPEDIA OF VAMPIRES

Theresa Cheung

Dedicated to the memory of Montague Summers
(1880–1948)

HarperCollins*Publishers*
77–85 Fulham Palace Road,
Hammersmith, London W6 8JB

www.harpercollins.co.uk

First published by HarperCollins*Publishers* 2009

10 9 8 7 6 5 4 3 2 1

A catalogue record of this book is
available from the British Library

ISBN 978-0-00-731279-5

Printed and bound in China

Contents

Acknowledgements

Researching and then writing the 900+ entries for this encyclopedia was a vampiric task in itself, draining almost all my physical and emotional energy. But it was also one of the most challenging, rewarding, and stimulating projects I have ever had the privilege to work on. I've been fascinated by vampires ever since I first read Anne Rice's *Interview with the Vampire* in my late teens, and to be given the opportunity at this stage in my writing career to indulge my fascination and explore the vampire myth in all its fantastic and gory detail was beyond delightful.

In addition to the numerous vampire experts, fans, and researchers I spoke to along the way, I would like to thank some individuals personally because without them this massive undertaking simply would not have been possible. Among them are my editor Jeannine Dillon, for her vision and enthusiasm for this project from start to finish; Katy Carrington for her support; Andy Paciorek for his stunning artwork; Charlotte Ridings for her assured, accurate, and always insightful editing; and Simon Gerratt for making sure that everything came together at the right time. Finally, I would also like to thank my partner, Ray, and my children, Robert and Ruth, for their love, patience, and support during the many long hours I went "out of this world" to complete this encyclopedia.

Introduction: Can Such Things Be?

For, let me tell you, the vampire is known every-where that men have been. In old Greece, in old Rome, in Germany, France and India, even in the Chersonese; and in China, so far from us in all ways, there even he is and people fear him to this day. He has followed the wake of the beserker Icelander, the devil-begotten Hun, the Slav, the Saxon, the Magyar. The vampire lives on and cannot die by the mere passing of time; he flourishes wherever he can fatten on the blood of the living. He throws no shadow, he makes in the mirror no reflection. He has the strength of many in his hand. He can transform himself into a wolf or become as a bat. He can come in mist which he creates, or on moonlight rays as elemental dust. He can, when once he finds his way, come out from anything or into anything, no matter how close it be bound. He can see in the dark – no small power this in a world which is one half shut from the light.

Ah, but hear me through. He can do all these things, yet he is not free. Nay, he is even more prisoner than the slave of the galley, than the madman in his cell. He cannot go where he lists; he who is not of nature has yet to obey some of nature's laws. He may not enter anywhere at the first, unless there be someone of the household who bids him come. His power ceases at the coming of the day. It is said, too, that he can only pass running water at the slack or the flood of the tide. Then there are things which so afflict him that he has no power, as the garlic and things sacred, as this symbol, my crucifix. The branch of the wild rose on his coffin keeps him that he may not move from it; a sacred bullet fired into the coffin will kill him so that he be true dead; and as for the stake through him, or the cut-off head that giveth rest, we have seen it with our eyes.

Professor Abraham Van Helsing,
in Bram Stoker's *Dracula*

Dracula: Since its publication in 1897, perhaps no other novel has inspired more movies, books, television shows, and continued fascination. Literary critics often like to remind us that *Dracula* is not particularly well written but there is no doubt that it is a masterpiece of story telling; the idea of vampires has become pretty much universal and hugely popular largely because of it.

More than a century later *Dracula* shows no sign of running out of steam and on all levels, from the sublime to the ridiculous, vampires continue to be endlessly reinvented. Today, the lure of the vampire is stronger than ever, with books such as Anne Rice's *Interview with the Vampire* and Stephenie Meyer's Twilight Saga series becoming international bestsellers; movies such as *Blade* and *I Am Legend* smashing box-office records; and TV shows like *Buffy the Vampire Slayer* achieving cult status. Vampire appreciation societies and fan clubs are booming. Also thriving is a darkly inclined Goth subculture of individuals who choose to model their lifestyles and personalities around the vampire myth. Moreover, there are those who believe that vampires are not the undead creatures of folklore or fiction, but are actual living creatures who feed on the "life force" of others – and those who ignore them do so at their peril.

And, of course, all these reinventions only bear a vague resemblance to the truth, for the vampire is far more complex than any researcher, writer or film director would like us to believe. Trapped in a twilight world between the living and the dead, fact and fiction, the elusive nature of the ever-changing vampire continues to mystify, captivate, and draw us in.

What is a Vampire?

No other word in the world of horror conjures up more fear and foreboding, or more fascination than "vampire." But what is a vampire? And what is it about vampires that has intrigued and terrified so many for so long?

A vampire in the traditional sense of the word is a creature who has "died" but who returns from the grave to remain among the living. Endowed with the ability to assume human form and live for centuries, it stands outside of – and therefore threatens – society. It feeds on the life force, the blood, of humans and animals, and is capable of transforming its victims into equally horrific creatures.

Preventing the return of a dead person's soul to the world of the living has been a preoccupation of people through the centuries – even headstones that we still use today all over the world were originally intended to stop the dead from sitting up. The undead vampire was especially feared because of its compulsion to kill, and over the centuries a vast body of information and research surrounding vampires and their habits – in particular, how to recognize, repel, and if necessary kill them – has grown up. Some of this information is still well known today. For example, vampires are weakened by sunlight; they suck blood by night and sleep in coffins by day, and driving a stake though their heart will "kill" them. Other facts, however, are less well known. For example, there are both male and female vampires; some vampires can change shape; some are invisible; some do not shun daylight; and some are not animated corpses but living vampires who do not suck blood from their victims but drain them of other things of value to human beings, such as energy, love, youth, creativity, and hope.

Perhaps the greatest weapon the vampire has is its power over our imagination, its ability to draw us in and lure us toward either a path of transformation or a path of despair. This power over our minds does not, however, mean that vampires exist only in our

The Element Encyclopedia of Vampires

imagination. In the novel *Dracula*, Van Helsing begins a lecture on the undead with the words, "There are such beings as vampires." Clearly novels like *Dracula* are works of fiction, and most people today believe vampires to be creatures of fiction. There is, however, enough evidence from eyewitness accounts and reports over the centuries to suggest that there may be such beings as "real" vampires, although they don't necessarily emerge in the guise most of us would expect.

When attempting to define exactly what a vampire is it is important to understand that, in general, they can be divided into three categories – vampires of folklore, vampires in fiction, and modern vampirism – and each category differs from the others by appearance, behavior, and even definition. Let's begin with the vampires of ancient folklore.

Long before *Dracula*, folklore depicted vampiric entities as spirits or ghosts that sometimes resided in the corpses of the deceased. Vampire mythology is ancient, with most cultures having some version of the vampire in their folklore. During the third millennium BC the Babylonians possessed a complex vampire tradition, and more than 5,000 years ago the Mesopotamians feared a ghoulish creature called the *akhkaru*, an evil spirit said to roam the night in search of the blood of newborn babies and pregnant women. Ancient Hindu texts of India also contain a host of vampiric entities and supernatural beings similar to those found in Mesopotamia, for example the *rakshasas*, who also prey on the blood of infants and pregnant women. A thousand or so years later, the blood-sucking evil spirits of Mesopotamia reappeared again in ancient Greek culture. One of the most terrifying Greek vampires

was a witch called a *strix* who feasted at night on the blood of newborns.

The vampire of folklore is altogether different from the vampire most of us recognize from novels like *Dracula*. In general, the vampires of folklore are peasants who return from the grave to torment or drain the life force of the living, first attacking their family and then their community or village. Sometimes they are presented as revolting, decaying, animated corpses but they are also described as appearing much the same as they did in life, although in death their appetite for food, sex, and blood is insatiable. They can wander the streets and attack their victims by day or by night. Sunlight does not destroy them. Once a victim has been attacked typically he or she does not die straight away but is struck down with a slow, wasting disease that eventually leads to death. After death the victim will in turn rise from the grave as a vampire to attack the living. In this way whole communities could be infected with vampires, disease, and death.

At the beginning of the nineteenth century the image of vampires in folklore started to be replaced by the image of vampires presented in fiction. The aristocratic, sophisticated, fictional vampire who wakes from the dead to suck the blood of sleeping victims, typically young women, is the vampiric form most people recognize today. It was first made popular in a short story written by John Polidori called *The Vampyre*, published in 1819. Polidori's work paved the way for the publication of Bram Stoker's *Dracula* in 1897. This Gothic milestone continues to set the standard for representations of vampires today in plays, novels, and movies.

During the Victorian period, fictional vampires were presented as powerfully hypnotic creatures. With magical abilities to direct the elements, command animals, climb walls, and live forever, they are seductive and charming but dangerous and deadly creatures. Despite possessing superhuman powers they are far more furtive than their folklore counterparts. Instead of staying close to home they are citizens of the world, preferring to dart silently from the shadows to kill victims on a small rather than a large scale. Sometimes their bite will transform the victim into a vampire but more often than not it will kill their victims instantly. They have the ability to blend into the world of the living and are often hard to distinguish from humans. The only telltale signs of their non-human nature are that sunlight destroys them, they cast no shadow or reflection, they have no appetite for food and drink, and they have a certain unnatural presence which can make animals and sensitive people feel uneasy.

Moving away from folklore and fiction, the existence of modern vampirism is suggestive of a number of diverse psychological and occult theories. Psychologists argue that the vampire legend was the result of primitive fears and superstition about death and dying, and over the years it evolved into our darkest desires given form. However, there are people today who reject any such psychological theories that try to explain away vampires. For these people vampires are "real." They are not the stuff of folklore and fiction, or products of the imagination; they are predatory, supernatural creatures in human form that survive by feeding on the resources of others in a way that weakens or kills them.

Perhaps one of the most intriguing aspects of modern vampirism is the school of occult thought which suggests that vampires are people who intentionally or unintentionally have the ability to drain and absorb the life force of others. This kind of vampire doesn't feed on blood but on the energy of other people. They tend to be nocturnal creatures with a tremendous appetite for both food and sex due to their biochemistry. Physically, it is almost impossible to spot this so-called "psychic" vampire, and their telltale symptoms are often dismissed as merely eccentric behavior.

The evidence for the existence of "real" blood-sucking vampires, or "energy" vampires, is elusive but for those who believe in them, this elusiveness is simply in keeping with the nature of the vampire – a creature that can be seen and yet not seen. However, this trait also means that today anyone who wants to put forward a definition of what a vampire is can do so, even if it deviates from the so-called blood-sucking "norm." Today, there are people who believe in all different kinds of vampires, making vampirism less of a threat and more of an alternative lifestyle. Millions of people model their personalities after their own ideas of vampirism. There are emotional vampires, sex vampires, lifestyle vampires, blood-drinking vampires, energy vampires, and vampires who believe they have inherited the condition or caught it from a virus. Vampire societies devoted to the study of vampire lore continue to grow in number; countless clubs, books, movies, magazines, and websites celebrate vampires, while role-playing games like *Vampire: The Masquerade* enable players to inhabit virtual vampiric realities.

In whatever way vampires are defined or explained today there are two common themes that always emerge. First, however vampirism is defined by dictionaries or vampirologists, it is always linked to the practice of

The Element Encyclopedia of Vampires

"preying on others" in some way to prolong life or boost vitality. This does not necessarily mean preying on the blood of others, which suggests that in reality vampires are beings who feed on others for sustenance, and that sustenance may be blood but it may also be energy, ideas, hope, or love.

The second common theme is that the greater an individual's or a community's belief in the existence of vampires, the stronger and more powerful the hold a vampire will have over his or her victim. Most important here is the aspect of the vampire's will and the victim's vulnerability. A vampire cannot pass where you don't want it to. If you believe yourself to be Master or Mistress of your house, it cannot enter unless invited or allowed in.

So to return to the question initially posed – what is a vampire? On the one hand vampires are creatures of myth and folklore who feed on people, sometimes using them to create more of their own kind, and which over time have evolved into hugely popular fictional creations, or products of the imagination. On the other hand, vampires are creatures who prey on others for sustenance and they are as real and as dangerous as you believe or allow them to be.

A Short History of Vampires

For most people today vampires are creatures of legend and fantasy with no basis in reality, now or at any other time. However, to those who have studied vampire folklore and examined reports of vampirism that have appeared over the years, and which still occasionally appear, there would appear to be enough evidence to suggest that the construction of the vampire is not entirely fantasy. Although there is no denying that vampires may be understood as ways to access humankind's darkest and deepest fears, there is also a very real history, science, and reality to vampires that deserves serious attention.

The fear of the vampire does not arise only from fantasy, but frequently from substantial and documented reporting. The first written record of reference to vampires comes from a Russian priest in 1047, but by then the idea of a corpse rising from the dead to feed on humans was already thousands of years old. Centuries later, when waves of "vampire hysteria" seized Eastern Europe, visiting scientists and investigators discovered that vampires had an extensive history and were not, as previously thought, simply a local or recent phenomenon.

Throughout the ages, creatures with vampire-like qualities have been said to creep from their graves at night to prey on the innocent, sucking their blood or life force dry. Ancient legends from all over the world describe all manner of vile, life-sucking monsters sent to Earth by evil deities to commit unspeakable acts on innocent victims. These creatures are not like the vampires of popular fiction. They are supernatural predators – revenants – dead bodies that have come back to life, in the form of winged demons, half animals, decaying corpses, and even beautiful women.

The variety in ancient vampiric myth and legend is almost endless; from monsters with red eyes and green or pink hair in China to the night-flying, blood-drinking *lamia* of ancient Greek mythology, with the upper body of a woman and the lower body of a winged serpent; from blood-sucking foxes in Japan to a head with trailing entrails known as the *penanggalan* in Malaysia. The ancient Hindu texts of India contain a host of evil spirit and vampiric deities. For example, the *jigarkhwar* found in the Sind area of India (now part of Pakistan), a vampiric entity with an appetite for human blood and liver which it consumed by paralyzing its victim with a mesmeric stare. As already mentioned, the vampire myth dates back more than 5,000 years to the Mesopotamian culture, and according to vampirologists, ancient Egypt, with its mysterious death rites and passionate belief in, and fear of, the afterlife, could have been a possible early center of vampire lore.

Central to the history of the vampire phenomenon is the belief that the dead can continue to influence events on earth. This concept can be traced in ancient African cultures, where it was thought that deceased relatives could cause sickness and pain among the living if they were not buried properly with respectful rituals. It was also thought that magicians could retain their evil powers, even in death, and their corpses were chopped apart so that they could not return to haunt the living.

The ancient practice of cannibalism may also be associated with vampirism. Among primitive cultures in Australia, Africa, Asia, Melanesia, New Zealand, and North and South America, cannibalism was a common part of rituals that followed battles and the funerals of great warriors. It was thought that eating the flesh and drinking the blood of the victim would enable the living to partake of their vital essence, strength, or virtue.

Another central concept of vampirism is that blood equals life. The ancient Aztecs thought that drinking the blood of their enemies provided warriors with immortality, and to diminish or enhance the powers of the undead, people in some cultures would perform specific blood rituals at death, based on the belief that the spirits needed the life force of blood to remain alive in the next world. An early written record of this practice comes from Captain James Cook when he visited New Zealand in 1769. He noted that many of the native Maoris had self-inflicted ritual cutting scars on their arms, cheeks, or thighs. While the details may vary, a number of scholars believe there are similarities in all these ancient beliefs, rituals, and stories. Other scholars, however, reject the assumption that vampires are part of all world cultures, arguing that although evil spirits and the notion of the restless dead are commonplace, blood-sucking semi-human creatures are not. Native American traditions, for example, have their own creatures of the night, such as the skin walkers (restless spirits of the dead who sometimes make themselves visible), but these do not fit the blood-sucking profile of the vampire. A plausible case could therefore be made for a widespread fear of the dead and the belief that blood equals life in many ancient cultures, but not necessarily for a widespread belief in the blood-sucking undead. This belief was certainly present in some places early on, but it wasn't until the late seventeenth century that it began to express itself strongly.

The rise of the bloodsuckers

In twelfth-century Christian Europe, the concept of the dead coming back to life in order to feed from the blood of the living was recorded in accounts by an English historian, William of Newburgh. He narrates a number of instances

The Element Encyclopedia of Vampires

where "blood suckers" had come back from the dead to terrorize the living. The solution he offers is to unearth and burn the body of the accused.

In the New World in the early days of the European Colonists there were whispers of vampiric activity. In 1692, the Reverend Lawson, minister of Salem Village, Massachusetts, reported he had been attacked at night by an unseen creature that had attempted to bite him. Accounts, like those from Lawson and William of Newburgh, indicate that vampires were being discussed in England and the New World, but there are not enough records from this period to suggest any widespread belief.

It was in Eastern Europe, however, that vampire mania made its first official appearance. The Slavic and Romany peoples have the richest vampire and folklore legends. Some scholars believe that the Slavic and Romany concept of vampires (both living and dead) may have derived from legends brought to Romania by the Romans in the second century AD. Roman beliefs were in turn based on ancient Greek mythology. The ancient Greek blood-sucking witch, the *strix*, transformed into the Romanian *strigoi vii*, or live blood-sucking witch (while the *strigoii mort* were dead vampires). Over time the two types of vampires eventually merged into a foul vampiric creature called the *strigoi*, also known by the old Greek term *nosferatu*, *nosophoros*, or plague carrier.

Other experts believe that the Slavic vampire traditions stem from legends brought to Europe by Gypsies traveling from India. These nomadic people lived in Greece, Germany, Romania, and the Slavic-speaking nations of Hungary, Russia, Poland, Slovenia, and Serbia. Wherever they went they took their stories with them and some of these stories were adopted by other cultures; when Gypsy beliefs about vampires were meshed with ancient Greek and Roman beliefs, the modern image of the vampire as a blood-sucking revenant creature that drained the life force of its victims, or converted its victims into the undead, may have first taken form.

Whatever their initial source was, from ancient India, Egypt, Rome, Greece, China, Mesopotamia, Russia, Romania (or Transylvania), or anywhere else, there is no doubt that it was in Eastern Europe that widespread belief in "authentic" vampires first took hold. Over the centuries extensive traditions developed there concerning vampires. For example, being conceived on certain days, a violent death or unexplained death, death by suicide, excommunication from the Christian Church, and improper burial rituals were all thought to cause vampirism. If a baby was born with a red caul – a piece of bloody membrane covering the head – this could indicate a predisposition to vampirism.

Protective measures to repel vampires included: eating, wearing, or placing garlic in the coffin; placing a crucifix in the coffin; putting blocks under the corpse's chin to prevent the body from eating the shroud; nailing clothes to coffin walls for the same reason; placing millet or poppy seeds in the grave to distract the dead (apparently vampires found counting a riveting occupation); or piercing the body with thorns or stakes. Evidence that a vampire was at work in the neighborhood included the deaths of cattle, sheep, relatives, or neighbors; exhumed bodies being in a lifelike state with new growth of the fingernails or hair; or if the body was swelled up like a drum; or if there was blood on the mouth and the corpse had a ruddy complexion. Vampires could be destroyed by staking the corpse through the heart or by decapitating or burning it. Repeating the funeral service, sprinkling holy water on the grave, and performing an exorcism were other methods used to destroy the creature.

Dracula is, of course, the most famous vampire from Romania. According to some experts (although it is important to point out that others strongly disagree), this fictional character was based on a real person: Vlad III Tepes or "Vlad the Impaler." Vlad Tepes ruled a principality bordering Transylvania called Wallachia on three separate occasions between 1448 and 1476. The reigns of Vlad were notorious for bloodshed and brutality, and he was known to impale his enemies on long wooden stakes so that they bled to death.

While the concept of vampires was fast becoming ingrained in Eastern European folklore, in the West reports of vampires were still sporadic. All this changed, however, in the early eighteenth century when ancient superstitions about vampires exploded into a major vampire scare in Eastern Europe, and even government officials became involved in hunting and staking vampires.

It all began on January 7, 1732, when an official report was signed by members of the Austrian government detailing their investigations of vampirism in Serbia. This report was directly responsible for bringing vampires to the attention of the West, and for introducing the word *vampir* or *vampyr*, taken from the Serbian usage, into the English language. Two cases, in particular, stand out: those of Arnold Paole and Peter Plogojowitz. In the Arnold Paole case, an ex-soldier turned farmer, who had allegedly been attacked by a vampire years before, died while hay-making. After his death other people began to die too, and it was believed by everyone that

Paole had returned from the grave to prey on his neighbors. In the second case, a Serbian peasant called Peter Plogojowitz was said to have came back as a vampire after his death, sucking the blood of nine villagers. The Paole and Plogojowitz incidents were extremely well documented: government officials examined the evidence and the bodies, wrote up detailed reports, and accounts were published and distributed around Europe, including in the English periodicals *The London Journal* and *The Gentleman's Magazine.*

Even though the 1732 report results were inconclusive, their publication fueled other reports of vampires throughout the whole of Europe. In an age when medical understanding was limited, vampires suddenly became a way for people to explain away the death of large numbers of people during times of plague. The belief that the first victim could not rest but was compelled to return to destroy others was a more seductive explanation than the idea of contagious disease. To prevent further deaths villagers would dig up corpses and "kill" them again. At the height of the vampire frenzy countless eyewitnesses claimed to have seen vampires, and terrified villagers in Serbia, Prussia, Poland, and Romania invaded graveyards and dug up corpses in search of vampires.

The vampire frenzy caused a sensation and triggered a debate among European scholars eager to find theories to explain the phenomenon. The scholars discovered that the Slavic vampire or *upir*, as it was sometimes called, found an echo in similar creatures in Europe and in other far-off cultures such as China. The fact that the phenomenon was not restricted to one area but was found in a variety of cultures gave credence to the belief that vampires were everywhere. They were dead people who refused to remain dead and returned to bring death to their community.

The mutilation of the dead, especially those buried as Christians, certainly alarmed Church officials in Rome and they launched their own investigation into vampirism. After a five-year study of vampire reports and sightings, Giuseppe Davanzati, the archbishop of Trani, Italy, concluded that vampires were an illusion generated by mass hysteria. The Pope advised Church leaders to speak out against the desecration of the dead. However, even while Davanzati was writing his report, Dom Augustin Calmet, a well-respected French theologian and scholar, put together a carefully thought-out treatise in 1746, stating that vampires did exist since he could not find any alternative reason to explain the phenomena that had been occurring in Eastern Europe for centuries. The Calmet treatise had considerable influence on other scholars at the time. In his book, called *Essays on the Appearance of Angels, the Demons and the Spirits and on the Ghosts and Vampires of Hungry, of Bohemia, of Moravia and Silesia*, he writes:

Dead men, men who have been dead for several months, I say, returned from the tomb, are heard to speak, walk about, infest hamlets and villages, injure both men and animals whose blood they drain thereby making them sick and ill and at length causing death. Nor can men deliver themselves from these terrible visitations, nor secure themselves from these horrid attacks, unless they dig the corpses up from graves [and] drive a sharp stake through their bodies … the name given to these ghosts is Oupries or vampires, that is to say bloodsuckers.

Calmet's treatise became a bestseller in Europe and even though he had not intended to fuel the hysteria, his writing did exactly that by triggering an outbreak of panic in the Austro-Hungarian Empire. This infuriated the Empress Maria Theresa, who sent her personal physician to investigate. He quickly wrote a report denouncing vampires as "supernatural quackery" and the Empress swiftly passed laws prohibiting the opening of graves and desecration of bodies. These laws marked the end of the vampire hysteria in Eastern Europe, but by then everyone knew about vampires and nobody would forget about them.

The rest, as they say, is vampire history. In 1819 John Polidori published *The Vampyre*, the first widely circulated full work of fiction about a vampire written in English, and toward the end of the nineteenth century the novel *Dracula* by Bram Stoker initiated the popular era of vampire fiction. *Dracula* has ensured the immortality of the vampire – our fear of and fascination with this creature simply refuses to die.

Whether vampires are creatures of our imagination or the result of age-old fears or, as some believe, as real as the trees in the forest, one thing is crystal clear to those studying the history of vampires: vampires have "lived" and will probably continue to "live" forever.

A BRIEF INTRODUCTION TO THE SCIENCE BEHIND VAMPIRES

There have been a number of theories with which scientists have attempted to explain the vampire phenomenon, but more often than not these seem as elusive as the nature of vampirism itself. Moreover, all these theories have failed to explain away every reported case of vampirism, and so they remained just that – theories.

According to one prominent idea, the common practice of grave-robbing in centuries past would have contributed to the illusion that bodies had risen from their graves overnight. Other rational explanations for the disappearance of bodies, or the strangely life-like appearance of corpses, include animals digging up bodies from shallow graves; flooding uncovering bodies from shallow graves; gases forming in the corpse, sometimes causing post-mortem movement; and the slow decomposition of corpses for various reasons, such as cold temperatures or death by poison.

Medical reasons to explain vampirism have been suggested too. There is a rare condition known as catalepsy that puts people into a deathlike state, even though they are not actually dead. Centuries ago, when medical science was not as advanced as it is today, these people may have been buried and, when they awoke from their deathlike sleep they would find themselves trapped inside a coffin. Sounds of knocking from coffins may not have been the corpse trying to rise from the dead but the victim trying to escape. Eventually, of course, the victim would die of starvation or suffocation, which would explain why, when the coffin was opened, the corpse looked gnarled, contorted, and dramatically altered from when the poor person was initially buried.

Iron-deficiency porphyria, a congenital blood disorder, has been put forward as another scientific/medical explanation for the vampire phenomenon. People who suffer from this condition have a chronic iron deficiency that can result in skin discoloration and sensitivity to sunlight. Drinking other people's blood would increase iron intake in times when iron supplements didn't exist, giving rise to talk of vampirism.

One popular theory is that our ancestors knew very little about the way that bodies decayed or decomposed, and so bodies that were only partially decomposed or were slow to decompose for a number of reasons, such as temperature and soil quality, were believed to be vampiric. This theory has its supporters, but recently it has been criticized by those who point out that our ancestors were not as ignorant as has been suggested and were very familiar with the stages of death. It was, after all, a part of their daily lives, and they were therefore fully aware that bodies decayed in different stages.

It has been argued too, that vampire beliefs arose as part of very strong religious and philosophical principles of how the world worked; the rules and laws which kept everyone and everything in their right place. If any of these rules or laws were violated – if, for example, funeral rites were not performed correctly – it was feared that this would unleash all kinds of unnatural events: the dead would rise from their graves as vampires. In other words, vampires were a symbol of the world order turned upside down, and for community leaders they became a way to impose tight moral order and social control.

Another modern explanation is that those who believe in vampires find it impossible to conceive of their own death and the death of others, so they seek answers in a world that is no longer human. Although psychologists and scientists can offer compelling arguments that vampires aren't real but simply creatures of myth and legend or the imagination, this still can't explain why belief in the existence of vampires lingers on. It also can't fully explain real-life cases of unexplained vampire attacks.

The Element Encyclopedia of Vampires

Any scientific approach to the vampire phenomenon will indicate that it is often difficult to distinguish vampire reality from vampire legend. In fact, vampires of legend are often based on real people, and real people in turn model their behavior on vampire lore, so the possibility that vampires do actually exist in some form is one that cannot be ignored. For example, the protagonist in Polidori's *The Vampyre*, Lord Ruthven, was loosely based on the aristocratic and exotic poet Lord Byron. At the time Polidori was writing his story, rumors were flying that Byron had murdered his mistress and had drunk her blood from a cup made from her skull.

As we've seen, the fictional character Dracula may have been modeled on the historical fifteenth-century Slavic prince Vlad the Impaler and his bloodthirsty ways. Vlad remains the most well-known "real life" vampire, even though he was never associated with vampirism prior to Bram Stoker's *Dracula*, but there are many other so-called "historical vampires," including Ersabet (Elizabeth) Báthory, a seventeenth-century Hungarian countess who became known as the "Blood Countess" because she drank and bathed in the blood of young girls in an attempt to stay young. In the late nineteenth century a Frenchman, Victor Ardisson, "the Vampire of Muy," became sexually aroused by the corpses he dug up from the cemetery, and in the 1920s and 30s there was Peter Kürten, a blood-drinking serial killer known as "the Vampire of Düsseldorf." In New York a man committed several murders in 1959 dressed in a Dracula costume. At his trial he told the court he was a vampire. And in San Francisco in 1998 a man called Joshua Rudiger claimed to be a two-thousand-year-old vampire and went around town slashing the necks of the homeless with knives. He insisted he was driven by the need to drink human blood.

Fast forwarding to the twenty-first century, in 2002 a German couple were tried for killing a friend in what appeared to be a vampire ritual. Manuela Ruda, aged 23 and her husband Daniel, aged 26, stabbed Frank Haagen 66 times, drank his blood, and left his rotting body next to the oak coffin in which Manuela liked to sleep. In court Manuela described how she had had her teeth fashioned into fangs and how she drank blood from corpses buried in the local cemeteries. She and her husband admitted the killing and a psychiatrist testified to their mental illness.

Vampiric behavior has now been recognized as a psychiatric disorder, called vampire personality disorder or Renfield's syndrome, after one of the victims in *Dracula*. Symptoms include drinking blood, drinking one's own blood (known as auto-vampirism), necrophilia, necrophagia (the urge to eat corpses), cannibalism, sadism, and vampiric fantasies.

Although opinion is divided, most people accept that vampire behavior is a psychiatric problem and that these people are not actual vampires but deluded and disturbed individuals. However, as far as the science behind vampires is concerned the question of whether or not vampires do exist is still a valid one, because there are just too many cases of unexplained vampirism to account for. Although rare, these real-life vampire stories are not confined to the distant past; they continue to occur and mystify both skeptics and believers to this day. You'll uncover all the chilling facts in the pages of this encyclopedia, but for now here's a brief taster:

 On April 16, 1922, on Coventry Street in the West End of London, three men were attacked on the same day by an unknown assailant who

left puncture marks in their throats. All the men were admitted to hospital and all claimed that they were attacked at exactly the same spot, seized by an invisible presence and bitten on the neck. They felt as if their blood was being sucked out. Despite police investigations, no one was caught. Doctors confirmed that the men appeared to have been bitten or stabbed by a thin tube. The assailant was said to resemble a huge bat.

Perhaps the most famous alleged attack by a "real" vampire in the twentieth century was carried out by the "Vampire of Highgate," in North London. In this case a tall, red-eyed phantasm was often seen lurking behind the main gate of Highgate Cemetery during the late 1960s and early 70s. It was described as a black, menacing mass and its presence was reported by many witnesses at the time to the local Hampstead and Highgate Express *newspaper. The mysterious death of several foxes in the local area was also recorded at the time. The animals reportedly were lacerated around the throat and drained of blood, and reporters drawn to the area spoke of being psychically drained by an unseen entity.*

As recently as 2008, a blood-sucking vampire dog, often referred to as a chupacabra, *was blamed for the death of 30 chickens in a farm in Texas. The animals were found drained of blood with two puncture marks in their otherwise uninjured bodies. This was no isolated incident. In fact reports of sheep, cattle, and other livestock being found drained of blood date back over a hundred years, and the mystifying nature of their deaths continues to fuel speculation that a blood-sucking vampire is on the loose.*

Such reports of animals or people found with unexplained bite wounds and blood loss suggest the very real and chilling possibility that vampires *do* actually exist – and those who study the real science behind vampires focus on how indeed this phenomenon could be possible. Numerous theories have been put forward to explain how vampires could exist on a diet of blood, and how a human body can transform into that of a vampire. Some vampirologists think the answer to these questions might be found in the study of cellular mechanisms, or molecular changes within the body. Others attempt to find answers in the study of psychoimmunology and a so-called vampire virus. Some focus their speculation on the powerful influence the mind has over the body, or the subtle energy transfers that occur whenever people interact. Moreover, assuming that vampires can exist, the scientific study of vampires also attempts to discover what the rules for their existence would be. How long could they live? Would they always need to shun sunlight? How would their digestive system work? How would you kill a vampire? How would they have sex? How could they hide in the modern world of forensic science? And so on.

This brief introduction to the history and science behind vampires has barely skimmed the surface of the seductive but insidious influence vampires have had over the centuries. It's given you the bare bones, the very simplest and basic foundation or starting point for an understanding of what vampires are, or could be, and what lies behind our seemingly insatiable fascination with them. For the flesh and blood – and the crucial information that can

The Element Encyclopedia of Vampires

help you discover the truth about vampires for yourself – you need to explore and ponder the entries in this book.

Whether you decide to dip in and out of this encyclopedia or read it from start to finish, remember the most important thing here, as with everything in this life and the next, is your belief and your will. In *Dracula*, vampires are presented as a terrifying force of evil that must be conquered at all costs, and yet despite this many characters in the book, including even the vampire hunter Van Helsing, develop an intense, often fatal attraction to vampires. In much the same way as the characters in *Dracula* struggle to resist, it could be said that the undying legend and lure of the vampire today is almost vampiric in itself, with more and more people becoming absorbed by, and seemingly powerless to release themselves from, the captivating quest for more information, once they have been "bitten."

Anyone who has ever been drawn to vampires, or studied the history and science behind vampires, will know that the attraction can be all-consuming. But however deep you decide to delve into the world of the vampire, you should never lose sight of the fact that this attraction does not have to be dangerous or deadly. As stated previously, vampires are as real and as powerful as you believe and allow them to be. You are the one in charge here.

LIVING THE MYSTERY

There is never going to be a simple answer to the question of what a vampire is, just as there is never going to be a single answer to the question of what lies behind our fascination with the image of the vampire, because, as this introduction has illustrated, the vampire defies definition. In both reality and fiction he, she, or it is a shape-shifter who can take on the form of society's fears at any given time. For instance, during the 1920s women who were assertively sexual were denounced as "vamps," implying that they had the ability to drain the essence of manhood from their lovers. Years later, in movies, the vampire came to represent many other things: addiction in Abel Ferrara's 1995 *The Addiction*; the rebellious outsider in Joel Schumacher's 1987 *The Lost Boys*. In fact, this ability to shape-shift goes some way to explain the growing trend today for the vampire to be depicted in an appealing, even desirable way. Edward Cullen's vampire status in Stephenie Meyer's bestselling *Twilight*, published in 2005, is not so much a curse but a quality that makes him utterly irresistible to Bella, the novel's heroine. In many ways Edward is an old-fashioned hero more suited to romantic melodrama than the primitive and savage Dracula myth.

Yet, despite being the ultimate shape-shifter, the image of the vampire somehow never manages to lose its humanity, and herein the reason for their widespread, undying appeal may perhaps be found. Vampires, whatever shape or form they take, embody so many aspects related to the human condition: death, desire, control, sex, intimacy, violence, romance, a fascination with mystery, and the feeling of being an outsider or of not fitting in. In short, vampires are erotic because the constant presence of death they embody or symbolize provokes a need within us for an intense affirmation of life.

The Element Encyclopedia of Vampires will provide a rich and sustaining source of illumination into the elements of vampires and the mysterious world they live in. As you explore, be aware that vampires break down the barrier between life and death, between desire and fear, and by so doing they hold out the promise – and the risk – of transformation. Uncovering the truth about them could change you forever, a reality that is both terrifying and inspiring in equal measure.

Could it be then, that our endless fascination with the image of the vampire results from a desire for knowledge, excitement, and intimacy that is far more consuming and far stronger than our fear of evil, death, and the unknown? Could it be that the more fascinated we are by the undead, the more human and intensely alive we feel ourselves to be?

Let's take the lid off the coffin and find out!

The Element Encyclopedia of Vampires

A–Z

OF THE

UNDEAD

"I am neither good, nor bad, neither angel nor devil, I am a man, I am a vampire."

Michael Romkey, *I, Vampire*

Abhartach

The story of Abhartach, an ancient Celtic warlord, could be the oldest vampire story in Western Europe. It comes from a remote place called Slaughtaverty, which lies in the Glenullin valley in Northern Ireland. In the fifth and sixth centuries AD this valley was divided into a number of tiny kingdoms, each ruled by their own chieftain or warlord. Abhartach was one of these warlords. Little is known about him except that he was small in stature and deformed, and that he ruled his people in the manner of a merciless tyrant. He also had an evil reputation for sorcery. His people wanted to get rid of him but they were too afraid of his alleged dark powers to kill him themselves. So they persuaded Cathan, a neighboring chieftain, to kill him for them instead.

Cathan killed Abhartach and he was duly buried standing up, as befitted an Irish chieftain; but within a day Abhartach returned from the dead and demanded a bowl of blood, drawn from the wrists of his subjects, to sustain his corpse. Cathan "killed" and buried Abhartach a second time, but the next day the vile corpse came back once more with the same terrifying demand. Not knowing what else to do, Cathan consulted either a local Druid or a Christian saint – the story has variations – and he was told that Abhartach had become one of the *neamh-marbh* (the undead) and a *dearg-diulai* (a drinker of human blood). It was impossible to kill him, but he could be prevented from rising again if he was destroyed with a sword made of yew wood and then buried upside down surrounded by thorns and ash twigs, with a great stone placed directly over the grave. Cathan followed these instructions to the letter and created a great *leacht* or sepulcher over the

creature, which gave the area its name: Slaughtaverty or Abhartach's leacht.

The grave can still be found in Slaughtaverty in the middle of a barley field. Known locally as the "giant's grave," even today local people remain reluctant to approach it after nightfall. In 1997, attempts were made to clear the land. Allegedly the workmen who tried to cut down the thorn tree arching across Abhartach's sepulcher found that their chainsaw malfunctioned three times. While attempting to lift the great stone, a steel chain snapped, cutting the hand of one of the laborers, and, ominously, causing blood to soak into the ground.

The tale of Abhartach was included (and taken as fact) in Geoffrey Keating's *History of Ireland*, written between 1629 and 1631. It was also recounted by Patrick Weston Joyce in his *Origin and History of Irish Names of Places*, published in 1885:

There is a place in the parish of Errigal in Londonderry, called Slaghtaverty, but it ought to have been called Laghtaverty, the laght or sepulchral monument of the abhartach [avartagh] or dwarf. This dwarf was a magician, and a dreadful tyrant, and after having perpetrated great cruelties on the people he was at last vanquished and slain by a neighbouring chieftain; some say by Fionn Mac Cumhail. He was buried in a standing posture, but the very next day he appeared in his old haunts, more cruel and vigorous than ever. And the chief slew him a second time and buried him as before, but again he escaped from the grave, and spread terror through the whole country. The chief then consulted a druid, and according to his directions, he slew the dwarf a third time, and buried him in the same place, with his head downwards; which subdued his magical power, so that he never again appeared on earth. The laght raised over the dwarf is still there, and you may hear the legend with much detail from the natives of the place, one of whom told it to me.

According to Bob Curran, lecturer in Celtic History and Folklore at the University of Ulster, Coleraine, the Irish writer Bram Stoker may have been influenced by the tale when writing his landmark vampire novel *Dracula* in 1897. There is no evidence that Stoker based *Dracula* on Abhartach but, according to Curran, Stoker was familiar with the writings of Joyce and the legend of Abhartach was well known and widely circulated around Ireland. It is therefore certainly possible that the legend of Abhartach, the blood-drinking warlord who returned from the dead, formed at least part of the inspiration for *Dracula*.

Ackerman, Forrest J (1916-2008)

Born on November 24, 1916 in Los Angeles, Forrest J Ackerman was a science fiction and horror writer and editor and the inspiration behind *Famous Monsters of Filmland*, an important magazine for fans of the horror movie genre that started up in 1958. Until this time there had been no monster movie or vampire clubs and magazines. However, it was the creation of the comic book character Vampirella that was Ackerman's most significant contribution to the field of vampires.

Vampirella was a young and sexy female vampire from outer space, partly inspired by the 1968 movie *Barbarella*, starring the Oscar-winning actress Jane Fonda. *Vampirella* first appeared in 1969 and went on to become one of the most successful vampire comics ever. It ran for 20 years and was revived again with great success in the 1990s by Harris Comics.

See also: COMICS

Aconite

An extremely poisonous plant, aconite (*Aconitum napellus*) is also known as monkshood or wolfsbane. Aconite is one of the most toxic herbal substances known and must only be used in minute medicinal amounts. Its potential to heal and also to poison probably helped to create an aura of magic and superstition around the herb. In medicine the plant's roots provide the chemically active ingredients; in vampire folklore the leaves are thought to be enough to repel vampires and other evil entities.

The generic name for aconite may be derived from the Greek *akontion* meaning "dart" or "spear," referring to the fact that this plant once provided poison for the arrows of some tribes. There are many legendary accounts of aconite being used as a poison. In the thirteenth and fourteenth centuries it was used as poison bait for wolves and this association may explain the use of the name wolfsbane. Another possibility is that the name commemorates the hill Aconitus in Pontica, where Hecate, an ancient goddess of magic and the underworld, is said to have created aconite from the spittle in the mouths of Cerberus, the three-headed dog who guarded the entrance to the underworld.

Aconite is widely associated with witchcraft and was noted as the traditional ingredient in a witch's flying ointment. Medieval witches were reputed to have used chips of flint coated in the plant extract to throw at intended victims. The victims would probably not notice anything at the time, except a scratch, but would shortly become ill and die. These darts were known as "elf-bolts." With such a deadly, dark, and magical reputation, small wonder then that aconite makes an appearance under the name wolfsbane as a magical potion with terrifying powers in the Harry Potter novels.

Addams Family, The

Originally a cartoon series created by Charles S. Addams (1912–88) that first appeared in the 1930s in the *New Yorker* magazine, *The Addams Family* eventually became a popular US television sitcom in the mid-1960s. It aired from 1964 to 1966 on ABC. In 1991 Oscar-winning actress Angelica Huston stared in a highly successful movie version, *The Addams Family*. This was followed up in 1993 by *Addams Family Values*, again starring Angelica Huston.

The Addams family is presented as a bizarre but close-knit family descended from witches and vampires. They are morbid and gothic in their appearance and behavior and their neighbors do not understand their strange habits. To this day, the Addams family remain one of the most notable and eccentric fictional families in American popular culture, demonstrating as had previously been done in *Abbott and Costello meet Frankenstein* (1948) – considered to be the first and one of the most successful vampire comedy movies – that stories involving vampires could be successfully transferred from the world of horror to the world of popular entertainment.

See also: MUNSTERS, THE

Addiction

Vampire lore tends to take on the form of each generation's fears and the rise of drug and alcohol addiction in the late twentieth century has influenced many contemporary vampire accounts. The vampire can be a metaphor for drug addiction through vein puncturing and the contamination of blood, and the self-destructive behavior of an alcoholic can suggest being enslaved by the curse of the vampire.

The association between vampirism and alcoholism actually predates the modern age by more than a century. In Eastern European lore alcoholics were thought to be prime candidates for revenants – or the restless dead. An 1897 report (A. Löwenstimm, *Aberglaube und Strafrecht*, Berlin) contains accounts from Russians that state that bodies were unearthed simply because the people were alcoholics when they were alive: "*In the year 1889 the peasants of the village Jelischanki, in the Saratow District, opened the grave of a man who had died of alcoholism and had been buried in the general churchyard, and they threw his body in the nearest river.*"

Vampire historian Montague Summers records the "*frantic teetotal tract*" *Vampyre: By the wife of a medical man*, published in 1858 and quotes the ravings of its victim: "*They fly, they bite, they suck my blood, I die. That hideous Vampyre! Its eyes pierce me thro' they are red, they are bloodshot. Tear it from my pillow. I dare not lie down. It bites. I die! Give me brandy, brandy – more brandy.*"

In the late twentieth century, the association between vampirism and addiction to violence and evil is strongly expressed in Abel Ferrara's grim, black and white/color movie *The Addiction* (1995). In the film a young philosophy student develops a thirst for blood after being attacked by an aggressive female vampire. The movie crafts a harrowing tale of urban vampirism, violence, and drug addition.

Adze

A vampire spirit thought to dwell in tribal sorcerers and to assume the shape of a firefly. It was traditionally greatly feared by the Ewe people of southern Togo and south-eastern Ghana. If caught it changed into a humanoid figure, hunchbacked with sharp talons and black skin, and it is in this guise that it was believed to be at its most dangerous and deadly, preying on children (especially attractive ones), drinking their blood and gorging on their tender hearts and livers.

Africa

There is not sufficient evidence to support widespread belief in vampires throughout ancient Africa. There is, however, enough evidence to suggest that ancient Egypt, Africa's center of mysticism, may in fact be the origin of vampire stories. It's also possible that African beliefs in witches, witchcraft, and creatures with vampire-like tendencies may have spread to the rest of the world and influenced the development of vampire folklore in Europe during the Middle Ages.

A particular species of creature with vampire-like tendencies that is believed to have its origins in Africa is called the obayifo. This creature is not undead like most vampires, but is a witch who can leave her body at night to damage crops and feed off the blood of living children. Other significant vampire-like species found in African folklore include the adze, asanbosam, impundula, mau-mau, tikoloshe, and ramanga.

Literal vampirism is rare in Africa but African beliefs about witches and witchcraft do share strong similarities to the vampire folklore of Eastern European traditions. For example, witches were thought to have tremendous powers, including the ability to transform into animals. They also fed on corpses and drank the blood of the living. (What's intriguing is that these attacks probably had more in common with psychic vampirism, making the obayifo intentional psychic vampires.) In addition, the idea that witches could rise from the dead and that destroying the corpse of the witch could prevent the spirit from continuing its activity on earth is also closely linked to European notions of vampirism. African witches also had the power to capture a departed spirit and enslave it to do whatever the witch commanded, thus turning it into a zombie-like creature, known as the isithfuntela.

See also: **PSYCHIC VAMPIRE; VOODOO**

African American Vampires

African beliefs in vampires and, more commonly, witches and witchcraft may have made their way to the United States by way of the voodoo traditions of Haiti. A number of accounts of vampires can be found in the folklore of late nineteenth-century African Americans. Some of these accounts are traditional in that vampires are believed to be bloodsuckers draining the life force of the living and dead.

Perhaps the most well-defined vampire figure among African American folklore was the feu-follet, or fifolet, a mysterious ball of light thought to be the vengeful soul that returned to earth to create trouble and occasionally to suck the blood of children. Unhappy spirits of the dead were believed to bring disease into households and even today in Louisiana, many families still practice a custom called "sitting up with the dead." When a family member dies, someone within the family, or perhaps a close family friend, will stay with the body until it is placed into a grave. The body is never left unattended. There are many reasons given for this practice today, most commonly, respect for the dead. This tradition however, may actually date back to vampire folklore, originating from Africa or Eastern Europe, where it was thought that watching for signs of paranormal activity would help prevent the corpse from returning from the dead.

African American vampires have largely been absent from vampire novels and movies, but in 1972 one African American vampire character broke the mold in the film *Blacula*. In the film a curse from Count Dracula turns African Prince Mamuwalde into Blacula. Another less well-known African American movie is the 1973 *Ganja and Hess*. Set in New York it is the story of Dr. Hess Green who becomes a vampire after being stabbed by an ancient African dagger by his assistant. Black actors haven't prominently featured in the role of the vampire or vampire hunter, but Teresa Graves in *Old Dracula*, also known as *Vampira* (1974), Grace Jones in *Vamp* (1986), Wesley Snipes as the day-walking vampire hunter in the *Blade* trilogy (1998, 2002, 2004), Eddie Murphy in *Vampire in Brooklyn* (1996), and Will Smith as the semi-human vampire hunter in *I Am Legend* (2007) suggest that this trend is definitely changing.

Afrit

According to Arabian folklore, an afrit is a vampiric ghoul or spirit who seeks revenge from beyond the grave. King Solomon, who reigned in the tenth century BC, was said to have tamed an afrit, and made it submissive to his will. The afrit is said to rise up like smoke from the spilt blood of murder victims. They are believed to bring unspeakable terror, and because of the unjust and brutal nature of their own death they are ruthless toward their victims. Sometimes they are said to appear in the form of the Christian Devil with horns on their head. It was thought that the only way to prevent their formation was to drive a nail into the blood-stained ground.

Afterlife Beliefs

The idea of the vampire is closely associated with a belief in the afterlife, because bloodsucking vampires are, quite literally, believed to be the living dead.

Across the centuries people have believed in life after death and wondered what lies on the other side of death. Where do the dead go? What is the afterlife like? Can the dead intervene in the affairs of the living? And almost every society known has tried to answer these questions, and the answers vary widely.

For the ancient Celts the afterlife is called the Otherworld, a place of the dead and other supernatural creatures. From the Otherworld the dead could watch the affairs of the living and from time to time return to the living in order to intervene with the affairs of our day-to-day existence. The dead did not return in the form of a spirit but in the form of a solid entity, similar to when the person was still alive. They returned for all sorts of reasons but primarily to warn the living or complete unfinished business, and occasionally to take revenge. By contrast, for the ancient Hebrews the dead made a journey to a place called Sheol. Here the spirits wandered aimlessly in rivers, lakes, and mist, unaware of what was happening in the world of the living. The ancient Egyptians believed the afterlife to be very similar to the world of the living. Servants were murdered when their masters died so they could continue to serve them in the afterlife. According to the Vikings the afterlife was a great hall called Valhalla, or the Hall of Heroes. It was a warriors' paradise of feasting and drinking that could only be entered by those who died with a sword in their hand.

Christian folk traditions suggest that the souls of good people become angels after death. However, a more orthodox reading of scripture suggests that the dead are not transformed until the Last Judgment, which is followed by a resurrection of the faithful. Another afterlife concept, found among Hindus and Buddhists, is reincarnation. Reincarnation is the belief that when a person dies their body decomposes, but their spirit or soul is reborn in another body, and that body can be human or animal. It is the belief that we have lived before and can live again in another body after death. Both Hindus and Buddhists interpret events in our current life as consequences of actions taken in previous lives.

Interpretations of the afterlife differ not just from culture to culture but from person to person. One source of belief in the afterlife, however, that continues to this day to be held up as "proof" that there is an afterlife, is the testimony of individuals who claim that they have:

- *Died and been sent back to life (a near-death experience)*

- *Visited the afterlife when they were unconscious (an out-of-body experience)*

- *Seen the afterlife in a vision*

- *Remembered the afterlife from a previous existence (reincarnation)*

- *Been visited by representatives of the afterlife such as angels or spirits*

- *Heard the testimony of intermediaries between the living and the dead (mediums)*

- *Been visited, or attacked by, or witnessed a vampire*

In centuries past it could be said that vampire stories were simply an offshoot of primitive attempts to explain the mystery of death and demonstrate the possibility of an afterlife. Now that science has unraveled so many of the mysteries of the universe it is no surprise that belief in the existence of an afterlife has dwindled. However, large numbers of people continue to believe that there is an afterlife, and despite the fact that science has attempted to prove the contrary, growing numbers of people continue to believe that undead vampires can and do exist.

Aging of Vampires

According to most accounts vampires are not immortal, but they can defy death and live for several hundred years. Their superhuman powers of speed, strength, and telepathy not only make them highly skilled hunters of human blood but may also explain their longevity. According to vampirologist Katherine Ramsland (*The Science of Vampires*, 2002), being a vampire positively affects the body's endurance and vitality. She believes this is because the body of a vampire is made up of "immortalized" cells, or microscopic cells that resist aging when fed on a diet of human blood. However, when vampires are unable to obtain this blood they can become ill with flu-like symptoms. If they continue to be starved of blood, they will die. This is why, in order to survive, vampires must learn how to acquire a steady supply of blood without drawing attention to their addiction. To do this they must learn new skills and fine-tune old ones all the time.

One vampirologist who has studied at length the aging experience of vampires is Hugo Pecos, overseer of an organization called the Federal Vampire and Zombie Agency (FVZA). According to Pecos ("Vampire biology," www.fvza.org, 2007) vampires are only ageless in that they do not age in the same way that humans do. Their longevity is not the result of some virus or pact with the Devil, but rather their unique ability to ward off the DNA damage that occurs during cell division in normal humans. Somehow the protective caps on the ends of chromosomes, known as telomers, get destroyed over time in humans, but not in vampires.

Therefore, according to Pecos, vampires do not age on a molecular/genetic level, but their appearance can change over time. They can also die. Their life of hunting and hiding can lead to injuries to their bodies and curvature of the spine. They can lose eyes, ears, and noses and sustain horrific injuries during fights, and older vampires are often heavily scarred from these activities. The older they get the more their fat stores disappear, leaving their skin thin and transparent with a dried, pale, and withered appearance, and as their injuries and exhaustion take their toll they may lose their ability to hunt, resulting in death from malnourishment.

Most vampires are destroyed long before they reach the upper limits of their lifespan because they represent such a threat to society. Ancient history does, however, give us some clues as to what that lifespan is. In ancient China, there was said to be one vampire in the emperor's court through the entire (eastern) Zhou Dynasty, which would put his age at 550. More recent records have noted vampires of over 200 years old.

While the promise of longevity, or even immortality, is an alluring and reoccurring theme in vampire lore, another theme that constantly reappears in vampire fact and fiction is the use of vampiric practices to try to hold back the passage of time. Historically, one of the most famous people to seek eternal youth was Elizabeth Báthory (d. 1614), a Hungarian countess who was convinced that bathing in, and drinking, the blood of freshly slain virgins would restore her youth.

See also: **BIOLOGY OF VAMPIRES;**
SOCIOLOGY OF VAMPIRES

AIDS

In centuries past, vampire lore was perhaps fueled by terrified responses to poorly understood medical conditions. Plagues and contagions were often attributed to the acts of the undead. In much the same way the modern epidemic of Acquired Immune Deficiency Syndrome, or AIDS, has sent waves of panic through society. As the symptoms of AIDS strangely echo the classic motifs of vampirism – a blood-borne, wasting malady with each victim capable of creating others through unconventional sex or blood-letting – it's easy to see why associations have been made between AIDS and vampirism.

A literal vampire must feed on blood to survive. Blood is a vampire's life, but what about the implications of AIDS or other lethal blood-borne viruses? Vampire lore suggests the spread of some evil disease of the blood transmitted through a bite. AIDS is a virus that is transmitted by blood and the bodily fluids involved in intercourse. Small wonder then that a number of vampirologists, vampire authors and modern-day vampires have not only made associations between AIDS and vampirism but been forced to consider the implications of this deadly and dangerous threat to vampire fact and fiction. Some vampirologists see AIDS as a way to deliver a potentially fatal blow to the vampire, others use it to emphasize their immortality; still others stress the fact that the super-senses of the vampire can tell when a person's blood is healthy enough to feed on. Some simply ignore the issue, arguing that vampires are creatures of fantasy not fact, while academics argue that vampirism can be seen as a metaphor for AIDS. For modern-day blood drinkers, however, who feed on the blood of willing donors, the age of AIDS has ensured that there is typically a very powerful (and sensible) emphasis on making sure any blood used is clean and safe.

In much the same way as the AIDS epidemic has imprinted itself in the vampire myth other sexually transmitted diseases have also left their mark. For example, toward the end of the nineteenth century syphilis struck in London, triggering fears of blood contamination, the damnation of prostitutes, and a frenzied hunt for signs of vampire attack.

See also: **CONTAGION; DISEASE;**
HOMOSEXUALITY

Albania

Several types of vampire are found in the traditions of Albania, a country situated in the Balkans, with the countries of the former Yugoslavia to the north and east and Greece to the south. Albanian vampire lore is similar to that of other Eastern European states.

Vampire species include the vrykolakas, also found in Greece, the sampiro, a derivation from the Slavic vampire, and the kukudhi, also known as the lugat. The kukudhi may be one of the most terrifying vampires of Eastern Europe and is extremely hard to "kill" in the traditional way of dispatching vampires. In many parts of Albania, there was a tradition that those who were guilty of a crime that went unpunished in this life were condemned to become vampires at their deaths. There was also a belief that vampires not only drank the blood of victims but also spread disease and sicknesses through communities. In some areas in the late eighteenth century plagues and epidemics were put down to the activities of the vampiric sampiro, and in other areas high instances of infant mortality were linked to the vampiric activity of a witch-like creature called the strigoi. According to vampire lore, the best way to kill such vile creatures was to pierce the heart with a stake. Hamstringing was also considered highly effective in the case of the kukudhi.

Even though Albania has become a more modern society, many Albanians today living in rural areas continue to believe in vampires and their insatiable appetite for human blood.

Alchemy

In Bram Stoker's *Dracula*, Van Helsing states that Dracula had been an alchemist in his mortal life, so along with necromancy, alchemy can be added to the vampire's skills in the occult arts.

The term "alchemy," commonly believed to refer to attempts to change base metals into gold, covers a wide range of topics – from the discovery of a single cure for all diseases to the quest for immortality, from the creation of artificial life to straightforward descriptions of scientific techniques. Broadly, one could describe alchemy as the art of converting that which is base, both in the material and spiritual world, into something more perfect. Symbolically therefore, alchemy is the mystical art of human spiritual transformation into a higher form of being.

Spiritual teachings

The spiritual teachings of alchemy were based on the idea that humans have a spirit or soul as well as a physical body, and it was thought that if the spirit could be compressed or concentrated, the secret of changing one aspect of nature into another could be discovered. The elusive catalyst that allowed this change to take place is known as the philosopher's stone, which is not actually a stone but a powder or liquid that turned base metal into gold and, when swallowed, broke down the limitations of the soul, giving it everlasting life. Alchemists are often pictured as stirring a bubbling concoction of base metal on a fire, attempting to turn it into gold. However, they would also keep a record of changes they observed within themselves – mood changes, significant dreams, physical symptoms, and such like. Some of the best minds of the last twenty or so centuries have studied alchemy as a way to unlock the secrets of nature and develop greater self-knowledge.

The alchemist's quest for transformation parallels the search for the philosopher's stone. The first phase for the alchemist is the *nigredo*, or black phase. In this phase the alchemist would use techniques such as hallucination and meditation to surrender to the dark or repressed aspects of himself in order to develop greater self-knowledge. He would also try to break down physical substances to their basest form. In the second phase, the *albedo* or white phase, the alchemist would try to purify himself and the material elements he was working with. Next came the yellow phase, called *citrinitas* and then the final phase, the red phase or *rubedo*. This last phase was one of the highest self-awareness and purification and was considered to be the stage of rebirth and enlightenment, and the creation of the elusive philosopher's stone.

Alchemy, which integrates chemistry and religion, originated in ancient Egypt and China. Before the scientific revolution, alchemists were respected figures on the European scene, and kings and nobles often supported them in the hope of increasing their revenue. But alongside the sincere were charlatans and swindlers, and their fraudulent activities led to alchemy getting a bad name. Even as late as 1783 a chemist called John Price from Guildford, England claimed he had turned mercury into gold. When he was asked by the Royal Society to perform the experiment in public, he reluctantly agreed. On the appointed day he drank the poisonous mercury and died in front of the invited audience.

In the sixteenth and seventeenth centuries, many practical alchemists, like Paracelsus, the first in Europe to mention zinc and use the word "alcohol," turned from trying to make gold to preparing medicine. After the scientific revolution in the seventeenth century, alchemy became marginalized, and interest in transmutation became limited to astrologers and numerologists. Nevertheless, the scientific facts that had been accumulated by alchemists in their search for gold became the basis for modern chemistry.

In the West, interest in the spiritual dimension of alchemy was rekindled in the mid-twentieth century through the work of psychiatrist Carl Jung. Today there are few practicing alchemists. Scientists have discovered how to change base metals into gold, but the process is uneconomical and so alchemy today is a spiritual rather than a practical quest. For sincere alchemists the search for spiritual perfection takes precedence over the quest for easy riches. The symbolism of turning base metal into gold represents what alchemists are trying to do within themselves, which is to refine themselves spiritually.

Alchemy represents two elements that are central to vampire lore. First, there is the quest for eternal life or the possibility to defy death using magic. The vampire's quest for red blood that will bring him eternal life can be seen as similar to the alchemist's quest for the philosopher's stone, which was described as a red liquid that could prolong life indefinitely. The second element, turning base metals into gold, is reflected in many works of vampire literature. Stoker's *Dracula* is a fine example. Unlike the vampire of folklore, Stoker describes Dracula as an intelligent, rich aristocrat and, apart from magic or occult sources there is no other convincing explanation for his wealth, influence, and intelligence.

Aldiss, Brian (1925–)

One of the most important voices in modern science fiction writing today, Brian Aldiss, OBE, was born in Norfolk, England in 1925. He wrote his first novel while working as a bookseller in Oxford and shortly afterward gained international recognition. Admired for his innovative literary techniques, evocative plots, and irresistible characters, he was awarded an honorary doctorate by the University of Liverpool in recognition of his contribution to literature.

Aldiss turned his literary talents to the vampire legend and, in the opinion of many of his fans, successfully persuaded readers to suspend scientific belief when writing *Dracula Unbound* (1991). In this book, which involves time travel and Dracula sending assassins to kill Bram Stoker before he can write his vampire novel, Aldiss suggests that vampires are evolutionary descendants of prehistoric reptiles.

Algul

An Arabian term, literally translated as "horse leech," for a vampire that was thought to live in cemeteries and drink the blood of dead children. In Western usage the algul became more commonly known as a ghoul, typically a female demon that lives in cemeteries and feasts on dead babies.

See also: **AMINE**

Alien Vampires

In 1894, in *The Flowering of the Strange Orchid*, English author H. G. Wells explored the possibility of space aliens taking over a human body in order to live off the life energy of others. Since then, vampires have become a favorite space alien in science fiction and fantasy. As their name suggests, these alien vampires are vampires from outer space. The most famous alien vampire is Vampirella, the femme fatale from the planet Drakulon.

See also: **ACKERMAN, FORREST J**

Allatius, Leo (c.1586–1669)

Leo Allatius (also known as Leone Allacci) was a seventeenth-century Greek writer who compiled information on the Greek species of vampire, the vrykolakas, in his study of Greek superstitions, *De Graecorum hodie quorundam opinationibus* (On certain modern opinions among the Greeks), published in Cologne in 1645. In this study Allatius, possibly the first author to write a whole book about vampires, found himself most drawn toward and convinced by stories of the undead from his native island of Chios. His work offers a fascinating insight into the traditions and beliefs concerning the vrykolakas – undecomposed corpses that had been taken over by demons – as well as the ordinances of the Greek Church (*nonocanons*) against vampires and vampirism. He also mentioned his own belief in the existence of vampires. According to Allatius the vrykolakas was:

the body of a man of evil and immoral life – very often one who has been excommunicated by his bishop … Into such a body the devil enters and proceeding from the tomb goes about mainly at night, knocking on doors and calling one of the house. If one answers he dies the following day. A vrykolakas never calls twice and the people of Chios insure their safety by waiting for a second before replying.

Allatius's book has ensured that the connection between Greece and vampires and vampirism has remained strong over the centuries. And according to vampirologist Gordon Melton in *The Vampire Book* (1998), when Allatius cited the three conditions for the existence of vampires – a corpse, the Devil, and God's permission for the Devil to reincarnate the corpse – the first connection between Satan and vampirism was made. This meant that from then onward symbols of God, such as a cross or crucifix and holy water could be used to identify, repel, and kill or destroy vampires.

All Souls' Day

A day for Catholics to commemorate and say masses for the faithful dead that falls on November 2 (or November 3, if November 2 is a Sunday). This date is the day after that of the ancient Celtic festival of Samhain, which was also a day for remembering the dead.

All Souls' Day dates back to the very origins of the Christian era, and by the tenth century it was firmly established in many Benedictine monasteries. A number of vampirologists have suggested that the notion of All Souls' Day within the Christian religion played a significant part in the creation and popularization of the vampire motif, and may even explain why the notion of the angry and vengeful dead caught on so quickly in the Christian world. With the endorsement of All Souls' Day, the Church now indicated that God permitted the departed to return to remind the living of their obligations to them. If their families neglected these obligations the angry dead might take physical revenge on them. Moreover, the dead who had not been correctly buried according to Church rites might return and punish those who had neglected them in this way. It was thought that the returning dead might attack the property or livestock of their remaining family. The returning dead might also drink blood from the necks of animals and, occasionally, in the ultimate act of revenge, the blood of their family.

Many different kinds of traditions have been found throughout Europe concerning the return of the dead on the night of All Souls' Day. In Germany, Austria, Bohemia, and the Low Countries food offerings were left in the churchyard or on tables for the returning dead. Soul cakes, baked on November 1 and eaten the following day by the living (and, allegedly, by the dead), were particularly common. The Mexican Day of the Dead is a holiday celebrated mainly in Latin America and by Latinos (and others) living in the United States and Canada. The holiday, which occurs on November 1 and 2 in conjunction with All Souls' Day, focuses on gatherings of family and friends to pray for and remember friends and family members who have died.

See also: **HALLOWEEN**

The Element Encyclopedia of Vampires

Alnwick Castle Vampire

A vampire revenant that terrorized people living in the area close to Alnwick Castle in Northumberland, England and whose activities were recorded by the twelfth-century English chronicler William of Newburgh. This famous case of a real vampire was told to Newburgh by a *"very devout priest of high authority and most honourable reputation."*

The term "vampire" was not used in the account because it had not yet entered the English language. However, the revenant described displayed characteristics that were later attributed to vampires. According to the *"very devout priest,"* the undead in question was a Yorkshire man who had been cruel and wicked in his lifetime. He escaped the law and came to Alnwick, to take up a position with the local lord. He married but rumors circulated that his wife was cheating on him. One night, while on the roof spying on his wife in the act of adultery, in a state of shock he fell and landed right beside his wife in bed with a local youth. The youth escaped and the man rebuked his wife, threatening to punish her. His injuries from the fall, however, were so severe that he fell ill. A priest visited the man and urged him to confess his sins, but he delayed and died impenitent.

The man was given a Christian burial but, said William of Newburgh, who paints a nightmarish picture, it was to no avail as he soon reappeared and began to attack villagers, spreading plague in his wake:

> For by the powers of Satan in the dark hours he won to come forth from his tomb to wander about all the streets, prowling around houses, whilst on every side the dogs were howling and yelping the whole night long … nor did anyone between the hours of dusk and dawn fare to go out on any business whatsoever, so greatly did each on fear that he might haply meet this fellow monster and be attacked and most grievously harmed.

Unlike the traditional literary vampire, rather than the body remaining uncorrupted William describes the body of the undead as in a state of decay. A foul and suffocating stench (which, along with the bloated and hideous appearance of the undead's victims strongly suggests an outbreak of plague) was said to accompany the wanderings of the revenant. As the victims multiplied the village emptied:

> The air became foul and tainted as this foetid and corrupting body wandered abroad, so that a terrible plague broke out and there was hardly a house which did not mourn its dead, and presently the town, which for a little while before had been thickly populated, seemed to be well nigh deserted, for those who survived the pestilence and those hideous attacks hastily removed themselves to other districts, lest they should also perish.

The elders met and a group of brave survivors, which included two young men who had lost their father to the plague, decided to march to the cemetery so they could dig up the man's corpse and burn it. The two brothers found the man's body in a shallow grave looking gorged and swollen, with a florid face and red, puffy cheeks. The shroud was dirty and torn. They pierced the corpse and warm blood flowed out, proving to them that the revenant was feeding on the blood of its victims. They dragged the body out of the cemetery and burned it to ashes on a pyre. Almost immediately the air was cleansed and the plague stopped.

This chilling account is a fine example of epidemics and plagues being attributed to the undead.

Alp

The alp is a shape-shifting, cannibalistic, blood-drinking, vampire-like demon or revenant from German/Austrian folklore that is often associated with the bogeyman and incubus. The origins of superstitions concerning the alp are uncertain, but in 1679 a German theologian, Philip Rohr, published a treatise entitled *De Masticatione Mortuorum* (On the chewing dead), which discussed beliefs concerning the dead who return to bite and chew. The text illustrates how widespread beliefs in vampiric entities were throughout Germany.

Characteristics

The alp is a strange and confusing vampire type, displaying a number of different characteristics. According to tradition, the alp normally terrifies women at night and in their dreams as nightmares, although men and children could also be attacked. Children were thought to be at risk of becoming alps if their mothers had committed a sin during pregnancy that remained unforgiven, or had eaten something, like a berry from the bushes, that was unclean, or had used inappropriate measures to ease the pain of childbirth. These measures were not often specified, but if they were they refer to superstitions and folk remedies. Hair on the back of the hands of an infant could also signal future vampirism or that the child might become a werewolf.

Sometimes the alp took the form of a little old man with a thirst for blood, but it was also said to appear as a bird, pig, cat, white stallion, butterfly, or a lecherous, black demon dog – which also links this legend to the legend of the werewolf. There is no consistency regarding this creature. In parts of Germany it was a living being, while in some areas of Austria it was the evil spirit of a dead person. In some areas it was a little old man and in others it appeared as a powerful, shape-shifting wizard. In all of its manifestations, however, it was said to wear a wide-brimmed soft hat, which obscured most of its face and was probably used as a disguise. The alp must safeguard this hat because, if it is lost, much of the creature's invisibility and strength disappears with it. The eye of the alp also matters greatly because it is the eye that torments the nightmares and dreams of its victims.

Curiously, in many traditions the alp never forced itself violently on its victims, and is credited with a certain gallantry before it drinks blood from the nipples of sleeping women, men, and children. It could also enter the mouth of its victim by becoming a mist or a snake. Once entered, however, a victim experienced untold suffering, and sexual relations with the creature were said to be vile.

The alp allegedly tormented people's minds and wills in their sleep and was said to be impossible to destroy, although there were a number of methods to protect against it. It was said that the sight of a crucifix, or some holy relic would drive the alp away. Salt sprinkled across the doorstep of a house

The Element Encyclopedia of Vampires

would also keep an alp or their kind from entering. Women were told to sleep with their shoes against the sides of their beds, with the toes pointing toward the door. If a community was being attacked by the alp, and it was believed that the creature was the spirit of a dead person, then the body would be dug up and burned to destroy it. If, however, the alp was thought to occupying a living person, then that person would have some blood drawn from them from an area just above their right eye, which was believed to take away whatever evil powers the alp possessed.

Alpha Vampire

In vampire communities, an alpha vampire is a vampire who asserts dominance over other vampires with his or her superior skills, strength, and intellect. According to vampirologist Hugo Pecos, who oversees scientific research into the undead, an alpha vampire is the strongest and oldest vampire.

Over 200 years old, alpha vampires are said to be 10 times stronger than humans and typically they have also acquired considerable wealth. Since they have the greatest amount of skill and experience they are able to lead packs of younger vampires who do most of the hunting. When younger vampires catch a victim, the alpha vampire drinks the blood first, which gives him or her superior strength. It is not just physical strength which sets the alpha vampire apart though, it is also intellect. According to Pecos (www.fvza.org), *Physical size and power are important but [are] by no means the only determinant of alpha status. In fact intellectual capacity* *is more important than physical prowess in determining the success and longevity as a vampire."*

See also: FEDERAL VAMPIRE AND ZOMBIE AGENCY

Alter Ego

An alter ego (Latin: "the other I") is a second self, a second personality or persona within a person. The term was first used in the early nineteenth century when schizophrenia was first described by early psychologists. A person with an alter ego is said to lead a double life and it is not uncommon for modern vampires to say that a vampire is their alter ego, or darker side of their personality.

Alucard

Alucard is "Dracula" spelled backwards. The name was first used by actor Lon Chaney, Jr. as the name of the vampire in the 1943 film *Son of Dracula*. It is often used by writers and filmmakers as an obvious plot device to show how little regard the vampire has for the intellect of humans; it typically takes the human characters a lot of time to unravel the name's true meaning. This inability to comprehend the vampire's true identity, despite it being blindingly obvious to readers and viewers, illustrates why the vampire's contempt for humans is justified.

America

Those who are fans of vampire movies might be forgiven for thinking that America was the birthplace of the vampire. However, there are only scattered accounts of vampire mythology in tribes that were native to America and in the African American community, although traces of African vampire myths have featured strongly in the South. The practice of blood-drinking did appear among the cannibal tribes of Native Americans and there were some vampires in their folklore. The Cherokee, for instance, believed in witches who ate the livers of the dead, and the Ojibwa believed in vampires who drank the blood of the living. It can be said, however, that vampires were largely a European import and for the most part European settlers who came to the New World brought their vampire beliefs with them. For example, settlers from Poland kept vampire mythology alive in their Canadian settlements.

It's often been said that when the electric light was invented this was the end of evil spirits, because people became less afraid of what lurked in the shadows and the dark, but alleged cases of vampirism are still alive and well in America and American culture. Highly successful contemporary TV series such as *Buffy the Vampire Slayer*, and international bestsellers like the Twilight Saga series by American writer Stephenie Meyer, are a sure indication that the image of the vampire has firmly secured its place in modern American culture. In addition, American Goths rank among the liveliest followers of modern vampiric activity in the world, and US vampire authors, vampire fan clubs, websites, magazines, trading cards, video games, and movies play a huge part in keeping the image of the vampire constantly in the spotlight.

In 1989 vampirologist Norine Dresser published *American Vampires*. In this insightful book she examined a culture rich in vampire lore and suggested that vampire tales flourished in the last century in the United States because they exploit the American obsession with three things: sex, power, and youth. *American Vampires* was also the first mainstream book to examine the growth of blood fetishism in the 1980s, when people who were sexually aroused by the sight or taste of human blood began to romanticize their practice in vampire films and fiction.

For vampires in Central America, see: CIVATATEO; LA LLORONA; MEXICO

For vampires in North America, see: BELL WITCH, THE; NATIVE AMERICANS; NEW ENGLAND; RAY FAMILY VAMPIRES; RHODE ISLAND VAMPIRES

For vampires in South America, see: AFRICA; JARACACA; LOBISHOMEN; VOODOO

Amine

Amine is an Arabian ghoul or algul, whose story appears in the *Thousand and One Nights*, a collection of folk stories collected over many centuries by various authors, translators, and scholars in various countries across the Middle East and South Asia. In the story Amine is a beautiful girl who marries a young man called Sidi Numan. Amine eats virtually nothing in the day and Sidi become suspicious. He follows her one evening and sees her feasting on a corpse. The next day he confronts her and she turns him into a dog. Eventually, Sidi is returned to his human form by a woman skilled in white magic who gives Sidi a potion to transform Amine into a horse. The ghoul is then taken to the stables.

"Amsworth, Mrs."

Written by English author E. F. Benson, "Mrs. Amsworth" was first published in London in *Visible and Invisible* in 1923, and was often reprinted in collections of vampire tales. It tells the chilling story of a small English village and the arrival of a friendly widow from India, where her husband has died. She is sociable and attractive by day but a blood-sucking vampire at night. Everybody likes her and falls under her spell with the exception of Professor Francis Urcombe, who eventually manages to expose her.

The tension between science and superstition are brought together in this story in the character of Urcombe, an impressive academic who resigns from his post because his interests in the occult increasingly put him at odds with the scientific community. Urcombe is an avid student of the occult and instinctively recognizes Mrs. Amsworth as a vampire. In his final confrontation with her he simply has to trace the sign of a cross with his fingers and this is enough to overcome her.

See also: **LITERATURE**

Andrew, Feast of St.

The feast day of St. Andrew, held on November 30, is considered in Romania to be one of the most dangerous times of the year as far as vampires are concerned, along with the feasts of Easter and St. George's Eve. Today, in some villages of Bukovina and Moldova ancient rituals to protect against vampires are still performed by many individuals, families, and communities on the eve of St. Andrew's Day. The main weapon used against vampires and other evil spirits is garlic and it is often eaten in abundance, either as cloves or garlic sauce at dinner on November 29. Garlic cloves may also be placed at doors, windows, and chimneys as a symbolic mark to ward off vampires.

Anemia

Anemia is a medical condition that has long been associated with vampirism. The most common disorder of the red blood cells, anemia is believed to affect close to four million Americans. Anemia is not a disease but a condition characterized by below normal levels of hemoglobin in the red blood cells. Hemoglobin is the iron-containing pigment of the red blood cells that carries oxygen from the lungs to the tissues. A diet deficient in the mineral can cause anemia, but there are many different kinds of anemia, each with its own cause; the more severe types of this condition are often inherited. Symptoms typically include a pale complexion, fatigue, dizziness and fainting spells, and loss of appetite. In both folklore and fiction all these symptoms are also associated with the bite or attack of a vampire.

In centuries past it is easy to see why the presence of anemia in both animals and people was thought to suggest vampirism. When the symptoms appeared suddenly or after a death in the family, and especially if they were accompanied by nightmares, nervousness, and an aversion to sunlight, a person would be closely examined for the telltale bite marks of a vampire. Speed of examination was essential because it was thought that a victim would not be able to find the marks themselves, or even recognize their symptoms until the life blood had been drained out of them.

In animals, symptoms of anemia accompanied by bite marks could indicate the feeding of vampire bats. A need fire could be used to save animals suffering from blood loss. Humans could be saved by the removal of the vampire feasting on the victim and by bathing the wounds in holy water. In cases of emergency a red-hot iron bar could be used to apply the holy water. Garlic, strung around the victim's bed could also offer protection and purification. The possibility of anemia is discussed in Bram Stoker's *Dracula* when Lucy Westenra becomes ill. Later it is agreed that Lucy is not suffering from the loss of red blood cells or anemia but from the loss of whole blood.

This firm association between vampirism and anemia illustrates how folklore can successfully weave itself around medical fact. In addition, anemia tends to affect more women than men, due to the blood loss caused by menstruation, so the image of the vampire preying on vulnerable and weakened young women is reinforced.

See also: **DISEASE**

Angel

A vampire character cursed with a human soul, who is also Buffy's ex-boyfriend on TV's *Buffy the Vampire Slayer*, who featured in his own spin-off TV show called *Angel*.

Angel first aired on the WB network on October 5, 1999, and ran for five seasons until 2004. The series focused on the character of Angel (played by actor David Boreanaz), a vampire over two hundred years old. Angel was known as Angelus during his rampages across Europe. He was cursed with a soul, which gave him a conscience and a sense of guilt for centuries of murder and torture. The character left the successful 1997 television show *Buffy the Vampire Slayer* at the end of Season 3 to move to Los Angeles in search of redemption.

In *Buffy the Vampire Slayer* the relationship between Buffy and Angel is compelling but also tragic, as Buffy is a slayer and Angel is a vampire, yet they fall in love. They make love but this proves to be Angel's undoing as a curse placed on him by the family of a Gypsy girl he murdered in his horrible past ensured that not only would he feel the guilt and horror of what he had done, but if he ever found happiness as a result of having a soul, he would lose it again. So after consummating his love with Buffy he once again turns into a vicious vampire, and Buffy realizes that she needs to destroy the evil vampire with whom she has fallen in love. The stage is set for numerous confrontations. Angel's viciousness is gradually modified in the episodes and seasons that followed because his character proved extremely popular with viewers, and he went on to have his own series.

Angel proved to be as popular, and at times even more popular, than *Buffy the Vampire Slayer*. It had similar themes to Buffy – the agony and ecstasy of love, the ambiguity of good and evil within each person, and the difficult and dangerous journey to redemption – but it was far darker in its presentation of

The Element Encyclopedia of Vampires

these themes. Angel is a vampire demon and his story is one of doom and resurrection. Throughout the series he craves redemption more than anything else but his tragedy is that he can see no easy path to that end. He chooses harsh lesson after harsh lesson and suffers blinding guilt and pain because the path of true love and happiness leads him only to evil. There is, however, a glimmer of hope in that he never stops fighting the evil within him, in the belief that by paying off his karmic debt by saving the lives of others, he will eventually regain his full humanity.

See also: **TELEVISION**

Anima/Animus

See: **JUNG, CARL**

Animal Vampires

Animals have figured strongly in vampire lore all over the world. Sometimes animals, in particular wolves, bats, dogs, rats, owls, moths, and foxes, are controlled by vampires, and on rare occasions they become vampires themselves. Vampires can also feed on the blood of animals and achieve transformation into a variety of animal disguises. The Slavic tradition included vampire cats, dogs, rats, fleas, birds, frogs, and insects.

The vampires of folklore regarded animals as potential prey and would often attack a village's livestock to feed on blood. In fact, one of the first signs of a vampire attack was the sudden death of livestock. Virtually any animal could also become a vampire; it was said that horses, snakes, sheep, dogs, cats, wolves, birds, and even butterflies could return from the dead to intimidate the living. These animals transformed into vampires when they became victims of a vampire but they could also transform through interaction with the dead. For example, it was thought in many Eastern European countries that if a dog or cat jumped over a corpse the soul of the deceased could enter into the animal. Just as animals were feared, they were, however, also sometimes used to locate and combat vampires. Horses, for instance, were used in cemeteries to find the graves of the undead; black crows and black dogs were also believed to be trustworthy vampire hunters.

Vampire dogs

On a number of occasions stories of animal vampires have appeared. These stories fall into a different category altogether from stories of vampires changing into animal form. Perhaps the best reported are stories of so-called vampire dogs. In 1810 stories emerged from the borders between Scotland and England concerning blood-drained corpses of sheep. Whatever the creature was that attacked the sheep, it bit the necks of the animals and sucked the blood through their jugulars, often leaving the animal completely devoid of blood. It was not unusual for eight to ten animals a night to be slaughtered in this manner.

In 1874 another spate of killings occurred, this time in Cavan, Ireland, where up to 30 animals a night were allegedly killed by a vampire dog. The method was similar: their throats had bite marks and their blood was drained. The creature left behind long tracks, dog-like, yet larger and deeper than might have been expected from a dog. The menace spread to other counties and villages, while bands of angry farmers scoured the country-side, shooting at stray dogs everywhere. By April the monster was prowling the hamlet of Limerick, nearly one hundred miles from Cavan, only by now it was attacking humans as well. According to the *Cavan Weekly News* for April 17, several people were attacked and bitten by it. The paper went on to state that some of the victims had been placed subsequently into an insane asylum because they were *"labouring under strange symptoms of insanity."*

Another infamous case of animal vampirism took place at Croglin Grange, an estate in Cumberland, England, in the summer of 1875. According to reports a Miss Amelia Cranswell was lying awake in bed when a shadowy beast broke through her window. Her brothers, Edward and Michael, heard her screams and broke down her locked door to reach her. They found her lying unconscious in a pool of blood, with blood pouring from wounds to her neck and shoulders. They saw the beast loping across the lawn and pursued it, but were unable to catch it. Other women in the neighborhood were attacked by what was described as a "grisly, bony apparition."

In 1905 a similar spate of sheep killings occurred, this time near Badminton, England. Again, the animals were attacked at the throat, lost large amounts of blood, and no flesh was eaten. By December 1905 over 30 sheep had had the life blood sucked out of them in Kent, and a police sergeant in Gloucestershire who talked to a reporter for the London *Daily Mail* is on record as saying, *"I have seen two of the carcasses myself and can say definitely that it is impossible to be the work of a dog. Dogs are not vampires, and do not suck the blood of a sheep, and leave the flesh almost untouched."*

Once again, the killings stopped suddenly, and the creature responsible could not be found. This is an important characteristic of these types of incidents, which continue to be reported on rare occasions today. In 2007 and 2008, for example, Internet news sites and the tabloid press were full of tales of "vampire dogs" running amok in the town of Cuero, South Texas. When a local rancher, Phylis Canion, discovered the corpse of a road kill victim, she believed the cause to be an elusive vampire-like creature called a chupacabra or "goat-sucker." Her theory proved popular with local residents. However, Texan scientists who investigated the case, and the carcasses of three strange animals Canion had preserved in her freezer, said the animal was likely to be a coyote, possibly crossed with a gray fox.

Fiction and film

In fiction the vampire's command over the animal kingdom features strongly in Bram Stoker's *Dracula*. As early as chapter one, when Jonathan Harker is traveling to Dracula's castle, he finds himself suddenly surrounded by a ring of threatening wolves. In movies the vampire's ability to transform into different forms, in particular that of a wolf or bat, has remained an essential ingredient of the vampire story (although in recent years, in an attempt to make the vampire more believable vampires have been denied the ability to shape-shift). Anne Rice's novels, for example, allow the vampire to have supernatural qualities but not the ability to lose its human form. And during the last decade, as the vampire has become a more appealing figure to identify with in fiction and film, the blood of animals has been used as a substitute for the blood of humans.

See also individual animals.

Animated Corpse

According to the classic definition, a vampire is an animated corpse that survives by drinking the blood of the living. It also has a demonic nature and is dedicated to spreading its evil throughout the world. Bram Stoker added many more traits to the vampire through his fiction, and over time the myth has been explored and refined by numerous vampirologists, writers, and philosophers.

The body of a vampire is technically dead by human standards. It can therefore be said that a vampire's body is in a state of arrested decay, animated by a supernatural force or spirit residing in its corporeal form, and kept vital by the magical energy of blood. By contrast, living vampires are not animated corpses. They are, in fact, very much alive. They choose to practice vampiric acts, which may or may not include blood drinking, and to model their personalities on classic vampires, to satisfy an emotional need.

Anita Blake Vampire Hunter

Written by American author Laurell K. Hamilton, Anita Blake Vampire Hunter is a series of 16 erotic fantasy novels narrated by the title character, Anita Blake. The Anita Blake novels have become *New York Times* bestsellers.

The series began in 1993 with *Guilty Pleasures* and titles have followed almost every year since, with the latest, *Blood Noir*, published in 2008. In the series the main character, Anita, lives in a fictional St. Louis similar in many respects to the present day – except that vampires and shape-shifters are real, and everyone knows they are real. The books chart Anita's ongoing attempts to solve a variety of supernatural mysteries, her struggle to come to terms with her own abilities, and her difficulties navigating an increasingly complex series of paranormal, romantic, and political relationships.

Anne Rice's Vampire Lestat Fan Club

Founded in 1988, Anne Rice's Vampire Lestat fan club formed as a response to the widespread popularity of the vampire novels written by Rice. There are a number of Anne Rice fan clubs but the Lestat club is recognized as the official one. Anne Rice herself suggested the addition of the name "Lestat de Lioncourt" to the club since most of the public response to her novels seemed to be to that fictional vampire character. The club stayed active until 2000 and then dissolved for a number of reasons, despite the fact that it had several thousands of members all over the world. Then in 2007, in true vampire style, the Lestat club came back to life and started to accept members again.

See also: **RICE, ANNE**

Anomalous Biological Entities

Anomalous Biological Entity (ABE) is the name given either to the pets of aliens, or to creatures that are created by aliens as a result of experiments that have gone wrong. Some believe that the vampire-like creature known as "goat-sucker" or chupacabra, believed to be responsible for a series of attacks on livestock, is an ABE, and that the wounds on the dead animals indicate an alien presence.

ABEs have been linked to UFOs (Unidentified Flying Objects) or secret US biological experiments, and some people in UFO circles are convinced that there is a deliberate US government conspiracy to keep ABEs from public attention to prevent widespread panic. The source for this belief is a Puerto Rican journalist called Jorge Martin, who describes himself as a *"leading UFO expert."* To date Martin remains absolutely convinced that the US and Puerto Rican governments have captured two of the creatures. Martin also suggests that *"genetic manipulations"* caused by government experiments have produced vampire-like creatures. He cites the work of several genetic scientists and claims he has proof of their experiments.

The US and Puerto Rican authorities have dismissed Jorge Martin's arguments out of hand, and experiments conducted at the Autonomous National University of Nicaragua have revealed that a supposed chupacabra carcass was nothing more than a common dog.

Despite this, alleged sightings of chupacabra have continued. Since 1994 there have been more than 2,500 reported cases of animal mutilations in Puerto Rico attributed to the chupacabra, and the sightings have spread to Mexico as well as to Texas, Northern Florida, Chile, and Brazil.

In April 2006, *MosNews* reported that the chupacabra was spotted in Russia for the first time. Reports from Central Russia beginning in March 2005 tell of a beast that kills animals and sucks out their blood. Thirty-two turkeys were killed and drained overnight. Reports later came from neighboring villages when 30 sheep were found dead with their blood drained. The bizarre and unexplained nature of incidents such as this, which continue to be reported to this day, has restarted speculation about vampire-like creatures and the possibility of ABEs.

Anspach Werewolf

A chilling werewolf case with overtones of vampire lore, in that a rampaging wolf was thought to have been a recently dead person, who returned not in human form but in the form of a wolf.

In 1685 the inhabitants of Anspach (now Ansbach), Germany, were terrorized by a wolf that had allegedly killed a number of women, children, and domestic animals. The victims were found torn apart with their flesh partly eaten. The wolf/werewolf was thought to be the town's detested and recently deceased Burgomeister or master of the town. A great hunt was mounted and a wolf was chased, caught, and killed. The townsmen then took the wolf's carcass, dressed it in a flesh-colored suit, and adorned its head with a mask, wig, and beard, giving the dead beast the appearance of the Burgomeister. Later the carcass was displayed as a werewolf in a museum to prove that werewolves did indeed exist.

Anthesteria

Held in Athens and many other Ionian cities in spring time, the Anthesteria was an ancient Greek festival associated with the god Dionysus in which it was thought that the dead returned to the city from the afterlife and wandered in the streets. The festival was probably celebrated from before 1500 BC until the Christian purges of pagan rites under the later Roman emperors.

To placate the dead and ward off evil spirits, the Athenians made gifts of food and wine, chewed the leaves of the whitethorn, and smeared tar on their doors. Such customs were continued by the Romans and still linger on today in the superstitions surrounding such festivals as All Souls' Day.

Apollonius of Tyrana

Apollonius was a first-century AD philosopher whose life is recorded in *The Life of Apollonius of Tyrana* by Philostratus. The story could easily have been written by Bram Stoker himself. It tells of a good-looking young man, Menippus Lycius, a pupil of Apollonius, who falls in love with a *"good looking and extremely dainty"* foreign-looking girl. Apollonius, an ancient precursor of Van Helsing in *Dracula*, warns

Menippus that she is too good to be true and may be a vampire. Eventually, Apollonius gets a confession from the girl that she was fattening Menippus up in order to eat him, because she likes nothing better than to *"feed upon young and beautiful bodies"* with blood that is so pure and so strong. Through the centuries this story has influenced many vampire writers and was the basis of the famous poem by Keats, *Lamia*.

Apotropaics

A term used to describe methods of turning away evil or to stop a corpse becoming a revenant or a vampire. These methods are numerous and diverse and include decapitation or mutilation of the corpse; specific funeral rites, such as burying a corpse face down; placing objects, such as a small cross with the corpse; and providing food for the corpse so it will not find it necessary to feed off the living.

Although the methods used by different countries and cultures vary, most apotropaics fall into four general categories.

1. *Pacifying apotropaics* attempt to pacify the vampire and remove its urge to kill.
   The practice of placing food with the dead to prevent the corpse becoming restless can be found all over the world throughout history, as it was assumed that the world of the dead was similar to the world of the living. In medieval Germany a number of different granular substances were put into graves or strewn around the graveyard, including poppy seeds, sand, mustard seeds, oats, linen seeds, and carrot seeds.

Here it seems the vampire was compelled not to eat the seeds but to count them one at a time, as it was thought that vampires had a compulsion to count things.

In *Macedonian Folklore* by G. F. Abbot (1903), there is a case described where a vampire hunter lured a vampire (a vrykolakas) into a barn where there was a heap of millet grains. The vampire became so preoccupied with counting these grains that the vampire hunter was able to nail him to a wall without any resistance on the part of the vampire. This belief that vampires were compelled to count may have once been used as a folk remedy against witchcraft. It was thought that if you were chased by a witch and scattered rice on the ground, she or he would have to stop and pick up every grain because it was nourished by God. A similar practice to deter both witches and vampires was to lay a dead dog or cat on one's doorstep, as it was believed that the witch or vampire would have to stop and count every hair on the animal. In Northern Germany it was also thought that the undead were obsessed with untying knots; often nets were buried with the corpse to provide it with hours of apparently riveting knot-untying entertainment.

2. *Countering apotropaics* use a natural substance with similar but more powerful properties, such as garlic, to repel the vampire. In some parts of rural Romania, windows and thresholds were smeared with garlic juice or decked with garlic flowers to ward off vampires. Goods that were placed in graves to prevent or counter vampirism include coins, candles, and religious objects. Across medieval Europe, the cross, holy water, and other symbols of the Church were almost universally held to be powerful weapons against vampires.

Modern authors appear to be moving away from the use of religious objects to control or prevent vampires. Anne Rice's vampires, for example, have no fear of priests and can kill them if they desire. The consensus seems to be that the power of the symbol comes from the faith of the person using it, and occasionally from the belief of the vampire, rather than from any intrinsic power in the object itself. So if a person tries to use a cross against a vampire but has no belief, the cross will be useless. Religious symbols can be altered to reflect the belief system of the person using them. In other words, any symbol that a person truly believes is a source of light and goodness can manifest itself into a force powerful enough to drive away the undead.

3. *Restrictive apotropaics* work by constricting the vampire so it cannot move or leave its grave. It was thought that vampires do not like sharp objects because injuries weakened them. Therefore to ward off vampires it was thought advisable to place sharp objects like knives on the threshold of a house or under a pillow. Sharp objects were also placed in graves. The placement of sharp objects in graves, such as a sickle in Romania and Hungary, daggers made of iron, silver, and steel in Morocco, and iron knives and hair pins by the ancient Slavs may have also been to prevent the movement or swelling of the corpse. (In Eastern Prussia in the late nineteenth century the placing of a bowl of cold water under the board on which the body was lying and putting tin spoons on top may have been for the same reason.) In Eastern Serbia a small hawthorn peg was used. In the folklore archives of the

University of California at Berkeley, there is the recorded testimony of an immigrant from Eastern Germany stating that in his native land wolfsbane and silver knives were placed under mattresses to ward off the undead.

Thorns were sometimes put in the grave to prevent the dead from walking. In Romania there are reports of the head and the feet of a corpse being bound with thorny briars, or thorns simply being strewn in the casket. That way, if the corpse became a vampire and tried to rise from its grave, its shroud would get caught on the thorns and keep in firmly in its coffin. Among the Slavs the thorn was also inserted under the tongue of the corpse to prevent it sucking blood; such thorns (as well as nails and knives) have been found in skulls in medieval burial grounds. In addition to thorns and other sharp objects, the corpse was often prevented from returning by physical restraints. For example, the knees being tied together or the body tightly bound by ropes and placed in a constricted position.

4. *Lethal apotropaics* prevent vampires killing by "killing" them first. In Romania a needle or sharpened stake may be inserted in the navel or the heart to kill the vampire, or at least prevent it from returning. At one time it was the practice of Gypsies to make poles of such woods as ash, hawthorn, and juniper to drive them into suspected vampire graves. Sickles were also used to try to kill or prevent vampires. When the corpse is buried with the sickle over its neck, should the corpse become a vampire and try to rise from its grave the sickle will cut the head off. Another way of using the sickle involved piercing the corpse's heart with it, a custom probably inspired

by the use of the stake. A consecrated bullet fired through the coffin was also thought to kill vampires. Some vampire hunters used silver holy bullets to destroy the vampires they chased. A Serbian belief states that a silver coin inscribed with a cross, cut into quarters, loaded into a shotgun shell, and then fired at a vampire will kill it.

In some small localities in Eastern Europe, where much of the vampire traditions about apotropaics originate, vampire superstition is still rampant and sightings or claims of vampire attacks occur to this day. One notable example of this occurred in Romania, during February 2004, when the Toma family feared that one of their number had become a vampire. They dug up the corpse and tore out its heart to stop their relative returning from the dead.

Appearance of Vampires

The physical representations of vampires have changed drastically over the centuries. For most of us the image of the vampire is a clear and well-defined one that draws its inspiration from stage and screen adaptations. The male vampire is typically presented as a hypnotic and attractive aristocrat dressed in Victorian-style black evening wear with polished, black leather shoes and a black swirling silk cape. It was perhaps the 1920s actor Béla Lugosi who helped create the impression of a distinguished, well-dressed vampire in a cape. Female vampires are stereotyped as beautiful, deadly pale, irresistible women, often dressed in white.

The vampires of folklore are, however, very different from the creatures of fiction. In life they would have been like any other person, most typically a common peasant, who rarely traveled outside his or her community. But after death, according to European lore, they transformed into a terrible revenant that wore a shroud or burial clothes and carried with it the foul stench of dried blood and disease. The trigger for the transformation of their corpse could be anything from incorrect burial rites to being the first person to die of an illness that went on to kill many others. Although they were frequently described as grotesque, decayed, and bloated corpses with blood-smeared fangs, extended fingernails, and hyp-notic blood-shot eyes it is important to point out that this was not always the case. There are also numerous accounts of revenants appear-ing in much the same form as they did when they were alive, but this time their appetite for food, sex, and blood is insatiable.

In other cultures the vampire was only par-tially human. The African adze could change from a human into a hunchbacked dwarf. The Chinese chiang-shih had green fur. Then there were traditional vampires who were not human at all, such as the vampire butterflies of Asia and the deathly vampire watermelons of Yugoslavia. This last vampire form clearly demonstrates how the appearance of vampires simply cannot be categorized. Vampires it seems can also take on the form of fruits, insects, plants, and animals.

Somewhere between the hideous vampire of folklore and the image of the vampire pre-sented in fiction and film lies the Dracula of Bram Stoker's novel. The Count is described in gorgeous detail in the book's second chapter:

Within, stood a tall old man, clean shaven save for a long white moustache, and

clad in black from head to foot, without a single speck of colour about him anywhere…

His face was a strong, a very strong, aquiline, with high bridge of the thin nose and peculiarly arched nostrils, with lofty domed forehead, and hair growing scantily round the temples but profusely elsewhere. His eyebrows were very massive, almost meeting over the nose, and with bushy hair that seemed to curl in its own profusion. The mouth, so far as I could see it under the heavy moustache, was fixed and rather cruel-looking, with peculiarly sharp white teeth. These protruded over the lips, whose remarkable ruddiness showed astonishing vitality in a man of his years. For the rest, his ears were pale, and at the tops extremely pointed. The chin was broad and strong, and the cheeks firm though thin. The general effect was one of extraordinary pallor.

Hitherto I had noticed the backs of his hands as they lay on his knees in the firelight, and they had seemed rather white and fine. But seeing them now close to me, I could not but notice that they were rather coarse, broad, with squat fingers. Strange to say, there were hairs in the centre of the palm. The nails were long and fine, and cut to a sharp point.

In recent years the vampire of fiction and film has demonstrated a trend toward a nor-mal human appearance that allows it to fit into society and hunt its prey undetected. With the possible exception of fangs which are retractable and show only when they are feeding, they have no definable characteris-tics. Similarly, psychic vampires appear as totally normal human beings, apart from their insatiable desire to consume not flesh or blood but the "life energy" of their victims.

Today modern vampires have the freedom to assume any social appearance they choose, from a distinguished business man to a metal head wearing all black and leather. This is a world away from the tux and cape of the Hollywood vampire of the early twentieth century, but in its own way resembles that of the very first written accounts of alleged revenant vampires from Eastern European lore, who in life were ordinary people who did not stand out from the crowd. After death, or their transformation to a vampire, however, it was a different story entirely.

Aptyrgangy

See: **DRAUGR**

Apuleius

Apuleius was a second-century AD writer and philosopher and native of North Africa who is often cited as an early writer who recorded tales of vampires in *The Golden Ass*. One vampire story in *The Golden Ass* clearly illustrates the link that is often made between witchcraft and vampirism. It tells the story of two young friends called Aristomenes and Socrates. Socrates is pursued by a witch called Meroe and her sister Panthia. The witches seize Socrates and draw the blood out of him but he manages to escape and staunch the wound with a sponge. The next day, when Socrates stops on his journey with Aristomenes to drink some water, the sponge falls off. As soon

as the running water touches Socrates' lips he collapses and dies – an emaciated heap of skin and bone.

Archetypes

Those who follow the work and writings of twentieth-century psychiatrist Carl Jung may view vampire personality disorder or vampire-like behavior as part of a pattern of behaviors – or archetype – which is a product of universal primal instincts. In other words an archetype is a human experience which is based on universally shared developmental biology.

Archetypes include the child, the father, the mother, the lover, the teacher, and so on. Those who choose to develop their personality through the vampire archetype may be expressing their desire for power. There is a dark and a positive side to every archetype and the vampire is no exception. On the dark side the vampire survives and gains power by destroying or controlling others; on the positive side the vampire gains power through renewal or transformation. The vampire archetype may also suggest society's tendency to project away from ourselves aspects of being human that we wish to deny or eradicate.

See also: **AUTO-VAMPIRISM; JUNG, CARL**

Ardisson, Victor

Dubbed the "Vampire of Muy," in southern France, Victor Ardisson was arrested in 1901 for violating graves. Ardisson differed from other alleged vampires in that he was not a murderer. He was, however, a necrophiliac, digging up corpses – often women he had known in life – in order to satisfy himself with them, which led people to believe that there was a vampire in the area. Ardisson was eventually caught and admitted to being the Vampire of Muy. The courts found him irresponsible for his actions, so he was sent to an asylum for the insane.

See also: CRIME; NECROPHILIA

Armenia

An ancient land in Eastern Asia Minor situated between Russia and Turkey and the first land to make Christianity a state religion. Armenia is an area of colorful history but also of constant strife. For most of the twentieth century it was part of the Soviet Union, gained its independence in 1991.

Among the many stories of vampires in Armenia the most well known is an account in an 1854 text by Baron August von Haxthausen of the Dakhanavar. This creature from the mountains of Ultmish Alotem would suck the blood from the soles of the feet of anyone who tried to cross its territory. According to folklore, two travelers managed to outwit the monster by sleeping with their feet under each other's head. The vampire, confused by a creature with two heads and no feet, left the region muttering about the injustice. This tale undoubtedly reassured all those that heard it that being quick witted could provide protection against vampires.

Art

Vampires offer a rare blend of seduction and danger and it is no surprise that artists have long been attracted to them. The earliest vampire known is that depicted upon a prehistoric Assyrian bowl, some 2,400 years old, where a man copulates with a vampire-like entity whose head has been severed from the body. Here the threat of cutting off her head is supposed to frighten the vampire away. Pictures of animal/human hybrids thirsting for human blood have also been found on cave walls in prehistoric sites discovered in Spain, France, Australia, and South Africa, in the tombs of the Egyptian pharaohs, in Chinese drawings on porcelain vessels, and in sculptures produced by the ancient civilizations of Central and South America. It wasn't, however, until widespread interest in vampires emerged (due in part to the vampire frenzy reported in eighteenth-century Europe) that the image of the vampire began to play a more significant role in Western art. Initially the vampire was first depicted as a decaying monster that spread disease, death, and evil, but over time artistic depictions of vampires evolved into the sexual deviate, the anti-hero, the hero, and even into the ordinary human being who is simply misunderstood.

Today, it could be said that artists are largely responsible for shaping our image of the vampire. There are many forms of artistic expression that illustrate the vampire tradition; some of these have psychological intent but others are more commercial. The artistic depiction of the vampire on mass-market paperbacks and comics, as well as in movie publicity shots, has played a huge role in establishing the popular image of the vampire as terrifying but hypnotic and sensual. The dark and perverse images and grotesque erotica of English artist Aubrey Beardsley (1872–98) are considered to be superior examples of Gothic, vampire-inspired art that illustrated books and stories. Lurid images of the bloodsucker attracting its prey, a dark figure lurking in the shadows or a body lying in a coffin are all examples of these familiar images. Just as the vampire is after eternal life, our fascination with the image of the vampire means they will continue to be seen in mass-market books, comics, and movies.

Subtler approach

A more subtle approach is favored by artists who prefer to focus on the psychological aspects of vampirism. One of the best-known landmark paintings of a vampire was Norwegian Edvard Munch's *Love and Pain*, also known as *Vampire* (1894). In the painting the lovers, locked in their dark and deadly embrace, evoke love's paradox as a source of tenderness and pain. *Vampire* remains popular today and is probably Munch's most famous work other than *The Scream*. In November 2008 after being in private hands for 70 years it sold for a staggering $38 million at Sotheby's, New York, setting a record for the artist. This was by no means the first depiction of a vampire, but earlier works were mostly engravings or ink drawings, and Munch's brooding work depicting a beautiful red-haired woman bending over a man's neck represents one of the early paintings of what we consider the modern-day vampire. Today, it remains a source of inspiration for vampire fantasy art and Goth-inspired art.

The Vampire (1897) by Philip Burne-Jones depicts an alluring female vampire crouched over a male victim and this painting is thought to have inspired a poem of the same name by Rudyard Kipling. Other famous paintings of vampires include Istvan Csok's 1893 study of Elizabeth Báthory and a study titled *The Vampires* in 1907, and *Vampire Nightmare* by German painter Max Klinger (1857–1920).

See also: FILMS; LITERATURE; POETRY; STAGE; TELEVISION

Asanbosam

A vampire from African folklore known by the Ashanti of southern Ghana and by people in areas of the Ivory Coast and Togo, the asanbosam is thought to live in the depths of the forests where it is often encountered by hunters. It has a human shape, and can take the form of a man, woman, or child but its teeth are made of iron and it has hooks for feet. Anyone who walks by a tree from where it dangles will be scooped up and stored among the high branches. When required, blood will be drawn from the victim's thumb to feed the vampire.

See also: **AFRICA**

Asema

The asema is a kind of living vampire from Brazilian folklore that is often confused with witches and witchcraft. It is, however, a vampire that frequently takes the form of an old man or old woman during daylight hours. When darkness falls it assumes the form of a blinding ball of light which travels over the land in search of prey. Once it has found a victim, the asema takes human form again in order to feed. When it has drained the blood of its sleeping victim it once again takes the form of a light ball to return home, where it leads an apparently normal human life. In some stories the asema can take off its skin to become a ball of light. In order to feed it can take its human form or remain as a ball, but if it remains in this form it is not blood that it feeds on but the life force or energy of its sleeping victims.

The color of the light ball is believed to be very significant. A pale blue light is not considered dangerous as long as the sleeper is not preyed upon for long periods of time. A deep red is thought to be more dangerous, and more deadly still are balls of dark blue or aquamarine light.

Certain precautions against attack by an asema could be taken, for example, eating herbs such as garlic that "taint the blood" and render it unpalatable to the vampire. Another remedy is to place small white stones or seeds outside one's front door. Like Eastern European vampires the asema were thought to be obsessive about counting, and it was believed they would not enter a house until everything had been counted and arranged tidily into piles. Whoever found the skin of the asmea had it in their power, and the skin could usually be found in the house of the human it inhabited in its human form. The best way to destroy the skin, and the vampire, was to burn it and scatter the ashes so that it could not reassemble.

Ash

A tree often used in Europe, especially in Prussia and along the Baltic coast, for the creation of stakes used in the destruction of vampires. According to the Roman writer Pliny the Elder, all evil things feared ash-wood and according to Norse myth Yggdrasil, the tree which bound together heaven, earth, and hell, was made of ash and the wood was therefore sacred. The name probably originated from the Norse *asha* (man) in the belief that Odin, the great god, used it to create humankind.

Ashes

In vampire lore, the ashes of the burned corpse or organs of a suspected vampire, mixed in a drink and taken as a medicine, were thought to have the power to heal victims of vampires. In some areas the smoke of vampire organs was believed to ward off evil and villagers would pass through the smoke to acquire protection. In Slavic lore eating the ashes of a burned caul was thought to heal victims of vampire attacks.

One Romanian account from the late nineteenth century tells the story of a crippled bachelor from Cujmir who died. Soon after his death his relatives fell ill. Some died and others felt their legs weakening. This association with withered legs suggested to the relatives that the crippled man was to blame, so they dug his body up. They found the body gorged with blood and curled up in the corner of the grave. They cut it open, removed the heart and burned the organs to ashes. These ashes were mixed with water and given to all the relatives who were weak or ill, including the dead man's sister. All recovered their health.

When consumption (tuberculosis) took hold in a family, some people in the outlying areas of New England in the eighteenth and nineteenth centuries would open the graves of their deceased relatives, looking for signs that they considered out of the ordinary such as liquid or "fresh" blood in the heart. The heart would be cut from the body and burned to ashes. Often the ashes were administered, in water or some medicine, to sick family members. The belief supporting these practices seemed to be that there was some sort of evil, perhaps a vampire, residing in one of the bodies, which was draining the life from others in the family.

Aspen

Believed to be the wood used to make Christ's cross, aspen in folklore was thought to protect against all evil things, including vampires. In the Middle Ages it was the wood of choice to make stakes to destroy vampires, and branches of aspen laid on the graves of vampires were thought to stop them rising up at night.

Assier, Adolphe d'

Member of the Bordeaux Academy of Sciences and author of *Posthumous Humanity* (1887), which suggested that a vampire attack could be explained by the presence of an astral body. According to d'Assier, the "inert corpse" of a vampire stayed in its coffin while the astral body left the coffin to feed on the living. The blood it consumed, or rather its quintessence, would then flow from the astral body (via an astral umbilical cord) to the moribund corpse, sustaining its continued existence.

Assyria

Ancient Mesopotamian empire believed by some vampirologists to be the birthplace of the vampire tradition (other suggestions include Babylonia, Egypt, India, and Ireland). Assyrian traditions had a complicated ranking of spirits, especially evil ones. Perhaps the most feared classes of Assyrian evil spirits were the ekimmu and the utukku. The name ekimmu translates literally as "that which is snatched away," suggesting a violent or sudden death; the utukku were believed to be wandering spirits. Exactly what the distinctions between the two were are unclear and there may have been very little difference. Some experts believe that the utukku were ghosts of individuals who had died before their time, which made them bad tempered and violent, as well as indecisive, weak, and insubstantial spirits, whereas the ekimmu are regarded as more muscular and solid revenants.

It was in Assyria that early writings, inscriptions, and incantations about the undead were first uncovered. One of these, dating back to 2000 BC, was translated in *The Cuneiform Inscriptions of Western Asia*, published by Sir Henry Rawlinson and Edwin Morris in 1866.

The phantom, child of heaven,
Which the gods remember,
The Innin [hobgoblin] prince
Of the lords
The …
Which produces painful fever,
The vampire which attacks man,
The Uruku multifold
Upon humanity,
May they never seize him!

Astral Body

Various esoteric traditions talk about the different levels of consciousness and existence that each person has. Some people think of these different aspects as "subtle bodies" or selves that exist in a parallel plane but are all part of a larger consciousness. A commonly recognized "extra" self is the astral body, also known as an energy body or the vehicle of a person's life energy.

The word "astral" is derived from the Greek for "star." The astral body can also be called a double or doppelgänger, because it is thought to be a duplicate of the physical body. The astral body exists on the astral plane, also known as the astral realm, astral world, or astral sphere, and in metaphysical terminology the astral plane is contiguous in space, if not in time, with the material world. The astral realm is the one that the spiritual part of a person or astral body enters during periods of sleep, under the action of anesthetics or drugs, by accident when a person is unconscious, or immediately after death. The astral realm is not normally visible to ordinary sight, yet it is regarded as the proper dwelling place of a person's spiritual body. As the astral body survives long after the physical body's death it can become a ghost, spirit, or vampire.

According to shamans, the astral body or second self resembles the physical body but is made up of a subtle field of shining and flexible light that encases the body, visible only by a psychically sensitive person. It is thought that when you are sleeping the astral body can separate from the physical body, which results in flying dreams, out-of-body experiences, and the experience of disorientation experienced if you wake suddenly and the astral body hasn't had time to line up with the physical one. Driven by emotions, passions, and desires, the astral body is believed to be a bridge between the physical brain and a higher level of mind.

According to some occultist explanations of vampirism, the corpse does not rise from the grave but instead sends an astral double out to do the work of bringing blood back to the grave to sustain the vampire's corpse. The astral vampire has the ability to shape-shift, and to pass under doors or enter a person's house through a keyhole. There is also a belief that there are evil beings in the astral plane and they can take over someone's astral body and compel a person to perform vampirism. Similar to this belief is the idea that a strong enough evil entity from the astral plane can enter a corpse and create a vampire by feeding it with blood. Noted spiritualist Adolphe d'Assier had a different theory. He argued that vampires were astral beings that drank blood, and by some process of spiritual blood transfusion then transferred the blood back to the corpse.

Modern occultists suggest that a psychic vampire, especially one responsible for night-time attacks, may be an astral body or astral vampire.

Astral Vampire

According to occultists "astral vampire" is the term used to describe the spirit shape or out-of-body projection of a corpse or a living vampire. In other words they are a kind of thought form or astral body. Vampire researcher Vincent Hillyer suggested that an astral body might be a vampire in cases of the restless dead. According to his theory, the astral body of a corpse might be able to project itself from the corpse, feed on the living, and return the blood to the corpse to sustain it. Hillyer developed a unique theory, called the "hemolytic factor," to explain how the spirit vampire could draw blood from the living. This theory revolves around the process of hemolysis, or the destruction of red corpuscles which leads to the release of hemoglobin. According to this theory, the astral vampire penetrates the victim's aura and physical body, and because the vampire is in need of blood and has few red blood cells, the process of hemolysis occurs. This allows the vampire to suck up the red corpuscles in the victim's blood. These are then taken back to the corpse and infused into it.

Modern occultists suggest that both an intentional and unintentional psychic vampire may be an astral body or astral vampire.

Aswang

Perhaps one of the most complex and confusing vampire figures, the aswang originates in the Philippines. The traits of the aswang differ according to the lore of the different islands, but most typically they are female and are believed to be a beautiful maiden or an old woman by day and a flying, ferocious creature at night. The nighttime transformation may take place with the use of special oils and potions. The aswang can marry, live in a home and have children, and is a seemingly normal human being in daylight hours. When night falls, however, the creature follows the crying kikik (or kakak) – night birds that lead the creature to the houses of potential victims. In some traditions the kikik are a type of aswang themselves.

The aswang feeds on blood and it has a long, hollow, thin tongue that it can insert through the cracks in the roofs of the victim's house. For reasons unknown the aswang prefers to feed on people, especially babies and children, who sleep on the middle rather than the edge of mats. After feeding the creature looks bloated. At first light the creature returns to its human form.

Salt is considered protection against aswang of many kinds, especially the aswang mannannagel, a blood-sucking creature with a tongue that can suck a fetus out of a womb. In some remote areas, a small bowl of salt is left near the cribs of sleeping babies to protect them, or a small bag of salt may be tied around the neck of children while they sleep. Garlic rubbed under the armpits is also thought to prevent an aswang attack. Pregnant women can protect themselves by wearing necklaces made of bullets and by smearing coal and dust on their abdomens.

Other aswang species

In folklore from other islands the aswang more closely resembles the traditional vampire in that is no longer a living person but the spirit of someone who has died violently or in childbirth. This entity is said to look like a dragon with wings and a long nose, and through this nose it extends its thin and spiky tongue to drink the blood of its victims. It typically rests during daytime but when night falls, somehow sensing its victims' fragile or more vulnerable energy, it will fly to the roofs of houses where children, the unwell, or the aged are sleeping. Another type of aswang can separate the upper half of its body from the lower. The torso can then grow wings and fly

in search of sleeping pregnant women. Once it has found one, it will rest its long, pointed, hollow tongue on the stomach of the woman and, without waking her, it will slowly draw out the life and the blood of the fetus. Once the creature has satisfied itself it will fly away and reconnect with its lower body. This horrific act can be stopped, however, if the unattached lower body is found and salt is sprinkled onto it. The aswang cannot abide salt and will be unable to reassemble itself, and so will wither and perish.

In some cases the Filipinos refer to the aswang as *tik tik* or *wak wak*. This is the name for a small nocturnal bird that resembles an owl. Some superstitions say that this bird is not an aswang but the familiar of the aswang. It does not appear to be as malevolent as its master though as it has been known to give a warning to humans with its screeching. Other superstitions confuse matters even further by suggesting that the tik tik is the spirit of the dead aswang.

Another curious aswang species found in the folklore of the Tagalog people, who live near the main island of Luzon, is called the mandurago. This vampire is a beautiful female who appears lifelike but is dead. It is said that her body is kept youthful and fresh by an evil spirit that animates her.

Aswang tales today

To this day tales of the aswang are used by Filipino parents and nannies to discipline children. In the 1950s belief in this creature was used by the American-backed government of President Magsaysay against a group of insurgents. Familiar with the aswang legend and aware that many Filipinos believed it,

American CIA operatives spread rumors that an aswang had preyed on people in a village where the insurgents were active. After waiting a few days for the rumors to spread, government troops silently kidnapped one of the insurgents, killed him, punctured his neck, hung him up by his feet, and bled him dry. The drained corpse was then placed on a busy pathway where it would be found. The plan worked instantly and the insurgents left right away. Many civilian villagers also left as they were too frightened to live in the area.

In the late 1980s researcher Norine Dresser found that tales of the aswang were very much alive in the Filipino community in California. In late 2004 16-year-old Tata Porras, of Barangay Cabuling in Tantangan, claimed that his 14-year-old brother Michael had been attacked by an aswang, which he said took the form of a big black dog with red, glowering eyes. According to Porras he and his younger brother were sleeping in a small makeshift hut near their rice field one evening, guarding their farm ducks, when the incident happened. A local Californian radio station carried the story on air; many listeners refused to believe it and dismissed it as a figment of the boy's imagination. Others, however, did believe the tale, citing personal accounts and stories they had heard from their friends and relatives living in the allegedly aswang-infested localities in the southern Philippines.

Attack

How a vampire attacks its victim depends on the type of vampire it is. The vampires of folklore that were believed to be revenants, or dead bodies that had come back to life, were thought to suck blood from humans or animals to keep their bodies from decomposing. They do this by biting the jugular vein in their victim's neck or veins in other parts of the body, something that is often referred to as the "kiss" of a vampire. Once bitten, the victim transforms into a vampire who must then also seek out human or animal prey to survive. Vampire folklore contains a huge variety of different methods of attacking humans and animals, from the traditional bite in the neck to an extended tongue that can suck the fetus out of a mother's womb, to the passing on of an infection or contagion.

Dopamine

The attacks of revenants are violent and unsubtle, but the vampire of fiction attacks his or her prey in a subtle, secret way, thus avoiding detection. These vampires are often described as highly intelligent and privileged members of society. Unlike revenants they live in a mansion or castle, sleep in a coffin by day, have a heightened sense of smell, are allergic to daylight, and may be centuries old. These vampires do not simply bite a victim at random. Instead they carefully nurture and seduce their victims, teaching them the ways of the vampire until they are simply unable to resist or escape. They do, however, eventually bite their victims in much the same way as revenants, using their teeth and body to drink from the veins of their victims.

Some vampirologists speculate that when vampires drain their victim's blood, dopamine, the feel-good chemical in the body, is released so that the victim feels no pain. According to vampire author Anne Rice, the process can *"only be described in human terms as a kind of falling in love."* On the other hand, sanguinarians (people who have a physical thirst, perceived need, or craving for blood) prefer to drink blood safely and with the willing consent of a donor. They don't typically bite the necks of people or animals to obtain blood. They drink it from a glass instead.

Psychic attack

The way a psychic vampire attacks is completely different to that of the traditional blood-sucking vampire. These vampires feed on a person's energy rather than their blood. Some psychic vampires can drain a person's energy through the power of touch or sometimes by simply being in the same room as their victim. Other psychic vampires attack their victims at night using the power of thought. In some instances the sensation is so strong that the victim fears they might be having a heart attack. Through the fear that the person gives off the psychic vampire takes energy, and when the person wakes the next morning they will feel drained, tired, depressed, and nauseous. Headaches, muscle tension, dizziness, and disorientation are also common. These attacks can go on nightly, but psychic vampires can also attack at any time of the day. A very strong psychic vampire can attack a person from great distances as well.

See also: **BITE; PROTECTION; TRANSFORMATION**

Australia

Inhabited since prehistoric times by Aborigines, who believed in the concept of the restless dead, Australia is the Pacific island continent. Although vampires do not play a huge part in Aboriginal folklore, a number of vampire-like creatures were feared, most especially the *mrart*, the ghost of a dead person who attacked victims at night and dragged them away from campsites. In some tribes there also existed a belief in a vampire-like being called the yara-ma-yha-who. This creature was described as a little red man just over three feet tall, with a large head and mouth and suckers for fingers and toes. It lived in the top of wild fig trees and did not hunt its prey, preferring to wait until unsuspecting victims took shelter in the tree and then pounce on them. It had no teeth but could drain the blood from the victim, rendering it helpless, before returning later to eat its prey whole. After all this exertion the creature would take a nap. On waking it would vomit, and in some cases the person would come out of its mouth still alive. Some people could be captured and "eaten" over and over again, until they shrank and started to resemble the yara-ma themselves.

Many Australian tribes considered blood to be the best remedy for a sick and weakly person. The Aborigines may also have believed that the corpse had a kind of astral body that could inhabit another person's body or live in the bush and attack its living relatives. To prevent this happening, corpses were often weighed down in their graves or their legs were broken.

Austria

Austria is a country in Europe that is rich in vampire lore, and reports from Austrian-controlled Serbia prepared by Austrian officials between 1725 and 1732 may have first introduced the word "vampire" into European consciousness. "Seen and Discovered" by a number of Austrian officers is an incredible document describing horrific events in a village near Belgrade in 1732. It's certainly worth reproducing extracts of the original here:

> After it had been reported that in the village of Medvegia the so-called vampires had killed some people by sucking their blood, I was, by high degree of a local Honorable Supreme Command, sent there to investigate the matter thoroughly along with officers detailed for that purpose and two subordinate medical officers, and therefore carried out and heard the present inquiry in the company of the captain of the Stallath Company of haiduks [a type of soldier], Gorschiz Hadnack, the standard-bearer and the oldest haiduk of the village, as follows: about five years ago a local haiduk by the name of Arnold Paole

> broke his neck in a fall from a haywagon. This man had during his lifetime often revealed that, near Gossowa in Turkish Serbia, he had been troubled by a vampire, wherefore he had eaten from the earth of the vampire's grave and had smeared himself with the vampire's blood, in order to be free from the vexation he had suffered. In 20 or 30 days after his death some people complained that they were being bothered by this same Arnold Paole; and in fact four people were killed by him.

> In order to end this evil, they dug up this Arnold Paole 40 days after his death – this on the advice of Hadnack, who had been present at such events before; and they found that he was quite complete and undecayed, and that fresh blood had flowed from his eyes, nose, mouth, and ears; that the shirt, the covering, and the coffin were completely bloody; that the old nails on his hands and feet, along with the skin, had fallen off, and that new ones had grown; and since they saw from this that he was a true vampire, they drove a stake through his heart, according to their custom, whereby he gave an audible groan and bled copiously.

> Thereupon they burned the body the same day to ashes and threw these into the grave. These people say further that all those who were tormented and killed by the vampire must themselves become vampires. Therefore they disinterred the above-mentioned four people in the same way. Then they also add that this Arnold Paole attacked not only the people but also the cattle, and sucked out their blood. And since the people used the flesh of such cattle, it appears that some vampires are again present here, inasmuch as, in a period of three months, 17 young and old people died, among them some who, with no previous illness, died in two or at the most three days. In addition, the haiduk Jowiza reports that his step-daughter, by name

of Stanacka, lay down to sleep 15 days ago, fresh and healthy, but at midnight she started up out of her sleep with a terrible cry, fearful and trembling, and complained that she had been throttled by the son of a haiduk by the name of Milloe, who had died nine weeks earlier, whereupon she had experienced a great pain in the chest and became worse hour by hour, until finally she died on the third day.

The document goes on to describe how the graveyard was visited again in order to open suspicious-looking graves and to examine the bodies. Up to 10 corpses were found to be in condition of vampirism. The heads of these corpses were cut off and burned along with their bodies. It is difficult to discount this report as it was signed by no fewer than five officers in the army of Charles VI, Emperor of Austria, and three of them were doctors familiar with corpses. It's worth noting also that this report was written five years after the Arnold Paole case, following investigation into this fresh outbreak of vampirism. It clearly shows that Paole was believed to be the original cause of these later events.

In 1755 the town of Olmutz in Austria was also the scene of several vampire reports, and in the region of Styria there were also two cases of reported vampire killings. One of these was the case of Countess Elga, which first appeared in a 1909 edition of the *Occult Review*. Another involved an attack by a psychic vampire and occurred late in the nineteenth century. In this case a cruel and greedy man had gained control of his niece's inheritance. When the niece and her husband secured the services of a lawyer the man vowed revenge. The lawyer fell ill and the uncle, whose health had been failing previously, became robust and

strong. However, when the lawyer eventually died and the uncle achieved his goal of thwarting his niece's attempt to reclaim what was rightfully hers, the man had a relapse and died because this source of strength was gone.

See also: **ALP**; **GERMANY**; **PAOLE, ARNOLD**

Auto-vampirism

The practice of drinking one's own blood, for sexual pleasure or as a form of self-mutilation. Auto-vampirism is classed as a symptom of clinical vampirism, sometimes called Renfield's syndrome or vampire personality disorder. In the 1960s the Jungian analyst Robert McCully, of the Medical University of South Carolina, studied and documented in the *Journal of Nervous and Mental Disease* (1964) a case of auto-vampirism, where a young boy drank his own blood. The subject was examined and underwent numerous medical tests. McCully described how the boy would cut veins on his body while looking at himself in a mirror. He would save the blood in a cup and drink it. Sometimes he would force the blood to spurt out in such a way that he could catch it and drink it in his mouth and this gave him erotic pleasure. When he cut and drank he became sexually excited and had an orgasm. He sometimes fantasized about drinking the blood of other boys, although he never did.

The boy underwent an ink-blot test, also known as a Rorschach test, and was asked to make a series of drawings. The results of the test suggested that he was depressed, lonely, and underdeveloped emotionally, although he was well developed intellectually. He was not delusional but aware of his behavior. McCully tried to explain the case from a Jungian perspective by relating it to ancient myths associated with blood drinking: the ancient Tibetan Buddhists drank blood to help them manage and control their emotions, and the boy drank his blood to compensate for his emotional underdevelopment by participating in the kinds of acts that allowed him to drop his emotional restraints and become bound to larger forces. McCully went on to theorize that the vampire image has been an archetypal image since the dawn of history, representing both transformation and survival at the expense of others.

It is important to point out here that auto-vampirism is not seen as providing sanguinarians with any energy, since the energy is just being recycled back into the system of the person. In fact, the practice is frowned upon by many in the blood-drinking community, who see it as a destructive act that provides no benefit.

Awakening

A term used by vampirologists to describe the physical and mental changes or transformation that occurs when someone awakens to their latent vampire nature. These changes, which sound fairly similar to average teenage feelings and behavior, often include an increased sensitivity to light (particularly sunlight) and a growing affinity for night and darkness. Many experience acute feelings of isolation, fatigue, and alienation during this process, as their changing nature distances them increasingly from their "normal" family and friends.

Aztecs

The vampiric idea that blood equals life played a strong part in the beliefs of the Aztecs, in what is now Mexico. It was thought that drinking the blood or eating the hearts of enemies provided warriors with immortality. The ancient Aztecs also had their own version of the vampire-like person/evil spirit found in many parts of the world. These were the cihuateteos, women who died in childbirth and returned to terrorize the living by drinking the blood of young children and seducing young men. They practiced magic and in true vampire style shunned sunlight because it could destroy them.

Awaken to darkness on this place we call Earth,
One vampire's bite brings another one's birth.
A vampire wakes with blood thirsty needs
On the warm rich sensation he feels when he feeds.
He stalks in the night like a disastrous beast,
And what once was alive will soon be deceased.

Victoria Boatwright

Babylonia

Babylonia was an ancient Mesopotamian empire centered on the city of Babylon in modern Iraq that flourished in the third millennium BC. The Babylonians developed a complex and elaborate mythology with a vast array of blood-sucking demonic and spirit hierarchies. The earliest inhabitants of Babylonia were the Sumerians, who believed in the existence of ghosts, demons, and devils; vampire-like creatures, such as the utukku and ekimmu, were later added to the supernatural hierarchy. Of these two, the ekimmu – the spirit of an unburied person or a person who had died violently – was the most feared because it hunted without mercy, and could only be dispelled by exorcism.

It was Babylonia that produced what may have been the first depiction of a vampire, found on an ancient cylinder seal, and some experts, taking their lead from vampire historian Montague Summers, believe that the origins of the vampire tradition, or the closest equivalent of the vampire, may be traced back to ancient Babylonia. Other experts disagree. They argue that the evidence for this – the last few lines on tablet 12 of the famous Babylonian *Epic of Gilgamesh* – was mistranslated by scholars keen to push the text in the direction of a vampire interpretation.

The Epic of Gilgamesh is, perhaps, the oldest written story in the world. It dates back to somewhere between 2740 and 2500 BC and is about the adventures of the historical King of Uruk. At the end of tablet 12 there is an account of the state of the person who has died alone and unburied. Instead of suggesting, as was previously thought, that the spirits of those who were unburied were con-demned to roam the earth, more recent translations and detailed study of the context of the Gilgamesh story make it clear that the line *"The spirit resteth not in the earth"* should be translated to mean that those who died uncared for (i.e., the ekimmu) roamed restlessly not on earth but in the Netherworld, the abode of the dead. Thus, while the idea of blood-sucking vampires did exist in ancient Babylonia, it may not have been as prominent or as influential as has previously been suggested.

Bad Lord Soulis

A member of the de Soulis family, who occupied Hermitage Castle in Roxboroughshire in the Scottish borders sometime between the early thirteenth to mid-fourteenth century, Bad Lord Soulis was reputed to be an evil man with vampiric tendencies. It is not clear which Lord Soulis carried this evil reputation, but many believe it was Sir William de Soulis, who was a contemporary of Robert the Bruce (1274–1329).

With the help of a blood-drinking familiar he called Robin Redcap – which had some similarities with redcaps that were thought to haunt the region – Bad Lord Soulis allegedly kidnapped, tortured, and murdered many people, including children in Hermitage Castle. Tradition also states that he used the blood of his victims in diabolic rites that may have included blood drinking. Eventually, local people realized what was going on and stormed the castle. They captured Soulis, took him up to Nine Stane Rigg, a stone circle crowning a nearby hill top, wrapped him in lead and boiled him in a brass cauldron.

> *The Boiling of Bad Lord Soulis*
>
> *On a circle of stone they placed the pot,*
> *On a circle of stones but barely nine,*
> *They heated it up red and fiery hot,*
> *Till the burnished brass did glimmer and*
> *shine.*
> *They rolled him up in a sheet of lead,*
> *A sheet of lead for a funeral pall,*
> *They plunged him in the cauldron red,*
> *and melted him lead bones and all.*

Some versions of the story say that Soulis was wrapped in lead to prevent his master the Devil from rescuing him; others say it was to stop his corpse returning from the dead to terrorize the countryside again. Other traditions state that the local people finally petitioned King Robert to *"dispose of him."* The Bruce, already extremely annoyed at the stories he had heard about the happenings at Hermitage Castle, readily agreed saying, *"Boil him if you must, but let me hear no more of him."* Locals took the king's words as marching orders.

There were no sightings of his corpse but to this day there are sightings of the ghost of Bad Lord Soulis wandering in the castle. Reportedly, the ghost of Soulis is a malevolent specter, whose nebulous meanderings are often accompanied by demonic laughter and the heart-rending sobs of children echoing along the crumbling corridors.

Bad Signs/Omens

In many parts of medieval Europe it was said that if a person was "born under a bad sign" they would become vampires after they had died. In many cases these bad signs were simply birth defects or abnormalities. It is important to remember that people had little or no scientific or medical knowledge in this period, and so anything that appeared ugly or out of the ordinary was regarded with suspicion as an evil omen. In Romania, for instance, "bad signs" believed to predispose a person to vampirism after death included being born with a split lower lip, a tail at the base of the spine, fused fingers and toes, excessive hair, a large birthmark, teeth, or an extra nipple. Writing in 1639 two English writers, James Shirley and George Chapman, described a newborn believed to be destined for vampirism in *Chabot, Admiral of France, V, 2:*

> *He was born with teeth in his head … and hath one toe on his left foot crooked and in the form of an eagle's talon … What should I say? Branded, marked and designated from his birth for shame and obloquy which appeareth further, by a mole under his right ear, with only three witches hairs in it; strange and ominous predictions of nature.*

A fire was lit in the town square, and the poor baby was taken there and the soles of his feet placed in the flames in the belief that this would prevent him walking when he grew up, and becoming a vampire later in life or after death.

If a child was born with a red caul, a thin membrane that covers the face of newborns, this was also considered to be a bad sign in Eastern European tradition. However, it wasn't just babies born with red cauls or birth defects that were regarded as potential vampires; in some remote country districts any person who was deformed was treated with suspicion, especially if the deformity was particularly unsightly. Adults with birth marks on their faces were often suspected of being vampires. Cholera outbreaks were regarded as a sign of vampires spreading disease and death, and if proper burial rites were not given to epileptics it was widely thought they would return from the dead as vampires.

Although many "signs" of vampirism were based on medical ignorance, a number of others were based simply on rumors and superstition. In many Southern European countries, for instance, people with blue eyes were considered more likely to become vampires, as were people born with red hair, based on the belief that Judas Iscariot who betrayed Jesus was thought to have had red hair. *It is believed in Serbia, Bulgaria and Romania,*" wrote English author Jon Wodroephe in 1623, *"that there are certain red [haired] vampires who are the children of Judus, and that these, the foulest of the foul, kill their victims with one bite or kiss which drains the blood if it were a single drought.*"

Vampires might also be traced to the seventh son born to the seventh son in a family, and to the actions of mother during pregnancy. For example, if a black cat crossed the path of a pregnant women or, worse still, if she conceived her child outside the bonds of marriage, the child she bore would surely become a vampire.

Outsiders

People who bore the marks or signs of a vampire were often either shunned, or tortured, and it is not surprising that many of them turned to a life of crime outside society. This only served to condemn them further as it was widely believed that thieves and prostitutes, along with witches and sorcerers, were potential vampires. Not even suicide offered relief, because of all the signs indicating vampirism, suicide was considered to be the most damning. It was thought that those who took their own lives would never find rest and would almost certainly become vampires after death.

Another widespread belief was that those who had led a sinful life were doomed to become vampires when they died. The case of 60-year-old Johannes Cuntius who on his deathbed admitted that he was guilty of many grievous sins – sins too dark and foul to be pardoned by God – illustrates well the belief that a generally sinful life is a prerequisite for becoming a vampire.

See also: **MODERN VAMPIRES**

Baital

Indian folklore is rich in tales of unearthly beings, many of whom resemble vampires. The baital, also known by the older term "vetala," was believed to be the spirit of a long-dead person that can inhabit and reanimate corpses. Its form is that of a four- to five-foot tall half human, half bat, with iron-like skin that makes it impervious to blows, and bat-like wings. According to some traditions, it also has a goat's tale. The baital can sometimes be found hanging upside down from trees in graveyards.

A baital is a central character in a collection of Indian tales, *Baital Pachisi* or *25 tales of a Baitai*, originally written in Sanskrit and dating back to the first century BC. They were translated by Sir Richard F. Burton and published in 1879 under the title *King Vikrum and the Vampire*. The baital who narrates the tales is more mischievous, wily, and clever than bloodthirsty. Using his supernatural powers, he is able to mock the king and teach him valuable lessons about humility in ways that human beings cannot.

See also: **INDIA**

Bajang

Found in Malaysian folklore, the bajang is a demonic vampire who is male and who can take a number of forms, most commonly that of a mewing polecat. Unlike a vampire that had formerly been a living person, the bajang was created by magic. According to tradition the bajang is compelled by spells and incantations to come out of the corpse of a stillborn child.

If it is caught the bajang can be turned into a kind of servant or familiar that stays with a family for generations. The only requirement the bajang has for its loyal service is that it is fed on blood, eggs, and milk. If it is not properly fed it can attack its master. The bajang's master, typically a magician or sorcerer, can command the creature to attack his enemies with a mysterious and often fatal illness. Most of the bajang's victims were women and it was said to be very active and savage at nightfall. Once it had drained its victim's blood it would return to its master and rest in a special chest that would be disguised or hidden away out of sight.

There were a number of methods for identifying the owner of a bajang as, according to tradition, the only way to destroy such a creature was to hunt its owner down and force him to destroy the bajang through magic and incantations. For example, it was thought that if experts called *pawang* (individuals skilled in dealing with wizards) scraped an iron vessel with a razor the guilty party's hair would fall out. Witch doctors would also be called in to investigate, questioning the suspected owner while he was in a state of potion-induced delirium. In many villages people suspected of owning a bajang were killed or driven away. As a precaution, stillborn fetuses were burned to prevent their falling into the hands of a wizard, magician, or sorcerer. Wearing amulets was thought to protect children from the attack of the bajang.

See also: **LANGSUIR**

Balkans

See: **ALBANIA**; **SERBIA**; **YUGOSLAVIA**

Banks, Leslie (1959–)

Philadelphia-born, African American *New York Times* bestselling author who writes the exotic and hugely popular Vampire Huntress series of books under the pseudonym L. A. Banks.

The series of books is based on the never-ending struggle between good and evil, but it is also about the strong bonds of love that exist between man and woman, within families and groups of friends, as well as love of oneself and the world or environment. Religion is also an intense subject matter in the series.

The first book in the series, *Minion* (2003) introduces the character of Damali, a 20-year-old African American woman with the heart of a warrior and an attitude to match, who is Neteru (the huntress). Damali's guardian team is also introduced and each member of the group possesses some kind of paranormal ability to help them banish evil from the world. In *Minion* and the books that follow the pace is fast, furious, and intense as Damali and her team grapple with a number of unusual but deadly breeds of vampires, who differ from the "regular" ones in appearance and exude a foul stench. These creatures are actually hybrids created by the evil vampire Fallon Nuit, who refers to them as his minions.

See also: **LITERATURE**

Banshee

In Irish folklore the banshee is an undead female spirit or evil fairy with vampire-like characteristics, in that she, like the vampire, is strongly associated with blood, disease and death. Thought to be the undead spirit of a young woman who died in childbirth, the banshee attaches herself to families and strikes terror into the hearts of those who encounter her, as she only manifests when there is to be a death in the family.

The Irish playwright, poet, and expert in Irish folklore William Butler Yeats wrote about the creature:

The banshee … is an attendant fairy that follows the old families, and none but them, and wails before a death. Many have seen her as she goes wailing and clapping her hands. The keen (caoine), the funeral cry of the peasantry, is said to be an imitation of her cry. When more than one banshee is present, and they wail and sing in chorus, it is for the death of some holy or great one. An omen that sometimes accompanies the banshee is the coach-a-bower (cóiste-bodhar) – an immense black coach, mounted by a coffin, and drawn by headless horses driven by a Dullahan. It will go rumbling to your door, and if you open it … a basin of blood will be thrown in your face. These headless phantoms are found elsewhere than in Ireland. In 1807 two of the sentries stationed outside St. James's Park died of fright. A headless woman, the upper part of her body naked, used to pass at midnight and scale the railings. After a time the sentries were stationed no longer at the haunted spot. In Norway the heads of corpses were cut off to make their ghosts feeble. Thus came into existence the Dullahans, perhaps; unless, indeed, they are descended from that Irish giant who swam across the Channel with his head in his teeth.

(From *A Treasury of Irish Myth, Legend, and Folklore*, ed. W. B. Yeats)

There are variations in the way she appears. According to Irish lore the banshee is known as Bean Si and is a beautiful young woman with long, flowing hair, wearing a gray cloak over a white, red, or green dress. Her eyes are always red and sore from crying. In both Scottish and Irish lore she is also known as Bean Nighe or "little washer by the ford." The Bean Nighe is thought to signal an imminent death by washing bloodstained clothes in a stream but, unlike the Bean Si, who is beautiful, the Bean Nighe is evil and ugly, with just one nostril, buck teeth, pendulous breasts, and red webbed feet.

A few banshee stories entered into American folklore with the arrival of immigrants. One of them comes from the American South, where a crying banshee with long flowing yellow hair is thought to haunt the Tar River in Edgecomb County, North Carolina.

Baobhan-sith

According to Scottish folklore, Baobhan-sith is a blood-sucking female spirit often described as something between a ghost, a fairy, a demon, and a witch who drinks the blood of men. This vampire-like creature has a history that stretches back hundreds of years. The name actually means "spirit woman," and the term "sith" clearly suggests great antiquity as it referred to the "people of the

mounds" who were believed to have inhabited Scotland in pre-Christian pagan times.

In the seventeenth and eighteenth centuries the distinctions between fairies, witches, and demons in Scottish folklore became blurred: all were regarded as dark and evil spirits. Descriptions of the Baobhan-sith vary. There are stories of her appearing as a small, dark woman with a human body and the hindquarters of a goat, suggesting her association with the Devil, but she is more commonly described as a tall, pale woman with ice-cold breath who likes to dance in the moonlight. In some regions she is portrayed almost as a skeleton wearing long, flowing robes and with vampire-like teeth, dancing alone in the shadows under the trees or the empty hills waiting for someone to pass by. For this reason her victims, shepherds and herders of the Scottish hills and mountains, would often avoid isolated, empty moors or deserted hollows.

The Baobhan-sith was most likely to manifest in the far Highlands and coastal west of the country, but she could also appear in the east and the Lowlands. She was said to have some form of control over the elements and could conjure up heavy fogs to disorientate her victims and make it easier for her to creep up on them unseen. There are also stories of her changing shape and manifesting in the human form of someone the victim knew. Then when the victim drew close she would pounce on them and draw their blood, like a wild animal.

Carrying a piece of iron or a holy medal thought to ward off evil was believed to offer protection against the Baobhan-sith. The belief that a holy medal could offer protection led some Scottish Presbyterian reformers from the Lowlands to declare that the Baobhan-sith were only associated with

Catholics living in the Highlands, and that a strong Presbyterian faith was the best protection against them of all.

The four hunters

One well-known folktale concerning the Baobhan-sith speaks of four young hunters who didn't return home once the moon rose. They lit a fire and entertained themselves; one of the hunters played music while the other three danced around the fire. While they were dancing one man wished he had a female partner to dance with. Suddenly, out of the shadows his wish was granted and four very beautiful women appeared. Three of the women danced while one stood quietly by the music maker. When the musician noticed blood falling from his three friends he panicked and ran away, hiding himself among the horses. The vampire was unable to claim her prey because of the iron shoes the horses wore. The angry Baobhan-sith was eventually forced to disappear at dawn. The hunter returned to the place where he and the other hunters had taken shelter and was horrified by what he found. His friends were dead and drained of all their blood.

The origins of the Baobhan-sith are very ancient and it is virtually impossible to say whether this vampire-like entity is the returning dead, a fairy, a demon, a witch, a vampire, the last vestiges of an ancient goddess cult, or a way for the wives of hunters and shepherds to make sure their men came home in time for supper at night and stayed faithful. Perhaps the best explanation is that she is a combination of all these, and that stories about the Baobhan-sith survive to the present day because, as they are handed down the centuries, they constantly change and adapt.

Barber, Paul

One of the foremost contemporary scholars on the subject of superstitions and beliefs surrounding the existence of vampires, Paul Barber was a research associate at the Fowler Museum of Cultural History at UCLA when he presented his theories about vampires in *Vampires, Burial, and Death* (1988).

According to Barber, reports of vampires can be explained by the ignorance of ordinary people about irregularities of the decomposition process in corpses – such as blood around the mouth, and hair and fingernail growth – before the age of forensic pathology. He states that the vampire tale is *"an ingenious folk hypothesis"* to explain observed phenomena that seemed impossible at the time. Barber's theory can explain some of the irregularities of buried corpses that were reported during the vampire scares of the eighteenth and nineteenth centuries, but for those who believe in the existence of vampires it cannot fully explain other irregularities, such as missing objects, holes in the coffin, and the family of the suspected vampire being ravaged at night.

Baron Blood

The name of a number of fictional vampire super-villains in the Marvel Comics universe, Baron Blood was created by Marvel Comics to be a worthy adversary for the Marvel super-heroes.

Baron Blood possesses all the powers of a standard vampire, but with greater strength and potency than most vampires. He can hypnotize victims, lift at least 1,500 lbs, command certain types of animals such as vermin, and control the weather. Baron Blood can walk in sunlight for about half an hour without feeling pain or burning up, and unlike other vampires he can fly without transforming into a bat. He also has the power to change his shape, although the extent of this power has never been determined.

The first Baron Blood, John Falsworth, appeared in *Invaders* (No. 7) in 1976 as a frequent foe of Union Jack. He was born in the late nineteenth century as a British nobleman. He traveled to Romania planning to gain control of Dracula, but he underestimated the Count's powers and was turned into a vampire himself. He returned to England as Dracula's agent of death. After a series of adventures, Baron Blood was eventually entombed by a team of super-heroes in a chapel with a stake through his heart and his coffin surrounded by garlic.

In 1981 Baron Blood appeared again as Kenneth Crichton, the grandnephew of the first Baron Blood. Eventually Captain America kills Blood and burns his body, but it wasn't too long before Blood reappears again from the ashes, this time in the form of Victor Strange, the brother of the sorcerer Doctor Strange. Victor Strange assumes the name Baron Blood and satisfies his lust for blood by attacking criminals. However, in 1993, realizing how violent and bloodthirsty he has become he commits suicide by plunging a knife into his chest. This uncharacteristic act of self-sacrifice is, however, no reason to think that Baron Blood can't and won't rise again to prominence in the Marvel Comic world.

See also: COMICS

Báthory, Elizabeth (1560–1614)

Frequently described as "Countess Dracula," Elizabeth (Erzsebet) Báthory was born into a troubled Transylvanian family in 1560. She became known as one of the "true vampires" of history and in her own way she may have been as influential in the creation of the vampire legend as the equally bloodthirsty Vlad the Impaler.

The Báthory family was one of the oldest families in Transylvania, and traced its ancestry back to a legendary and mighty warrior called Vid Báthory, who had allegedly slain a dragon with a mace. Elizabeth's mother, a devout Catholic, was the sister of King Stephen of Poland and her father, George, held several administrative posts. Elizabeth had at least one elder brother and two younger sisters called Klara and Sofia. Before Elizabeth was born a number of incestuous unions were alleged to have occurred between members of the Báthory family, and there were rumors of monster babies and madness running in the family.

Early life

As a child Elizabeth was subject to seizures and uncontrollable fits of rage. She was, however, a great beauty and a gifted linguist, and in 1571 at the age of 11 she was promised in marriage to the 15-year-old Count Ferenc (Francis) Nadasdy, one of the richest and most eligible bachelors in Europe. In 1574 Elizabeth fell pregnant as the result of an affair with a peasant. This did not stop the marriage going ahead, however, and on May 8, 1575, Elizabeth and Francis were married. Francis, clearly wanting to acquire the illustrious name of Báthory, changed his own name to that of his wife's family.

Elizabeth went to live with her husband at Csejthe (pronounced Chay-tay) Castle. Count Francis was a soldier in the Hungarian army and his fighting skills and courage earned him the title "The Black Hero of Hungary." Elizabeth found herself left alone for longer and longer periods of time and it was around this time that she began to fall under the influence of some of her servants who were knowledgeable in witchcraft. There are many who believe that an old servant woman called Darvulia, an elderly maid called Dorothea Szentes – known locally as Dorka the witch – and Elizabeth's majordomo Ujvary played a large part in the horrific acts that were later to earn Elizabeth her evil and twisted reputation.

Elizabeth allegedly entertained herself by being sadistic to her servants. On the advice and with the approval of her husband, she would discipline servant girls by tying their hands behind their backs and putting pieces of oiled paper between their toes and setting the paper on fire. The wild attempts of the girls to rid themselves of the papers were called "star kicking" and it seemed to have greatly amused her. She would also stick pins in various sensitive body parts, such as under the fingernails, and in winter she would execute people by having them stripped, laid out in the snow, and doused with water until they froze.

Legendary crimes

In 1604 Elizabeth's husband was killed in battle and she became the mistress of Csejthe. The loneliness and boredom of her life began to take its toll and she started to age prematurely. It is at this point that the line between history and hearsay, fact and fiction, becomes blurred.

One well-known account states that a young maidservant was combing Elizabeth's hair and accidentally pulled it. Elizabeth became angry and struck the girl so sharply across her face that she drew blood. Later when the Countess looked at the skin on her hand where the girl's blood had fallen she thought that the skin looked younger than the skin around it. Elizabeth consulted with her servant Darvulia and heard that it was believed in the countryside that the blood of young virgins could restore youth if the blood was taken when dark spells and rites were performed. This was the beginning of Elizabeth's bloody campaign. With the help of her accomplices she would recruit young girls from local villages to work as servants in the castle of Csejthe. Once there the Countess and her accomplices would subject the girls to the most depraved acts of sadism. Some were kept in cages suspended from the ceiling and the Countess's accomplices would use sharp blades to draw blood from them so that she could stand under the cage and be showered with it. Other girls were hung by their heels over the countess's tub, and when the time came for her to take her daily bath their throats were slit.

There are no exact figures for the number of her victims; some accounts put the number at 610, others put it lower at around 50. For a while the disappearance of the girls did not worry the local authorities – the girls were merely peasants from the minority Slovak population. For approximately 10 years between 1601 and 1611 the Countess murdered freely without any official enquiry. Rumors circulated about cannibal feasts and blood-drinking orgies going on in the castle but people were too scared of the Countess to do anything about it.

The Countess's reign of terror eventually ended in late 1610. According to one popular story, one of the girls managed to escape and raise the alarm. Another story tells of a Lutheran pastor who spoke out against her. Yet another account states that on the advice of her accomplices, Elizabeth decided that peasant blood was not powerful enough and she needed the blood of beautiful young noblewomen. She invited them to the Castle under the pretence that she was offering jobs as maids of honor; up to two dozen young maidens disappeared in this way. Eventually, rumors about the Countess grew and grew until they reached the Hungarian king, Matthias. He had no option but to investigate.

On December 29, 1610, the king and his provincial governor, Count Gryorgi Thurzo, entered Csejthe Castle and discovered evidence of the murder and depravity that had been taking place within its walls. A series of trials took place conducted by the king him-self. Báthory's accomplices were all found guilty and executed but Elizabeth was saved from the trial and criminal proceedings by her noble rank. The king commanded that she remain for the rest of her life at Csejthe. Stonemasons walled her up in the apartments where she had committed her atrocities. Only a small gap was left through which food could be passed. There were no windows and she spent the last years of her life alone and in darkness. According to legend, whenever her guards tried to look at her through the aperture she was still the most beautiful woman in Hungary.

Elizabeth died in her dark, silent prison on July 31, 1614. She left what remained of her property and holdings to her children. Records concerning her were sealed for a hundred years and her name was forbidden to be mentioned throughout Hungary. The name Csejthe became a swear word and the Slovaks within the borders of the country referred to her as "the Hungarian whore."

In addition to her reputation as a sadistic killer, Elizabeth was accused of being a vampire and a werewolf. During her trial there were accusations that she would bite the flesh of the girls while torturing them, which formed the basis of her connection to the werewolf. The connection between Elizabeth and vampires is less obvious, but by all accounts she was an attractive woman and her use of blood to create a more youthful self certainly qualifies her to be a vampire by metaphor, at the very least.

Impact on vampire history and literature

Although she died close to four centuries ago the memory of the Countess was kept alive over the centuries by legends and tales and later by novels, stories, and eventually films. There is no reason why Bram Stoker would not have known about Elizabeth Báthory when he wrote *Dracula*. According to historian Raymond McNally, author of *Dracula was a Woman* (1983), Dracula appears to get younger as the novel progresses, and Stoker could well have got this idea from reading about the Hungarian Countess. Her story may also have inspired Sheridan Le Fanu to write *Carmilla* (1872), the story of an older vampiric girl who influences the impressionable mind of a younger girl. In this story undertones of blood lust and depravity echo the story of Elizabeth.

Today, the influence of the Countess lingers on in popular imagination and in books and movies, including *Countess Dracula* (1972), a Hammer Horror movie in which a countess discovers a fountain of youth in flowing blood; *Thirst* (1988), a film in which a descendant of the Hungarian Countess visits a science lab where human subjects are drained of blood; *Daughter of Night* (1992), a novel by Elaine Bergstrom based on the Countess; and *The Blood Countess* (1996), a novel by Andrei Codrescu that weaves Báthory's story together with the story of a fictive modern-day descendant involved in a murder in Hungary.

Although in a minority, some historians believe that Elizabeth was not a bloodthirsty murderer of young women but the victim of a political conspiracy. They argue that trial processes in the seventeenth century included intimidation and torture, so any testimony to her thirst for blood and sadistic lifestyle may not be as reliable as previously thought. It is also worth noting that following her trial, all records of her activity were sealed and it was not until a century later that the story appeared in print. A Jesuit priest, Laszlo Turoczy, located copies of the original trial in 1729 and gathered stories circulating about her. It was Turoczy who initially suggested that the Countess bathed in blood in his book about the history of Hungary, which appeared during the wave of vampire hysteria that swept through Eastern Europe at the time. Other writers would later pick up on the story and continue to embellish it.

It's impossible to know whether Elizabeth was as sadistic and vile as her reputation suggests, but, rightly or wrongly, the legacy she leaves behind is that of the "Blood Countess" renowned for her multiple murders and obsession with blood.

See also: **HISTORICAL VAMPIRES**

Bats

As a premier symbol of vampirism, the bat has a rich place not just in vampire folklore but in world folklore with its associations with darkness, death, and the supernatural. Today, the bat has become an integral part of the vampire tradition.

Bats are the only mammals that can fly. There are almost one thousand species of bats and the largest have a wingspan of several feet. They typically spend much of their time hanging upside down asleep. The vampire bat comprises a small proportion of the bat world and is distinguished from other bats by its feeding habits. Whereas other bats feed on fruit and insects or plants, the common vampire bat, *Desmodus rotundus*, feeds on the blood of other mammals.

Vampire bat

Quite hideous in appearance, with razor-sharp incisors, the home of the vampire bat is Central and South America. They have an extraordinary sense of smell and vision and are extremely agile, able to walk, run, fly, and hop. Rather than sucking the blood of their sleeping victims they nick them painlessly on areas such as the neck and allow the blood to flow, then lap it up like a cat with their tongue. Their saliva contains a strong anti-coagulant for optimum blood flow and they feed for about 20 minutes until they are bloated. Just like the vampire they are named after, the vampire bat hunts at night and often feeds on its victims when they are asleep. It rarely kills those it feeds from – usually pigs, horses, or cattle, and in a small number of cases, people – but there have been isolated reported of deadly vampire bat attacks. As recently as June 2007 at least 38 people in Venezuela, including several children, were thought to have died after being attacked by vampire bats. Although the precise cause of the deaths has not been confirmed, experts say that it was almost certainly due to rabies carried by the blood-sucking creatures. It is thought that the bats were probably disturbed by nearby mining, logging, or damming projects, and were forced to find new prey – in this case, members of the Warao tribe.

Bats and the vampire legend

Although the bat was not firmly tied to the vampire legend until the nineteenth century, in many cultures it came to be associated with the dark, sinister aspects of life. For example, in Classical mythology they were sacred to Proserpina, the wife of Pluto, god of the Underworld, and in the Middle Ages they were often believed to be bad omens or signs of death. Demons with bat-like wings were common symbols of darkness and evil. They conjured up images of fallen angels, and the motif of wings on a human figure conjured up the idea of flight into unknown and forbidden realms. Europeans first discovered and described vampire bats in the sixteenth century. One of the earliest descriptions was written in 1565 by historian and explorer Girolamo Benzoni, who observed them in what is now Costa Rica: *"There are many bats which bite people during the night ... While I was sleeping they bit the toes of my feet so delicately that I felt nothing, and in the morning I found the sheets and mattresses with so much blood that it seemed that I suffered from some great injury."* The pres-

ence of bats increased in European vampire folklore after Spanish conquistadores returned from the New World with stories of these blood-drinking vampire bats. In Romania, for example, it was reported that a bat flying over a corpse could create a vampire. The fact that bats are also common vectors for spreading rabies did nothing to improve their dark image.

Although the vampire bat is not found in Slavic countries, it finally got its name in the eighteenth century around the time when the Slavic vampire frenzy was making its mark on the rest of the world. Over the next century the association between bats and vampires grew stronger, and the first theatrical use of a bat-like cloak probably occurred in 1852 in a play by Dion Boucicault called *The Vampire*. It wasn't until Bram Stoker's novel *Dracula* (1897) however, that bats became firmly associated with vampires; in the story Dracula appears in bat form at night. The first convincing on-screen bat transformation was accomplished by Lon Chaney Jr. in *Son of Dracula* (1943), and ever since then bats have been a staple of vampire and horror film and fiction as one of the favorite disguises of the vampire. The creation of the DC Comics character Batman, and the incredibly successful movie franchise spin-offs must also to some extent be credited to *Dracula*. Although Batman is not a vampire there is a clear association between him and Dracula.

Today even the medical community has latched on to the Dracula–bat connection. A Venezuelan research team has isolated a previously unknown anticoagulant substance from the saliva of the common vampire bat. Named *draculin*, this anticoagulant agent promises to be significant in the development of improved drugs to fight heart disease and stroke.

The menacing reputation of bats is undeserved, as bats have an important part to play in the ecosystem; they are essential to the control of insects. Naturists who study bats have repeatedly carried out bat PR programs because they believe the bats' close association with vampires has given them a bad name.

See also: ANIMAL VAMPIRES

Baudelaire, Charles (1821-67)

In the 1857 original edition of *Flowers of Evil*, the influential French poet Charles Baudelaire wrote two poems, "The Vampire" and "Metamorphoses of the Vampire," which deal explicitly with vampirism. Both poems were censored from the 1857 edition and Baudelaire was convicted on obscenity charges. In these two poems Baudelaire describes female sexuality in terms of vampirism, rot, and prostitution and the images he conjured up had a profound influence on the development of the femme fatale motif in late nineteenth-century art. The following is a translation of "Metamorphoses" by Edna St. Vincent Millay.

Meanwhile, from her red mouth the woman,
in husky tones,
Twisting her body like a serpent upon hot
stones
And straining her white breasts from their
imprisonment,
Let fall these words, as potent as a heavy scent:
"My lips are moist and yielding, and I know
the way
To keep the antique demon of remorse at bay.
All sorrows die upon my bosom. I can make
Old men laugh happily as children for my
sake.
For him who sees me naked in my tresses, I
Replace the sun, the moon, and all the stars
of the sky!
Believe me, learned sir, I am so deeply skilled
That when I wind a lover in my soft arms,
and yield
My breasts like two ripe fruits for his
devouring — both
Shy and voluptuous, insatiable and loath —
Upon his bed that groans and sighs
luxuriously
Even the impotent angels would be damned
for me!"
When she drained me of my very marrow,
and cold
And weak, I turned to give her one more
kiss — behold,
There at my side was nothing but a hideous
Putrescent thing, all faceless and exuding
pus.
I closed my eyes and mercifully swooned till
day:

Who seemed to have replenished her arteries
from my own,
The wan, disjointed fragments of a skeleton
Wagged up and down in a new posture
where she had lain;
Rattling with each convulsion like a
weathervane
Or an old sign that creaks upon its bracket,
right
Mournfully in the wind upon a winter's
night.

Baudelaire's poetry was shaped by the writing of Edgar Allan Poe, an American poet and short-story writer obsessed with the dark side. From 1852 to 1865 Baudelaire introduced the French-speaking world to the work of Poe though his translations, which included the vampirish story "Berenice." Baudelaire, in turn, inspired numerous writers who imitated his convention-challenging decadent Gothic style.

Bavaria

A region in southern Germany, Bavaria developed a number of customs and superstitions concerning vampires. Although German territory, it's likely that concepts concerning the undead were absorbed from Slavic immigrants as well as from contact with the Slavs in neighboring Bohemia.

The most common name for vampire in Bavaria is "blutsauger," which literally means bloodsucker. As recently as the 1980s, belief in the blutsauger was found to still exist in rural parts of Bavaria. The blutsauger was described as being an animated corpse with pale flesh, and the best way to protect against it was to rub doors and windows with garlic. After death a person might become a blutsauger if they had not been baptized, had led a sinful life, were involved in witchcraft, or died by suicide. A person who was already dead might become a blutsauger if an animal jumped over his or her corpse.

One of the most well-known revenant tales from the folklore of Bavaria is a specter who appeared near the village of Kodom. In this story a vampire-like ghost who had been a herdsman during his life began to appear to other villagers. One of the villagers died and his death was blamed on the specter. Fearful that the same fate might befall other villagers the corpse of the herdsman was dug up and pinned to the ground. This didn't stop the ghost and it reappeared and suffocated several villagers. The body was then taken to the local executioner and stakes were driven into the corpse. According to tradition, the corpse howled and gave up great quantities of blood. The corpse was then burned in a field next to the cemetery and the revenant never appeared again.

See also: **GERMANY**

Bebarlangs

A Filipino tribe, the Bebarlangs supposedly had members who could send out their astral bodies to feed not on the blood but on the vitality or life force of others. In this way they could be said to have practiced a kind of psychic vampirism.

See also: **PHILIPPINES**

Becoming a Vampire

According to vampire folklore there are a number of methods by which a person can become a vampire. Certain predispositions at birth can increase the risk of becoming a vampire, as can certain actions taken in life. The circumstances of death or what happens to the corpse after death can also be significant.

Aside from being attacked by a vampire, actions taken in life that can lead to vampiric transformation include:

- *Committing suicide, practicing witchcraft or sorcery*

- *Leading a sinful life, or eating sheep killed by a wolf*

- *Being a werewolf*

- *For priests, saying Mass while in a state of mortal sin*

In folklore a vampire's attack or bite could cause the victim to become a vampire but more generally the vampiric state occurred after death. Fear of vampire infestation led not to persecutions of the living but to corpse mutilations. Death or after-death causes of vampirism include:

- *A cat or other animal jumping over the corpse*

- *A shadow passing over the corpse*

- *No burial rites or improper burial rites*

- *A violent death or murder*

- *Murder that is not revenged*

- *A candle being passed over the corpse*

- *Death by drowning*

- *Being buried face up in the grave*

- *Death at the hands of a vampire or werewolf*

Vampirification

Moving away from the traditions and customs of folklore over the centuries, a number of writers, scientists, doctors, and vampirologists have attempted to explain the physical transformation that takes place when a human becomes a vampire. This process is sometimes referred to as "vampirification."

Typically, when a person dies the heart and brain stop working, the joints become stiff with rigor mortis, making body parts hard to move, and the skin turns white. Within a few days the process of decomposition occurs, fingernails and hair are shed and facial features become unrecognizable. Vampires, according to tradition, remain intact, their limbs remain supple and their bodies do not decay. Hair and nails continue to grow and they do not decompose. The only change at death that stays the same is that their skin turns a deathly white. In 1616 the Italian scientist Ludovico Fatinelli tried to explain this process in his *Treatise on Vampires*.

Fatinelli states that when a person becomes a vampire the body does not decompose but enters a vampiric coma where pulse slows, breathing is shallow, and the pupils dilate to a point that the person is believed to be dead and is buried. If the person is old or ill they will probably die. If, however, they are young and healthy they awake after 24 hours transformed into a vampire. Fatinelli did not explain how the vampire managed to escape from his or her coffin buried underground, but when his book was published he was charged with heresy and burned at the stake for encouraging the notion of vampires.

In recent years a number of authors have picked up where Fatinelli left off and have written books that attempt to combine forensic science with biology and folklore to try to explain the process of vampirism. Some of the most notable include forensic psychologist Katherine Ramsland, who investigates the myths and realities of vampires in *The Science of Vampires* (2002), and psychiatrist Philip D. Jaffe in *Clinical Vampirism: Blending Myth and Reality* (1994). According to these authors, the process of becoming a vampire begins in the brain when a chemical or neurotransmitter called dopamine is released to produce a feeling of well-being. Changes then begin to occur in the vampire's sense organs; pupils are superdilated, which gives them eyes that appear black but which have brilliant night vision. These superdilated eyes make it impossible for the vampire to see in the daylight which is why they are likely to shun it. The whites of their eyes appear red or bloodshot. Extra receptor cells appear in the nose and throat and also the ears, heightening the vampire's sense of smell and hearing.

Another change is that the vampire's blood turns black due to the lack of a certain protein in the red cells called hemoglobin. Vampire experts believe that this black blood is not

The Element Encyclopedia of Vampires

pumped by a heart, as it is thought vampires probably don't have hearts (and if they do it they are too withered to be of real use). Instead their blood is pumped by contractions of skeletal muscles in the chest.

Another obvious change is the growth of upper and lower canine teeth; there are stories that these teeth can retract so they look normal when not used. Fast-growing and long fingernails can also appear to help them grab their victims. Other physiological changes include a yellowing of skin color; as the skin ages it becomes more translucent and blue from the veins under the skin. Within those veins the blood runs cold and a vampire's body temperature is also described as much lower than a human body temperature. Some researchers state that a vampire over the age of 100 may have a body temperature as low as 65°F or 18°C and this temperature decreases with age and might even drop to 60°F or 15°C. As far as the vampire's bones and muscles are concerned, those who study vampires say that they become stronger with age, which would allow vampires to gain incredible strength.

See also: **Aging, of Vampires; Biology of Vampires; Birth of a Vampire; Burial Customs; Decomposition; Sociology of Vampires; Transformation**

Beheading

According to the folklore of many countries, beheading a corpse was thought to ensure that it did not return from the grave in the form of a revenant or vampire.

The vampire hunters of old knew that consciousness resided in the head, as it is the part of the body that possesses the majority of our sensory stimulation. Therefore even if decapitation didn't kill it, the creature would be unable to see, smell, or hear its victim. For this reason the head of the vampire was often placed by the corpse's feet or behind its knees, making it impossible for the vampire in a small coffin to pick it up. Another practice was to place the head backward on the corpse's head so it would not be able to see where it was going. There are many tales of vampire beheadings in Eastern European folklore similar to the case of Franz von Poblocki below, which is a fine example.

In 1870, a citizen of the town of Neustatt-an-der-Rhoda (now known as Wejherowo) in Pomerania (then a part of West Prussia), named Franz von Poblocki, died of consumption (tuberculosis). Two weeks later, his son Anton died, while other members of his family experienced illness and terrifying nightmares. The family consulted a local vampire hunter named Johann Dziegielski and with the consent of the family Dziegielski decapitated Anton's corpse and buried it with the head placed between the knees. The body of Franz was then exhumed, decapitated, and re-buried with the head placed between the legs. The family and the vampire hunter were put on trial for exhuming the bodies, but later a court of appeal dropped all charges.

Not all vampire hunters believed that this act was enough to really kill the vampire – it was considered more of a hindrance to it. To be sure that the vampire would not return from the dead many thought it wise to take the further precaution of burning the corpse and scattering the ashes.

Belgrade Vampire, The

The name given to a vampire case that took place in Belgrade, Serbia in 1732. The case was recorded by Dr. Herbert Mayo in his esteemed 1851 work: *On the Truths contained in Popular Superstitions.*

A vampire was thought to have caused several deaths. Fear and panic spread through the city of Belgrade and the surrounding area. It was believed that the vampire was creating more vampires. To prevent the vampire attack corpses were exhumed and destroyed. When the coffin of the vampire was eventually opened the body was allegedly found leaning to one side. Its skin was fresh and ruddy, the nails grown long and crooked, and blood still dribbled from its mouth. A stake was driven into the corpse, whereupon the vampire screamed and fresh blood oozed out. The corpse was then burned to ashes and the "facts" of the case were witnessed and attested to by three regimental surgeons, a lieutenant, and a second lieutenant. The document must have been extremely convincing because even Dr. Mayo stressed that the document was above suspicion, stating that "*No doubt can be entertained of its authenticity, or its general fidelity; the less that it does not stand alone, but is supported by a mass of evidence to that same effect. It appears to establish beyond question, that where the fear of vampirism prevails, and there occur several deaths, in the popular belief connected with it, the bodies, when disinterred weeks after burial, present the appearance of corpses from which life has only recently departed.*"

Bell Witch, The

The Bell Witch incident took place in 1817 and involved an evil spirit that terrorized the historical Bell family of Adams, Tennessee. The story is the basis of the films *An American Haunting* (2006) and *The Bell Witch Haunting* (2004), and may have influenced the production of *The Blair Witch Project* (1999).

The story of the Bell witch shares many similarities to the reported vampire cases that occurred in Eastern Europe in the first half of the nineteenth century, in that it was thought that the undead had returned to terrorize the living by bringing disease, unhappiness, and destruction. It differs, however, in that there is little emphasis on blood-sucking and the exhumation of corpses to "kill" the spirit. Today, it is most often described as the "greatest American ghost story."

The story

According to folklore, John and Lucy Bell lived with their nine children on a farm, and the phenomena started with noises and scraping and progressed to clothes being pulled off people and furniture and stones being thrown about. Two of the children, Elizabeth and Richard, had their hair pulled one night, and Elizabeth was slapped, punched, and pinched. Elizabeth was eventually sent to stay with a neighbor and the disturbances followed her to her neighbor's house, indicating that she was the focus of the activity.

The strange events continued over the next few years. Later activity included strange lights appearing outside the house, stones thrown at Elizabeth's brothers and sisters, and visitors receiving slaps from invisible hands.

The entity also began to speak using foul language. According to reports, a voice would appear from nowhere and with no identifiable source. The voice claimed to be various different people but eventually settled on the name of Kate Bates, a woman who had been dissatisfied with business dealings with the Bells. From then on the voice was called Kate.

A committee was formed to investigate and the Bell family became the object of much curiosity: General Jackson even paid a visit with a "witch layer," a professional exorcist. According to legend, just outside Bell Lane their carriage got stuck. Kate's voice could be heard promising to appear that night, and the carriage became unstuck. Later in the evening the witch layer tried to shoot Kate with a silver bullet but was slapped and chased out of the house.

Elizabeth's father, John Bell, began to suffer from repeated bouts of illness, and Kate claimed she was the cause. He couldn't eat, his tongue was swollen, and Kate declared that she would torment him for the rest of his life. Unfortunately, this is exactly what she did. Finally the ordeals and cursing wore John down, and on the morning of December 19, 1820, he fell into a stupor, dying a day later. A bottle was found in the medicine cabinet, and when the contents were given to an animal the animal died. Kate declared with delight that she had poisoned John with the liquid while he was asleep.

After John Bell's death the activity diminished. However, it started again some time later when Elizabeth got engaged to a Joshua Gardener, who apparently did not meet the poltergeist's approval. The entity told Elizabeth not to marry Joshua and the couple could not go anywhere without the entity following them

and persistently taunting them. In 1821 their patience finally snapped and they broke off their engagement.

Elizabeth eventually married a man called Dick Powell, and Kate finally disappeared with the words, "I will be gone for seven years." John's widow, Lucy Bell, and two of her sons who stayed at the farmhouse, did hear manifestations seven years later, but they kept quiet about it this time and the torment stopped after two weeks. Apparently the spirit promised to return in 1935 but failed to do so, or wasn't noticed by anybody.

Theories

The most commonly accepted explanation is that this is a classic case of poltergeist activity. There are several theories as to what a poltergeist really is. Some believe that poltergeists are not ghosts at all, but are instead telekinetic abilities, or the power of mind or thoughts to influence people and move objects, manifested by a living person in turmoil. According to this explanation, this is why the focus of any activity is typically a single person, and frequently an adolescent. The turmoil of puberty alone could make some people manifest telekinetic incidents, or abused children or teens might use telekinesis as a way of protecting or avenging themselves. In the Bell Witch scenario the activity focused on Elizabeth, who was the right age, around puberty, for sexual guilt and tension. It has also been suggested that there was some kind of incestuous relationship between Elizabeth and her father, which would have seriously disturbed the young girl. This theory, however, does not account for poltergeist activity that took place when she was not around, such as that with General Jackson.

Another explanation that has been put forward is that the Bell Witch may have been a type of astral vampire, the astral body of a dead or living person attacking and draining the life force of others. Another school of thought suggests that Elizabeth may have been a psychic vampire with the ability to consciously or unconsciously influence the feelings and actions of those around her. Skeptics dismiss the case as pure superstition and speculation, arguing that no credible first-hand accounts exist of the events related to the legend. The only reported first-hand documentation is the diary of William Bell, who was six years old when the events started and who allegedly wrote his diary 25 years later. No record of this diary exists. It is simply referenced in 1894 in *An Authenticated History of the Bell Witch of Tennessee* by Martin Van Buren Ingram.

Benson, E. F. (1867-1940)

Edward Frederic Benson was a British writer noted for his horror tales and regarded as one of the foremost authors of the vampire short story in the early twentieth century.

Benson's short stories have a wonderfully malevolent feel and are regarded as classics in their field. Two of the best known are "Mrs. Amsworth" (1923) – a vampire story about a middle-aged jolly woman who preys on innocent victims in a sleepy English village – and "The Room in the Tower" (1912) about an evil old lady called Julia Stone, strongly believed to be a vampire.

My awaking was equally instantaneous, and I sat bolt upright in bed under the impression that some bright light had been flashed in my face, though it was now absolutely pitch dark. I knew exactly where I was, in the room which I had dreaded in dreams, but no horror that I ever felt when asleep approached the fear that now invaded and froze my brain. Immediately after a peal of thunder crackled just above the house, but the probability that it was only a flash of lightning which awoke me gave no reassurance to my galloping heart. Something I knew was in the room with me, and instinctively I put out my right hand, which was nearest the wall, to keep it away. And my hand touched the edge of a picture-frame hanging close to me.

I sprang out of bed, upsetting the small table that stood by it, and I heard my watch, candle, and matches clatter onto the floor. But for the moment there was no need of light, for a blinding flash leaped out of the clouds, and showed me that by my bed again hung the picture of Mrs. Stone. And instantly the room went into blackness again. But in that flash I saw another thing also, namely a figure that leaned over the end of my bed, watching me. It was dressed in some close-clinging white garment, spotted and stained with mold, and the face was that of the portrait.

The Element Encyclopedia of Vampires

Overhead the thunder cracked and roared, and when it ceased and the deathly stillness succeeded, I heard the rustle of movement coming nearer me, and, more horrible yet, perceived an odor of corruption and decay. And then a hand was laid on the side of my neck, and close beside my ear I heard quick-taken, eager breathing. Yet I knew that this thing, though it could be perceived by touch, by smell, by eye and by ear, was still not of this earth, but something that had passed out of the body and had power to make itself manifest. Then a voice, already familiar to me, spoke.

"I knew you would come to the room in the tower," it said. "I have been long waiting for you. At last you have come. Tonight I shall feast; before long we will feast together."

(From "The Room in the Tower" by E. F. Benson)
See also: LITERATURE

"Berenice"

Short story written by Gothic horror writer Edgar Allan Poe in 1835 about a man's obsession with the teeth of a beautiful, cataleptic woman. "Berenice" is often associated with vampire fiction.

Although the story is a tale of madness and no vampires actually appear, Poe manages to evoke in just a few thousand words a chilling atmosphere of necrophilic fantasy. The story also uses features and allusions that are typical of vampire stories – in particular the appearance of the woman who is reminiscent of a vampire: tall, slender, pale, with raven-black hair and large, hypnotic eyes.

Bertrand, Sergeant François

A nineteenth-century Frenchman who took great delight in digging up and tearing apart corpses. His case was examined by Dr. Alexis Epaulard in a 1901 treatise on vampires.

In 1848 a number of mysterious grave desecrations took place in Paris, including one at the prestigious Père Lachaise Cemetery. The graves had been opened and the corpses torn to pieces. Animals were initially blamed but human footsteps were discovered at the scene. Watches were set up at the cemetery but nobody was caught and the desecrations stopped. This did not, however, stop guards and caretakers from spreading hysteria by claiming to see shadows darting among tombstones and declaring that the walls and the iron gates should have been strong enough to keep out moral prowlers.

The culprit struck again in March 1849 at the Montparnasse cemetery. This time, however, he set off a spring gun trap. Guards ran to the scene in time to see a man in military uniform jump over the cemetery wall and escape. He left behind a trail of blood, which suggested that he had been wounded by the spring gun. Police searched nearby barracks extensively looking for a man with gunshot wounds, and they eventually found a junior officer called Sergeant François Bertrand. As soon as Bertrand recovered from his wounds he was court-martialed and confessed to everything.

Bertrand was known among his companions as a refined and quiet man, prone to fits of depression. Prior to entering the army at the age of 20 he went to a theological seminary. In February 1847 he said in his confession that a fit of madness seized him. He was walking with a friend in the countryside and they came upon a graveyard. He noticed a grave that had not been completely filled due to a rainstorm and saw a pick and shovel lying beside it. He was overcome with a desire to dig up the corpse. He made excuses to get rid of his friend, returned to the graveyard and exhumed the body. He testified:

I dragged the corpse out of the earth and I began to hash it with a spade, without well knowing what I was about … When I rose, my limbs were as if broken, and my head weak. The same prostration and weakness followed each attack … two days later I returned to the cemetery and opened the grave with my hands. My hands bled, but I did not feel the pain: I tore the corpse to shreds, and I flung it back into the pit.

Four months later, when his regiment was sent to Paris, Bertrand experienced another episode. One day he was walking through Père Lachaise Cemetery and an urge to dig up a corpse and tear it apart came over him again. That night he returned to the graveyard and exhumed the body of a seven-year-old girl. A few days later he dug up a woman who had died in childbirth and had been buried only 13 days earlier. On November 16, 1848, he dug up a 50-year-old woman, tore her body apart, and rolled in the bits.

Bertrand went on to give other accounts of exhumations. Sometimes the desire came upon him after he had had a glass of wine. Other times it came upon him for no reason at all. He dug up both men and women but only mutilated female corpses. Sometimes he hacked the corpse to pieces with his bare hands. Other times he used a spade. He opened stomachs, tore mouths open, and pulled off limbs.

During his hospitalization and trial, Bertrand said that he had not had any more urges and that he was cured. The authorities must have believed him as he was given a light sentence of just one year's imprisonment. He disappeared into obscurity after his release.

The sudden urge to tear corpses apart, followed by exhaustion draws parallels with vampirism, but is perhaps more characteristic of necrophilia or the medical symptoms of a condition called lycanthropy, a clinical condition in which a person believes they have been transformed into a wolf.

See also: **HISTORICAL VAMPIRES**

Berwick Vampire, The

A vampire case reported by the twelfth-century historian William of Newburgh in *Historia rerum Anglicarum*, which took place in the far north of England in the town of Berwick.

According to Newburgh, a wealthy man with a reputation for evil died and was buried. He emerged from his grave soon afterward to wander the streets of the town at night. He did not attack anyone but his state of decomposition and the foul stench that accompanied him sent waves of panic and hysteria through the townspeople, afraid that a plague would spread. The corpse was exhumed and cut into pieces and burned by 10 young men. There were no further disturbances.

Bhuta

Also known as bhut or bhuts, this vampire species from India is believed to be the restless souls of people who have suffered a violent death or died by accident, suicide, or execution. It can also be people who were not buried with proper funeral rites or someone who was insane, disabled, or diseased in their lifetime.

The bhuta are thought to live among the shadows in cemeteries, deserted regions, and abandoned buildings. They are flickering lights or misty apparitions that cast no shadow and hover above the ground. They can be avoided by lying down. As they wander the night the bhuta can enter corpses and bring them to life in a zombie-like state. The re-animated corpses have long, lolling black tongues and they stalk the night, slitting open dead bodies, devouring intestines, and drinking spilled blood.

Bhuta are also shape-shifters and can transform into bats and owls; this latter may explain why Indians believe it is unlucky to hear an owl hoot in a cemetery. If someone is attacked by a bhuta, severe sickness will follow, and in some instances death. Like the European vampire, the bhuta are blamed for blighted crops, diseased livestock, accidents, plagues, natural disasters, and insanity, although some bhuta, such as the bhuta of Awadh, prefer to play jokes on travelers and hinder their journey.

To placate the bhuta shrines are built. These shrines are thought to be places where the bhuta can rest without touching the ground, which they cannot do because the earth is sacred. Flowers and bowls of water are often placed by the shrine, as are cradles hanging from ropes or chains. *Bhutastan* are large shrines built to honor several bhutas or one of special importance. They are often more decorated and have a bronze statue representing the bhuta residing within it. Festi-vals and blood sacrifices may also take place within these temples and the bhuta, regarded more as spirits within the Hindu pantheon than as vampires as known in the West, is believed to speak to the villagers through a dancer who appears naked and painted in yellow, red, and white.

See also: **CHUREL; INDIA**

Binding a Corpse

The practice of tying down the arms and legs of a corpse immediately after death to prevent it from becoming a revenant or vampire and leaving its grave.

The method of binding varied from region to region and depended on local customs. The Finns tied the knees together, for example, but in other countries, such as Romania, people preferred to tie the feet. According to the Slavs a corpse with an open mouth is likely to be a vampire, and so the mouth was also often bound shut to prevent the deceased from chewing or biting; sometimes coins, garlic, or cotton were placed in the mouth for the same purpose. In some regions the ropes were cut before burial so as not to hinder the dead person's journey to the afterlife; this was a very old practice handed down from the ancient Greeks. In Romania, prior to burial the ropes were buried nearby; if they were stolen and used in black magic the corpse would become a type of vampire known as a strigoi.

See also: **APOTROPAICS; BURIAL CUSTOMS; PREVENTION**

Biology of Vampires

By combining forensic science with biology and folklore to describe the process of vampirification, a number of writers have written books that attempt to prove that the existence of vampires can be explained rationally. These publications include *Five Books on the Structure of the Vampire Body* written in the sixteenth century by Flemish physician Andreas Vesalius, and, more recently, *Clinical Vampirism, Blending Myth with Reality* by Philip D. Jaffe (1994) and *The Science of Vampires* by Katherine Ramsland (2002). The following is an overview of vampire biology according to these sources.

The vampire's nervous system is believed to be fairly similar to a human's but a number of changes take place in the brain. These changes include lower levels of the neurotransmitter serotonin. In humans studies have shown that lower levels of serotonin have been linked to aggressive and violent behavior. Another feel-good chemical neurotransmitter, dopamine, is released whenever the vampire feeds and has a narcotic effect. Circadian rhythms in the vampire brain are also altered, so that instead of feeling awake when there is sunlight vampires feel sleepy and fatigued.

There are also remarkable changes in the vampire's sense organs. The iris in each eye becomes hyperdilated and although this gives them excellent night vision it also gives them eyes that appear black and renders them virtually blind in daylight. There is also inflammation of the sclera, which makes the whites of the eyes appear red. The vampire's sense of smell and hearing is heightened. They can smell or hear their prey long before they see them because they have double the receptor cells in their nose and ears compared with humans.

During vampire transformation both the upper and lower teeth experience growth and additional enamel is deposited on the crown of the teeth. Nails may also grow longer and sharper. Within ten years of becoming a vampire all body hair will be lost, and the vampire's skin will have turned from a deathly pale to yellow, and then to translucent blue, with veins clearly visible.

Body temperature is considerably lower in vampires than it is in humans, typically about 60°F (15°C) compared with 98°F (36°C) in humans. Vampire bones, ligaments, and tendons are thicker and stronger than those in humans, and about 90 percent of vampire muscles are of the fast-twitch variety (compared with 50 percent for the average human). Fast-twitch muscles are for short bursts of action and force, ideal for capturing and overpowering their prey.

Finally, contrary to what is often thought, the vampire's ability to live for several hundred years is not because they have sold their soul to the Devil, but is the result of their ability to ward off the aging DNA damage that occurs during cell division in normal humans.

See also: **AGING, OF VAMPIRES; BECOMING A VAMPIRE; SOCIOLOGY OF VAMPIRES; TRANSFORMATION**

Birds

Birds have long been associated with vampires because of their ability to fly and their predatory habits. Vampire finches are small birds native to the Galapagos Islands that occasionally feed by drinking the blood of other birds, pecking at their skin with their sharp beaks until blood is drawn.

Birds can become servants or familiars of the undead or actual vampires themselves. Some species of vampire, such as the aswang and bruxsa, can transform themselves into birds when night falls.

See also: **Bats; Flying Vampires; Fowl; Owl**

Birmingham Vampire, The

In January 2005, a vampire scare erupted in the UK in Birmingham. Although police dismissed it as a myth, reports of a vampire prowling the streets struck terror into the locals.

According to eyewitness reports, a vampire was on the rampage in Glen Park Road, Ward End. The attacker reportedly bit a male pedestrian and then bit neighbors who had come to the man's aid. One woman had "chunks" bitten out of her hand. The *Birmingham Evening Mail* was flooded with calls from terrified families, community leaders, and schools. Oliver Luft of the Birmingham news agency Newsteam reported:

As the sun dips below the rooftops of sleepy terraced streets, residents rush home, quickly gathering up playing children, because after night falls a vampire hungry for blood stalks.

Reports of a Dracula-style attacker on the loose biting innocent people has spread terror throughout neighbourhoods in Birmingham, causing many to fear the darkness of the night.

Police in Birmingham did not investigate the case as no one reported injuries from biting to them, and hospitals did not receive unusual numbers of admissions. However, even though officials declared the Birmingham vampire to be an urban myth fueled by rumors, to this day a number of locals continue to believe that something sinister prowls their streets at night.

Birth of a Vampire

Evidence suggests that in the great majority of cases, vampires are creatures who are originally human before undergoing a process of transformation, and that the vampire body is dead but it remains somehow active and able to function for hundreds of years unless killed again. The evidence also suggests that the victims of vampires can become vampires themselves.

Vampires are therefore born when a person dies and becomes a vampire, or they are created when a person is bitten by a vampire and transforms into one. This, however, is not the whole story. In some cultures it is believed that there are certain predispositions to vampirism, or certain "rules" which state that some individuals are more likely to become vampires than others. Sometimes people become vampires through no fault of their own – for example, due to carelessness in carrying out funeral rites, or by being born under a bad sign, such as with a red caul. And sometimes the likelihood of transformation is increased because of certain actions committed during a person's life; for example, leading a sinful life was thought to increase the risk, as was death by suicide.

Vampires that are revenants – dead bodies that have come alive – need to suck blood from humans and animals to stay alive. They do this by biting into the jugular vein in the neck, a process known as the kiss of a vampire. This bite transforms the victim into a revenant who must also seek out blood to survive. However, sophisticated vampires (like those described in Bram Stoker's *Dracula*) do not simply bite their prey, drink their blood, and leave them to die. Instead they carefully nurture their victims and teach them the ways of the vampire.

The process

Those who believe in vampires say that the birth of a new vampire begins when a vampire drains its victim's blood until he or she is almost dead. The following night the vampire reappears and explains to the victim – who is by now completely hypnotized by the vampire – why he or she has been chosen to be a vampire. With the victim's consent (almost always given thanks to the victim's hypnotized state) the vampire completes the process of vampirism by drinking more blood from the victim. After this the vampire bites his or her own wrist and allows the disciple to drink blood for the first time. This is described as a profound awakening as the new vampire is exhilarated with his newfound super senses and superior strength and awareness. In time, however, the elation typically wears off, and the new vampire begins to feel remorse, guilt, and depression over an existence that is unbearable and intolerable.

Drawing on her extensive knowledge of vampire folklore and legend, the novelist Anne Rice gives an extraordinarily detailed account of the birth of a vampire in her best-selling book *Interview with the Vampire*. In the book, the vampire Louis tells his tale of initiation to a young journalist in present-day America. He declares that he was reborn as a vampire at the age of 25 in the year 1791, when the vampire Lestat drained his blood to the point of death. The ritual transformation is completed a few nights later when Lestat attacks him again. Louis recalls that the movement of Lestat's lips raised the hair all over his body and sent shocks of sensation through him that were "*not unlike the pleasure of passion.*" Then Lestat bit his wrist and gave it to Louis to drink, for him to enjoy a vampire's pleasure for the first time. "*I drank, sucking the blood out of the holes, experiencing for the first time since infancy the special pleasure of sucking nourishment, the body focused with the mind upon one vital source.*"

After this powerful experience Louis is fully reborn as a vampire. He has left his earthly life behind and now sees the world around him through the eyes of mystery. The account below is the first account in fiction of how a vampire sees, hears, and feels after his transformation. It shows that once reborn as a vampire, Louis is endowed with a heightened sense of reality.

I saw as a vampire ... It was as if I had only just been able to see colors and shapes for the first time. I was so enthralled with the buttons on Lestat's black coat that I looked at nothing else for a long time. Then Lestat began to laugh and I heard his laughter as I had never heard anything before. His heart I still heard like the beating of a drum, and now came this metallic laughter. It was confusing, each sound running into the next sound, like the mingling reverberations of bells, until I had learned to separate the sounds, and then they overlapped, each soft and distinct, increasing but discrete, peals of laughter.

Bite

Although some vampires, most notably psychic vampires, do not take blood through biting, according to many traditions a vampire must bite its victim in order to drink the blood it needs to survive.

In folklore, although a vampire's attack might cause a victim to become a vampire in some cases, generally the vampiric state did not manifest until after death. Fear of vampire infestation led to the exhumation of corpses and their treatment as vampires rather than to the persecution of the living. It was not until the early twentieth century that greater emphasis was placed on the bite of a vampire as a method of attack. In nineteenth-century vampire fiction victims of vampires did not become vampires; they either died or survived the attack. In *Dracula* those bitten by Dracula die but survive as a vampire. The Count does kill Renfield but not by draining him of blood.

The jugular

The bite of a vampire is usually a two-pronged one in the neck, but the location can vary. For example, in the nineteenth century, vampires were believed to bite over the heart, where they left a sickly bruise. As the seat of love, biting close to the heart added a certain poetic resonance to the blood-sucking act, which may explain why vampires made breast incisions in such works as *Carmilla* (1872) by Sheridan Le Fanu.

In addition to the chest a vampire might also bite a person's limbs or their wrist, but it was Bram Stoker's *Dracula* (1897) which confirmed the jugular as the vein of preference for a vampire; perhaps because the jugular is both a sensual and accessible place from which large amounts of blood could be drawn. The first visible bite marks in a motion picture appeared in 1931 in a Spanish-language version of *Dracula* and resembled a snake bite. Over the years the "two hole" puncture-style bite was replaced by seductive love bites that leave both upper and lower bite marks. The vampire bat leaves a two-prong bite mark on its victims' skin and this may go some way to explain why they have became associated with the vampire myth.

In some vampire lore the bite of a vampire is instantly healed after an attack and there are no bite marks left behind. If, however, bite marks are left behind, from the point of view of a forensic scientist a vampire bite mark would be considered unusual because fangs are involved. Human beings don't have fangs so the bite may initially be identified as coming from an animal. If, however, the bruising of human teeth is identified, alongside puncture wounds or fang marks, then it might be possible to put forward a case for a vampire attack – assuming, of course, that vampires retain some of their mortal teeth.

Black

Colors have different meanings in different cultures. These meanings have altered over the centuries, but in Western art, religion, and folklore, because it is associated with darkness and an absence of light black is the color most often associated with the powers of darkness and of evil. It's small wonder, then, in literature and film, villains and vampires, like Dracula, typically dress in black.

Our emotional reaction to color is instantaneous and although this response will vary from person to person, consciously or unconsciously we are aware that some colors – such as green and yellow – are warm and inviting, whereas other colors, like red and black, are more menacing and threatening because of the associations they trigger in our minds. Red, for example, is the color of blood and black is a symbol of darkness or the night. Our reaction to black can therefore be overwhelming because the absence of light or color, the primordial void, evokes strong emotions.

Symbolically, black is the color of the night and by association death, hate, fear, and evil in Western culture. However, many color experts and folklore traditions suggest it can also represent power, sexuality, sophistication, style, intelligence, formality, and wealth. In pagan cultures black represents the absence of negativity, and in other cultures it is associated with fertility. But even if black is given a more positive spin, it is still strongly associated with mystery, the depths of the unknown, and with a different world from that of everyday reality – making it the ideal color for the vampire. Other images and emotions it may conjure up include sadness, depth, aloofness, remorse, and hidden anger. It can also mean sorrow or mourning, in the Christian tradition of wearing black to funerals, and submission; priests wear black to express their complete dedication to God.

Black Blood

According to those who study the science and biology of vampires, vampire blood is said to be black because it lacks a certain protein in the red blood cells called hemoglobin.

William of Newburgh, a twelfth-century English monk and chronicler describes perhaps the earliest record of black blood in 1196. The incident took place at Melrose Abbey in Scotland and concerned a dead priest who had supposedly risen from his grave at night to harass a woman he knew when he was alive. The woman reported the revenant to the Church officials and two guards were assigned to watch over the grave. One of the guards witnessed the revenant rise up from the grave and he struck at it with an axe, leaving a wound in its body before it disappeared again into the grave. The following day Church officials opened the grave and witnesses reported a fresh, open wound with thick, black blood flowing out of it. The corpse was removed and burned and the revenant was never seen again.

The black blood of a vampire is also thought to have excess amounts of adrenaline in it. Adrenaline is the "fight or flight" hormone released to give us increased alertness and energy when under threat, and this profusion of adrenaline helps the vampire move with incredible speed and power.

See also: **BIOLOGY OF VAMPIRES; BLOOD**

Black Dagger Brotherhood

The Black Dagger Brotherhood is a bestselling vampire romance series by author J. R. Ward, a pseudonym for contemporary American writer Jessica Rowley Pell Bird. The series focuses on six vampire brothers and their warriors, who live together and defend their race against lessers, de-souled humans who threaten their kind.

Dark Lover (2005) is the first book in the series. It tells the story of Wrath, the last pure-bred vampire left on the planet. Blaming himself for not intervening when his parents were killed, Wrath descends into self-hatred and emotional distance, but when the lessers kill one of his best fighters, he is left with the responsibility to help the warrior's half-human daughter, Beth, through her transformation. It is through Beth that Wrath learns to feel and look toward the future of his life and of the species as a whole.

See also: **LITERATURE**

Black, Jacob

A fictional character in the international bestselling Twilight Saga book series by vampire author Stephenie Meyer, Jacob Black is described as a Native American of the Quileute tribe in La Push, near Forks, Washington.

Jacob Black has a small role in the first book in the series, *Twilight* (2005). He is the son of the heroine Bella Swan's father's friend and he introduces her to the idea that her mysterious boyfriend Edward is a vampire by telling her Quileute legends. During *New Moon* (2006), the second book in the series, Jacob undergoes a transformation that enables him to shape-shift into a werewolf, and he develops into a central character in the series.

Black Magic

Frequently associated with vampirism and vampires, black magic is the use of supernatural and psychic power for evil ends. It is the opposite of white magic, which is concerned with healing and promoting what is good.

Through the centuries the term "black magic" has been used with a wide variety of meanings, and it evokes such a variety of reactions that it has become vague and almost meaningless. It is often synonymous with three other terms with multiple meanings: witchcraft, the occult, and sorcery. The only similarity among its various uses is that it refers to efforts to manipulate the supernatural with negative intent and the selfish use of psychic power for personal gain. Workers of black magic are thought to have but one goal – to satisfy their own desires at whatever cost to others. Therefore any vampire who uses his or her supernatural powers to satisfy their desires at the expense of others could be said to be practicing the art of black magic.

Black and white

Magic, good or evil, is universal, with no ethnic or racial association, and it is unfortunate that not just in Western civilization but many cultures around the world, good and evil have for centuries been denoted as white and black. White often designates healing, truth, purity, light, and positive energy, while black is darkness, falsehood, evil, and negative energy. To understand why black and white and not other colors became significant, you need to go back into prehistory and imagine how terrifying the night was for humans before we learned to use fire. The black of night was full of unseen threats, a dangerous time you might not survive. The white light of day brought illumination and safety.

In modern times probably the most popular synonym for black magic is the occult. Originally the term meant hidden, hence mysterious, and was routinely used by classical and medieval scholars to refer to "sciences" such as astrology, alchemy, and kabbalah; however, from the late nineteenth century, when magical sects such as The Order of the Golden Dawn emerged, the term began to take on the meaning of evil or satanic. Perhaps the best-known occultist and black magic practitioner was Aleister Crowley (1875–1947), who dubbed himself the Antichrist. More than any other person Crowley gave the occult an evil connotation.

See also: **BLACK; BLACK MAGICIANS; MAGIC; OCCULT; SATANISM; SORCERER; SUPERNATURAL; WITCHCRAFT**

Black Magicians

In medieval times black magicians were believed to be wizards who had the power to raise the dead from their graves. In some parts of the Nordic world it was said that black magicians could also steal the breath of anyone they took a disliking to. The process was known as *mundklem* and it has strong similarities to psychic vampirism, in that the vital energies of a person were drained away from a distance until the person got weaker and weaker and eventually died.

In some cases these magicians had previously been men of the Church who had switched their allegiance from Christ to the Devil so they could practice black magic. One noteworthy black magician was Gottstkalk the Evil of Holar (1497–1520). Gottskalk was a Scandinavian bishop who wrote a grimoire or manual of black magic called the Raudeskin, which contained spells for raising the dead and controlling them so they could attack the living. The Raudeskin also included instructions and diagrams for making magic staves – wooden staves believed to hold magical powers. One of these staves was carved with the runic symbol Aegishjalmur, or "helm of awe." This was believed to have the power to summon blood-drinking devils from hell to transform a body into an animated corpse.

See also: **BLACK MAGIC; OCCULT; SATANISM; SORCERER; SUPERNATURAL; WITCHCRAFT**

Black Mass

A black Mass is a blasphemous imitation of the Roman Catholic Mass. It is performed by Satanists and the basic proceedings of a normal Mass are reversed or twisted.

Vampirism has been connected to this ceremony from the Middle Ages onward, when it was thought that people who dabbled with the black arts or black magic would inevitably return from the dead because they had made a pact with the Devil. There is disagreement among historians about how the rites were performed but typically a naked woman's back was used as an altar and a priest desecrated the consecrated host and made blood offerings. Through its spells and sacrificial blood offerings a black Mass was thought to be an effective ritual for reviving a vampire.

See also: **SATANISM; WITCHCRAFT**

Black Stallion

According to Slavic folklore, a black stallion that has no spots or marks can detect the grave of a vampire. The stallion is walked around a graveyard, where it will refuse to step over a grave if it is the grave of a vampire.

See also: **HORSE**

Blackthorn

According to tradition, blackthorn – a shrub belonging to the *Prunus* genus and found throughout Europe – was thought to offer powerful protection against vampires and vampire attack. Belief in the supposed supernatural power of blackthorn (and other thorny woods) dates back to the time of Christ and the crown of thorns he wore at the crucifixion. The Romanians were so convinced of its effectiveness they sewed it into their clothes. In the case of the Lastovo Island Vampires, blackthorn was believed to be the only shrub strong enough to destroy them.

See also: **THORNS**

Black Veil, the

Devised by the Sanguinarium movement, a loosely based organization for people who fashion their lives and their lifestyles around vampires, the Black Veil is a set of rules for vampire etiquette. The rules were compiled by occultist and psychic vampire Michelle Belanger and COVICA (the Council of Vampyric International Community Affairs) in 2000 as a voluntary standard of common sense, ethics, and ideals for the Sanguinarium and the greater vampire community.

The rules of the Black Veil, also known as Rules of Community, all have the same goal, which is to foster mutual respect, discretion, and safety among community members. The Black Veil is embraced by some vampire lifestylers and disliked by others, due to its apparent status as a forced authority. It was, however, designed as an ethical code that can be adopted by anyone in the community, and was not designed to instruct people on how to become vampires.

Blackwood, Algernon (1869–1951)

An English-born horror writer, Algernon Blackwood was regarded as one of the foremost horror writers of his generation. BBC radio listeners came to know him as the "Ghost Man" who read stories over the radio. Educated at Cambridge University before moving to Canada and eventually becoming a reporter in New York City, his first book, *The Empty House and Other Ghost Stories*, was published in 1906 and a series of books followed, mostly with a supernatural or horrifying theme.

Blackwood's vampire short stories include: "With Intent to Steal" (1906), "The Terror of the Twins" (1910), "Descent into Egypt" (1914), and his most famous vampire story, "The Transfer" (1912). "The Transfer" features not one but two "vampires," the first of which is a predatory psychic vampire called Mr. Frene:

> *a man who drooped alone, but grew vital in a crowd. He vampired, unknowingly, no doubt, everyone with whom he came in contact; left them exhausted, tired, listless … he took your ideas, your strength, your very words, and later used them for his own benefit and aggrandizement … His eyes and voice and presence devitalised you.*

The rival vampire in the story is a barren patch of earth in an old rose garden that hungers for life, and it represents the larger, devouring, inescapable, and cruel aspects of nature.

See also: **LITERATURE**

Blacula

A 1972 American film, released by American International Pictures and directed by William Crain about an African American vampire, Prince Mamuwalde, played by William Marshall.

Although criticized for being a rather formulaic vampire movie, *Blacula* became a cult favorite, due in part to the fact that Marshall, a Shakespearean actor of considerable talent, added great depth to the vampire character. It was also the first attempt to convert the vampire genre to popular black cinema. In the film an African prince travels through nineteenth-century Europe to campaign against the slave trade. He is turned into a vampire when he meets Count Dracula. After numerous decades locked in a coffin in Dracula's castle he is transported to modern-day Los Angeles and released. He kills to feed on his victim's blood but is plagued with regret, and eventually commits suicide by walking onto a sunlit roof. An uninspired and less successful box office sequel, *Scream, Blacula, Scream*, was released in 1973.

Blade the Vampire Hunter

Blade is a fictional vampire hunter in the Marvel Comics universe that later became a character in both films and television.

Comic books

Created by writer Marv Wolfman and cartoonist Gene Colan, Blade's first appearance was in the comic book *The Tomb of Dracula* #10 (July 1973) as a supporting character. In this issue Blade appears on the London docks where he proceeds to kill several vampire members of Dracula's legion. The character reappeared through 70 further issues of *The Tomb of Dracula*. He disappeared in the 1980s and reappeared again in issue 10 of *Dr. Strange: Sorcerer Supreme* (November, 1989) and the revived *Tomb of Dracula* series (1991–92). Eventually the character was given his own comic book series, *Blade the Vampire Hunter*, which ran for 10 issues between 1994 and 1995. For several years Blade did not appear, until a new *Blade* series was launched in March 1998 to coincide with the release of what was to be a highly successful movie version from New Line Cinema.

Movie

Blade, the movie released in 1998, was critically acclaimed and grossed $70 million at the US box office, and $130 million worldwide; this success is often credited with starting the current superhero revival in American cinema. Two sequels – *Blade II* (2002), which was even more successful, making $80 million in the United States and $150 million worldwide, and *Blade: Trinity* (2004), which grossed $130 million overall – were subsequently produced. Although box office takings for the two sequels were strong, neither was as well received by the critics as the original movie. In all three films black actor Wesley Snipes plays the titular character, a half-man, half-vampire superhero vampire hunter who becomes the protector of humans against the vampires. The cinema film diverges a little from the comic series in the character of Blade. In the comic series Blade is presented as a boastful, eloquent, and confident character, but in the film his character is stoic and quiet, almost monosyllabic. At the end of the first movie, Blade also proves himself to be remarkably heroic and self-sacrificing when he chooses to forgo a cure for vampirism in order to continue protecting humans by hunting vampires with their own powers.

TV series

In June 2006 the first in a series of 13 American television films based on the Marvel comic character and popular *Blade* movie trilogy was released. Kirk Jones starred in the title role. The two-hour pilot for a *Blade* TV film series was directed by Peter O'Fallen from a script by David S. Goyer (who also wrote the three feature films) and noted comic writer Geoff Johns. The plot in the TV movie series began where the Blade movies ended. Although the series premier had 2.5 million viewers it failed to hold its numbers, and in September 2006 the press announced that no second series of the show would be commissioned.

Blavatsky, Madame Helena (1831–91)

Helena Petrovna Blavatsky, the daughter of Russian aristocrats, was a key figure in the nineteenth-century revival of occult and esoteric knowledge. A highly intelligent and energetic woman, she helped to spread Eastern philosophies and mystical ideas to the West and tried to give the study of the occult a scientific and public face.

Life and teachings

Blavatsky became aware of her psychic abilities at an early age. She traveled through the Middle East and Asia learning psychic and spiritual techniques from various teachers, and she said that it was in Tibet that she met the secret masters or adepts who sent her to carry their message to the world. In 1873 she traveled to New York, where she impressed everyone with her psychic feats of astral projection, telepathy, clairvoyance, clairsentience (a form of extra-sensory perception by which a person acquires psychic knowledge primarily by means of feeling) and clairaudience (extra-sensory auditory perception).

Blavatsky's powers were never tested scientifically, but her interests were always more in the laws and principles of the psychic world than psychic power itself. In 1874 she met and began a lifelong friendship with Colonel Henry Steel Olcott, a lawyer and journalist who covered spiritual phenomena, and a year later they founded a society "to collect and diffuse a knowledge of the laws which govern the Universe." They called this society the Theosophical Society, from theosophy, a Greek term meaning "divine wisdom" or "wisdom of the gods."

Traveling to India, Blavatsky and Olcott established themselves at Adyar, near Madras, and a property they bought there eventually became the worldwide headquarters of the society. They established the nucleus of the movement in Britain and founded no fewer than three Theosophical Societies in Paris. Throughout her life Blavatsky's powers were dismissed as fraud and trickery, but this did not stop the Theosophical Society from finding a home among intellectuals and progressive thinkers of her day. The society was born at a time when spiritualism was popular and Darwin's theory of evolution was undermining the Church's teachings, so the Society's new thinking flourished. Many people appreciated the alternative it offered both to Church dogma and to a materialistic view of the world.

Blavatsky drew her teachings from many religious traditions: Hinduism, Tibetan Buddhism, Platonic thought, Jewish Kabbalah, and the occult and scientific knowledge of her time. Her teachings are difficult to read but were absorbed by many people and then simplified into a worldview that was taken up by many later New Age groups. This worldview includes a belief in seven planes of existence; the gradual evolution and perfecting of spiritual principles; the existence of nature spirits ("devas"); and belief in secret spiritual masters or adepts from the Himalaya, or from the spiritual planes, who guide the evolution of humanity.

Isis Unveiled

In her writings Blavatsky presents esoteric views on the origins of vampires on earth and also examines the question of psychic vampirism, describing it as a kind of "occult osmosis." Her principal work, *Isis Unveiled*, a two-volume compendium of theosophical lore, contains an intriguing story of a Russian vampire, supposedly reported by an eyewitness earlier in the century. In the story a cruel governor weds and then abuses a beautiful young girl. When he falls ill he makes the girl swear she will never remarry, promising to return from the dead and kill her if she does. After his death the girl marries the man she has always loved and the governor duly returns from the grave. Each night his risen corpse rides in a black coach drawn by six black horses to her house. He enters her house and drains her blood, bringing death closer with each nightly visit. Local officials try to save the woman by exhuming the governor's body. They find his corpse perfectly preserved and bloated with blood. A stake is plunged through his heart, followed by an exorcism, and the girl is saved.

In the same book, Blavatsky also makes it very clear that the corpse of the future vampire is in a "magnetic stupor," and in this state the soul may be attracted back into the body, in which case,

> *either the unhappy victim will writhe in the agonizing torture of suffocation, or, if he has been grossly material (i.e. having an overpowering affinity for physical existence), he becomes a vampire.*
>
> *The bicorporal life begins; and these unfortunate buried cataleptics sustain their miserable lives by having their astral bodies rob the life-blood from the living persons. The æthereal form can go wherever it pleases; and so long as it does not break the link which attaches it to the body, it is at liberty to wander about, either visible or invisible, and feed on human victims.*

Blessed Objects

Vampire folklore contains a number of references to the use of blessed objects or weapons to repel or kill vampires. For example, in Eastern Europe, it was common practice to bury the dead with a crucifix to sanctify the corpse and to prevent it from turning into a vampire. A sacred bullet could also be fired into a coffin of an alleged vampire to kill it. There is very little detail about how a bullet could be made sacred, but the assumption is that it had been blessed by a priest or simply sprinkled with holy water.

From a religious point of view the use of any blessed object has a powerful effect. A blessing is thought to charge or endow an object with the belief of the person doing the blessing, and it is this belief and devotion to God that has the power to damage a supernatural creature in both physical and unseen ways. That is why exorcism uses objects such as holy water and crucifixes because the essence of these objects can work on unseen levels. However, on an occult or mystical level, an object does not necessarily have to be a religious one to be effective against a vampire; any item that agrees with the vampire hunter's belief could work in the same way as an extension of the hunter's will, and many vampire movies, TV films, and books contain the idea that a crucifix can only work to repel or kill a vampire if the victim truly believes it can work.

See also: **APOTROPAICS**

Blood

There are many definitions of what a vampire is but, with the exception of psychic vampires, essentially the traditional vampire is a blood drinker, a creature who feeds on the blood of humans or animals. In this way the relationship of the vampire to blood could be said to define it.

Mystery and religion

Since primitive times, blood has been connected with mystery and religion, as well as with life, illness, and death. When blood is lost a person feels weak, and when too much blood is lost a person will die. This is probably why blood came to be considered a person's life force, with sacred, even magical properties. Blood was thought to be soul, strength, and rejuvenating force, and blood sacrifices of humans and animals were performed to unleash these powers and appease the gods with the greatest gift that humankind can offer.

Across cultures blood has been used or referred to symbolically in religious rituals – from blood sacrifices to the goddess Kali in India, to the symbolic drinking of Christ's blood in Christianity. In the biblical tradition the ancient Jewish leaders made a firm connection between blood and life. In the Old Testament book of Genesis (9:4), God tells Noah that he *"must not eat the flesh with the life, which is the blood, still in it."* The book of Leviticus contains detailed rules for a system of blood sacrifice in which animal blood is shed as an offering to God. It also contains one of the most quoted phrases in vampire literature, *"for the blood is the life."*

Christianity took Jewish belief in blood as life a step further in that Jesus, the incarnation of God who was crucified by the Romans, was the ultimate human sacrifice to God. In the Gospel of St. Matthew (26:28) Jesus takes a cup of wine and tells his disciples to *"drink from it, all of you. For this is my blood, the blood of the covenant, shed for many for the forgiveness of sins."* Centuries later the blood of Christ, in the form of red wine in the Eucharist, became the most sacred of objects in Christianity. This may go some way to explain why the blood-sucking vampire, directly defying all that was sacred, was especially feared in Christian Europe.

Sacred fluid

Since ancient times blood has been drunk, rubbed on bodies, and used in ceremonies for religious or ritual reasons. When blood is drunk a small amount gets broken down in the stomach into iron and proteins, but ingestion of blood generally tends to provoke vomiting and has no real nutritional or health benefit. However, most blood drinking reported in history has little to do with nutrition and more with the belief that drinking blood can enhance power in some way. Warriors of many cultures drank the blood of their enemies to symbolically enhance their power and absorb the strength of their enemies. In seventeenth-century Yorkshire, in England, there were reports that women drank the blood of their enemies to boost their fertility.

The distinct red color of blood as it flows out of the body also endowed anything red with sacred powers. Red objects and red wine, for example, were identified with blood, and in ancient Greece drinking red wine was a symbolic ritual drinking of the god Dionysus' blood – the god of fertility and new life. To a lesser degree, blood was associated with other bodily fluids, notably semen. Men do not supply blood when they create a baby, only semen, and so it was thought that male characteristics passed to the child via the semen.

Blood as a metaphor

Blood – like the vampire itself – has the power to assume almost endless metaphorical forms. "Bad blood" suggests tension and rivalry between people; "blood brother" suggests the strong bonds of kinship; someone who is "hot blooded" is angry or passionate; "red blooded" indicates someone who is full of energy, while someone who is "cold blooded" is calculating and cruel. Belief in the power of blood to heal and destroy evil reveals itself in the misguided medical practice of blood letting, which was thought to purify the blood of evil or disease-causing properties. The strongest oath is a blood oath, in which the parties mingle their blood. It is used in many initiation rituals as many people believe that exchanging blood joins them in an unbreakable bond. Blood is also associated with sex and fertility because it is shed when a virgin loses her virginity, when a woman menstruates, and when a woman gives birth. Finally, the blood of a mother is passed to a child, therefore the virtues and defects of the parents were thought to be passed to their offspring. Thus, blood was thought to carry the characteristics of family, clans, nationalities, and races – bloodlines.

To sum up, blood is the vital fluid held in awe since prehistoric times, and in vampire folklore the belief that blood is the reanimating factor for the corpse joining the ranks of the undead remained strong for centuries. Blood is our connection to our ancient past and modern scientific explanations of the vital functions played by blood in the human body have, if anything, given it an even more mystical and revered place in human life. Vampires who drink blood therefore steal the most precious substance a person can have, essentially robbing the living of life. By consuming a person's blood, vampires wield not only the power of life and death over them but they establish an unbreakable bond. With that bond, and through the use of that person's blood, they can offer their victims ecstasy and transformation, but also anguish and pain.

See also: **BLACK BLOOD; BLOOD DISEASE; SYMBOLS**

Blood Disease

Vampire folklore arose long before the birth of modern medicine, but at the beginning of the twentieth century a dramatic shift began to occur in the vampire myth.

The novel *Dracula* (1897) mixes traditional lore about vampires with new medicine when Van Helsing uses a blood transfusion as a scientific remedy to counter the vampire's attack against Lucy Westenra. The remedy fails but the suggestion that vampirism may be a disease of the blood, caused by a germ or a chemical disorder of the blood, either of which may be passed on via the vampire's blood, rather than a supernatural state, is debated.

Hints that vampirism was a blood disease continued to appear in novels and films in the decades that followed, but it wasn't until 1954 that the idea was presented boldly in Richard Matheson's novel, *I Am Legend.* In this novel narrator Robert Neville is the only human left among an entire population transformed into vampires. Neville reads *Dracula* but finds no answers, but he does find answers in scientific study and analysis. Eventually, he discovers that the creation of vampires is the result of a contagious disease and manages to isolate the cause.

This shift in literature and film from vampirism as a supernatural state to a disease of the blood that can be explained and dealt with scientifically was mirrored in the world of science and medicine. In the mid 1960s there was serious medical speculation that vampirism could be explained by either misdiagnosed porphyria, a rare blood disorder that causes people to become sensitive to sunlight, or misdiagnosed anemia, a disease of the blood that causes a reduction in red blood cells, weakness, and pale skin. However, an examination of vampire folklore and eyewitness accounts disproves both the porphyria hypothesis and the suggestion that anemia may have been the cause. Some of the symptoms of vampirism are akin to porphyria and to anemia, but not all of them – in particular, puncture wounds on the neck or other body parts. Nonetheless, to this day people continue to associate vampirism with some physical disease, such as a blood disease or a virus, or, if no physical cause seems likely, a psychological disorder such as Renfield's syndrome.

Is vampirism a disease, a virus, a personality disorder, a diabolical experiment gone wrong, or a manifestation of pure evil? Questions like these, raised by scientists, doctors, philosophers, and writers have added a dimension of scientific reality to the vampire myth.

Blood Drinkers

According to vampire folklore, a vampire must drink blood to transform into a vampire and overcome death. There are two types of blood drinkers: immortal and mortal.

Immortal blood drinkers

In folklore there are numerous instances of immortal blood drinkers, vampires that have returned from the grave or cheated death in some way. The cases of Arnold Paole and Peter Plogojowitz are fine examples. Although there is a lot of evidence from folklore and testimony from witnesses and vampire hunters that these creatures actually do exist, many believe that much of this evidence is not convincing.

"Facts" reported many years ago, before modern science and medicine had developed, are not verifiable and cannot always be relied upon because they may have been based on superstition and ignorance. It is important, however, to take into consideration the fact that just because the existence of immortal vampires or the undead cannot be proved, does not mean that they do not exist. Although immortal vampires do not seem to be active today a number of theories have been put forward to explain how they might exist. Ancient explanations include demonic possession, a restless soul reanimating a corpse, and witchcraft, in that a corpse is magically sustained by blood. Vampire attack was regarded as another possible cause.

Mortal blood drinkers

Not all blood drinkers are the undead. Throughout history right up to the present day, there are human beings with a definite need to drink or share human blood. These people drink blood for a number of reasons, ranging from ancient beliefs in the sacred power of blood, to the use of blood for sexual excitement (blood fetishism), to a form of insanity known as Renfield's syndrome. Famous historical vampires of the past include notorious murderers, such as Elizabeth Báthory and Gilles de Rais, but there are also mortal blood drinkers who do not want to kill to obtain blood. The sanguinarian movement is for modern blood drinkers who wish to drink and share blood safely and painlessly with willing donors, known as blood dolls. Some mortal blood drinkers find blood-drinking to be an erotic experience, and others find that it makes them feel empathically linked to their donor, cementing bonds between vampire and donor that are emotional and spiritual in nature.

A number of vampire authors who don't want their fictional vampires to be brutal murderers have attempted to substitute animal blood for human blood. However, according to the American National Heart, Lung, and Blood Institute, *"There is no substitute for human blood,"* and many people in the vampire subculture claim that human blood tastes better and gives more energy. For "real" vampires, animal blood is therefore an inadequate substitute. Other authors have had their vampires rely on blood banks or willing blood donors for sustenance.

Digestion

As far as digestion is concerned, those who study the science of vampires suggest that the vampire's digestive process would need to adapt to digest blood and to keep it down without vomiting. The process of transformation or becoming a vampire might involve some kind of mutation of the digestive system. Others suggest that an understanding of the way that blood-sucking creatures such as bats and leeches digest blood can help explain the process. The problem is the excess amount of iron in blood, and some vampirologists have suggested that vampires have enzymes that can filter excess iron and a more finely developed net of capillaries to absorb it from the gut, or whatever the gut has turned into. In addition, vampires, like vampire bats, are equipped with a chemical called draculin. This is an anticoagulant that inhibits blood clotting.

None of these theories can be proved, but whatever the mechanism of transformation undergone in order to survive entirely on a diet of blood, the vampire's body would somehow need to adapt to using only the proteins and nutrients carried in blood in its digestion.

Blood Fetishism

A blood fetishist is someone who is erotically attracted to the sight, taste, or smell of blood; he or she generally has no physical need to consume it, and will usually be happy with small amounts. Blood fetishism, also sometimes referred to as blood play, is often accompanied by other sexual fetishes, including sadism and masochism, and the blood is usually taken during sexual or fetish play, as in a bondage or domination situation.

Sexual gratification though blood drinking has been a well-documented clinical phenomenon since 1876 when Richard von Krafft-Ebing wrote *Psychopathia Sexualis.* In the standard psychological interpretation blood can become an erotic fixation for children born into abusive families or who are victims of abuse, where the emotions of love, pain, and powerlessness can often trap them in an infantile state of insatiable emotional hunger. Not all blood fetishists are victims of abuse, but for the majority blood, as a potent symbol of warmth and belonging, carries an erotic charge. For some the act involves self-bleeding or self-mutilation, but for others it is a way of establishing intimacy or trust with another person.

Although blood fetishism is not a new phenomenon it is only in the last few decades that blood fetishists have cultivated a sense of belonging with the vampire lifestyle. A contributing factor, no doubt, has been the mass rejuvenation of the vampire image by best-selling authors such as Anne Rice and Stephenie Meyer, and the image presented in their novels of the vampire as a sensitive and intelligent outcast, craving meaningful human relationships.

Blood Letting

The physical act of cutting or piercing the flesh in order to extract blood. Blood letting was a common medical practice in the West for centuries, thanks largely to the medical theories of a second-century Greek physician, Galen, who stated that illnesses stemmed from "bad blood" and could be cured by letting out this bad blood. Blood letting continued as a medical practice well into the nineteenth century. The veins or arteries of patients would be cut with knives and bled into a bowl, or live leeches would do the work instead. Thankfully blood letting is no longer common practice, but it is still used by blood drinkers for feeding, and in blood play or fetishism.

Sanguinarians are modern-day mortal blood drinkers who do not have long or sharp fangs. Some of them claim the reason for this is dilution via the prolonged interbreeding of vampires and humans. Others say the fangs are retracted when not in use. Either way, sanguinarians rarely if ever actually bite their donors in order to draw blood. Aside from the risk of infection, as the human mouth is full of bacteria, human teeth are far too blunt for blood sucking, so sterilized instruments are often used to make the incisions instead, such as razor blades, needles, syringes, or pen-knives. Although the neck and wrist are popular locations for blood letting, sucking blood directly from fleshy areas, such as the pad under the thumb, just above the shoulder blades, or the thigh area can help minimize pain. Blood can also be extracted and poured into a glass or cup to drink.

In this age of AIDS, the practice of blood letting involves considerable risk, and sanguinarians stress how important it is for all blood donors to have a CBC – complete blood count – and general health check to eliminate any risks such as anemia, any blood clotting problems, and any blood-borne diseases. They should also be tested for viruses like HIV and hepatitis. Any razor blades or knives used should be clean and sterile, either boiled or from an airtight sealed package.

Blood Play

Term used to describe rituals, rites, fetishes, and eroticism that are based on drawing blood. Those for whom blood play involves drinking blood for sexual, spiritual, artistic, or for any other reason are often called "real" or "blood" vampires. Lifestyle and psychic vampires, on the other hand, do not drink blood.

The motivation for blood play is complex and deep seated. It can satisfy a desire for sexual excitement and it can be an outlet for emotional trauma or self-loathing. Ritual blood play can be an intimate way of sharing in and understanding the emotional pain or experiences of others. For some, blood play and real vampirism is an extension of sadomasochist sexual activity, the erotic inflicting and receiving of pain.

Some blood players are discrete, and apart from blood play episodes they lead ordinary lives. Others are more open and flaunt visible scars. Some cut only themselves, others cut only others; some are blood donors, some are only blood drinkers, others do both. There are no real rules or standard practice for becoming a blood vampire or engaging in blood play, although those who are involved stress the need for a safe and respectful approach to the practice. They say that blood play must be strictly consensual among willing adults. Sterile, sharp instruments should be used, and when blood drinking is involved rigorous blood testing is need to avoid the spread of AIDS.

See also: **BLOOD FETISHISM**

Bloodsucker

Term given to animals, such as bats and leeches, who must feed on the blood of other animals and humans to survive; bloodsucker is also a term used to describe a person who preys on another person in some way. The vampires of folklore and fiction, who can only survive by literally sucking out the blood of their victims, as well as modern-day blood drinkers, are often referred to as bloodsuckers.

Blood Tears

Vampires do not typically weep tears of blood in vampire folklore, although blood is often seen to be oozing from their mouths and other orifices, but by the end of the 1980s vampires in fiction and film had acquired the ability to weep blood tears. This notion makes Gothic and romantic sense because of its association with stigmata, but not biological sense. From a scientific point of view, there is no reason why the ingestion of blood would produce blood tears.

Blood Transfusion

See: **TRANSFORMATION**

Blood, of a Vampire

In magical spells blood is a powerful ingredient. A drop of a person's blood is believed to bring that person under the power of the spell-caster. In folklore the blood of an evil person is thought to be very potent and a powerful protector against disease, because of the energy of resentment and fury that is released on death. In East Prussian lore, the blood of executed criminals could be drunk for luck. In much the same way the blood of vampires was believed to have great magical potency in Eastern European folklore. It could either be a powerful protector or a curse. When the corpses of suspected vampires were dug up, humans had to take great care not to be sprayed by their blood, because it was thought to drive humans mad. Thus vampire corpses were often covered before they were mutilated and onlookers would stand well away from the body.

In typically contradictory style, as well as being considered a curse, vampire blood was also believed to have great healing powers. Centuries ago in the folklore of Russia and Poland, the blood of vampires was believed to protect against vampire attack. Blood bread was made by gathering blood from the corpse of a destroyed vampire. This blood was then mixed with flour and baked into bread, which was eaten to protect against vampires.

As well as drinking the blood of a vampire or baking it into a bread, people would also smear themselves with vampire blood to release themselves from the curse. The notion was that the vampire would avoid the taint of its own blood when looking for victims. According to accounts, however, this technique often failed spectacularly, as the Arnold Paole case, reported from eighteenth-century Serbia, illustrates.

Blow Vampire, The

Myslata of Blau, more commonly referred to as the Blau or Blow Vampire, was an alleged fourteenth-century vampire. According to folklore, Myslata was a herdsman who lived in a village called Kadam, in Bohemia. Soon after his death he appeared in public and called out the names of people he recognized. These people died mysteriously a few days later.

Myslata's corpse was exhumed and a stake plunged in the heart, but this did not stop it appearing again the following night. The corpse taunted the villagers; it suffocated some people and terrified others to death. The corpse was exhumed again and given to an executioner who pierced it with a whitethorn stake and then burned it. Throughout the process the vampire allegedly screamed.

A version of the story was recorded by an abbot named Neplach in a chronicle that dates back to 1336:

In Bohemia about one mile from Cadanus in a village called Blow a certain shepherd called Myslata died. Every night he rose and went about every farm in the area and spoke to frighten and kill people. When he had been impaled with a stake, he said: They hurt me much, as they gave me a staff to defend me from the dogs; and when he was exhumed for cremation, he swelled up like an ox and roared terribly. When he was placed in the fire, someone grabbed a stick and put it into him, and immediately blood poured out from him as from a vessel. Furthermore, when he had been dug up and was being put on a cart, he drew his feet to himself as if alive, and before he was cremated, anyone whom he called by name at night, died within eight days.

The case was also recorded in *Magia Posthuma* by Charles Ferdinand de Schertz in 1706.

There is no mention of blood-sucking in the story and blood is only mentioned in connection with the state of the dead body. It also appears that the malice is confined to haunting the neighborhood and naming people who consequently die within eight days, so this story might be more accurately described as a revenant or living corpse story, rather than as a vampire story. However, the means that are used to destroy him are very similar to those used against vampires – stakes and fire – so there are certain similarities.

Blue

In Greek lore, blue is a color that is thought to repel vampires and other evil creatures; blue paint around windows and doorframes was thought to prevent vampires from entering a house. In Eastern European folklore, however, a person born with blue eyes was thought to become a vampire after death, or even already be a vampire. This belief probably derived from the fact that people with blue eyes were a rarity in the area, and so any traveler or stranger with blue eyes would have been regarded with suspicion. It may also have derived from the misguided belief that it was impossible for a blue-eyed child to be born to brown-eyed parents, and so there had to be some supernatural cause to explain this phenomenon.

See also: **BLACK**; **RED**

Boden, Wayne (1948–2006)

Wayne Clifford Boden was a Canadian serial killer and rapist active from 1969–71. He earned the nickname "the Vampire Rapist" because he would feast on the breasts of his victims in what some investigators thought was a vampire-like embrace, a penchant that led to his conviction following forensic dental evidence.

On October 3, 1969, the body of Shirley Audette was found dumped at the rear of an apartment complex in downtown Montreal. Although she was fully clothed, she had been raped and strangled, and showed savage bite marks on her breasts. Then on November 23, a jewelry clerk named Marielle Archambault left work at closing time with a young man whom she introduced to her co-workers as Bill. When she did not report for work the following morning, Archambault's employer went to check on her in her apartment. She was discovered dead on the couch. The killer

had raped her, and left his telltale teeth marks on her breasts.

"Bill" waited two months before he struck again, on January 16, 1970, killing a 24-year-old woman called Jean Way. The city was gripped by fear but this was to be the last attack in Montreal. Boden moved to the city of Calgary, where, on May 18, 1971, a 33-year-old high school teacher named Elizabeth Anne Porteous did not report to work. As with Marielle Archambault, she was discovered dead in her apartment. Raped and strangled, her breasts were likewise mutilated with bite marks. Two of Porteous's colleagues had spotted her in a blue Mercedes on the night of her murder. The car was reported as having a distinctive advertising bull-shaped decal in the rear window and the following day it was spotted at a gas station. Boden was arrested half an hour later. He admitted that he had been on a date with Porteous on the night of her murder but insisted that she had been fine when he left her.

The police turned to a local orthodontist, Gordon Swann, to prove that the marks on Porteous's breasts and neck were Boden's bite marks. This orthodontic forensic evidence, along with a broken cufflink Boden left behind at the scene of the crime, was enough for the jury to find him guilty of murder, for which he was sentenced to life imprisonment. He died in 2006 of skin cancer.

See also: **HISTORICAL VAMPIRES**

Body-snatching

The practice of stealing a freshly buried corpse from its grave, body-snatching, also known as grave-robbing, is believed to have originated in France; it spread elsewhere in Europe when people realized how profitable a venture it could be. The business of body-snatching flourished between the seventeenth and nineteenth centuries and was probably the cause of a number of cases of vampire hysteria, especially as the corpses tended to disappear soon after they were buried.

Bodies were snatched from their graves for a number of reasons, ranging from necrophilia to the more lucrative custom of selling corpses to medical research institutions. Medical schools were not allowed to use many corpses, but because they needed them regularly to ensure that the study of human anatomy kept moving forward they would buy corpses from body-snatchers, known as "resurrection men." When the number of stolen corpses grew larger and larger, guards were placed at burial sites. Unable to use corpses from graveyards some resurrection men took to murdering vulnerable people, such as prostitutes and the dying, to keep their business going.

Burke and Hare

Two of the most well-known body-snatchers are William Burke and William Hare. In 1827 these Ulster immigrants moved to Edinburgh, Scotland, and killed up to 30 guests in a boarding house owned by Hare, selling the bodies to Dr. Robert Knox. After they were caught Burke was hanged on January 28, 1829, but not enough evidence could be found to convict Hare and Knox and they were spared. In a fitting end to the story, Burke's body was donated to a medical school for "useful dissection." His skeleton is still on display at the Anatomical Museum at the University of Edinburgh.

Body Temperature

According to vampirologists, a vampire's core body temperature is only about 60°F (15°C), compared with over 98°F (36°C) for humans. This lower-than-normal body temperature could theoretically prove useful to modern vampire hunters, as it would make a vampire easily distinguishable from humans when viewed through heat-sensitive infrared devices.

See also: **BIOLOGY OF VAMPIRES; TRANSFORMATION**

Bogeyman

Also referred to as a bogey in British folklore, the bogeyman is said to be an evil spirit and in some instances synonymous with the Devil. The term is also used metaphorically to refer to a person or thing of which someone else has an irrational fear. The threat of calling the terrifying bogeyman was often used by parents – and probably still is – to frighten children into good behavior. Vampires are often grouped together or associated with bogeymen, and some experts believe that fear of the dead returning may in fact be the origin of the bogeyman.

The precise origins of the bogeyman legend are unknown, but it is possible that it derived from the old European pagan gods. The Slavic for god is "bog" and after Christianity came to Europe many deities in the old religions were regarded as evil spirits. It is possible that the gods of pre-Christian Britain became known as horrible, frightening beings.

Bohemia

According to vampire historian Montague Summers, who wrote *The Vampire in Europe* in 1929, Bohemia was the main centre of vampire activity in Eastern Europe from as early as the fourteenth century, more so even than Transylvania.

From the beginning of Slavic settlements in Bohemia (possibly anytime from the beginning of the sixth century) the Slavs brought their vampire stories and legends with them. A number of ancient graves uncovered by archeologists in the province are considered to be "vampire graves," in that the remains are decapitated and the body chained to the ground to prevent the possibility of a vampire attack. Dom Augustin Calmet included reports of vampires in Bohemia in his famous 1746 treatise. He noted that in 1706, another treatise on vampires – *Magia Posthuma* by Charles Ferdinand de Schertz – reported a number of incidents of vampires who appeared as troublemaking spirits, attacking their neighbors and the village livestock. One of the earliest cases from Bohemia recorded by Schertz was that of the so-called Blow Vampire, which may date back to the fourteenth century.

In the eighteenth century vampire hysteria in Bohemia took on such proportions that the Empress Maria Theresa commissioned her personal physician, Gerard van Swieten, to scientifically examine the reports of vampire rituals. His paper, *Remarques sur le Vampirisme* (Remarks on Vampirism), examined vampire superstition in Bohemia and surrounding provinces and the dreadful rituals associated with it. In 1755, on the basis of his report, which concluded that "*vampires appear only where ignorance still rules,*" Maria Theresa had a decree drawn up regarding the persecution of vampires, forbidding all defense measures such as decapitation, impaling, or cremation. This did not, however, stop widespread belief in vampires, pockets of which still linger today in rural areas.

See also: **Slovakia**

Borgo Pass

A passage though the Carpathian Mountains in Transylvania (located now in Romania but which was in Hungary at that time), the Borgo Pass is the location in Bram Stoker's *Dracula* of Count Dracula's castle. *Dracula* opens with the journey of Jonathan Harker from Bistritz to the castle via the Borgo Pass. Through description of the journey Stoker immediately builds an initial atmosphere of claustrophobia and foreboding: "*mighty slopes of forest up to the lofty steeps of the Carpathians themselves. Right and left of us they towered … an endless perspective of jagged rock and pointed crags, til those themselves were lost in the distance, where the snowy peaks rose grandly.*" Eventually, the tunnel-like road leads to a "*vast ruined castle, from whose tall black windows came no ray of light, and whose broken battlements showed a jagged line against the moonlit sky.*"

The real Borgo Pass is much tamer than the description given by Stoker, which is perhaps more reminiscent of Switzerland, a region he was more familiar with. The Borgo Pass lies in the middle of the 900-mile crescent of the Carpathians that extend from Romania into Slovakia. The elevation of the peaks rise up to 8,000 feet. The road to the Borgo Pass winds gently through woods and open fields and today the Castle Dracula Hotel can be found situated at the top of the pass. Even though the location is remote, and Stoker clearly added a great deal of imagination to his description of it, it is still the place of choice for organizations like the Transylvanian Society of Dracula to meet.

Bori

A spirit with vampiric qualities in West African lore, the Bori are thought to be able to kill humans by slowly sucking out their life force so that the person dies of a wasting illness.

According to the Hausa people, all illnesses are caused by specific bori, who live in forested areas and can appear in human form, either with hoofed feet or without a head. The bori can also shape-shift into animal form and the only telltale signs of its true nature are a dreamy look and footprints in ashes that look like claws. If placated with respect and ritual dance, performed in a trance-like state, the bori will not harm people; however, if its name is spoken in vain, or if someone is careless and the sparks of a fire hit it, the bori can become angry and attack humans. These attacks can be warded off by charms and prayers. Iron is also thought to repel it.

See also: **AFRICA**

Borneo

Borneo is the third largest island in the world and is located at the center of maritime Southeast Asia. Its vampire tradition is largely a product of cultural diffusion from Malaysia, but in some areas of the island there are unique folklore beliefs about what happens to the body and spirit after death. It is thought that the spirit can only leave the body when the corpse has rotted completely down to dry bones. This process takes some time and while the body is gradually decaying, the spirit lurks miserably on the fringes of human habitation and its discomfort may affect the living with illness. The spirit only stops feeling drawn to the living when its body is finally reduced to bones.

Some tribes in Borneo today still carry this belief. They would be dismayed by burial practices in America and Europe which do not separate the bones of a body from the flesh, believing that such lack of attention could create an army of potential zombies.

Bottling a Vampire

In Bulgarian lore, bottling a vampire is believed to be one of the most effective ways to trap, imprison, and destroy vampires. It can, however, only be accomplished by a sorcerer or someone with a powerful will and an excellent sense of balance.

In *The Vampire: His Kith and Kin* (1928) Montague Summers gives a description of the bottling process. His description betrays a certain degree of sympathy for the vampire's predicament:

The sorcerer, armed with a picture of some saint, lies in ambush until he sees the vampire pass, when he pursues him with his icon; the poor vampire takes refuge on a tree or on the roof of a house. But his persecutor follows him up with the talisman, driving him away from his shelter, in the direction of a bottle specifically prepared, in which is placed some of the vampire's favourite food. Having no other resource, he enters this prison and is immediately fastened with a cork, on the interior of which is a fragment of the icon. The bottle is then thrown into the fire and the vampire disappears forever.

Boucicault, Dion (1820–90)

Irish-born actor and playwright, Dion Boucicault's plays on the vampire theme played an important part in the spread of vampires in the consciousness of mid-nineteenth-century England and America.

Best known for *Love in a Maze, London Assurance, The Shaughraun, The Vampire, A Phantasm in Three Dramas*, and *The Phantom*, as a playwright Boucicault had an uncanny knack for anticipating the fickle tastes of his audiences on both sides of the Atlantic and providing them with just the novelty they wanted. In *The Vampire* (1852) three acts follow a set of characters through their descendants. The heroine learns of her danger through a dream in which the portraits of her ancestors come to life to warn her that the vampire seeks both the love and the blood of a virgin to give him new life in another century. *The Vampire* was not well received by critics or the public, but Boucicault found a fan in Queen Victoria who attended the benefit pre-

miere in London and returned the following week to review the drama a second time. Although the Queen found the second viewing fairly tedious she did commission a watercolor portrait of Boucicault in the role of the vampire.

In its more simplified and realistic transatlantic incarnation, *The Phantom* (1856), the play seems to have fared much better with the public. According to its producer, Samuel French, the 1856 production at Wallack's Theatre, New York *"was crowded to excess, and the enterprise netted ten thousand dollars in a run of eleven weeks, unprecedented in the history of the New York stage."*

See also: **STAGE**

Brahmaparush

A cruel vampire species found in parts of northern India, the brahmaparush is said to drink the blood and eat the flesh from the skulls of its victims, and to perform a ritualistic dance with the body's intestines wrapped around its head.

See also: **INDIA**

Bram Stoker's Dracula

One of the most memorable, but also the most heavily criticized, film adaptations of Bram Stoker's novel, *Bram Stoker's Dracula* from Columbia Pictures opened on November 13, 1992. Directed by one of Hollywood's top directors, Francis Ford Coppola, with a screenplay by James V. Hart, the film stared Gary Oldman as Count Dracula, Anthony Hopkins as Van Helsing, Keanu Reaves as

Jonathan Harker, and Winona Ryder as Mina Harker.

Coppola's intention was to make an accurate version of the story and the film is faithful to Stoker's intent, but not to the letter as there are a number of significant departures from Stoker's novel. For example, *Dracula* does not open in 1462 as the film does with the story of Vlad the Impaler, the fifteenth-century Romanian ruler who serves as an historical reference for Dracula's character. Neither is *Dracula* the novel a love story, with the unspoken "love is stronger than death" subtitle of the film.

After the prelude, in which Vlad curses God and becomes a vampire after the love of his life, Elizabeth, dies, the movie opens with Jonathan Harker, an English solicitor's clerk, leaving his fiancée, Mina to travel to Castle Dracula in Transylvania so that the count can sign some real estate papers. Although both novel and film show Dracula becoming progressively younger after arriving in England and drinking the blood of his victims, the movie diverges most notably from the novel when instead of Dracula's attack on Mina being one of predatory supernatural horror, it becomes one of longing and love. Dracula falls for Mina because she is a mirror image of his former love Elizabeth. In the final scene Mina visits the dying Dracula and through her love Dracula finds redemption.

None of the scenes in *Bram Stoker's Dracula* were shot on location; all the scenes were filmed on specially prepared sets in Hollywood. The release of the movie was accompanied by a massive advertising campaign, which included hundreds of souvenir items, comic books, trading cards, jewelry, posters, and games. Despite mixed reviews it was a box office success and grossed more than $132 million.

Brazil

See: ASEMA; IARA; JARACACA; LOBISHOMEN; PISHTACO

Breaking Dawn

Released on August 2, 2008, *Breaking Dawn* is the fourth novel in the Twilight Saga series by Stephenie Meyer. From its initial print run of 3.7 million copies, 1.3 million were sold in the first 24 hours of its release, setting a record in first-day sales for the Hachette Book Group USA.

Breath of a Vampire

In Bram Stoker's *Dracula* (1897), Count Dracula's breath is described as terrible, and this is in keeping with European vampire folklore where one of the means of identifying a vampire or revenant is by his or her foul breath. The breath of a vampire is often remarked upon and described as foul or reeking like rotting food. The reasons for this are fairly obvious: a vampire's diet consists of blood and there is no need for dental hygiene. The increasingly sophisticated vampires of recent fiction and film, however, generally don't suffer from halitosis.

Any discussion of vampire breath begs the question: Do vampires, or indeed any creature that is undead, breathe? Some vampirologists suggest that vampires only breathe lightly because they get all the oxygen they need from blood and their need for oxygen from the air is far lower than it is for humans. Other vampire experts state that because vampires don't have a beating heart to pump oxygen around their body, they don't actually need to breathe at all. They can, however, choose to breathe to appear normal to humans and to allow air to pass through their voice box so they can speak.

Breslau Vampire, The

The Breslau Vampire was the name given to a revenant that allegedly terrorized the city of Breslau, Poland in 1591–92. The story was recorded by the seventeenth-century writer Henry More, in his *Antidote to Atheism*. The case demonstrates folklore belief that a revenant could be created by suicide and by improper burial rites.

The story

In Breslau, one of the chief towns of Silesia, on Friday, September 20, 1591, a shoemaker killed himself by slitting his own throat with a knife. His wife discovered his body and to avoid the shame of suicide washed him and dressed his corpse in such a way as to claim he had died of some sort of disease. The man was given a Christian burial despite the rules forbidding the religious interment of suicides. However, within weeks rumors started circulating that the shoemaker had killed himself.

The relatives were questioned by the authorities and made up more lies. The authorities persisted and the council considered what action to take. The widow and her friends pleaded for the body not to be exhumed or moved to unhallowed ground. Meanwhile a restless ghost that looked like the shoemaker began to appear day and night.

According to vampire historian Montague Summers in *The Vampire in Europe* (1929):

> *For this terrible Apparition would sometimes stand by their bed-sides, sometimes cast itself upon the midst of their beds, would lie close to them and pinch them, that not only blue marks, but plain impression of the fingers would be upon sundry parts of their bodies in the morning.*

The ghost also began to appear during the day and no one in the city felt safe. After eight months of suffering, the authorities eventually ordered the body to be publicly exhumed on April 18, 1592.

> *In the opened grave they found the body entire, not at all putrid, no ill smell about him saving the mustiness of the grave-cloths, his joints limber and flexible, as in those who are alive, his skin only flaccid . . . the wound of his throat gaping, but no gear nor corruption in it.*

The corpse was kept unburied until the 24th and lots of people came to see it. Then it was reburied under the gallows, but this did not improve the situation. The dead man's attacks became more violent. Finally, the widow broke down and admitted that he had committed suicide and said the city could do with him what they thought was best.

On May 7 the body was dug up again and reported to have grown *"more sensibly fleshy"* since its previous interment. They cut off the head, legs, and arms of the corpse and – through the back – cut out the heart, which looked as fresh as the heart of a newly killed calf. They burned the various parts, gathered the ashes in a sack, and poured them into the river. After this the dead man was never seen again.

There were also reports of the shoemaker's maid who died after him also returning from the grave to assault people at night, sometimes in the shape of a woman, at other times as a dog, a cat, a hen or a goat. After her corpse was disinterred and burned, she was never seen again. Unlike reports of the shoemaker's appearance, which appear to be more authentic, the reports concerning the maidservant sound like the telltale signs of a group of people whose imagination is being fed by hysterical fear.

Brides, of Vampires

"Vampire bride" is the term sometimes used to describe the relationship between a male vampire and his female victims. Sometimes this relationship has developed by implication in novels and films in a manner similar to a Middle Eastern harem.

The idea probably derived from Bram Stoker's 1897 novel *Dracula*. In the opening chapters Dracula is depicted as living alone in his castle with three young women, described as *"ghostly women"* and *"weird sisters."* Later in the novel, there is the suggestion, following the death of Lucy Westenra, that the sharing of blood between Dracula and Lucy created a kind of husband–wife-like bond between them. The notion of vampire brides emphasizes the sexual nature of the vampire's relationship to his victims. The vampire, usually male, attacks his victims, rapes them, and then makes them his slaves. In the twentieth century this notion was developed further in vampire novels and films, most notably *The Brides of Dracula* made by Hammer Films in 1960.

Brite, Poppy (1967–)

American author Poppy Brite achieved considerable success in the 1990s as a literary representative of the Gothic horror genre. She also highlighted the role of vampires within this genre.

Brite's first novel, *Lost Souls* (1992), traces the modern adventures of a small group of vampires and focuses on Nothing, the offspring of Zillah, a 100-year-old vampire and another vampire with whom Zillah had a one-night stand. The alienated Nothing searches for his roots and the meaning of his existence. Brite returned to the theme of vampires a few years later with two critically acclaimed collections of contemporary vampire literature: *Love in Vein* (1994) and *Love in Vein II* (1996).

See also: LITERATURE

British Isles, The

The British Isles do not have a reputation for contributing prominently to vampire folklore and mythology but there have been a number of hugely significant contributors to the development of the fictional vampire, most notably Bram Stoker with his 1897 novel *Dracula*.

Early reports of vampire-like beings, which are similar to vampire tales of Eastern Europe, can be found in Oxford archdeacon Walter Map's 1190 *De Nugis Curialium* ("On the Courtier's Trifles," a collection of anecdotes, stories, and gossip which preserves early medieval folk traditions), and in William of Newburgh's *Historia rerum Anglicarum* (1196).

Map's *De Nugis* discussed fairy people and the dead who returned to life, among them the Shoemaker of Constantinople, a vampire demon who murdered three children. It also mentioned the story of a knight whose wife gives birth to a son. The son is found dead one morning with his throat cut. The same thing happens to the next two children. When the fourth child is born a stranger stays awake while the family falls asleep and notices a woman come to the baby and bend over it. Before she can hurt it the stranger seizes the woman. It turns out that the captured woman is a demon who has assumed the form of a woman. Once released from the stranger's grasp she flies away screeching. William of Newburgh was the source of many famous vampire stories including those of the vampires of Melrose Abbey and Alnwick Castle. Although mention of blood drinking is missing from both the work of Map and Newburgh, their reports illustrate how vampires easily fall into the category of revenants returning to the land of the living.

In Scotland and Ireland several vampiric folklore figures can be found, such as the Scottish baobhan-sith and the Irish dearg-diulai. Welsh folklore boasts perhaps the most unusual vampire – a chair with a thirst for blood. However, such beliefs, which appeared to be widespread around the twelfth century, did not gather strength. During the seventeenth century when reports of vampires in Eastern Europe surfaced they were greeted as if a totally new phenomenon was being described.

The word "vampire"

The word "vampire" was introduced into English in 1741 when it appeared in a footnote in a book entitled *Observations on the Revolution*, which, although written in 1688, did not get published until nearly 60 years later. The term did not refer to the blood-sucking undead but was used in a comment on contemporary society, with the implication that the meaning of the term was already well known: merchants are described as *"vampires of the Publick, and Riflers of the Kingdom."* Perhaps a more influential reference appeared in the 1810 publication *Travels of Three English Gentlemen from Venice to Hamburgh, Being the Grand Tour of Germany in the Year 1734.* The reference is more significant because it was written during the height of the vampire epidemics reported in the Austro-Hungarian Empire, and describes an encounter with a vampire. An English edition of Dom Augustin Calmet's 1746 treatise on vampires was published in 1759.

In the years after Slavic vampires became well known in England the most widely reported incidents were the case of the vampire of Croglin Grange in the 1890s and the Highgate Vampire in the 1970s.

For information on British literary and film vampires see also: BYRON, LORD; COLERIDGE, SAMUEL TAYLOR; GOTHIC; HAMMER FILMS; LEE, TANITH; POLIDORI, JOHN; SOUTHEY, ROBERT; TREMAYNE, PETER; VARNEY THE VAMPIRE

Brown, James

In 1892 the *Brooklyn Daily Eagle* newspaper reported on the strange and unusual case of "James Brown," an alleged sailor vampire who was imprisoned in Washington, D.C.

According to the *Daily Eagle*, the incident occurred in 1867 when Brown, a Portuguese sailor, left Boston on a fishing smack. When two of his crew went missing, the ship's captain searched the fishing boat and discovered Brown in the hold sucking blood from the corpse of one of the missing crew members. The other crew member was also found dead, his body drained of blood. Brown was convicted of murder and sentenced to be hanged. However, his sentence was commuted to life in prison when President Andrew Johnson intervened. Brown was jailed in Ohio and in 1892 was transferred to an asylum in Washington, D.C.

It's certainly possible that the *Daily Eagle* report is accurate, but a number of experts believe that Brown was unjustly accused of murder and of being America's first "human vampire," because no evidence has been found to support the newspaper's claims of either. One explanation is that the story of James Brown was confused or combined with another story of a human vampire, that of Mercy Lea Brown, which was reported in the same year. Apart from the year, there are another two points in common: they share New England settings, and both feature apparent vampires with the surname Brown.

It would be interesting to know why President Johnson commuted Brown's death sentence. Grounds of insanity are likely, but whatever the reason, Johnson remains the only President of the United States to have saved a vampire from hanging.

Brown, Mercy, Lea (1871–92)

The most famous alleged vampire from America, the case of Mercy Lea Brown of Rhode Island dates to the late nineteenth century. By this time news of alleged vampires in eighteenth-century Europe had filtered over to the American colonies in New England, in particular Rhode Island. There, just as in Eastern Europe, the nature of infectious disease was not understood and vampirism was an easy explanation for deaths from highly virulent diseases, such as smallpox. Bodies were exhumed and mutilated in much the same way as they had been for many centuries in the Balkans.

The reports

On January 18, 1892, Mercy Lea Brown of Exeter, Rhode Island, daughter of George Brown, died of tuberculosis at the age of 19. She followed her mother, Mary, and her sister Olive, who had also died from tuberculosis, to the grave. Her brother Edwin also showed signs of lung trouble, and after Mercy's death he became critically ill. According to an article in the *Providence Journal* on March 19, 1892, George Brown was besieged by people who told him that the only way to save Edwin was to dig up the bodies of his dead wife and two daughters to see if their hearts were full of blood, and if so to burn the hearts and feed Edwin the ashes. Two days later another article in the *Providence Journal* gave a detailed explanation of vampires and the vampire cult and how the tradition had come to New England from the Slavic people of Russia, Poland, and Bohemia.

George did not believe in vampires but there was little help from the medical community and he agreed to the exhumations at Chestnut Hill Cemetery. Medical examiner Dr. Harold Metcalf – who did not believe in vampires either – was on hand when the corpses of

Mary, Olive, and Mercy were exhumed. The corpses of Mary and Olive were both decomposed, but the corpse of Mercy was judged by some to be in exceptionally good condition, even though Metcalf said there was nothing unusual about the state of her nine-week-old corpse. Some witnesses were convinced that her body had shifted in the coffin.

Dr. Metcalf removed Mercy's heart and liver. Clotted and decomposed blood dripped from the organs, which onlookers took to be a sure sign of vampirism. The organs were taken to a rock and burned. The ashes were saved and mixed with a small amount of medicine prescribed by Dr. Metcalf and given to Edwin to drink.

Edwin followed the instructions but still he died. Despite this, over the years the story of Mercy Lea Brown has grown and grown. There have even been claims that there were other girls in the Brown family who died before Mercy was exhumed and they bore the mark of a vampire on their throats. To this day Mercy's grave continues to attract visitors, and there have been reports of hovering lights seen near her grave and the faint whisper of a girl's voice begging to be let out.

See also: RHODE ISLAND VAMPIRES

Bruxsa

In Portugal, witchcraft was believed to be the cause of vampirism. The bruxsa is a much-feared vampire witch in Portuguese folklore that shares many of the same characteristics as the aswang from the Philippines. At night the bruxsa can use witchcraft to transform into the shape of a large bird or other animal and feed on the blood of infants while they sleep in their cribs. Protection against the bruxsa was supplied by a variety of methods, including magical amulets, incantations, a nail hammered into the ground, and a pair of scissors placed under the pillow. Garlic was also sown into children's clothes to protect them.

Buckinghamshire Vampire

The case of the Buckinghamshire Vampire was recorded by the twelfth-century English chronicler William of Newburgh, from an oral account told to him by Stephen, the archdeacon of the diocese of Lincoln, England. The term "vampire" wasn't widely used in England until the eighteenth century and the alleged vampire in this story was a restless ghost of a dead man who acted in a vampire-like way.

In this case a man died in 1192 in Buckinghamshire and was buried in a proper way. The night after his death, however, he returned to attack his wife and family. His attacks were repulsed so he took to attacking pets and animals. Local villagers also spotted him during the day. His presence became so unsettling that Archdeacon Stephen was appealed to for help. Stephen convened a synod or Church council and wrote a letter to St. Hugh, the bishop of Lincoln, asking for advice. The bishop consulted priests and theologians and learned that this was not an isolated incident as similar attacks had occurred elsewhere. Although he was told that peace could only be found if the corpse was dug up and burned, the bishop rejected that option as unbecoming and wrote an absolution for the man instead. He told the archdeacon to open the tomb and place it on the corpse's chest and then close the tomb.

The tomb was opened and the body was found to be incorrupt. The absolution was laid on the dead man's chest and the ghost never troubled anyone again.

Buckthorn

According to European vampire lore, branches of buckthorn hung on the gates of houses are believed to be a way of warding off evil and vampire attack. In ancient Greece buckthorn was used to protect homes from the restless dead during the festival of Anthesteria and this may explain its association with protecting homes against vampires.

See also: **APOTROPAICS; PREVENTION; PROTECTION; THORNS**

Buffy the Vampire Slayer

In 1992, *Buffy the Vampire Slayer* was a moderately successful American movie. The Buffy concept then transformed itself into a hit Warner Bros. television series, which aired between March 1997 and May 2003. The Buffy TV series generated a huge fan base that still exists today.

The movie

In the 1992 action, comedy, horror movie, actress Kirsty Swanson played the role of Buffy, a Southern California cheerleader interested only in boys and shopping. Fate takes her life in a different direction when she meets mysterious Merrick (Donald Sutherland), who explains to her that she is the Slayer and her destiny is to destroy vampires. The film was considered a modest success, grossing around $16 million in America, and it received mixed reviews from critics.

The TV series

Now immersed in popular culture, the Buffy TV series was created by Joss Whedon. It was about the adventures of *"the One Girl, the Chosen One of each generation,"* selected as the Slayer responsible for ridding the world of vampires, and generated a wide fan base, especially among teenagers in the 1990s. The show's sharp writing and attractive cast, and gripping, universal theme of good against evil, gave rise to numerous Internet sites and merchandise – and even scholarly discussion about the themes and issues tackled by the show.

The character of Buffy develops over the seven seasons the series lasted, from a girl who is young and naïve into a woman with considerable courage and self-belief. In the beginning she has more in common with the typical victim of a vampire, such as Bram Stoker's Lucy Westenra, than a vampire hunter, but the tables gradually turn and the victim grows up and transforms before the viewer's eyes into the Slayer, who is the Chosen One. Buffy has to deal with problems on a worldly level and on a supernatural level at the same time, and although she often longs to forget she is the Slayer, she manages to overcome and defeat most, but not all, of the challenges and forces of darkness sent to oppose her. Over the years of the series she somehow emerges triumphant and stronger despite making mistakes, enduring defeat and heartache, and losing her friends and family, and even her own life – twice.

The Buffy *vampires*

In the first episode of the TV series vampires are introduced and explained as demons inhabiting human corpses. According to the show's mythology, when the ancient demons known as the Old Ones were banished from earth, the last one fed on a human and mixed their blood, creating the first vampire.

The *Buffy* vampires have superhuman physical abilities such as incredible strength and agility, as well as acute hearing and sense of smell, and remarkable powers to self-heal after injury. They do not require oxygen, food, or water and feed only on blood. If they are deprived of blood for too long their brain functions slow down and they become living skeletons. They can shape-shift into monstrous form and into human form, but in human form they can still be detected by their lack of heartbeat and body heat. They cannot be killed except by decapitation, fire, or staking through the heart. Their flesh burns in sunlight and when they come into contact with blessed objects, such as holy water, recently consecrated ground, or a crucifix.

The vampires in *Buffy the Vampire Slayer* are evil and terrifying most of the time, and it is regularly established on the show that they do not have a soul and therefore lack any conscience. But they also have an appealing side and some, like Buffy's vampire lover/enemy Angel, even do good deeds on occasion. Angel and Spike, two vampires who have had their souls returned to them, are shown to feel remorse for their previous actions and to feel conflicted by their residual humanity. They establish relationships with humans and these relationships can distract them at times from their evil agenda. Sometimes they hire human blood donors, and the show suggests that when humans give blood they feel a kind of erotic attraction for the vampires who feed from them.

Popular appeal

Buffy the Vampire Slayer generated a huge fan base among people of all ages, with countless spin-off fan clubs, websites, comics, novels, and memorabilia.

Much of the show's wild popularity was down to clever writing dashed with plenty of hip, trendy humor, highly dramatic storylines, the use of popular music to contribute to the Gothic mood, and an attractive young cast with cool, edgy fashion sense. But there is no doubt that the show's timeless themes of good versus evil, the ambiguity of good versus evil, the agony and ecstasy of love, the close bonds of friendship, the voyage of self-discovery, female empowerment, the importance of sacrifice for redemption, and, of course, the enduring allure of the vampire theme, also played a huge part in securing the show's massive and long-lasting appeal. In addition, the show constantly offered its viewers lessons in keeping problems in perspective with a sense of humor, whether these problems were emotional and interpersonal, or supernatural and world-threatening.

Bulgaria

A country in the Balkans and one of the oldest areas of Slavic settlement dating back to the sixth century, Bulgaria is located south of Romania, between the Black Sea and Macedonia. In the seventh century the Bulgars, a semi-nomadic people of Turkish descent, arrived and claimed military authority over the Slavic tribes in the region, establishing the first Bulgarian kingdom in 681. Christianity arrived in the ninth century when Pope Nicholas sent missionaries into the country. From 1018 onward, over the centuries Bulgaria suffered successive invasions and subjugation by the Byzantine emperors, Serbians, and Ottoman Turks. It did not regain its independence until 1908.

The country's violent and varied history is reflected in the people's equally violent and varied beliefs concerning vampires and the undead. Many of these beliefs are associated with Bulgarian beliefs about life after death. It was thought that the dead went on a 40-day journey immediately after their death and traveled to all the places they had visited in their lives. At the end of the 40 days the spirit journeyed to the next life. If, however, the burial was not done properly, or the corpse was not washed properly, or a cat or a dog jumped over the body, or a shadow fell on it before burial, this could interfere with the spirit's journey to the next life. With entry to the next life blocked, the spirit might return as a vampire.

There were certain other conditions which made a person more likely to return from the dead as a vampire. Those who died a violent death or who had died excommunicated from the Church were vulnerable, as were thieves, murderers, alcoholics, people who committed suicide, and witches. Signs of a potential or developing vampire were believed to be a hole in the tombstone above the grave, and severe bloating and bleeding noticed on the corpse after burial.

Bulgarian vampires

A number of vampire species originate from Bulgaria. It is believed to the home of the ubour, an undead creature that has only one nostril and a sting at the end of its tongue. The ubour was believed to be a ravenous blood drinker and tormentor of the living. Protection from it could be obtained by leaving it rich offerings or excrement. Another type of vampire was the ustrel, which was believed to be the spirit of a child who was born on a Saturday but that died before being baptized. The ustrel was believed to work its way out of its grave on the ninth day after burial and feed on the blood of local livestock. After ten days the ustrel was thought to have become so strong it did not need to return to its grave at night. It found a new home between the hind legs of a cow or on the horns of a ram and would work its way steadily though a whole herd. If an ustrel was believed to be present, the owner of the herd would seek out the services of a vampire hunter or vampirdzhija, a person with the ability to see vampires. Once a vampire was detected, the village would perform a ritual known as the lighting of the need fire, where the village animals were guided between two bonfires at a crossroads. It was thought that this ritual would force the vampire to leave the animals and remain at the crossroads where it would be torn apart by wolves.

Other vampires that originated from the corpses of people who had been improperly buried, or who had died a violent death, were "killed" by the traditional stake. Protection could also be gained by building a fence around the grave or filling the hole in the tombstone with dirt and poisonous herbs. A ritual, which was actually a second burial, could also be tried. The most dramatic process of destruction was bottling, during which a vampire hunter forces a vampire into a bottle that is then burned in a fire.

Vampires in Bulgaria did not always appear as revenants or decaying corpses or malevolent spirits; there are numerous stories of vampires blending into the community, even getting married and fathering children. With the exception of nightly departures in search of blood, the vampire appeared totally normal. Such vampires were often only detected after an unusual series of unexplained deaths in their village had occurred.

Some of these beliefs were still current among superstitious Bulgarians in the early twentieth century, and to this day many locations in the country still have their "own" vampire stories. As recently as 2003, in Serbia, Bulgaria, and Romania there was said to be a clan of vampires called the Children of Judas, who supposedly were the immortal spawn of Judas Iscariot. Judas, the betrayer of Jesus, was paid 30 pieces of silver for his betrayal. The Children of Judas were said to leave a scar resembling three Xs – XXX, denoting the Roman numeral 30 – on the victims they kiss, and are noticeable by their red hair, which Judas supposedly had.

Bullet

More commonly used to destroy werewolves than vampires, sacred bullets (sacred, presumably because they had been blessed by a priest) shot into the graves of vampires were believed to be an effective way to dispatch the undead in Eastern European folklore. Originally the folklore bullet did not need to be made of silver, as silver was beyond the reach of most villagers. Gunshots fired into the air were also thought to repel vampires in some regions.

See also: **DESTROYING VAMPIRES; KILLING VAMPIRES**

Bundy, Ted (1946–89)

American serial killer, Ted Bundy murdered numerous young women across the United States between 1974 and 1978. After more than a decade of vigorous denials, he eventually confessed to 30 murders, although some estimate that the total may have been closer to 100. Bundy aligned himself to the vampire image by biting his victims, and it was this biting that eventually led to his arrest.

Bundy began killing young women in the Pacific Northwest before moving on to Colorado and Utah. He was arrested in Utah but escaped and fled to Florida. On January 15, 1978, he attacked and killed two women, Lisa Levy and Martha Bowman, in their sorority house at Florida State University. A month later he abducted, raped, and strangled 12-year-old Kimberly Leach and left her body in woods. On her left buttock two bite marks were found, which became a key piece of evidence when Bundy was arrested and tried in Florida. The impression his teeth made was clear enough for a match to be made to a dental impression of Bundy's own teeth.

On July 23, 1979, Bundy was convicted of two counts of murder and sentenced to death.

He received another death sentence for the murder of Kimberly Leach. Before his execution he confessed to 30 murders in 6 separate states, dating back to 1973. Again aligning himself with the image of a vampire, he said that he killed to fill an empty void within him. Inside of him there was a thirst and a hunger for power and control over others that craved satisfaction. He regarded his victims as sex objects that he owned and could do anything he liked with.

Bundy was executed by electric chair on January 24, 1989.

Bunnicula, the Vampire Rabbit

A 1979 book for children written by Deborah and James Howe, *Bunnicula* tells the story of a vampire rabbit called Bunnicula that is still in print today. The rabbit does not suck blood but the juice from garden vegetables, so his predatory nature is not traditional. However, he is a charming example of how the pervasive vampire/Dracula image can be introduced to children early in life.

See also: **LITERATURE**

Bunson, Matthew

Matthew Bunson is an American author whose chief contribution to vampire research and literature is his 1993 *Vampire Encyclopedia*, an A to Z of over 2,000 vampire-related entries. His work was published around the same time as Gordon Melton's massive vampire study, *The Vampire Book*, and some vampire enthusiasts believe it did not get the recognition it deserved as a result.

Burial Customs

In European folklore the time between death and burial was believed to be a dangerous one, when the corpse was especially vulnerable to evil contamination. The Slavs observed many superstitions about how people should be buried and what would happen if all the rules were not followed. An unburied corpse or improperly buried body was considered to be at high risk of becoming a vampire or revenant. Some scholars say that the Slavs inherited this idea from the ancient Greeks, but there are similar beliefs all over the world.

There were numerous customs and rituals for the treatment and burial of corpses to prevent their undead return. Some of the most common are mentioned below:

- Covering mirrors in the house: *According to lore, mirrors are soul stealers and if a corpse is seen in a mirror the soul will not rest and will be at risk of becoming a vampire.*

- Stopping the clocks in a dead person's house: *This practice was thought to protect the corpse from evil because it suspended time and put the corpse into a protected state until burial ensured its safety.*

- Painting a cross *with tar on the door of the deceased's house.*

- Cleansing the corpse: *Washing the corpse and keeping it clean with soap, water, and sometimes wine was thought to purify and protect it. In parts of Greece, folklore dictated that the walls of the room in which the death occurred must also be cleaned and whitewashed.*

Restraints: *The soul was thought to escape through the mouth of a body, so tying the mouth closed would prevent the soul from returning to reanimate the corpse. Stuffing the mouth with coins, garlic, or dirt also prevented the soul from returning. It would also prevent the corpse chewing – a sure-fire sign of vampirism. Once buried, tying the knees, feet, or hands together was also thought to prevent the corpse leaving the grave.*

Lighted candles: *Putting a lighted candle on or near the corpse was thought to prevent the soul from wandering away and becoming lost in the darkness and vampirism.*

Watching a corpse: *The practice of sitting with a corpse until it was buried was to prevent any bad signs thought to increase the risk of vampirism (such as an animal jumping over the corpse) occurring before burial. In fact, passing anything over a corpse was considered unlucky.*

Traveling to the grave: *Customs varied from region to region, but corpses were not typically removed via the front door because this was thought to increase the risk of the revenant or vampire returning to taunt the living through the front door. In some cases corpses were taken out feet first, in others head first, and in others they were taken out through the back door or a window or a hole in the wall cut especially for the purpose. Great care was also taken concerning the direction the coffin traveled in. To avoid the risk of evil and misfortune, it needed to be taken in an east-to-west direction, following the sun, to its grave.*

Burial garments: *The garments clothing the corpse were pinned to the coffin to keep the*

corpse in its grave, and shrouds were not allowed to touch the corpse in case it tried to eat them and rise from the grave.*

Face-down burial: *Burying a corpse face down (also known as prone burial) was thought to prevent the vampire finding its way back to the surface, and if they started biting it would cause them to bite firmly into the earth. If the corpse needed to be exhumed it would also protect the living, as the gaze of a vampire was thought to be fatal. Sometimes the corpse was believed to turn over by itself, as in the popular saying that someone would "turn in their grave." The modern meaning refers to the corpse objecting if he or she were to learn something disagreeable, but the original meaning is that the corpse was turning so that it could prepare to return from the dead as a vampire.*

Location: *Burying a corpse at a crossroads, boundary or at a remote location far away from the village was thought to prevent the likelihood of vampirism. The unhallowed ground of crossroads and boundaries was thought to trap the vampire, and burying the corpse far away was thought to make it difficult for the vampire to find its way back.*

Mutilating the corpse: *Decapitating a corpse, staking it through the heart, or cutting out the heart were all thought to destroy the physical vehicle of the vampire. Other measures included driving nails into the feet and slashing or cutting off the limbs. In Romanian lore, three stakes driven into the grave of a vampire were thought to kill it if it tried to leave.*

Wrapping corpses in a net: *According to lore, vampires are forced to untie the knots of a net* before they can leave their grave. In some parts of Germany it was thought that it took a vampire a year just to untie one knot. Filling the coffin with sand, grain, or seeds, most typically poppy, mustard, linen, carrot, millet, or oats, was also thought to keep the vampire busy, as it would be forced to collect all the grains or seeds one at a time, at a rate of one a year, before being able to leave its grave.

- Weighing down the corpse: *Heavy stones would often be used to weigh down the corpse, coffin, or grave to prevent the corpse from getting up and leaving. Tombstones were not only for the purpose of remembering the dead, but for keeping the dead in their graves. Food and drink could also be left on top of the corpse to weigh it down if it felt the need to leave as a vampire.*

- Sharp objects: *Daggers, nails, needles, spikes, thorns, and other sharp objects would often be buried with a corpse to prevent it from leaving the grave. In Romanian lore a sickle was placed around the corpse's neck so that if it tried to rise it would behead itself.*

- Blessed objects: *Burying a crucifix or other blessed object with the corpse was another preventative measure.*

- Scattering the ashes: *According to vampire lore, the most certain way to prevent vampirism was to burn the corpse and scatter the ashes, so that there was no physical vehicle for the vampire to use.*

- Second burial: *According to some Serbs, disinterring a corpse one or three years after death for a ritual cleansing of the bones and reburial would ensure that it would not return as a vampire. In many Eastern European countries the color of the bones is significant: white bones suggest a soul in peace and that the spiritual transition of the dead individual has been completed; dark bones suggest the need for prayers because the soul is in turmoil.*

See also: **APOTROPAICS; COFFIN; CORPSE**

Burning

According to vampire lore, burning the corpse of a revenant or vampire and scattering the ashes was believed to be the best way to destroy a vampire, because it annihilated the vampire's physical entity completely. However, in earlier times, because the actual process of burning a corpse to ashes was a major undertaking, requiring a lot of wood, high temperatures, and constant heat, in many cases before the burning option was considered other preventative measures were used first, such as piercing a vampire with a stake or beheading it. If, however, the attacks continued, then burning was believed to be the only way to ensure that the vampire stopped.

See also: **BURIAL CUSTOMS; CREMATION**

Butcher of the Balkans

In 2007, the body of Slobodan Milošević (1941–2006), the former President of Serbia who was known as the "butcher of the Balkans" for his role in genocide and crimes against humanity during the Balkan wars of the 1990s, suffered the indignity of having a wooden stake driven through its heart.

In early March 2007, days before the first anniversary of Milošević's burial in his home town of Požarevac, Serbian vampire hunters acted to prevent the former dictator returning from the grave as a vampire by driving a three-foot hawthorn stake through his heart. The first anniversary of a man's death is a significant date in local tradition as it is thought that striking a corpse before it has been buried a year will pre-empt its return to earth. Miroslav Milošević (no relation), a self-described vampire hunter and member of the local opposition party was arrested after leading the group, who told police that they had driven *"a three-foot-long wooden stake into the ground and through the late president's heart"* to prevent him from *"returning from the dead."*

It is unclear whether the group actually believed in vampires, or if the act was politically motivated, but their desecration of the former president's corpse is an indication of the continuing prevalence of belief in vampires in twenty-first-century Serbia.

Butterfly

Since ancient times the butterfly has been associated with death and the undead in folklore and legend all over the world. The amazing process of change from a caterpillar to a butterfly captivated many ancient cultures, which regarded it as a symbol of a soul's journey from an earthly body to a heavenly body. The ancient Greeks often symbolized the human soul with butterfly wings in art. In Japanese legend the butterfly is a symbol of the souls of the dead.

In Slavic lore, it was thought that the soul took the form of a butterfly when it left the body in sleep or at the point of death. It was

also thought that a vampire could turn into a butterfly. When a corpse was impaled, if a butterfly appeared it was said that the vampire was trying to escape its destruction and attempts were made to catch the butterfly and burn it in a fire. If it was not caught many believed the vampire would return to the village. In parts of Asia there is also a legend that vampires can transform into butterflies, a belief probably originating from stories about a blood-sucking moth from Malaysia. This notion that both vampires and souls can transform into butterflies seems confusing, but perhaps some form of analogy is operating here indicating that the transformation into a vampire was regarded in some way as akin to that whereby a caterpillar is transformed into a butterfly.

See also: ANIMAL VAMPIRES; DEATH'S HEAD MOTH; MOTHMAN

Byron, Lord (1788–1824)

George Gordon Byron, sixth Baron Byron, is generally considered to be one of the most influential English Romantic poets. However, his firm association with vampiric literature was established not so much through his writings but through his connection with John Polidori.

In 1813 Byron composed the well-known poem *Giaour* and within this poem his familiarity with the Greek vrykolakas, a corpse animated by a devilish spirit which returns to attack its own family, can be seen. *Giaour* is his only mention of the vampire in his vast literary output, but it set the scene for what was to be the most famous vampiric episode in his life.

In 1816, Byron traveled with a young physician and writer called John Polidori to Switzerland. (Interestingly, the relationship between Polidori and Byron was somewhat parasitic. Byron was a famous, wealthy, and charismatic aristocrat and Polidori enjoyed basking in Byron's glory, but there was a price to pay as Polidori seems to have felt disrespected.) Once in Switzerland, Byron and Polidori stayed at a villa overlooking Lake Geneva and were joined there by Mary Godwin, the creator of *Frankenstein,* and her soon-to-be-husband, the Romantic poet Percy Bysshe Shelley. On June 15, bad weather forced everyone to remain inside for a few days and Byron suggested that they all write ghost stories to keep themselves entertained. Byron's story about two traveling companions, which he never finished, bears strong resemblances to Byron himself and his companion Polidori. Byron lost interest in the story but Polidori reworked it, and a few years later, in April 1819, a story called *The Vampyre* appeared in *New Monthly Magazine*, under the name of Lord Byron. Byron denied that he was the author. In the next issue Polidori declared that he was in fact the true author and that the story had been written from notes he had taken from the tale told by Byron in Switzerland in 1816.

Many critics at the time suggested that the character of Lord Ruthven, the malevolent vampire in the story, was loosely based on Byron. Byron was a remarkably flamboyant character with an extravagant lifestyle and numerous lovers. There were even rumors at the time that he had murdered his mistress and drunk her blood from a cup that was made from her skull. In this way Byron could be said to be a highly significant influence on the development of the literary representation of the aristocratic vampire in the nineteenth century, not just because of his contribution to *The Vampyre* – which is one of the most important and least recognized vampire stories ever written – but because his decadent lifestyle inspired the creation of a main character who is a vampire.

Byron never returned to the subject of vampires in his writing, but many literary critics have seen vampirism as a metaphor in nineteenth-century Romantic treatment of destructive relationships. Psychic vampires suck the very life force out of those they love and the Romantic poets frequently discussed longing and lust in terms of illness, pain, and exhaustion, even if they never explicitly mentioned vampires.

Ironically, Byron's death on April 19, 1824, may have been caused by a series of bleedings or blood lettings after he succumbed to an illness. Bleeding was still common medical practice at the time. Although his body was returned to England to be buried, the idea that Byron did not die but lives on as a vampire was put forward by novelist Tom Holland in an intriguing book (*Lord of the Dead: The Secret History of Byron*) written in the mid 1990s.

See also: LITERATURE

The Element Encyclopedia of Vampires

"Vampires provided a perfect mirror of the worst fears of the pious and perfect."

Manuela Dunn-Mascetti, *Vampires: The Complete Guide to the World of the Undead*

Caligula

Gaius Julius Caesar Germanicus (AD 12–41), more commonly known as "Caligula" or "Little Boots," was the third emperor of Rome. He ruled in a demented and cruel way from AD 37 until his assassination on January 24, 41.

According to rumors (which eventually became legend), Caligula returned as a revenant or wandering undead and haunted the Lamia Gardens and the Esquiline Hill where his corpse had been hastily and unceremoniously buried in a shallow grave after his assassination. Although Caligula's body was eventually exhumed and cremated, stories continued to circulate for centuries about his ghost haunting the gardens and the hill. Caligula's violent death, his evil life, and the lack of a proper burial are three classic signs that were thought to make it impossible for the dead to find rest in earlier times.

Callicantzaro

Recorded by the seventeenth-century writer Leo Allatius, the callicantzaro is a terrible vampire-like creature from Greece. According to Greek lore, the callicantzaro is a child born during the time between Christmas and Epiphany who must leave his or her family for most of the year to live in the underworld. However, from Christmas to Epiphany (January 6), the child comes back to the earth and attempts to devour the flesh of humans. It was said that the first victims were the creature's brothers and sisters.

The characteristics of the callicantzaro differ from region to region. It can be big or small but often has long, sharp fangs, donkey ears, a black face, and red eyes. One method believed

to prevent a child from becoming a callicantzaro was to singe the unfortunate child's toes over a fire. The callicantzaroi are actually closer to werewolves than they are to vampires – there is no direct connection with blood drinking – but they are frequently mentioned in non-fiction books about vampires.

Calmet, Dom Augustin (1672–1757)

The first scholar to systematically examine vampire superstitions, the Benedictine monk Augustin Calmet lived at the same time as the vampire hysteria that swept Central and Eastern Europe in the early part of the eighteenth century.

Born on February 26, 1672, at Ménil-la-Horgne in Lorraine, France, Calmet joined the Benedictine order at Saint Mansuy Abbey in Toul and was ordained in 1696. Most of his life was devoted to biblical studies and teaching philosophy and theology at the abbey of Moyenmoutier. He became one of the most respected biblical scholars of his day.

Vampire hysteria

When news of the vampire hysteria in Hungary, Moravia, and Silesia reached Calmet he was intrigued by the detailed and corroborative testimonies of eyewitnesses, believing that they should not simply be dismissed. For all practical purposes vampirism did not as yet exist in France and was largely unknown to the scholarly community. Calmet began collecting information about it in the belief that it was necessary to understand the phenomenon in light of the Church's view of the world. In 1746 he published a two-volume work about the vampire cult, *Dissertations sur les Apparitions des Anges, des Démons et des Esprits, et sur les Revenants, et Vampires de Hongrie, de Bohème, de Moravie, et de Silésie,* which became an instant bestseller. It went through two French editions in 1746 and 1749, and the third edition of 1751 appeared under the title *Traité sur les Apparitions des Esprits et sur les Vampires ou les Revenants de Hongrie, de Moravie, etc.* It appeared in a German edition in 1752 and was translated into English in 1759. The English translation was republished and edited by Reverend Henry Christmas in 1850, with the title *The Phantom World.*

Calmet approached the subject of vampires with an academic, open-minded attitude that confounded his critics. *"There are so many natural things which take place within and around us,"* Calmet wrote, *"of which the cause and manner are unknown to us."* He defined vampires in the traditional way as people who had lived and died and then returned from the grave to suck the blood of the living. With this definition as his basis, Calmet collected as many accounts and as much data as possible from newspapers, official reports, travelogues, and eyewitness reports.

He then cast a critical eye over all these reports. He gave consideration to the idea that demons were responsible for the vampire's ability to exit and re-enter the grave but rejected it, concluding that it was impossible for a corpse to leave the grave.

How a body covered with four or five feet of earth, having no room to move about and disengage itself, wrapped in linen, covered in pitch, can make its way out, and come back upon the earth, and there occasion such effects as are related of it; and how after that it returns to its former state, and re-enters underground, where it is found sound, whole and full of blood, and in the same condition as a living body? This is the question.

He was also troubled by the supposed incorruption of vampire corpses as evidence for the existence of vampires as, in the eyes of the Church, incorruption was a state enjoyed only by deceased saints as a testimony from God to the degree of their sacredness. He condemned the mutilation of exhumed bodies and examined all known folklore about premature burial and bodily changes after death, pointing out problems and inconsistencies. While Calmet struggled to reconcile the contradiction that a vampire can be both a physical entity and a supernatural entity, he never seemed to have made the analogy to the flesh/spirit paradox of his own religion.

Calmet could not bring himself to conclude that the reports he had examined proved conclusively that vampires existed, but despite his skepticism and exposure of vampirism as superstition, he could not dismiss the reports entirely and left the matter open. On occasion he even seemed to favor the existence of vampires, suggesting that *"it seems impossible not to subscribe to the belief which prevails in these countries that these apparitions do actually come forth from their graves and they are able to produce the terrible effects which are so widely and so positively attributed to them."*

Critics

Calmet was immediately attacked by intellectuals and Church officials for taking vampires seriously when the first edition of his study was published. In later editions he responded to this criticism by reaching a far more skeptical conclusion, but these were never circulated as widely as the first edition, and by then everybody was talking about vampires. When a new outbreak of vampirism was reported in Silesia, Empress Maria Theresa dispatched her personal physician to examine the case and his report decisively dismissed the outbreak as superstition and hysteria. In 1755 and 1756 Maria Theresa issued laws to prevent the spread of vampire mania; these included placing the matter of dealing with reports of vampirism with civil authorities instead of the clergy. From this time on, interest in vampires among Western Europeans gradually shifted to focus on literary creations, and vampire scares subsided. Nonetheless they continued in isolated regions of Eastern Europe well into the twentieth century.

In the generations after his death in 1757, Calmet was repeatedly condemned by French intellectuals for indirectly fueling vampire hysteria by not being more assertive in refuting the existence of the creatures. He was, however, favorably cited by twentieth-century vampire historian Montague Summers, for recording and preserving for future genera-

tions texts and eyewitness accounts from the vampire hysteria that might otherwise have been lost forever.

Candle

Since ancient times and in many cultures a lighted candle has traditionally served as a potent way to ward off evil and the threat of vampires. It is not so much the light or flame of the candle that terrifies the undead but the fact that it symbolically represents the rays of the sun and the light of goodness and, in Christian ceremonies, the light of Christ. Throughout Slavic regions candles were placed on graves to provide protection and illumination for the dead as they passed over to the next world. In Romania, a candle, along with a coin and a towel, were believed to be the main source of protection against vampires. In Bulgaria, too, it was considered a disgrace or a sin to neglect to put a candle at the head of a sick person or in their hands, because it was believed that the soul would need a light in order not to get lost in the darkness.

See also: **APOTROPAICS**

Cannibalism

Some experts believe that the origins of vampirism may relate to cannibalistic rituals among primitive cultures in Africa, Melanesia, Australia, New Zealand, North and South America, and Asia. Cannibalism, the practice of eating human flesh and drinking human blood, was pursued in these cultures when meat from animals was scarce, but it was more commonly an aspect of ceremonies and funerals of great warriors. It was thought that if members of the community ate the flesh and drank the blood of a warrior they would acquire the strength, courage, and other qualities of that warrior.

The ceremonial consumption of the dead practiced by primitive cultures was commonly conducted with great honor and respect for the dead, and is called endocannibalism. It is very different from the savage form of cannibalism practiced by individuals who eat their victims for deranged or occult reasons. However, it's conceivable that the vampire-like beings, witches, zombies, and ghouls of folklore, who feast on the flesh of corpses as well as the blood of the living, could be transitional figures between the cannibal and the vampire.

See also: **BERTRAND, SERGEANT;**
            HISTORICAL VAMPIRES;
            LYCANTHROPY; WEREWOLF

Carmilla

A seminal work of vampire literature written in 1872, *Carmilla* is a short story written by Irish author Sheridan Le Fanu and published in his collection of short stories, *In a Glass Darkly*. *Carmilla*, which influenced Bram Stoker when writing *Dracula*, tells the story of a young woman's susceptibility to the dangerous attentions of a female vampire. It has been adapted many times for cinema.

The story

Carmilla begins with the heroine, Laura, who lives in a castle in Austria, remembering how when she was a child, a woman who caressed her and caused puncture wounds in her neck would visit her nightly. The story then jumps forward 12 years to Laura at the age of 19. While on a walk one day with her father she witnesses a coach accident that injures a beautiful young woman, called Carmilla. At Laura's prodding, the father invites Carmilla to stay with them at the castle until she recovers fully from her ordeal. Carmilla is given a room in the castle and it isn't long before Laura recognizes Carmilla as the woman who used to visit her at night when she was a child; she also bears a strong resemblance to a portrait of Countess Mircalla Karnstein at the castle, which was painted many years ago in 1698.

Carmilla soon enchants Laura, despite her odd habit of declining food and her aversion to religious objects. She visits Laura every night with kisses and professions of love, but the closer the two women become the weaker Laura gets. Laura is also haunted by strange dreams and panic attacks. Her death is prevented by the arrival of a general, a family friend, whose daughter died at the hands of a woman called Millarca. It soon becomes obvious that Millarca and Carmilla are the same woman, and that Carmilla is an anagram of the vampire's true name – Countess Mircalla who died 150 years previously.

The vampire is hunted down to the ruins of her castle at Karnstein and her coffin is found. Inside lies the body of the Countess, with her eyes open and apparently in perfect health. The coffin is saturated with blood. Immediately, the general and Laura's father take action to ensure that Carmilla never rises from the grave again.

The body, therefore, in accordance with the ancient practice, was raised, and a sharp stake driven through the heart of the vampire, who uttered a piercing shriek at the moment, in all respects such as might escape from a living person in the last agony. Then the head was struck off, and a torrent of blood flowed from the severed neck. The body and head were next placed on a pile of wood, and reduced to ashes, which were thrown upon the river and borne away, and that territory has never since been plagued by the visits of a vampire.

Le Fanu's description of the destruction of Carmilla indicates that he was probably familiar with vampire reports that had circulated from Europe in the early eighteenth century, such as that of Johannes Cuntius.

The story concludes with Laura relating bits of vampire folklore. She also makes it clear that even though Carmilla's ashes have been scattered, her memory continues to haunt her. *"To this hour the image of Carmilla returns to memory … and often from a reverie I have started, fancying I heard the light steps of Carmilla at my drawing room door."*

Contribution to vampire literature

In *Carmilla*, the development of the vampire myth to that point in time can be seen. Le Fanu recognized the vampire as a dead person returned, rather than a demonic spirit. This dead person is confined to an area close to their grave and tends to attack loved ones and family. Although pale in appearance and with strange habits, the vampire can slip in and out of society without being detected. Carmilla sleeps in a coffin and has nocturnal habits, but she also has superior strength and can transform into different shapes, her favorite being a cat. And in much the same way as would later occur in *Dracula*, the bite of a vampire does not instantly kill its victim, but weakens them until they slowly wither away.

With its undertones of daring lesbian vampirism, sensuality, and timeless Gothic style, *Carmilla* introduced the female revenant vampire to Gothic literature and gave new life to tales of the undead. The story went on to influence many supernatural writers, including Bram Stoker, who noted his debt to Le Frau when he wrote *Dracula* in 1897. It is also largely thanks to *Carmilla* that the figure of the female vampire developed in nineteenth- and twentieth-century literature from being merely a slave of the male vampire to being a supernatural power in their own right.

See also: **LITERATURE**

Carnolia Vampire

Also known as Grando, the Carnolia Vampire was a terrifying revenant, or undead person, that was thought to wander the district of Carnolia (Kranj) in Yugoslavia.

The story first appeared in a commentary by Erasmus Francisci for a 1689 work entitled: *Die Ehre deß Herzogthums Crain* by Baron Janez Vajkard Valvasor. According to the story, a peasant landowner called Giure Grando died in

1672 and was buried. He allegedly returned from the grave shortly after to have sexual relations with his widow. He also ran up and down village streets knocking on windows; inside the homes of the windows he knocked on someone died. Grando's terrified widow appealed to the village head for help and several brave villagers opened his grave. Inside they found Grando's smiling corpse to be remarkably preserved. The grin soon disappeared, however, and turned into a frown when a crucifix was held over it. Tears also rolled down its cheeks. According to Valvasor's account:

> In it they found Giure Grando intact. His mouth was very red. He laughed at them and opened his mouth. At first the companions fled, but soon they came back again and set about driving a sharpened hawthorn stake through the belly of the corpse, which recoiled at each blow. Then the priest exorcised the spirit with a crucifix, "Behold you vampire [strigon] here is Jesus Christ who has delivered us from hell and has died for us; and you vampire can have not rest." At these words tears flowed from the corpse's eyes.

After commending Grando's soul to God, the body was decapitated, and the trouble stopped forthwith.

Carpet

In parts of the Balkans and among some Slavic peoples, carpets and other strong fabrics were often used as a form of protection or preventative measure against vampirism during burial. The logic behind wrapping a corpse in a carpet was to restrain it and restrict its movements. As a form of corpse binding, carpet wrapping was also found in Russia and Bulgaria and its use may have stemmed from Turkish or Asian origins.

Carrickaphouka Castle

The legend of the vampire of Carrickaphouka Castle, near Macroom, County Cork in Ireland dates back to 1601 when a former high sheriff of County Cork, called Cormac Tadhg McCarthy, allegedly returned from the grave to attack and drink the blood of passers-by. When a feature about Carrickaphouka appeared in *The Irish Monthly* in 1874, the term *derrick-dally* was used to describe the evil entity that haunted it. The original meaning of this term is unclear but it may be related to the ancient Irish name for ghosts – dearg-diulai – and translated as "one who drinks blood."

Long before rumors about the vampire sheriff began to circulate, mysterious and dark stories were already associated with Carrickaphouka. The name Carrickaphouka means "rock of the pouka," the pouka being an Irish demon that could appear in many forms – a horse, an eagle, a goat, or in forms that were indescribably terrible. Carrickaphouka Castle was said to have been built on a rock inhabited by a pouka.

Cormac Tadhg McCarthy was said to be a fierce and violent man. He got help from the English to subdue the lands around Cork and hunted down any rebels without mercy. One of these rebels, James Fitzgerald, led a band of disaffected Irish lords. Pretending that he wanted to talk peace, McCarthy invited Fitzgerald to a banquet, where he poisoned him, cooked and ate his flesh, and drank his blood in front of his English supporters to show his loyalty to them. This depraved act sent shock waves throughout Ireland and blackened the McCarthy name for centuries to come. Even the clan tried to distance itself from McCarthy's behavior, by explaining that he had been possessed by a pouka when he committed the crime.

When McCarthy died his corpse, animated by the power of evil, was said to return to the castle to attack and drink the blood of passers-by – which effectively makes this not just a ghost story but also a vampire story. The castle was destroyed and reduced to ruins during the Williamite wars in Ireland, but even today, four centuries later, superstitious locals still cross the road to avoid passing the fallen castle late in the evening. There have also been recent reports in local magazines of eerie screaming coming from the ruins, and fresh blood splattered on the gateway in the morning.

Carrot Seeds

In some parts of medieval Europe carrot seeds were thrown in the grave or along the road to the cemetery as protection against vampires. It was thought that the undead had an endless fascination with counting and would be compelled to stop and count every seed, at a rate of one seed every year, before leaving the cemetery.

See also: APOTROPAICS

Castle Dracula

There is no actual castle called Castle Dracula, which in Bram Stoker's novel *Dracula* (1897) is the Transylvanian abode of Count Dracula, but this has not stopped the attempts of Dracula enthusiasts to try to identify a real castle with the fictional one. Castle Bistrita, Castle Bran, Castle Poenari, and Slains Castle have all been suggested.

In *Dracula*, Stoker places Castle Dracula in the Borgo Pass in the Carpathian Mountains of Transylvania, and the first section of the novel describe Jonathan Harker's trip to Castle Dracula and his experiences there. Harker journeys to the castle at night and he reaches it by horse-drawn coach. His first glimpse of the castle comes when moonlight illuminates it as a *"vast, ruined castle from whose black windows came no ray of light."* In the light of day Harker discovers that the castle sits on a rock overlooking the surrounding forest and river gorge. It is built to be almost impregnable to attack and during his stay the *"frowning walls"* of the castle have the feel of a prison.

Castle Bistrita

Given the accuracy with which Stoker described the Transylvanian landscape in *Dracula*, it would seem logical to look for a real Castle Dracula near the Borgo Pass. There is a castle near the Borgo Pass road, called Castle Bistrita, which was built in the 1440s by John Hunyadi, the governor of Hungary and a contemporary of Vlad the Impaler. There is, however, no evidence to suggest that this was ever Castle Dracula and it was destroyed at the end of the fifteenth century. Another castle located close to the Borgo Pass is Hunedoara Castle, which although built in the thirteenth century still exists today. Vlad was thought to have visited this castle at least once, but once again there is not enough evidence to suggest that it was Castle Dracula.

Castle Bran

Another place to search for Castle Dracula is south of Transylvania, in the territory of Vlad, who was also known as Dracula the "son of Dracul," ruler of Wallachia. In the Carpathian Mountains near Brasnov lies Castle Bran. Built in 1382, Castle Bran was an important trading post. It was never occupied by Vlad Dracula, though he may have visited on occasion. With its winding staircases and spooky corridors, Gothic chapel and underground passageway, there is certainly a strong similarity to the fictional castle in *Dracula*. In their 1972 bestseller, *In Search of Dracula*, researchers Raymond T. McNally and Radu Florescu state that, *"The analogies between Stoker's description of Castle Dracula and the real Castle Bran are simply too close to be coincidental."* Touted by the Romanian Tourist Board as the real Castle Dracula, today the castle remains one of Romania's major tourist attractions.

Castle Poenari

Although it is certainly possible that Castle Bran inspired Stoker's description of Castle Dracula, it is more likely that if the real Castle Dracula actually ever existed it was the castle built and inhabited by Vlad Dracula himself during his years as ruler of Wallachia. This castle, built in the fourteenth century and known by several names, including Castle Argeş and Castle Poenari, was constructed near the Transylvanian border on a hill to the north of the town of Curtea-de-Argeş, the original capital of Wallachia. It passed through several hands until in 1456 it came into the possession of Vlad Dracula.

Deciding to rebuild the castle, Vlad used slave labor to provide stones from the remains of another castle across the Argeş River. The rebuilding process has become one of the most famous stories of Vlad, where his nickname the Impaler is first mentioned. When Vlad discovered that the Boyars, the elite families of Wallachia, had been responsible for the deaths of his father and brother, he decided to get his revenge. He arrested all the Boyars during their Easter celebrations and, still dressed in their fine clothes, men, women, and children were forced to march to Poenari and rebuild the castle. The Boyars were forced to work until their clothes fell off and then they had to continue working naked. According to legend thousands died in this enforced construction work.

With three towers, thick walls, and, according to legend, a secret passageway to the bank of the river (although no evidence with this secret passage has ever been found), Vlad's castle was fairly small in comparison with Castle Bran – about 100 feet by 120 feet (30 × 36 meters) – and it was severely damaged in 1462 when the Turks attacked and captured it. After Vlad's death the castle was used mainly as a prison. In the sixteenth century it fell under the control of the Hungarians before being abandoned and left to the ravages of time. In 1912 and 1940 earthquakes seriously damaged the ruins, but in the 1970s the Romanian Tourist Board, responding to interest in the Dracula legend, carried out a partial reconstruction and built a walkway up to the previously inaccessible castle.

In the 1960s historians McNally and Florescu set out in search of the historical roots of Bram Stoker's Castle Dracula. Although they acknowledged that Castle Bran had more similarities with the fictional depiction, they identified Castle Poenari as the real Castle Dracula. In 1977 American adventurer, author, and vampire researcher Vincent Hillyer spent a night alone in the castle, which he recounts in his book *Vampires* (1988). During the night Hillyer claimed to have been bitten by a strange presence. He also maintained that after being bitten he became permanently sensitive to sunlight, burned easily, and developed keratoses, a precancerous condition of the skin. Hillyer related his experience to other vampirologists and a theory was put forward that over the centuries the castle had become a magnet for evil because of its bloody history and the number of corpses buried on the mountain top.

Other possible sites

Vlad's small castle may well be the real Castle Dracula, but it is unlikely to have been the model that inspired Stoker's description because, like Castle Bran, it was probably not known by Stoker, who never visited Romania. As Stoker gives no specifics concerning his inspiration for Castle Dracula, one possibility is that no castle in Eastern Europe was the model and that his inspiration was perhaps closer to home in the castles of his native Ireland. Another suggestion is that Stoker was inspired by Slains Castle, a manor house that sits on craggy rocks near Cruden Bay in Scotland. Cruden Bay was visited many times by Stoker when he was writing Dracula, but again this may be a false lead as evidence suggests that the section of the novel concerning the castle was probably written long before he traveled to Cruden Bay.

The search for the model for the home of Count Dracula illustrates the problem of trying to reconcile Stoker's fictional Dracula with history. It's far more likely that there was no model and Stoker's memorable descriptions of Dracula's castle, which emphasize its inaccessibility, loneliness, and gloomy ambiance of Gothic terror, were simply a product of Stoker's imagination; an imagination fueled by descriptions he had read of castles in Gothic fiction and European folklore.

Cat

Often associated with witchcraft and magic – and revered as gods in ancient Egypt – cats were regarded as direct links to or expressions of evil in the Middle Ages, serving as familiars or demonic servants to witches. They were rounded up and tortured for their supposed crimes. Given their dark history it's not surprising that suspicion also fell on cats during the vampire crazes that swept Europe in the seventeenth and eighteenth centuries. It was thought that vampires could transform themselves into cats, and if a cat jumped over a corpse before it was buried this was thought to transform the deceased into a revenant or vampire. Cats are carnivorous predators so this makes some sense from a biological point of view.

The association between cats and vampires is well illustrated in the story of the Pentsch vampire related by Henry More in 1653. A prominent citizen of Pentsch, Silesia called Johannes Cuntius died after being kicked by a horse. Before his death he confessed to leading an evil life and said he believed that his soul was in danger. A black cat attacked him before he died and soon after his burial rumors that he had returned from the grave swept the town. His body was exhumed and found to be a state of perfect preservation.

Throughout Asia similar associations between cats and vampire lore can be found. For instance, in China a cat that jumped over a corpse was thought to transform the deceased into the undead. The vampire-like bajang of Malyasia appeared as a polecat and the victims of the pelesit, another vampire-like species, often announced that they had been attacked by a cat. The chordewa of Bengal could also assume the shape of a black cat.

Vampire cat of Nabeshima

In Japan there is the tale of the erotic vampire cat of Nabeshima, which has some similarities to the influential fictional tale of *Carmilla*, with the vampire assuming the form of a cat.

According to legend, a demon in the form of a cat took the life of the favorite concubine of the Prince of Hizen, a member of the honored Nabeshima family. The vampire cat then took the form of the dead concubine and in this guise carried on sleeping with the prince. The prince had no idea that the beautiful woman he slept with at night was in fact a demon who was draining his life blood. Day by day the Prince of Hizen's strength dwindled; his face became both pale and livid, as he appeared to be suffering from a fatal illness. He took all the medications prescribed by doctors, but none did any good.

Since his sufferings always increased at night, a guard was placed over his quarters. One of the guards, Soda, was particularly vigilant and because of him the demon was unable to enter the bedchamber and began to lose its influence over the prince, who soon began to recover from his ordeal. One night Soda noticed a beautiful woman enter the prince's apartments and, recognizing her to be a force of evil, attacked her. The woman turned into a cat and escaped into the mountains. Determined to destroy the vampire cat, a great hunt was launched and the cat was slain, although this did not end all stories of the vampire cat. According to a report from Japan published in Britain in the *Sunday Express*, July 14, 1929, *"The vampire cat of Nabeshima is once more about its nightly business, bewitching the beautiful wives of the descendants of the old two-sworded fighting Samurai."*

See also: ANIMAL VAMPIRES; SOUL-RECALLING HAIR

Catalepsy

Catalepsy is a state of suspended animation and muscular rigidity that has sometimes been mistaken for actual death. A person suffering from catalepsy can see and hear but cannot move. Their breathing, pulse, and other regulatory functions are slowed to the extent that, to an untrained eye, it would seem as though they were dead. The cataleptic condition can last from minutes to days. In earlier times, there were few diagnostic tests that could be done on a body to ensure it was in fact dead, and so it is possible – even likely – that persons suffering from catalepsy could have been declared dead and buried prematurely.

It has been argued that catalepsy gave rise to many stories of vampires and vampirism. If the unfortunate cataleptic woke up in the coffin, the naturally desperate attempt to escape would result in torn clothes, ripped fingernails and contorted positions and expressions before eventual death from suffocation. All this would present a grotesque post-mortem appearance when the grave was finally opened, and could be taken as "evidence" that the dead are restless in their graves.

See also: **CLINICAL VAMPIRISM; PREMATURE BURIAL**

Cattle

Domesticated animals found all over Europe, cattle that died through severe blood loss would often provide evidence to their owners that a vampire was at work. One solution to the problem was to use a need fire, a ritual which involved running cattle through flames.

In the 1990s a series of cattle mutilations in Puerto Rico were attributed to the activity of the chupacabra, a vampire-like creature that drained the blood of its victims. Reports of the creature primarily occur in Puerto Rico, however in recent years sightings have been reported in areas of Texas, Florida, and even in Russia.

Cattle are susceptible to the feeding of vampire bats, whose presence can be detected by the amount of ammonia in the cattle's urine after feeding. In 2007, when the South American rainforests were being cleared to make way for livestock pasture, researchers confirmed that vampire bats were sinking their fangs into cattle instead of wild forest mammals.

Caul

The caul is the membrane of the amniotic fluid sac that sometimes still covers the body or head of a newborn at birth. Folk beliefs about the caul varied widely around the world. For the most part it was a sign of good fortune – for example, sailors considered them a protection against drowning at sea – but in some regions it could also be a very bad sign.

A belief repeatedly recorded from the sixteenth century down to the present day is that when a baby is born with a caul covering the face (also called a "mask," "veil," or "sillyhow"), the caul must be kept for luck; whoever has one will never drown. Even as late as the 1870s, British newspapers carried advertisements from would-be purchasers of a caul, offering large sums of money. Midwives sold them to sailors as charms or amulets.

In the cultures of Northern and Eastern Europe, the caul, which marked babies out as different, was associated with vampirism. A child born with a caul was thought to become a vampire after death. To prevent such a fate, the caul was removed, dried, ground into fine particles, and fed to the child on its seventh birthday. In Romanian lore the caul of a newborn had to be broken and washed away immediately. If the baby swallowed it, he or she would be doomed to vampirism. Among the Kashubs, a Slavic tribe in the Ukraine, a red caul was regarded as presumptive evidence that the child was destined to return from the dead. Normally a caul is a clear or gray-white membrane but in the event of a hemorrhage it can turn red. The reason red cauls were regarded as suspicious was probably due to the belief that blood, or anything red in color, tends to predispose someone toward vampirism.

Causes of Vampirism

A number of theories – some based in folklore or superstition, others in occult theory, and others still in the scientific or medical study of vampires – have been put forward over the centuries for the causes of vampirism. However, as the existence of real vampires has yet to be proved conclusively, all of these theories remain just that – theories.

Possible causes of vampirism generally fall into the following loose categories:

- Bad signs/omens: *In some parts of medieval Europe people believed that certain individuals were destined to become vampires by the conditions of their birth. For example, in Romania, children were expected to return as vampires if they were born with teeth, an extra nipple, excessive hair, deformed limbs, a split lower lip, a caul, or a large birthmark on the face. Those who generally led a sinful life, those who were diseased or deformed, and those who committed suicide or died a violent death were also doomed to a harsh existence in the afterlife. Other bad signs included incorrect burial customs. In Slavic and Chinese traditions, any corpse which was jumped over by an animal, particularly a dog or a cat, was feared to become one of the undead. A body with a wound that had not been treated with boiling water was also at risk. In Russian folklore, vampires were said to have once been witches or people who had rebelled against the Church while they were*

alive. *It is now generally accepted that such beliefs were the product of superstition and ignorance, and few if any of them are taken seriously today.*

- Medical: *As the twentieth century progressed, many people turned to science to explain how a person could be mistaken for a vampire and how someone could appear to have been the victim of a vampire attack. Certain medical conditions – in particular anemia, catalepsy, and porphyria – have been offered as explanations. But as convincing as these explanations are from a medical point of view, none of them can fully explain all aspects of the vampire legend, and in particular bite marks or puncture wounds on the neck or other body parts.*

- Rational: *According to one prominent theory, the common practice of grave robbing or body-snatching in centuries past would have contributed to the illusion that bodies had risen from their graves overnight. Other rational explanations for the disappearance of bodies, or the strangely lifelike appearance of corpses, include animals digging up bodies from shallow graves; flood waters uncovering bodies from shallow graves; gases forming in the corpse, sometimes causing post-mortem movement; and the slow decomposition of corpses for various reasons, such as cold temperature or death by poison. Once again all these theories are convincing but they cannot explain eyewitness accounts or how vampires were allegedly able to get in and out of their graves to carry out their attacks.*

- Psychiatric disorders: *Vampire-like behavior in individuals has now been recognized as a*

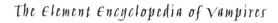

psychiatric disorder, called vampire personality disorder or Renfield's syndrome. Symptoms include drinking blood, drinking one's own blood (known as auto-vampirism), necrophilia (attraction to dead bodies), necrophagia (the urge to eat corpses), cannibalism, sadism, and vampiric fantasies. Although opinion is divided, most people accept that vampire behavior is a psychiatric problem and that sufferers are not actual vampires but deluded and disturbed individuals.

Genetic: *According to this theory a vampire is a vampire because there is a vampiric gene that makes that person biologically different from people without this gene. If this is the case, the vampire gene would probably be recessive and would lurk in family lines, only occasionally revealing itself. This theory could explain the commonly reported physiological differences, sensitivities, and physical reactions that many vampires are reported to have, but at present the theory remains completely unproven.*

Spiritual: *This occult theory suggests that a vampire possesses a non-human soul or astral body, which is contained within a human body but is vampiric in origin, and can leave the body at death and during periods of sleep or unconsciousness. Generally, the nature of the vampiric soul stays dormant until the body has transformed into that of a vampire, at which point, a secondary wave of changes occur, bringing on an awakening to the vampire's true, inner nature. This theory is unproven now, and for the foreseeable future.*

Parasitic/Symbiotic entity: *This theory states that the vampiric person is actually a host to a completely separate entity. The person is fully human in soul/spirit and genetics, but there is a secondary vampiric life form within the host body (either parasitic or symbiotic, depending on your point of view). Many people who uphold this theory do in fact believe the condition to be curable by the removal of the entity through exorcism, though some believe exorcism to be fatal to the host (as they are now linked to the second entity). Once again such a theory is completely unproven.*

Energy deficiencies: *This theory states a vampiric person is a person with an energy deficiency, who requires supplemental sources of energy from the life force or energy of others. This theory could explain the needs of psychic vampires, but not of the traditional blood-sucking type.*

Biological: *This theory states there is a virus or other similar biological explanation for a vampire-like disease/condition which is contracted, and which either alters the physiology of the person, or causes cascading changes in some unknown ways. This theory might explain how vampirism can suddenly appear in individuals with no prior warning signs, but it would also suggest that vampirism is somehow transferable or catchable, which is a controversial suggestion.*

Many causes of vampirism have been explored and fleshed out in vampire fiction and movies but, as fascinating and at times convincing as all these theories can be, none of them really stand up to critical thinking. At this time there is no correct answer and no single cause. And until and unless people who believe they are vampires allow themselves to be seriously studied by scientists, there is never going to be a definitive answer.

Celákovice Cemetery

A fascinating vampire burial ground in the town of Celákovice, which is situated a few miles from Prague, the cemetery of Celákovice is unique in that it is the sole Czech necropolis where vampires only are buried, or, to be more exact, those who were supposed to be vampires by their contemporaries.

In medieval Europe many bodies of suspected vampires were not completely destroyed but buried in separate graveyards, often with their heads lopped off and facing the ground so that the vampires could not find their way back. Their bodies were also tied or weighed down to further prevent any movement. Such sites had been found in Moravia and neighboring Slovakia, but the one discovered in Celákovice is one of the most notable as it contains the remains of alleged vampires which may date back to as early as the tenth or eleventh centuries. Archeologist Jaroslav Spacek oversaw the excavation of the site in 1966 and eventually had the 14 bodies from this small burial ground removed for research. There were no stakes through the bodies but they had been decapitated and their mouths had been stuffed with rocks and sand – all common anti-vampire measures of the time. Whoever or whatever these adults had been in life, their neighbors feared that they would return after death.

See also: **Burial Customs; Cemetery; Coffin; Corpse; Grave**

Celts

The Celts were one of the first great peoples of continental Europe, Britain, and Ireland. At their strongest, around about 300 BC, their lands stretched from the west of Ireland to Turkey and from the Baltic Sea to the Mediterranean. Some experts believe that Irish vampire legends and vampire legends from other parts of Europe are derived from ancient Celtic beliefs about the dead.

The ancient Celts believed in the existence of an Otherworld, where the dead and supernatural entities co-existed. They also believed that the dead were very much aware of the affairs of this world and could intervene in the lives of humans if they so desired. When they intervened they did not do so in spirit form but in a solid, corporeal form that was very similar to the way they had appeared when they were alive. It was thought that the dead had similar emotions and needs for food, drink, and sex as the living, and that they would often return to take their revenge on their enemies or to complete unfinished business.

Mikulovice

In July 2008, a 4,000-year-old vampire grave, believed to be the first such burial in Europe, was discovered during a routine archeological dig of an early Bronze Age burial site in Mikulovice, Eastern Bohemia, in the Czech Republic. Archeologists believe this grave bears a resemblance to Celtic tombs discovered in the British Isles designed to prevent blood-sucking revenants from rising from their graves and preying on the living. During their explorations, the archeologists found the grave of a man whose skeleton showed the unmistakable telltale signs that his community had believed him to be a vampire and had carried out specific rituals designed to keep the corpse in its grave after death. On opening the grave, which was set well apart from others nearby, the archeologists found that the skeleton had been weighted down to prevent it returning to haunt the living. The only people in Europe to carry out similar rituals on suspected vampires at that time were the ancient Irish.

The similarity of the rituals seems to imply that there may be a link between the Bohemian grave and the Irish burials, and it is certainly possible that migrating Celtic tribes, traveling westerly through Europe toward Ireland and Scotland, brought their anti-vampire traditions with them to the British Isles.

See also: **IRELAND**

Cemetery

A place where dead people are buried. The word "cemetery" is derived from the Greek and actually means "a place of rest or sleep." Despite being sacred ground, in addition to castles, tombs, and swamps, cemeteries or graveyards are considered to be the traditional places where vampires can be found. Folklore and fiction abound with tales of vampires stalking through deserted burial grounds and cemeteries in the dead of the night.

If an animal jumped over a grave in medieval Europe it was thought that the corpse would become a vampire – even today it is considered unlucky to step over a grave. It was also considered unlucky to disturb a grave unless hunting for vampires, which required the exhumation and mutilation or destruction of the corpse if it was found in a vampiric condition. Cemeteries could also be scattered with seeds, garlic, or grains to prevent vampire attacks and, for the same reason, stakes or iron nails were also used to pierce gravesites.

See also: **BURIAL CUSTOMS; CELÁKOVICE CEMETERY; CHARNEL HOUSE; COFFIN**

Chaney, Lon (1883–1930)

An American actor, known as the "Man of a Thousand Faces" because of his ability to twist his features into nearly unrecognizable shapes, Alonso "Lon" Chaney starred in over 100 silent movies during the first decades of the twentieth century and was the first actor to play a vampire in an American feature-length movie, *London After Midnight* (1927).

In *London After Midnight*, Chaney played a police inspector in the disguise of the undead. He was director Tod Browning's first choice to play the part of Dracula for the screen, but he died of cancer before he could be signed for the part and the role went to Béla Lugosi. Chaney's son, Lon Chaney Jr., stared in *Son of Dracula* (1943).

Characteristics of Vampires

Defined as dead humans who return from the grave to feed on the blood of the living for sustenance, through the centuries vampires have been known by their distinctive characteristics.

Descriptions of vampires from Eastern Europe, and in particular from Transylvania and Romania in the seventeenth century, set the scene for endless debates about their existence and defining characteristics in the eighteenth century, and also became the basis for the development of the vampire as a literary creation in the nineteenth. Bram Stoker drew heavily upon these early vampire stories when he wrote *Dracula* in 1897. Toward the end of the nineteenth century and through the twentieth century researchers began to discover that vampire-like creatures, similar to those defined by European folklore, could be found not just in Europe but in the folklore and mythology of other cultures around the world. Ancient Asian, African, and Indian cultures, for example, all had their vampire-like beings. And in the twenty-first century researchers, archeologists, historians, and vampirologists continue to uncover intriguing information about the defining characteristics of vampires in folklore, fact, and fiction all over the world.

When attempting to define the characteristics of a vampire it is important to understand that, in general, they can be divided into four categories: vampires of mythology, vampires of folklore, vampires in fiction, and modern vampirism. Each category differs from the others.

 Mythology: *Vampire mythology is ancient, with most cultures having some version of the vampire in their traditions. During the third millennium BC the Babylonians possessed a complex vampire tradition and more than 5,000 years ago the Mesopotamians feared a ghoulish creature called the akhkaru, an evil spirit said to roam the night in search of the blood of newborn babies and pregnant women. Ancient Hindu texts of India also contain a host of vampiric entities and supernatural beings similar to those found in Mesopotamia, for example, the rakshasas who prey on the blood of infants and pregnant women. Several thousand years later the blood-sucking evil spirits of Mesopotamia reappeared again in ancient Greek culture. One of the most terrifying Greek vampires was a witch called a strix who feasts at night on the blood of newborns.*

In general, the vampires of mythology are evil spirits or the restless dead, who return from the dead to torment or drain the life force of the living. They have the power to direct the elements and bring death and destruction on a small and large scale; but there is not always a strong emphasis on blood-sucking.

 Folklore: *The characteristics of the vampire of ancient folklore are altogether different from the vampire most of us recognize from modern novels. The typical vampire or revenant of Europe did not wear a cape or stylish clothing. They would look as corpses would appear if they had been dragged from the ground – decayed, foul-smelling and revolting. A revenant was typically recognized by villagers as being one of their deceased neighbors and it had one purpose: to attack and spread disease by drinking the blood of the living for sustenance.*

Fiction: *At the beginning of the nineteenth century the folkloric image of the vampire*

started to be changed in fictional vampire stories. The fictional vampire who wakes from the dead to suck the blood of sleeping victims, typically young women, is the vampiric form most people recognize today. During the Victorian period, fictional vampires were presented as powerfully hypnotic creatures. With magical abilities to direct the elements, command animals, climb walls, and live forever, they are seductive and charming but dangerous and deadly creatures. Despite possessing superhuman powers they are far more furtive than their folklore counterparts. Instead of striking whole communities they prefer to dart silently from the shadows and kill individuals. Sometimes their bite will transform the victim into a vampire but not always. They have the ability to blend into the world of the living and are often hard to distinguish from humans. The only telltale signs are that sunlight destroys them, they cast no shadow or reflection, they cannot appear in photographs, and they have a certain unnatural presence which can make animals and sensitive people feel uneasy.

Modern vampirism: *Moving away from folklore and fiction, modern vampirism has evolved in countless different but equally fascinating directions. Perhaps one of the most intriguing is the school of occult thought which suggests that vampires are people who, intentionally or unintentionally, drain and absorb the pranic energy, or life force of others. These kinds of vampires don't feed on blood but on the energy of other people. They tend to be nocturnal creatures with a tremendous appetite for both food and sex due to their biochemistry. Physically, it is almost impossible to notice defining characteristics*

of this psychic vampire and their symptoms are often dismissed as merely eccentric behavior.

One thing is clear: vampires are beings who prey on others in some way. This does not necessarily mean preying on the blood of others. The defining characteristic of a vampire is the need to feed on others for sustenance; that sustenance may be blood but it may also be ideas, energy, hope, youth or love.

See also: **APPEARANCE OF VAMPIRES; BIOLOGY OF VAMPIRES; SOCIOLOGY OF VAMPIRES**

Charnel House

A charnel house is a vault or building where human skeletal remains are stored. They were often built near churches for depositing bones that were unearthed while digging fresh graves. The term can also be used more generally as a description of a place filled with death and destruction.

A charnel house differs from graveyards and cemeteries in that those buried in them did not always require formal burials. Although some charnel houses were used for the burial of monks or clerics, many others were used as places to bury those considered unclean or unworthy of a formal burial. In Russia, suicides, murder victims, people who had drowned, and even victims of stroke were disposed of differently to other people because it was thought that Mother Earth would object to their burial and spew them out. They could not be left unburied (as the authorities would object) so until the early nineteenth century pits, similar to charnel houses, called *ubogie doma*, were used for the *inovercy* or unclean dead.

Not surprisingly, charnel houses were often breeding grounds for disease, and in medieval Europe, because of the absence of religious symbols, they were often considered to be the ideal dwelling place for the vampire with its love of death, decay, and darkness.

Chase, Richard (1950–80)

Convicted vampire murderer, Richard Trenton Chase of Sacramento, California, killed six people in the 1970s because he believed that his blood supply was disappearing from his veins, and that it was the duty of his victims to sacrifice their lives to replenish his life force.

Life and crimes

Born on May 23, 1950, by the age of 10, Chase showed signs of what psychiatrists would later term chronic paranoid schizophrenia. In his adolescence, he was known as an alcoholic and a chronic drug abuser. He developed hypochondria as he matured and in early adulthood he began to have a number of bizarre beliefs about his health. For example, he thought his cranial bones were moving about on his head, so he shaved his head to stop this happening. He also held oranges on his head, believing vitamin C would be absorbed into his head via diffusion.

Eventually, Chase left his mother's house and rented an apartment with friends. His flatmates complained that he was constantly intoxicated by drugs and alcohol. He also boarded up his bedroom door. His roommates demanded that he move out; when he refused, they moved out instead. Once he had the apartment to himself Chase began to kill and disembowel various animals, which he would then eat raw, sometimes mixing the organs with Coca-Cola in a blender and drinking the concoction like a milkshake. Chase believed that eating animals would prevent his heart from shrinking.

He was committed to a mental institution in 1975 after being taken to a hospital for blood poisoning, which he seems to have contracted after regularly injecting rabbits' blood into his veins. When dead birds were found outside his hospital window, staff discovered that he was drinking their blood and nicknamed him "Dracula."

After investigation Chase was, for some bizarre reason, deemed not to be a danger to society and was released in 1976. His mother decided on her own that her son did not need to be on the anti-psychotic medication he had been prescribed. She thought it was turning him into a zombie and weaned him off it. By now Chase felt that no one was going to help him get the blood he believed he needed. He bought dogs, killed them, and ate them raw. One day he became convinced that one of his neighbors had deliberately poisoned a dog he had eaten. In anger, he purchased a shotgun and on December 29, 1977, committed his first murder. He shot and killed at random Ambrose Griffin, a 51-year-old engineer and father of three.

A month later, Chase decided animal blood was not enough and that he needed human blood to sustain him. His next victim, again chosen at random, was a pregnant woman. Chase shot her three times; he then had sex with the corpse, mutilated it, and bathed in the dead woman's blood. A few days later, on January 27, Chase went on his final rampage. He murdered three people in one house and drank the blood of the female victim, after mutilating her body. His final victim was an infant from the same house. He took the infant in his car, shot it, and put the body in the trash. Then he went to sleep.

Upon entering the murder scene, police discovered that Chase had left perfect handprints and perfect imprints of the soles of his shoes in the blood of his victims. His house was raided and blood-caked evidence was found all around his house. In 1979, Chase stood trial on six counts of murder and on May 8, the jury found him guilty. He was sentenced to death.

In subsequent interviews, including sessions with doctors, Chase claimed not to remember the murders. Later he claimed that he might have done them, but they were blanked from his memory. Disturbed by the gruesome details of his crimes, other prisoners tried to talk him into killing himself. Whether it was the constant suggestions or just his own tortured mind, Chase managed to collect enough prescribed antidepressants and on December 26, 1980, prison officials discovered him dead in his cell from an overdose. Considering folklore beliefs about the association between vampires and suicide, his death was strangely suited to the man that had become known as the "vampire of Sacramento."

See also: **CRIME; HISTORICAL VAMPIRES**

Chi

The Chinese term for life-energy. It is also often referred to as pranic energy, psychic energy, prana, life force, or the bio-electrical energy that runs our bodies on a subtle level. Psychic or energy vampires believe that they can manipulate chi and feed upon it to sate their hungers. It is believed by some that, to a certain extent, blood vampires also feed upon chi, for a great deal of this subtle energy is believed to be concentrated in the blood.

See also: **ENERGY VAMPIRES; PSYCHIC VAMPIRE**

Chiang-Shih

In Chinese mythology vampires are called "hopping corpses" – chiang-shih or jiang-shi. The name may come from a practice in Chinese folklore whereby a family who could not afford to travel to a place where a relative died to bring back the body would hire a Taoist priest to animate the corpse so it could hop back home.

Traits

Usually a chiang-shih was thought to be created after a particularly violent death, such as a suicide, hanging, drowning, or smothering. It could also be a result of an improper burial, as it was thought that the dead would become restless if their burial was postponed after their death. Like Slavic vampires, the chiang-shih was a nocturnal creature thought to feed on the living, but unlike its Slavic cousin, the chiang-shih stole a person's breath, rather than their blood. The influence of Western vampire stories did eventually bring a blood-sucking aspect to the Chinese myth in modern times, but traditionally chiang-shih killed and sustained their energy by stealing breath.

The chiang-shih could appear normal but at other times it could take on a hideous aspect. In this form the chiang-shih had long, sharp fingernails and superhuman strength, and could kill people just by breathing on them. The chiang-shih was said to be particularly vicious, ripping the head or limbs off their victims. They were also said to have a strong sexual drive which led them to attack and rape women. After a period of growing stronger, the vampire could gain the ability to fly, grow long white hair, and possibly change into a wolf.

Protection and prevention

It was said that these vile creatures could be evaded by holding one's breath, as they are blind and track living creatures by detecting their breathing. People also protected themselves from chiang-shih by using garlic or salt. They could be driven away with loud noises, and it was also thought that thunder could kill them. Brooms were used to sweep the creature back to its resting spot, while iron filings, rice, and red peas were used as barriers. If, however, a chiang-shih reached its flying, white-haired stage, it could only be killed by a bullet or thunder. Its body then had to be cremated.

Villages that were believed to be infested with vampire occurrences would usually recruit a Taoist priest to perform a ceremony to exorcise the negative energy. The priests traditionally relied on talismans – yellow paper strips with illegible characters written in red ink or blood. It was commonly believed that with incantations the priest could activate the talisman, which when applied to the vampire's forehead area, would put the creature under a spell. Although Taoist priests no longer perform such ceremonies, it is still conventional Feng Shui wisdom in Chinese architecture that a threshold, a piece of wood approximately six inches high, be installed along the width of the door to prevent a hopping corpse from entering the building.

Strange Tales from China

Over the centuries the chiang-shih has been the subject of many legends and stories in China. One well-known story was written during the Ch'ing dynasty by P'u Sung-ling (1640–1715) in a collection of stories called *Liao-chai chih-i* or *Strange Tales from China*. In this story four travelers, unable to find a bed anywhere else for the night, have no option but to sleep in a room in an inn where there is a corpse lying behind a curtain. The innkeeper tells them it is the body of his daughter-in-law. The four travelers, exhausted from their journey, fall asleep but soon one of them is awakened by the loud snoring of the other three. The traveler then sees the pale corpse of the innkeeper's daughter-in-law draw back the curtains and stand above the snoring sleepers one by one. Each time she stands above a sleeper, the snoring stops. The terrified traveler tries to keep quiet but the chiang-shih hears him and tries to catch him. The traveler runs out of the room and the chiang-shih follows. The chiang-shih is faster and eventually catches up with him as he falls in front of a tree and faints.

The next morning the traveler awakes to find the corpse of the chiang-shih standing over him with her long fingernails stuck into the tree. She had dug them in so deeply that she could not pull them out. Eventually, the fingernails had to be cut off to free the corpse which was swiftly buried. Unlike Eastern European vampires, once a chiang-shih is buried it cannot claw its way out of the grave. The three snoring travelers were found dead and were buried too. The remaining traveler suffered from panic attacks for many months after, and never fully recovered from his ordeal.

See also: **CHINA**

Chikatilo, Andrei (1936–94)

Ukrainian Andrei Chikatilo, known as the Forest Strip Vampire, called himself a "mistake of nature" and "a mad beast" after being arrested for the murders of over 50 people, mostly women and children, in the former Soviet Union from 1978 to 1990. He admitted to eating their body parts and drinking their blood. Despite his odd and disruptive behavior in court, he was judged fit to stand trial and was found guilty of 52 murders. He was executed on February 14, 1994.

"This one was no madman," reflected one Moscow investigator who joined the manhunt to catch Chikatilo. *"Sometimes he did not even seem human at all, a specter rising out of Russia's blood-drenched soil, a Soviet vampire."*

See also: **CLINICAL VAMPIRISM; CRIME; HISTORICAL VAMPIRES**

Children of Judas

Found in remote areas of Bulgaria, Serbia, and Romania, the Children of Judas were said to be a dangerous clan of vampires distinguished by their red hair. They were thought to be the immortal descendants of Judas Iscariot who was said to have been a redhead and believed to have been the first vampire. The Children of Judas would drain the blood of their victims and kill them with a single bite or kiss that left a mark in the shape of three crosses – XXX – the Roman numeral 30, representing the 30 pieces of silver Judas "earned" for betraying Jesus.

See also: **BULGARIA; CURSE; JUDAS; ORIGINS, OF VAMPIRES**

Children of Vampires

Throughout the world in vampire mythology, folklore, and fiction, children, especially babies and infants, are often the preferred victims of numerous vampire species, such as the aswang and civatateo, and all kinds of blood-sucking witches, because they are so defenseless and their young blood so potent. However, when returning from the grave as the undead, child vampires are anything but innocent and defenseless. Although their lust for blood is tinged with a poignant longing for their lost lives, they are ruthless killers.

In folklore, vampire children are feared when a child is born out of wedlock or with a deformity, such as a birthmark, or with a red caul, or when a child dies before it has been baptized, as it is thought that these children are likely to transform into vampires after death. Vampires can turn children into vampires if they choose, but they don't tend to as children can be too uncontrollable and demanding. In fiction, one of the most harrowing and memorable child vampires of the twentieth century is Claudia, the little girl with a lust for blood in Anne Rice's *Interview with the Vampire* (1975).

Many experts state that a vampire cannot biologically reproduce, but there are instances in folklore when this can occur. For example, in Slavic Gypsy lore, a dhampir is a half-breed, the mortal child born of a vampire father and human mother. In vampire fiction, children born in this way often have the dark power but not the will to destroy humans, and will often dedicate their lives to hunting down vampires. The Marvel comic character Blade, who first appeared in 1973, is an example of the half-breed dhampir figure.

See also: **DHAMPIR; REPRODUCTION; SEX**

China

In the nineteenth century when Western scholars began to study vampire folklore in China they soon encountered tales of revenants or animated corpses. The most feared vampire-type was the chiang-shih, distinguished by its glaring red eyes, sharp talons, and white, long hair. It could fly and after attacking its victims in the most savage way, it could suck the very life force out of them.

Of the many vampire-like creatures that are believed to menace people around the world, the chiang-shih is one of the few who are without doubt undead. The transformation into a vampire takes place prior to burial – they are not known to rise from the grave. It was essential to avoid this at all costs. If a corpse was not buried quickly it could become a vampire; animals jumping over the corpse could also cause it to become a vampire; and direct sunlight and moonlight were to be kept away from the corpse as this was thought to infuse the vampire with a supply of energy which then required human breath to keep the body sustained. Similar to European vampire traditions, garlic and strong pungent odors were believed to protect against vampire attacks.

Belief in vampires in China seems to have derived from the idea that every person has a higher soul and a lower soul. At death the higher soul left the body to join with the ancestors but the lower soul, called the *p'ai* or *p'o*, sometimes remained within the corpse. The *p'ai* was thought to be able to absorb energy through both sunlight and moonlight if the corpse is left exposed to open air, and in this way it could gain the strength to rise again. It was only when the *p'ai* left the body that the corpse disintegrated.

The shepherd and the vampire

Numerous stories can be found in Chinese folklore concerning vampires. One of the most chilling allegedly took place in 1741. A shepherd asked and obtained permission to spend his nights in the shelter of the local temple, dedicated to three heroes. Many people told him that it was haunted, but this didn't seem to concern him and he moved in anyway. Around midnight he heard a noise coming from under the pedestal of the three statues. Out of the ground arose a hideous creature with glowing eyes, sharp talons, and a body covered in matted green hair.

The shepherd rushed outside and clambered up a large tree in the courtyard. Looking down he saw that the horrible figure was standing in the doorway glowering with rage, but it did not seem able to cross the threshold. All night the shepherd clung to the tree branches, and as the day broke the specter vanished into the recesses of the building. The local magistrates, summoned by the shepherds, discovered a creature of most hideous appearance with green hair, just as the shepherd had described. The magistrates immediately commanded that a pyre should be built and the corpse burned. As it burned the creature writhed and whistled with a screeching sound and blood poured from it in streams.

See also: **CHIANG-SHIH**

Cholera

Cholera is an infectious disease caused by a bacterium that affects the absorption of water in the small intestine. In severe cases it produces violent diarrhea within only a few days. The dangerous aspect of cholera is the vast loss of fluid that can occur in a short space of time. If untreated, the loss of fluid can be fatal.

From 1730–35 Hungary, the Balkans, Poland, Bulgaria, and Bohemia (now the Czech Republic) had a seeming epidemic of vampire cases. Many historians believe that this was most probably caused by outbreaks of cholera, rather than vampires. In the days when people had no idea how to treat and prevent the spread of infectious diseases like cholera and whole communities were wiped out within weeks, it is easy to see how vampirism was blamed. In addition, many cholera victims were buried prematurely and tried to escape from their coffins – a sign of vampirism. The United States also has had many outbreaks of vampirism in New England, in 1854, 1888, and 1890, which can all again be attributed to cholera.

See also: **DISEASE**

Chordewa

A witch capable of turning herself into a black vampire cat. According to vampire historian Montague Summers, tales of the chordewa could be found among the Oraon hill tribe of Bengal. In cat form the creature can come into the homes of people who are sick and dying and lick their lips, thus dooming them. The chordewa can be identified by its odd mewing and the strength needed to capture her. Any injury inflicted on the cat will be discovered on the witch as well; and if the cat was captured the witch would faint or fall into a coma. Often women suspected of being a chordewa were burned.

Christianity

Belief in vampires predates the introduction of Christianity into Eastern and Southern Europe but ironically it wasn't until Christianity completed its conquest of Europe that belief in vampirism became widespread. Rather than suppressing vampirism, it appears that Christianity's insistence that vampires were creatures of the Devil actually helped to promote and popularize the idea of vampirism in Europe.

Early documents

One of the earliest documents published concerning witches and witchcraft, the *Malleus Maleficarum*, dates back to 1486 and it clearly states that the Devil used corpses to cause injury to humans. In this way theologians and Church officials collected folklore, rumor, and superstitious beliefs and turned them into fact. Moreover, Church officials were thought to be the only people to turn to for help and protection in times of vampire crisis.

During the thirteenth and fourteenth centuries pagan beliefs were systematically suppressed and viewed as the work of Satan or the Devil. By 1645, when Leo Allatius wrote the first book to systemically study the subject of vampires, it was obvious that much thought

had been given to the subject and Allatius himself promoted the idea that vampires were real; they were bodies reanimated by the Devil. There were a number of other ways in which medieval Christian doctrine contributed to the spread of vampirism. It was thought, for example, that if someone was not baptized before they died they were at risk of becoming vampires, as were people who were excommunicated, people who committed suicide, people who renounced the Church or sinned against the Church, and people who did not receive a Christian burial. Christianity also possessed the most effective weapons against vampires, in the shape of crosses or crucifixes, incense, holy water, prayers, the Mass, absolution, confession, and the faith of ordained priests.

Vampires condemned as fantasy

During the seventeenth-century vampire crazes in Eastern Europe, Church officials became increasingly concerned about cases where the bodies of people buried as Christians, and presumably awaiting resurrection, were exhumed and mutilated. The Pope commissioned Archbishop Giuseppe Davanzati to study the problem, and in 1744 Davanzati published a report condemning vampires as pure fantasy. Around the same time, however, biblical scholar Dom Augustin Calmet published his report on vampires, which went on to become a bestseller all over Europe. In this work Calmet called upon his peers to give reports of vampire cases in Eastern Europe serious consideration. Although in later editions Calmet came to the conclusion that vampires did not exist, by leaving open the possibility in his first edition – which was the

The Element Encyclopedia of Vampires

one most translated and read – that vampires were corpses animated by the Devil, belief in vampires began to spread far and wide. Eventually, in 1755 and 1756 the Empress Maria Theresa passed laws to stop the disturbance of graves, and in the decades that followed the accepted opinion among Church officials has remained the same: vampires are not real.

Role of Christianity challenged

The struggle against the undead became more secular during the eighteenth and nineteenth centuries when people started to take matters into their own hands. But even though Christianity declined as the main bulwark against vampires, its weapons, in particular the crucifix, remained essential symbols in the fight against evil. Vampire hunters were not necessarily priests or men of the Church now, but, like Van Helsing in Bram Stoker's *Dracula*, were educated men with a conscience and supporters of good in general.

In the twentieth century, vampire writers began seriously to challenge the exclusive role of Christianity as the only effective force against vampirism. In the novels of Anne Rice, for example, vampires are not affected by Christian symbols. They can handle crucifixes with no negative reaction. Following Rice's lead, in recent years an increasing number of vampire writers no longer attribute any power to Christian symbols, unless the individual's belief in them is unshakeable.

See also: **CHURCH; EXCOMMUNICATION; EXORCISM**

Christmas

Not a holiday typically associated with vampires and the undead in modern times, but centuries ago the Christmas and New Year period was widely believed to be a time of magic and possibility. Different rituals grew up around these "moments of sacredness" when it was thought that the laws of everyday life were temporarily suspended and the boundaries between the physical world and the world of spirits dissolved.

The pre-Christian pagan winter solstice (December 21) was seen as an especially problematic time, when the boundary between this world and the next could be breached, allowing harmful spirits to seep through to perhaps claim a victim or two. It became customary to put up decorations and hold loud, cheery celebrations in the hope that the noise and color would convince the lurking demons and evil spirits that there was too much brightness and too many humans gathered in one place to take them on. From this vantage point of pagan folk beliefs a number of Christmas customs, such as decking the halls with holly, singing carols, lighting candles, and flinging open the door at midnight on Christmas Eve to let the evil spirits out can be better understood.

Those born during the Christmas period were usually considered to be especially blessed, because they would have nothing to fear from spirits and were protected from death by drowning. However, in some Greek legends (of the callicantzaro and vrykolakas), children born on December 25 were destined to become vampires after they had died.

Father Christmas

Santa Claus, also known as St. Nicholas, Father Christmas, Kris Kringle, or simply Santa, is the figure who, in most of Western culture, is described as bringing gifts on Christmas Eve, December 24, or on his Feast Day, December 6 (St. Nicholas's Day). The legend of Santa Claus can be traced back hundreds of years to a monk named St. Nicholas. It is believed that Nicholas was born sometime around AD 280 in Patara, near Myra in modern-day Turkey. Much admired for his piety and kindness, St. Nicholas became the subject of many legends. It is said that he gave away all of his inherited wealth and traveled the countryside helping the poor and sick.

Some Christians believe that the present-giving tradition of Santa Claus detracts from the true message and meaning of Christmas, which is to celebrate the birth of Christ and his message of humility, sacrifice, and love. Still others oppose Santa Claus as a symbol of the commercialization of the Christmas holiday. And then there are those who believe that Santa is something far more dangerous and sinister – a vampire in disguise.

There are several different legends and folktales that make up the modern-day depiction of Santa Claus, and many of these folktales can be traced back to the Europe of several centuries ago when vampire hysteria began to emerge, which coincidentally was about the same time that the figure of Santa Claus was becoming popular. The real Santa Claus only comes out one day a year. He is nocturnal. Is this by choice or a dire need to avoid the burning rays of the sun? Could the big beard and padded moustache perhaps be hiding sharp fangs, and the thick coat a bone-thin frame? The red costume doesn't show any spilled blood and his face is always unnaturally puffy, bloated, and ruddy.

Then there is the question of how Santa enters homes. Not through the front door. The chimney is available but only if he can somehow transform into something small enough to fit down a chimney and then somehow fly back up – the form of a bat, for example. And what about the present-constructing elves? Could they perhaps be children who never age, early victims trapped in a loop of undying servitude? As for the argument that Santa leaves presents, some have argued that Santa may be a reformed vampire, trying to make up for the foul deeds of his past.

There is certainly enough circumstantial evidence to argue that the Santa tradition may be inspired, at least in part, by belief in vampires. Although Santa does not appear to suck blood when he visits children at night, or harm them in any physical way, it could be said that by encouraging young people to focus on their material needs rather than the spirit of loving and giving at Christmas, he is feeding on and stealing for himself a part of their soul.

Chupacabra

The chupacabra, from the Spanish words *chupar*, meaning to suck, and *cabra*, meaning goat – literally "goat-sucker" – is a vampire-like creature prominent in the folklore of Puerto Rico and Central and South America and which has also been reported in Europe and the United States.

The name comes from the creature's reported habit of attacking and drinking the blood of livestock, especially goats. Animals attacked by chupacabra have clean puncture wounds on their neck, forehead, and genitals and they are typically found drained of blood. Some autopsy reports show damage to internal organs such as the liver, without any local exterior damage. Mutilations are performed with surgical precision. One report speaks of a cow, completely skinned from head to hoof, and drained of blood.

While the creature seems to prefer animals and generally tries to avoid people, it can also attack humans. In 1996 a chupacabra attack was reported by a woman in Mexico. She managed to escape but her description of the creature matches those given by others who have had face-to-face encounters. Physical descriptions vary but it is typically said to be a heavy creature, the size of a small bear or large dog that stands erect on powerful hind legs. It is covered in fur, has hypnotic red eyes, bat-like wings, and a row of color-changing spines reaching from the neck to the base of the tail. It is said to smell of sulfuric acid and to run, jump, and fly with supernatural speed.

Reported attacks

The first reported attacks occurred around 1992, when the Puerto Rican newspapers *El Vocero* and *El Nuevo Dia* began running stories about the killings of many different types of animals, such as birds, horses, and goats. (The first killings, however, may date back to the 1970s when a clutch of similar, sinister killings of blood-drained animals with puncture wounds occurred in the small town of Moca.) For a time the carnage seemed to be confined to the island of Puerto Rico, but in the late 1990s other Caribbean islands began to report similar killings and there were also several reported sightings of the creature in Mexico, Chile and some of the southern US states such as Arizona and Texas. Whole packs of stray dogs were found dead in Texas, some drained of blood, others without internal organs. Livestock in both Texas and Arizona were attacked and killed; again tiny puncture wounds were found in their necks. There were also similar killings of dogs and sheep in northern Florida, and cattle were savaged in Baja, California.

In July 2004, a rancher near San Antonio, Texas, killed a hairless, dog-like creature that was attacking his livestock. The creature, which later became known as the Elmendorf Creature, was determined by biologists to be a coyote of some sort. In October of the same year two similar creatures were found. Once again biologists in Texas declared them to be canines of undetermined species with facial deformities.

In 2005, Isaac Espinoza spent millions of his own money trying to hunt down the chupacabra. He lived in the jungles of South America for eight months with a team of researchers, video and print journalists, and local guides. During the course of the expedition the team allegedly had several close encounters with a creature that the researchers were not able to identify, and discovered skin and hair samples that do not match any known species in the world.

In April 2006 *MosNews* in Russia reported the first eyewitness sightings of chupacabra in Europe. From March 2005 onward, rumors in Central Russia of a beast killing animals and sucking their blood were circulating among farmers. At least 32 turkeys and 30 sheep were killed in this way.

In August 2006, Michelle O'Donnell of Turner, Maine, described a dog-like creature with fangs found alongside a road, apparently struck by a car, but it was otherwise unidentifiable. Photographs were taken and several witness reports seem to be in relative agreement that the creature was canine in appearance, but unlike any dog or wolf in the area. The following year, a woman called Phylis Canion found three strange animal carcasses in Cuero, Texas. She took photographs of the carcasses and preserved the head of one in her freezer before handing it over for DNA analysis. Researchers concluded that the animal in was a gray fox suffering from extreme mange. In November 2007, researchers from Texas State University San Marcos determined that the DNA samples belonged to a coyote.

On January 11, 2008, there was a sighting at the province of Capiz in the Philippines. Eight chickens were killed and their blood drained and the owner said he saw a dog-like creature attacking them. While in August 2008, a De Witt County deputy filmed an unidentifiable animal along the back roads again near Cureo, Texas. The animal was about the size of a coyote but was hairless with a long snout, short front legs, and long back legs.

Theories

A number of theories have been put forward to explain reports of chupacabra sightings. Among the hill people in Puerto Rico the folklore explanation for chupacabra is that they are the souls of evil men who come back in the form of ugly dwarves to torment the living. Another more "scientific" explanation is that the chupacabra is a real creature that somehow survived the age of the dinosaurs. Others suggest that the creature is an illegally imported exotic animal that has somehow managed to breed or cross-breed. Others have blamed the livestock deaths on human beings who might have carried them out for occult purposes. All sources, agree, however, that the creature is vampire-like and that it needs blood to survive.

An alternative explanation, and one most rigorously defended by the authorities, is that the creatures are not real at all, and the sightings are either products of superstition and imagination, or they are simply other animals that have been wrongly identified. Like many cases of such animal mutilations, it has been argued that they are not as mysterious as they might first appear; some biologists believe that the mutilation can be explained by either people killing the livestock or, more likely, other animals eating them. The loss of blood may be explained by insects drinking it.

Another theory is that this creature is simply an unusual-looking dog. In 2001 an alleged corpse of the animal was found in Tolapa, Nicaragua, and forensically analyzed at UNAN-Leon. Pathologists at the university found that it was just a dog. There are very striking morphological differences between different breeds of dog, which can easily account for the strange characteristics.

There is of course the alien theory put forward by UFO enthusiasts, which suggests that the chupacabra is a pet belonging to some careless aliens who let it out. The weakness of this theory is that UFOs are a global phenomena, but the chupacabra is restricted largely to Latin America. And then there is the government conspiracy theory. Several military research labs are located in Puerto Rico and some suggest the chupacabra is an escaped genetic experiment. Finally, another theory suggests that chupacabra attacks are linked to vampire bats. Three species of blood-sucking bats inhabit Latin America, the largest of which is the vampire bat. However, a vampire bat attacks its victims in a completely different way, without killing them. It makes an oval-like incision and laps up the blood. It cannot suck a cow dry.

Alleged sightings of chupacabra continue to grow over an increasingly wide area, and at this point in time none of the theories presented by researchers, scientists, and biologists can fully explain all the reported sightings and the bizarre nature of the killings. Today, the mystery of their existence (or not) is still very much with us.

See also: **ANOMALOUS BIOLOGICAL ENTITIES; CHUPA-CHUPA**

Chupa-chupa

Named after the chupacabra, a mysterious entity that allegedly attacks creatures and drains them of blood, chupa-chupa is the name given to a so-called vampire alien or UFO. Sometimes reports of chupa-chupa and chupacabra are grouped together, but the distinctive feature of chupa-chupa attacks is that they are associated with red or white UFO lights appearing in the sky, and these lights can burn and injure people and leave them weak and anemic, as though their blood has been drained. Some vampirologists have suggested that the chupa-chupa phenomenon represents a modern version of the vampire myth.

Reports of chupa-chupa attacks first occurred in the 1970s in Puerto Rico and South and Central America, often coinciding with reports of chupacabra attacks. Between July 1977 and November 1978 a number of these attacks occurred in Colares, Brazil, killing people and leaving others seriously ill. Around 40 people were admitted to hospital with severely burned chests. Blood tests indicated that all the victims had very low levels of hemoglobin. Some died directly from the burns but others suffered a slow and agonizing wasting death over a period of many months.

One doctor who treated the victims of the alleged UFO attacks in the late 1970s said that she found small puncture wounds on the arms of people who were struck by the mysterious beams of light that burned them. She believed blood had been taken and many people in the area believed that the UFOs had come to suck the blood or energy from humans. The chupa-chupa victims who survived never fully recovered from their trauma and continued to report weakness, dizziness, and headaches as well as fear and paranoia for the rest of their lives.

Other cases of alleged chupa-chupa attacks were reported in Brazil in the 1980s and 1990s and to this day "vampire lights" remain a much talked about and feared phenomenon in Brazil. Although it has repeatedly been suggested that chupa-chupa are simply products of superstition, or that vampire bats may be the cause, the search for definitive answers to this mystery continues.

Church

In seventeenth- and eighteenth-century European vampire folklore, the inside of a church or place of Christian worship was believed to be a sanctuary where a person was safe from vampire attack. Churches are also filled with some of the most effective weapons against vampires: crucifixes, holy water, prayer books, the Bible and candles. However, just as a consecrated church is impossible for vampires to penetrate, if the church is desecrated, neglected, or ruined, vampires can gain access. Neglected and abandoned cemeteries, graveyards, and charnel houses outside or near churches were also believed to be magnets for attracting the undead.

In the twentieth century many vampire authors began to move away from the church-as-sanctuary-against-vampires theme. This can be explained by a growing awareness of the variety of religious experiences available around the world, and the recognition that there are many people (including vampires) to whom Christian religious symbolism is meaningless. For example, in the 1970s Anne Rice's

vampires have no fear of holy symbols; they can sleep under altars and kill priests as any other victims.

Today the consensus seems to be that the power of religion to offer protection against vampires derives from the faith of a person in the Church, rather than any intrinsic power of the Church itself. If a person tries to escape from a vampire by hiding in a church but has no faith, the building cannot offer safety and protection.

See also: **CHRISTIANITY;**
 EXCOMMUNICATION

Churel

In Indian folklore, a churel, also called a churail, is a vicious and vengeful vampire-like entity created from women who die unnatural deaths through murder, suicide, or accident, or women who die while pregnant during the Diwali festival. If the corpses of these women are not treated with respect by their relatives, their spirits will return to drink the blood of men.

Descriptions of the churels vary from region to region, probably because of confusion between the undead and wholly demonic entities. In some they assume the disguise of a beautiful woman, but this disguise is not always effective as it is said that the feet of the churel face backward. They prowl graveyards, attempting to lure passers-by to them; they may also prowl roadsides, still in the guise of a beautiful maiden. Once they manage to get travelers in their clutches they draw off blood and semen and discard the drained corpse.

In other folktales the churel are hideous creatures, though still female. They are described as having a demon-like form with huge fangs, claws, pot belly, pendant breasts, and a pig's face. They are said to dwell in cemeteries, coming out at dark to attack any passers-by. In other accounts the churel have human faces but with razor-sharp teeth, which they use to eat the flesh of their victims, as well as drinking their blood. In still other accounts the churel work with the goddess Kali, a deity with black skin, fangs, and four arms who wears a garland of corpses and skulls. Known as "the destroyer," Kali hunts battle grounds and drinks the blood of the dying and dead.

Prevention is possible by cremation, or by burying the corpse of a potential churel face downward, or by filling the grave with stones or thorns and strewing the ground with mustard seeds. Prior to the corpse's burial, small nails are also driven through the forefingers and thumbs and the big toes are bound together with iron rings.

See also: INDIA

Civatateo

Among the Aztecs of Mexico, a civatateo was a kind of vampire witch that first came to the attention of Europeans in the sixteenth century during the Spanish conquest. The civatateo, also known as civapipiltin or "princess," was described as hideous, with a white ghastly face, shriveled body, and arms and hands covered in white chalk, wearing a tattered dress covered with painted crossbones.

Personifying the fear of death during childbirth, they were believed to be the evil spirits of noblewomen who had died in labor and who returned to the land of the living to take revenge upon other children by attacking them at night and killing them with a wasting disease. They could also mate with human men and produce children born as vampires. The civatateo lurked in temples and held sabbats, or meetings, at crossroads. Offerings of food were left at shrines at crossroads to placate the creature, and if the civatateo remained there until morning they would be killed by the sunlight.

Classifications of Vampires

The traditional vampire from Slavic folklore is a dead, reanimated corpse of a former human being who returns to attack the living. But the vampire tradition is a living one and over the centuries the vampire concept has evolved and developed in countless different ways. Today, different vampire species can be roughly divided into five categories: spirit vampires, undead vampires, living vampires, alien vampires, and animal vampires. It is important to bear in mind that these categories are not set in stone; some vampire types may fall into two or more categories, and not all vampirologists use the same terms.

1. *Spirit vampires*: Spirit vampires are vampires that can exist without physical bodies. They can float, fly, appear and disappear at will, and are generally considered immortal and indestructible. Some have the power to take on human or animal form. Some are the restless souls or spirits of human beings who remain on earth. Others are blood-sucking demon or witch spirits. Mythological vampire species, like the churel or civatateo,

tend to fall into this category, as do astral vampires.

2. *Undead vampires*: Undead vampires are not spirits but former human beings who have become vampires. Dracula and vampires like him fall into this category. These creatures are the traditional vampires of European legend. They appear human but they most certainly are not. They can become vampires immediately after death, but they can also be born as a vampire or change into a vampire while alive after being bitten by a vampire, or they can achieve transformation by some other supernatural or medical explanation.

3. *Living vampires*: Living vampires are not spirits or the undead but people who consider themselves to be vampires or who resemble vampires in many ways. Historical vampires with a thirst for blood, like Countess Elizabeth Báthory, fall into this category, as do psychotic serial killers like Richard Chase and people like the sanguinarians who drink blood. From a metaphorical point of view, anyone who uses or drains another person in some way, be it of money, hope, or energy – as is the case with psychic vampires – can be described as a living vampire.

4. *Alien vampires*: Alien vampires are vampires from outer space. They appear mainly in comics and movies, merging science and horror, and in works of fiction like *The Space Vampires* (1976) by Colin Wilson, but they can also manifest in real life, as eyewitness reports of the chupa-chupa vampire manifestation attest.

5. *Animal vampires*: Animal vampires are allegedly supernatural creatures that suck the blood of both humans and animals to sustain themselves; the chupacabra falls into this category. Even though they are real creatures rather than supernatural ones, vampire bats can also fall into this category.

See also: BECOMING A VAMPIRE; BIOLOGY OF VAMPIRES; HISTORICAL VAMPIRES; TRANSFORMATION; VIRUS

Clinical Vampirism

A pathological condition in which a person feels compelled to drink blood, clinical vampirism is also known as Renfield's syndrome, a term coined by clinical psychologist Richard Noll after the character Renfield in Bram Stoker's 1897 novel *Dracula*, who believes he cannot survive without consuming blood.

Clinical vampirism is not the same as the consensual blood-drinking practiced by living vampires or sanguinarians. It also varies in intensity; some individuals appear normal in every respect, apart from occasional bouts of desire to drink blood, while other cases involve paranoia, schizophrenia, violence, and aggression toward others. According to Noll, the craving for blood typically arises from the idea that it conveys life-enhancing powers. The condition starts with a key event in childhood that causes the experience of a blood injury or the ingestion of blood to be exciting. After puberty and into adulthood this excitement translates into sexual arousal and also a sense of power and control. The condition often begins with auto-vampirism – the drinking of one's own blood – and progresses to the consumption of the blood of insects and animals, and finally culminates with true vampirism, the drinking of the blood of other humans.

In addition to auto-vampirism and vampirism, in psychiatric and medical literature since the nineteenth century the term "vampirism" has also been used to cover necrophagia or the eating of the flesh of corpses, necrosadism, the abuse of corpses, necrophilia or sexual excitement over corpses, and cannibalism. One of the earliest cases of clinical vampirism was that of Antoine Léger, a nineteenth-century French vineyard worker. The case was described by Richard von Krafft-Ebing in a seminal work called *Psychopathia Sexualis* (1886), which linked blood lust and sexuality and influenced Bram Stoker and many other vampire-story authors since. Although Léger raped, killed, and drank the blood of a 12-year-old girl, he was the first criminal in France to be treated as a mental patient. Instead of being executed or sent to prison, he was confined in an asylum.

See also: **CHASE, RICHARD; CRIME; HISTORICAL VAMPIRES; KÜRTEN, PETER**

Cloak and Cape

From the 1820s onward, when vampires first emerged as characters in plays and operas, black velvet cloaks and capes have been firmly associated with the image of the vampire. It's easy to understand why. Cloaks and capes suggest secrecy and the darkness and insecurity of the night. They can also resemble the wings of a bat encircling its prey.

In the twentieth century the opera cloak with red satin lining – to hide drops of blood – and large collar became the stereotypical vampire "look." The collar was first introduced by playwright Hamilton Deane in 1924 for the purposes of a stage illusion. The actor playing Dracula needed to disappear on stage, so a collar large enough to hide the actor's head when he turned his back on the audience and vanished from behind the cloak through a trap door was used. The image was so striking that it has become part of the stock costume for vampires ever since.

See also: **APPEARANCE OF VAMPIRES**

Clocks

According to European folklore a person's house can be protected from a vampire attack by stopping the clocks at the time of death. Stopping a clock is said to put the corpse into a sort of suspended animation, preventing demonic forces from entering the body until it is ready for burial.

See also: **APOTROPAICS; PREVENTION; PROTECTION**

Cockerel

In many cultures, the cockerel is associated with the sun or sun gods and is a symbol of light and goodness and therefore the enemy of evil spirits and vampires. The nocturnal potency of the vampire traditionally disappears when the cock crows at dawn, as it signals the vampire's destruction under the first rays of the sun.

See also: **ANIMAL VAMPIRES; BIRDS**

Coffin

A burial container for a corpse, in vampire literature and folklore the coffin is the traditional daytime rest place for the vampire. Apart from protecting the vampire from the destructive rays of the sun, the coffin has a number of symbolic meanings. Containers and boxes suggest secrets and concealment but also the promise of revelation. And as an enclosure of the human form the coffin is also a womb-like symbol of the mysterious transition between life and death and the separation of life from death.

Brief history of coffins and vampires

Although now a part of the contemporary image of the vampire, it should be noted that the coffin was not an essential ingredient for the vampire myth. Vampire lore originated in an era prior to the use of coffins – until the end of the seventeenth century it was only the wealthy who could afford them; the poor were simply wrapped in a burial shroud and placed in a shallow grave. To keep wild animals away a flat rock would be placed on the body and the practice of piercing the body with a stake may have simply originated as a means to fix the corpse to the ground.

By the early eighteenth century it was becoming more common to bury the dead in coffins, and a number of anti-vampire measures would be taken to hold the body in place in the coffin. Coffins would be filled with stones to prevent the corpse from leaving its grave, or they would be filled with seeds, which the vampire was compelled to count one by one before being allowed to leave. One widely held tradition was that no item of clothing belonging to a living person should be placed in the coffin as the vampire could use that clothing to somehow "vampirize" the living. In Bram Stoker's *Dracula* (1897) the count does not need to sleep in a coffin but he does need to rest on Transylvanian earth, and he fills boxes with that earth. There is no folklore tradition that sleeping in a box filled with native earth is the vampire's preference, so it is possible that Stoker simply made it up.

The popular image of vampires sleeping in their coffins probably derives from the 1931 *Dracula* movie, in which the vampires are shown rising from their coffins. While many twentieth-century movies and novels tended to use coffins to build atmosphere and immediately suggest the presence of a vampire, in recent years the coffin has become less of a necessity and simply a way of providing protection from the sun's rays. In the novels of Anne Rice, for example, the vampires can sleep in coffins if they choose to do so, but they can also return to the earth or stay in a sealed chamber that protects them from sunlight.

See also: **BURIAL CUSTOMS**

Coins

According to the ancient Romans and Greeks the dead had to cross the river Styx and travel to the underworld on a ferry steered by the feared boatman Charon. Coins would be put in the corpse's mouth or on the eyes to pay for the trip. It was also believed that coins could prevent an evil spirit entering the body through the mouth or the eyes. In Romanian lore this custom continued and a coin was placed in the grave, and sometimes in the mouth to prevent the undead from chewing.

See also: APOTROPAICS; BURIAL CUSTOMS

Coleridge, Samuel Taylor (1772–1834)

The English Romantic poet and philosopher Samuel Taylor Coleridge was an associate of William Wordsworth. Together the two poets published the most important work of the Romantic movement, *Lyrical Ballads* (1798). Included in the *Lyrical Ballads* is the famous "Rime of the Ancient Mariner," which some literary critics believe may have influenced Bram Stoker's description of the count's journey by sea in *Dracula*.

Christabel

In *Christabel* (published in 1816), which is the first and perhaps the greatest example of the vampire motif in British poetry, Coleridge may have relied upon the imagery of Gottfried Bürger's *Lenora* (1773). In *Christabel* the vampiric motif of a young maiden attacked by another beautiful maiden is presented in sumptuous Gothic style. Although never mentioning vampires directly it is generally conceded that vampirism is the theme.

From the outset the young, beautiful, and vulnerable Christabel is presented as a potential victim in need of protection from evil. Lady Geraldine is first seen basking in the moonlight which traditionally revives vampires. She faints at the threshold of the castle and needs to be assisted by Christabel to step inside. Again this is in keeping with the vampire theme as vampires cannot enter a person's house unless invited. Geraldine also has a negative effect on the castle dogs, which vampires are prone to do.

Once inside the castle Lady Geraldine begins her vampiric seduction. The two women share a bottle of wine, and with clear lesbian undertones Christabel falls into a trance when Lady Geraldine partially undresses, revealing her breast and half her side.

> But through her brain, of weal and woe,
> So many thoughts moved to and fro,
> That vain it were her lids to close;
> So half-way from the bed she rose,
> And on her elbow did recline
> To look at the lady Geraldine.

At this point we are not told what Geraldine's naked body looked like, although later Coleridge suggests that her bosom was both "cold" and "old." Christabel falls into a trance and the two women sleep together. The next morning Geraldine awakes refreshed and rejuvenated but Christabel wakes feeling guilty and conflicted.

The air is still! through mist and cloud
That merry peal comes ringing loud;
And Geraldine shakes off her dread,
And rises lightly from the bed;
Puts on her silken vestments white,
And tricks her hair in lovely plight,

And nothing doubting of her spell
Awakens the lady Christabel.
"Sleep you, sweet lady Christabel?
I trust that you have rested well."

And Christabel awoke and spied
The same who lay down by her side —
O rather say, the same whom she
Raised up beneath the old oak tree!
Nay, fairer yet! and yet more fair!
For she belike hath drunken deep
Of all the blessedness of sleep!
And while she spake, her looks, her air,
Such gentle thankfulness declare,
That (so it seemed) her girded vests
Grew tight beneath her heaving breasts.
"Sure I have sinned!" said Christabel,
"Now heaven be praised if all be well!"
And in low faltering tones, yet sweet,
Did she the lofty lady greet
With such perplexity of mind
As dreams too lively leave behind.

The vision of fear, the touch and pain!
She shrunk and shuddered, and saw
again.

Christabel takes Geraldine to her father after having a brief and terrifying flashback of Geraldine's body when she first disrobed.

Christabel begs her father to send Geraldine away but it is too late. The baron is enraptured and, forgetting his age and his daughter, turns away from his daughter with a triumphant Geraldine by his side.

Coleridge never finished the poem but the fragment went on to have a remarkable influence on vampire and Gothic fiction, and is largely considered the main source of inspiration for Sheridan Le Fanu's vampire short story *Carmilla* published in 1872. Geraldine is often cited as the first vampire in English literature but it should be noted that Geraldine lacks many or most characteristics normally associated with vampires; for example, she doesn't drink blood, nor is she identified as undead. The life-draining vampire (and demon) metaphor is, however, pervasive throughout and whatever creature Geraldine is, she is seductive, predatory, and dangerous. Her malign influence gathers strength as the story progresses, and toward the end she seems altogether unhuman.

See also: LITERATURE

Collins, Nancy (1959–)

American horror fiction writer, Nancy Collins is best known for her critically acclaimed and bestselling vampire novels. In *Sunglasses after Dark* (1989) – which received the Horror Writers' Association Bram Stoker Award – Collins introduces the heiress

The Element Encyclopedia of Vampires

Denise Thorne, who is raped and vampirized and emerges from her experience as the vampire Sonia Blue. As soon as she adapts to her new existence Blue begins searching for the man who attacked her and her adventures continue in three sequels: *In the Blood* (1992), *Paint it Black* (1995), and *A Dozen Black Roses* (1996).

Comics

Comic books, a combination of literature, plays, and movies, have created vampire images, characters, and storylines that are far more complex and interesting than simply that of the blood-sucking undead.

Comic books emerged as a new form of entertainment in the 1930s, arising from comic strips that had become a regular item in newspapers. An early comic book title, *More Fun*, seems to have carried the first vampire character when ghost detective Dr. Occult faced a creature called "Vampire Master" in issue 6. In 1939 Batman encountered a vampire in issues 31 and 32 of *Detective Comics*. In 1948 in response to the enthusiasm showed during the 1940s for adventure, crime, and horror stories the first and most successful horror comic, *Adventures into the Unknown*, was established. It wasn't long before over 100 other horror comic books emerged, most of which ran vampire stories; one of the most memorable was "Midnight Mess," which appeared in the 1953 issue of *Tales from the Crypt* by EC Comics. Also in 1953, Bram Stoker's *Dracula* was transferred to the illustrated form with issue number 8 (August) of *Erie* by Avon Periodicals.

Comics Code

The surge of enthusiasm for horror comics and vampire tales did not go unnoticed by the American Comics Code Authority of the 1950s who found the material morally objectionable. In 1954 the CMAA or Comic Magazine Association of America issued a Comics Code in response to criticisms of the horror genre, such as graphic portrayals of violence and the glamorizing of crime. One paragraph of the Code deals in particular with vampires and other major characters associated with horror stories, and vampires were banned from future publications: *"Scenes dealing with, or instruments associated with walking dead, torture, vampires and vampirism, ghouls, cannibalism and werewolfism are prohibited."*

At the same time as the comic book controversy in America, a similar controversy occurred in England. The Children's and Young Person's Harmful Publications Act was passed in 1955 and horror comics disappeared from shops.

In true vampire style, Dracula rose again in 1962 when Dell Comics, which did not adhere to the Code, issued a new work on Dracula in a single October/December issue. A second issue never appeared, but by then vampires were already discovering new ways to return to the comic book world via movie fan magazines. In 1958 the horror movie fan magazine *Famous Monsters of Filmland*, published by Warren Publishing Company, appeared and, being a new type of magazine, it was not subject to the same regulations of the Comics Code. Horror comics were interspersed with movie stills and features. In 1964 Warren published a black and white horror movie comic called *Creepy* that featured characters and storylines banned by the Code. In 1965 *Eerie* appeared and followed a similar format. Then in 1966, Dell released a second issue of *Dracula*, which continued the storyline of the original 1962 issue.

Vampires take the lead

By the end of the 1960s there was growing pressure to liberalize the Comics Code. Gold Key issued *Dark Shadows*, the first comic book to feature a vampire as a leading character, and that was later joined by Warren Publishing's hugely popular *Vampirella* featuring a female vampire from outer space. Finally, on January 1, 1971, the Code was formally revised, reflecting not just the changing times but the inability of horror comic critics to back up with evidence their assertions that these publications were a direct cause of juvenile delinquency and crime. Excessive gore, sadism, and torture were still discouraged but *"vampires, ghouls and werewolves shall be permitted to be used when handled in the classic tradition such as Frankenstein, Dracula and other high caliber literary works."*

A number of companies immediately responded to the new situation. In 1972 Marvel Comics led the return of the vampire to the comic book genre with *Tomb of Dracula*, which placed Dracula in the modern world. Other companies also established a sizeable variety of bloodsuckers, often noted for their charm, beauty, and frequent absence of clothing. Along with Dracula, who over time began to bear less and less resemblance to Stoker's creation, other memorable comic book vampires include Vampirella, Satana, the Devil's daughter, and Morbius – the living vampire.

Due to market saturation in the 1980s, sales of horror comics began to slow and vampire comics all but died. However, the situation changed again in the 1990s due to improved technology in producing comic books and a new adult readership. No longer were comic books just for young people. The huge popularity of Anne Rice's bestselling vampire novels and the 1998 box office blockbuster *Blade* also played a significant part in the vampire comic revival and a host of horror and vampire comic books emerged, most notably *Midnight Sons* by Marvel Comics. The 1990s also saw the emergence of "Bad Girls" – female superheroes who are both feminine and deadly – and vampire erotica trends reflected in comics such as the revived *Vampirella* by Harris Comics.

Although there have been natural ebbs and flows over the years, sales of vampire comics have never completely died and with interest steadily growing again in recent years, thanks in part to Stephenie Meyer's worldwide bestselling Twilight Saga books, it's clear that vampires will continue to be an established part of comic book art for the foreseeable future. It seems that the comic book industry has finally understood that readers of all ages appear to have an insatiable appetite for stories about vampires.

See also: **PULP MAGAZINES**

The Element Encyclopedia of Vampires

Contagion

From the plagues of the Old Testament to the modern fear of AIDS, humans have always understandably feared contagion for the sickness, suffering, and death it can cause. Many experts believe that during the vampire hysteria of eighteenth-century Europe, when outbreaks of plague destroyed whole communities, belief in the existence of vampires was this rational fear of contagion personified.

This theme of vampirism as a deadly contagion can often be seen in vampire fiction, where an attack by a vampire is followed by symptoms of wasting and disease. It also reappears in a more literal sense in novels and movies, such as *Blade* (1998), when the spread of vampirism is caused by an airborne virus.

See also: **TRANSFORMATION**

Corpse

Traditionally, a vampire was believed to be a reanimated corpse who left the grave to feed on the blood of the living to sustain its "life." According to vampire lore it was possible to stop a vampire attack by identifying a corpse for the telltale marks or signs of a vampire. Today we now understand that most of these so-called signs were due to the process of natural decomposition, but in medieval times any of the following natural post-mortem conditions could have been misinterpreted as evidence of vampirism:

- Bloating: *This is caused by a natural build-up of gases in the tissues, but in earlier times it was regarded as a sign that the corpse was filled with fresh blood.*

- Blood seepage: *The blood inside a corpse can seep out, and the gases generated by decomposition can force blood up through the nose and the mouth. In earlier times it was thought that corpses could not bleed and any spots or trickles of blood were seen as proof that the vampire had been feeding on the blood of the living.*

- Ruddiness: *A natural phase of decomposition, corpses can turn from gray and pale to pink and red after a few weeks. This is caused by the pooling of blood in capillaries but in earlier times it was thought that the "healthy" appearance of the corpse was proof of vampirism.*

- Movement: *Many bodies were buried hastily while still in a state of rigor mortis, but this stage is followed by flaccidity later on. The expanding gases of decomposition can also make corpses shift naturally but any signs of movement or flaccidity within the grave were taken as signs of vampirism. A corpse with an erection was also taken as proof but again normal decomposition can cause penis inflation. Some experts have also suggested that premature burial may account for movement within the grave – people awoke in their graves and unsuccessfully tried to claw their way out.*

- Warmth: *Heat can be generated by the process of decomposition but any corpse that felt warm to the touch was regarded as a vampire in earlier days.*

- Growth: *Decomposition exposes raw skin and nail beds; in earlier times this was taken as new skin or nail growth and a sign of vampirism.*

Chewing: *In Slavic lore, before attacking livestock and living people, vampires could first chew on their clothes or their hands and feet. "Chewed" limbs, however, were simply limbs that had decomposed at a different rate and "chewed" clothes were garments that had simply been consumed by bacteria.*

Incorruption: *Corpses that were not decomposed enough were thought to be vampires; however, the rate of decomposition varies according to a number of factors, such as the ambient temperature, the presence of insects, air, and moisture, and so on.*

Stench: *Some vampire accounts tell of corpses giving off the foulest of smells, which is simply a normal part of the decomposition process.*

Noise: *In some accounts, when a vampire is staked it was said to shriek or moan. This was most likely caused by gases forced by the pressure of staking to make their way out through the glottis, an opening in the windpipe.*

Destruction: *Once identified as a vampire, a corpse would need to be destroyed so that the vampire had no physical vehicle. Destruction of the corpse would often involve slashing, cutting up, or decapitation and inevitably the gases of decomposition would spill out, which was again take as further proof of vampirism because the stench and sight of decaying flesh and rotting blood is truly foul.*

Although many experts believe that ignorance about the decomposition process led to the popularization of the vampire myth, other experts disagree. There are those who believe that our ancestors were not as ignorant as has often been suggested and were instead fairly knowledgeable about the way that bodies decomposed. Death was a fact of life, and for these experts the vampire myth became widespread because it originated from a very firm religious belief in the rules and laws which kept everyone and everything in the world in their right place. If any of these rules or laws were violated – for example, if someone committed suicide – this would unleash any number of unnatural events. In other words, vampires were seen as a symbol of the world order turned upside down, and for community leaders belief in vampires became a way for them to reinforce the idea that there was an urgent need for tighter moral order and social control.

Methods of destruction

According to Slavic lore the best way to destroy a corpse and prevent it turning into a vampire was to drive a stake through its heart (or through its head, belly, or back) with a shovel. It was thought that this would pin the soul to the corpse and stop it leaving the grave. Extra precautions included scorching the corpse with a hot iron and washing it with boiling water or wine. Decapitating a corpse with a gravedigger's shovel or a sexton's shovel was another popular method of destruction. The corpse would be covered with a cloth to prevent any blood spilling, as the blood of a vampire was thought to cause death. Once the head had been cut off its mouth would be stuffed with stones or coins to prevent it chewing, and before reburial the head would be placed under the corpse's arm, at its feet, or behind its knees. In some places the head and corpse were buried separately.

Burial at a crossroads or some remote place as far away from the community as possible was another preventative measure.

When staking and decapitation didn't stop a vampire, the most effective method of destruction was believed to be burning a body to ashes. Centuries ago the main method of burning was a bonfire, but cremation would often prove difficult as corpses need intense heat to burn. Failure to burn was taken as further proof of vampirism, so often the corpses would be cut into small pieces and then burned.

See also: BODY-SNATCHING; BURIAL
    CUSTOMS; DECOMPOSITION;
    MANDUCATION; PREVENTION;
    PRONE BURIAL

Corpse Candle/Light

In European lore, sometimes the grave of a revenant or potential vampire can be indicated by glowing lights known as corpse candles, also called jack-o'-lanterns, ignis fatuus, fetch-candles, or corpse lights.

Corpse candles are believed to be phosphorescent lights in white, red, or blue that can appear not only near a vampire's grave but almost anywhere, inside or outside a house, on the ground, on the roof, or over a person. They are said to vanish when approached and as well as marking the location of a vampire's grave they were also said to warn of death. In Welsh folklore a pale bluish corpse candle is said to presage the death of a child, a bigger candle the death of an adult, and multiple candles a multiple loss. Although corpse candles have been witnessed all over Europe their origin is supposed to date back to fifth-century Wales.

Legend says that St. David, the patron saint of Wales, was concerned that the people he served were always unprepared for death, so he prayed that they might have some kind of warning. He received a vision in which he was told that the Welsh people would always be forewarned of a death by the dim light of mysterious candles.

In folklore there are numerous reports of the seemingly mysterious and supernatural appearance of corpse lights near the location of a vampire's grave. A number of natural explanations have been put forward to explain this phenomenon, ranging from atmospheric conditions and gaseous emanation from the ground to the effect of bioluminescent organisms, such as *Photobacterium fischeri*, on the corpse, and, in more recent years, car headlights.

Corwin Vampire, The

According to New England folklore, in 1834 the eldest son of the Corwin family of Woodstock, Vermont, died from a mysterious wasting disease. When another son became ill, the townspeople of Woodstock advised the Corwins to take precautions against a vampire.

According to legend, the eldest brother was disinterred from the Cushing Cemetery and burned. His ashes were buried in an iron container beneath the Woodstock village green. Supposedly, a few local boys decided to get together late one night and dig up the burned ashes. They quickly abandoned their grisly task when they heard unearthly screams and voices all around them. Unfortunately the town register does not contain any records about a Corwin family in the Woodstock community, so there is no telling whether or not this story has any grounding in fact.

The Woodstock Vampire

The case of the Woodstock Vampire, as it came to be known, first appeared in print in 1889 in the *Journal of American Folklore*. The story, recorded some fifty years after the event, was based on recollections from an anonymous "old lady" who claimed to be an eyewitness. In 1890 the story appeared again, this time in the *Vermont Standard* and with considerable embellishment to *"fill in with further details what she* [the old lady] *has left incomplete."* This second account reads like a bizarre horror story and is rich in fantastic details that may have been heavily fictionalized but nonetheless it falls into a category of its own among documented cases in America. In New England there are accounts of exhumations and hearts being cut out, but nowhere are there other accounts of roaring noises, earthly, hellish disturbances, sulfurous fumes, and several prominent physicians *"clearly of the opinion that this was a case of assured vampirism."*

Count Dracula

See: **DRACULA**

Count Dracula Fan Club

Founded in 1965 by animation filmmaker Dr. Jeanne Keyes Youngson, the Count Dracula Fan Club is dedicated to the promotion and study of the work of Bram Stoker's *Dracula* (1897) and vampirism in general. With an extensive library and headquarters in New York, the club reported over 5,000 members in 1998. In 2000 it was renamed Vampire Empire and is still alive and thriving today, with its own small press and dedicated team of vampire researchers.

Counting

In Eastern and Central Europe in the seventeenth and eighteenth centuries, following the burial of a person that was thought to be a potential vampire, various seeds and organic grains, such as millet, oats, mustard seeds, linen seeds, carrot seeds, and poppy seeds, were sometimes placed in the coffin, in the grave, over the grave, on the paths from the cemetery to the homes of the living, and on the thresholds and roofs of the homes to protect the inhabitants. However, the vampire is not repelled or pierced by the objects; rather the creature is compelled to eat them or count them one at a time, at a rate of one seed or grain a year.

Poppy seeds were believed to be especially useful because their inherent narcotic nature would make a vampire want to rest in its grave instead of walk abroad. Chinese narratives about vampires also state that if a vampire comes across a sack of rice it will have to stop and count all of the grains. There are similar myths recorded on the Indian subcontinent and even in South America. Another way to prevent vampires was to lay a dead dog or cat on the doorstep as it was thought that the vampire would be compelled to stop and count every hair on the animal. In northern Germany the vampire was believed to be similarly obsessed with untying knots, and nets and stockings were often buried with the corpse to provide it with centuries of apparently riveting occupation.

This belief in the preventative power of counting may have originated with an ancient folk remedy against witches that was later applied to vampires. It was thought that if a witch chased a person and they scattered rice on the ground, the witch would be compelled to stop and pick up every grain, because the rice was a grain nourished by God (or sunlight) and as such the witch had to pick up every grain to be sure of not stepping on any and thus being destroyed.

See also: **APOTROPAICS; BURIAL CUSTOMS**

Coventry Street Vampire

In 1922 a vampire scare took place in London. The first sighting occurred in early April, when an enormous black bat-like creature with a wing span of six feet was seen flying around West Drayton Church during the night of a full moon. A number of witnesses said they saw it dive into the cemetery and roam around the tombs. A couple of policemen chased after it and reported that it let out a loud, blood-curdling screech before flying away. An old man who claimed to have seen the giant bat 25 years previously stated that it was the spirit of a vampire who, in the 1890s, had murdered a woman in Hammersmith, West London, to drink her blood.

On April 16, at around 6 a.m. an office clerk walking down Coventry Street in the West End of London felt something seize him and pierce his neck. The man felt as if blood was drawn and he fainted. When he woke up in hospital he told the staff what had happened to him. Doctors said that he appeared to have been stabbed with a thin tube, but the man disagreed. He was certain that there had been no one close enough to deliver such a blow.

Two and a half hours later on the same day a second unconscious man was brought to the hospital, bleeding heavily from the neck. When he regained consciousness he also told of being attacked by an invisible presence when walking down Coventry Street, at the very same corner where the office clerk had been attacked. Later that evening a third victim was admitted to the hospital with the same wounds. All three men said they had been attacked at the same turning off Coventry Street.

Rumors of a vampire at large swept across London and an investigation was launched. One police spokesman interviewed by a newspaper reluctantly admitted that the injuries sustained by the three men on Coventry Street defied rational explanation, and there had been no headway in finding the bloodthirsty attacker. Another rumor, which may have originated in a Covent Garden pub when an off-duty policeman discussed his part in the vampire hunt with the landlord, suggested that the police had hired a vampire hunter who had followed the creature to Highgate Cemetery and driven a stake through its heart.

The attacks on Coventry Street have not been repeated to date and the mystery remains unsolved.

See also: **MOTHMAN**

COVICA

COVICA, the Council of Vampyric International Community Affairs, is a (now apparently defunct) consortium dedicated to the standardization of beliefs, terminology, and the exchange of information between people who fashion their lives and lifestyles around vampires and the wider vampire community. It was set up in the late 1990s to help unify the various diverse vampire communities. It did not attempt to be a governing body, rather a group which provided resources and assisted in the direction of the greater community, setting up standards or codes of conduct such as the Black Veil.

Creating a Vampire

There seems to be no general consensus about how a vampire is created, either in folklore or fiction. In some cultures vampires are made by a supernatural curse. In others all it took to create a vampire was to die unbaptized, to live a sinful life, or to commit suicide. The circumstances of a birth, for example, if a baby was born deformed or with a caul, could create a potential vampire. The undead could also be created by any number of bad signs in this life or by the neglect of correct burial procedures. It was also thought that vampires could be made by something as innocent as an animal jumping over a corpse, or something as sinister as spirit or demon possession.

Sometimes a single bite or a series of bites over a period of time can drain a mortal of blood and give them vampire blood. Sometimes drinking the blood of another vampire is the charm. In recent years it has been suggested that a vampire is created by some kind of virus.

The most popular notion in vampire fiction is that a vampire is made through the bite of another vampire. However, there does seem to be some degree of choice on the part of the vampire as, among all the prey from which the vampire drinks blood he or she can decide which of his or her victims are simply food and which are potential companions. Once a potential companion has been chosen, the vampire sets about luring them, forcing them, or, in some instances, responding to their request to become a bloodsucker.

In Anne Rice's book *Interview with the Vampire* (1975), the vampire Lestat decides to turn Louis de Pointe du Lac into a vampire. What this means is that after a period of initiation, during which Louis feels what it is like to be on the edge of death and realizes he does want to live, Lestat drains Louis to the point of death and then gives him his own vampire blood to drink. As the blood works on him Louis "dies" and feels the pain of his death. But once this process is complete he experiences the world differently and sees the world through the eyes of the undead. A vampire has been created.

See also: **BECOMING A VAMPIRE; BURIAL CUSTOMS; TRANSFORMATION**

Cremation

By burning a corpse and reducing it to ashes, cremation was considered to be the most successful way to destroy a vampire. Despite this, cremation was often the last resort used against a vampire, not just because the Church taught that bodies should not be burned but also because a corpse requires intense heat to burn, and many villagers did not have the large supplies of wood required. If, however, staking and prayers proved not to work against a vampire, cremation was applied. In Greece cremations were often used for suspected revenants as a form of prevention. The Russians would capture and kill any insect or animal that emerged from the flames, for they believed it was the spirit of the vampire trying to escape. In Bulgaria the "benefits" of staking and intense heat were combined by plunging a red hot stake into the corpse's heart.

See also: **BURIAL CUSTOMS; BURNING; CORPSE**

Crime

Over the centuries there have been people who have imitated vampires through crime. Most of these individuals – labeled as so-called "real" vampires – manifest symptoms of what psychologists call clinical vampirism, which means a compulsion to drink blood. This compulsion can be psychological and/or sexual, and on occasion these "vampires" consume human flesh as well.

Vampiric crime had its precedent in the bloody career of Elizabeth Báthory (1560–1614), who is alleged to have killed hundreds of young women for their blood. Notoriously bloodthirsty serial killers such as Jack the Ripper are often labeled vampiric murderers, but there is a difference between those who kill others because they have a sadistic desire to do so and those who kill to drink blood.

As the vampire archetype evolved in popular awareness in the nineteenth century, the vampire criminal emerged alongside. One of the earliest and most well-known cases was that of Sergeant Bertrand, who was arrested in 1849 for opening graves and eating the flesh of corpses. Another well-known case from the nineteenth century was that of James Brown, who was arrested in 1867 on board a ship allegedly sucking the blood from the body of a crewman he had murdered. Brown was eventually sent to the National Asylum in Washington, D.C. Other famous vampire killers include Fritz Haarmann (1879–1924) and Peter Kürten (1883–1931). Prior to his 1924 execution, Fritz Haarmann had killed and cannibalized at least twenty people. Peter Kürten, also from Germany, was a serial killer who got satisfaction from drinking the blood of his victims. He was executed in 1931.

A number of vampiric crime reports surfaced in the twentieth century (and continue to surface in the twenty-first century) and a few of them, such as John George Haigh (1909–49) who after killing his victims drained their corpses of blood, and Richard Chase (1950–80) who drank the blood of his victims, have became famous. Many other cases, however, have received little attention, even though the details surrounding them are equally bloodthirsty and repulsive. Listed below is a representative sample of some of the less well-known vampiric criminal cases that have occurred in the last two centuries.

- 1861: *Martin Dumollard of Montluel, France. Executed for murdering several young girls whose blood he drank.*

- 1872: *Vincenzo Verzeni of Bottanuco, Italy. Sentenced to life imprisonment for two cases of murder. He stated that he got tremendous satisfaction from drinking the blood of his victims.*

- 1897: *Joseph Vacher of Bourg. Executed for killing up to 12 people and drinking their blood from bites in their neck.*

- 1959: *Salvatore Agron, a 16-year-old resident of New York City. Convicted of several murders that he carried out at night while dressed as a vampire. He claimed to be a vampire in court and was executed for his crimes.*

- 1960: *Florencio Roque Fernandez of Manteros, Argentina. Arrested for entering the bedrooms of more than 15 women and then biting them and drinking their blood.*

- 1969: *Stanislav Modzieliewski of Lodz, Poland. During his trial one of his victims said that the only way she survived was to feign death while he drank her blood. Modzieliewski stated that he found blood drinking extremely pleasurable; he was eventually convicted of seven murders and six attempted murders.*

- 1973: *Kuno Hoffman of Nuremberg, Germany. Confessed to murdering two people and drinking their blood.*

- 1979: *Richard Cottingham of New York. Arrested for raping and slashing a young prostitute and drinking her blood.*

- 1980: *James P. Riva of Massachusetts. Killed his grandmother with a gun and then drank the blood coming from the wound. Later he stated that the voice of a vampire had promised him eternal life if he killed his grandmother.*

- 1985: *John Crutchley of Pittsburgh was arrested for rape and for drinking the blood of a woman. He later confessed to an insatiable desire for human blood and to drinking the blood of willing donors for years.*

- 1988: *Unsolved case. Six men said they were picked up by a woman in the Soho area of London. This woman allegedly slipped drugs into their drink, cut their wrists, and sucked their blood while they were unconscious.*

- 1991: *Marcelo da Andrade of Rio de Janeiro. Killed 14 young boys and sucked their blood.*

- 1991: *Tracy Wigginton of Brisbane, Australia. Stabbed a man and then drank his blood.*

- 1996: *Vampire cult arrests. The cult was led by 17-year-old blood drinker Rod Ferrell from Murray, Kentucky, who was charged with the murders of Richard and Naomi Wendorf. Ferrell said that he killed the Wendorfs because he wanted to consume their souls.*

- 2002: *Manuela and Daniel Ruda of Germany. Tried for killing a friend in what* appeared to be a satanic vampire ritual. Manuela and her husband Daniel stabbed Frank Haagen over 60 times, drank his blood and left his decomposing body next to the oak coffin in which Manuela liked to sleep.

🖤 2003: Allan Menzies of West Lothian, Scotland. Confessed to killing a friend and drinking his blood. The jury was told that police had found a horror book in his home, with handwritten notes stating, "I have chosen my fate to become a vampire."

🖤 2008: Jeremy Allan Steinke of Calgary, Canada. Found guilty of the gruesome murder of an Alberta couple and their eight-year-old son. On April 23, 2006, police found a crime scene awash in blood, the walls smeared with bloody handprints. During his trial it was alleged that Steinke was fond of drinking blood and once ate a batch of cookies that a friend had made with blood.

Croglin Grange

Recorded in Victorian England, the case of the vampire of Croglin Grange, an ancient house located in Cumberland, England, is often cited as an example of "real" vampirism.

The incident was recorded in vivid detail by Dr. Augustus Hare, a well-respected clergyman who lived in a Devonshire rectory, in his autobiographical book, *Memorials of a Quiet Life* (1871). The details of the story sound convincing but to date the account has not been verified historically and there is no record of a Croglin Grange.

According to Hare, Croglin Grange was an old family estate owned by the Fisher family who rented a one-storey house to two brothers and a sister: Edward, Michael, and Amelia Cranswell. The Cranswells settled into the district and soon became popular with their neighbors. During one summer the district experienced a hot spell and when the Cranswells retired at night, Amelia decided to sleep near the window to stay cool. She closed the window but not the shutters. Unable to sleep she spotting a figure approaching. This figure eventually reached the window and began scratching at it.

Suddenly, she could never explain why afterwards, the terrible object seemed to turn to one side, seemed to be going round the house, not to be coming to her at all, and immediately she jumped out of bed and rushed to the door, but as she was unlocking it, she heard scratch, scratch, scratch upon the window, and saw a hideous brown face with flaming eyes glaring in at her. She rushed back to the bed, but the creature continued to scratch, scratch, scratch upon the window. She felt a sort of mental comfort in the knowledge that the window was securely fastened on the inside. Suddenly the scratching sound ceased. And a kind of pecking sound took its place. Then, in her agony, she became aware that the creature was unpicking the lead! The noise continued, and a diamond pane of glass fell into the room. Then a long bony finger of the creature came in and turned the handle of the window, and the window opened, and the creature came in; and it came across the room, and her terror was so great that she could not scream, and it came up to the bed and twisted its long bony fingers in her hair, and it dragged her head over the side of the bed, and — it bit her violently in the throat.

The woman screamed and her brothers rushed to her side. One brother stayed with his sister and the other ran after the creature and saw it disappear over the wall of a nearby church.

A doctor who attended to the woman's wounds suggested a change of scenery so the trio set off to Switzerland for an extended holiday. Eventually they returned to Croglin Grange convinced that the incident was the activity of an escaped convict. However, the following spring the creature reappeared. This time one brother shot it in the leg and chased it to the vault of a nearby cemetery.

The next day the brothers summoned all the tenants of Croglin Grange, and in their presence the vault was opened. A horrible scene revealed itself. The vault was full of coffins; they had been broken open, and their contents, horribly mangled and distorted, were scattered over the floor. One coffin alone remained intact. Of that the lid had been lifted, but still lay loose upon the coffin. They raised it, and there, brown, withered, shrivelled, mummified, but quite entire, was the same hideous figure which had looked in at the windows of Croglin Grange, with the marks of a recent pistol-shot in the leg; and they did – the only thing that can lay a vampire – they burnt it.

Today, the story of the Croglin Grange vampire is still very much alive in Cumbrian folklore, despite being attacked many times by critics as pure fantasy. In 1924, Charles G. Harper based his criticism of the story on a visit to the area. Harper could find no place named Croglin Grange. There was a Croglin Low Hall and a Croglin High Hall but neither fitted Hare's description. Nor could Harper find a church or vault close enough to either to match the description of the one given in Hare's account.

At a later date Harper's conclusions were challenged by F. Clive Ross, who visited the area and interviewed a number of residents. Ross came to the conclusion that Croglin Low Hall was the house in Hare's story and that a chapel had once existed near it for many years. Ross also suggested that there may have been a mistake in Hare's account and that the story took place not in the 1860s but in the 1680s.

Cross

One of the oldest and most traditional weapons against evil and the undead, the cross predates the crucifix of Christianity by many centuries. In ancient times it was associated with the sun and the heavens and represented divine protection. It is still deemed to be one of the most potent forms of protection against evil.

Crosses have been found all over Europe in burial grounds, to block the entry of evil entities or placed around the neck as a personal amulet or shield. They were also used to exorcise demons and devils and force the undead to leave. In the Middle Ages inquisitors wore crosses and made the sign of the cross in the presence of accused witches to ward off evil. To ward off vampires gold crosses would often be placed in the corpse's mouth or laid on the body.

The cross features strongly in vampire literature, film, and popular culture, but not all fictional vampires shrink away from crosses. The vampires of Anne Rice, for example, are not affected by holy objects. Vampire hunters of

The Element Encyclopedia of Vampires

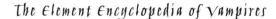

history, literature, and film often point out that it is not the cross itself which has power but the will and faith of the person using the cross. Without firm belief that good can triumph over evil the cross is ineffective, and theoretically this means that any holy or sacred object, such as the Star of David, the Buddhist prayer wheel, or Tibetan mandala is as potent as the cross if the believer has faith in them.

See also: **CHRISTIANITY; CRUCIFIX; GARLIC; PROTECTION**

Crossroads

For Jonathan Harker in Bram Stoker's *Dracula* (1897), a crossroad is the point where his journey into the terrifying world of the undead begins. To reach Dracula's castle he must travel toward the "*extreme east of the country, just on the border of three states, Transylvania, Moldavia and Bukovina, in the midst of the Carpathian mountains, one of the wildest and least known portions of Europe*" – the crossroads between three countries. The border he has to cross is not just between countries but between this world and the next.

Crossroads – places of meetings and partings of ways – have long been regarded as likely places for evil activity. They are unhallowed ground haunted by vampires, demons, the Devil, witches, fairies, ghosts, spirits, and other evil entities. In Russian folklore the undead were thought to wait at crossroads, drinking the blood of passers-by. In Romanian lore, living vampires, people who are destined to become vampires after death, send their souls out of their bodies at night to wander at crossroads. Crossroad superstitions can

also be found in Europe, India, Japan, and among Native Americans, perhaps because in some parts of the world, murderers, sorcerers, and suicides who were not allowed to be buried in the consecrated ground of the church, were buried at crossroads. A stake or nail was driven through the corpse in these cases in an act known as "nailing down the ghost" designed to prevent the corpse's return as a vampire or as a ghost. Crossroads were also places where territories, routes, or villages collided, and they therefore became symbols of the meeting place between earth and spirit.

Superstitions vary from place to place concerning crossroads. As previously mentioned, vampires were thought to haunt crossroads but, conversely, crossroads were also thought to offer some form of protection against vampires – perhaps because of the cross shape they form. One German superstition holds that if you are chased by a ghost or demon, you should head to a crossroads for protection. On reaching the crossroads the spirits will vanish with an unearthly shriek. Theoretically, this is because vampires are thought to find the choice of four different paths confusing. They therefore stand in the middle of the road pondering which direction to take until dawn, when they must hurry back to their grave.

Crow

Crows are intelligent and curious birds. They often follow people around and watch them just out of curiosity. In earlier times this stalking would have created superstitious fears about them and in most, but not all, cultures they have become symbols of evil. Often considered the harbinger of death, because they are black, predatory, and carrion eaters, in European folklore crows were thought to be controlled by vampires and, according to Gypsy tradition, they can actually become a vampire. In vampire literature vampires are sometimes described as having the body or the appearance of a crow.

Crowley, Aleister (1875–1947)

Described by the media as "the wickedest man in the world," Aleister Crowley courted controversy all his life with his fascination for sex, magic, and blood. Despite his excesses there are some who believe this English occultist was a truly great magician.

Life and crimes

Born Edward Alexander Crowley on October 12, 1875, in Leamington Spa, Warwickshire, Crowley was drawn to blood and torture at a young age and was branded "the Beast" or Antichrist by his mother when he rebelled against the fundamentalist Christian sect called the Plymouth Brethren that he had been brought up in. After leaving Trinity College, Cambridge, without a degree but fluent in occultism, Crowley began to pursue his occult interests full time in London. Stories soon circulated about his alleged supernatural powers, including psychic attacks on his enemies with demons and vampires. A number of Crowley's contemporaries, including Bram Stoker, author of *Dracula*, were in awe of him. It was said that he could "will harm" on other people; a rival occultist, Samuel Mathers, engaged in a battle of psychic vampirism with him and lost.

Whether the rumors that circulated about Crowley were true or not, one thing is clear; he had great charisma and a huge sexual appetite, and a seemingly unending stream of women were attracted to him despite his well-known fascination for blood, torture, and sexual degradation. It was said that he would sharpen his teeth so that he could give blood-drawing "serpent kisses." He also made several attempts to create a "magical" child, none of which were successful.

Crowley was alleged to have had at least one encounter with a human vampire. An account of this meeting is given by one of his early biographers, J. F. C. Fuller, and is quoted by Crowley in his own autobiography. In that account, which is presented as a true experience by Crowley, the person is referred to as "Mrs. M.," a vampire and a sorceress. Crowley is asked to help free a woman who was being attacked by this vampire, and although she tries to bewitch him with her beauty, she is no match for Crowley and is forced to leave the room as the wrinkled, decrepit, cursing old woman she really is.

Crowley lived in the United States from 1915 to 1919 before visiting Italy, where he lived in his hillside villa called the Sacred Abbey of the Thelemic Mysteries. The villa became the site of sexual orgies and magical rites, and his excesses led him to be expelled from Italy in 1935 by Benito Mussolini.

In his later years Crowley was a victim of poor health, financial trouble, and drug addiction. He earned a meager living from his writing, much of which is incoherent, although many continue to read his work today. His most important work, *The Book of Law*, was allegedly communicated by the Egyptian god Horus's spirit messenger Aiwass. Central to the book is the law of Thelema, "Do what thou wilt shall be the whole of the law," which Crowley maintained meant doing what you must do and nothing else. His other significant work is *Magick in Theory and Practice* (1929), which many practitioners consider to be a fine work on ceremonial magic.

The writings of Crowley hint that he could draw sexual energy from young male and female prostitutes and that he sacrificed a black cat during a magical ritual in Paris, in order to drink its blood. These incidents, like his meeting with the mysterious "Mrs. M.," may or may not be true, but Crowley was a master of illusion and would have delighted in spreading unsettling rumors about himself.

Crowley died on December 1, 1947, in a boarding house in Hastings. One of the many attractions of Crowley's magic was his advice to follow your own way, become your own self, and create your own lifestyle – you don't need a priest or a judge to tell you how to act; you can work it out for yourself. Unfortunately, it is easy to see how such teaching can be misinterpreted and become dangerous in unscrupulous or impressionable hands.

See also: **MAGIC; WITCHCRAFT**

Crucifix

The crucifix, a cross with the form of the crucified Christ on it, is the most easily recognized symbol of Christianity. It carries the same principles of protection against vampires as the cross, but because of the intensity of the symbolism of the crucifixion it is believed to be even more powerful.

Although many priests involved in destroying vampires may have worn a crucifix, it is not mentioned consistently in vampire lore, and really only became a standard element of vampire lore through Bram Stoker's novel *Dracula* in 1897. One example in folklore of the power of the crucifix is found in the story of the Yugoslavian Carnolia Vampire, which first appeared in print in 1689. In the story, a landowner called Grando died but returned soon after as a vampire. He attacked a number of people and the Church was called upon to destroy him. His corpse was dug up and officials noticed it was smiling. However when a crucifix was held over it, the smile soon turned to tears.

In *Dracula*, Stoker combined popular Roman Catholic ideas about the supernatural power of holy objects with the medieval identification of vampirism with Satanism. Therefore, for Stoker the crucifix, a symbol of Christianity and goodness, causes Dracula, a creature of Satan, to lose his power, and in vampire literature, plays, and movies in the decades that followed, the crucifix retained its power to unsettle or destroy the vampire. If a victim wore a crucifix the vampire would not be able to attack him or her unless the crucifix was removed. The strength of the crucifix, however, rests not on its substance but on the will and the faith of the believer.

In other words a crucifix in the hands of a non-believer would be totally ineffective against a vampire.

In the later part of the twentieth century, vampire writers such as Anne Rice began to challenge the effectiveness of the crucifix and protest against the authority of one particular religion over the vampire. In Rice's Vampire Chronicles supernatural beliefs about the power of holy objects, such as crucifixes, are cast aside as they offer no protection against the overpowering force of vampirism.

See also: **CHRISTIANITY; CHURCH; GARLIC; PROTECTION**

Cullen, Edward

Edward Cullen is a fictional character from Stephenie Meyer's Twilight Saga series. He features in the international bestselling novels: *Twilight, New Moon, Eclipse,* and *Breaking Dawn* (2005–8). Edward is a vampire who, over the course of the Twilight series, falls in love with, marries, and has a child with Bella Swan, a human teenager who also later chooses to become a vampire. In the 2008 *Twilight* film, Edward is played by British actor Robert Pattinson.

See also: **MEYER, STEPHENIE**

Cuntius, Johannes (The Pentsch Vampire)

The case of Silesian revenant Johannes Cuntius was recorded by religious scholar Henry More in *An Antidote Against Atheism* (1653). The case demonstrates the belief that a person who had led a generally sinful life was doomed to become a vampire after death.

The account

According to More's account, Cuntius was a 60-year-old alderman in Pentsch, Silesia, in the sixteenth century. He was accidentally kicked in the head one day by a horse on his way home from work. He was not killed immediately but as he lay dying he confessed that he had made a pact with the Devil and that his sins were far too grievous to be pardoned by God. Several days after his death a black cat attacked and scratched his face, and immediately the sky filled with clouds and a violent storm created chaos until he was buried.

Within days of his burial Cuntius was said to have risen from the grave and to have molested several village women. In the weeks that followed, Pentsch officials were inundated with vampire stories. In some of these stories he seems to operate in incorporeal form, appearing and disappearing like a ghost, but in others he seemed to have tremendous physical strength. It was said that Cuntius charged through the village bashing the heads of dogs on the ground, devouring chickens, and pulling up fence posts. There were also reports of milk turning to blood and terrible smells and the sensation of foul, icy breath in the Cuntius house. Cuntius also appeared to have had violent encounters with former friends and acquaintances, and he even demanded to share his bed with his wife.

Village officials inspected the grave of Cuntius and found mouse-like holes around it. The holes were filled but reappeared again within hours. Eventually villagers dug up the corpse and discovered that it was flexible, soft, and lifelike.

> *His skin was tender and florid, his joints not at all stiff, but limber and flexible, and a staff being put into his hand, he grasped it with his fingers very fast: his eyes also of themselves would be one time open, and another time shut; villagers opened a vein in his leg and the blood sprang out as fresh as in the living; his nose was entire and full, not sharp, as in those that are ghastly sick, or quite dead: and yet Cuntius, his body had lain in the grave from Feb. 8 to July 20, which is almost half a year.*

Cuntius's corpse was taken to court and a judgment of vampirism made. The judge ordered that the body be burned. Wood was piled on the corpse and set alight but the resulting flames did not burn the body sufficiently. A hook was used to pull the body out and an executioner called to cut it into pieces. However, according to More this task was far from easy and took much effort. Eventually, Cuntius was chopped into pieces, burned, and the ashes thrown into the river. When this had been done, in the words of More *"the spectre never more appeared."*

Curran, Bob

A contemporary expert in vampire myth and folklore, Dr. Bob Curran lives and works in Northern Ireland. A psychologist and historian, he has written extensively on the dark and mysterious and is the author of *Vampires: A Field Guide to Creatures that Stalk the Night* (2005).

Curse

A verbal invocation or appeal for misfortune, injury, evil, disease, or death to befall a person or place, a curse normally involves the intervention of God or the Devil but it can also involve black magic or witchcraft.

Christianity could be said to practice the most damning form of curse in the rite of excommunication, an act by which a person is denied participation in the sacraments of the Church and the soul cursed to eternal damnation. In European vampire lore a priest's curse was thought to create revenants. Curses were also used as weapons against the undead. In Romania, for example, Gypsies would attempt to destroy a vampire, by chanting, *"God send you burst."*

The vampire's existence is, of course, one that is cursed as he or she is doomed to live in the shadow world between life and death, feeding on the living to survive. A number of biblically inspired legends have attempted to explain the origin of this curse, from the fallen angel theory – vampires are angels cast out of heaven as punishment for turning against God – to the theory that the curse dates back to the Old Testament murder of Abel by his brother Cain.

> *What hast thou done? The voice of thy brother's blood crith unto me from the ground. And now art thou cursed from the earth, which hath opened her mouth to receive thy brother's blood from thy hand; When thou tillest the ground, it shall not henceforth yield unto thee her strength; a fugitive and a vagabond shalt thou be in the earth … And the LORD said unto him, Therefore whosoever slayeth Cain, vengeance shall be*

taken on him seven fold. And the LORD set a mark on Cain, lest any finding him shall kill him. (Genesis 4:10–15)

According to this legend, after being banished and eternally marked for his crime Cain, the first-born child of Adam and Eve, met Lilith, who in Hebrew legend was the first wife of Adam, and Lilith taught him to suck blood. Together Cain and Lilith spawned a host of vampires and demons.

Judas Iscariot

Another legend suggests that the curse dates back to Judas Iscariot. Because Judas betrayed Jesus to the Romans, he and his family were cursed for all eternity for this evil deed. The Bible states that Judas committed suicide because of his guilt and vampire folklore claims that those who commit suicide are doomed to come back as vampires. Judas was said to have had red hair and this was the identifying trait of his descendants. It was also said that the reason vampires detest silver is because Judas betrayed Jesus for 30 pieces of silver.

See also: **CHILDREN OF JUDAS; ORIGINS, OF VAMPIRES**

Czech Republic

See: **SLOVAKIA**

The Element Encyclopedia of Vampires

"I raised the lid, and laid it back against the wall; and then I saw something which filled my very soul with horror."

Jonathan Harker, in *Dracula* by Bram Stoker

Dakhanavar

According to ancient Armenian legend there was once a vampire called Dakhanavar who preyed on anyone who happened to wander in the valleys around Mount Ararat where he lived. He allegedly killed his victims by sucking their blood in their sleep – not from their necks but from the soles of their feet. One day two surveyors discovered a way to trick the vampire. After counting all 366 valleys they prepared to go to sleep. To protect themselves they each lay with their feet underneath the other's head, so when the vampire came to them he could not find their feet. Frustrated and confused by the bizarre sleeping position of the surveyors, the vampire went off and was never heard of again.

See also: **ARMENIA**

Danag

According to some experts, and to author Stephenie Meyer who mentions the Danag in her 2005 novel *Twilight*, a danag is a Filipino vampire that is believed to be one of the most ancient of the species. Although there are few if any documented sources or accounts, the danag, which presumably resembled a human being, was said to work alongside humans for many years, helping them to plant targo. Unfortunately, the vampire–human partnership ended abruptly one day when a woman cut her finger. The danag sucked her wound and enjoyed the taste so much that it drained and killed her.

See also: **PHILIPPINES**

Daniels, Les (1943–)

American author best known for a series of novels, rich in historical detail, about the reprehensible vampire Don Sebastian de Villanueva: *The Black Castle* (1978), *The Silver Skull* (1979), *Citizen Vampire* (1981), *Yellow Fog* (1986), and *No Blood Spilled* (1991). Don Sebastian is a cynical, amoral, and misanthropic Spanish nobleman and, according to some literary critics, one of the most evil fictional vampires ever to be created in vampire literature.

Dark Energy

For those who study the science behind vampires, the structure and patterns of the universe may answer questions about why our fascination with the image of the vampire endures. In the words of vampirologist and forensic psychologist Katherine Ramsland, in her critically acclaimed book, *The Science of Vampires* (2002), *"Our very notions about dark energies, dark entities and parasitic forces may well be influenced by the rhythms of the universe itself."*

According to cosmologists, when the universe came into existence at the "Big Bang," it expanded rapidly, with the gravitational pull of matter eventually slowing this expansion down. However, research in the 1990s indicated that the rate of expansion is actually faster than previously believed and that some invisible force is offsetting the force of gravity. What this force is no one knows, hence the term "dark energy," but if this dark energy continues to push the universe outward the danger is that the universe will be depleted of energy to sustain itself. In this context dark energy appears to have parallels with vampirism in that it is the force that sucks energy out of the world. Ramsland suggests that this may explain why the image of the vampire possesses an eternal, universal quality and why as long as there are humans on earth there will also be stories about vampires.

Dark/Darkness

Since ancient times darkness has been associated with evil, nightmare visions, and the attack of a vampire. In Bram Stoker's *Dracula* (1897), as well as in the numerous vampire novels and movies that followed, this concept continues to be exploited. Although the vampires of contemporary imagination typically reside in darkness or dark places, such as coffins, windowless mansions, castles, or other dank and dreary places, it is important to note that the vampires of ancient folklore were not necessarily destroyed or even weakened by light or sunshine. The medieval vampires of Russia and Poland, for example, could appear anytime between midday and midnight.

See also: **NIGHT**

Dark Shadows

One of the most successful television series to feature the character of a vampire, *Dark Shadows* ran on the ABC network in the US between 1966 and 1971 and was revived briefly on NBC from 1990 to 1991. *Dark Shadows* initially focused on the wealthy Collins family who lived in Collinwood, a gloomy mansion in a New England seaport town called Collinsport.

This Gothic soap opera-style show, the first of its kind, debuted on daytime television in June 1966. It endured poor ratings until April 1967 when the producer, Dan Curtis, introduced the character of Barnabas Collins, played by actor Jonathan Frid. Collins, a 175-year-old vampire, rejuvenated the show and an audience of mainly school children and housewives were held spellbound. When Barnabas was first introduced he awoke from a long period of slumber to find himself in modern times. With the addition of a vampire, the storyline became permanently supernatural in nature, and ratings soared.

Frid played Barnabas more like a tragic hero than a villain and the viewing audience adored him. A number of episodes flashbacked in time to historic Collinsport to explain why Barnabas became a vampire; other episodes focused on his efforts to cure himself of his vampirism. Other plotlines included witches, warlocks, ghosts, reincarnation, werewolves, zombies, black magic, time travel, and virtually every other major Gothic, horror, and fantasy theme.

Although *Dark Shadows* went off the air in 1971 the popularity of the series was maintained by a number of devoted fan clubs as well as comic books, novels, video releases, and two movies – *House of Dark Shadows* (1970), and *Night of Dark Shadows* (1971). In 1990 NBC attempted to revive the show with actor Ben Cross playing the part of Barnabas, but low ratings led to the show's cancellation in 1991.

Now regarded as something of a classic, *Dark Shadows* continues to enjoy cult status. In July 2007, Warner Bros. announced that they had purchased the film rights of the *Dark Shadows* television series from the estate of Dan Curtis, and filming is planned to begin in mid 2009.

Barnabas Collins

Dark Shadows was memorable for its vivid melodrama, action-packed storylines, adventurous music score, Gothic atmosphere, and endearing inclusion of gaffs in the shows that were aired. The scenes were never re-shot because editing was too expensive and time-consuming for the lean budget. Perhaps the most significant effect of the series, however, was that it transformed for a television audience the character of the vampire from the force of evil depicted in Bram Stoker's *Dracula* into a sympathetic character who longs to be human again and to lead a normal life. Collins is the archetypal outsider, the lonely misfit who desperately wants to fit in. He is good at heart but has the misfortune to have something terrible in his blood that drives him to do things he does not want to do. There seemed to be a truth about his angst-ridden, flawed character that made fans not only embrace but strongly identify with him. The development of Barnabas's storyline and character in the series illustrates perfectly how the strict good versus bad scenario of Bram Stoker's novel had flowed into a more ambiguous interpretation of good and evil.

Darwin, Charles (1809-82)

Charles Darwin was an English naturalist who propounded the theory that every living species has evolved over time from common ancestors through a process he called natural selection. Darwin's revolutionary theories would undoubtedly have influenced Bram Stoker in the composition of his classic vampire novel *Dracula* in 1897.

Darwin's theory of evolution – the suggestion that humans evolved from animals and were not created by God as a separate, superior species – was a profoundly disturbing notion to many people at the time, but it very likely influenced the receptivity of the Victorian public to the vampire theme. Some literary critics have asserted that *Dracula* can be read as a tentative refutation – or even parody – of Darwin's theory. Throughout the novel there is an anxious blurring of distinction between human and animal, as the evolutionary order appears to reverse itself toward our basest human instincts.

Davanzati, Giuseppe (1665-1755)

A respected theologian and Archbishop of Trani, Giuseppe Davanzati was the author of a famous vampire treatise published in Naples in 1744, entitled *Dissertazione sopra i vampiri*.

Davanzati studied theology at the universities of Naples and Bologna, eventually becoming a papal representative to Emperor Charles VI and then an archbishop. His *Dissertazione* was a response to concern from Rome about allegations of vampirism in the diocese of Olmutz. Davanzati studied a number of "factual" cases that had been reported, mostly in Germany, from 1720 to 1739 and concluded that all these cases were the product of superstition and fantasy and should be dismissed. A major component of Davanzati's argument was that vampire attacks tended to occur more often in communities where people were poorly educated and therefore more likely to be deceived by appearances than by more educated people. Davanzati emerged as a leading authority on vampires, and his opinion that vampires were unreal but that belief in them may be demonic and inspired by the Devil came to be generally accepted not just by the Church but by the civil authorities.

Dawn and Daytime

In vampire folklore – although there are exceptions, for example in Polish and Russian lore – dawn is traditionally the time when vampires must return to their grave or resting place. The signal for this retreat is typically the first crow of a cockerel. As vampires are destroyed by sunlight and weakened by day the best time for humans to destroy them is therefore after dawn. In Stephenie Meyer's internationally bestselling Twilight Saga series of novels there is a shift from the traditional "vampires only come out at night" theme. Although Meyer's vampires are weakened by daylight they are not destroyed by it. In fact, their true nature is revealed and their skin sparkles like diamonds.

Although vampires traditionally can't attack humans by daylight, it is possible for an astral vampire or a psychic vampire to intentionally or unintentionally feed on the dreams or energy of others at any time of day or night.

See also: SUNLIGHT

Dearg-diulai

Also known as a *dearg-due* or *dearg-dul*, a dearg-diulai is an ancient vampiric creature from Ireland dating back to very early Celtic times. This much-feared creature would usually take on the shape of a pretty woman so she could haunt lonely places and drink the lifeblood of weary travelers. The term, translated literally, means "red bloodsucker."

According to legend, the only way to defeat the dearg-diulai is to pile stones on top of her grave. While this will not "kill" her, it will prevent her from rising from the dead. The most famous story of the dearg-diulai is the tale of a beautiful woman who was supposedly buried in Waterford, in a small churchyard near Strongbow's tree. Several times a year she would rise from the grave and lure unsuspecting men to their deaths with sexual enticements. There is also a well-known legend in Antrim of a dearg-diulai who cannot find peace as a corpse until she finds another female to take her place. In County Kerry there is a legend of a dearg-diulai who haunted a stretch of road until a drunken man blessed and prayed for her and by so doing released her from her fate.

In Slaughtaverty, County Derry, there is a legend of a male dearg-diulai, called Abhartach, whose story – according to vampirologist Bob Curran in *Vampires: A Field Guide to Creatures that Stalk the Night* (2005) – may have been the inspiration behind Bram Stoker's *Dracula.* Dearg-diulai theorists argue that

Stoker never traveled to Eastern Europe and that he may have taken the name Dracula from dreach-fhoula, pronounced droc'ola, which means "bad blood" or "tainted blood." The Du'n Dreach-Fhoula, or the Castle of Bad Blood, is supposed to be a fortress guarding the pass in Macgillycuddy's Reeks in Kerry and was once believed to be inhabited by blood-drinking fairies.

See also: **CARRICKAPHOUKA CASTLE**

Death

Almost every culture has its stockpile of mythic undead characters, such as ghosts, demons, zombies, and vampires. Pale and wasted, a vampire is the personification of death but it also embodies the concept that human beings can have life after death, again a belief shared by almost every culture. Herein could lie both our eternal fascination with and abhorrence of vampires, as in order to sustain their existence they need to feed on the blood of the living. Cultural historian Paul Barber, in his book *Vampires, Burial and Death* (1988), has postulated that belief in vampires resulted from people of pre-industrial societies attempting to explain the natural, but to them inexplicable, process of death and decomposition.

See also: **AFTERLIFE; BECOMING A VAMPIRE; BURIAL CUSTOMS; TRANSFORMATION**

Death's Head Moth

In the folklore of parts of Romania, it is said that the souls of vampires can be incarnated in death's head moths, and in this form they can bring disease into the house. If such a moth is captured and impaled to a wall with a pin it is believed that the vampire will be trapped.

See also: **BUTTERFLY**

Decapitation

In Eastern European folklore, decapitation or beheading was believed to be one of the most effective ways to destroy a vampire. When a suspected vampire was reported in a village and its identity determined, the body would be disinterred and the head cut off. It was thought that decapitation would prevent the head from directing the corpse. This belief may originate from the ancient idea that a vampire needs both a head and a heart to regenerate. The vampire would usually be decapitated with a sexton's shovel after the corpse had been covered with a sheet and warnings given to onlookers to keep their distance, in case the stored-up blood in the vampire splashed on them and caused disease. Sometimes the head was reburied separately from the corpse, but if buried with the corpse it would be separated from the body by a layer of dirt, or placed at the body's feet, behind the knees or buttocks – anywhere away from the arms to prevent reattachment or the vampire returning with its head under its arm.

The discovery of a tenth- to eleventh-century vampire burial ground in Celákovice, near Prague in 1966 shows what an ancient practice decapitation was for the supposed corpse of a revenant or vampire. All the skeletons discovered showed the telltale signs of anti-vampire rituals. Some were weighed down, others had a nail driven through their temple, and all had had their heads cut off.

See also: **BURIAL CUSTOMS; DESTRUCTION**

Decomposition

In his 1988 book *Vampires, Burial and Death*, cultural historian Paul Barber proposed the theory that belief in vampires may have resulted from an attempt by people of pre-industrial societies to explain the process of decomposition after death. In other words, people suspected vampirism if a corpse did not look as they believed it should look. Rates of decomposition vary according to ambient temperature and soil composition and this variation probably led many vampire hunters to the conclusion that a corpse that had not decomposed was a vampire, or, ironically, to wrongly interpret natural signs of decomposition as vampirism.

The decomposition process

A brief examination of what happens to a person's body when they die will illustrate how the natural process of decomposition could have breathed new life into the vampire myth. (Warning: what follows is not for the faint-hearted!)

When the heart stops beating there is no more pressure to move blood through the body, so it settles according to gravity in whatever parts of the body are closest to the ground, and after about ten hours discolors into a pink, purple color. With no oxygenated red blood cells in the capillaries the skin turns pale and waxy, the eyes flatten, and the extremities turn blue. While the body's temperature cools the muscles relax but then stiffen into rigor mortis, which was first documented scientifically in 1811. Many people mistakenly think that a corpse remains rigid, but after approximately two days it relaxes again as the muscle fibers decompose.

A foul and unmistakable stench develops as the skin detaches from the body and the internal organs liquefy and ooze out of the body's orifices. Nails drop off, leaving fresh skin underneath them, and hair falls out in clumps. As bacteria multiply and parts of the corpse putrefy, the face becomes swollen, discolored, and unrecognizable. Liquids and blood also come out of the nose, mouth, and ears. Bacteria in the intestines produce gases that bloat the body to almost twice its size and eventually turn the skin mostly black. Bloating also makes the tongue and eyes protrude, the lips curl back to reveal gums and teeth, and the genitals and breasts swell in size.

The corpses of suspected vampires could have been exhumed at any time, which meant that vampire hunters got to see a wide variety of corpses at different stages of decomposition. If they saw the corpse's lips curled back into a gnarled smile, or liquids and blood oozing from the mouth, these perfectly natural stages of decomposition could all have been given a sinister interpretation. A corpse that looked bloated would have been described as "plump," "well-fed," or "ruddy" – changes that were all the more striking if the person was pale or thin in life – and any blood found in the coffin would have given the false impression that the corpse had recently been engaging in vampiric activity. If the corpse had shifted position because of bloating this would again look like the work of a vampire.

The staking of a swollen, decomposing body could produce a groan-like sound when the gases moved past the vocal cords or a sound reminiscent of flatulence when they passed through the anus. And when the skin and nails fell away to reveal new skin beneath and the hairline receded to give the appearance of longer hair this could produce the illusion that hair, nails, and teeth had grown. Even more alarming was the disappearance of rigor mortis, as this would have led vampire hunters to believe that the corpse had regained flexibility to get around. Add to all this certain soil conditions that may preserve corpses for longer than was expected and it is easy to see how this might have suggested vampirism.

Incorruptibles

Corpses that are well preserved or have lasted many years with little evidence of decomposition are known as incorruptibles. There are a number of well-documented cases in which people have been exhumed years or even centuries after their deaths and have been found to be inexplicably preserved. For example, in 1927 a coffin washed into a Kentucky river; the body inside it looked as if it had only been buried the day before, but it later proved to be over a hundred years old. Ironically, as well as being a sign of vampirism, the Church also viewed incorruptibility as a measure of sanctity, and incorruptibles – people whose bodies mysteriously thwart decay – were canonized by the Catholic Church.

The causes of incorruptibility are disputed. The argument for a spiritual cause may include a belief that the pious nature of the individual in some way permeated the flesh (a metaphysical cause having a physical effect), or a belief that decomposition was prevented by the intervention of an external divine entity. The argument for an occult cause includes the belief that decomposition was prevented in some way by the process of transformation into a vampire, or other evil entity. And the argument for a physical cause, which is the one most likely to be championed by scientists, includes the belief that the corpse has been subjected to environmental conditions that retard the process of decomposition.

See also: **MANDUCATION; PREMATURE BURIAL**

De Launay, Gabrielle

The story of Gabrielle de Launay, a lady whose case was tried before the High Court of Paris in about 1760, sent shockwaves through the whole of France at the time. Some vampirologists believe Gabrielle's story is not so much a desperately sad and romantic story about a revenant returning from the grave but a desperately sad story illustrating how common an occurrence premature burial may have been at the time.

Gabrielle de Launay was a beautiful 18-year-old and the daughter of the president of the Tribunal of Toulouse. She fell in love with an army officer, Maurice de Serres, but was forbidden to marry him by her father who refused to let her travel with Maurice to the Indies where he was being posted. The lovers parted broken-hearted, and two years later word arrived that Maurice had been killed.

Convinced that Maurice was dead, Gabrielle was persuaded to marry President du Bourg, a man 30 years her senior. Five years passed and Gabrielle finally died of unhappiness. Around the same time, Maurice, who was not actually dead as reported, returned to Paris and learned of her passing. Overcome with grief he bribed the sexton of St. Roch Cemetery where she was buried to let him see her body one last time. In a fit of passion Maurice seized her body and ran off, forcing the flustered sexton to re-inter the empty coffin and keep silent, lest the authorities learn that he had committed sacrilege by accepting gold from Maurice to open the coffin.

Another five years passed and du Bourg was passing through a somewhat unfrequented street in the suburbs of Paris when he came face to face with a lady he recognized immediately to be his dead wife. She drove past him swiftly in her carriage, but du Bourg saw the coat of arms of de Serres upon the door. Du Bourg immediately set about proving that his wife was still alive and impersonating the spouse of de Serres, Julie. When the empty broken coffin of Gabrielle was discovered suspicion turned into certainty.

The whole city was astounded when du Bourg demanded from the High Court the dissolution of the illegal marriage between Captain Maurice de Serres and the pretended Julie de Serres, who was Gabrielle du Bourg, his lawful wife. The High Court, convinced that Gabrielle had not died but had been in a catatonic state when she had been buried, dismissed her plea to enter a cloister and ordered her to return to her first and lawful husband. Two days after the High Court declaration President du Bourg awaited Gabrielle's arrival in the great hall of his mansion. She appeared, but could scarcely totter through the gates, for she had a few moments previously drained a swift poison. Crying, "I restore to you what you have lost," she fell dead at his feat. At that same instant, de Serres was said to have killed himself, thus reuniting the lovers at death.

De Lioncourt, Lestat

Lestat de Lioncourt was the central vampire character in the majority of Anne Rice's best-selling series of Vampire Chronicles, which became a key element in the revival of interest in vampires toward the end of the twentieth century. Lestat's suave and deadly character inspired the creation of a rock band, a role-playing game – Vampire: the Masquerade – and Anne Rice's Vampire Lestat Fan Club.

In the first two novels in The Vampire Chronicles, Rice describes in some detail Lestat's two-century-old existence and his transformation into a vampire in France around 1760. An atheist before his transformation into a vampire, he does not fear crucifixes, holy symbols, or churches. In the 1998 movie, *Interview with the Vampire*, actor Tom Cruise played the role of the Vampire Lestat to critical acclaim.

See also: **RICE, ANNE; VAMPIRE CHRONICLES, THE**

De Masticatione Mortuorum

Translated roughly as "On the Masticating Dead," *De Masticatione Mortuorum* was the name given to two vampire treatises, one written by Philip Rohr, published in Leipzig in 1679, and one by Michaël Ranf, published in 1728, also in Leipzig. Like the treatise written by Dom Augustin Calmet in 1746, the publication of both treatises did much to spread European vampire hysteria in the seventeenth and eighteenth centuries.

Dementors

Dementors are vampire-like creatures in the phenomenally popular Harry Potter fantasy novels by British author J. K. Rowling. The Dementors suck the joy out of a person and make them feel like they will never be happy again. With their vampiric draining of happy memories, these soulless wraith-like entities leave their victims in the hell of their most terrible memories. In this way, life becomes devoid of goodness and meaning and eventually the victim loses their soul, which is the ultimate fate of all victims of vampires.

The "cousins" of the dementors are the "black riders," the closest thing to vampires in J. R. R. Tolkien's epic fantasy *The Fellowship of the Ring*, published in 1954. The "black riders," which some literary critics believe may have been the inspiration for Rowling's dementors, were once human but their souls and their memories have been drained by the evil of the rings that gave them unearthly power.

Demons/Demon Possession

In ancient times demons were thought to be evil spirits who brought misfortune, terror, misery, and chaos to humans. Vampires were often alleged to be reanimated corpses inhabited by demons.

Overview of demon belief

For centuries in mythology, folklore, and religion demons were said to be non-physical creatures of a (usually) malign nature. In Christian terms demons were generally understood as fallen angels, formerly of God but now in league with the Devil. They were blamed for a host of ills and misfortunes including demonic sexual molestation, where a demon masquerades as a man or woman to molest its victim. Many possession cases in the Middle Ages involved sexual molestation by demons, although this may have been more to do with repressed humans than supernatural activity. In many cultures and religions demons have been exorcised. In Catholicism cases of demonic possession, in which demons battle for a person's soul, are dealt with by formal exorcism rites that date back to 1614.

Demons, like vampires, can be found in virtually every ancient culture, including those of Assyria, Babylonia, Egypt, Greece, and Rome and every religious system, including Judaism, Hinduism, and Buddhism. Some vampire species in the world, in particular Asian vampires like the chiang-shih, langsuir, and mmbyu are even considered to be actual demons. To the ancient Greeks daemons, from the Greek word *daimon* meaning "divine power," "fate," or "god" were intermediary spirits between the gods and humankind, rather like guardian spirits. They could be either good or evil. Good daemons were supportive and encouraging but evil daemons could lead people astray with bad counsel. However, by medieval times, the Christian Church had completely condemned pagan beliefs in daemons and though people still believed in them, the very definition of daemon was transformed into demon, traditionally associated with evil.

Keen to discredit pagan beliefs, a number of medieval theologians studied the hierarchy of demons and their powers, attributes, and derivations. Religious leaders taught that demons were the messengers and followers of the solitary agent of evil – Satan or the Devil. St. Thomas Aquinas (1225–74) further perpetuated this belief by blaming natural disasters and even bad weather on demons, while Pope Eugenius IV (1383–1447) referred to demons as "agents of Satan." Demons were said to be extremely evil and terrifyingly clever, masters in the art of persuasion. Humans had to be constantly on their guard against them. In 1580 philosopher Jean Bodin claimed in *De la Demonomanie des Sorciers* that:

> It is certain that the devils have a profound knowledge of all things. No theologian can interpret the Holy Scriptures better than they can; no lawyer has a more detailed knowledge of testaments, contracts and actions; no physician or philosopher can better understand the composition of the human body, and the virtues of the heavens, the stars, birds and fishes, trees and herbs, metals and stones.

The vampire/demon link

The link between vampires and demons may have first developed out of the highly developed system of demonic belief established by the Assyrians and Babylonians of ancient Mesopotamia, as they were frequently ranked together as agents of sin. Much of Judaic and

Christian demonology may also have come from this ancient tradition. In official medieval Church doctrine, Devil worship, witchcraft, vampirism, and demonology were typically grouped together as evils to be purged by mankind.

Belief in demonic possession as an explanation for vampirism was popular in medieval European folklore. According to this explanation a demon could create a vampire by entering and taking possession of a corpse, but to maintain the corpse as a host it would need some kind of physical substance, and that substance was blood. This theory could explain why holy symbols, such as crosses, repel vampires. It could also make it easier to understand why the reanimated corpse would find it so easy to kill loved ones and family members when it became a vampire. The once-living individual would no longer be controlling the corpse. Instead it would be the mind of the demon that controlled the actions of the corpse. The weakness of this theory for modern-day vampirologists is that it is difficult to prove demonic possession exists in the living, let alone in a corpse.

Today, in religion and parapsychology, demons have evolved into meaning entities which appear to have malicious intent, and are possibly of a non-human origin; differentiated from a spirit or ghost which proceeded from a once-living person. Some occultists believe that human thoughts can generate such negativity that a person's soul can somehow degenerate into a form of that which we name a demon.

See also: **EXORCISM; INCUBUS/SUCCUBUS; NECROMANCY; SHAMAN; WITCHCRAFT**

De Rais, Gilles (1404–40)

Gilles de Rais, also known as Gilles de Laval, was a fifteenth-century French nobleman and a national hero of the Hundred Years War. However, his alleged cruelty, sadism, sexual perversions, and cannibalism earned him a place in history as one of the most notorious murderers or historical vampires of all time. He was also the basis for the fairy story about the bloodthirsty, serial-killing villain Bluebeard.

A fine soldier, Gilles fought alongside Joan of Arc against England and became a marshal at the age of 24. He inherited a vast fortune but his extravagant tastes and an interest in black magic and Satanism brought him close to financial ruin. He was eventually accused of numerous murders, especially of young boys who had disappeared from the area. At the resulting trial he was tortured and "confessed" to charges of murder and vampirism, and was executed for his crimes. Many historians believe that he may not have been guilty of the crimes he was accused of, and that his bizarre sexual habits and extravagant lifestyle made him an easy target for his political enemies.

Destruction/Destroying Vampires

In almost every culture, vampires have been regarded as evil creatures and as soon as the identity of the vampire was confirmed, people would attempt to locate and destroy it to prevent the evil spreading and infecting humans with death, disease, evil, and misfortune.

Although methods of dispatching vampires varied from region to region, for example in Albania the preferred method of dispatch was a stake through the heart whereas in Poland burying a corpse face down was thought to be sufficient. According to most vampire hunter lore however, there are really only two sure-fire methods of destroying a vampire. The first method, popular in early vampire folklore, was to stake the corpse and then behead the vampire. The head and body should then be burned in two separate places, with the ashes scattered in separate locations. The second method, which is a more modern addition to the vampire myth, is to expose the vampire to sunlight and then scatter its ashes.

In the folklore of Eastern Europe, vampire activity would typically be traced to a graveyard and to the corpse of a particular individual who had died recently. The corpse would be disinterred and studied for signs of vampirism, such as blood around the mouth. If the corpse was confirmed as a vampire it would then be staked or shot with a sacred silver bullet blessed by a priest. Originally the logic behind staking a corpse through the stomach, back, or heart was to hold the body to the ground so it could not get up, but in the nineteenth century this ancient tradition was modified when it was said that a stake driven into the heart would stop the blood of life flowing through the vampire's veins. In keeping with the belief that vampires are the undead, it was thought that if the stake was removed the vampire would spring to life.

Decapitation, ideally with a gravedigger's shovel (because it was thought to possess certain supernatural powers due to its association with the dead) or a sexton's shovel (potent because of its association with God), was then often used. Killing a vampire in this way was thought to be dangerous because anyone sprayed with a vampire's blood might go insane or die, so slayers who used this method would cover the corpse with a cloth before beheading it.

The severed head had also to be treated with caution. As well as avoiding blood, the slayer would fill the mouth with garlic, coins, or stones to prevent the vampire from biting. The head would then be buried separately from the body, or buried under the feet of the corpse to prevent the possibility of re-attachment.

Another method of destroying a vampire was to bury a suspected vampire at a crossroads, or the place where two rural roads intersected. Centuries ago crossroads were used by the Germanic Teutons as places for human sacrifices and executions to be conducted. After Christianity was adopted in Europe, officials continued to bury outlaws and suspected criminals at crossroads. It was thought that even if the vampire rose from the dead at a crossroads its demonic brain would be bewildered by the choice of direction offered it. If decapitation or burial at a crossroads did not work, the last option was to burn the body.

Vampire hunters

In some instances, villagers or Church officials would be involved in the detection and destruction of a vampire, but in others it was thought that vampires could only be destroyed by professional vampire hunters. In Serbia it was said that a vampire hunter, called a dhampir, had almost magical powers. These slayers were said to play music that caused the blood-sucker to lose concentration so it could be easily shot or stabbed with a wooden stake. Other methods included playing on the weaknesses of a vampire. For instance, vampires were thought not to possess the ability to swim. They were also said to be very attached to their clothing, such as hats and coats. The slayer would try to steal the vampire's clothes and throw them in a lake, causing the vampire to drown when it attempted to recover them. Vampires could also be lured to dangerous places, such as the edges of high cliffs.

It is also a known "fact" in vampire hunter lore that when a vampire is destroyed, the body releases a kind of spectral energy that is so strong it can shatter glass and move objects. In cases where older or more powerful vampires were dispatched, enormous discharges of this energy were reportedly experienced by vampire hunters. There was also the danger of this energy escaping. In Serbian lore, when the corpse of a vampire was impaled, witnesses would watch anxiously for the appearance of a butterfly or moth, which would indicate that the vampire was trying to escape its destruction. If detected, the insect had to be caught and killed as soon as possible to ensure that the vampire was completely destroyed.

Vampire destruction in fiction and film

Once the vampire of folklore became the subject of popular fiction, staking a vampire through the heart was often seen as an adequate method of dispatch. However, by typically staking the vampire through the heart, rather than the stomach or back, a change in the myth was confirmed. Staking was no longer for the purpose of confining the vampire to its grave to prevent it leaving but to attack the heart, the organ that pumped blood, and therefore "life" into the vampire. Another change to the vampire myth was the idea that the vampire could be killed by sunlight. Previously, although the vampire's powers were more enhanced at night, its actions were not limited to it. Daylight protected the living from vampire activity but the idea that sunlight killed vampires was not widespread. However, once the negative effects of sunlight on vampires had been suggested – most memorably in the death at dawn scene in the 1922 vampire movie classic *Nosferatu* – it soon became an established part of vampire stories in fiction and film.

During the twentieth century the vampire myth was restructured again in fiction and film, and although vampires still face three deadly threats – fire, a stake in the heart, or sunshine – the possibility of the vampire being revived in some way by a magical spell, or by adding blood to the ashes of a burned vampire, is raised. And if the stake or blade is removed, even if the creature's body has crumbled to dust, the vampire's supernatural vitality will restore its body in the condition it had before it was destroyed, returning it to "life."

In the novels of Anne Rice vampires are not affected by crucifixes or other traditional methods of dispatch. Although fire is dangerous and potentially deadly, some vampires can survive the most intense burning and older vampires gain immunity to sunlight. In Stephenie Meyer's 2005 novel, *Twilight*, decapitation and burning are the preferred methods of dispatching a vampire, but the teenage vampire Edward Cullen is not destroyed by sunlight. His skin simply glistens like diamonds and he grows more beautiful when exposed to it.

See also: **BOTTLING A VAMPIRE; DHAMPIR; PREVENTION; PROTECTION; VAMPIRE HUNTERS**

Detecting/Detection of Vampires

In most societies in medieval Europe, it was simply townsfolk or villagers who grouped together to detect or look for telltale signs or clues to the presence of the undead.

If the vampire could be traced to a grave telltale signs included:

- *Finger-sized holes or disturbed earth around the grave*
- *Corpse lights*
- *Disturbed coffins*
- *Fallen or moved tombstones*
- *Footprints leading to and from the grave*
- *An absence of birdsong*
- *Dogs barking at graves or refusing to enter the cemetery*
- *Horses shying away from a grave*
- *Groaning sounds coming from underneath the earth*

Signs of a vampire corpse included:

- *Open eyes*
- *Ruddy complexion*
- *Bloated body*
- *New nails or long hair*
- *Flexible limbs*
- *Lack of decomposition*
- *Blood around the mouth or in the coffin or tomb*

In Eastern Europe the task of detecting vampires was often turned over to professional vampire hunters, called dhampirs.

Over the centuries, vampires seem to have acquired the ability to blend virtually unnoticed into the world of the living, and therefore the task of detecting a vampire has grown harder and harder for vampire hunters, fictional or otherwise. The suave and sophisticated vampires of modern fiction are very different from the vampires of ancient folklore, which were often described as looking and smelling just like a decomposing corpse would if it had risen from the grave. There are, however, a number of telltale signs which modern vampires generally appear to manifest and these include:

- *Fangs or sharpened teeth which extend when feeding*
- *Red eyes or eyes that change color*

- *Paleness*

- *Bad breath*

- *Long nails and hairy palms*

- *A reluctance to enter a house without invitation*

- *Remarkable strength and dexterity*

- *An enormous sexual appetite but no appetite for food*

- *Weakness or fatigue during daytime*

- *An aversion to sunlight and religious discussion*

It is important to point out, however, that these signs tend to apply to blood-drinking vampires, and not necessarily to psychic vampires.

Signs of a possible vampire attack in a victim generally include sleeplessness, nightmares, anemia, bite marks, fatigue, nervousness, mood swings, sleepwalking, difficulty breathing, no appetite, weight loss, and an aversion to garlic and sunlight.

Devil

See: **FALLEN ANGELS; OCCULT; SATAN**

Dhampir

In the lore of the Slavonic Gypsies, dhampir is the name given to the child of a union between a human female and a male vampire; such a person was regarded as possessing unique abilities to detect and destroy vampires. Although the tradition dates back many centuries, dhampirs have been reported in modern times in rural areas. One of the last known dhampir ceremonies was held in 1959 in Kosovo.

Vampire hunters are common in Gypsy lore. It was thought that vampire men were irresistible to women and many children were produced. As a result a large number of men in Eastern Europe were said to be the offspring of vampires. The dhampir were said to have the incredible powers of seeing vampires, even if invisible, and the speed, agility, and strength that made them more than equipped to kill vampires. Although the dhampir were greatly feared by the Romany they were also respected and were often hired to rid the village of vampires and to protect them from all manner of evil.

Before declaring the vampire finally dead the dhampir would perform a number of bizarre rituals, which included using a shirt sleeve as a telescope to spot the invisible vampire, running around and wrestling with an invisible foe, or "shooting" it with a silver bullet consecrated by a priest. If the vampire was traced to a cemetery the body would be exhumed and either burned or a hawthorn stake pounded into its heart or stomach.

One of the most unusual tricks employed was a ritual called "bottling the undead." This method involved the hunter holding a bottle with a few drops of animal blood in it in one hand and a picture of a saint to terrify the blood-sucker in the other hand. The hunter would then chase the vampire up a tree or onto the roof of a house. Once trapped in a high place the hunter would tempt the creature with the bloody snack in a bottle. With no other means of eating the vampire would crawl into its prison, which the hunter fastened tightly with a cork. The bottle was then thrown on the coals of a blazing fire.

If for any reason the hunter could not destroy the vampire, he was still thought to have the power to send it away. A large fee was then collected by the dhampir for his services to the community.

Not surprisingly, the trade drew its fair share of charlatans and frauds who, vampire-like, preyed on the fears, superstitions, and trust of the public. These charlatans would often work in groups. They would travel the Balkans, "sniffing" out or "sensing" vampires in a village. They would sometimes check for a recent death, or drain the blood from livestock and then blame a village or town's bad luck or illnesses to the presence of a vampire. After they had instilled fear and suspicion among the villagers, they would then profess to have the power to command a vampire to leave, but their services were never cheap.

Fiction and film

In modern fiction and film half-human, half-vampire dhampirs can be created from vampire and human procreation, a vampire bite to a pregnant woman, scientific crossbreeding, or any other hundreds of ways. The limit to the dhampir's creation in fiction is only the writer's imagination. Whatever their back story, the half-breed dhampir figure, such as the Marvel comic superhero Blade, or more recently the half-vampire, half-human daughter of Edward Cullen in Stephenie Meyer's 2008 novel *Breaking Dawn*, often represent the pinnacle of vampire and human strengths combined, defeating all others, and especially hunting other vampires without much remorse.

> *See also:* **BOTTLING A VAMPIRE;**
> **DESTROYING VAMPIRES;**
> **DETECTING VAMPIRES; MULLO;**
> **REPRODUCTION; VAMPIRE**
> **HUNTERS**

Disease

Over the centuries certain people have been accused of being vampires or the victims of a vampire attack because their physical characteristics resembled the traits of these blood-sucking monsters. Modern medicine has shed some light on the vampire myth by highlighting certain medical and psychological conditions that may well explain why some people were mistaken for vampires in the past.

Anemia

Anemia is a disorder in which there is not enough of a certain protein in the red blood cells. The most common type of anemia is iron deficiency anemia caused by low levels of iron in the blood. Symptoms of anemia may include fatigue, pallor, dizziness, headaches or migraines, depression, and on occasion cravings for blood – all indications of an inadequate oxygen supply as red blood cells transport oxygen around the body. However, it is not hard to see how a severely anemic person could be mistaken for a vampire victim in centuries past.

Porphyria

Porphyria is a rare hereditary blood disease and, like anemia, it causes symptoms that are similar to those considered characteristic of a vampire. People suffering from porphyria cannot produce heme, an essential component of red blood, and this makes them sensitive to sunlight. They may also have tightened skin around the lips and gums, thus making the teeth more conspicuous.

Other diseases where sufferers can become sensitive to sunlight (and which may have been mistaken for vampirism) include xeroderma pigmentosum, a rare genetic defect that causes extreme sensitivity to the sun's ultraviolet rays, and rabies. Symptoms of rabies include hypersensitivity to light and mirrors, frothy, bloody fluid in the mouth, ferocious aggressive behavior, and excessive thirst.

Catalepsy

Catalepsy is a dysfunction of the nervous system that causes a slowing down of the body's regulatory functions, so much so that to the untrained eye the person appears dead. Sufferers can see and hear but cannot move or speak. If someone was buried in a cataleptic state and awoke days later in their coffin, their attempts to claw their way out may have led people to believe that a vampire was attempting to return from the grave.

Sleep paralysis

Sleep paralysis is not a disease but a condition in which someone about to drop off to sleep, or just upon waking from sleep, realizes that he or she is unable to move, or speak, or cry out. People suffering from episodes of sleep paralysis frequently report feeling a presence that is often described as malevolent, threatening, or evil during these episodes.

Contagions

Rabies is a condition that has been associated with vampirism. The symptoms of consumption or tuberculosis, which include fatigue, pale skin, loss of appetite, blood in the sputum, bad breath, and weight loss, were also quite similar to the symptoms believed to denote vampire attack. In fact, there are a number of documented cases in both Europe and the US in which a family or town viewed a person who had died from consumption as a vampire. The epidemic allusion is obvious in the classical cases of Peter Plogojowitz and Arnold Paole, and even more obvious in the Mercy Brown case and in the vampire outbreaks of New England, where the tuberculosis/vampire link is clear.

Finally, there is the unproven theory suggested by some vampirologists that there is some strange virus that may alter the DNA of normal humans so that they transform into blood-sucking monsters. Vampire virus theories have as yet no scientific basis.

See also: **Dolphin Hypothesis**

Dissertatio de Vampyris

The *Dissertatio de Vampyris* or *Vampris*, translated as *Dissertation on the Vampire* and published in 1733, was one of the most popular and authoritative scientific treatises on the undead in the eighteenth century. Written by Johann Heinrich Zopfius and Francis von Dalen it contains the following well-known statement about vampire infestations reported in Serbia:

> *Vampires issue forth from their graves at night, attack people sleeping quietly in their beds, suck out all the blood from their bodies and destroy them. They best men, women and children alike, sparing neither age nor sex. Those who are under the fatal malignity of their influence complain of suffocation and a total deficiency of spirits, after which they soon expire. Some who, when at the point of death, have been asked if they can tell what is causing their disease, reply that such and such persons, lately dead, have risen from the tomb to torment and torture them.*

Dog Rose

Rosa canina, or dog rose, is a wild rose with thorns and white and pink flowers that can be found in parts of Europe and Asia. Like many other rose varieties it was used as a preventive method against vampirism. The Wallachians thought that placing dog rose thorns and vines on the corpse's shroud and inside the grave or coffin would pin the corpse down and stop it rising from the grave.

See also: **APOTROPAICS; PREVENTION**

Dogs

According to Eastern European lore, if a dog jumped over the corpse of the recently deceased person this might create a revenant or vampire. Black dogs were also believed to be capable of detecting the presence of vampires and attacking and destroying them.

The use of dogs for detecting and hunting vampires may go back as far back as 2000 BC, when rulers of the Hittite Empire in Asia Minor were said to keep vampire-fighting dogs "as large and fierce as lions." And according to the Federal Vampire and Zombie Agency (FVZA), in 1863 the German authorities, dissatisfied with existing breeds of vampire-hunting dogs, contracted dog breeder Louis Doberman to create a breed of dog specifically for the purpose. The Doberman Pinscher breed was born, and "*with its unique blend of speed, ferocity and intelligence, the Doberman became the gold standard in vampire control.*" However, the FVZA is not generally taken seriously as an accurate historical resource by most vampire experts and researchers.

As well as being enemies of the vampire, dogs could also be their allies. Vampires were said to be able to control dogs or transform themselves into them. In addition, dogs could become vampire-like beings themselves. Vampire dog attacks have been reported throughout history, and this has led some vampirologists to suggest that the supposedly recent chupacabra or vampire dog phenomenon may actually date back several hundred years.

An early reported case of a suspected vampire dog occurred in Ireland in 1874, when some creature began to kill and drain the blood of as many as 30 sheep a night in Cavan, Ireland. The creature left behind long dog-like tracks, and when the menace spread to other villages and counties bands of angry farmers scoured the countryside, shooting at stray dogs everywhere. Another infamous case took place at Croglin Grange, an estate in Cumberland, England, in the summer of 1875 when a dog-like beast allegedly attacked a woman. In 1905, a rash of sheep killings, which again prompted attacks on stray dogs, was reported near Gravesend, England. As before, all the sheep were attacked at the throat, lost large amounts of blood, and no flesh was eaten. Once again, the killings stopped suddenly, and the creature responsible was nowhere to be found.

See also: ANIMAL VAMPIRES

Dolphin Hypothesis

On May 30, 1985, David Dolphin, Ph.D., Professor of Chemistry at the University of British Columbia gave a memorable presentation to the American Association for the Advancement of Science. According to Prof. Dolphin, blood-drinking vampires were in fact victims of a disease called porphyria, an incurable genetic disease affecting at least 50,000 patients in the United States that causes sudden symptoms of severe pain, sensitivity to light, respiratory problems, skin blisters and lesions, blood in the urine, aversion to garlic, hairiness, elongated teeth, and which sometimes results in death. He suggested that people with porphyria, desperately drinking fresh blood to try to alleviate their symptoms by introducing its required element (heme) to their system, were responsible for the spread of the vampire legend and hysteria.

Dolphin's hypothesis received a great deal of attention from both the medical community and the media because of the suggestion that there were parallels between vampirism and this blood disease. However, it was quickly discounted by numerous experts because Dolphin based his idea on vampire fiction, in particular Bram Stoker's *Dracula*, and film, rather than on folklore and mythology. The idea that vampires became blistered and ulcerated in the sun is not prominent in vampire folklore and the hypothesis totally ignores the most significant parts of the vampire tradition – the undead state.

For a few years after Dolphin's theory was presented, porphyria patients felt unfairly singled out for attack because their condition was momentarily and incorrectly linked to vampirism. Several patients reported that people who had had no problem with their condition before began to "avoid them like the plague." The perpetuation of such beliefs, despite medical evidence to the contrary, indicates the emotional power of contemporary folklore about vampires.

Doppelsauger

Also known as a *duppelsauger*, the doppelsauger is a type of vampire found in the Hanover region of Germany among the Slavs. Translated literally the name means "double-sucker" and refers to the belief that a baby or child once weaned will become a vampire if he or she nurses again. After death the doppelsauger will transform into a vampire, and while still in the grave or coffin will eat the fleshy parts of its chest. As a result, by some kind of sympathetic magic, their living relatives will become vampirized of their life essence.

The presence of a doppelsauger was believed to be able to be detected if a living relative started to waste away, and by certain telltale signs on the corpse, such as lips that would not decay. To prevent a doppelsauger from leaving its grave, a gold coin or gold cross was stuck between the teeth of the corpse. A semicircular board could also be placed under the chin to separate the lips from the breast. In addition, the burial garment was not to come into contact with the lips. When moving the corpse of a doppelsauger out of a house the front doorsill was removed; after the coffin had been taken out it was tightly replaced to make sure the body did not return, for it was thought that it needed to enter by the same method it departed.

Despite these precautions it was still possible for a doppelsauger to escape from the grave and if this was the case relatives would need to go to the cemetery in the middle of the night and exhume the body. Its destruction was ensured by slicing off the back of the neck with a spade, and if it was a real doppelsauger the corpse would let out a chilling scream.

Doyle, Sir Arthur Conan (1859–1930)

Scottish-born author famous all over the world for his fictional detective, Sherlock Holmes, Arthur Conan Doyle was a graduate of the University of Edinburgh and practiced medicine until 1891, by which time Holmes was appearing regularly in the *Strand* magazine. Holmes only investigated one alleged vampire case, in *The Adventures of the Sussex Vampire*, but Doyle was intensely interested in the paranormal and also wrote two vampire-theme tales, both in 1894: *John Barringon Cowles* and the more well-known *The Parasite*.

The Parasite is a dark and chilling tale of a psychic vampire. The protagonist, a young professor named Gilroy, has no means of defense against Miss Penelosa, a crippled old maid with "*a pale, peaky face*" who gradually saps the professor's vitality. Gilroy eventually realizes that Penelosa is a "*monster parasite*" and shuts himself away from her. This only offers temporary relief and when he emerges from his self-imposed seclusion, the attack resumes. Knowing that no one will believe the truth about what is happening to him, Gilroy descends into despair, madness, and crime. His misery only ends when Penelosa dies due to outside circumstances.

See also: LITERATURE

Dracula

Count Dracula, as presented in Bram Stoker's 1897 novel *Dracula*, is the prototypical blood-sucking vampire of Gothic horror; a villain with an insufferable ego and an utterly diabolical and evil nature. Even though he has seemingly unappealing characteristics and is absent for large portions of the novel, Dracula's menacing presence dominates the story. His character is a demonstration both of the hypnotic, compelling, and timeless attraction of evil and (in the Victorian age) the potentially overwhelming power of repressed sexuality.

Description

In Stoker's novel, Count Dracula (we never learn his first name) is described as a centuries-old vampire, sorcerer, and Transylvanian nobleman, who claims to be a Székely descended from Attila the Hun. In his youth, he studied at the academy of Scholomance in the Carpathian Mountains, overlooking the town of Sibiu and became proficient in the black arts and magic. Later he took up a military profession, fighting the Turks across the Danube. Using black magic Dracula has managed to evade death for several centuries and now lives in his decaying castle in the Carpathian Mountains near the Borgo Pass with three vampire women for company.

Dracula first appears in chapter one of the novel, but the reader does not learn until later in the book that the driver who met Jonathan Harker and took him to Castle Dracula was none other than the Count himself. In the second chapter he is presented to readers as a brooding figure of a man dressed entirely in black, with a strong face, long white moustache, thin nose, sharp teeth, pointed ears, hairy palms, long nails, and foul breath.

He was a tall man, clean shaven save for a long white moustache and clad in black from head to foot, without a single speck of colour about

him anywhere … His face was a strong, a very strong, aquiline, with high bridge of the thin nose and perfectly arched nostrils, with lofty domed forehead, and hair growing scantily round the temples but profusely elsewhere. His eyebrows were massive, almost meeting over the nose and with bushy hair that seemed to curl in its own profusion. The mouth, as far as I could see it under the heavy moustache, was fixed and rather cruel looking, with particularly sharp, white teeth. These protruded over the lips, whose remarkable ruddiness showed astonishing vitality in a man of his years. For the rest, his ears were pale, and at the tops extremely pointed. The chin was broad and strong and the cheeks firm though thin.

In superb English but with a strange accent, Dracula welcomes Harker to his house, urging him to *"Enter freely and of your own will."* Once inside the castle Harker notices that the hand Dracula offered to shake seemed as cold as ice, *"more like the hand of a dead than a living man,"* and later this combination of elegance, horror, and crudeness that Dracula embodies is once again brilliantly brought out by Stoker's description of Dracula's hands:

Hitherto I had noticed the backs of his hands as they lay on his knee in the firelight, and they had seemed rather white and fine; but seeing them now close to me, I could not but notice that they were rather coarse — broad, with squat fingers. Strange to say there were hairs on the centre of his palm. The nails were long and fine and cut to a sharp point. As the Count leaned over to me and his hands touched me, I could not repress a shudder.

Unlike the vampires common to Eastern European lore, which are often described as bloated, repulsive, corpse-like creatures, Dracula exudes a veneer of aristocratic charisma which masks his predatory evil and violent temper. Despite Dracula's "charm" his unusual nature becomes a matter of grave concern to Harker, who notices that he has yet to see the Count eat or drink and recalls that all the people at Bistritz and on the coach had some terrible fear for him. In chapter three the suggestion that there may be some link between the Count and the historical Vlad the Impaler is made, but as the novel progresses the reader's attention is drawn not to Dracula's history but to his supernatural qualities, which are akin to some of those typically considered to be attributes of the undead. The Count has superhuman strength, equivalent to twenty men according to Harker. Harker also observes Dracula scaling the castle walls *"with his coat spreading out around him like great wings."* Eventually, Harker discovers Dracula asleep in a box filled with earth, looking as if his youth has been restored by drinking fresh blood.

Characteristics

Later in the novel we discover that drinking the blood of his victims helps Dracula grow younger. He also casts no shadow and has powerful hypnotic and mind-control abilities that enable him to control both humans and animals, including bats, owls, moths, foxes, wolves, and rats, as well as the elements, such as thunder and fog. He can shape-shift and travel as elemental dust or mist. He also uses necromancy, which involves the use of corpses to acquire special knowledge, and as a mortal has learned every branch of knowledge available in his day. Despite such

impressive physical and mental abilities the Count does have his limitations. Being nocturnal his movements and strength and ability to shape-shift are limited by daylight. Crosses, garlic, and holy water make him recoil; he must sleep in a box filled with his native soil and he can only go where he is first invited. This last fact means that his entry into a person's life is inextricably linked with their desire, which forms the basis of the symbolism of sexual prowess that the Count embodies.

Perhaps his most mysterious and terrifying power is his ability to transfer his condition to others via a bite in the throat, and then to complete the process of transformation by encouraging his blood-drained victims to drink his own blood. His preference for companionship appears to be women, as there is no mention of the men aboard his ship the *Demeter* becoming undead.

Revenge

As the action of the novel shifts to England, the Count declares that his revenge has just begun. It is not, however, clear what offence Dracula is seeking revenge for, but the clue may come in the opening section of the book when he speaks about the distinguished but disappointing history of his family. His warlike glory days are long behind him, and as he discusses the crowded streets of London there is a sense that he lusts for power and conquest again. *"I long … to be in the midst of the whirl and rush of humanity, to share its life, its change, its death, and all that makes it what it is. But alas!"* In this light, Dracula is not just a vampire of incalculable evil; he is a more human – more sympathetic – creation, eager to subject the world to his dark brutality and recapture his family's lost power. He is a monster with the unique combination of supernatural powers and extraordinary human characteristics that makes him a chilling threat to humans everywhere.

Destruction

Contrary to popular belief, Dracula is not impaled with a stake at the end of the novel, or exposed to the rays of the sun. He is stabbed in the heart by a knife wielded by Quincey Morris, the only American in the book, and then has his throat slit by a knife wielded by Jonathan Harker. This omission of the proper rituals of destruction, for example cremation, has led some to express doubts whether Dracula has really been finished off. Dracula, it is suggested, may rise again.

In fiction, a number of writers have taken on the challenge of revisiting Dracula or bringing Dracula back from the dead but, with the notable exception of *Count Dracula and the Unicorn* (1978) by Jeanne Youngson and the works of Raymond Rudorff and Peter Tremayne, few are viewed to be of any lasting significance.

Dracula

Ranked among the greatest works of Gothic literature, *Dracula* was written by Bram Stoker and published in London in 1897 by Archibald Constable and Co. and in the US two years later. Critical reviews were mixed on publication, but it was a success with the reading public who applauded its message of good triumphing over evil. Its appeal has not waned over the years and the novel has never been out of print. After Stoker's death in 1912 it went on to inspire countless plays, movies, books, comics, scholarly treaties, crucial interpretations, and imitations.

Synopsis

The story begins with Jonathan Harker, a newly qualified English solicitor, journeying to Count Dracula's remote castle which is situated in the Carpathian Mountains on the border of Transylvania and Moldavia. The purpose of Harker's visit is to offer legal support to Dracula for a real estate purchase overseen by his employer in England. Once he has arrived at the castle, despite being impressed by his host's gracious manner, Harker soon feels like a prisoner. He also notices the increasingly weird nocturnal behavior of the Count, which includes wall climbing and not eating or drinking. One night after being warned not to leave his room by Dracula, Harker falls under the spell of three female vampires. He is saved by the Count who for some reason wants to keep Harker alive, perhaps because he needs his legal advice. The picture of Dracula as a vampire is finally completed when Harker discovers the Count in his daytime sleep.

The storyline now moves to England where Dracula intends to move to and establish himself. Leaving Harker imprisoned in the castle, Dracula travels to the Black Sea and secretly boards, with 50 boxes of his native soil, a Russian ship, the *Demeter*. Aboard the *Demeter* he rises from his box each night and feeds on the sailors until the ship runs aground on the shore at Whitby during a fierce tempest. Dracula transforms into a large dog and leaves the derelict ship.

Through the rest of the novel Dracula, although a constantly disturbing presence, only makes fleeting appearances as the storyline shifts to Harker's devoted fiancée, Wilhelmina 'Mina' Murray, and her vivacious friend, Lucy Westenra. Dracula attacks Lucy first and she begins to waste away. She receives a blood transfusion from her doctor, John Seward, who calls in his old teacher, Professor Abraham Van Helsing from Amsterdam, to give his opinion. Van Helsing immediately suspects the vampiric cause of Lucy's condition but it is too late to save her from her fate and she dies. Soon afterward the newspapers report children being stalked in the night by a beautiful strange lady. Van Helsing, knowing that this means Lucy has definitely become a vampire, confides in Seward, an American Quincey Morris and Arthur Holmwood, Lucy's fiancé, and together they track her down, stake her heart, behead her, and fill her mouth with garlic.

Around the same time as Lucy's destruction, Jonathan Harker, who barely escaped from Dracula's castle with his life, arrives home from recuperation in Budapest where he has married Mina. He and Mina join the coalition of vampire hunters. The Count continues his campaign of revenge by visiting

and biting Mina at least three times. However, instead of draining her blood and killing her he feeds her his blood, presumably the first step into transforming her into a vampire and an act that creates a telepathic bond between them. The coalition realize that the only way to counteract Mina's descent into a vampire is to kill Dracula, and Mina's telepathic connection with Dracula is used by them to hunt him.

Dracula flees back to his castle in Transylvania, followed closely by Van Helsing's group, who manage to track him down just before sundown and destroy him by cutting his throat, decapitating him, and stabbing him in the heart with a knife.

Literary analysis

Although Dracula owed a debt to preceding works of vampire fiction, namely the writings of Polidori and Le Fanu, it became the template for the wealth of vampire literature that followed after it and, despite being imitated and pastiched many times, to this day it remains the definitive and most memorable vampire yarn. In the novel Stoker took the sometimes vague and contradictory vampire folklore that had emerged from earlier times and established forever the vampire as part of popular folklore in the West. Today the Dracula-inspired character of the vampire has assumed almost mythic status in popular culture. Incarnations of the Count can be found in comics, such as *The Tomb of Dracula*, numerous screen adaptations, as well as in plays, musicals, ballet, opera, commercials, greetings cards, and websites.

In the style of the nineteenth-century English novelist Wilkie Collins, Stoker presents the story through a series of reader-friendly journal entries, diary accounts, newspaper reports, and letters. Such a narrative required Stoker to write in a number of different styles to suit each character. The novel is full of surprises but it is generally agreed that the beginning journal entries of Jonathan Harker, which detail his introduction to Castle Dracula, are superior in terms of pace, content, and terrifying description. The middle section of the novel slows down in pace and intensity as Dracula, planning world domination, moves to London. In this middle section Stoker develops the world of the other major characters, but the novel returns to form and climaxes with the pursuit of Dracula from England to his homeland where he is destroyed in the shadow of his own castle.

Dracula is of ongoing interest to literary critics and remains the subject of much commentary, analysis, and critique. The sexuality expressed in Dracula is of particular interest to modern scholars – the sexuality of vampirism itself; the sexuality of women in the novel; the homoerotic undercurrents between Harker and Dracula (why does Dracula keep Harker imprisoned in his castle when he travels to England?); the eroticism of blood; and the strange relationships between the characters (why are Seward, Holmwood and Quincey so keen to offer Lucy their blood?) Also significant is that the vampire is eventually brought down by a woman – Mina – who emerges from her ordeal with an independence that can no longer be controlled by men.

Scholarly analysis of the text also indicates that Stoker gave a lot of thought to making vampires seem scientifically possible but at the same time he also wants to show that there are some things science cannot explain. Vampirism is presented as a disease, echoing familiar nineteenth-centuries maladies like consumption, but the novel also takes great pains to describe the phenomenon alongside popular conceptions about Darwinism, in particular the notion of evolutionary degeneration or a throwback. On a deeper level the novel taps into late Victorian anxieties about the conflict between religion and science, and because both science and faith must be used to overcome Dracula, the underlying suggestion is that the two are not incompatible.

Though *Dracula* is certainly not a literary masterpiece there is no doubt that it is a masterpiece of story telling and deserves its continuing cult status. It continues to flourish today because it touches on everlasting questions of spiritual meaning, and sexuality, and humanity's constant questions about the nature of good and evil. Last, but by no means least, it is simply a great page-turner, appealing to the perverse pleasure we take in being scared.

Genesis and development

Stoker's notes do not indicate his exact inspiration but they do show that he started writing the novel in March 1890 when he visited Whitby in England for a holiday. His research in Whitby led him to use the name Dracula for his vampire. Between 1893–6 he continued work on the novel while on several vacations to Cruden Bay, a fishing village in Scotland. Stoker was tenacious in his research and his notes show that he consulted numerous sources of information. They also show that he originally set the work in Styria, Austria, but then moved it to Transylvania. He did not, however, ever visit Transylvania – his descriptions are derived from his imagination.

Dracula went through numerous changes right up to submission, judging by the number of corrections, changes, and additions to the manuscript. The original title of the book at submission to the publishers was *The Undead*, but somewhere along the line either the editor or Stoker changed the title to *Dracula*.

In writing *Dracula*, it is often suggested that Stoker was inspired by stories about the fifteenth-century bloodthirsty Wallachian prince known as Vlad the Impaler, but he may also have been inspired by the story of Countess Elizabeth Báthory, who allegedly bathed in and drank the blood of young virgins in an attempt to preserve her youth, which may connect to the element of the story in which Dracula appears younger and revitalized after feeding. *Dracula* also has strong similarities to an earlier Irish writer, Sheridan Le Fanu's classic of the vampire genre, *Carmilla*. The most probable explanation is that a number of influences – from literature, ancient history, Eastern European folklore, as well as contemporary events (for example, Jack the Ripper terrorized London in 1888) – fired Stoker's rich imagination and contributed to the creation of *Dracula*. Despite this the connection with Vlad the Impaler remains fixed, and even though Dracula researchers have proved otherwise, many people continue to think of the historical man and the fictional vampire as one and the same.

Stoker was not a historian or a researcher but a novelist. Like any novelist he embellished his research and knowledge, took ele-

ments and transformed them or invented his own. For example, there is no record in folklore of vampires needing to sleep on their native earth; this was Stoker's invention. In folklore vampires reside in their graves and always return to them but in Stoker's novel the Count sleeps in boxes of earth – note boxes not coffins, that was a later invention by others. Another invention is that Dracula casts no reflection in a mirror and that he cannot cast a shadow. Stoker's vampires cannot cross running water, another invention. He also changed the vampire's color, making Dracula pale and turned him from a bloated corpse into a creature who erotically preys on the blood of humans, especially beautiful young women.

Dracula, on screen and stage

Prior to publication Stoker staged a single performance of *Dracula* at the Lyceum Theatre in May 1897. The stage dramatization was part a reading and part a full-scale theatrical production. Stoker was very aware of the book's dramatic potential but the first reading of the book was described as "dreadful" by actor Henry Irving.

On publication the novel received mixed reviews and although it stayed in print it may well have fallen into obscurity with Stoker's other works if it had not been constantly adapted for stage and screen in the twentieth century. In an attempt to gain acceptance from the middle classes, early film and stage versions of *Dracula* softened the appearance of the character of Dracula as presented in the original novel. The vampire lost his hairy palms, bad breath, and unsociable habits and over the years the character portrayed on stage and films started to become more and more removed from the character created by Stoker.

In 1924 Irish-born actor-manager Hamilton Deane bought the stage rights to *Dracula* and the Count came to the London stage in a production that romanticized the vampire, giving him a red-lined black cape and a high collar. (The high collar that has now become such a familiar part of Dracula costumes was to hide the back of the actor's head as he slipped through a stage door leaving others holding an empty cape.) In 1927 Deane's version was rewritten for a Broadway production, with actor Béla Lugosi in the title role.

The first feature film of note for Americans to be made from Dracula was F. W. Murnau's 1922 silent black-and-white *Nosferatu*. Then along came the 1931 Universal release, *Dracula*, starring Béla Lugosi who famously donned an opera cape and tuxedo for the role. The movie inspired countless others, including the Hammer Horror films of the 1950s and 60s, most notably *Horror of Dracula* (1958), which starred the charismatic actor Christopher Lee. Following these, hundreds of movies featuring Dracula, or vampires who are slightly disguised version of Dracula, have been made over the decades, with varying degrees of success. In recent years, a number of cinematic efforts have been made to adhere as closely to the novel as possible – most notably *Bram Stoker's Dracula* (1992) – but in the opinion of many *Dracula* experts there has yet to be a definitive representation.

See also: **COMICS; FILM; LITERATURE; STAGE; TELEVISION**

Dracula / Draculea

More correctly spelt as Draculea, Dracula is the name of both the title character in Bram Stoker's novel, *Dracula*, and the Transylvanian ruler, Vlad Tepes, "the Impaler." There is no actual link in Romanian folklore between Vlad the Impaler and vampirism but the name is involved in continuing debates among scholars trying to distinguish Dracula history from Dracula legend.

The name, Dracula, came from the title Dracul, given to Vlad's father, Vlad II, to describe his activities. Dracul meant "dragon" or "Devil" and some experts believe that the term was used to mean "Devil" by Vlad's enemies. Others suggest that the name may have come from Vlad's membership of the chivalric Order of the Dragon. Vlad II's son, who became known locally as Tepes, the Impaler, may simply have earned the name Dracula because he was his father's son and not perhaps for his crimes – Dracula simply means "son of Dracul." Although he also wrote his name as Drakulya and Dragulya, Draculea was Vlad's signature of choice.

The name was virtually unknown in the West until Bram Stoker used it to name his title character in his 1897 novel. As it was so closely associated with cruelty, evil, and the bloodthirsty fifteenth-century ruler of Wallachia, it was the perfect name for his vampire. In their 1972 book, *In Search of Dracula*, researchers Radu Florescu and Raymond McNally make much of the supposed connection between the historical Vlad the Impaler and Stoker's fictional Dracula. They suggest that Stoker came across the name Dracula in his reading on Romanian history and chose this to replace the name – Count Wampyr – that he had originally intended to use for his villain. It's not clear how much Stoker actually knew about the harsh and cruel exploits of Dracula of Wallachia, but Florescu and McNally stress that notes on the original manuscript of the novel show that he did appear to have some knowledge, and urged the public to see the "obvious" association.

Others, however, have questioned this alleged connection, stating that Stoker in fact knew very little of the historic Vlad III except for his name. They argue that although there are sections in the novel where Dracula's background is discussed, only one quote directly ties Stoker's vampire to Vlad III, namely *"that Voivode Dracula who won his name against the Turks"* (a reference to Vlad's infamous battles with the Turks over Wallachian soil). In addition, Vlad III was an ethnic Vlach, while in the novel Dracula claims to be a Székely; Vlad was from Wallachia and not Transylvania, and Dracula's aversion to holy objects is uncharacteristic of Vlad, who was in fact part of a Christian knightly order.

Few would argue that Vlad was a cruel and ruthless ruler, but he was never accused of vampirism and local legends are in distinctly short supply as far as evidence of any supernatural powers are concerned. Many people are also unaware that Stoker's *Dracula* was banned in Romania until 1989 as representative of the decadent West, and that the real Dracula, Vlad Tepes, is thought of by Romanians as something of a hero, considered to be the founder of Bucharest, Romania's capital city. (The clear financial rewards of increased tourism due to enthusiasts in search of the real Dracula has however caused the authorities to gradually incorporate vampire folklore into their historic accounts, rather than play it down.)

We do know from Stoker's note-taking that he probably got the name from a book by William Wilkinson, the British consul in Bucharest in 1820, called *Account of the Principalities of Wallachia and Moldavia*. In this book Wilkinson wrote a short account of the historical Dracula, but it is in a footnote to this brief description that Stoker's debt to Wilkinson can be found. This gives the origin of Vlad's nickname: *"Dracula in the Wallachian language means Devil. The Wallachians at that time, as they do at present, used to give this as a surname to any person who rendered themselves conspicuous either by courage, cruel actions or cunning."* Here we have an explanation for the attraction of the name. For Stoker it was synonymous with cruelty, cunning, and courage and linked to the Devil. What better title for the villain of his novel? But that is all that exists in Stoker's working papers to give evidence of any link to the historical Dracula, suggesting that it was the name that interested Stoker rather than the actual figure.

The Element Encyclopedia of Vampires

"Dracula's Guest"

Originally intended for inclusion in the final version of *Dracula* published in 1897, "Dracula's Guest" is the title for an early chapter of the novel omitted because of limitations on word count. It was published posthumously by Bram Stoker's widow, Florence Stoker. Although not a short story in the traditional sense it can be read as a standalone story and was eventually published in 1914 in *Dracula's Guest and Other Weird Stories*. Despite its title Dracula never actually makes an appearance in the story.

In the chapter, an anonymous narrator is stranded in a snowstorm on the night of April 30, a time when the forces of evil are said to be active in the world. The narrator takes shelter from the snowstorm in the ruins of a village where no one has lived for hundreds of years because vampires had been unearthed and people fled for their lives. The narrator stumbles across the tomb of the Countess Dolingen of Gratz with a great iron stake driven through its marble slab and an eerie inscription upon it: *"The dead travel fast."* A terrible hailstorm erupts and after a fleeting vision of a beautiful woman he loses consciousness; he then awakes to a gigantic wolf with flaming red eyes lying on top of him licking his throat. The narrator is paralyzed with fear, but suddenly armed men arrive and shoot at the wolf, which flees. The chapter ends with the narrator feeling frightened and uneasy, but grateful for his rescue and protection.

The narrator is often assumed to be Jonathan Harker, the narrator of the first chapters of *Dracula*, but experts note that the style of the narrator is different – much

bolder – than the style of Harker's journal entries in *Dracula*. In addition, the story is not written in the diary style that characterizes *Dracula*. There is considerable debate among literary critics as to whether it would have been better to include the chapter in the 1897 book or not, but whether read on its own or as part of the novel it is a wonderfully atmospheric introduction to the supernatural themes explored in the novel.

Dracula Societies

Dracula has become one of the most recognized images in popular culture so it is no surprise that a number of clubs, societies, and organization have formed over the years to promote and celebrate him. Societies which are still thriving today include:

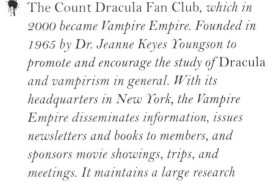

- The Count Dracula Fan Club, *which in 2000 became Vampire Empire. Founded in 1965 by Dr. Jeanne Keyes Youngson to promote and encourage the study of* Dracula *and vampirism in general. With its headquarters in New York, the Vampire Empire disseminates information, issues newsletters and books to members, and sponsors movie showings, trips, and meetings. It maintains a large research library, opened in 1970, which includes books on vampires and of the horror genre. The 5,000-member club continues to grow and thrive.*

- The Dracula Society. *The primary organization in the UK was originally founded in 1973 by Bernard Davies and Bruce Wightman, to cater for lovers of the vampire and his kind. Based in London, the society aims to keep the study of* Dracula *alive by sponsoring lectures, meetings, parties, and tours. The society maintains an archive related to Dracula and literary vampires in general, as well as publishing a quarterly magazine for its members,* Voices from the Vaults.

The Bram Stoker Society. *Founded in 1980 by Dublin-based author Leslie Shepherd, the aim of the Bram Stoker Society is to encourage the study and appreciation of the works of Bram Stoker, the author of* Dracula. *The society publishes a newsletter and an annual journal.*

See The Vampire Directory for further details about these and other active Dracula and vampire organizations and societies.

Dragon, Order of the

The Order of the Dragon was an elite medieval society established in 1408 to honor Christian kings and nobility of Central and Eastern Europe who had proven themselves against heretics, Turks, and other enemies of Christianity.

Founded in 1408 by Sigismund, King of Hungary, Croatia, and Bohemia and later Holy Roman Emperor, members of the Order were known as Draconists. According to a surviving copy of its statute, the Order required its initiates to defend the Cross and fight the enemies of Christianity and face certain obligations, such as the wearing of dark colors on Fridays as a sign of their devoutness. The public face of the Draconists was of a chivalrous society dedicated to defending Christianity from the infidel, while promoting fraternal loyalty between members. But there was another shadowy side to this Order which some believe was more of a secret society dedicated to dark and deadly conspiracies than a benevolent brotherhood of pious knights dedicated to the holy crusade.

In 1431, Vlad II of Wallachia, the father of Vlad the Impaler, joined the order and subsequently used the dragon symbol on his coins and banners. Some experts believe that this may be the origin of the name Vlad Dracul, which can also be translated as Vlad the Devil or the holder of the Devil's symbol, because in Romanian *drac* means dragon or Devil. When Vlad III came to power he was therefore known as Vlad Dracula or Draculea, the son of Dracul, and it seems that he inherited his father's lust for bloodshed, dark conspiracy, and cruelty. It's certainly possible that the name Vlad Dracul was the inspiration for the name Dracula in Stoker's 1897 novel.

Draskylo

The Greek term *draskylo* means "to step across" or "stepping across" and it refers to the fear of animals jumping over corpses, an act believed to turn a corpse into a vampire.

See also: **BURIAL CUSTOMS; GREECE**

Draugr

A draugr or draug (draugar in the plural) is a vampire-like undead creature from ancient Norse mythology. The draugar were believed to live in the graves and bodies of dead Vikings. Those who lived near the mounds or tombs of dead warriors were often said to be fearful of their undead "neighbors" as it was thought the draugr could rise from its grave and attack the living at any time.

A draugr could be easily recognized by its deathly pale or blue skin and the unmistakable reek of decay that accompanied it. These creatures were also believed to have remarkable strength and could increase their body size at will. Victims were crushed and killed and then the draugr would eat the flesh and drink the blood of its prey. In some cases the blood-drained victim was likely to become a draugr.

The only way to defeat one of these creatures was to return it to its tomb as it was thought that they were virtually indestructible. Prevention was far better than a cure. It was essential that the walking dead were stopped from rising from their graves and a number of precautions were therefore taken at funerals. For example, a pair of open iron scissors would be laid on the chest of a corpse, sharp twigs or pieces of straw would be concealed in the clothing, needles would be run into the soles of the feet or the toes would be tied together, presumably to make it hard for the corpse to move and walk. When the coffin was taken out of the house, the bearers were required to raise and lower it in different directions – in the form of a cross – to confuse the "sleeper" within.

The most effective method of preventing the draugr was the "corpse door." A special door was added to a building and the corpse was carried, feet first, out to the grave; the entrance would then be bricked up again so the corpse would not return. The reason for this practice was that it was widely believed in the Norse world that the undead could only re-enter a house in the same way they had left it. If the door was bricked up the undead would therefore not be able to re-enter.

Devil of Hjalta-Stad

According to contemporary vampire lore expert Bob Curran, one of the most well-known examples of a blood-drinking, walking draugr from Norse folklore is the so-called Devil of Hjalta-Stad. The creature is first mentioned in a letter written by Sheriff Hans Wium to Bishop Haldorr Brynjolfsson, in the autumn of 1750. The draugr was said to have been the corpse of an old, balding man, wrapped in ragged grave clothes, who haunted the ancient burial ground at Hjalta-Stad and a nearby house. Little is known about the life of this old man but it was probably someone with an evil reputation, perhaps suspected of witchcraft. The creature allegedly threw stones and called out obscenities at terrified passers-by.

According to Nordic law at the time, the secular authorities could summon the creature and compel it to explain its actions. The letter of Sheriff Wium gives a detailed account of the summons, during which the creature addressed onlookers with, *"words the like of which eye hath not seen nor ear heard."* Attempts were made to explain the phenomenon away as a hoax but the Sheriff later dismissed such explanations, stating that no human voice could have produced the terrifying screams of the Devil or been able to answer correctly the number of personal questions which were asked.

Whether the Devil of Hjalta-Stat was the malignant corpse of an old man or simply an elaborate hoax, the story serves as a fine example of a draugr from Icelandic folklore – a vampire-like, evil presence that lurks in the darkness and spreads fear and terror throughout the community.

Dream Sending

A form of psychic vampire attack that has existed for centuries, dream sending is a means of influencing, attacking, draining energy, or even killing a person through their dreams. It is based on the widely held magical or occult belief that dreams are not imaginary but real experiences. In the novel *Dracula* impending physical vampire attacks are often first conveyed through disturbing dreams and nightmares. When Dracula begins his attack on Lucy Westenra in the novel she has bad dreams and nightmares of red eyes and flapping sounds at her bedroom window.

The ancient Greeks and Egyptians had dream-sending rituals to cause a person to act or think in a certain way, and Egyptian magicians were thought to have the power to summon the dead to appear in the dreams of others. The dead were also thought to have great power in a person's dreams, with the ability to enforce a curse or spell. Among the Azande people of Africa bad dreams are thought to cause illness, death, and misfortune.

See also: **INCUBUS/SUCCUBUS; NIGHTMARE; SLEEP PARALYSIS**

Dreams, About Vampires

In many cultures around the world the soul is considered to have the ability to detach from the body during sleep, unconsciousness, or death and one of the reasons why the dead are believed to live on is their continuing presence in a person's dreams after death. It is considered unwise to awaken people suddenly from sleep because the soul may not have a chance to find its way back to the body, in which case the person will die.

Interpretation

In European folklore, dreaming of someone who was dead was regarded as a visit from beyond the grave. However, when such dreams about the departed turned into terrifying nightmares about the undead they were typically associated with evil, distress, and torment, and the impending attack of a vampire. Today, such dreams are no longer taken literally and interpreted very differently. According to modern dream interpretation – which suggests that dreams are symbolic messages from a person's unconscious designed to help them understand and cope better with challenges in their waking life – dreams about blood-sucking vampires can be interpreted in countless different ways, depending on the context of the dream and the circumstances of the dreamer's waking life. Listed below are some common themes that typically emerge when interpreting vampire-related dreams from a modern psychological perspective.

Vampires are the parasites of the supernatural realm; they share a world with ghouls (creatures that prey on the dead) and the succubus and incubus that take on human form to have sexual intercourse with sleeping people, and they are also repelled by simple, natural things like daylight and turned away by religious symbols. Dreaming of these parasitic creatures can therefore signify that a part of your existence is having the life sucked out of it, that you need to take a closer look at the more tiresome aspects of your life and dispel the worries connected with them, and that you need to employ some kind of self-protection or preservation. It may be that someone you know is holding you back, or trying to control every aspect of your life so that your energy is being drained away. It is also possible that you are the one behaving in a parasitic manner and are subconsciously quite disturbed by it.

Alternatively, to dream of seeing a vampire may also indicate that you are feeling seductive, powerful, and very sensual. In addition, perhaps there is a need for you to be more adventurous and open-minded in your waking life, or that some change of attitude is needed.

Dark forces

Both vampires and werewolves have been regarded as symbols of dark forces since medieval times. Both drain their victims of their vital essence. To imagine either in your dream could also be interpreted as a warning to distance yourself from someone in your waking life who doesn't have your best inter-ests at heart. It could also refer to some activity or habit that is having a negative effect on you. Bear in mind that while werewolves are believed to have a particular preference for young women (suggesting dangerous sexual predators), vampires, their fanged fellow fiends of the night, are opportunistic killers who take their sustenance from any kind of human blood whether it be a man, woman, or child. So if you had a dream in which someone you know came too close for comfort before baring a set of needle-sharp fangs, your dream may be alerting you to someone who is feeding off your energy, or else sponging off your finances and thriving at your expense.

Sleepwalkers

It's also worth pointing out in this entry on dreams that according to some experts, one possible explanation for alleged vampire attacks is that they are simply living humans, unconsciously acting out their vampiric dreams or fantasies. Interestingly enough, there is an explanation of vampires in folklore that uses the more common definition of "sleepwalker," that is, one who really walks about while asleep, usually acting out dreams in the process. Some experts believe there may actually have been two species of vampires, one kind being those who were dead and returned, and the other kind being those who were alive but in some kind of trance or dream-state. The latter could be spotted roaming at night, especially when the moon was full.

According to this "sleepwalker" theory, those who claimed they experienced the onslaught of a vampire attack honestly believed they experienced something ferocious, unearthly, and tangible, but it's possible some of these experiences were actually encounters with individuals who were not in their normal waking minds, but were physically acting out their dark desires in their sleep as they moved about in the world of their dreams. Seen in this light, vampires could quite literally be "the stuff that dreams are made of."

Drowning

According to Slavic folklore, death by drowning was one of the ways in which a person could become a vampire after death. In a similar way to suicide or murder, death by drowning occurs suddenly and takes the soul by surprise, making it easier for an evil spirit or demon to enter the corpse and use it to become a vampire or revenant.

See also: **WATER**

Drunken Boy

According to Asian legend, the Drunken Boy is a giant ogre, dressed in scarlet, who feasts on blood, especially the blood of young women, like a vampire. However, he may never have been human and is considered more of a demon than a vampire.

In Japan a story is told of Raiko or Yorimitsu, a great hero of medieval times who disguised himself and his companions as priests and managed to get into the Drunken Boy's lair, where a blood-drinking party was in progress. The hero managed to slip something into the drinks of the ogres, threw off his disguise and set upon them. A fierce battle ensued, and according to legend the Drunken Boy's head kept on battling even after it had been decapitated. In the end Raiko won and bore the

female captives he had saved and the trophy head back in triumph to the imperial capital.

Dumas, Alexandre (1802-70)

French novelist and playwright Alexandre Dumas, also known as Dumas père, is best known as the author of the fast-paced adventure yarn *The Three Musketeers* and the Gothic romance, *The Count of Monte Cristo*. But he is also important in the development of the modern vampire myth for writing a play called *Le Vampire*, which opened in Paris on December 20, 1851. *Le Vampire* was based on Polidori's, *The Vampyre* (1819) and featured Polidori's infamous vampire creation, Lord Ruthven. Dumas also wrote a short story, "The Pale-faced Lady" (1848) about a vampire in the Carpathians.

See also: **LITERATURE**

Dummolard, Martin

Known as the Monster of Montluel, Martin Dummolard was a nineteenth-century mass murderer, and is ranked as the most reprehensible of the so-called historical vampires. Dummolard was a young man when he met and fell under the spell of Justine Lafayette when he moved into her Lyon boarding house. Both Justine and Dummolard were necrophiles. Dummolard would kill and drink the blood of his victims and bring the flesh home to serve to his mistress Justine. Despite causing terror in the streets of Montluel he was allegedly able to murder up to 80 women in the 1860s. Following a sensational trial, Justine, regarded as the real instigator of the crimes, was guillotined and Dummolard, regarded as her puppet, was confined to an asylum for the rest of his life.

Dust

According to traditional vampire lore and vampire fiction, vampires burn in sunlight and turn into dust. This belief may or may not originate from ancient Hebrew folklore, which suggests that the original vampire-witch – Lilith – was created from the dust of her husband, Adam.

In medieval European vampire lore the only sure-fire method of destroying a vampire was believed to be burning the suspected vampire completely to ashes and then scattering the dust to the wind. In the 1897 novel *Dracula*, vampires have the ability to transform themselves not just into animals and mist but also into a cloud of dust, but this ability has not become a prominent part of modern vampire lore.

Dybbuk

The dybbuk is a vampire-demon from Hebrew folklore and a manifestation of the ambivalent distinction that exists between demons and vampires in some cultures. Although in Christian tradition, demons are regarded as always evil, it is important to understand that the word demon comes from the Greek word for "spirit," which also means inspiration. As a result, in some cultures demons can be ambivalent in nature, spurring individuals on to acts of great good as well as great evil.

Among the early Hebrews, spirits or souls that lingered on earth after death were sometimes referred to as "clinging souls" or dybbuk. These spirits were thought to have the power to not only draw vitality from the living but to occupy or possess a person's body, drawing energy from within like a parasite. The dybbuk was thought to swarm everywhere. They could enter a person's body through the nose or mouth, through food or drink, or through impure air or fumes. Once they had entered a human body they were believed to dwell specifically in the fingers or toes.

Traits and activities

There is no clear definition of the traits and activities of the dybbuk before the fifteenth century when rabbis became increasingly concerned about attack from supernatural forces and ways to protect against it. In writings from the rabbinical school of Isaac Luria (1534–72) for example, a clear picture of the dybbuk as an evil entity first emerges, but before that medieval Jewish literature, especially the works of Hasidei Ashkenaz, are rich in detail and advice about avoiding and dealing with the attack of "wandering souls." From the seventeenth century the dybbuk, as a clinging soul that possessed individuals and fed on their life energy for sustenance, became an established part of Jewish folklore.

There seem to have been two types of dybbuk; the "wandering soul" who took up habitation in a still-living person, and the wandering entity who had never lived but was just pure evil and very dangerous. Death before atoning for one's sins or not being buried in accordance with Jewish sacrament was thought to turn the spirit of a Jew into a "wandering soul." Being cursed by a rabbi, breaking Jewish law, leading a sinful life, speaking harshly, or not washing properly, as well as death by suicide, were also believed to be prerequisites for turning a dead soul into a dybbuk. The second-century BC *Testament of the Patriarchs*, which details the lives of the heroes of the Old Testament, suggests that the origin of the form of dybbuk that had never lived as a human but was simply a malignant and dangerous force may have been the children of Lilith, the first wife of Adam, who gave birth to hundreds of demons. The *Testament* also seems to suggest that evil entities could be conjured from dust and menstrual blood, which was considered "unclean" and therefore cursed by God. Another type of dybbuk may have been the Yezer Hara, a vampire demon that attacked the faithful as they left synagogues at night and filled their minds with lustful thoughts.

Possession

One of the first signs of dybbuk possession was believed to be fatigue, followed by violent mood swings and vomiting of white foam. Rabbis would frequently point to the story of the dark creature that took possession of King Saul (I Samuel 16:14), which caused him to have violent mood swings and rages. Such dark creatures were thought to spread disease and death, and local communities would typically associate bouts of plague and sickness as well as diseases as epilepsy with the attack of the dybbuk. It was thought that the dybbuk fed on its host, causing him or her to waste away and die. There was no point offering the victim food or drink because the dybbuk would repel any nourishment or goodness offered it. Another sign of dybbuk possession was the ability to prophesy or see the future.

Prevention

Prevention was believed to be better than exorcism and men, women, and children were urged to do all they could to protect themselves from the attack of a dybbuk. Circumcision was believed to be an especially vulnerable time and garlic and ribbons were hung around a boy's crib to ward off an attack. Sweets were also placed beside a crib as it was thought the vampire demon could be distracted by sweet temptations. The sound of breaking glass was thought to frighten a lurking dybbuk away. Dybbuks were said to dislike the light and smoke of lighted candles. Amulets made of wax or iron might also be worn or hung from doorposts as protection.

Fragments of rabbinical works on exorcism from all centuries have been discovered in the Middle East and Europe indicating that there were a number of different rites and rituals to expel each type of dybbuk, but these could only be performed by a rabbi who had been trained in exorcism. Prior to the exorcism a hole had to be made in the building to allow the creature to escape in the shape of a moth or fly. If this precaution was not taken it was thought that the dybbuk would not leave and instead would find another victim to drain the life force out of. The most common method of exorcism used involved speaking directly to the dybbuk to determine its identity during its earthly life, because once the name was discovered it could be used in invocations, chants, and rituals to expel it. The dybbuk, however, would be aware of the danger of giving its name and would attempt to mislead the rabbi.

The dybbuk certainly has vampiric characteristics in that it draws energy from the victim it occupies, causing them to waste away and die, but it is also part demon, part ghost, and part parasite, and therefore remains like many vampiric entities from folklore, a contradictory and complex creature.

"I decided as long as I was going to hell, I might as well do it thoroughly."

Edward Cullen, in *Twilight* by Stephenie Meyer

Earth

Earth, because of its ancient association with death, was sometimes placed in a corpse's mouth in ancient burial rites to prevent it from chewing its way out of the grave. This was especially important in the case of the Jewish estrie. According to Eastern European folklore a vampire typically returns to its grave at least once a day, normally at dawn, but there is no evidence to support the widely accepted notion that this return is compulsory, or the idea that vampires are compelled to sleep by day in a coffin filled with their native soil. This idea was introduced in the novel *Dracula* in 1897, when Bram Stoker stressed the importance of Dracula's need to sleep in a box filled with his native earth from Transylvania.

See also: **DUST**

Eastern European Legends

It is important to bear in mind that Eastern Europe is an overarching geographic term for regions that may be more specifically classified or described in other ways. However, from the point of view of vampire folklore and tradition, "Eastern Europe" generally refers to the European countries of Albania, Belarus, Bosnia, Bulgaria, Croatia, the Czech Republic, Estonia, Hungary, Latvia, Lithuania, Macedonia, Poland, Romania, Serbia, Slovakia, Slovenia, and Ukraine.

The word "vampire" was first used in the countries of Eastern Europe, especially among the Slavic peoples. Experts are uncertain of the origin of the Slavic vampire. It could have derived from many different sources including Greek and Roman legend or legends brought to Eastern Europe by Gypsies from India or Egypt. Whatever its origin it was in the Eastern European countries that widespread belief in vampires first took hold.

Revenants

The revenants or vampires of Eastern European folklore were very different from the sophisticated, seductive vampires presented today in contemporary fiction. They would typically come from peasant stock and although there are stories of revenants that appear in much the same form as when they were alive, there are also stories of revenants appearing as revolting walking corpses in a plague-infested condition, bloated with blood and reeking of the stench of decay and death. These early vampires were thought to plague people with disease, physical violence and supernatural evil. Instead of sucking the blood from their victim's throats with fangs they would draw blood from other areas of the body with sharp pointy tongues.

Medieval Slavic vampire legends probably grew up as an explanation for why so many people died during times of plague. When the death of one person was followed by the death of others from a contagious disease, it was believed that the first person had become a vampire and was intent on destroying those closest to it – family, friends, and neighbors. Graves where suspected vampires were buried were identified and the bodies dug up and "killed" again, by decapitating them with a shovel or by driving a stake into the corpse, thus preventing them from leaving the grave.

Vampire mania

Until late in the seventeenth century, when a flurry of official reports was written by the authorities describing the vampire scares of Eastern Europe, and the methods of hunting and destroying them, the Slavic vampire legends were unknown to the rest of the world. However, a number of "real" vampire scares in Eastern Europe were carefully documented by visiting officials and clergymen, and these reports sparked a vast amount of debate throughout Europe about whether vampires were actually real or not. Vampire mania continued throughout the eighteenth century, but by the mid-nineteenth century belief in vampires was no longer as widespread and the matter was laid to rest, with the exception of a few isolated Slavonic regions where locals continued to believe in "real" vampires.

See also: **SLAVIC VAMPIRE, THE**

Eclipse

Eclipse is the third book in Stephenie Meyer's hugely successful Twilight Saga. It is preceded by *Twilight* and *New Moon* and followed by *Breaking Dawn* and continues the story of 18-year-old Bella Swan and her vampire lover, Edward Cullen. Released on August 7, 2008, the book sold more than 150,000 copies in the first 24 hours alone.

See also: **MEYER, STEPHENIE; TWILIGHT SAGA**

Egypt

Egypt in Northern Africa was one of the world's first great civilizations. According to some vampirologists it may also have been the birthplace of the vampire because of its complex but highly positive view of death and the afterlife. Numerous vampire authors, most notably Anne Rice in *Queen of the Damned* (1988), have incorporated the mysteries and rites of ancient Egypt into their writing.

Belief in the afterlife

The ancient Egyptians believed in post-mortem life and this belief protected them from much of the fear and terror of death experienced by other cultures. Corpses were called "beloved Osirises" after Osiris, the god of the underworld, and, according to some scholars, the embalming of corpses, the beautiful tombs, and offerings of food and wine to the dead, suggesting that the dead were thought to have a hearty appetite, along with the recitation of the names of the dead, could perhaps be the first hints of vampirism.

The ancient Egyptians feared that they would be forgotten by future generations and the recitation of the names of the dead was an attempt to ensure that the dead kept active in eternity. If a person's name was forgotten it was feared that the individual would perish forever, and in some parts of Egypt even today family members will visit a tomb and talk to the person. Another important Egyptian belief that may have promoted the idea of vampirism is that of the Ka, an astral being that was a companion to a person while they were alive, but once they died the Ka became more powerful and guided the soul, the Ba, into the afterlife. Offerings of food and drink in the tomb were for the Ka. And like virtually every other ancient culture, Egypt had its fair share of tales of supernatural vampiric beings sucking the blood out of the living. One example is the warrior goddess, Sekhmet, who drank blood offerings.

After 1070 BC the New Kingdom became weaker, eventually splitting into five separate kingdoms. Foreign kings and their armies occupied Egypt: the Nubians, the Assyrians, the Persians, and the Greeks. With each occupation other customs and beliefs were incorporated into Egyptian beliefs, but despite this the spirits, rites, and mysteries that characterized ancient Egyptian belief in the afterlife remain enduring.

Ekimmu

Found among the ancient Assyrians and Sumerians, the ekimmu were vampire-like creatures believed to be the restless spirits or souls of dead people denied entry to the underworld and so doomed to wander the earth forever, attacking humans in anger and revenge.

Ekimmu means "that which is snatched away," and there were a number of ways that a corpse could become an ekimmu, including violent death; incorrect burial rites or no burial at all; lack of proper attention to the dead by the living, especially concerning the leaving of food and drink to sustain the spirit on its journey to the underworld; death by drowning or starvation; dying during pregnancy; and dying before love was fulfilled.

Descriptions of the ekimmu vary from legend to legend. Sometimes they are portrayed as winged demons, sometimes as a rushing wind, sometimes as a walking or winged corpse, sometimes as dust, and sometimes as a shadow. Some legends state they were creatures of the night, but according to others they could appear at any time of day, but especially favored times were when the sun was high in the sky. This was when they were believed to be at their most dangerous and travelers were urged to avoid journeying through lonely places, where such spirits were said to dwell.

Traits of the ekimmu

The ekimmu were said to attack humans not by drinking their blood, but by attaching themselves to them. The fearsome creature was also believed to be invisible and could follow a person home where they would torment them. At first they would hurl objects around the house and create trouble, but eventually they would leech away all the victim's energies, eventually killing them. Once attached to a person they became virtually impossible to exorcise, and could only be removed by extreme prayer and fasting. Tales of ekimmu entering houses in this way date back at least to 2000 BC, making them among the oldest supernatural entities.

While not overtly described as vampires, these traits of the ekimmu make them appear to be psychic vampires. Blood-drinking is not mentioned in connection with the creature (unless they manifested in the vicious form of the alu, see below), but there are often mentions of "evil wind gusts." This is significant because in Sumerian mythology wind was often depicted as a manifestation of magical or psychic power.

Alu

The most deadly form the ekimmu could manifest in was the alu or alus; these hostile demon-like creatures could take on less substantial shapes, such as wind, dust, or smoke, although they were often described as skeletal thin and deathly pale, with lips covered in scabs. Among the Assyrian undead the alu was perhaps the closest to the traditional vampire because it drank the blood of the living. They were nocturnal entities who spread disease and death wherever they went. They could be repulsed by fire and distracted with pieces of bloody animal meat, but the best form of protection from them was to wait until they returned to their graves so that their corpses could be dug up and either reburied correctly or burned.

Protection

Apart from avoiding lonely places and paying attention to correct funeral rites, little is known about other forms of protection against the ekimmu and alu, except perhaps the use of magically prescribed bowls, jars, and bottles. The idea was that if an exorcist could coax an ekimmu into its dust or spirit form, it might be lured into a bowl and then trapped when the bowl was upturned. Bait might be used to tempt the ekimmu or alu into the bowl, such as blood or raw meat, and the spells written on the side of the bowl were thought to trap the creature there. The main way of destroying an ekimmu, however, was to burn its body and dispose of the ashes far away from human habitation.

Over time the power and craftiness of the ekimmu and alu began to grow, and eventually in the Middle Eastern tradition they merged into blood-drinking and flesh-eating ghouls.

See also: **ASSYRIA; BABYLONIA**

Elga, Countess

A report published in the *Neues Wiener* paper in Vienna on June 10, 1909, detailed how villagers, suffering the deaths of many of their children, had decided that a certain Count B. who had recently died had returned as a vampire and was residing in his castle, a fortress built as a defense against the Turks in a wild and desolate part of the Carpathian Mountains. The angry lynch mob burned down the castle. In September 1909, vampirologist Franz Hartmann offered a theory in the *Occult Review* that it was not the count but his beautiful daughter, Elga, who was the vampire. Elga had died in a riding accident sometime before her father's death.

Emotional Vampires

This term is used interchangeable with the terms psychic vampire and energy vampire, and typically refers to people who intentionally or unintentionally drain the emotional energy of others.

Codependency is a state of emotional parasitism, originally used to describe the psychological state of a partner trapped in a relationship with an alcoholic. With its compelling evocation of vitality-draining relationships, codependency resonates strongly with both the traditional idea of the vampire and the idea of emotional vampirism and the unsatisfactory, draining human relationships associated with it.

See also: **ADDICTION; LIVING VAMPIRES**

Empusa

Usually translated into English as "vampire," even though it is actually a demon that enters a corpse to feed on its flesh and drink its blood, the empusa is a vile vampire-like creature from Greek mythology.

Usually members of the supernatural entities who served Hecate, goddess of witchcraft and magic, the empusas can appear in a variety of different disguises, sometimes in the form of a woman. The most well-known account of their activity appears in *The Life of Apollonius of Tyana* by Philostratus, a biography of the first-century philosopher and miracle worker. The story tells of a handsome youth called Menippus, who is met by an apparition – an empusa – in the guise of a Phoenician woman. He falls in love with her, not realizing she is actually an empusa and is fattening him up so she may devour him and feed on his flesh and blood. The young man is eventually saved from his fate by Apollonius who recognizes the true nature of the creature.

Energy Vampires

The term energy vampire is used interchangeable with the terms psychic vampire and emotional vampire and typically refers to people who intentionally or unintentionally drain the energy, vitality, or "life force" of others.

See also: **LIVING VAMPIRES**

England

Early accounts of the undead in England remain largely unrecorded, but there were certainly influences in ancient times from the Celts and the Romans. Some experts believe that the first poem concerning the undead may have been the Anglo-Saxon *Vampyre of the Fens*. The work and when it was written are largely unknown, but it could date back as early as the eleventh century.

Alongside Norse influences derived from the Vikings, many Germanic traditions of the undead were introduced by the Anglo-Saxons, and once introduced to the British Isles vampires were mentioned fairly consistently in the work of medieval chroniclers, such as William of Newburgh and Walter Map.

The first use of the word in a literary work can be found in the account of *The Travels of Three English Gentleman*, published in 1745, where the following passage occurs:

> *We must not omit observing here, that our landlord [at Laubach] seems to pay some regard to what Baron Valvasor has related of the Vampyres, said to infest some Parts of this Country. These Vampyres are supposed to be the Bodies of deceased Persons, animated by evil spirits, which come out of the Graves, in the Night-time, to suck the blood of many of the Living, and thereby destroy them.*

The word and the idea started to become quite familiar after that, and in his *Citizen of the World* (1760–2) author Oliver Goldsmith writes in a matter of fact, everyday way, *"From a meal he advances to a surfeit, and at last sucks blood like a vampire."*

By the end of the eighteenth century belief in the existence of vampires had become widespread with English translations of vampire stories from Eastern Europe. From then onwards a number of fascinating vampire cases have been reported in England, including that of the late seventeenth-century vampire of Croglin Grange, and the Highgate Vampire.

Literary figures

A number of notable English literary figures, such as Samuel Taylor Coleridge and Lord Byron made significant contributions to vampire literature, while two very important Irish writers, Bram Stoker and Sheridan Le Fanu, had their famous works, *Dracula* (1897) and *Carmilla* (1872) published in London. In addition, in the later part of the twentieth century England was the birthplace of the musical and vampire-inspired lifestyle Goth cult movement.

See also: **EUROPE; IRELAND; WALES**

Epidemic

Throughout the Middle Ages, and well into the seventeenth century, a number of epidemic diseases, often referred to as "the plague," caused severe depopulation in Europe and in parts of the Middle East. One of the most well-documented outbreaks was the Black Death (bubonic plague), which began in 1347 in Constantinople and spread throughout Europe over the following three or four years. It came to an area of the countryside as if like a dark, deadly storm, killing hundreds of innocent people in a matter of weeks, and then floated away.

The idea of pestilence and epidemic was strong in the medieval mind, and the creation of the vampiric legend relied for at least one of its characteristics on this. Epidemics and vampirism are linked in many accounts dating right back to medieval times where the undead are blamed for bringing disease into a region, and of all the fears existing concerning the undead, the most frightening was that associated with the epidemic nature of vampire attack. The first victim of an epidemic was often believed to be the vampire, and it was thought that staking and burning the corpse of the first victim and others who had died from the plague would end the epidemic. An example of this is the case of the Berwick Vampire reported by the twelfth-century English chronicler William of Newburgh.

It is interesting to note that many of the original characteristics of traditional vampirism seem to have arisen in China and Assyria and, coincidentally, so also did the first epidemics of bubonic plague.

Erestun

A vampire in Russian lore, the erestun was an ordinary person, most likely a robber, villain, or someone depraved, who while he was alive, or possibly after death, had his body invaded by evil. The transformed person

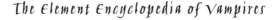

becomes a vampire that stalks and then devours the family of the victim before moving on to attack and kill others. To prevent the erestun from rising out of the grave, a stake made of aspen is driven through his back between his shoulders. The erestun could also be destroyed by whipping the corpse with a horse whip.

See also: **RUSSIA**

Eretica

In Russian lore, the eretica is a vampire-like creature, strongly associated with witches. The ereticy (plural) are women who during their lives have offered their souls to Satan in return for magical powers, and they are an explicit illustration of the frequent association between women and sin in vampire lore. After death, they return to earth, disguised as ugly old women who roam the earth turning people against Christianity. They are only active during spring and autumn. At other times they sleep in the coffins of those who have led un-Christian lives. If someone fell into the grave of an eretica or saw an eretica, then they would slowly wither and fade away. The eye of the eretica is extremely dangerous and can act on its own as a psychic vampire and send the evil eye, again causing humans to waste away and die. Like other vampires, the eretica can by destroyed by burning or the use of a stake.

See also: **RUSSIA**

Eretik/eretnik

A type of cannibalistic vampire in Russian lore associated with heretics. Heretics were associated with sorcery, and sorcerers were believed to become vampires after death. The eretik is a corpse that leaves its grave and eats people. When exhumed it can be found lying on its stomach and the only way to destroy it is to plunge a stake made of aspen through its back or to burn it. The term "eretik" became a substitute for the older Russian term for vampires, upir.

See also: **RUSSIA**

Estonia

Estonia, a region situated along the Baltic Sea to the north of Latvia, had vampire species in its folklore, but these beliefs were not very developed and were largely the product of

Russian influences. The Estonian species, the veripard, which means "blood beard," was a nightmare vision that tormented people during the night by smothering them. The rarest type of the undead was called the vere-imeja, which means "bloodsucker."

Estrie

The theme of the demonic preying upon the innocent and the breaking of the bonds of trust can be found in Hebrew culture with the estrie, a female demon that takes on human form. Vampire-like it lives among humans, feeding on their blood to sustain itself. It particularly likes the blood of young children.

In medieval Jewish lore it is difficult to determine whether the estrie was regarded as a true demon or as a witch, as it was described, sometimes in the same source, as both. Included among the incorporeal spirits, it was nonetheless always a woman, a flesh-and-blood member of the community. In either guise her character was that of the vampire whose particular prey was little children, though she did not disdain at times to include grown-ups in her diet. The sense of surviving descriptions about the estrie appears to be that she was an entity who adopted a woman's form and spent her life among men, the more readily to satisfy her gory appetites, and that she was best known in her human form.

Traits

The estrie could change its appearance at will but when flying at night reverted to her demon shape. If an estrie was wounded by a human being, or was seen by one (in her demonic state), she would die unless she could procure and consume some of the person's bread and salt. According to one report, a man who was attacked by an estrie in the shape of a cat and beat her off, was approached by the witch in the form of a woman the next day and asked for some of his bread and salt. When he was innocently about to grant her request, an old man intervened and scolded him sharply for his generosity: *"If you enable her to remain alive, she will only harm other men."*

When prayers at religious services were offered for a sick woman suspected of becoming a vampire, no one in the congregation should say "Amen." Dead women deemed to be at risk of being an estrie were examined before burial. If their mouths were open, it was though they would become a vampire. By placing dirt or earth in their open mouth it was believed the transformation could be stopped.

Ethics, among Vampires

By any system of law every single vampire is a multiple-murderer without ethics. But if there is such a thing as a real vampire it is for all intents and purposes a different species to humans; a species that requires fresh blood, preferably human, in order to survive, and as such, a species that should perhaps be judged by its own standards. The ethics for real vampires are therefore a matter for them. However, when it comes to sanguinarians, people who have a need to drink blood, psychic vampires, people who feed on the energy or life force of others, and modern vampires, people who simply like to model their lives on the vampire lifestyle, there is without doubt a place for a code of vampire ethics.

In 2000 Michelle Belanger, a sanguinarian psychic vampire, and COVICA (the Council of Vampyric International Community Affairs) set up a voluntary standard of common sense, etiquette, and ideals for the Sanguinarium or the greater vampyre/vampire community, called the Black Veil. This is not a text to instruct someone on how to be a vampire, but rather a code of ethics for those who are and wish to adopt it as their own personal code. It was based on an earlier version written in 1999.

Black Veil

The Black Veil, also known as the rules of the community, contains 13 principles for modern vampires to follow. These principles include the following ethical guidelines:

- Discretion: *Respect yourself so that others respect you. Take care in revealing your true nature only to those with the wisdom to understand and accept it.*

- Diversity: *There are many different points of view and no single one has all the answers to who and what vampires are. Find the path that is right for you and uphold that freedom for others.*

- Control: *Vampires are more than their hunger and can exercise control. Do not be reckless and exercise control and ensure the safety and well-being of others.*

- Behavior: *Understand that every action has consequences. Respect the rights of others*

and treat them as you would wish to be treated.

- Donors: *Feeding should only occur between consenting adults. Donors should be allowed to make informed decisions before they give of themselves. Respect the life that is fed upon and do not abuse those who nourish you.*

Eucharist

The Eucharist, also called Holy Communion, is the holiest ritual of Christianity commemorating, by consecrating bread and wine, the Last Supper, the final meal that Jesus Christ shared with his disciples before his arrest, and eventual crucifixion, when he gave them bread saying, *"This is my body,"* and wine saying, *"This is my blood."* In the Roman Catholic Church and the Eastern Orthodox Church, it is believed that in the elements of bread and wine, the body and blood of Christ are somehow mystically present. Among Protestants the sacramental elements are not considered the actual body and blood of Christ but are seen as symbols of them.

Typically at the end of Mass, the service in which bread, most often in the form of small wafers, and wine were consumed, some wafers would be left on the altar with a lighted candle. In his treatise on vampires, Dom Augustin Calmet, an eighteenth-century Roman Catholic priest and scholar, collected a number of old stories about the use of these wafers as effective weapons against vampires. In one of these Pope Gregory the Great (c.540–604) told the story of two nuns who died in a state of excommunication. After death they were seen in church. St. Benedict sent consecrated bread over to their former nurse so that it might be offered to the undead nuns. From then on the nuns remained quietly in their graves. In other stories a consecrated wafer is placed on the corpse or in the mouth of a suspected vampire.

Dracula

In the story of *Dracula*, the Eucharistic wafer is used as a means of protection against vampires; a wafer is placed on Mina Harker's forehead after she has been forced to drink Dracula's blood. The wafer brands itself onto her skin, leaving a red mark until Dracula is killed. In dramatizations of *Dracula* that followed, the Eucharistic wafer was used rarely and was replaced instead by the crucifix. The vampires of modern fiction don't generally tend to be affected by sacred objects such as the Eucharistic wafer and the crucifix, unless the vampire hunter has strong belief in their powers. This is largely due to the belief and acceptance in modern life that Christianity is but one religion among many.

See also: APOTROPAICS

Europe

Perhaps no other region in the world has as much vampire lore as Europe, in particular the countries of Eastern Europe. Among the many countries of Europe stories and legends about the undead have traveled, which means that the vampire lore of different European countries often shares strong similarities and these similarities can make it hard to know what the exact origin was of a country's vampire legend.

Greece

The best starting place is Greece, one of Europe's oldest civilizations. Perhaps the oldest vampire story from ancient Greek myth is that of Lamia, the beautiful mortal queen of Libya that the Greek god Zeus fell in love and fathered children with. Zeus' jealous wife, Hera, found out about Lamia and took away all of Lamia's children. Being a mortal, Lamia could not take revenge on Hera, but she decided that other mortal mothers would suffer as she did. She wandered the world drinking the blood of young children. She was considered demonic for her actions and not long after the race of lamiae was named after her; vampire-like creatures with serpent-like bodies.

In Greece today, some people still believe in vampires known as vrykolakas. A person could become a vrykolakas through violent death, improper burial, or excommunication. These formidable creatures could be killed by decapitation and by driving a stake through the body.

Romania

Romania is the country most people today associate with vampires because it contains the district of Transylvania. Although it is true that people in Transylvania have many beliefs about the undead, contrary to popular belief Transylvania is not the home of the so-called "real" Dracula, Vlad the Imapaler, who was the fifteenth-century ruler of another Romanian district, Wallachia. In

Romania vampires, called strigoi, if male and strigoaica, if female, are thought to be living vampires who can leave their bodies to attack others. (Italy also has an ancient belief in a living vampire, the strega, which behaves in a similar way to the Romanian strigoi.) Immortal blood-drinkers are called strigoi morti and these creatures are most like "traditional" vampires in that they can leave their graves at night and feed on the blood of the living. These vampires can be destroyed by staking and decapitation. In addition, belief in the nosferatu – a blood-drinking vampire that can have sexual relations with humans – also comes from Romania. It was thought that illegitimate children were doomed to become nosferatu.

Poland

In Northeastern European counties, such as Poland, there is folklore concerning the upyr, a vampire-like creature that roams and sucks the blood of the living from noon to midnight – meaning that at least half its activity occurs during daylight hours.

Western Europe

Vampire species resembling those found in Eastern Europe and Greece can also be found in the West. In Germany, the nachzehrer is fairly similar to the vrykolakas, although the nachzehrer can feed on the blood of both the dead and the living. England, Ireland, Scotland, and France don't tend to have original vampire folklore, although a number of well-known vampire cases have emerged from these countries over the years.

Evil

Terrible acts that are combined with lack of remorse or consideration for the feelings of others are considered by many experts to be the definition or hallmark of evil. Glance over the evolution of the "traditional" blood-sucking undead vampire and it appears chaotic, but there is at least one consistent, conceptual thread; the vampire, however sympathetically humanized as a tortured romantic or manifestation of alternate spirituality, is evil. Like Satan, vampires embody evil.

It's probable that the concept of evil has existed since humankind began. It may even be an innate part of us that we will never be able to understand or remove. Today experts approach the capacity for evil within a person as a manifestation of a number of different elements, including an imbalance in biochemistry or mis-wired neurology; insurmountable social problems and lack of role models; or personality disorder and a failure of control and free will. Some experts look at evil acts as part of the fabric of nature. In other words, the behavior we see in murderers and sadists reflects natural principles. These people are not monsters as such but a manifestation of a system that is out of balance in some way. Others argue that the criminal's way of thinking is different from other people in that they view crime as a way to stave off feelings of emptiness and have no conception of the impact of their actions on others. Another school of thought suggests that evil is caused by the healthy development of the personality being disrupted in some way by traumatic events, brain injury, brainwashing, or physical or emotional abuse.

Nature v. nurture

Central to the debate of what makes a person "evil" is the question of genetics versus environment, or whether a person is born or made evil. The answer most often given is that it is both. Each factor modifies the other in such a way that the manner of processing a situation is unique to the individual, as is his or her choice to become cruel or violent. In short, the development of an evil person is a unique combination of events, as is their response to evil.

While the whole notion of evil may be irrelevant to "real" vampires – they are not bound by any mortal ethics or moral code – it is still relevant for those who want to understand their universal appeal and why so many people continue to sympathize and identify with them. The truth probably is that vampires appeal to us because of their mystery, daring, and their passionate longing and willingness to serve their own needs, regardless of the consequences of their actions. Through them we can feel what it is like to be different, dangerous, powerful, sensual, and sexual and through them we can feel what it is like to surrender to our deepest longings.

See also: **SEX**

Evil Eye

The ancient and greatly feared belief that certain people can inflict bad luck, misfortune, illness, or wasting death simply with a glance or intense stare, the power of the evil eye is thought to lie in the negative, destructive energy that can be transmitted to another person with a glance or lingering look from a malevolent person. Living vampires, such as witches, with the power to drain away their victims' life force are thought to be capable of withering any living or non-living thing with their look.

The evil eye superstition was known as far back as 3000 BC, appearing in the cuneiform texts of the Sumerians and Assyrians. There is also evidence that the Babylonians and ancient Greeks believed in it. Women in ancient Egypt would paint their eyes and lips with makeup to keep the evil eye away. Most tribal cultures are aware of it and it is mentioned in both the Bible and the Koran. Even today in Mexico and Central America superstitions about the evil eye still exist.

A form of psychic vampirism, the curse of the evil eye can either be involuntary or deliberate. When it is involuntary the person casting it may not be aware of the sickness and exhaustion a jealous or envious look from them can cause others. When the evil eye is deliberately cast, the action is called "overlooking," and it is a form of witchcraft that can cause misfortune, illness, loss of property, and even death. In the Middle Ages witches, sorcerers, magicians, medicine men, and witch doctors were said to cast the evil eye. Native American shamans often combine the menacing look with a pointing stick, finger, or wand. A person may also be cursed with the evil eye at birth and not know it. Pope Leo XIII (1810–1903) was said to possess the evil eye.

Deflecting techniques

All those who believe in the evil eye must constantly be on their guard against it, as a malevolent stare could come from anyone, even a stranger in the street.

The evil eye is most likely to strike when an individual is at the height of his or her happiness and success, although for some unknown reason children and cows seem to be special targets of the evil eye. Being humble could deflect it, and admired infants would be smeared with dirt before being taken out. If a person was hit by the evil eye various superstitions offer protection against disaster striking. Phallic-shaped objects and spittle are believed to protect against the evil eye. If a witch or sorcerer is not available to offer a counter-spell, the "fig hand" – a clenched fist with the thumb stuck through the first two fingers – and the "horned hand" – a fist with the first and last fingers stuck out to signify horns – are said to offer protection. Other protective amulets include bells, brass objects, red ribbons, blue beads, garlic, horseshoes, or hanging charms in windows to confuse a witch's gaze. Touching wood was also thought to offer protection against the curse of the evil eye.

Evil Omens

See: **Bad Signs/Omens**

Evolution, of Vampires

Vampires today have come a long way from the animated corpses or revenants (restless dead) of medieval folklore. They have evolved in countless different directions, moving away from epitomizing the notion of pure evil and brutal aggression, as embodied by Bram Stoker's Count Dracula, to sexy, intelligent seducer, and even to conscience-bound hero – Stephenie Meyer's Edward Cullen. Today we have vampires who do not need to kill anyone, avoid the sun, or even drink blood. Anyone who wants to put forward a definition of a vampire can do so, and plenty have done just that. In centuries past the definition of a vampire was clearer, but now everyone seems to want to have their own interpretation of vampires, ranging from the traditional view of immortal, blood-sucking creatures to sex vampires, emotional vampires, psychic vampires, vampires suffering from blood disorders or viruses, and people who call themselves vampires, simply because they model their lifestyle on vampires and vampire fiction.

Part of the reason for the evolution of the more sympathetic image of the vampire is the general questioning of absolutes that characterizes modern life and which has led to a relativist blurring of the boundaries between good and evil. The vampire has evolved from a metaphor of pure evil to a metaphor of the "other," or the part of an individual they want to suppress or will not allow themselves to express. For some the problem with this romanticizing of the vampire – as authors such as Stephenie Meyer have done – is that the horrific intensity of the confrontation of pure evil that the original vampires represented is lost.

However, despite the chaos of interpretation, certain key themes do emerge to unite contemporary vampire culture. First of all, vampires manifest an alternative approach to life that sets them apart. Second, vampires have a dark and secret side to them; and finally, despite all attempts to prove otherwise, vampires have the potential within them to be evil, if they so choose.

See also: **EXPLANATIONS OF VAMPIRISM;**
ORIGINS OF VAMPIRES

Ewers, Hans Heinz (1872-1943)

Hans Heinz Ewers was a German writer of horror fiction who made a number of contributions to vampire fiction. Although opposed to anti-Semitism, in later life he was known for his sympathetic views toward Nazism. Although the graphic and grisly portrayal of vampires that characterizes his writings has rendered them largely unappealing, they take their place among the most shocking and gruesome of all vampire literature.

His first noteworthy vampire novel was *Alraune* (1911), the story of Alraune, the result of experimental insemination of a British prostitute by a rapist and murderer. The beautiful Alraune is a vampire who attacks men sexually and then feeds on their blood. The antihero, Frank Braun, becomes her victim, but survives because she dies before killing him. *Vampire* (1922) also features Frank Braun. On this occasion Braun suffers from a mysterious illness and his only relief from it is in the company of women. Only one, an older woman, stays with him for more than a few days; he drinks small amounts of her blood while in a trance.

See also: **LITERATURE**

Excommunication

As defined by canon law, excommunication is the most serious punishment that can be inflicted upon an individual by the Church. It is the exclusion of someone from participation in communion, which means they cannot be a part of church activities or receive sacraments or, according to some traditions, find peace in the afterlife until absolution has been granted. Some doctrines, especially those in the Orthodox nations, stated that a corpse would remain incorrupt and its soul doomed to eternal suffering until absolution was granted. Some vampire experts have speculated that such beliefs may have helped encourage stories about vampires because a logical development from here is that incorrupt corpses are perfect vehicles for possession by evil entities, who seek to inhabit and reanimate the corpse and use it to seek blood from the living as nourishment. An excommunicated soul unable to gain entry to God's kingdom would also probably be full of resentment and hatred, which could trigger the reanimation of the corpse and manifest itself in the creation of a deadly, dangerous vampire.

See also: **CURSE**

Exhumation

Exhumation is the digging up or disinterring of a corpse, once believed to be the first step in detecting a vampire. After being exhumed the corpse would then be examined for so-called signs of vampirism and numerous medieval documents and reports mention accounts of exhumation in connection with suspected cases of vampirism. In general, if a corpse had deteriorated "properly" then it was thought that the soul was at peace, but if the corpse appeared preserved, was flexible, had shifted in its grave, or contained blood, it was thought that the corpse was feeding on the blood of others and that it was necessary to destroy it by decapitation or burning.

Although contact with the exhumed corpse was kept to a minimum by the use of sheets – it was believed that the blood of the corpse could infect others – there were exceptions. Where the corpse was exhumed by order of a public authority, rather than by a group of individuals, public fascination might compel it to be displayed; in 1591 the corpse of the Breslau Vampire was put on display for 20 days.

Another common practice was to examine the exhumed corpse's heart. If it was fresh and contained blood it was thought that the deceased was vampirizing the life of a sick person. It was reported, for example, that the heart of a man was burned in Woodstock Green, Vermont, sometime around 1829. He had died six months previously of consumption and was buried. When his brother became ill within a short time (also with consumption), the family exhumed the body and examined the heart. Finding that it still contained liquid blood, they were convinced that the dead man was the cause of the disease. They removed the heart and burned it to ashes in an iron pot.

See also: **CORPSE; DESTROYING VAMPIRES;
DETECTING VAMPIRES**

Exorcism

Exorcism is the process by which an evil spirit, demon, or possessing entity is driven out of a human host, object, or place. According to one school of thought, and some vampire hunters, a vampire is a demonically possessed corpse that must have an exorcism performed upon it. Exorcism is not a cure for vampirism but is essential to the survival of the individual possessed.

Possession and exorcism

The concept of possession by evil spirits and the practice of exorcism are very ancient and widespread, and may have originated in prehistoric shamanistic beliefs. In some shamanic traditions it is thought that possessing spirits can steal souls, and the shaman enters a trance to search for the soul and force the evil spirit out. The word derives from the Greek *exorkizein*, meaning "to bind by oath," or to invoke a higher power to make a spirit act in a certain way. Rituals of exorcism exist universally in societies where evil spirits are thought to interfere with earthly affairs and cause misfortune. Typically exorcisms are performed by trained individuals, usually religious officials or magical or occult adepts known as exorcists. Rites vary from simple requests to leave to complex rituals involving trance and techniques including fasting, prayer, sacred herbs, and blessed water. Whatever method is used, the ritual is often believed to be extremely dangerous for both the performer and the victim of the possession, sometimes resulting in the death of either individual.

Demonic possession

Jewish rabbinic literature refers to exorcisms. The best-known rite concerns that of the vampire-like entity, the dybbuk. Christianity also associates exorcism with demonic possession. The Christian New Testament includes exorcism among the miracles performed by Jesus. Because of this precedent, demonic possession was part of the belief system of Christianity since its beginning, and exorcism is still a recognized practice of Catholicism, Eastern Orthodoxy, and some Protestant sects. The Roman Catholic Church offers a formal rite of exorcism, the *Rituale Romanum*, dating back to 1614. In order to "qualify" for an exorcism, the victim must display certain symptoms including superhuman strength, levitation, and speaking in tongues (glossolalia). Some Protestants also perform exorcisms. Pentecostalists practice "deliverance ministry" where healers drive out evil spirits by the laying on of hands.

Possessing spirits

In Hinduism, Buddhism, and Islam, possessing spirits are blamed for a number of misfortunes and can be cast out of people and places, but unlike in Christianity, such conflicts are not considered battles for the person's soul. Typical Hindu exorcism techniques include offering copper coins, candy, or other gifts, and pressing rock salt between the fingers. In China, ghosts are exorcised from houses by Taoist priests in a complex ritual involving a mystic scroll placed on an altar, a cup, a sword, and mystical signs, repeated to all four corners of the room.

Unfinished business

A more moderate but equally controversial view on exorcism and possession was put forward in the twentieth century by American psychologist Carl Wickland, who believed that possessing spirits were not evil but simply confused, and were trying to finish their worldly business in a living person. This could cause any number of mental problems. Wickland recommended using mild electric shocks to help the spirits leave in his controversial book *Thirty Years Among the Dead* (1924). This view still has a number of supporters, among them psychiatrist Dr. Ralph Allison, who wrote in his book, *Minds in Many Pieces* (1980), that various of his patients exhibited signs of demonic possession and required exorcism as well as conventional treatment.

According to the scientific point of view, the fact that exorcism appeared to have worked on people in the past who were experiencing symptoms of possession or vampirism (and continues to work today in some societies) can be attributed to the placebo effect and the power of suggestion. No doubt those who believe that vampires are demonically possessed corpses would disagree.

See also: **DEMONS; DESTRUCTION; POSSESSION**

Explanations of Vampirism

From the late eighteenth century onwards, when eyewitness accounts and reports of exhumed corpses manifesting signs of "vampirism" or continued life after death filtered into Western and Central Europe from Eastern Europe, a number of academics and Church officials attempted to find explanations for the phenomenon. Some scholars dismissed the reports as the product of superstition and ignorance but others took the accounts seriously and attempted to offer "rational" explanations.

Superstition and ignorance

One plausible explanation is that belief in vampires is simply an ancient and cultural response to primitive fears about death and the afterlife. Finding it impossible to conceive of their own death and the death of others, people throughout time have tried to find answers in a world that is no longer human. In other words, vampire stories were a product of superstition and ignorance. For example, one commonly held belief was that vampirism was caused by demonic possession: a demon or evil entity entered a corpse and forced it to rise from the grave and seek blood for nourishment.

Premature burial

A popular explanation put forward was premature burial, caused by catalepsy, a disease in which the person appeared to be dead but was not actually dead when they were buried. In *The Vampire: His Kith and Kin*, respected vampirologist Montague Summers suggested that premature burial *"may have helped to reinforce the tradition of the vampire."* When the unfortunate person woke up in their coffin, their frantic attempts to escape would have accounted for changes in the appearance of the corpse once exhumed, as well as noises coming from the grave.

Decomposition

Another explanation, which like that of premature burial remains popular today, is that continued changes in the body after death, such as loss of rigidity, which most people were unaware of in earlier times, led to accusations of vampirism. Put simply, the eighteenth-century observers saw bodies in different stages of normal decay and reported what they believed to be signs of continuing life from a perspective of limited understanding of the normal process of decomposition. For example, rational explanations for the disappearance of bodies, or the strangely life-like appearance of corpses, include animals digging up bodies from shallow graves; flooding uncovering bodies from shallow graves; gases forming in the corpse, sometimes causing post-mortem movement; and cold temperatures or lack of air or moisture preserving corpses. Trapped air would have caused the corpse to "shriek" when staked. In addition, the practice of grave robbing would have contributed to the illusion that bodies had risen from their graves overnight.

Social and moral control

According to some experts, vampire beliefs cannot be explained away by ignorance about the decomposition process because our ancestors would have been very familiar with death and its stages, as it was an inevitable part of their daily lives. They argue that vampire beliefs arose as part of very strong religious and philosophical principles of how the world worked and the rules and laws which kept everyone and everything in the world in their right place. If any of these rules or laws were violated – if funeral rites were not performed correctly, for example – this would unleash all kinds of unnatural events and the dead would rise from their graves as vampires. In other words, vampires were a symbol of the world order turned upside down; for community leaders, therefore, this belief in vampires became a way for them to enforce moral order and social control.

Virus

Another notion was that vampirism was some form of disease or virus. The spread of plague germs could account for the reported spread of vampire symptoms – an epidemic of plague occurred around the same time as the vampire outbreak in East Prussia in 1710 – and in the nineteenth century vampirism was used as an explanation for infectious diseases like consumption or tuberculosis. In 1616, Italian scientist Ludovico Fatinelli published his *Treatise on Vampires*, in which he speculated that vampirism was caused by a microscopic pathogen. This theory has been dismissed by scientists and doctors over the centuries, but even today there is speculation among those who study the science of vampires that the source of vampirism is the "Human Vampiric Virus."

Medical explanations

Other medical explanations offered include anemia, rabies, and porphyria. In Bram Stoker's *Dracula* (1897), iron deficiency anemia is put forward as an explanation (although it is dismissed), and some experts believe that anemia, with its symptoms of paleness and extreme fatigue, is a credible explanation for reports of vampirism. During the twentieth century rabies was offered as an explanation. People with rabies often manifest animal-like behavior and an unquenchable thirst, and in eighteenth-century Hungary there were outbreaks of rabies. In the 1960s porphyria, a congenital blood disorder was put forward as a medical explanation. Like people with anemia, people who suffer from this condition have a chronic iron deficiency, which can result in skin coloration and sensitivity to sunlight. Drinking the blood of healthy people would increase iron intake at times when iron supplements didn't exist, giving rise to talk of vampirism.

Vampire behavior

Vampire behavior, as exhibited by blood-drinking serial killers, such as Elizabeth Báthory (1560–1614) and Richard Chase (1950–80), has now been recognized as a psychiatric disorder, also called vampire personality disorder or Renfield's syndrome, after one of the victims in *Dracula*. Symptoms include drinking blood, drinking one's own blood (known as auto-vampirism), necrophilia (being aroused by dead bodies), necrophagia (the urge to eat corpses), cannibalism, sadism, and vampiric fantasies. Although opinion is divided, most people accept that clinical vampirism is a psychiatric problem and that these people are not actual vampires but deluded and disturbed individuals.

As far as the science behind vampires is concerned, the question of whether or not vampires do exist remains a valid one, because there are still cases of vampirism that cannot be explained away rationally.

Although rare, real-life vampire stories, such as that of the Highgate Vampire, reported in the 1970s and the chupacabra "goat-sucker" attacks reported as recently as 2008, are not confined to the distant past; they continue to occur and mystify both skeptics and believers to this day. Such reports of animals or people found with unexplained bite wounds and blood loss suggest the very real and chilling possibility that vampires could actually exist. And if they do exist, the question of what they are, and how they came to be, remains a tantalizing and unanswered one.

Extraterrestrials

According to some vampirologists, extraterrestrials are a type of modern vampire because many reports of encounters with alien life forms bear a strong resemblance to encounters with or reports of vampires.

There have been reports of extraterrestrials, or ETs, and UFOs (unidentified flying objects) since ancient times, but from the early 1960s onwards many ET encounters have became darker and more sinister. Victims have reported being attacked, missing time, and experiencing terrifying abductions where they are physically and sexually assaulted, sometimes aboard a spaceship. Although reports of benign encounters continue, in general encounters with ETs are feared.

Typical characteristics of stories concerning so-called alien abductions mirror those of reported vampire attacks in that they usually occur at night, while the victim is asleep. Abducting ETs can cause nightmares and appear to have supernatural powers over humans and animals, as well as the ability to be invisible, to shape-shift, and to paralyze victims while they attack or sexually assault them. They also leave their victims weak, confused, and exhausted.

Some phenomena reported alongside UFO sightings are clearly vampiric in nature. From the 1970s onwards, mysterious mutilations of livestock have been reported. The wounds left on these animals are too precise to be explained away as attacks by predators or humans and often show signs of intense laser-type heat. Intense heat is also experienced by victims of the so-called chupa-chupa or alien vampires in the sky. In such cases victims report being attacked by beams of red light that leave them feeling as though they are drained of energy.

Not all reports of alien encounters parallel reports of encounters with vampires, and ETs have also been compared to other supernatural beings, such as fairies, demons, and angels. However, there is a case for arguing that they are a species of modern vampire because, in true vampiric style, they symbolize fear and the mystery of the unknown, and have the power to steal life away.

See also: **ORIGINS, OF VAMPIRES**

Eye/eyebrow

In German and Russian folklore the eye of a corpse has the power to draw the living into the grave, and for that reason the eyes are immediately closed at the point of death. In some gypsy lore, the eye of a living vampire also has the power to act as a vampire on its own, causing others to waste away. The evil eye cast by the Russian eretic possesses such powers.

Perhaps because it makes a person's face look menacing, there is a belief in vampire folklore that people with overgrown eyebrows that meet in the middle are not to be trusted, and are associated with bad luck, foul temper, and vampires and werewolves. In Greece, eyebrows that meet are a sign of being a vampire, and in Ireland, Denmark, and Germany, of being a werewolf.

"The blood is the life."

Count Dracula, in *Dracula* by Bram Stoker

Fairy / Fairies

In European folklore, fairies are said to be non-human, immortal earth spirits with supernatural powers who occupy a limbo between earth and heaven. From the Latin *fata* meaning fate, the term comes from the Fates of Greek and Roman mythology – three sisters who spun the thread of life and determined the fate of all. In archaic English, fairies were also known as *fays*, a term which means enchanted or bewitched, and is in recognition of the skill fairies were thought to have in predicting and even controlling human destiny. Fairies were believed to bring both good and bad luck and to possess magical powers. They were sometimes said to be witches or their familiars.

Fairies and vampires

There are associations in folklore between fairies and vampires. Both creatures are immortal, often nocturnal, and have the ability to shape-shift, and both can manifest blood-sucking tendencies. For example, the malign and succubus-like baobhan-sith from the Scottish Highlands and the leanhaum-shee of the Isle of Man are two fairy spirits with decidedly vampiric tendencies. Like vampire folklore, fairy legends are universal and there are a number of theories about how fairies originated. One is that they are fallen angels. Others suggest stories about fairies arose to explain misfortunes or natural disasters, while others say they are simply small humans. Another theory that reinforces the association between vampires and fairies is that they are spirits of the restless dead.

Traits and characteristics

Regardless of how they originated, getting involved with fairies is never considered to be straightforward. They can be benign, but numerous superstitions also suggest a darker side. For example, it is thought that fairies may steal away babies and turn them into changelings, or they might curse a person to ill-health or a household to poverty. If they fall in love with a human that person may be blessed with immortality, but this also brings the curse of living forever and watching loved ones die. In order to stay in favor with the fairies, some superstitions suggest that humans should leave out food, drink, and gifts for them.

Fairies, also known as the good people, the little people, elves, or good neighbors, come in all shapes and sizes; however, traditionally they are tiny, resemble humans, and have wings. It is said that they are only visible to those with clairvoyant sight but if they wish they can make themselves visible to anyone. Some are said to be fearsome creatures with awesome powers, while others, like leprechauns or brownies, are more benign. Whatever their shape or appearance, fairies are thought to have great affinity for nature. They are said to live in the Land of Fairy or Elf Land, which is believed to exist in a timeless underground world. At night they allegedly step out from Elf Land to dance, sing, travel, and have fun or make mischief.

Some traditions claim that certain types of fairies have a group consciousness, while other types of fairies are individual, exalted beings very close to the angelic kingdom. The fairies with a group consciousness have a fairy queen that serves as their spokesperson. Other traditions emphasize the immortality of fairies. Due to this immortality, the fairies have a different perception of time than humans. In the story of Rip Van Winkle, for example, Rip thought he had been gone only a short time but when he returned to the realm of mortals, nearly one hundred years had passed in his absence.

Celtic folklore

Fairies are mainly associated with Northern European cultures, and especially the Celtic folklore of Ireland, Wales, Brittany, and Cornwall. In Ireland they are known as Tuatha de Danaan, or people of the goddess Danu, a divine race that once ruled the island. The Tuatha are thought to be strong and beautiful and skilled in magic. Celtic folklore was transported to the American colonies and to Asia, while Native Americans have their own "little people" fairy lore. The little people live in the Pryor Mountains of Montana and are said to have powerful medicine and strong teeth.

From the eighteenth century onwards stories report that the fairies have departed, or are fading away. Some people believe that they are disappearing because humans have stopped believing in them. Others say pollution, urbanization, and technological advances are the main cause of their decline. Yet, however often they are reported as gone, belief in fairies still lingers on, reports of sightings still occur, and the traditions continue. Today, many people believe that fairies and other elemental spirits are making themselves known through visions or photos or fairy lights or orbs to urge us to treat the natural world more kindly. Skeptics may argue that fairies are alluring creatures of myth and/or the imagination, but fairies are as real as vampires are to those who believe in them.

Fallen Angels

Inspired by the Book of Enoch, which dates back to the third century BC, some vampirologists claim that vampires are the offspring of the union between the Watchers (fallen angels, those expelled from heaven for plotting against God) and humans.

The Book of Enoch is a Jewish pseudepigraphic work (a work that claims to be divinely inspired). It was not included in either the Hebrew or most Christian biblical canons, but could have been considered a sacred text by various Jewish sects. The original Aramaic version was lost until the Dead Sea Scroll fragments were discovered between 1947 and 1956 in 11 caves in and around the Wadi Qumran near the ruins of the ancient settlement of Khirbet Qumran, on the northwest shore of the Dead Sea.

According to the Book of Enoch, when the Children of the Watchers had consumed all of the food available, they began to eat the flesh and drink the blood of humans. In another adjunct, vampires are held to be the offspring of the daughters of Eve (female humans) and the Angel of Death, and their mission is to thwart the demonic offspring of the fallen angels.

Few vampirologists today take the fallen angel theory seriously.

Familiar

A "familiar" is the term used for a spirit that takes on the shape of an animal to serve or become the companion of a witch or sorcerer. It serves only the master or mistress it has been created by or with whom it has bonded, and is sometimes fed by blood from their thumb, fingers, or breasts.

In many cultures all over the world the familiar can be found assisting its master or mistress in spell-casting or undertaking errands. During the medieval witchcraft trials, witches were accused of having familiars in the shape of cats, toads, rats, birds, and dogs. These familiars were said to be the gift of the Devil to help the witch in her evil work, and any unusual markings on a witch's body were said to indicate the place where the familiar sucked and drank blood.

See also: **ANIMAL VAMPIRES**

Fan Clubs

Due in part to the huge popularity of television shows such as *Dark Shadows* and *Buffy the Vampire Slayer*, and the runaway success of vampire novels, such as Anne Rice's

Vampire Chronicles, from the late 1970s onwards the image of vampires in popular culture was rejuvenated. Images of vampires began to appear everywhere, from cereal boxes to playing cards to greetings cards, and while vampires were spreading from books and film to other venues, academics were busy researching natural explanations for vampire folklore.

The boom in interest in vampires led to the formation of a number of different vampire fan clubs. Some of these clubs were for people who had been so affected by the vampire image to the point of filing their teeth into a fang shape, avoiding the sun, exchanging blood with a willing donor, and dressing in black, but the great majority were for people inspired by a particular vampire author, character, game, TV show, film, or comic, and/or those who found themselves irresistibly drawn to the vampire mythology. Some of the most notable vampire fan clubs formed in the latter part of the twentieth century include:

- *The Vampire Information Exchange (VIE)*
- *The Vampire Studies Society*
- *The Count Dracula Fan Club*
- *Anne Rice's Vampire Lestat Fan Club*
- *The Bram Stoker Society*

Information and contact details for these organizations, and others, can be found in the Vampire Directory. Many fan clubs formed in the 1970s and 80s continue to thrive today as the vampire boom shows no sign of abating, especially now that public interest has been rejuvenated once again by Stephenie Meyer's bestselling Twilight Saga novels and accompanying box-office hit movie, released in December 2008.

Fangs

Considered in popular culture to be one of the hallmarks of the blood-sucking vampire, the elongated canine fangs of the vampire are often revealed in a hideous grimace as they bite into a victim's neck to suck their lifeblood. But fangs are a classic example of the way in which authors and film directors have transformed a relatively obscure aspect of vampire folklore into one of the most recognizable. In folklore there is infrequent mention of fangs. It is the tongue, which is usually pointed or barbed, which is typically used to suck blood in traditional Eastern European vampire folklore. It wasn't until the nineteenth century that authors started to use fangs as a way to emphasize the vampire's animal-like savagery and cruelty.

Writing in the 1840s, author James Malcolm Rymer mentions *"fang-like teeth"* when he describes the attack on Flora Bannerworth by the vampire Varney in *Varney the Vampyre*, and in Sheridan Le Fanu's 1872 tale *Carmilla* a wandering peddler notes that Carmilla had the *"sharpest tooth – long thin, pointed, like an owl, like a needle."* In Bram Stoker's *Dracula* (1897) Jonathan Harker notices that Dracula's mouth was *"fixed and rather cruel looking, with peculiarly sharp, white teeth; these protruded over his lips,"* and the three women in the castle also possess extended canines. In the 1922 film *Nosferatu*, Count Orlok has rodent-like fangs, but it was in the late 1950s and 1960s that the vampire's fangs really came into their own in the world of movies, thanks to the Hammer Horror films.

A new feature introduced into modern vampire novels and films has been the retractable fangs of the vampire. The teeth of vampires appear normal, allowing them to interact with humans, and they show their fangs only at the moment they want to feed.

Conventional canine fangs do create a problem for vampire cinema in that they appear to be used more for tearing and ripping flesh, rather than for inflicting the precise and tidy puncture wounds usually depicted. Therefore it has become common for the canine teeth to curve together and to be more pointed and refined than real canine teeth. Contradicting the traditional Freudian interpretation of the phallic nature of fangs, some experts believe that the puncture wounds made by vampire fangs could unconsciously refer to ancient myths that associated a snake's bite to the onset of menstruation. After being bitten, a girl would become more sexual. This means that the bite of a vampire can be associated with the anxieties both of men (fangs are textbook phallic symbols) and women.

Farciennes, Vampires of

According to Paul de Saint-Hillaire in his 1980 book *Liège et Meuse Mystérieux*, in 1851 when the old chapel of Tergnée, near Farciennes in Belgium was demolished, the workmen discovered five old coffins. In each of these coffins a large nail had been driven though the coffin lid at the place where the heart of the corpse would have been. The nails, which were up to 68 inches long and inscribed with the initials of the Batthyány-Waldstein family, were taken to the Archeological Museum of Charleroi. The Batthyány-Waldsteins were said to have inherited the Château de Farciennes some time around the middle of the eighteenth century. Unfortunately, the nails subsequently were lost while at the museum, but researcher Paul de Saint-Hillaire is convinced that the coffins must have been those of five former inhabitants of the Château de Farciennes – Count Karl-Joseph of Batthyány, said to be a descendant of Vlad the Impaler, his wife, Anna von Wald-stein, the daughter of a Bohemian nobleman, and their three children. It appears to have been tradition in the Batthyány-Waldstein family to nail down the dead in order to prevent their return as vampires.

The nailing down of corpses was a fairly commonplace way to prevent the dead rising from their graves, but what makes this case special is its location. Belgium is not one of the traditional vampire locations and the case illustrates how this Hungarian family brought their traditions and customs with them to Farciennes.

See also: Burial Customs

Fealaar, Vampire of

A Scottish story, the tale of the vampire of Fealaar was reported in *Selected Highland Folk Tales* by R. Macdonald Robertson, published in 1961. The story tells of two poachers who take refuge in an ancient house near Fealaar, a few miles from Braemar. As the door was locked the two men entered by a window. One of the men needed some water and as he put one leg over the windowsill to leave he felt something seize and bite his leg and drink blood. The man pulled his leg away and searched the area for an animal. He did not find anything but in the distance he saw blue lights and a white winged object. As a result the man carried a scar for the rest of his life on the leg that was bitten, and the rumor circulated that the house was haunted by a vampire.

Federal Vampire and Zombie Agency (FVZA)

The Federal Vampire and Zombie Agency was an organization that between the years of 1868 and 1975 allegedly controlled America's vampire and zombie population while overseeing scientific research into the undead.

According to the FVZA website (www.fvza.org/index.html), which was *"set up as a tribute to the men and women who served in the FVZA, especially the over 4000 Agents who lost their lives fighting to keep our country safe,"* vampires supposedly arrived in America with the first European settlers. During this time fighting vampires was a task left to local militias, known as the Vampire National Guard. However, as the country became more urbanized the need for an organized, well-trained force to combat the growing plague of vampires became evident. *"The Civil War delayed implementation until 1868, when President Ulysses S. Grant officially formed the Federal Vampire and Zombie Agency."*

The website goes on to state that at first the FVZA was a specialized branch of the Armed Forces and the troops were known as the Vanguard, a contraction of Vampire National Guard. However, when the huge surge of immigrants coming to America increased the vampire population to 300,000 by the turn of the century, President William McKinley moved the FVZA into the Department of Justice. In addition to hunting down vampires and zombies, the agency had an important role in aiding the medical community's understanding of vampire physiology and the spread of the infection.

The FVZA website, overseen by the enigmatic Dr. Hugo Pecos, who claims to have seen vampires, also contains a timeline of significant events in vampire history, reports of vampire sightings, past and present, as well as interesting information about the biology and sociology of vampires, zombies, and werewolves. The lack of historical accuracy in the FVZA website and the unsubstantiated nature of the claims it makes has led few vampire experts to take it seriously.

Feehan, Christine

Christine Feehan is an American romance/paranormal writer, born in California, who has numerous bestselling, award-winning novels to her credit. Some literary critics believe that she reinvented the vampire novel with her bestselling Carpathian series of novels, which launched in 1999 with *Dark Prince*; the twentieth novel in the series, *Dark Slayer*, is due to be published in 2009.

In Feehan's novels the Carpathians are a powerful and ancient race with the ability to shape-shift and live for over a thousand years. Although they feed on human blood, for the most part they don't kill their human prey and manage to live among humans undetected. Despite their gifts, the Carpathians are on the edge of extinction. Only a few children have

been born in recent centuries and the ones that are born are male and die young. It has been several centuries since a female was born and in the absence of female company, known as "life mates," male Carpathians lose their ability to see in color and feel emotion. The only feeling left for them is the thrill of making a kill, but once they do this they lose their soul and become the monsters of vampire legend, the "undead." With so few females left, males must choose between committing suicide or transforming into a vampire. However, if they do find a "life mate," their ability to feel and see in color is restored, and their souls are saved.

See also: **LITERATURE**

Female Vampires

Although the dominant form of the male vampire who preys on vulnerable females has tended to overshadow the role of the female vampire in the creation of the vampire myth, female vampires, also known as vampira, and vampiress, are mentioned in centuries-old folktales from all over the world.

Female vampires in folklore

Many vampire-like females, such as Kali, the dangerous goddess of India, can be found in polytheistic cultures. In some cultures the oldest vampires were female. They included the Greek lamia, the Jewish Lilith, and the Malaysian langsuir. The stories and myths linked to these figures indicate that the origins of the oldest vampires in the world may well have been rooted in the savage hurt, pain, and anger caused by the loss of a child, and even though all these figures went on to develop unique characteristics, at some time or other they merged with the traits of the sexually aggressive woman or vamp. In addition, supernatural entities, like the succubus, behaved in a vampiric sexual way, attacking men at night in their beds and leaving them feeling drained and depleted in the morning.

In Europe there are several hundred reports of female vampires. In these the female vampire typically shares the same strange, physical and predatory characteristics as the male. One nineteenth-century report from Devon, England, states how rumors grew about the wasting disease of a farmer called Jack. It was said that Jack's wife had long, sharp fingernails and very pale skin, and when guests came to dinner she never ate. One night Jack witnessed his wife gliding towards him as he lay in bed. She tried to bite him and then changed into an eel and escaped.

In the nineteenth century the gathering of information about two historical figures was largely responsible for the creation of the modern view of vampires. The first of these figures was the fifteenth-century Wallachian prince, Vlad the Impaler, but the second was the seventeenth-century Hungarian countess, Elizabeth Báthory. An early account of the Countess's blood-drinking reign of terror was circulated in the 1720s and translated into English in 1865 in Sabine Baring-Gould's *The Book of Werewolves*. Many experts believed that Báthory's career directly influenced Bram Stoker when he created *Dracula* in 1897.

Literary female vampires

As far as vampire literature is concerned, virtually all of the first literary vampires were females. Goethe's *Bride of Corinth* (1797) is based on a story from ancient Greece about a young virgin who dies and returns from the grave to enjoy her sexuality. In English literature it is very possible that the first vampire figure to appear was a woman called Geraldine in Samuel Taylor Coleridge's poem, *Christabel*. However, after John Polidori introduced the character of Lord Ruthven in 1819, vampire literature tended to be dominated by the figure of the male vampire for about fifty years. Then in 1872, Sheridan Le Fanu wrote his novella *Carmilla* about a 200-year-old vampire who, like her male counterparts, preys on vulnerable young women.

In the twentieth century male vampires tended to dominate vampire fiction again but there were exceptions, mirroring the rise of feminism. In 1969, one of the most popular female vampire characters, Vampirella, appeared, not in a novel but in a comic. And in literature female vampires were gradually transforming from vamps into powerful figures with real leadership qualities. For example, in her bestselling Vampire Chronicles, Anne Rice introduces several powerful female vampires, including Akasha, a commanding female, and Lestat's mother, Gabrielle.

Although there have been notable and influential exceptions, in general it can be said that vampires tend to be stereotyped in literature as a personification of male desires for sex and power and in its most negative form the vampire story has a misogynistic edge. However, in recent years the females that the male vampire encounters have become much more complicated, powerful, and resourceful. For example, in Stephenie Meyer's *Twilight* (2005) Bella Swan is more than a match for her vampire lover. It has also been suggested by literary critics that the bite marks of the vampire resemble the fangs not of a canine but of a snake, and in ancient myth the bite of a snake is associated with the onset of menstruation and womanhood. As such the vampire myth could be said to be about the empowerment and discovery of sexuality not just in men but in women as well.

See also: **AMINE; ASANBOSAM; ASWANG; BRUXSA; CHORDEWA; CHUREL; CIVATATEO; DANAG; ESTRIE; HANNYA; HECATE; JIGARKHWAR; LA LLORONA; LEANHAUM-SHEE; LOOGAROO; MANDURUGO; MARA; MOROI; OLD HAG; PENANGGALAN; STRIX**

Ferrell, Rod (1980-)

Roderick Justin Ferrell was the leader of a gang of teenagers from Murray, Kentucky, infamously known as the Vampire Clan. Clearly unstable and mentally ill, he told people he had no soul and was a 500-year-old vampire named Vasago. In 1998, Ferrell pleaded guilty to the double slaying of a couple from Eustis, Florida, becoming the youngest person in the United States on Death Row.

On Thanksgiving Day in 1996, Ferrell, age 16 at the time, killed the parents of a former girlfriend. He had become obsessed with a vampire fantasy role-playing game Vampire: The Masquerade, but he did not find it sadistic

enough and formed what he called the Vampire Clan. His aim was to "open the gates of hell" by killing people and stealing their souls. Within a few days of the murders he was arrested, and although he told his arresting officers he was a vampire and too powerful for them to hold for long, he eventually pleaded guilty and was given the death penalty. In September 1999, the Florida Supreme Court reduced his sentence to life without parole.

See also: **CLINICAL VAMPIRISM; CRIME**

Feu-follet

The feu-follet, also known as the fifollet, is one of the most definable vampire figures reported among African Americans. Believed to be the soul of a child who had died before baptism, or the soul of a dead person who was sent back to earth by God to do penance (but instead attacked people), the feu-follet resembled the traditional will-o'-the-wisp. The great majority of reported attacks were merely to do with nuisance making, but on occasion they resembled the attack of the incubus/succubus figure or the attack of a vampire that sucked the life blood out of its victims.

Films

There are literally hundreds of vampire films or movies, with more coming out as each year passes, for every taste, style, and production budget. They range from the formulaic to the trashy and gross, to the weird and grim, to the scary and sexy, to the intelligent and original. In this Encyclopedia it would be impossible to cover every vampire movie released and this entry simply provides an overview of the best-known films made since the 1950s. It is important to bear in mind, however, that any discussion of the success, accuracy, or quality of a vampire movie will always be subjective.

Nosferatu

Nosferatu (1922), directed by F. W. Murnau, was an unlicensed version of Bram Stoker's *Dracula*, based so closely on the novel that the Stoker estate sued and won, with all copies of the film ordered to be destroyed. To this day it is still regarded by many vampire movie enthusiasts as the definitive vampire movie.

Dracula

The first official *Dracula* film adapted from Bram Stoker's 1897 novel was a Universal Pictures production released in 1931, directed by Tod Browning and staring Béla Lugosi. The film launched Lugosi into stardom and was a financial success for Universal, but the era of the vampire movie dynasty did not really begin in earnest until the 1950s when Universal sold the rights to *Dracula* to a low-budget, up-and-coming British studio called Hammer Films. Hammer reinvented the image of the vampire by giving its audience more explicit blood, violence, and sex than previous *Dracula* movies.

The first of many Hammer vampire movies was *The Horror of Dracula* (1958), starring Christopher Lee as Dracula and Peter Cushing as Van Helsing. Hammer Films immediately tried to build on the success and popularity of *Horror of Dracula* and released a number of equally bloody sequels, some of which were more successful than others. These sequels included:

- Brides of Dracula *(1960)*: *Van Helsing, played by Peter Cushing again, gets vampirized but manages to overcome the bite wound in the end.*

- Dracula, Prince of Darkness *(1965)*: *Christopher Lee returned in the title role to entertain and scare the life out of visitors to his castle.*

- Taste the Blood of Dracula *(1970)*: *Children are vampirized by Dracula and turn on their parents.*

- Vampire Lovers *(1970)*: *Screen adaptation of Sheridan Le Fanu's* Carmilla *starring Ingrid Pitt in the title role. In 1971 a sequel,* Lust for a Vampire, *starring Yutte Stensgaard as Carmilla was released.*

- Countess Dracula *(1971)*: *Story of the infamous, blood-drinking Countess Elizabeth Báthory, starring Ingrid Pitt in the title role.*

- Dracula, A.D., 1972 *(1972)*: *The story of Dracula set in 'hip' 1972 London.*

- The Satanic Rites of Dracula *(1973)*: *Christopher Lee reprised the role of Dracula for the final time. The film is set in London and is about a new strain of deadly bacteria.*

Hammer Films did not have a monopoly on successful vampire films during the 1960s and 70s. Italian director Mario Bava, who specialized in stylish, atmospheric horror films, produced several notable vampire movies, including *Black Sunday* (1960), *Black Sabbath* (1963), and *Blood and Black Lace* (1964). American International Pictures also had a good run of vampire movies that featured two new original American vampires, Count Yorga and Blacula. *Count Yorga, Vampire* (1970) dramatized the idea that there is nothing good people can do to stop the deadly proliferation of vampires. *Blacula* (1972) starred William Marshall as the noble but bloodthirsty and doomed African vampire prince.

Characteristics of film vampires

Vampires of film typically combine features of both the revenant or animated corpse of folk-lore and the seductive aristocrat of literature, but in the 1970s and 80s a new breed of younger "cool" vampires began to emerge on screen. These vampires were either good hearted or warped by evil. One of the first hip, young vampire movies to hit the screens was *The Hunger* (1983), which starred Catherine Deneuve and David Bowie as a vampire couple who seek out their prey in punk nightclubs. *Fright Night* (1985) was another movie featuring hip, young vampires and many regard it as one of the first quality horror comedies.

Coming-of-age vampire movies developed in 1987 when *Near Dark* and *The Lost Boys* – both films about the complications of growing up as a vampire – were released. These and other youth vampire movies set the scene for the 1992 movie, *Buffy the Vampire Slayer*, which paved the way for the hugely successful TV show of the same name.

Along the way a number of low-budget vampire movies, including *Andy Warhol's Dracula* (1974), about a vampire who can only drink the blood of virgins, and *The Addiction* (1995), about a philosophy student who is turned into a vampire, began to make up their own vampire rules. In addition, beginning with the absurd *Abbott and Costello Meet Frankenstein* (1948), a surprisingly high number of vampire movies were produced as comedies and spoofs. *Love at First Bite* (1979) was a farce directed by Roman Polanski; *Vampire's Kiss* (1989) starred Nicolas Cage as a New Yorker who believes he is a vampire; *Dead and Loving It* (1995) was a spoof directed by Mel Brooks; and *Vampire in Brooklyn* (1995) starred comedian Eddie Murphy as a vampire from the Caribbean.

Blockbusters

Although art-house films and spoofs have their audience, it was the big-budget Hollywood vampire films with lots of action and special effects that tended to be more financially successful for film makers and reliably entertaining for the viewing public. In 1992, *Bram Stoker's Dracula*, directed by Francis Ford Coppola, arrived in cinemas. Although it was a box-office success, many vampirologists protested that the movie was not faithful to the novel as the title suggests because it introduced many variations, including an opening sequence about Vlad the Impaler battling the Turks. In 1994 Anne's Rice's bestselling novel *Interview with the Vampire* was transferred to the screen, becoming one of the highest grossing movies in the US that year. Then in 1998 the box-office smash hit *Blade*, starring Wesley Snipes as a half-vampire/half vampire hunter, exploded onto the screen with ninja-style fighting and, quite literally, a shower of blood.

In the years that followed, although a number of vampire films or films featuring important vampire characters or vampire hunters appeared, including *The League of Extraordinary Gentlemen* (2003) and *Van Helsing* (2004), it was not until 2007 that the film world was set alight again with *I Am Legend*, a post-apocalyptic science-fiction film directed by Francis Lawrence and starring Will Smith.

In 2008 *Let the Right One In*, an acclaimed Swedish animated horror movie based on the novel of the same name, appeared and was greeted with much enthusiasm by fans of vampire cinema. The movie *Twilight*, based on Stephenie Meyer's bestselling Twilight Saga series, was also released in 2008. In the book and movie a human, Bella Swan, falls in love with the "vegetarian" (he drinks the blood of animals not humans) vampire Edward Cullen. *Twilight* was released in American cinemas on November 21 and grossed $35.7 million on its opening day, the biggest opening-day take for a non-sequel and non-summer movie. The record-breaking success of *Twilight* has once again breathed new life into vampire movies and set the stage for other vampire-related movies with sizeable budgets and bankable stars to appear in them.

Must-see vampire movies

The following list of must-see vampire films is arranged in no particular order and is by no means definitive as taste in vampires movies differs from person to person but, hopefully, it will help introduce anyone or serve as a starting point to some of the greatest vampire movies of all time.

Interview with the Vampire (1994)

Twilight (2008)

Let the Right One In (2008)

Fright Night (1985)

Bram Stoker's Dracula (1992)

Cronos (1993)

Horror of Dracula (1958)

Nosferatu: The Vampyre (1979)

Dracula (1931)

Black Sunday (1960)

Blacula (1972)

The Addiction (1995)

Blade (1998)

Near Dark (1997)

I Am Legend (2007)

The Lost Boys (1987)

From Dusk till Dawn (1996)

Underworld (2003)

Nosferatu, eine Symphonie des Grauens (1922)

See also: COMICS; LITERATURE; STAGE; TELEVISION

Finding Vampires

When the identity of a vampire was not known to its victims or to others certain procedures could be used to identify its grave. In Eastern Europe professional vampire hunters or dhampirs might be employed to find, and then destroy a vampire.

Methods used to find and identify a vampire included the scattering of ashes or salt around graves to reveal the imprint of vampire feet. A blue light hovering around a grave at night was a telltale sign, as were graves with holes in them, graves that were sunken, and graves that had crooked crosses or tombstones. A white horse that refused to step over a particular grave was another sign as the horse was considered a symbol of purity. Finally, if there were no obvious external signs of vampire habitation, vampire hunters would simply dig up graves and examine corpses.

See also: **Detecting Vampires**

Fingernails

In Bram Stoker's *Dracula* (1897), to enhance his animal-like quality the Count is depicted as having long, sharp, and fine fingernails. Long nails were often said to be a typical characteristic of the undead of folklore. The association of long fingernails with vampires probably developed in parts of Europe during vampire hunts, when bodies were exhumed from their graves and corpses with long nails — nails look as if they have grown after death because the skin recedes — were declared to be vampires. Fresh nails were a common item mentioned in Eastern European and German vampire reports.

Finland

One of the northernmost countries in the world, situated between Sweden and Russia, the myths and legends of the ancient Finns were gathered together in the nineteenth century and recorded in the *Kalevala*, the national epic poem of Finland. It reveals a mythology that has a highly developed concept of the underworld, called *Manala* or *Tuonela*. Death in Finn mythology was personified by a figure called *Kalma*, which means "god of the tombs." Guarding *Kalma* was *Surma*, a monster with sharp fangs who, like his mistress, drinks the blood of humans. In Finland there was also an ancient tradition of impaling corpses to prevent them from leaving their graves, as it was believed that the spirits of the restless dead could spread disease and death.

Fire

Since ancient times, fire has been regarded as a symbol of the purifying force of goodness and light against the force of evil and darkness. It was also a sign of sacredness and divinity, illustrated by God appearing to Moses in the Old Testament in the form of a burning bush to send him to Egypt to free his people. Just as fire was used to save towns and villages from the plague, in Eastern Europe it was also used to burn witches and heretics, and was considered the most effective tool to stop the undead. From Bulgaria and Romania to Russia and Poland, if lesser means failed (i.e. impaling the corpse with a stake or decapitation) the body of a suspected vampire was burned.

Fire that is applied as an act of defense can threaten a vampire but it is often not enough to destroy the vampire completely. This is why cremation – the total reduction of the vampire's body to ashes – is always preferred. In the words of vampirologist Montague Summers in *The Vampire in Europe* (1929):

To burn the body of the Vampire is generally accepted to be by far the supremely efficacious method of ridding a district of this demonical pest, and it is the common practice all over the world. The bodies of all those whom he may have infected with vampirish poison by sucking their blood are also for security sake cremated … Any animals which may come forth from the fire – worms, beetles, birds of horrible and deformed shape – must be driven back into the flames for it may be the Vampire embodied in one of these, seeking to escape so that he can renew his foul parasitism of death. The ashes of the pyre should be scattered to the winds, or cast into a river swiftly flowing into the sea.

Although Bram Stoker made no mention of fire in his novel, there are few other literary works or films that do not. In Anne Rice's Vampire Chronicles, along with exposure to sunlight, cremation was the only known way to destroy a vampire, or for a vampire to destroy him or herself.

Fishing Nets

In some Gypsy villages fishing nets were dropped over the doors of houses to prevent the attack of a vampire. It was thought that vampires who tried to enter the house would be compelled to count all the knots in the nets before feeding. The placing of fishing nets is associated with the idea that vampires have obsessive compulsive traits and that if they were presented with knots, or seeds, or grains, it would distract them from the business of spreading disease and death.

See also: **APOTROPAICS; PREVENTION**

Flea/flies

In Slavic folklore fleas and flies were forms that a vampire could transform itself into. Possible explanations for this belief include the blood-sucking activities of fleas, as well as the association with dirt and disease. Although many would not have been aware of it at the time, the flea was indeed a carrier of disease and plague and in this way it could be said that insects fueled the eighteenth-century vampire hysteria. In Russia, it was believed that when the corpse of a vampire was burned, any insect that escaped had to be caught and killed, even one as small as a flea or a fly, as it could be the vampire escaping. Flies are not blood-suckers, but in much the same way as the flea they were associated with disease, dirt, death, and the undead.

See also: **ANIMAL VAMPIRES; BUTTERFLY**

Flückinger, Johann

Johann Flückinger was an eighteenth-century Austrian army surgeon who documented several vampire cases in Serbia and it was his research that led to the spread of the word "vampire" into the English language.

While stationed in Belgrade, Flückinger was sent with other medical officers to investigate reports of vampire attacks around

Medvegja. On January 7, 1732, Flückinger published his report, *Visum et Repertum*, which contained a number of detailed accounts of vampires, focusing on individual cases, including that of Arnold Paole. It was quickly translated into other languages, including French and English, and created a sensation around Europe because it stated categorically that vampires did exist and were poised to spread like a plague throughout the German-speaking world. The report also prompted other researchers, Dom Augustin Calmet among them, to investigate the phenomenon.

On March 4, 1732, the *London Journal* printed an almost exact translation of the account, marking the introduction of the word "vampire" into common English.

Flying Vampires

Often associated with witchcraft and sorcery, flying vampires are part of vampiric lore all over the world, but they are especially common in Asia. And although there are flying males, flying is traditionally linked to female vampires, for example the aswang and danag of the Philippines and the langsuir of Malaysia. As some Chinese vampires aged they transformed into flying creatures. In many cases flying is the means by which the vampire reaches her victim, landing on rooftops or entering through windows.

In general, European vampires cannot fly, though they can levitate and some vampire-like entities – such as the banshee and bruxsa – can fly. However, one way a vampire was said to fly in European vampire lore was by transforming itself into a bird, butterfly, insect, or bat. In the nineteenth century, when the vampiric condi-

tion was increasingly attributed to a disease or blood condition or personality disorder, the vampire's ability to fly and shape-shift was increasingly regarded as unbelievable. Most twentieth- and twenty-first-century vampires in fiction and film fly by transforming themselves into a bat, although the vampires of Anne Rice and Stephenie Meyer are exceptions and appear to be able to fly under their own steam.

Folklore

The vampire originated with the folklore associated with revenant beings, the restless dead or corpses that returned from the grave to harm the living for reasons of revenge or malice. Being a reanimated corpse or evil spirit, however, was not enough to be classed as a vampire; a "true" vampire must drain the blood or vital essence of its victim. In vampire lore blood is highly symbolic, and is associated with the soul or life force or personality of a person as well as with innocence and sexuality, and these associations make the vampire a timeless creature of folklore and myth.

There is folklore in almost every culture about vampires. Some experts think that the vampire concept dates back to the civilizations of ancient India, China, and Egypt, however, it is the vampire lore of Europe, and in particular Eastern Europe, that has had the most impact on Western popular culture, because in non-Western folklore vampires tend to be blurred with other malevolent spirit beings.

Characteristics of folklore vampires

In general, the vampire of European folklore was very different from the sophisticated,

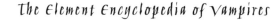

aristocratic vampire familiar to us through fiction and film. It typically appeared in the form of a reanimated, foul-smelling, decaying, bloated corpse with rancid breath, long finger-nails and hair, sharp teeth, and red eyes, but it could also appear in much the same form as it did in life, although with an insatiable desire for food or sex or blood (sometimes for all three). It could also appear in the form of a ghost who ethereally transported blood back to the corpse it inhabited. This phantom-like creature, which is found in some famous cases of vampirism, including that of Peter Plogo-jowitz (1725), could feed on living people while they were asleep at night. Whatever form it assumed, the vampire was said to be most active and deadly at night. Sunlight was not necessarily a threat but it could weaken the vampire; the theme of destruction by sun-light was, however, not fully introduced into vampire mythology until 1922 in the land-mark film *Nosferatu.*

According to various European traditions, suicides, criminals, blasphemers, and children born with cauls, hair, or teeth could become vampires, and in some regions red-haired or left-handed children or children born out of wedlock were regarded as suspect. A vampire could be repelled or kept in its coffin by a num-ber of different objects including crucifixes, holy objects, and wild roses and substances such as garlic. Sometimes it was said that the vampire could be thwarted by his or her com-pulsive need to count seeds or untie knots, and in some traditions a vampire cannot enter a place where it is not invited or cross running water. The destruction of a vampire could be accomplished by burning the corpse or by decapitation or, most commonly, by impaling it with a wooden stake.

Food

The practice of providing food for the dead is common throughout the world and throughout history, either to prevent corpses from becom-ing restless or, more simply, because it was assumed that the world of the dead was similar to the world of the living and the dead would need to eat. In parts of Romania in the seven-teenth and eighteenth centuries it was custom-ary for a relative of the deceased to carry wine and bread to the grave. It was believed that the presence of food would relieve the strigoi or vampire of the need for human flesh and blood.

It is often assumed that vampires only drink blood but some vampires of folklore enjoy a varied and sometimes disgusting diet. For example, the Indian bhuta will eat manure or excrement, and the ekimmu of Assyria can eat ordinary food. In addition, psychic vampires feed on the psychic energies of those around them. In general, though, in folklore and literature and film, blood remains the vampire's favored source of nourishment.

Forever Knight

Forever Knight was a Canadian television show about a modern-day vampire who worked as a police detective in Toronto. It enjoyed some ratings success during the early 1990s.

The television series originated in 1989 as *Nick Knight*, a made-for-television movie with rock star Rick Springfield in the title role. Despite his desire to be part of the human community, Knight must still consume blood to survive. The movie aired on the CBS net-work but was not regarded as having enough ratings to warrant a TV series. In 1992, CBS tried again, renaming the series *Forever Knight*. From the outset the series suffered from low budgets and major cast and time-slot changes, and although it earned a dedicated and enthusiastic fan base – some of whom remain dedicated to the re-runs of the show to this day – it was canceled after three seasons.

"For the Blood is the Life"

"For the Blood is the Life" is a short story written by American author Frances Marion Crawford and published posthumously in 1911. Functioning on many levels of sinister and supernatural horror it is regarded as a classic in traditional vampire literature.

The story is set in Italy and tells the story of a young Gypsy girl called Cristina who is rejected by a handsome boy called Angelo. She later dies at the hands of thieves and the violent and sudden manner of her death, and her unrequited love for Angelo, bring her back from the grave to feed on him until her destruction.

At twilight, when the day's work was done, instead of hanging about in the open space before the church with young fellows of his own age, he [Angelo] took to wandering in lonely places on the outskirts of the village till it was quite dark. Then he slunk home and went to bed to save the expense of a light. But in those lonely twilight hours he began to have strange waking dreams. He was not always alone, for often when he sat on the stump of a tree, where the narrow path turns down the gorge, he was sure that a woman came up noiselessly over the rough stones, as if her feet were bare; and she stood under a clump of chestnut trees only half a dozen yards down the path, and beckoned to him without speaking.

Though she was in the shadow he knew that her lips were red, and that when they parted a little and smiled at him she showed two small sharp teeth. He knew this at first rather than saw it, and he knew that it was Cristina, and that she was dead. Yet he was not afraid; he only wondered whether it was a dream, for he thought that if he had been awake he should have been frightened.

Besides, the dead woman had red lips, and that could only happen in a dream. Whenever he went near the gorge after sunset she was already there waiting for him, or else she very soon appeared, and he began to be sure of her blood-red mouth, but now each feature grew distinct, and the pale face looked at him with deep and hungry eyes.

(From *For the Blood is the Life by* F. Marion Crawford)

Fortune, Dion (1890–1946)

Dion Fortune was the occult name of Violet Mary Firth, considered by some to be one of the most important occultists of the twentieth century. An exponent of the concept of psychic vampirism, Fortune wrote several important works including *Psychic Self-Defence* (1930), in which she set out her theories concerning the subject of psychic attack and psychic self-defense and recounted her own experience of a psychic attack. She also wrote the vampire short story "Blood Lust" (1926).

Fortune was born in Llandudno, Wales, on December 6, 1890. Her mother was a Christian Scientist and her father a solicitor, and the family motto, which Fortune later used as her magical motto and the inspiration for her magical name, was "Deo, non Fortuna," meaning "By God, not by chance."

Fortune's interest in magic and the occult were not sparked until the age of 20, when she went to work in an educational institution and was under the supervision of a woman who had studied occultism in India. According to Fortune, this woman was a bully with a foul temper, who used hypnosis and the projection of negative thoughts, called psychic attack, to get her own way and destroy Fortune's self-confidence. Fortune managed to survive these psychic attacks but experienced a three-year-long nervous breakdown.

The experience stimulated Fortune's interest in the human mind and, while she was recovering, she began to study psychology and Freudian analysis. By the age of 23 she had become a psychoanalyst and was convinced that many of her patients were not mentally ill but victims of psychic attack.

At the end of the Great War, after serving in the Women's Land Army, Fortune met Theodore Moriarty, an Irishman, occultist, and freemason, who gave her training in the occult. Her learning experiences with Moriarty are featured in her occult autobiography, *Psychic Self-Defence*. In *Psychic Self-Defence* Fortune, drawing on her own experiences of psychic attack, describes the elements of psychic attack as vampirism, nervous exhaustion, and a wasting of the body into a *"mere bloodless shell of skin and bones."* Fortune suggested that occult masters had the unconscious or conscious power to separate their psychic self from their physical body and to attach it to another and drain that person's energy. Symptoms of psychic attack could manifest as bite marks on the neck, ear lobes, and breasts.

Dion Fortune was a prolific author. As well as *Psychic Self-Defence*, considered by many to be the definitive text on the subject, and *The Mystical Qabalah*, in which she outlines how the kabbalah can be used by Western students, she also wrote on the occult and published a number of novels. She was well known in her day and attracted many devoted followers. In 1927 she married Welsh physician and occultist Penry Evans, who brought a new pagan element to her work. The marriage was stormy and they divorced in 1939.

See also: **ASTRAL BODY; OCCULT**

Forty Days

A period of time that has been associated in European folklore with the life span of a vampire, perhaps because it recalled the forty days Christ spent being tempted by the Devil in the wilderness.

According to Bulgarian lore, a corpse took forty days to transform into the undead; during this period the corpse remained bloated and the bones were like jelly. After the forty days the undead (ubour) took a skeleton form again and could emerge from the grave looking like normal human beings. It was also said that vampires haunted cemeteries and grave sites at night, but only for forty days.

See also: **LIFE OF A VAMPIRE**

Fowl

Hens or cocks are domesticated birds that figure in certain rituals to appease vampires or to help cure a victim of vampirism. In India a person believed to be bitten or attacked by a vampire would have the blood of a cock rubbed all over his or her body. The Russians also used the blood of a fowl to cure vampirism. The aim in both these rituals was to appease the vampire so that it would be satisfied with the death of the fowl and leave the victim alone. Other European traditions held that if a fowl jumped or flew over a corpse the dead person was doomed to vampirism, and it was also thought that fowl could become vampires themselves, or that vampires could shape-shift into hens or cocks to prey on the living.

See also: **BIRDS**

Fox

See: **ANIMAL VAMPIRES; KITSUNE**

France

France possesses few original vampire traditions, although it does have a number of shocking cases of living vampires – sadistic murderers who drank the blood of their victims. Heading the list is Gilles de Rais. De Rais was a respected soldier who fought against the English during the Hundred Years War, but he was also a murderer who took sexual pleasure in torturing and killing young children. It was a struggle to bring him to trial but he was eventually convicted and strangled before his body was burned. Other famous so-called living vampires from France include: Sergeant Bertrand, Antoine Léger, and Victor Ardisson.

According to respected vampirologist Montague Summers, who conducted extensive research on vampires in the early part of the twentieth century, the absence of a specific body of beliefs in France is intriguing and perhaps deliberate given the fact that Roman and Germanic influences shaped Gallic culture.

The idea of the vampire was introduced into France at the end of the seventeenth century, but without a firm basis in folklore and legend it remained a neglected topic. The subject seems to have been raised in 1693 by a Polish priest who asked the faculty of the Sorbonne to give him advice on how to deal with corpses suspected of being vampires. In 1737, the *Lettres Juives* (Jewish Letters) included accounts of some famous Serbian vampire cases but the subject did not become an issue for the French public until the publication in 1746 of Dom Augustin Calmet's research on vampires, which considered the reports of vampires in Eastern Europe and called for further study. Calmet's refusal to dismiss vampires as the product of superstition and ignorance earned widespread scorn among French scholars.

Viscount de Morieve

Alongside notorious historical vampires like Gilles de Rais, the interesting historical case of the Viscount de Morieve, a French nobleman who was fortunate enough to keep his estates during the French Revolution, deserves special mention. He was assassinated shortly after the

Revolution, but not before he had executed many of his employees as revenge for the ridicule he suffered during the turmoil. After his burial, according to reports, a number of young children died unexpectedly. These accounts continued for over 70 years. Eventually his grandson decided to investigate the allegations and had the vault opened. While all the other corpses were decayed the Viscount's was still fresh and free of decay, and blood was found in the heart and chest. New nails had also grown and the skin was soft. The body was removed and a whitethorn stake driven into the heart; allegedly the corpse made a groaning sound. The corpse was then burned and from that day on there were no more reports of unusual deaths.

Mélusine

There are also two traditions from French folklore which deserve mention. The first concerns the *mélusine*, a creature who is not a vampire as such but does indicate the direction of some vampire traditions in folklore and literature.

Mélusine, the daughter of King Elianas and his fairy wife, reportedly was turned into a serpent from the waist down by her mother after she and her sisters turned their magic against their parents. Mélusine was forced to remain this way until she found a man who would marry her on the condition he would never see her on a Saturday, when her serpent body reappeared. Raymond of Poitou accepted Mélusine's terms. The two married and Mélusine helped him build a kingdom. Sadly, their children were born deformed and deranged. In anger Raymond declared that he knew Mélusine's secret and from that moment

Mélusine was condemned to fly forever through the air in pain. Until the kingdom fell it was said she would appear before the death of each of Raymond's heirs, and after that before the death of a French king, to wail and lament like a banshee.

Le Grand Bissetere

The second tradition from French folklore is an entity known as *Le Grand Bissetere*, which has clear vampiric tendencies. This creature was said to be a beautiful but gaunt figure that hovered around forest roads and woodland pools in rural Provence making moaning sounds like a screech owl and dancing in the moonlight, beckoning passers-by to their doom. Meeting this entity was considered extremely unlucky as it was thought capable of drawing the life from those it encountered and leaving them dead.

Frankincense

Frankincense is an aromatic resin taken from different types of trees found in East Africa and then turned into a kind of incense. It is clearly associated with the birth of Christ. In Dalmatia and Albania frankincense was used by the clergy to bless the knives and stakes used in destroying vampires.

Freud, Sigmund (1856–1939)

Sigmund Freud was an Austrian psychiatrist who founded the psychoanalytic school of psychology. He is best known for his theories of the unconscious mind and the defense mechanism of repression, and for creating the clinical practice of psychoanalysis for curing psychiatric and emotional disorders through dialogue between a patient and a psychoanalyst. Freud is also well known for the way he redefined sexuality as the major motivational energy of human life, as well as for his therapeutic techniques, including the use of free association, his theory of transference in the therapeutic relationship, and the interpretation of dreams as sources of insight into the unconscious mind. According to vampire expert David Skal, although the father of psychoanalysis did not write directly about vampires, his theories on hysteria, phallic symbolism, sexual repression, oral gratification, and the death wish have given vampirologists and commentators on vampire literature their critical compass over the years.

Sex and death

A strong tie to the Freudian doctrine of the oral stage of psycho-sexual development is quite obvious in the comfort and pleasure derived from taking nourishment through the sucking of blood. Freud also felt that sex and death were intertwined and indeed the death of many famous literary vampires can be viewed from a sexual perspective in that the most common method of killing female vampires is through the insertion of a stick, knife, or stake through the heart, all of which can be seen as pointed, phallic symbols.

Freud also studied the phenomenon of sexual arousal through sado-masochistic action, and there is often a strong sense in much vampire fiction that the vampire not only sucks its victim's blood but seduces them as well. This erotic scene from Bram Stoker's *Dracula* (1897) illustrates just such an event:

The girl went on her knees, and bent over me, simply gloating. There was a deliberate voluptuousness which was both thrilling and repulsive, and as she arched her neck she actually licked her lips like an animal, 'till I could see in the moonlight the moisture shining on the scarlet lips and on the red tongue as it lapped the sharp white teeth … There she paused, and I could hear the churning sound of her tongue as it licked her teeth and lips, and could feel the hot breath on my neck … I could feel the soft, shivering touch of the lips on the super-sensitive skin on my throat, and the hard dents of two sharp teeth, just touching and pausing there. I closed my eyes in languorous ecstasy and waited … waited with a beating heart.

See also: **PSYCHOLOGICAL EXPLANATIONS OF VAMPIRISM; SEX**

Funeral

See: **BURIAL CUSTOMS; CORPSE**

"I am the shadow on the moon at night, filling your dreams to the brim with fright."

The Nightmare Before Christmas

Games, Vampire

Since the 1960s vampire board, role-playing, and computer games have become increasingly popular. The games were at first spin-offs from vampire novels, films, and TV shows but as public appetite for vampires grew, novels became spin-offs from the games.

Board games

One of the first vampire board games to appear was the Barnabas Collins "Dark Shadows" game, inspired by the Gothic TV soap opera *Dark Shadows*. In the game players must assemble a skeleton on a scaffold. The winner gets to wear Barnabas's fangs. Other board games featuring vampires, vampire hunting, and vampire murder mysteries followed in the 1970s and 80s. In 1992 the movie *Bram Stoker's Dracula* inspired a spin-off board game, computer game, and role-playing game.

Role-playing games

For many years board games were the only vampire games, but in the 1990s role-playing games joined them. Role-playing games establish a complete fantasy world with a history, characters, and rules of engagement, but what makes them unique is that they enable players to enter the story they also tell. Largely as a result of the success of *Dungeons and Dragons* – a magic and fantasy game which featured vampires – role-playing games became extremely popular.

In 1991, White Wolf Inc. introduced *Vampire: The Masquerade*, a game created by Mark Rein-Hagen, which soon established itself as one of the most popular role-playing games, with tens of thousands of players all over the world. The success of the game owes much to the dark allure of the virtual world on which it is based, a world of darkness, in which vampires run things, compete with each other for power, and hunt for human prey while keeping their identity a secret. Although *Vampire: The Masquerade* has been the most popular vampire-themed role-playing game, it was not the only one released in the 1990s. Others included *Nightlife* (1990), *Vampire Kingdom* (1991), and *Bram Stoker's Dracula* (1992).

Computer games

The 1990s was also the decade when the world of computer games discovered vampires. The very first vampire-themed computer game appears to have been *Elvira, Mistress of the Dark* (1990), and this was soon followed by many others, including *Dracula Unleashed* (1993) and *Vampire: Master of Darkness* (1993). In the years that followed, vampire computer games continued to develop and by so doing they offered a new way for game makers and players to consider the role of the vampire and speculate about the nature of vampiric existence.

Computer games featuring vampires were soon joined by Nintendo, PlayStation and X-box video games. Some of these games, such as *Underworld*, released on PlayStation 2 in 2004 and *Buffy the Vampire Slayer*, released on Nintendo in 2009, are spin-offs from popular movies and TV shows; others, for example, *Vampire Rain: Altered Species*, released on PlayStation 3 in 2009, are dark and violent virtual worlds where players can make up their own rules. In the twenty-first century the continued appearance of vampires in video games once again demonstrates the indestructible nature of the vampire story and its ability to endlessly reinvent itself for each new generation.

See also: VAMPIRE: THE MASQUERADE

Garlic

Garlic, a member of the *Alliaceae* family of plants, which includes onions and chives, has been used since ancient times as an herb and a medicine. Over the years it developed a reputation as a form of protection against supernatural evils, such as witches and demons, and it is virtually universally regarded as a protective weapon against vampires. The highly pungent scent of garlic was believed to be deadly to vampires, who were said to be repelled by it and unable to enter a threshold over which it has been hung or rubbed.

Origins of garlic's use

The origins of garlic's beneficial reputation stretches back to ancient Egypt where it was thought to have potent healing powers. In China and Malaysia it was rubbed on the heads of children to protect them from evil creatures. In Filipino folklore, one rubs the armpits with garlic as a form of protection. Garlic also appears in the folklore of Mexico and South America to ward off evil. In Southern Slavic regions and Romania it was hung on doors or worn around the neck to ward off vampires. The mouths, ears, and nostrils of a corpse would be stuffed with cloves of garlic, or they would be placed in a coffin to prevent the corpse rising as a vampire. Vampires hiding in the community could be spotted by

their reluctance to eat garlic. St. Andrew's Eve and St. George's Eve, religious holidays with supernatural associations, were believed to be especially active times for vampires and on those days windows and doors were rubbed with garlic to keep them away. Cattle and livestock might also be rubbed with garlic.

The reason that vampires, in particular, were thought to have such an intense aversion to garlic is probably associated with the proven healing and blood-cleansing powers of the herb. As it was thought that vampires could contaminate their victim's blood, any healing substance that appeared to purify the blood would have been associated with magical powers. Another obvious reason is that garlic has an extremely strong smell. Not only would its pungent aroma be a counterbalance to the awful smell of rotting flesh so often associated with vampires, but wearing it, eating it, and rubbing it on a person or on the walls of a house would keep not only animals and vampires away, but everyone else as well! Perhaps one of the reasons there is not such a strong vampire mythology in France as there is in other places in Europe is down to the French tradition of eating garlic.

Literature

Garlic was introduced into vampire literature through Bram Stoker's *Dracula.* When Lucy Westenra is in peril because of the Count's attentions, Van Helsing immediately prescribes large numbers of garlic plants as protection so that *"every whiff of air that might get in would be laden with the garlic smell."* Throughout the twentieth century garlic became central to the developing vampire myth, gradually replacing the crucifix as the most well-known vampire detection/repellent substance, most probably because it does not have religious connotations.

Modern beliefs

Belief in the efficacy of garlic against possible vampires lasted well into the twentieth century. On February 15, 1912, the British newspaper the *Daily Telegraph* referred to the death of a 14-year-old boy in Hungary. He had worked for a farmer and after his death the farmer said the body continued to visit him. To put a stop to this the farmer and some of his friends went to the cemetery where the boy was buried. They dug up his body, placed three stones and three cloves of garlic in his mouth and drove a stake through his body.

Today many vampirologists regard the vampire-repelling powers of garlic as ancient superstition but as recently as the 1970s Romanian officials sanctioned the use of garlic during church services. Those who refused to eat it were regarded as potential vampires. And on St. George's Eve, to this day some Eastern European villagers follow the ancient traditions of eating garlic, hanging heads of the herb around their windows and doors, and giving their cattle garlic rubdowns.

See also: **APOTROPAICS; PROTECTION**

Gautier, Théophile (1811–72)

A French Romantic poet, novelist, and critic, Théophile Gautier was an important figure in nineteenth-century French literary circles and the author of many well-known novels, such as *Mademoiselle de Maupin* (1835). In the *Chronique de Paris* on June 25, 1836, Gautier contributed a tale called "*La Morte Amoureuse,*" translated literally as "the dead woman in love," but titled "The Beautiful Vampire" in a 1927 English translation. This tells the story of a young priest, Romuald, who becomes infatuated with a beautiful courtesan, Clarimonde. She dies but returns from her grave and visits Romuald every night as a wild, passionate, blood-drinking lover. After three years an older priest learns of the nightly visits and leads Romuald to Clarimonde's grave. The body is exhumed and after being sprinkled with holy water it crumbles into dust.

Gayal/Geyel

A gayal is an Indian vampire ghost, believed to be the spirit of a man who dies unmarried or before having a male heir, and who therefore does not have a son to perform his funeral rites. The creature is therefore created when the funeral rites are not performed correctly, which is also a common theme in European vampire lore. When the gayal returns from the dead it focuses on the sons of other people as well as the dead man's own relatives, but it could also disrupt the wider community. The gayal could also act like a demon and possess individuals by entering their bodies through their mouths while they were eating. Once in possession of someone they were said to draw the good from within, causing the person to sicken and waste away – a common vampiric theme.

There was no way of destroying this type of vampire; the only remedy was to prevent it being created in the first place. The best way of dealing with it was therefore to ensure that proper funeral rites according to Hindu custom were strictly observed. Fear of a visit by the gayal meant that the dead man's distant kin or even his neighbors would ensure all the necessary rites were carried out.

See also: **BURIAL CUSTOMS; INDIA**

Gay Culture

As a creature of secrecy, sensuality, otherness, and shape-shifting, the vampire has long been regarded as a symbol of the transgressive sexuality of gay culture. In vampire literature a gay and lesbian undercurrent can be found as early as Samuel Taylor Coleridge's poem *Christabel* (1816), and in *Carmilla* (1872) and *Dracula* (1897). In film the tradition of lesbian vampires goes back at least as far as *Dracula's Daughter* of 1936, while the first gay male vampires appeared in Roman Polanski's *Fearless Dracula Hunters* (1966).

It was not until the 1970s, however, that the vampire myth and lifestyle began to attract a really big gay following, largely thanks to the writings of Anne Rice. Although her novel *Interview with the Vampire* (1976) was not overtly gay, the undercurrents of homoeroticism were unmistakable as the vampires Lestat and Louis traveled the globe devoting special attentions to their exsanguinations of young men, and eventually cohabiting in a non-traditional living arrangement that included the child vampire Claudia.

Attraction of the vampire myth

According to psychologist and vampire researcher Katherine Ramsland, part of the attraction of the vampire myth for a gay audience is that the vampire's dark sexuality sets them apart from the rest of the world as an outsider – a threatening presence to the mainstream. The vampire story isn't just about drinking the blood of other humans to survive but about fulfilling an intense need; a need that is sensual and overpowering but also dangerous, subversive, and often misunderstood. The element of risk is important. Many gay people see and experience the world and their sexuality in a different way to heterosexuals and although this difference separates them from the mainstream, at the same time it gives them a kind of transcendent power that is both threatening and seductive to others.

See also: **AIDS; HOMOSEXUALITY; LESBIAN VAMPIRES; SEX**

Gelnhausen

In 1597 in Gelnhausen, a small town near Frankfurt in Germany, a woman by the name of Clara Geisslerin collapsed and died after confessing that she was a blood drinker and a witch. The case is interesting because it shows that witches were also accused of blood drinking and because, just like the vampire, suspected witches were burned for their alleged "crimes." In the case below, Clara's corpse was burned but unfortunately, of course, the majority of suspected witches were burned alive rather than after they had died.

Clara Geisslerin was accused of prostitution with three devils. She was also accused of countless murders and of digging up the graves of children in order to drink their blood. She was tortured in the most ghastly manner in order to get her to confess, but no sooner had she been taken off the rack she claimed to be innocent. So she was tortured again until she had confessed to consorting with the Devil, who visited her in the shape of cats, dogs, and worms. She also confessed to giving birth to somewhere in the region of 17 children (the exact figure is unclear) conceived with her devil lovers, murdering them, and drinking their blood. This time, Clara had no chance to retract her confession, because she died when she was taken off the rack. The judicial report concluded: *"The devil would not let her reveal anything more and so wrung her neck."* On August 23, 1597, her corpse was burned.

George, Feast of St./St. George's Eve

An important religious celebration in Eastern Europe, the Feast of St. George is celebrated on or around May 6 in Eastern Europe (April 23 in the Western Gregorian calendar) in honor of St. George, the patron saint of England and the enemy of vampires and witches.

The night before the feast of St. George, St. George's Eve, was believed to be one of the most dangerous nights of the year, when the powers of evil and darkness were heightened and vampires and other evil entities met *"at a place where a dog does not bark and a cuckoo does not sing."* People would hide in their houses with every form of protection against vampire attack they could think of. Thorns would be placed on doorsteps, tar painted on the doors, bonfires would be lit, and garlic spread everywhere. In parts of Romania lights would be extinguished, knives placed under pillows, and prayers chanted all night. If the night passed without incident St. George's Day would be celebrated enthusiastically with a sumptuous

feast and houses would be decorated with roses. Bram Stoker was clearly aware of such superstitions concerning St. George's Eve when he wrote *Dracula*, as in the novel peasants warn Jonathan Harker that *"all evil things in the world will have full sway"* on St. George's Eve. Today, the Feast of St. George is still celebrated in Europe, and in rural parts of Romania precautions are still taken against the threat of a vampire attack in the night.

Gerard, Emily (1849–1905)

Emily Gerard was an Englishwoman whose articles for English periodicals on the lore and superstitions of Transylvania were used by Bram Stoker when he did his research for his novel *Dracula*.

In 1888 Gerard, who was married to an officer in the Austro-Hungarian army and spent two years living in Transylvania, published a book about her experience there called *The Land Beyond the Forest*, which is the actual meaning of Transylvania. In her book Gerard describes the place as like an exotic island rich in superstitions and strange customs. She also wrote articles about Transylvania, including "Transylvanian Superstitions" (1885), for English newspapers and periodicals. In her writings Gerard discussed Transylvanian history, clothing, food, superstitions, customs, and the lore of vampires with considerable warmth and affection.

The old-world charm still lingers around and about for many things. It is floating everywhere and anywhere – in the forests and on the mountains, in medieval churches and ruined watch towers, in mysterious caverns and in ancient gold-mines, in the songs of people and in the legends they tell.

Germany

The vampire tradition in Germany and Austria is very diverse as it reflects the different cultures that have helped form the concept of the vampire character there. In addition, German vampire myths borrow from a rich vein of traditional folklore that includes elves, dwarves, and blood-drinking witches. The influence of the Slavic vampire can be found in eastern regions, but the Germans also have a number of particularly vicious vampire species of their own, such as the nachzehrer or "afterwards devourer" of northern Germany, and the zombie-like blutsauger or "bloodsucker" of southern Germany.

Like the Slavic vampire, the nachzehrer was a recently deceased person or revenant who returned from the grave to attack the living, usually family. Also like the Slavic vampire, the nachzehrer was believed to be created if a person committed suicide or died from an accident. In the grave nachzehrern were known to chew on their clothes and extremities before rising and eating the bodies of others.

In Bavarian folklore, people became vampires if they had not been baptized, were involved in witchcraft, ate the meat of an animal killed by a wolf, lived an immoral life, or committed suicide. Corpses could transform into vampires if an animal jumped over the grave, and, curiously, a nun stepping over a grave could have the same effect.

Schrattl

In some parts of the Alps the name schrattl was given to a violent type of vampire that attacked both animals and humans and spread disease through a region. These vampires were said to have extraordinary mental powers and could render those they attacked insane. They were considered to be "shroud eaters" – corpses that transformed into some form of foul life while in the grave and had eaten their way out of their funeral sheets. Typically the schrattl attacked members or property belonging to their own families first, before moving on to others. Also feared was the alp, a shape-shifting evil spirit of a dead person who could again manipulate the will of its victims before sucking their blood and life energy.

Prevention and protection

A number of anti-vampire traditions were upheld, including the placing of fishing nets in the grave of a suspected vampire in northern Germany where it was thought that vampires were compulsive undoers of knots. To effectively kill a vampire, a stake through the heart and garlic in the mouth were recommended. The Silesians buried corpses face down to avoid the dangerous gaze of a vampire. Salt sprinkled across a doorstep was thought to prevent an alp from entering, and if a community was subject to attack from an alp it was thought that the only way to destroy it was to find the corpse or living person that the alp had attached itself to. The corpse should be burned, and if the alp had attached itself to a living person then that person had to have some blood drawn from an area under their right eye to take away their evil powers.

Eighteenth-century vampire frenzy

In the early eighteenth century reports of Eastern European vampires began to filter into Germany, and between 1725 and 1732 areas of Austria and Germany were gripped by vampire frenzy. Epidemics of vampires were reported in 1710, 1721, and 1750. Churchyards were attacked and bodies exhumed as terrified villagers searched for the "shroud eaters" they believed to be attacking them. It is often suggested by historians that the hysteria was the result of a tuberculosis outbreak, but the hysteria was widespread and had not calmed down by 1755 when the town of Olmutz was involved in a full-scale vampire scare. In the 1790s an alp that took the form of a fierce dog with bloodshot eyes was reported to have disappeared only when a particular body was exhumed and burned. Fast-forwarding to the late nineteenth century, there were reports of either an individual alp or a group of alps allegedly drinking blood from the nipples of sleeping men in the Harz mountain region of Germany.

Treatises

The Germans made a significant contribution to the vampire myth in a number of treatises written by seventeenth- and eighteenth-century scholars and researchers on the undead. These include the works of Michaël Ranft, Johann Christopher Rohl, Johann Stock, and Johann Zopfius. Other notable treatises include *De Masticatione Mortuorum* (1679) by Philip Rohr, which discussed the feeding habits of the nachzehrer, and *De Miraculis Mortuorum* (1670) by Christian Frederic Garmann. A popular version of the Arnold Paole case in book form was the runaway best-seller at the 1732 Leipzig book fair.

Leading the attack on the existence of vampires was theologian Michaël Ranft's *De Masticatione Mortuorum in Tumilis Liber* (1728). Ranft stated that although the dead may be able to influence the living they could never reanimate corpses. Others suggested that the changes in the corpse offered as "proof" of vampirism could have natural explanations, such as premature burial or the natural stages of decomposition. The debate about the existence of vampires raged on for several decades in Germany until scholars finally agreed to relegate them to the realm of superstition.

Germany's contribution to the creation of the modern literary vampire is noteworthy. The short poem, *"Der Vampir"* (1748) by Heinrich August Ossenfelder and *The Bride of Corinth* (1797) by Goethe were both highly influential. Also from Germany, one of the finest vampire films of all time – *Nosferatu* (1922) by director F. W. Murnau – became an important signpost in the developing vampire myth of the twentieth century.

See also: **AUSTRIA**

Ghost

"Ghost" is the popular term for a supposed apparition of a dead person. In folklore, vampires share a lot of common ground with ghosts. Both are typically nocturnal entities who return to the world of the living from the world of the dead, and both frequently attack family members. And although ghosts are not a prominent feature of Slavic folklore, both can be found in the traditions of many cultures.

Background

The term "ghost" typically refers to the disembodied soul, which after death is thought to travel to the underworld or afterlife. Beliefs vary as to what happens to the soul after death but virtually every culture has a tradition that the ghost of a dead person can return to the world of the living, and when they return they can have either good or bad intent.

In the West, those who believe in ghosts sometimes hold that they are the souls of those who cannot find peace in death or do not realize they are dead, and so they linger on earth. Their inability to find peace is often explained as a need to deal with unfinished business, to deliver advice or information, to protect or stay close to loved ones, or simply to re-enact the moment of death. In some cases the unfinished business involves a victim seeking justice or revenge after their death. The ghosts of criminals are sometimes thought to linger to avoid purgatory, hell, or limbo.

In Asian cultures many people believe in reincarnation, and ghosts are thought to be souls that refuse to be reborn because they have unfinished business, similar to those in Western belief. In Chinese belief, ghosts can also become immortal, or they can go to hell and suffer forever, or they can die again and become a "ghost of a ghost."

Every culture has superstitions and beliefs about ghosts but both the West and the East share some fundamental ideas. There are often procedures and rituals for dealing with troublesome ghosts, such as exorcism. Ghosts may wander around places they frequented when alive, or where they died. Contrary to popular belief most ghosts are not reported at graveyards where the body may be buried but in houses and buildings where a person may have died, suffered, or lived for many years.

Many ghosts are reported when conditions are foggy and could well be explained as tricks of the light, just as those reported during thunderstorms may be caused by electrical charges in the atmosphere. Although there are reports of appearances during the day, the majority of ghosts do seem to appear at night — it's possible that a person is more sensitive to clairvoyance when relaxed or asleep at night. Many ghosts also appear during dreams. However, some believe that ghosts reported to have been seen at night when a person is wide awake may actually be hallucinations that occur when they are drifting off to sleep.

Ghosts and vampire

It's clear that there are certain similarities in folklore between ghosts and vampires but it is also important to point out that there are fundamental differences too. Ghosts are disembodied spirits typically described as fog-like, misty, silver, and transparent. They can be visible but they can also make their presence felt with strange noises, smells, gusts of cold air, the switching of lights on and off, and by the movement of objects. Vampires on the other hand are undead reanimated corpses or revenants that typically suck the blood of their victims. Although they can act like ghosts by making noises and breaking things they do these things through a physical body or through magic.

One of the reasons why the difference between ghosts and vampires has become less clearcut over time could be the emergence of the Spiritualist movement among many nineteenth- and early twentieth-century Americans and Europeans. Spiritualists promote the idea that it is possible to communicate with those who have passed to the other side, i.e. ghosts, and some spiritualists believe that vampires can communicate as spirits. Others believe in the concept of an astral body or psychic vampirism, in which spirits of the living and the dead can vampirize living people.

Another reason why the boundaries can sometimes blur is that ghosts and vampires both appear to be searching for answers to the same question: what happens when we die. A vampire exists somewhere between life and death and is eternally wandering and searching for peace. A ghost has presumably already demonstrated what happens when we die – a part of us lives on – but the restlessness of the ghost suggests that the search for answers does not end with death.

Ghoul

In Islamic legend, a ghoul, known in Arabic as *algul* – a name derived from the word for "horse-leech," a kind of blood-sucking insect – is a demon who feeds on the flesh and blood of humans, especially travelers and children, and corpses stolen from graves. Ghoul-like creatures (in that they lurk around graveyards, drink blood, and can pass themselves off as humans) can be found in a number of different areas and countries, including Japan and the Philippines. In the Philippines they are believed to chew on the recently dead; an interpretation which would seem to serve to explain sounds emerging from the grave and from the disintegration of the body.

Arabic lore

In Islamic tradition there are many different types of ghoul, both male (*ghul*) and female (*ghulah*). They were said to travel at night and to lurk around graveyards, deserts, and lonely, deserted spots where they lured travelers to their deaths. When in human and not monster form they could bear children but could be identified by their lack of appetite during the daytime and their habit of sneaking away to graveyards and cemeteries at nightfall, where they rested in secret graves and then awoke to feast on human flesh and blood, both living and dead. Ghouls could be destroyed if hit hard enough by a single blow, but a second blow could revive them.

Perhaps the most feared of the Arabic ghouls was the female variety that transformed themselves into women to entrap and feast on unsuspecting admirers. Montague Summers, in his 1928 book *The Vampire: His Kith and Kin*, recounts an Arabic folktale which gives a typical illustration of Oriental belief in ghouls blending with popular beliefs about vampires.

The tale tells the story of one Abdul-Hassan, newly married to a beautiful young woman called Nadilla. He presently noticed that Nadilla never ate an evening meal, but she explained that it was a consequence of her frugal upbringing. One night, however, Abdul-Hassan awoke to find himself alone in their bed, and to his concern his wife did not return until dawn. The next evening, when she got up from their bed, thinking he was asleep, and threw on a cloak to go out, Abdul-Hassan resolved to follow Nadilla to find out where she went.

To his surprise she soon left the main streets of the town and made her way to a remote cemetery which had a very ill repute as being darkly haunted. Tracking her very carefully he perceived that she entered a large vault, into which with the utmost caution he ventured to steal a glance. It was dimly lighted by three funerary lamps, and what was his horror to behold his young and beautiful wife seated with a party of hideous ghouls, about to partake of their loathsome feast. One of these monsters brought in a corpse which had been buried that day, and which was quickly torn to pieces by the company, who devoured the reeking gobbets with every evidence of satisfaction, recreating themselves meanwhile with mutual embraces and the drone of a mocking dirge.

Abdul-Hassan fled home, and said nothing about what he had seen to his wife the next morning. That evening, however, he insisted she ate with him. When she refused,

filled with anger and disgust he cried: "So then you prefer to keep your appetite for your supper with the ghouls." Nadilla turned pale, her eyes blazed, and she shook with fury, but she vouchsafed no reply and retired in silence. However, about midnight when she thought that her husband was fast asleep she exclaimed: "Now wretch receive the punishment for thy curiosity." At the same time she set her knee firmly on his chest, seized him by the throat, with her sharp nails tore open a vein and began greedily to suck his blood. Slipping from beneath her he sprung to his feet, and dealt her a blow with a sharp poniard wherewith he had been careful to arm himself, so that she sank down dying at the side of the bed. He called for help, the wound in his throat was dressed and on the following day the remains of this vampire were duly interred.

Unhappily for the young man, three nights later the ghoul returned with renewed strength and tried to attack him again. *"On the following day they caused her tomb to be opened, and the body was discovered apparently asleep since it seemed to breathe, the eyes were open and glared horribly, the lips were blub and red, but the whole grave was swimming in newly-spilled blood."* This time Abdul-Hassan took no chances; the body was exhumed, burned, and the ashes were scattered in the River Tigris.

Ghouls and vampires

Ghouls demonstrate the dualistic religious view from the Middle East that transferred itself to Slavic countries in the Middle Age. (This view, known as Manichaeism, holds that life is a big battle between good and evil. At death the good aspects of human nature leave the body, which as a corpse is evil and unclean.) Although ghouls tend to eat human flesh, while the vampire drinks blood, there are nonetheless certain similarities between the ghouls and vampires (as Summers' story above shows). Some experts believe that ghoul lore may have been imported into Eastern Europe sometime in the sixteenth century, where it influenced the development of the vampire legend.

See also: **ALGUL; BERTRAND, SERGEANT; WEREWOLF; ZOMBIE**

Girl and the Vampire, The

The story of *The Girl and the Vampire* is prominent in Romanian vampire lore and it has a number of variations. One version is found in *Ion Creanga (Romanian Folktales)* by Tudor Pamfile (1914).

Once in a village a young man hanged himself on a tree and became a vampire after the parents of a girl he loved repulsed his proposal of marriage to her. The vampire continued to visit and make love to the girl every night, but she did not want to have anything to do with an evil spirit and asked a wise woman for advice. The wise woman told the girl to fix a large ball of thread with a needle to the back of the vampire's coat the next time he visited. The girl should then hold on to one end of the thread and followed the vampire back to his grave. The girl did as she was told and the following night, again following the instructions given to her by the wise woman, she visited the grave to spy on the vampire. She saw him eat the heart of a dead man buried there and then set out to the village to visit her. She followed him as he left the churchyard.

The vampire asked her what she had seen that evening but the girl refused to tell him. The vampire told her that if she did not tell him her father would die that night. The girl still refused and her father died. The following evening the same thing happened but this time the vampire correctly predicted that her mother would die. On the third night when the girl refused to tell the vampire what she saw he told her that she would die.

On the advice of the wise old woman the girl called all her relations together and told them that she was going to die soon. When she was dead they were not to take her out by the door or by the window, but to break an opening in the walls of the house. They were not to bury her in the churchyard, but in the forest, and they were not to take her by the road but to go right across the fields until they came to a little hollow among the trees of the forest and here her grave was to be. And so it happened. The girl died, the wall of the house was broken down, and she was carried out on a bier across the fields to the margin of the forest.

After some time a wonderful flower, such as has never been seen, either before or after, grew up on her grave. One day the son of the emperor passed by and saw this flower, and immediately gave orders that it should be dug up well below the roots, brought to the castle, and put by his window. The flower flourished, and was more beautiful than ever, but the son of the emperor pined. He himself did not know what was the matter, he could neither eat nor drink. What was the matter? At night the flower became again the maiden, as beautiful as before. She entered in at the window, and passed the night with the emperor's son without his knowing it. However, one night she could contain herself no longer, and kissed him, and he awoke and saw her. After that, they pledged troth to each other, they told the emperor and empress, they were married, and they lived very happily together. There was only one drawback to their happiness. The wife would never go out of the house. She was afraid of the vampire.

One day, however, her husband took her with him in a carriage to go to church, when there, at a corner, who should there be but the vampire. She jumped out of the carriage and rushed to the church. She ran, the vampire ran, and just had his hand on her as they both reached the church together. She hid behind a holy picture.

The vampire stretched out his hand to seize her, when all at once the holy picture fell on his head, and he disappeared in smoke. And the wife lived with the emperor's son free from all danger and sin for the rest of her life.

The story of *The Girl and the Vampire*, which also exists in a Russian version, probably served as a warning against out-of-wedlock sexual relations, while at the same time confirming the Church as the best form of protection against the forces of evil and urging young people to listen to their elders.

See also: **ROMANIA**

Glamis Castle

A Scottish castle, Glamis was built in the fourteenth century and has been inhabited ever since. The castle has many supernatural legends associated with it and is allegedly the home of a monster, a vampire, and several ghosts, said to be former earls or unknown ladies and servants. In addition, the castle is said to have more exterior windows than can be located from the inside, suggesting some sort of secret chamber within the castle.

According to legend, the monster associated with Glamis Castle is the 11th Earl of Strathmore. Born deformed in the early 1800s, with an egg-shaped body, tiny arms and legs, and no neck, the child was sealed away in a secret chamber and left to die. Despite this treatment, he supposedly lived for a very long time, and is said to have died in the 1920s.

In a similar story which, like the story of the Glamis Castle monster, cannot be proven,

the Glamis Castle vampire is said to be a servant girl who was caught drinking the blood of her victim. She was allegedly sealed up alive within the secret chamber, where legend has it that she continues to sleep the sleep of the undead, until someone finds her and she is set free. A different version of the legend is that in every generation of the family, a vampire child is born, who is then walled up in this secret room.

Gleaner

Originally known as the *Galneur Hollandois*, the *Gleaner* was a Dutch journal that encouraged the spread of vampire stories in the eighteenth century by legitimizing the "scientific" writings of supposed vampire "experts." In 1732, it published a lengthy list of vampire cases in Eastern Europe and recommended that those who did not believe in vampires or who were interested in learning more about them should consult a number of treatises on the phenomenon written by respected German researchers, theologians, and scientists.

Glut, Donald Frank (1944–)

In 1972, Donald Frank Glut, an American author, produced his first vampire book, entitled *True Vampires of History*. It proved to be a major landmark in vampire literature and research as it was the first to gather together both real and legendary vampires in an historical narrative. This was followed in 1975 by *The Dracula Book*, a copious book exploring the character of Dracula as presented in novels, comics, on stage and screen. It has become the foundation stone of all vampire bibliographical and movie research.

Gods, Vampire

Merciless and terrifying deities that display vampiristic tendencies or characteristics; they are found in most cultures all over the world. Fear of the darkness and nightmares of an evil deity stealing a life away may have helped to give substance to circulating vampire tales.

The most powerful and terrifying vampire gods can be found in Asian traditions. They were typically depicted with red eyes, fangs, had an insatiable appetite for blood, and were dressed with human heads, skulls, and other organs as ornaments. Only a great Hindu or Buddhist saint could hope to defeat such dangerous and deadly deities. According to some scholars these deities may be found in the ancient Indus Valley civilizations, and may date back to as early as the third millennium BC. Once established, stories of vampire gods began to spread to other regions and over time, as religions established themselves, the power and influence of these stories grew. The most well-known ancient vampire goddess is Kali from India, who in the past could be appeased with offerings of blood from animal sacrifices.

Vampiric deities are symbols of the eternal and indestructible nature of the undead and also of the vulnerability of humankind against the forces of nature. Over the centuries the all-encompassing power of the ancient gods grew weaker as the understanding and knowledge of humans grew stronger. So instead of worshipping the undead, even-tually vampire hunters would seek out and destroy them.

Goethe, Johann Wolfgang von (1749–1832)

Johann Wolfgang von Goethe was a German poet, dramatist, novelist, and polymath who made vampires a legitimate subject for serious treatment in European literature when he wrote *Die Braut von Korinth*, translated as *The Bride of Corinth* (1797). The ballad, which features the first female vampire and male victim in Germanic literature, was based on the classical tale of the maiden Philinnion by Phlegon of Tralles, but in Goethe's version the girl dies of grief because her parents will not allow her to marry her lover, Machates. She returns as a corpse bride to enjoy the sexual and emotional freedom she was denied in her lifetime.

> *Gods, though, hearken ne'er,*
> *Should a mother swear*
> *To deny her daughter's plighted troth.*
> *From my grave to wander I am forc'd,*
> *Still to seek The Good's long-sever'd link,*
> *Still to love the bridegroom I have lost,*
> *And the life-blood of his heart to drink;*

It would be an exaggeration to say that the vampire entered German literature with Goethe's ballad, but it would be difficult to over-estimate the enduring influence and popularity of this piece.

Gogol, Nikolai (1809-52)

Nikolai Gogol was a Russian dramatist and novelist who made a significant contribution to the growing vampire theme in Russian literature with his 1853 story, *Viy*, a story that is more comedy than horror. *Viy* is a tale about the King of the Gnomes but there are a number of vampire characters, including a dog that can transform itself into a lovely maiden who steals babies and drinks their blood, and an evil woman who rides a phantom horse and lures men to their deaths.

Gold

Although it is used less frequently than silver, gold is a metal used as a protection against vampires, probably because of its association with sunlight, goodness, divinity, and purity and as such it acts as an antidote to the forces of evil and darkness. Crosses made of gold and gold coins would often be left on the corpse of a suspected vampire to prevent it from leaving the grave and disturbing the living.

See also: **APOTROPAICS**

Good Vampires

By definition, vampires are evil in folklore. However, from the 1960s onward a growing trend began to emerge in vampire fiction and film in which the vampire was presented as a more sympathetic character. So-called "good" vampires are vampires who act morally in their dealings with humans. They are still bloodsuckers but get blood from animals, blood banks, or willing donors. They do not

kill or attack their victims and they are also able to control their blood lust so that it does not override their moral perspective.

Among the first "good" vampires to emerge were the comic book heroine Vampirella, and Barnabas Collins from the TV series *Dark Shadows*. Through the 1980s, "good" vampires continued to appear in vampire literature and film and have now become an essential part of the revival of interest in vampires in the last decade. In 2005 Stephenie Meyer created the ultimate "good guy" vampire in the character of Edward Cullen in her international best-selling Twilight Saga series.

See also: **VICTIMS**

Gothan, Bartholomäus

Bartholomäus Gothan was a German printer who published an account about the activities of the fifteenth-century Wallachian prince Vlad the Impaler in the early 1480s. His account was written in Low German, which means it would have been accessible to the towns of the north German region. The full title of the work, which helped spread much of the accepted notion about Vlad's cruelty was: "*About an evil tyrant named Dracole Wyda MCCC-CLVI years after the birth of our Lord Jesus Christ, this Dracole Wyda Carried out many terrible and wondrous deeds in Wallachia and Hungary.*"

Gothic

A term derived from the name of an ancient Germanic tribe that helped bring about the fall of the Roman Empire, it was applied to a style of stark, unsubtle yet ornate medieval architecture and then to a literary genre. With regard to the latter, "Gothic" refers to a Romantic form of writing that was popular in the late eighteenth century and throughout the nineteenth. Gothic novels, stories, plays, and poems have played a major part in the formation of the modern vampire image.

In essence Gothic literature is the literature of the nightmare exploration of the hidden, irrational, chaotic, dark, or shadowy aspects of life and the inner self. It relies heavily on the use of terror, horror, mystery, and the supernatural to impose a sense of dread and to encourage readers to consider what is evil and unconventional in human life and within themselves. To accomplish this, Gothic literature developed its own set of conventions. Typically the action takes place on a stormy night in ruins, castles, monasteries, or graveyards, and the plot concerns the attack on a naïve innocent by supernatural forces in the form of ghosts, monsters, and other evil entities.

Horace Walpole's *Castle of Otranto* (1764) popularized the Gothic novel in England and this was soon followed by spectacularly atmospheric novels penned by the likes of Mrs. Ann Radcliffe and Charles Robert Maturin. Vampires were an obvious attraction for Gothic writers and early contributions included Gottfried Bürger's *Lenora* (1773) and Goethe's *Die Braut von Korinth* (1797). It was not until 1819, however, that vampires fully established themselves in popular Gothic literature with John Polidori's *The Vampyre: a Tale*.

Polidori's vampire character, Lord Ruthven, combines the characteristics of the cruel and rakish Gothic villain with those of the traditional blood-drinking vampire and remains one of the most influential vampires in literature. Prior to Lord Ruthven the vampire had been presented as an uneducated, dirty, and unappealing peasant, but the vampire described in Polidori's novel is educated, aristocratic, and financially comfortable. He was also very much at ease with his surroundings and his plausibility made him all the more terrifying; Bram Stoker would later use this combination of plausibility and sexual allure and charisma to great effect in *Dracula* in 1897.

Virtually every nineteenth-century Romantic writer, from Coleridge to Edgar Allan Poe, used the vampire theme in his or her work, but the next highly significant Gothic vampire work after Polidori's was James Malcolm Rymer's *Varney the Vampire*, published in 1847. The character of Varney is even more reprehensive than that of Ruthven. His need for blood and love of wealth and status reinforced the aristocratic nature of the Gothic vampire that remained a defining feature of nineteenth-century vampire literature. Sheridan Le Fanu's *Carmilla* (1872) is about a noblewoman but her attacks add a sensual and subtle dimension perhaps missing from earlier works of Gothic vampire literature.

All these works prepared the way for what is still regarded as the greatest work of Gothic vampire literature, Bram Stoker's *Dracula*. In *Dracula*, Stoker played on traditional Gothic themes by placing its opening chapters in a remote castle, and in the Count he created a classic Gothic villain who is also a supernatural being. However, Stoker took Gothic convention one step further by bringing the fantasy world of Dracula into the contemporary and familiar world of his readers when he unleashed Dracula's evil into the very heart of England. By so doing he suggested that the evil had spread through to the center of the civilized but unbelieving world.

Throughout the twentieth century vampire literature headed off in many different directions, although it did often return to its Gothic Romantic roots. In the 1970s it re-emerged again in strength with the novels of Anne Rice, who is widely regarded as the foremost practitioner of the Gothic style of literature for the modern age.

See also: LITERATURE

Goths

The word "Goth" was applied to adherents of a counter-cultural movement that appeared in most urban centers in the West in the 1980s.

The origins of the Goth movement can be traced to bands and nightclubs in the United Kingdom during the waning years of the punk movement in the late 1970s. Perhaps the most significant of these bands was Bauhaus, a gothic rock band formed in 1978 who released in 1979 the single "Bela Lugosi's Dead." Bauhaus was joined by other bands including: The Cult, The Cure, The Sisters of Mercy, and Siouxsie and the Banshees who often played in a London nightclub aptly named The Bat Cave.

Gothic rock music was explicitly non-conformist and anti-establishment. It articulated the dark and shadowy side of life and expressed a fascination with death and dying. The slow, heavy sound of gothic rock bands has often been described as gloomy and morbid, and in many ways Goths could be said to elevate despair to an art form, transforming dissatisfaction with everyday life into creative self-expression.

Gothic subculture

The movement spread to mainland Europe and North America in the 1980s. By the 1990s a new "underground" of gothic subculture was establishing itself in the United States. Perhaps the best example from this decade was the controversial gothic rock musician Marilyn Manson. Today the majority of large urban centers in the United States have at least one nightclub that features Goth music. From music, Goth activities have spread to other areas, including fanzines, books, and (of course) the Internet, where the privacy of the virtual universe is as effective a cover for the shadowy side of life as darkness.

Many Goths love fashion, the occult, and role-playing games, and inevitably found the vampire to be the perfect image for their culture with both men and women dressing in black and often looking as if they belonged to the pages of an Anne Rice novel. Pale makeup, tattoos depicting skulls and bats, costume jewelry shaped like spiders and snakes, badly cut hair, torn clothes, dark lipstick, and dark nail polish present an overall image of death and make it difficult for others to identify whether a person is male or female. Androgyny is an essential aspect of their image for many Goths, as it expresses an ideal of wholeness and opposites coming together and the blurring of boundaries between what is male and what is female.

In recent years a number of distinct Goth types have emerged, and these include the foppish and old-fashioned Romantic-looking Goths, who tend to wear Edwardian or Victorian period clothing; grunge Goths, who often dress in torn clothes; and fetish Goths, who like to wear skin-tight leather and pieces of metal pierced through body parts. Of course, not all Goths fit into any one category and combining different styles is common.

The Goth subculture is not a religion or a cult, but some people fear that it may encourage young people to turn toward violence and the occult. Some, but by no means all, Goths embrace the occult and Satanism but it is generally nothing more than a sinister role-playing device. Few believe they can truly gain supernatural powers by worshipping the Devil. They simply enjoy pretending to be evil and looking to the darker side of life.

Vampires, of course, fit especially well into the Goth subculture as they represent an ancient, supernatural, and powerful image of dark spirituality that can be tapped into and manipulated for creative self-expression. And Goths constitute some of the most enthusiastic "vampires" in the United States and Britain today. However, although it is easy to understand why Goths so readily identify with the image of the vampire, it is important to note that the gloomy and melancholic Goth worldview is not always shared by vampire enthusiasts.

See also: **MODERN VAMPIRES**

Grave

Typically a hole dug in the ground, although it can also refer to a tomb, a grave is a burial site for a corpse. In many Eastern European vampire traditions, the grave is the place where a corpse is believed to transform into a vampire and the place where vampires return to "rest" after their killing sprees.

A series of finger-like holes around a grave, although probably due to the action of scavengers, would in times past often be regarded

as a telltale sign that the grave was that of a vampire: it was thought the vampire would escape through these holes at night in a mist-like form. Earth that was disturbed around a grave was also regarded with suspicion, as it suggested that the vampire was moving in the grave below (again despite the fact that erosion, and the action of animals or grave robbers could offer a perfectly natural explanation). A Serbian schoolbook from the early nineteenth century also advises: "*If the grave is sunk in, if the cross had a crooked position, and* [if there are] *other indications of this sort,* [they] *suggest that the deceased has transformed into a vampire.*" And, of course, if any limbs or parts of the corpse had risen up to the surface, due to flooding or not being buried deep enough, this was regarded as a sign of vampirism.

If a grave was identified as suspect, vampire hunters would sometimes use a virgin horse as a way to confirm their suspicions – the horse would allegedly balk at stepping over the grave of a vampire. In parts of Germany sounds of moaning, groaning, or munching from the grave were also said to be the undead at work, eating their clothes, themselves, and other corpses. In the nineteenth century however, many people concluded that occasionally people were buried while still alive, and that this would account for the stories of vampires.

See also: **BURIAL CUSTOMS; CEMETERY; DESTROYING VAMPIRES; DETECTING VAMPIRES; PREMATURE BURIAL**

Grave Desecration

See: BERTRAND, SERGEANT; BURIAL CUSTOMS; GRAVE; NECROPHILIA; PREMATURE BURIAL

Greece

Greece is regarded as one of the oldest and most important sources for the vampire legend. Its concept of the vampire has passed through many phases of development but remains strong today.

Legends about the undead date back to the days of ancient Greece, with stories of such horrifying creatures as the blood-drinking lamiai, empusa, and the mormolykai. Although these creatures were known to be blood drinkers they were wholly supernatural beings rather than the revivified corpses of Eastern Europe.

The first idea of a distinct Greek vampire as a reanimated corpse seems to have developed around AD 580, after a migration of Turkish and Slavic peasants into the northern part of the region, who brought their traditions with them. However, Slavic beliefs concerning the undead did not take firm hold in Greece until about the seventeenth century, when precepts from the Greek Orthodox Church indicated that excommunication caused a corpse to remain cursed until the ban was lifted. Villagers believed that an incorrupt corpse was receptive to contamination by an evil entity; once contaminated the corpse was called a "vrykolakas," the Slavic word for werewolf, which gradually became associated with the word "vampire."

Vrykolakas

The Church attempted to clarify the situation concerning excommunication as a cause of vampirism by declaring that an incorrupted corpse was not the same as a vrykolakas; according to the Church a vrykolakas was created by demonic infestation. Declarations from the Church, however, had little effect and the general assumption among Greek villagers was that excommunicants, alongside suicides, immoral persons, the unbaptized, witches, and those who had a cat jump over their corpse, came back as a vrykolakas.

An interesting description of Greek beliefs about the process by which a victim of a vampire attack in turn became a vampire occurs in the writings, published in 1898, of a priest on the island of Crete:

It is a popular belief that most of the dead, those who have lived bad lives or who have been excommunicated … become vrykolakes; that is to say, after the separation of the soul from the body there enters into the latter an evil spirit which takes the place of the soul … it keeps the body as its dwelling place, and it runs swift as lightning wherever it lists … And the trouble is that it does not remain solitary, but makes everyone, who dies while it is about, like to itself, so that in a short space of time it gets together a large train of followers. The common practice of the vrykolakes is to seat themselves upon those who are still asleep and by their great weight to create an agonizing sense of oppression. There is great danger that the sufferer might himself expire, and himself too be turned into a vrykolakas … This monster, as time goes on, becomes more audacious and blood-thirsty, so that it is able to devastate whole villages.

Another interesting vampire species from Greece was the callicantzaro, a vampire discussed by Leo Allatius in his 1645 treatise, *De Graecorum hodie quorundam opinationibus*. The callicantzaros were unusual among vampires in that their manic activities and attacks on humans were limited to Christmas Day and the 12 days afterwards. Any person born during this period was also considered unlucky and believed to be destined to become a vampire after death.

Gwrach y Rhibyn

A Welsh version of the Irish banshee, the Gwrach y Rhibyn was somewhere between a fairy and a vampire, and manifested as an old hag who brought warnings of death and disaster to well-established Welsh families.

According to the folklore of rural Wales, the Gwrach y Rhibyn was said to linger at crossroads and isolated spots waiting to attack travelers as they passed by. The only means of removing her seems to have been physical force. At other times she was glimpsed beside rivers or as a ball of light (similar to a corpse candle) drifting between houses late in the evening. Like other evil entities, she was believed to draw magical powers and superhuman strength from the moon, particularly when it was full.

As well as warning families of pure Welsh stock of impending deaths, the Gwrach y Rhibyn was also said to drink the blood of humans as they slept. Her favorite victims were the vulnerable, in particular elderly people and babies, and she would drink their blood in small amounts, returning over a period of several nights. If a baby grew pale and ill it was said that this was caused by the Gwarch y Rhibyn.

According to vampire lore expert Bob Curran, in some images of the Gwarch y Rhibyn she appears covered in dried blood that she had drunk using a long, dark, sharp tongue. She would drink the blood of her victims on several occasions and each time they would grow weaker and weaker – a classic vampire theme.

See also: **WALES**

Gypsies

In the Middle Ages the vampires of Eastern mythology began to be introduced to the West by the Romany Gypsies who migrated from northern India via Egypt and North Africa into Europe about a thousand years ago. These nomadic people lived in Germany, Greece, Romania, and the Slavic-speaking countries of Hungary, Russia, Poland, Slovenia, and Serbia. They were well acquainted with Indian vampiric deities and beliefs about the dead and undoubtedly merged them with their own beliefs about the dead, disseminating them to others wherever they traveled.

Although it is likely they arrived much earlier – the tenth century according to some historians (and they were noted in Crete in 1322) – the first record of Gypsies in Europe comes from Germany in 1417. They claimed to be exiles from "little Egypt" and Europeans called them "Egyptians," which became corrupted to Gypsies. Their language, Romany, is related to Sanskrit and most of their customs are similar to Hindu customs.

Over the centuries the Romany people have often been unjustly viewed as social outcasts and widely blamed for a variety of crimes and evils without substantiation. They have also been unfairly stereotyped in vampire fiction and film, often depicted as ignorant and superstitious peasants. The Romany culture is, however, independent and resilient, and because of its preservation of vampire traditions and customs it has played a crucial part in both spreading and preserving vampire lore all over the world. Today, "Travelers" is a wider and more politically correct term for groups of people with a nomadic lifestyle, traditionally including but not restricted to the Romany people.

The Gypsy universe

The Gypsy universe is populated by numerous deities and spirits. Their relationship with death is a living one but it is also governed by fear, with numerous taboos, rules, and regulations governing the way the living deal with the dead and dying. The Romany in the Balkans believed that when someone died his or her soul hovered near the corpse in the burial ground and there was always a danger, as with the Indian bhuta, that the soul might become restless and re-enter the corpse, causing it to rise from the grave. To prevent this happening, the living would make regular trips to gravesites to talk to the dead through cracks in the earth and to offer presents of food and drink. Despite this attention to detail it was thought inevitable that some corpses might live on as vampires, called "mulo," meaning "one who is dead."

Gypsies and vampires

The Romany people have various beliefs about how vampires can come into being. Among others, if a person has led a sinful, ill-tempered or unsatisfying life they may return. If a dog, hen, ox, or ram jumps over a corpse, or if a corpse swells or turns black before burial, this is considered a bad sign. The most dangerous corpses are those of people who have died suddenly, unnaturally, by violence or suicide, and the corpses of still-born babies are also regarded with suspicion as it is thought they continue to grow inside the grave until they reach their eighth year and then become restless and want to leave their graves.

It was also thought that when a corpse became a vampire it could rise from the grave like a ghost and take on a human form that looked normal except for jelly-like limbs (the bones had been left in the grave) and an odd physical trait, such as a missing finger. Other vampires, however, looked revolting, with long hair and a partially decomposed body covered in filmy mist. Whatever their form the creature could either emerge at midnight or at noon, when no one could see they cast no shadow. These vampires made their presence known by destroying property and shrieking. Male vampires were said to sexually assault either their surviving wives or other women. Female vampires might appear normal but would drive their men mad with their insatiable demands.

Candidates for vampirism

According to Gypsy lore, certain parts of the body, especially the eye can become vampires on their own, and certain animals, vegetables, and tools can also become vampires. The most likely candidates for vampirism are snakes, horses, and lambs although cats, dogs, oxen, and chicken are also considered at risk; any animal could become a vampire under certain conditions, especially if it jumps over a corpse before burial. Pumpkins and watermelons kept longer than two weeks could be vampirized, although vampire vegetables were considered more irritating than dangerous as they tended to disturb people at night. Farm tools could also be vampirized if they were left unused for three years, and again would cause disturbances rather than serious harm.

Prevention

Preventative measures against vampires included fences of iron placed around graves to prevent vampires escaping. Stakes of ash or hawthorn could be driven into a grave or boiling water poured over it. Corpses could also be pierced with an iron or steel needle through the heart before burial, or be buried with iron or steel in their mouths. The heels of the shoes could be removed and hawthorn placed in a sock, or a hawthorn stake could be driven though the corpse's leg. Homes could be protected from vampires with fishing nets (vampires were compelled to count every knot before entering) or by a sprinkling of thorns. Crosses and holy water were also feared by vampires. Black dogs and wolves were thought to attack vampires. Some Romanian Gypsies believed that white wolves lingered around graveyards to attack vampires.

Dhampir

The victim of a vampire could also call upon the services of a vampire hunter called a dhampir, the son of a vampire. Gypsies believed that intercourse between a vampire and his widow might produce a male offspring and this child would develop unusual powers to detect and destroy vampires. In addition, Slavic Gypsies prized the presence of a set of twins born on a Saturday who were willing to wear their underpants inside out. It was thought that this odd spectacle would cause a vampire to flee immediately.

"Vampirism was one of the most demonic outbreaks of mass hysteria ever to sweep the world. Its origins are rooted at the beginning of time and almost all of them are founded on superstition."

Anthony Masters, *The Natural History of the Vampire*

Haarmann, Fritz (1879-1925)

Known as the "vampire butcher of Hanover," Fritz Haarmann, with the help of two accomplices, killed at least 24 and perhaps as many as 50 young men. Although he was not a vampire in the traditional folklore sense but a disturbed murderer with a blood fetish, he became known as a vampire because he would bite his victims on their necks and then eat their flesh and drink their blood.

Haarmann was born into a strict German household in 1879. He was a poor student and joined the military on leaving school. After his service he returned home to Hanover where he was accused of molesting young children and placed in an insane asylum. He escaped and took up a violent, crime-ridden life on the streets. In 1918 after a spell in jail he found a job as a butcher in a meat shop. Around this time he took to waking sleeping boys at Hanover railway station and asking to see their ticket. If they had none, he would offer them a place to stay for the night. The boys were never seen again after that.

In 1919 he met Hans Grans, who become his lover and partner in crime. Throughout the early 1920s victims were selected upon Grans' taste for their clothes. When killing the boys, who were aged between 12 and 18, Haarmann would bite into their throats and drink their blood. Another mysterious accomplice, called Charles, who was also a butcher, assisted by grinding and cutting up the bodies and disposing of them. The clothes were sold in the meat shop and, most grisly of all, it appears that some of the victims were sold as meat and sausages.

In 1924, when Haarmann was in jail on indecency charges, police discovered human remains in the mud banks of the nearby river. Officers searched his rooms and found human blood stains. Outside they found what was left of 22 corpses. Haarmann eventually confessed to his crimes in minute detail when a mother of one of the missing boys identified a scrap of clothing worn by her son which had been traced back to Haarmann.

In court Haarmann declared that he was sane but when he committed the murders he was in a trance and not aware of his actions. The court rejected this argument, based on Haarmann's lack of regret and the specific details he had given police concerning the manner in which he would kill his victims by biting them. With regard to his demeanor at the trial, one newspaper wrote, *"Throughout the long ordeal Haarmann was utterly impassive and complacent."*

Executed by decapitation in April 1925, Haarmann received a kind of immortality when his brain was removed by officials and given to scientists at Göttingen University for research purposes. The *Daily Express* headlined its report of April 17 with: *"VAMPIRE BRAIN. PLAN TO PRESERVE IT FOR SCIENCE."*

Charles disappeared and Grans was sentenced to life imprisonment.

In *The Vampire: His Kith and Kin* (1928), vampirologist Montague Summers summarized public opinion about the case as follows:

This is probably one of the most extraordinary cases of vampirism known. The violent eroticism, the fatal bite in the throat, are typical of the vampire, and it was perhaps something more than mere coincidence that the mode of execution should be the severing of the head from the body, since this was one of the efficacious methods of destroying a vampire. Certainly in the extended sense of the word, as it is now so commonly used, Fritz Haarmann was a vampire in every particular.

See also: **HISTORICAL VAMPIRES**

Habergeiss

In some parts of Austria and in the German mountains, the alp (a type of vampire specific to German and Austrian folklore) became known as the habergeiss, a three-legged creature that could move very fast. When night came the habergeiss was believed to attack cattle and livestock in the fields and drink their blood. It would not normally attack humans unless they prevented it from feeding, although when it did attack it did so with great violence.

See also: **GERMANY**

Hag Attack

Part witch, part demon, part vampire, and part ghost, the motif of the old hag with child-snatching vampiric tendencies, tangled hair, rotting teeth, a hooked nose, mad eyes, and claw-like fingers has permeated down across the years, taking on new shapes and identities. One of the most common forms of these crones is the Irish banshee. The hag is also related to the mara (from which the word "nightmare" is derived), a demon that likes to attack humans at night.

Victims of hag attack – also known as Old Hag Syndrome – report that they awake abruptly to find they cannot move, even though they can see, hear, feel, and smell. There is typically the feeling of a great weight on their chest and the sense that there is a sinister or evil presence in the room. Old Hag Syndrome has been documented since ancient times and modern research suggests that up to 10 percent of people will experience at least one hag attack in their lives. The name of the phenomenon comes from the superstitious belief that a witch – i.e. an old hag – sits or "rides" on the chest of the victims, rendering them immobile.

Explanations

Medical experts suggest that there is probably a medical or scientific explanation for Old Hag Syndrome, such as indigestion, sleep disorders, stress, or repressed tension. Some researchers believe that tales of encounters with the hag might be attached to the phenomenon known as sleep paralysis, a condition characterized by being unable to move or speak. Sleep paralysis occurs in the moments just before dropping off to sleep or just before awakening and is typically associated with the feeling of some sort of menacing presence. Although medical explanations, emotional tension, and sleep paralysis can explain the great majority of cases, it is important to point out that (just like a small fraction of reported vampire attacks) rational and scientific explanations are unable to explain them all.

See also: **OLD HAG**

Haigh, John George (1901-49)

Known as the "Vampire of London" and the "Acid Bath Murderer," John George Haigh was an infamous mass murderer.

Born in England in 1901, Haigh was raised in a strict Pilgrim Brethren family that filled him with the threat of eternal punishment for sin. He grew up repressed and fixated on religion and the image of the bleeding Christ on the Cross. He frequently dreamed about railway accidents with injured and bleeding people, and by the age of six he had started to wound himself so he could drink his own blood.

By the time Haigh had reached adulthood his compulsion for blood had grown so strong that he rented a storeroom and killed nine of his acquaintances, including a young woman, by shooting or clubbing them. He then cut their necks, drained their blood into a cup and drank it. Assuming that he could not be caught if there weren't any bodies, he disposed of the corpses in drums of sulfuric acid. By the time of his arrest and execution in 1949, he had murdered at least nine people, and in each case he appears to have drunk the blood of his victims.

What made Haigh's crimes so terrifying for the public was his seemingly normal appearance and his complete lack of remorse, which manifested itself in the matter-of-fact, detailed way he described his crimes. He was also unusual in that there was no sexual motivation in his crimes, a characteristic common among other serial killers. It is possible that Haigh made up the blood-drinking in order to appear insane and escape the death penalty, but the disturbing dreams he described before each killing suggests otherwise:

Before each of my killings, I had a series of dreams, I saw a forest of crucifixes that changed into green trees dripping with blood ... which I drank, and once more I awakened with a desire that demanded fulfilment.

See also: **CLINICAL VAMPIRISM; CRIME; HISTORICAL VAMPIRES**

Halloween

Observed annually on the night of October 31 and originally a pagan festival of the dead, Halloween (also known as All Hallows' Eve) is celebrated today as a night of supernatural fancy dress, trick-or-treating, and fun and games.

The origins of Halloween date back more than 2,000 years to the time of the Celtic druids who lived in the British Isles and in parts of Germany, France, and Scandinavia. The ancient Celts called this festival the festival of Samhain and it marked the end of summer and the harvest, and the beginning of the dark, cold winter – a time of year that was often associated with human death. It was thought that on this night the veil between the dead and the living was at its thinnest and the spirits of the dead could rise out of their graves to wander freely on earth. The living would disguise themselves so the dead would not recognize them, and huge bonfires would be lit in an attempt to rekindle the diminishing energy of the sun god in the winter. As time went on fairies, witches, demons, vampires, and werewolves as well as spirits of the dead and other forces of evil were said to come out in force on Halloween night.

When the Christian Church arrived, it could not completely obliterate the old pagan influences in Europe; instead it assimilated them into its own framework. So in the year 835, All Saints' Day was introduced and its eve, Halloween, replaced Samhain.

Similar traditions can also be found in Romania on St. Andrew's Night – a feast day held on November 30 when the spirits of the dead are believed to wander the earth. All kinds of pots are covered as vampires might hide in them, and one of the best ways to protect a house and its inhabitants is to rub garlic onto the door frames. Currently the tradition of Halloween is enjoying new-found popularity, not just in America where Halloween has been an established part of American folklore since the 1840s, when poverty-stricken Irish immigrants introduced the tradition to the United States, but in mainland Europe and England too.

Hamilton, Laurell K. (1963–)

Laurell K. Hamilton is an American author of the *New York Times* bestselling series about a female vampire hunter called Anita Blake and her relationships with vampires and werewolves. Blake's primary opponent is Jean-Claude, a 400-year-old master vampire who is destined to become her lover, but her enemies include zombies, werewolves, trolls, and other supernatural monsters. In the novels Hamilton builds an alternative history in which the United States has altered society so that vampires and werewolves have become accepted. Blake earns her living by reanimating the dead and gaining important information from them. The first Anita Blake novel, *Guilty Pleasures*, appeared in 1993; as of May 2008, the series has run to

16 novels and has sold more than six million copies worldwide.

In her novels, which are written with a touch of humor and the dialogue of a hard-hitting detective novel, Hamilton does not shy away from sex and violence. Blake is tough in talk and action and can fend for herself, but many readers have expressed dissatisfaction with Hamilton's increasing focus over the years on the character's infection with the *ardeur*, a psychic hunger that can only be satisfied via direct or vicarious sexual energy. However, despite often being criticized as an *"X-rated Buffy the Vampire Slayer,"* a number of fans have consistently expressed their approval of the series.

See also: **LITERATURE**

Hammer

A tool often used by vampire hunters to drive or pound a wooden stake into the heart of a vampire (or the corpse of a suspected vampire) to destroy it. The hammer may have derived its anti-vampire symbolism from its association with the Norse god Thor, whose powerful hammer was used to defeat all evil. The image of a hammer descending onto a stake is a recurring theme in Hammer Films, but one of the most powerful scenes of staking was in the 1992 movie, *Bram Stoker's Dracula*.

See also: **DESTRUCTION**

Hammer Films

Hammer Films, an English film studio that became synonymous with horror films involving vampires and monsters in the 1960s, was founded in 1934 by William Hinds, a comedian and businessman whose stage name was Will Hammer. The company went bankrupt after producing five films, including *The Mystery of the Marie Celeste* (1935) featuring Béla Lugosi.

In 1947 Hinds and Enrique Carreras, the owner of a chain of London-based cinemas, reorganized it as Hammer Productions and went on to produce a number of low-budget B movies. Public support for its increasingly graphic horror movies in the aftermath of World War II turned Hammer into a successful film company. The conservative film industry had neglected horror movies for several decades and Hammer's willingness to explore the genre was due to Carreras's and Hinds's understanding that motion pictures should above all entertain and tell a gripping story.

However, it was not until 1955 that Hammer's first significant experiment with the genre came, in the form of an adaptation of a highly successful BBC science fiction horror television series, *The Quatermass Experiment*, built around a character called Bernard Quatermass, a scientist who sent a rocket into space that returned with a new form of alien life on board, which had taken over the body of the surviving astronaut. This was soon followed by *X the Unknown* (1956) and *Quatermass II* (1957). The success of these monster movies indicated that films with a pure horror theme could be very successful and encouraged the company to buy the motion picture rights to *Dracula* and *Frankenstein* from Universal Pictures.

The Curse of Frankenstein was released in 1957. Directed by Terence Fisher and starring Christopher Lee and Peter Cushing the film emphasized the shock value of presenting realistically gruesome scenes to the audiences.

It was a massive hit, earning £6 million at the box office (having cost only £200,000 to produce). Flush with the success of *The Curse of Frankenstein*, the following year Hammer Films now turned their attention to *Dracula*, better known under its American title, *The Horror of Dracula* (see below).

Hammer reigned supreme as the leading horror studio for the next two decades, providing audiences with breathtaking, spectacular scenes that mixed the familiar formula of death and resurrection with liberal amounts of violence, sex, and seduction. However, as audience tastes became more sophisticated the popularity of Hammer films began to wane in the 1970s, and by 1975 the studio was bankrupt.

In the early 1980s Hammer Films was restructured and went on to produce a series for British television, *Hammer House of Horror*, which ran for 13 episodes. In 1983, it produced 13 made-for-television films under the banner of *Hammer House of Mystery and Suspense*. The series was made in association with 20th Century Fox and as a result some of the sex and violence was toned down considerably for US television. This series was Hammer's final production of any kind to date.

Dracula movies

Hammer's first entry into Dracula movies was *The Horror of Dracula* (1958), directed by Terence Fisher and starring Christopher Lee as Dracula and Peter Cushing as Van Helsing. It was shot in full color and the story was updated to include more graphic action, sex, gore, and blood. There were a few errors, for example some fans complained that Dracula casts a shadow in the movie, but it became an instant classic in horror film and influenced many vampire movies that followed it. Substantial changes were made to Bram Stoker's story to accommodate the low budget. For example, much of the action is set in an unnamed place in Central Europe and the story is transformed into an epic battle between Van Helsing and Dracula. The final battle between Dracula and Van Helsing is highly charged, with Dracula displaying superhuman strength, but Van Helsing eventually manages to open the heavy red draperies and let sunlight disintegrate Dracula into dust. British censors only allowed part of Dracula's decomposition to be shown.

Hammer produced eight other *Dracula* films between 1960 and 1974:

- *The Brides of Dracula* (1960)

- *Dracula: Prince of Darkness* (1966)

- *Dracula Has Risen from the Grave* (1968)

- *Taste the Blood of Dracula* (1969)

- *Scars of Dracula* (1970)

- *Dracula, A.D. 1972* (1972)

- *The Satanic Rites of Dracula* (1973)

- *The Legend of the 7 Golden Vampires* (1974)

The success of *The Horror of Dracula* was followed by four direct sequels, beginning with the vastly inferior but still profitable *The Brides of Dracula* (1960). This movie did not include Dracula himself, but Peter Cushing

repeated his role as Van Helsing to battle Baron Meinster (David Peel), a sinister vampire who can shape-shift into a giant bat with a human face.

Christopher Lee returned as Dracula in the following six films, which all found a number of intriguing ways to resurrect the Count, who had been "destroyed" in *The Horror of Dracula*. For example, in *Dracula: Prince of Darkness* (1965) Dracula's servant kills a man and allows his blood to drip onto Dracula's ashes, thus resurrecting him.

Hammer increased the graphic violence and gore with *Scars of Dracula* (1971) in an attempt to make the character appeal to a younger audience. The commercial failure of this film led to further re-imagining of the character and story with *Dracula, A.D. 1972* (1972) and *The Satanic Rites of Dracula* (1973), which were not period pieces like their predecessors, but set in a then-contemporary 1970s London. *The Satanic Rites of Dracula* was to be Christopher Lee's final appearance in the Hammer Dracula movies.

The world of Dracula created by Hammer finally came to an end with *The Legend of the 7 Golden Vampires* (1974), which unsuccessfully attempted to blend the world of vampires with the world of martial arts.

Other vampire-themed movies

In the early seventies Hammer produced a number of variations on the *Dracula* story. The first choice for a new direction was a screen adaptation of Sheridan Le Fanu's story *Carmilla*. *The Vampire Lovers* (1970) featured lesbian sex scenes and graphic violence and starred the voluptuous Ingrid Pitt as the vampire Carmilla of Karnstein. It is perhaps one of the most faithful adaptations of the story.

The film's success inspired *Lust for a Vampire* (1971), which again featured graphic violence and sex as Carmilla (this time played by Yutte Stensgaard) vampirizes men instead of women, and *Countess Dracula* (1971) starring Ingrid Pitt as Countess Elizabeth Nadasday, a movie based on the story of the Blood Countess, Elizabeth Báthory. The theme of violence in vampire movies peaked in *Vampire Circus* (1971), which was set in Serbia in 1810 and centers on the story of the vampire Count Mitterhouse (Robert Tayman) who is revived and vows revenge on the town that destroyed him one hundred years previously. *Twins of Evil* was released in 1972, a film that returned to the story of *Carmilla* for inspiration; *Captain Kronos – Vampire Hunter* was also released in that year.

Hammer movies inspired a worldwide boom in vampire movies in the 1960s but by the middle of the 1970s its era of dominance in horror film-making was over. The artistic and commercial failure of poorly made films like *Captain Kronos* and *The 7 Golden Vampires* eventually forced the studios into bankruptcy in 1975. However, over the decades love of Hammer movies has been kept alive by significant numbers of devoted fans, who have organized and created a world of fanzines, books, and memorabilia.

Hannya

The hannya is a vampire-like, demon-possessed entity from Japanese folklore. Its most common manifestation was in female form, but there were also male hannyas. It was said that hannyas were especially jealous women who became insane and demon-possessed when rejected by a lover. They would transform into a hideous creature to exact vengeance on an unfaithful lover or on men in general, drinking blood and eating children. Before attacking, a hannya was said to scream at her enemy, and attack with her claws and horns. Some of Japan's most disturbing forms of art feature the hannya demon in its many hideous forms.

One legend of the Hannya tells of a woman who fell in love with a priest.

Some versions of the story say she was rejected outright, while others have the priest returning her love, yet he was forbidden by his vows to touch her. Her tragic painful longing and desperation turned her into a monster consumed with rage and jealousy and determined to get revenge.

Hantu Langsuir / Hantu Laut / Hantu Penanggalan

Three vampiric demons from Malaysia. The hantu langsuir, also known as the pontianak, is the classic Malaysian female vampire, believed to be the demon spirit of a woman who dies in childbirth and returns to feed on the blood, milk, and the entrails of newborns, nursing mothers, and pregnant women. She drains her victim's blood through a hole at the base of its neck and is said to shape-shift into the form of an owl.

The hantu laut is a vampiric spirit that attacks fishermen and sailors. It either feasts on their flesh and blood or vampirizes their soul or living essence.

The hantu penanggalan are said to be female vampiric demons that fly about as a bodiless head with trailing entrails. They prey upon pregnant women and newborns, sucking their blood and eating their flesh.

See also: **MALAYSIA**; **PONTIANAK**

Hardman, Mathew

In November 2001 teenager Mathew Hardman stabbed to death at her home on Anglesey, North Wales, a 90-year-old widow, Mabel Leyshon. Hardman, who had lived just a few yards away from his victim, mutilated her body before placing pokers at her feet in the shape of a cross. He removed her heart, wrapped it in newspaper and placed it in a saucepan on a silver platter next to her body. Vampire-like, he then drank her blood.

Struck by the brutality of the murder scene, police decided to publicize the macabre elements of Mrs. Leyshon's death including the ritualistic nature of the crime. Among the calls received by the murder squad were two from people who had heard rumors that a young man had been arrested for asking people to bite his neck. That young man was Hardman. Two months before Mrs. Leyshon's murder, he had accused a 16-year-old German girl of

being a vampire. Claiming she was "one of them," he begged the student to bite his neck so that he too could become a vampire. When she refused, he became violent and began insisting, pressing his neck against her mouth. Eventually the girl had to summon help.

At his trial the prosecution said the teenager, who denied the charge, was obsessed with vampires and the occult, and had told others he wanted to kill someone in order to become immortal. Hardman denied being obsessed, and told that court that his alleged fascination with vampires was nothing more than a subtle interest. The jury disagreed and Hardman was found guilty.

See also: **CLINICAL VAMPIRISM**; **CRIME**; **HISTORICAL VAMPIRES**

Harker, Jonathan

A major character in Bram Stoker's novel *Dracula* (1897), Jonathan Harker's journal entries in the first part of the book serve to introduce readers to the pure evil that is Count Dracula.

In many ways Harker fulfills the central role of the Gothic hero in the novel. He is young, handsome, trustworthy, and in love. He manages to survive his ordeal in Dracula's castle and, with the help of his mentor Van Helsing, rescues his young wife from the evil clutches of the Count. He then goes on to play a leading role in defeating him. Harker is also the quintessential Englishman. He represents traditional values and the comfort, protection, and sense of security a firm belief in Christianity can bring against the forces of evil.

Some experts have suggested that the character of Harker was based upon Joseph Harker, a young artist who worked at the Lyceum Theatre where Bram Stoker was employed to create the stage setting for the theater's production of *Macbeth*. Stoker had known Harker's father who had been kind to him when he was younger, and Stoker returned the favor shown to him by helping Harker establish himself as an independent artist.

In many stage and film representations of the novel the character is presented as a good but naïve person, utterly out of his depth until he joins forces with the superior intellect and experience of Van Helsing.

See also: **DRACULA**

Harker, Mina

A leading female character in Bram Stoker's 1897 novel *Dracula*, Mina's story begins with her as Miss Mina Murray, a young schoolmistress (teaching etiquette and decorum) who is engaged to Jonathan Harker and is a friend of Lucy Westenra.

After Jonathan escapes from Count Dracula's castle, Mina travels to Budapest and joins him there to aid his recovery. The two return as husband and wife. Once home they learn that Lucy has died from a mysterious illness stemming from a wild animal – later they discover that the animal was none other than Dracula taking a different shape.

Mina and Jonathan join a coalition formed by Van Helsing, which is dedicated to destroying the Count. When Dracula learns about the coalition he takes revenge and tries to weaken it by visiting – and biting – Mina at least three times. The Count also feeds Mina his blood, intending her to become a vampire at her death. Mina slowly succumbs to the vampire blood flowing through her veins and switches back and forth from a state of consciousness to a state of semi-trance, during which she is telepathically connected with Dracula.

The coalition uses Mina's semi-trance states to track down Dracula's movements and eventually they catch up with and destroy him. Mina is thereby freed from her curse. The book closes with a note about Mina and Jonathan's married life and the birth of their first-born son, whom they name Quincey in remembrance of their American friend Quincey Morris, who was killed during the final confrontation.

Victorian womanhood

On one hand, Mina is an idealized vision of Victorian-era womanhood: she is pretty, virginal, gentle, and deferential but at the same time she also embodies traits of the "new woman," doing things considered "masculine" by Victorian standards – administration, shorthand, journalism, and traveling. She is also remarkably strong, resilient, and intelligent and plays an active role in defeating Dracula by allowing herself to be hypnotized by Van Helsing in order to track the Count's movements.

To some literary critics Mina represents the nurturing aspects of the mother who cares for the vampire hunters and is rewarded for her devotion by a child, in contrast to Lucy who rejects her nurturing instincts and is destroyed at the hands of her fiancé. Mina's child, however, may have Dracula's blood in him, and in later representations of the character, for example in the film adaptation of the comic series *The League of Extraordinary Gentlemen* (2003), Mina is portrayed as an actual vampire.

Harris, Charlaine

Charlaine Harris is a contemporary *New York Times* bestselling American mystery writer and creator of the on-going Southern Vampire series of novels, published by Ace Books, which began in 2001 with *Dead until Dark*. The series features a telepathic heroine, Sookie Stackhouse, who becomes increasingly immersed in the supernatural world when her boyfriend turns out to be a vampire. Her telepathic abilities do not appear to work on vampires however.

In September 2008, *True Blood*, an American television series based on the Southern Vampire novels and starring Anna Paquin as Sookie, premiered on the premium cable network HBO in the United States. The series has been critically acclaimed and won one Golden Globe and two Satellite awards for its first season, reportedly becoming the most watched show on HBO since the phenomenally popular *Sopranos* and *Sex and the City*.

See also: LITERATURE; TELEVISION

Harris, Rachel (d. 1793)

In 1790 Captain Isaac Burton, a naval officer of Manchester, Vermont, married Rachel Harris, the step-daughter of Esquire Powel

and the daughter of his second wife. Rachel contracted tuberculosis and died within a year and was buried in February, 1793. Burton then married Hulda Powel, Esquire Powel's daughter by his first wife. Soon after they were married Hulda also contracted tuberculosis. As she lay close to death, friends of the family suspected that she was the victim of a demon-like vampire who was sucking her blood. It was suggested to Burton that Rachel could be this demon vampire and that disinterring her corpse, burning it to ashes and then feeding the ashes to Hulda would cure her.

Burton organized a ceremony at the graveyard and there, according to some reports, a crowd of up to 1,000 onlookers watched Rachel's body being exhumed. Organs were removed from her body and burned. The bizarre cremation ritual did not save Hulda's life, however, and she died a few months later on September 6, 1793.

Franz von Poblocki

Given that vampire superstitions were rife in the eighteenth century, cases like that of Rachel Harris were far from unusual at that time. What is intriguing, however, is that even in the medically and scientifically "enlightened" twentieth century isolated reports of cases similar to that of Rachel Harris continued to occur. For example, on February 5, 1970, Franz von Poblocki from the Polish town of Kantrzyno was buried in the local graveyard. Two weeks later his son Anton also died, while other members of the family experienced illness and nightmares. To the locals the reason was clear: Franz had become a vampire and was feeding on the souls of his family. The family brought in a vampire hunter who beheaded Anton's corpse and then

Franz's corpse. The obvious cause of death for both father and son was tuberculosis. The family and the hunter were put on trial for exhuming the corpses but the court of appeal dropped all charges.

See also: **NEW ENGLAND**

Harrison, Kim

Contemporary American novelist Kim Harrison is best known for her Rachel Morgan urban fantasy series (also known as The Hollow series), which is set in an alternate history where a worldwide pandemic caused by genetic modification has caused the death of a large portion of the world's human population. At that point, the hidden "Inderlanders," creatures such as witches, werewolves, and vampires come forward to reveal themselves to the world.

The series, which is published by Harper-Collins and began in 2004 with *Dead Witch Walking*, tells the story in the first-person point-of-view of Rachel Morgan, a detective witch who works with local law enforcement agencies and faces threats both mundane and supernatural in origin. The series also focuses on Rachel's professional relationships with her partners, a living vampire and a pixy, as well as her personal relationships with males of different species.

Harrison's vampires are similar to traditional portrayals of blood-sucking vampires, with some exceptions. Their saliva contains neuro-transmitters that make the pain of a vampire's bite feel like pleasure. Vampires can also mentally control their victims. There are two kinds of vampires: living and undead. Living vampires are normal humans infected with the vampire virus. When vampires become undead, they gain the full physical benefits of the vampire virus, but lose their souls in the process.

See also: **LITERATURE**

Hartmann, Franz (1838–1912)

Franz Hartmann was an early twentieth-century German physician who was also a leading expert and author on the occult and the undead. Although he has often been dismissed by specialists as a crank, and his theories on the astral body are only considered credible today within a few occult circles, his work did help preserve many fascinating vampire tales from the nineteenth century.

Psychic vampirism

Hartmann investigated a number of contemporary vampire cases and reported his findings and conclusions in a series of occult journals. It was from these investigations that Hartmann developed his theory of the psychic vampire or psychic vampirism. According to Hartmann, vampires were real but they were not the blood-sucking undead. They were an instinctive force field of subhuman intelligence, a kind of mindless, malignant psychic cancer. Hartmann maintained that a psychic vampire could attach itself to the astral body of a living person, slowly draining that person of health and vitality. His theory was supported by his observations of a young boy with classic symptoms of vampire attack. The boy was emaciated but had a huge appetite. He also claimed that there was a force pressing down on his chest that paralyzed and drained the life out of him. The boy's employer claimed that he had grabbed an invisible but jelly-like substance resting on the boy's chest.

Premature burial

In 1895 Hartmann published a book about the phenomenon of premature burial. He detailed some 700 cases of premature burial and developed a theory first put forward in the 1860s by a French physician, Z.-J. Piérart. According to this theory when a person was buried alive their astral body separated from their physical body, and this astral body could vampirize others, feeding on both life and blood to nourish the corpse in the tomb. Hartmann suggested that the astral body could actually be severed completely from the physical body and continue as an earthbound vampiric spirit.

On a more "practical" note, after reviewing so many distressing cases of premature burial Hartmann also recommended that anyone interred without proper embalming should be provided with chloroform in the coffin, so if the unfortunate individual woke up a way out was available.

Haugbui

In Norwegian folklore the haugbui (meaning "sleepers in the mounds" or "barrow dwellers") could be dangerous and deadly, like the vampire-like draugr (meaning "one who walks after death"), but they would only attack if someone walked over the place where they were buried. It was said they could rise suddenly from the earth and then sink back into it, like smoke.

The haugbui could from time to time be unpredictable, and on occasion leave their tombs and attack those whose homes were nearby, or passers-by for no reason. *The Eyrbyggja Saga*, for example, tells the story of Thorolf Halt Foot, a man of foul temper when

alive and even worse when he returned as a haugbui, marauding and killing in the countryside around his tomb at certain times of the year. It was said that any animal that grazed close to his tomb howled piteously and went mad. In some instances, cattle, horses, and even dogs were found dead and drained of blood close by. Sometimes the creature would also attack shepherds and herders. No one could destroy him but he was eventually contained by building a stone wall around his tomb. Even then he still proved difficult to restrain, and after several deaths in the locality his body was dug up and burned.

See also: **DRAUGR; ICELAND**

Hawthorn

Hawthorn, a member of the rose family, is a hardy, thorny shrub or small tree with white or pink flowers that blossom in clusters before being followed by small red, blue, or black fruits. Hawthorn has been called a symbol of hope because it signals the end of winter and beginning of spring and, along with other thorny woods, was one of the favored woods used to make stakes for destroying vampires in parts of Europe, especially among the Slavs.

In ancient times hawthorn was considered by the Romans to be a charm against witchcraft, but in medieval times its association with Christ and his crown of thorns meant that it was considered effective against all evil entities, including vampires. Hawthorn would be sharpened into stakes and pounded into the ground near graves to pierce the vampire when it rose from its tomb. Thorns of the shrub would also be placed in shrouds or coffins to stab or pin the corpse down.

Hawthorn placed on a windowsill was thought to prevent a vampire from entering a house.

It is interesting to note that in Serbia the word for a hawthorn stake is also the word for a type of butterfly. The relation between the two is a confusing one for in Serbia a vampire was thought to be able to transform into a butterfly. Moreover in the Balkans generally, the human soul was believed to take on a corporeal form when it left the body and one of the forms reported is that of a butterfly.

In her book, *The Land Beyond the Forest*, Emily Gerard stated that the people of Transylvania would *"lay the thorny branch of a wild rose bush across the body to prevent it leaving its coffin,"* and it is possible that Bram Stoker learned of this practice when writing *Dracula*. Van Helsing mentions that a branch of wild rose on the coffin will keep the vampire inside.

In *Travels through Serbia* (1828), Serbian author Joakim Vujić records how hawthorn was used to destroy the corpse of an exhumed vampire in a village near Novi Pazar. The priest opened the "vampire's" clenched teeth with a hawthorn stick and then poured holy water into the corpse's mouth, placing another twig of hawthorn between its jaws. Another man struck the corpse on the chest with a sharpened hawthorn stick. The corpse opened its mouth and blood poured out and the vampire was declared destroyed.

Heart

While some regions prefer decapitation as a method of slaying a vampire, most regions in Europe adhere to the idea that the heart must be removed and destroyed. There is widespread belief in vampire lore in Romania that vampires have two hearts, the second providing the creature with its undead existence. (It was also thought that vampires had two souls or spirits, one of which departs at death leaving the other to animate the corpse and dedicate itself to the destruction of humankind. Moreover, it was also stated that one could recognize a vampire by the fact that he or she would talk to him or herself!)

In the past, people believed that the spirit resided within the heart, the accepted source of power for the undead, so that when killing the evil spirit of the vampire a stake should be driven through the heart; the heart would then be cut out and burned and the ashes scattered in flowing water. There were variations in how this procedure was carried out. Many people simply burned the heart, but in Serbia the heart was cut, boiled in wine, and placed back into the cavity. In areas where the Greek Orthodox Church was powerful, the heart would literally be ripped out – a custom that would have struck fear into Yugoslavian Gypsies who believed that any contact with vampire blood could cause madness. In Romania a stake was often heated and inserted into the heart, thus destroying it.

See also: **DESTRUCTION**

Hecate

Hecate was a goddess believed by the ancient Greeks to be the patroness of sorcery and magic and the Queen of the Underworld – the world of the sleeping and the dead. She was an influential figure in linking vampirism with witchcraft, sorcery, and the occult. She was often depicted with three bodies standing back to back so she could see in all directions from a crossroad. Her association with vampirism and blood-drinking probably originated from her involvement with sorcery as well as the actions of her evil servants: demons known as mormos and phantom-like vampires called empusas.

Hematomania

Most of these individuals, who may be titled real vampires in popular parlance, have manifested symptoms of what psychologists refer to as hematomania, a blood fetish, or clinical vampirism, a compulsion to consume blood; psychological and sometimes sexual needs require blood to be met and satisfied. Occasionally, the so-called vampires are also known to eat human flesh as well as consume the blood.

The condition is extremely rare but there are a number of historical and modern-day examples. Elizabeth Báthory (1560–1614) is a well-known historical example of a murderer with a blood lust, and today the sanguinarian movement is an organization of self-professed vampires or seemingly ordinary people who drink human blood from willing donors.

See also: **BLOOD; CLINICAL VAMPIRISM; DISEASE; HISTORICAL VAMPIRES; SANGUINARIANS**

Heretics

A heretic is a person who adheres to a theological teaching or doctrine condemned as false by religious authorities. Over the centuries, heresy has appeared in numerous religious systems but it has been most associated with the Christian Church. In medieval times heretics were excommunicated from the Church, and burned at the stake to save their souls.

Somewhere along the line, the idea that people who were excommunicated from the Church were likely to transform into vampires developed. This was especially the case in Russia where several heretic vampire types, such as the eretica, came from.

See also: **CHRISTIANITY; EXCOMMUNICATION**

Hermsdorf Vampire

In 1753 in the village of Hermsdorf, which, according to vampirologist Hermann Schreiber in *Es Spukt in Deutschland* (1975), is a place in Silesia close to the town of Troppau, near the Polish border, a woman known as the "Doktorin" who had spent her lifetime curing people with the help of mysterious potions she brewed at home died. Schreiber states that he has found the story about Frau Doktorin in issue 40 of the *Vossischen Zeitung*, dated 1755.

According to Schreiber, when the woman sensed that her life was coming to an end, she called her husband to her bedside and made him promise that after her death he would cut her head off before her corpse was buried. She also made him swear that he would not bury her in a Catholic churchyard.

After her death, her husband found that he simply did not have the stomach to carry out her request, and to make matters worse a local priest told him that only sinners were buried outside of the churchyard, so she was buried in the churchyard. It was not long before stories began to circulate that the Doktorin had returned from her grave as a vampire. One night when he got very drunk at a local inn the husband told his drinking companions about the gruesome requests his late wife had made before her death. The next day, the whole village had heard the story, and it did not take long before the authorities had heard about it too.

In 1755 the woman's grave was opened, along with those of another 30 corpses also suspected of being vampires. Of the 31 corpses exhumed 21, including the Doktorin, looked remarkably fresh and were declared to be vampires. The undead vampires were staked and cremated.

Hiadam Vampires

One of the best-documented vampire cases from the early eighteenth century occurred in a village called Hiadam, a location believed to be near the Hungarian border but never officially identified. Officials from the Holy Roman Empire were called in to investigate in 1720.

The case began one evening when a soldier billeted with a farming family witnessed a stranger come into the house and take a place at the table. The next morning the farmer was discovered dead. Eventually the family told the soldier that the stranger had been the farmer's father, who had died 10 years before. The soldier told his friends and it was not long before word reached the local general, Count de Cadreras, who instigated an investigation. Other people came forward to report other vampire attacks; one claimed that a vampire, dead 16 years, had sucked the blood and life out of his two sons; another claimed that a vampire, who died 30 years before, had killed several family members.

When the bodies of the suspected vampires were exhumed, they showed delayed decomposition, and fresh blood flowed when they were cut. The Count ordered that the bodies be beheaded and then burned. A full account of the investigation and outcome was sent to Emperor Charles VI, who was so alarmed that he ordered a second investigation, this time by theologians, surgeons, and lawyers. Although the paperwork given to the Emperor documenting these proceedings, along with a lengthy narrative given by the Count to an official at the University of Fribourg, survived, the town of Hiadam has never been identified, nor has a place by that name ever been recorded.

Hide

Animal skins or hides would be used by Gypsies to cover the body of a suspected vampire during the process of impalement, as it was thought that any contact with vampire blood would cause a person to go insane. The hide would either be placed over a suspected grave and then stakes would be pounded into the earth to impale the corpse, or it would be wrapped around the corpse while a hammer was used to drive a stake into the corpse's heart or stomach.

See also: **DESTRUCTION**

Highgate Vampire

At a cemetery in Highgate, London, between 1967 and 1983 a series of events took place which led many people to believe that a vampire had taken up residence at the cemetery. The cemetery, officially called the Cemetery of St. James, was consecrated in 1839. Its association with the vampire legend began with its use by Bram Stoker as the disguised burial place of Dracula's victim, Lucy Westenra in his 1897 novel.

The more recent story of vampires at Highgate, however, began in the late 1960s with reports of phantoms seen in the cemetery in the evenings. When a local occultist and author, Sean Manchester, heard reports of the dead rising from their graves from a schoolgirl, Elizabeth Wojdyla, and her friend he set out to investigate. Wojdyla also claimed that something malevolent was coming into her bedroom at night. Over the next few years Manchester collected other accounts of strange sightings in and around the cemetery. In 1969 Wojdyla, still suffering from nightmares, began to develop the symptoms of pernicious anemia and on her neck were two small puncture wounds. According to Manchester, when he and Wojdyla's boyfriend filled her room with garlic, crosses, and holy water her symptoms improved.

The vampire hunt

Around the same time there were reports that the cemetery and nearby park were being used for the ritual killing of animals; some of the animals were found drained of blood. Local newspapers began to speculate that their might be a "vampyre" in the area. Manchester then reported that he was in touch with another woman who had the same symptoms as Wojdyla. While sleepwalking this young woman had led him to some burial vaults in the cemetery, which encouraged Manchester to believe that the possibility of a vampire at Highgate cemetery was real. Newspapers picked up on the story and the cemetery soon became a focal point for journalists and the curious.

On March 13, 1970, a group of a hundred people led by Manchester made their way to Highgate cemetery. The hunt was not organized by Manchester but was entirely spontaneous, due to a television transmission about the suspected vampire on the same evening. The large iron door to the tomb would not budge and so Manchester and two helpers entered the vault through a hole. They found three empty coffins. In each coffin they placed a cross and garlic and sprinkled them with salt and holy water. In the words of Manchester himself, which would not seem out of place if found in Bram Stoker's novel:

> Two assistants followed and we searched the musty, damp interior for signs of the undead's resting place, brushing aside cobwebs and items of decay as we went. In all we found three evacuated coffins which we proceeded to line with garlic and a cross. A circle of salt was poured around, and holy water sprinkled inside, each.

In August the same year the body of a young woman was found at the cemetery. Her corpse had been decapitated and burned. Police treated it as an incident of black magic attributed to Satanists and did not directly relate it to the vampire hunt. Two local self-proclaimed vampire hunters called David Farrant and Allan Blood were, however, blamed for disturbing the earth around the graves. Farrant was arrested for trespass but acquitted on the grounds that the cemetery was open to the public.

As is typical of such incidents, stories based on rumor and unconfirmed sightings soon spread, and the tabloid newspapers ran a number of sensationalist features. One witness allegedly reported seeing a gaunt man dressed in black leave the cemetery at night. According to Manchester he did manage to enter another vault and discover what he claimed to be a real vampire. He did not mutilate the body but read an exorcism and sealed the vault with garlic-permeated scent.

Seven years later

Seven years later in 1977, Manchester started to investigate a mansion near Highgate cemetery that was said to be haunted. According to his account he discovered a coffin in the basement and when he opened it he allegedly saw the same vampire he had seen seven years before in Highgate cemetery. This time he staked the body, which then disintegrated into slime, and burned the coffin. Not long after the mansion was demolished.

Although Manchester believed he had destroyed the vampire, reports of animals drained of blood reappeared in the nearby suburb of Finchley in 1980. Manchester speculated that a vampire had been created by the bite of the Highgate vampire. He researched the case and came to the conclusion that a woman called Lusia was the culprit. Lusia had died and been buried in Great North London cemetery. One evening

in 1982, Manchester went to the cemetery and allegedly encountered a spider-like creature about the size of a cat. He staked it and as dawn approached it turned into Lusia. Manchester returned the remains of her body to her grave, and the case of the Highgate vampire was closed.

No vampire was ever publicly discovered, but Manchester wrote up his account of the events that took place there in *The Highgate Vampire* (1995) and *The Vampire Hunter's Handbook* (1987). Meanwhile his vampire-hunting rival, David Farrant, founded The Highgate Vampire Society and recorded his perspective on the story in the society's literature. According to Farrant in his bestselling book on the subject, *Beyond the Highgate Vampire* (1997), ley lines may be an important factor that has been left completely out of the Highgate equation. Ley lines are hypothetical alignments of a number of places of geographical interest, such as ancient monuments and megaliths, and Farrant claims that these lines can transmit psychic energy along their course and enable a vampire to materialize when the right conditions prevail.

It is important to bear in mind that the existence of the Highgate Vampire has not been proved to date, and both Manchester's and Farrant's accounts and insights are simply their perspectives on a series of unexplained events that took place at Highgate cemetery.

Hillyer, Vincent (1930–2000)

American author and lecturer Vincent Hillyer was best known for his research on vampires and for the account of his night spent in Castle

Poenari in Romania which he recorded in his book *Vampires* (1988).

Hillyer's interest in vampires began in his youth when he watched reruns of classic vampire films, such as *Dracula* (1931) starring Béla Lugosi, but it was not until 1977 that this interest was rekindled when he became the first Westerner to spend the night alone in the so-called Castle Dracula at Poenari. According to Hillyer, while he slept in the castle he received a large painful bite on his collarbone that made him ill; a local doctor identified it as the bite of a spider, but Hillyer claimed that after his experience he was more sensitive to sunlight. He also developed pre-cancerous skin lesions.

Out of his experience at Poenari and his study of vampires Hillyer wrote *Vampires* in 1988 and developed his own theory of psychic vampirism, which was based upon the existence of the astral body, a subtle duplicate of the physical body. The astral body needs the physical body as its home, and after the death of the physical body, the astral body tries to feed the physical body with the blood of living humans to keep it from decaying.

Metaphorically, Hillyer defined the process of the intake of blood by the astral body as the Hemolytic Factor. He propounded that the astral body perforates the physical body of the victim. The blood in the astral body then causes a process of hemolysis (the degeneration of red blood cells and the release of hemoglobin) within the victim. In the resulting expulsion of red corpuscles, the astral body collects the blood cells and transports them back to its own host body. Hillyer also believed that all living persons who are knowledgeable in occult practices can become intentional psychic vampires.

Hillyer took part in extensive vampire-related research all over the world, eventually becoming the vice president of the Count Dracula Fan Club and a board member of the American chapter of the Transylvanian Society of Dracula. He died in 2000 from complications of cancer.

His-hsue-kuei

His-hsue-kuei is a Chinese name for a vampire, which translates as "sucking blood demon."

See also: **CHIANG-SHIH; CHINA**

Historia rerum Anglicarum

Written around 1196 to 1198 the *Historia rerum Anglicarum* is a chronicle of England written by the English monk and historian William of Newburgh. Translated as *History of England* it attempts to cover the years 1066 to 1198. Although it has been criticized for being over-reliant on oral traditions, legends, and rumors, it is often cited as one of the primary medieval accounts of vampires, containing a number of interesting cases recorded in Buckinghamshire, Berwick, and Alnwick Castle.

Historical Vampires

Whether vampires did or do exist is a hotly debated issue, but throughout history there have been a number of bloodthirsty individuals whose activities have certainly provided a basis for the legend.

Vlad the Impaler and Elizabeth Báthory

First and foremost there is Vlad the Impaler, the fifteenth-century Wallachian prince whose favorite method of torture was to impale people. The end of the stake was oiled, but not quite sharpened and it would be slowly pushed into the body, starting from the buttocks of the victim and continuing until it came out from their mouth. It was said that in 1461 Sultan Mohammed II, the conqueror of Constantinople and a man not noted for his squeamishness, returned to Constantinople after being sickened by the sight of 20,000 impaled corpses rotting outside of Vlad's capital.

The second most well-known example is the sixteenth-century Countess Elizabeth Báthory, who was known as the Blood Countess. She allegedly tortured and killed over 600 servant girls and drank their blood and bathed in it. She is probably the most prolific female serial killer in history.

Other famous historical vampires

Other well-known historical figures frequently associated with vampires include the necrophiliac Sergeant Bertrand (mid nineteenth century), the bloodthirsty Gilles de Rais (1404–40), and the vampiric Antoine Léger (died 1824). In 1872 Vincenzo Verzeni, a so-called living vampire from Italy, was arrested and sentenced to life imprisonment for murder and corpse mutilation. He also drank human blood. His teeth were allegedly so sharp that the authorities feared he would bite through the steel bars in his jail and so he was placed in a special prison cell.

In more modern times, a number of blood-hungry serial killers have been dubbed vampires by the press. In the early twentieth century Victor Ardisson became known as the Vampire of Muy. Fritz Haarmann committed at least 24 murders in Germany between 1919 and 1924. He killed his victims by biting their necks. During his trial, which became a media circus, Haarmann was variously called a werewolf and a vampire. He was beheaded in 1925.

Haarmann wasn't the only "vampire" in Germany at that time; Peter Kürten, a serial killer who was beheaded in 1932, was known as "the Vampire of Düsseldorf." He was charged with nine murders and a variety of other offences, including sexual assaults. Kuno Hoffman was another vampire grave robber and murderer of Germany, called "the Vampire of Nuremberg." He was caught in 1973 after murdering a couple and drinking blood from their wounds. Although he declared that the blood of the living was much tastier than the blood of the dead, he would also break into graves and drink the blood of corpses, believing it would make him "good looking and strong."

In England, John George Haigh, the infamous Acid Bath Murderer, was also known as "the Vampire of London." Haigh, who was hanged in 1949, claimed to have drunk the blood of his victims before destroying their bodies in a vat of sulfuric acid.

In addition to individuals whose blood-thirsty lifestyles have fueled the vampire legend, there have also been a number of historical cases involving the dead bodies of suspected vampires, most notably the cases of Peter Plogojowitz (1725) and Arnold Paole (1727) – arguably the most famous vampire cases in history.

See also: **CLINICAL VAMPIRISM; CRIME; LIVING VAMPIRES; NECROPHILIA; REAL VAMPIRES**

Hockerill

In 2007 in Hockerill, Hertfordshire, England, a 43-year-old man was attacked by someone who tried to bite his neck when he was putting his garbage out at night. The attacker snarled like an animal when the man wrestled with him. The man immediately called the police. The incident became one of several similar attacks to affect this small community over a period of several months. Residents told visiting news reporters that several people in the community had nicknamed the attacker "Dracula." The case remains unsolved.

Local skeptics, the police, and the media downplayed the attacks as the work of a deranged, mentally ill person "pretending" to be a vampire, but those living in the community and those who were attacked were not so sure. The Hockerill incident and others like it, when small communities report unexplained and bizarre attacks, often fuel public curiosity and interest in whether or not vampires really could or do exist today.

See also: **REAL VAMPIRES**

Holes

In Eastern European vampire lore, vampires were said to exit and re-enter graves via holes in the ground, and one way to detect a vampire was to see a series of small holes on a grave or near it. In Bulgaria it was customary to place bowls of human excrement or poison by the holes to prevent the vampire leaving the grave. The vampire would eat the excrement instead of seeking out the blood of the living.

Holly

Holly is a spiky-leafed evergreen shrub or tree typically distinguished by red or black berries. The Christian custom of decorating houses and churches with holly may have originated from the ancient Roman use of the tree during the festival of Saturnalia or from the Teutonic belief in the beneficial nature of holly. Hung on doors and windows, it has been used as a form of protection against vampires for centuries.

See also: **PROTECTION**

Holmwood, Arthur

A fictional character in Bram Stoker's novel *Dracula* (1897). He is presented as a decent, honest character who becomes Lord Godalming when his father dies, and then Lucy Westenra's fiancé. He stakes Lucy the vampire on what should have been their wedding night.

Holy Objects

In vampire folklore there are a number of references to the use of blessed or holy objects as a form of protection against the vampire. In Eastern Europe, for example, a sacred bullet can be fired into the coffin of a vampire to kill it. It is not clear, however, how exactly the bullet was made sacred, although it is likely that it was blessed by a priest or simply sprinkled with holy water. It was also common practice in Eastern Orthodox Christian communities to bury the dead with a holy object, such as a crucifix. The idea was to sanctify the corpse and make it impossible for the undead to enter it.

From an occult perspective the use of holy or blessed objects can have a potent effect against the undead, because when an item is blessed it becomes charged with a form of will power. A similar principle would be at work if an item was blessed not by a priest but in a way that agreed with the vampire hunter's beliefs. The hunter's belief would have a psychic power of its own. Many contemporary vampire stories contain the idea that a person must believe in a crucifix or other holy object for it to work against vampires. In other words, it is the person's belief or will that is potent, not the object itself.

Holy Water

See: **WATER**

Homosexuality

The undead vampires or revenants of folklore appear to have little preference whether their victims are male, female, or even human, but, in the words of vampire expert David Skal, *"given that vampire stories create tension and interest through the presence of a sexual outsider it is not surprising that explicit and implicit homosexuality has been employed in film and fiction to evoke aspects of vampirism."* The images presented have ranged from the stereotype of the gay sexual predator to powerful evocations of liberation from sexual conservatism.

Literary critics have long been aware of a homosexual aspect to the very first pieces of vampire literature, but while works such as Sheridan Le Fanu's *Carmilla* (1872) set the scene for a recurring lesbian undertone in vampire literature, male vampires tended to prefer female victims. This male heterosexuality was emphasized in *Dracula* (1897), the first major work to include male vampire victims. Jonathan Harker is not vampirized by Dracula but left as a treat for his vampire brides when the Count departs to London. In the first vampire movies there was also an absence of male vampires attacking male victims. It was not until the sexual revolution of the 1960s and 70s that vampire movies with gay vampires, such as *Tenderness of Wolves* (1973), began to appear.

The most notable expression of homosexual vampire relationships in literature came in the novels of Anne Rice, which collapsed vampire gender boundaries and brought homosexuality to the fore. Her first novel, *Interview with the Vampire* (1975), focused on the intense relationship between Louis and Lestat de Lioncourt and the homosexual associations between them were clear. Although her vampires do not have sex as such, because their sex organs were dysfunctional, biting and sucking of blood is presented as an act superior to sex.

See also: **AIDS; GAY CULTURE; LESBIAN VAMPIRES; SEX**

Horror of Dracula, The

The Horror of Dracula was the first of the Hammer Films Dracula movies, released in 1958 as *Dracula* and re-titled *The Horror of Dracula* in the United States. Along with the Béla Lugosi version of *Dracula* (1931), it helped set the image of Dracula for contemporary popular culture in the twentieth century. The movie introduced actor Christopher Lee as the ultimate Dracula and made fangs, red eyes, large amounts of blood, and overt sexuality an essential part of vampire movie-making.

Two elements combined to make *The Horror of Dracula* a commercial success. First of all the film presented Dracula as a sexual and seductive predator, and by so doing made Lee into an international star with a legion of female fans. Second, it was the first *Dracula* movie to be made in Technicolor; color added a whole new bloody dimension to the horror movie.

The movie

The movie is a version of Bram Stoker's 1897 novel but it deviates from the original text in that Jonathan Harker is not a naïve English-man and real estate agent but a follower of Van Helsing, who is sent to Dracula's castle to investigate who and what the Count is. Harker is subsequently killed and vampirized, and then destroyed by Van Helsing when he arrives at the castle. Dracula leaves the castle to vampirize Lucy Westenra, who is recast in this reinterpretation as Harker's fiancée and Mina Murray's sister. Mina is married to Arthur Holmwood, who emerges as the dominant male.

Van Helsing, discovering that Lucy is biting others, takes the lead by killing her. An angry Dracula retaliates by seducing and attacking Mina. Her death is prevented by Holmwood and Van Helsing who chase Dracula back to his castle and confront him. The film climaxes quite spectacularly with Van Helsing jumping across a table to tear open a curtain, revealing the rays of the sun. Dracula dissolves into dust – a startling conclusion that created certain problems when attempting to resurrect Dracula in a sequel.

See also: **FILMS**

Horse/Horseshoes

In European vampire folklore a horse, most typically a stallion, was often used to help find the grave of a vampire. In Albania a white horse would be led into a graveyard and be forced to walk over the graves. If the horse refused to step over a particular grave then it was thought this was because a vampire lay underneath. In other areas of Europe the horse would be black. Whatever the particular color, it had to be monochrome. In some traditions the horse had to be ridden by a virgin or be virginal itself. In others it was thought that walking a horse several times over a suspected grave could destroy a vampire. Curiously, it was also said that vampires had the power to transform themselves into black horses.

One early twentieth-century Romanian case describes how a white horse was used to help identify the grave of a disease-causing vampire.

In the village of Vaguilesti in Transylvania a peasant by the name of Dimitriu Vaideanu married a woman and had many children with her. Seven of these children died within a few months of being born and the people of the village suspected that a vampire was in their midst. A white horse was taken to the cemetery at night to see if it would pass over the graves of all the wife's relatives. The horse jumped over all the graves except that of the wife's mother, Joana Marta, who had been suspected of witchcraft in her life. When it reached Marta's grave the horse refused to move and started to beat the earth with its hooves. A few nights later Vaideanu and a son went to dig up the grave and were horrified by what they saw. The corpse had red skin, long fingernails, and long hair and appeared to be sitting up. They burned the corpse and returned home. The attacks and the deaths of the children stopped.

Horseshoes

In a number of countries horseshoes are symbols of good luck because they are made of iron. All over the world iron has been regarded as a charm against evil spirits. They also evoke the shape of the crescent moon and invite the protection of pagan moon goddesses. In addition, the seven nails in a horseshoe invoke the traditionally lucky number seven. In England, for example, it was thought that a horseshoe on a door could protect against witches and witchcraft. Although originally used to keep witches at bay, horseshoes were also used to protect against vampires.

See also: **Animal Vampires**

Host, Consecrated

The consecrated Host is the blessed wafer or bread used in the Christian sacrament of the Eucharist, in which bread and wine are consumed in memory of the sacrifice of Jesus Christ. The wine either becomes or symbolizes Christ's blood and the bread becomes or symbolizes his body. For vampire hunters the Host is one of the most powerful weapons that can be used against a vampire, either as a shield or broken into four pieces to form a cross. Its use against vampires in history is, however, fairly rare as from the Middle Ages to the twentieth century it was usually well protected and kept locked away, for fear it would be desecrated.

In Bram Stoker's *Dracula*, Van Helsing places the Host on Mina Harker's forehead as a form of protection, but in more modern vampire literature and films the crucifix replaced the Host as the most potent religious symbol to be used against the vampire.

Huber, Ambrosius

Ambrosius Huber was a late fifteenth-century printer from Nuremberg. In 1499 he published a pamphlet on Vlad Tepes (Vlad the Impaler), which was one of several works that helped to present the image of Vlad to the West as a bloodthirsty, sadistic murderer. The pamphlet included a well-known woodcut showing Vlad eating in the middle of various impaled victims. The text added to the gore by stating that Vlad would impale people and roast their heads in kettles. It also stated that the tyrant cooked children and made their parents eat them.

Hubner, Stephen

The case of Stephen Hubner, who became known as "the vampire of Trautenau," a Slavic village, is interesting because his corpse was not only accused of attacking and strangling people, sometime between 1730 and 1732, but cattle as well. The case was investigated by the supreme court of the district and enough evidence was uncovered to warrant exhuming the body. It was found perfectly preserved with *"all the marks of vampirism,"* so the magistrates ordered it to be decapitated and burned, together with other corpses buried around him.

Huet, Pierre-Daniel (1630-1721)

Pierre-Daniel Huet, the French bishop of Soissons and Avranches, was a leading classical scholar of his day and one of the first Church writers to examine the undead, including vampires in his *Memoirs*. His views on the subject of vampirism were based on his theological beliefs and reports from Father François Richard who had spent many years on the island of Santorini, believed to be heavily infested with vampires. Huet's account examined the Greek customs of burning the dead, the belief that evil persons had their bodies taken over by the Devil, and the morbid preventative custom of cutting off a corpse's feet, nose, hands, and ears and then hanging them around the corpse's elbows.

Huli Jing

The huli jing ("fox fairy") is a much-feared spirit from Chinese mythology. It resembles the characteristics of a vampire and it takes the life force of its victims, albeit through sex.

This malevolent spirit is said to shape-shift from the shape of a fox into a seductive woman, old man, or scholar who can then seduce and vampirize the life force of its victims during orgasm. When the victim weakens and falls ill, the huli jing leaves to seek another victim. The huli jing can also shape-shift into the image of another person, living or dead, and has the ability to pass through walls and closed windows and haunt places. The creature can only been seen at night, where it is said to reside on the rooftops of homes. The huli jing is also thought to cause insanity and if several generations of the same family suffer from insanity it is said that an ancestor once injured a huli jing. Therefore great care is taken never to harm a huli jing. However, if its tail is cut off it will leave and never return, as the power of the huli jing resides in its tail.

A female huli jing is believed to especially like scholars of virtue, but if she is given wine to drink she will become drunk and vanish. One remedy against the huli jing is the burning of paper charms, or written prayers. The ashes are then mixed into a tea and drunk. In modern Mandarin and Cantonese, the term *huli jing* is a derogatory expression used to describe a woman who seduces a married man.

See also: CHINA; KITSUNE

Hungarian Hunter, The

In 1746 Dom Augustin Calmet published an influential treatise on vampires in Eastern Europe, which included the following description of a vampire hunter, known simply as "the Hungarian," who successfully dealt with a vampire problem in Liebava, Hungary. The following is quoted from Montague Summers' *The Vampire: His Kith and Kin* (1928).

A certain Hungarian who passed through the village at the time when the terror was at its height avowed that he could cope with the evil and lay the vampire to rest. In order to fulfil his promise he mounted the clock-tower of the church and watched for the moment when the vampire came out of his grave, leaving behind him in the tomb his shroud and cerements, before he made his way to the village to plague and terrify the inhabitants.

When the Hungarian from his coin of vantage had seen the vampire depart on his prowl, he promptly descended from the tower possessed himself of the shroud and line carrying them off with him back to the belfry. The vampire in due course returned and not finding his sere-clothes cried out mightily against the thief, who from the top of the belfry was making signs to him that he should climb and recover his winding sheet if he wished to get it back again. The vampire, accordingly, began to clamber up the steep stair which led to the summit of the tower, but the Hungarian

suddenly gave him such a blow that he fell from top to bottom. Thereupon they were able to strike off his head with the sharp edge of a sexton's spade, and that made an end of the whole business.

The priest who related this history to me, himself saw nothing of these happenings, neither was anything witnessed by the Right Reverend Canon who was acting as Episcopal Commissioner. They only received the reports of the peasants of that district, a folk who were very ignorant, very credulous, very superstitious, and brimful of all kinds of wonderful stories concerning the aforesaid vampire.

Hungary

On February 15, 1912, the *Daily Telegraph* newspaper in Britain contained the following paragraph:

A Buda-Pesth telegram to the Messaggero reports a terrible instance of superstition. A boy of fourteen died some days ago in a small village. A farmer, in whose employment the boy had been, thought that the ghost of the latter appeared to him every night. In order to put a stop to these supposed visitations, the farmer, accompanied by some friends, went to the cemetery one night, stuffed three pieces of garlic and three stones in the mouth, and thrust a stake through the corpse, fixing it to the ground. This was to deliver themselves from the evil spirit, as the credulous farmer and his friends stated when they were arrested.

Given the fact that some experts believe it was in Hungary that the undead first came to the attention of Europe, it's no surprise that reports of suspected vampires lingered on there well into the early twentieth century. The respected vampirologist Montague Summers once described Hungary as being a place *"heavily infested with vampires"* owing to the large number of cases reported in villages and throughout the countryside during the seventeenth and eighteenth century. The incessant nature of these cases forced both the secular and Church authorities to investigate, and reports of vampire outbreaks in Hungary were examined as fact by scholars, doctors, and theologians as well as in treatises by highly respected experts and theologians such as Dom Augustin Calmet. Notable cases reported in Hungary include the Hiadam Vampires, and the cases of Peter Plogojowitz and Arnold Paole.

Hungarian vampire species

The most talked-about species of vampire from Hungary was the *vampir*, which could be destroyed by driving a stake through the heart. There were, however, less well-known species such as the *liderc*, a shape-shifting creature that attacked and killed victims through exhaustion. Defensive measures included the use of garlic. Another vampire-like species was the *nora*, an invisible being that was said to jump on humans and suck their breasts, causing swelling. The antidote was to smear garlic on the breasts.

It has often been suggested that Hungary, the land of the Magyars, gave the world the word "vampire," which has its origins in the Magyar tongue. This theory, however, has recently been countered by Hungarian scholars who argue that the first appearance of the word "vampire" in print in Hungarian postdates its first published use in most Western languages by some 50 years. The question remains open to debate, but it is possible that the word was picked up in Hungary and transmitted to the West by travelers in the early eighteenth century. Other experts have reinforced the idea that, despite popular ideas to the contrary, there was no widespread belief in vampires among the Hungarians, arguing that, with the exception of the much-reported vampire outbreaks that occurred between 1725 and 1732, few reports of vampires actually come from Hungary. Most scholars, however, agree that Hungarian interaction with Gypsies and their Slavic neighbors would increase the likelihood of beliefs about vampires drifting into the countryside.

Hunger, The

The Hunger was a 1981 novel about vampires written by horror writer Whitley Strieber. In 1983 it was made into a visually arresting film featuring Catherine Deneuve, David Bowie, and Susan Sarandon.

The novel brings vampirism into the modern age but its central character, Miriam Blaylock, is an ancient vampire (she is old by the time of Christ) whose vampirism seems to be caused by a blood disease. She does not bite her victims but uses a knife to slice open their arteries. As she drinks she connects with them telepathically and the experience becomes an erotic one for her and her victim. After losing her vampire lover she sets out to find his replacement and chooses a female doctor involved in research on immortality to help her. Blaylock allows herself to be studied by the scientist but at the same time she gradually seduces her and draws her into her immortal life. The climax of the film is dramatic, shocking, and intense with a powerful focus on the circle of life, death, immortality, and love.

Hypnosis

Hypnosis is a state of intense concentration or altered state of consciousness when a person can be more receptive to new ideas and suggestion and display heightened psychic awareness. Even though there are accounts of vampires attacking victims while they sleep, and victims waking up to see a vampire hovering above them, hypnotic powers were not a prominent feature of vampire folklore. However, ever since Bram Stoker's *Dracula* (1897) – where the Count's mesmerizing powers are clearly evident from early on in the book, and become even stronger when he has bitten a victim and shares a telepathic bond with them – the vampire's hypnotic powers have become an essential part of his power in many vampire books, games, and films.

The technique of hypnosis has been known and used for centuries: it was practiced in ancient Greece and Egypt and even earlier in ancient India. The term itself comes from Hypnos, the Greek god of sleep, and was first used in 1842 by James Braid, a Scottish surgeon. However, the eighteenth-century German physicist and astrologist Franz Anton Mesmer (1734–1815) is often referred to as an early exponent of hypnosis. Mesmer believed he was using a mysterious force he called "animal magnetism" to heal his patients. His techniques included the laying on of hands and staring fixedly in the eyes. Animal magnetism became popular in Europe with magnetized patients, or "somnambules" as they were referred to, reporting that they felt no pain during surgery.

In the 1840s Scottish medical practitioner James Braid set out to expose animal magnetism as fraudulent. However, when he used the technique on his own patients with great success he was forced to revise his opinions. Braid noticed how similar the trance state and sleep were, and coined the term "hypnotism" to describe it. The name has remained even though hypnosis is actually a very natural state of mind that never involves sleep. Individuals do not even lose consciousness. Braid also discovered that Mesmer's techniques, the fixed stares and waving or laying on of hands, were not needed. Patients could enter a state of hypnosis by staring at a light or by suggestion alone.

Hypnosis is achieved when the brain waves slow down and the individual reaches such an intense level of concentration that he or she blocks out any interference or distraction to his or her focus. During this state of intense concentration certain innate abilities, such as memory and suggestibility, are heightened. Individual response to hypnosis can vary enormously but it is thought that the majority of the population – around 85 percent – can be hypnotized, although only a small percentage can achieve deep trance. Several steps seem essential to achieving an altered state. These include deep relaxation, concentration, turning inwards, focusing on specific sounds, words or images, and choosing to change one's conscious state. There also appear to be three major stages of hypnosis: light, in which the individual feels lethargic but is aware of what is going on around them; cataleptic, in which the muscles become tense; and somnambulistic, which is a state of deep trance where the subject's will can be manipulated by the suggestions of the hypnotist and/or vampire.

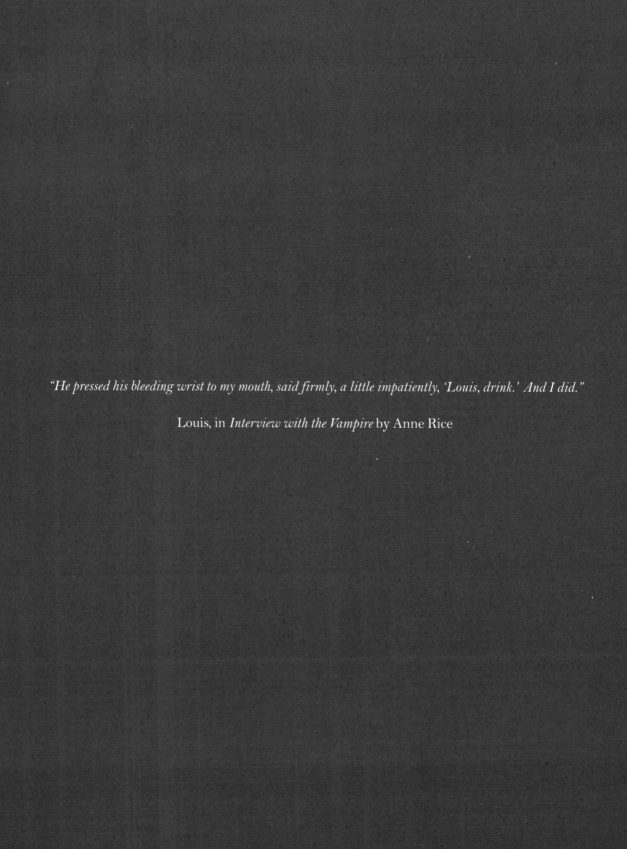

"He pressed his bleeding wrist to my mouth, said firmly, a little impatiently, 'Louis, drink.' And I did."

Louis, in *Interview with the Vampire* by Anne Rice

I Am Legend

Published in 1954, the novel *I Am Legend* by American author Richard Matheson is still in print today. Considered by many to be a classic in the science fiction and horror genre and the first "modern vampire novel," it was also the first novel to suggest that vampires were not creatures of pure evil but victims of an illness. The novel went on to influence many vampire tales in subsequent years.

The novel

The hero of the novel is Los Angeles resident Robert Neville, the last human on an earth that has been overtaken by vampires. The action takes place between 1976 and 1979. Vampirism is a bacteria-caused plague spread through blood infection, and the infection has destroyed the human race. Those who are not killed by the illness become vampires. Neville, however, appears to be immune to the plague. He becomes an outsider who spends his nights barricading himself away from the vampires. During the day he is a vicious vampire hunter, killing vampires without mercy.

As the vampires, who now dominate the planet, build themselves an increasingly sophisticated society, Neville must come to terms with his isolation and loneliness. All he has in the world is a store of frozen food and a selection of classical music. He bonds with a stray dog and a widow, called Ruth. The dog dies and Ruth turns out to be a vampire spy. Neville spends a great deal of time researching in libraries and archives for scientific information on the vampire plague, hoping it will help him discover an antidote, but his search becomes increasingly futile.

As the novel progresses and the world shifts from human to vampire, readers are forced to consider what "normal" really is, when Neville becomes more "alien" and the vampires more "normal." It throws up the intriguing proposition that perhaps vampirism is the logical progression of evolution.

The movies

I Am Legend has been adapted into a feature-length film three times. The first, released in 1964, was titled *The Last Man on Earth*, starring Vincent Price and the second, released in 1971, was called *The Omega Man* and starred Charlton Heston. In the later film the vampirism element is almost completely removed and replaced by a mutating plague.

In 2007, Will Smith starred in *I Am Legend*, the third film version. This movie deviates from the original novel in that the infection is caused by a virus originally intended to cure cancer, although some vampiric elements are retained, such as sensitivity to UV light and attraction to blood. The film also takes place in the year 2012. In addition, the ending is very different from the original novel: Neville discovers a cure and sacrifices his life to allow another immune person to take the cure to a hidden sanctuary. In an alternate ending, viewable only on the film's DVD, Neville realizes he has become an interruption to vampiric evolution rather than a savior of humankind, an aspect retained from the novel. The film was a critical and commercial success and in July 2008 it stood among the top 50 all-time highest grossing films both in the US and worldwide.

See also: FILMS; LITERATURE

Iara

The iara, also known as *mcboiacu*, are a vampire-like species said to dwell deep in the Brazilian forests. Some folklore experts have argued that they are actually the same as the Brazilian asema and that both names refer to a kind of shape-shifting witch that can take the form of a serpent.

Whether the iara is the undead or a living person who has sold their soul to the Devil, or is the spirit of someone who has died violently or as an unbeliever, this creature is greatly feared. It is said to glide through the jungle in snake form, attacking whoever it encounters. Its eyes are red and mesmerizing and capable of freezing anyone to the spot. On other occasions this entity can appear in the guise of a beautiful young maiden with an enchanting singing voice that can lure young men into the jungle to meet their doom. Once she has her victims in her clutches she will return to her serpent form and wrap herself around them, drawing their blood and semen with her sharp fangs. Men are said to be powerless to resist the voice of the iara when they hear it, and the legend of the iara was often offered as an explanation for the disappearance of those who ventured alone in the jungle.

In other versions of the myth Iara was a beautiful young mermaid, often described as having green hair and light skin, who would sit on a rock by the river combing her hair or dozing under the sun. When she sensed the presence of a man she would start to sing gently to lure him, but this was not always a bad thing: she would cater for all the needs of her lover for the rest of his life. Whether malevolent or benign in her actions, like the vampire figure she resembles, Iara is doomed to loneliness because she is immortal and her human lovers will age and die.

Iceland

In past centuries the Norsemen, who lived in the ice-cold climates of Scandinavia and Iceland, believed that ghosts and the walking undead prowled the woods and wastes between isolated farmsteads and hamlets with one intention – to harm the living. The majority of what is known about the Scandinavian undead can be found in ancient Icelandic stories, recorded by medieval monks who were the descendants of Norwegians who had settled down in Iceland hundreds of years before. In the writings of these monks sagas of the returning undead can be found and these types of stories, which include accounts of vampire-like creatures, such as the draugr, believed to be the malevolent wandering dead, the haugbui or "sleepers in the mounds," who attacked those who trespassed near their graves, and black magicians, said to have the power to raise or control the dead, were known as *eventyr* or *aeventyr* stories. Many of these tales were written from a Christian perspective and warn about the dangers of ancient pagan beliefs, because by then much of Scandinavia had been converted to Christianity.

See also: BLACK MAGICIANS; DRAUGR; HAUGBUI

Ichor

Some vampirologists have suggested that vampirism may be some kind of supernatural disease, where the bite of a vampire deposits a kind of enzyme, found in the vampire's saliva, into the bloodstream of its victim. According to this theory, which like most theories concerning the science of vampires remains just that, an unproven theory, when the vampire has drunk enough blood to kill its victim, this enzyme triggers a metabolic change in the victim's body. The metabolic change begins the production of a dark-green liquid called ichor within the victim's bloodstream.

In a few days there is enough ichor to nourish the victim's body the way that blood once did. If, however, the victim's blood loss is not significant enough to cause death, the victim will show signs of anemia but will not die. Until the enzyme has fully metabolized, the victim will be weak and sickly and will develop a telepathic link with the vampire. The only way to save the victim from becoming a vampire is to kill the original vampire before the transformation takes place.

See also: **BECOMING A VAMPIRE; BIOLOGY OF VAMPIRES; DISEASE**

Identification of Vampires

During the vampire epidemics of the eighteenth century a number of procedures or rituals were used to identify the grave of a vampire. Holes appearing around a grave were taken as signs of vampirism. Another method was to lead a virgin horse around a suspected grave – if the horse balked, the grave was regarded as that of a vampire. In some instances when graves of suspected vampires were opened, corpses that were well preserved or had blood on them were declared vampiric by villagers and Church officials. Evidence that a vampire was active in a community included the death of cattle, sheep, and relatives or neighbors of someone recently deceased. The vampires of folklore could also make their presence felt in nightmares and in wasting diseases.

See also: **CORPSE; CORPSE CANDLE; DETECTING VAMPIRES; DHAMPIR; FINDING VAMPIRES; VAMPIRE HUNTERS**

Ignatius Day

Ignatius Day is a feast held in memory and honor of the Christian martyr St. Ignatius of Antioch, who was eaten by lions in Rome's Colosseum in AD 107. The festival date varies from October 17 (previously February 1 in the West) to December 20 in the region of the Eastern Church. Among the Wallachians the day was typically celebrated with the killing of a pig. The animal's lard was then smeared over a person's body to prevent a vampire attack.

Ignis Fatuus

The term refers to spectral, phosphorescent lights that are believed to appear as bluish or yellow flames or candle lights in the countryside and graveyards at night. Translated literally, ignis fatuus means "foolish fire." It was considered foolish to follow these spectral lights because they were thought to be death omens, often playing tricks on those traveling alone at night by luring them away from their path until they lost their way. Ignis fatuus lights appear in folklore all over the world. They are also known as corpse candles, jack-o'-lanterns, will-o'-the-wisp, elf fire, friar's lantern, witch lights, or walking fire.

There are various legends to explain the lights. Typically they are believed to be the ghosts of souls who cannot rest, either because they were sinners on earth who did not repent or because some wrong done to them while they were alive stands uncorrected. In German lore the light is a wandering spirit who accompanies an invisible funeral procession. In Sweden the light is that of an unbaptized soul trying to lead travelers to water in the hope of being baptized. In parts of Africa, the lights are called "witch lights" and are believed to be sent by witches to scare wrongdoers.

Natural explanations for the phenomenon include: unknown energy from the earth; electrical and magnetic vibrations; or marsh gas or the igniting of gases escaping from rotting plants or animals. In folklore, however, the ignis fatuus became a living entity, often with malicious intent.

The associations of vampires with the ignis fatuus include the belief that some species of the Eastern European undead, such as the ubour of Bulgaria, give off sparks or appear as luminescent specks of light.

Ikiryoh

In Japanese folklore the ikiryoh is the name used to describe a vampire-like entity that is thought to be created by the evil thoughts and feelings of a person. When it is energized by someone's hatred, the ikiryoh becomes so powerful it can leave the person harboring the hateful thoughts and enter and possess the person who is the object of the hatred. Once inside it can kill the victim slowly by draining away that person's energy. The ikiryoh is thought to be extremely difficult to exorcise and there are numerous rites to drive it away, including the reading of Buddhist scriptures.

Immortality

Immortality is the promise of eternal life. The idea that vampires are immortal may be one of the reasons for their enduring hold over our imagination. The idea of living forever has great appeal for almost everyone. Throughout the ages the quest for eternal life has been taken up by magicians, alchemists, adventures, and sorcerers, but with the exception of semi-mystical figures it has proved elusive. The vampire, however, has found a way to defeat death even though it has to pay a terrible price for this existence – drinking the blood of the living to sustain itself. It is important to point out, however, that the immortality of the vampire is not universally documented in folklore. It is in vampire literature that their eternal nature became more established, with figures such as Dracula. However, in both fiction and folklore, even though the vampire's existence is dark and cursed it does appear to have gained some kind of victory over humans in that it has "overcome" the finality of death.

According to those who study the science of vampires, contrary to popular opinion, vampires are not actually immortal but they can live for several hundred years. One vampirologist who has studied at length the aging experience of vampires is Hugo Pecos, overseer of an organization called the Federal Vampire and Zombie Agency (FVZA). According to Pecos, vampires are only ageless in that they do not age in the same way that humans do. Most vampires are destroyed long before they reach the outer limits of their lifespan because they represent such a threat to society. Ancient history does, however, give us some clues as to what that lifespan might be. In China, there was said to be one vampire in the emperor's court throughout the entire (eastern) Zhou Dynasty, which would put his age at 550. More recent records have certified vampires of over 200 years old.

See also: AGING, OF VAMPIRES

Impossibility

In 2005, a physics professor from the University of Central Florida called Costas Efthimiou made the headlines by claiming that vampires are a mathematical impossibility.

According to the professor, on January 1, 1600, the human population totaled 536,870,911

people. If from that day vampires came into existence and bit one person a month, there would have been two vampires by February 1, 1600. A month later there would have been four, and so on. In less than three years, according to this assumption, every human would have been transformed into a vampire and there would be nobody left for vampires to feed on. "*In the long run, humans cannot survive under these conditions, even if our population were doubling each month,*" Efthimiou said.

Efthimiou's theory does seem to suggest that vampires are not just a biological but also a mathematical impossibility. However, those who believe in vampires argue that his theory is based on assumptions which are as speculative and unproven as the vampire legend itself. In addition, not all vampire victims become vampires, and there are ways, such as drinking animal blood or the blood of willing donors, for vampires to survive without killing and feeding on humans.

See also: BECOMING A VAMPIRE; BIOLOGY OF VAMPIRES

Impundulu

The impundulu is a mythological vampire-like creature, usually owned by a female witch, in the folklore of the tribes of the Southern Cape of Africa. In fact, the curse of the impundulu was usually passed genetically from mother witch to daughter witch. It would appear to its mistress in the form of a handsome young man who then became her lover. Merciless and relentless, it was believed to have an insatiable appetite for blood from both animals and humans, attacking the witch's enemies in the form of a black and white bird, the size of a human. Families, herds, and entire villages could be devastated by the creature and the wasting disease, coughing, sharp pains in the chest or head, and sudden deaths it was thought to bring.

In 2005, a South African man was convicted of culpable homicide after killing a two-year-old boy he believed to be an impundulu. So convinced was the court that the man had no intention of killing a human being that no expert witnesses were called to testify, and although originally charged with the murder of the toddler, a lesser charge was introduced after taking the man's beliefs into account. This case illustrates how belief in the impundulu remains widespread throughout Africa. In destroying a witch's agent, it is still widely believed that the witch who sent it can be destroyed as well.

Incense

Composed of grains of resins and spices that are burned or sprinkled on lighted charcoal to create a sweet or pungent odor, incense has been used in many religions over the centuries to drive out evil entities from a person or a place. In fighting vampires, it ranks alongside garlic as a preventative measure and as a way to counteract the stench of death. Vast amounts of incense would often be used to mask the smell of exhumed corpses suspected of vampirism, but incense would also have been used to repel the undead. In some regions of Romania, for instance, it was often pushed into the ears, eyes, and nostrils of a corpse to stop an evil spirit from entering and reanimating the body.

See also: **APOTROPAICS; PREVENTION**

Incorruptibility/Incorruptibles

A corpse that is extremely well-preserved and showing little sign of decomposition is known as an "incorruptible," and incorruptibles are a reoccurring theme in many factual accounts of vampirism. In vampire lore the transformation into a vampire leaves the corpse in a preserved state. Even though the Christian Church believed that incorruptibility was a sign of sanctity – and that the corpses of saints and martyrs remained well-preserved – if incorruptibility occurred in the corpse of an ordinary person the only explanation for it was that the Devil was at work. In medieval times there was a widespread belief in the idea that incorruptibility could be caused by excommunication, and that the corpses of people who had died excommunicated were likely to be reanimated by evil spirits to return as vampires.

Today scientists have proved that there are many natural causes for the preservation of corpses, from temperature and soil conditions to deep burials. We have corpses today that have reportedly lasted for hundreds of years with little evidence of decomposition. For example in early 2009 six perfectly preserved "pony-tailed" corpses were unearthed during construction work in Turfan, in China's far west Xinjiang region. The bodies are believed to be officials from the Qing Dynasty and to date back almost 400 years.

See also: **CORPSE; DECOMPOSITION**

Incubus/Succubus

In Western demonology, an incubus is believed to be a vampire-like male spirit or demon that disturbs the sleep of women, often subjecting them to nightmares or unwanted sexual intercourse that drains them of life and strength. Incubi (from the Latin *incubare*, "to lie in" or "to lie upon") were thought to press down on the chests of women and to be particularly fond of seducing/crushing nuns and other women committed to the celibate life. The incubi were thought to be able to father children who would be born as witches or demons or to be hideously deformed.

The female equivalent of the incubus is the succubus, a female demon or spirit who is said to disturb the sleep of a man and initiate sexual intercourse with him. This demon is quite similar to other female vampire spirits such as the mara and the mullo. Unlike the incubus, whose attentions are typically horrifying to women, in some cases succubi attacks were not always unwelcome, and the only evidence of their nocturnal visits was extreme (although sometimes fatal) fatigue.

The incubus/succubus is similar to the vampire in that it attacks its victims night after night and is sexually insatiable, but it does not suck their blood. In vampire lore, a male vampire was often believed to return to his wife or other women seeking sexual favors, and in some instances it is highly likely that living men masqueraded as vampire husbands in order to have affairs; any resulting children were passed off as those of the "vampire husband."

Explanations

Over the centuries various explanations have been put forward to explain the phenomenon of the incubus/succubus, from demons and witchcraft to nightmares and sexual repression/fantasy. In the thirteenth century Thomas Aquinas argued that children could be conceived through the intercourse of a woman with an incubus, and during the fifteenth century Church leaders believed they were instruments of the Devil and were closely tied to witchcraft. By the eighteenth century, however, a trend toward a more subjective understanding began to occur, with incubus/succubus attacks increasingly explained as an expression of repressed sexual feelings.

See also: **ALP; HAG ATTACK; NIGHTMARE; PSYCHIC VAMPIRE**

India

In India's religious world, which includes Buddhism, Islam, Hinduism, Christianity, and Sikhism, each with their own legends of the dead, there are a number of demonic entities with vampiric qualities. Although the theory has yet to be proved, some experts have suggested that the vampire myth may have originated in the bloodthirsty legends of the ancient Indian gods dating back to as early as the third millennium BC. The vampiric concept may then have shaped the development of the vampire tradition in surrounding lands, such as Tibet, China, and other parts of Asia. Wars, trade, and cultural diffusion would also have brought Indian tales to Europe. There is certainly evidence that the Gypsies brought vampiric beliefs with them from India when they migrated westward.

Vampire-like beings

Throughout the many regions of India there is an abundance of vampires and vampire-like beings. The word "bhuta" is often used to describe Indian vampires, although most vampirologists correctly refer to it as a type of vampire that on occasion can enter a corpse and use it to devour living people. Other types include the fearsome and nocturnal rakshasa, with their appetite for infants, the yatu-dhana (or hatu-dhana) – sorcerers who devoured what the rakshasa left, the pisachas (bloodthirsty eaters of raw flesh), the baital, supernatural beings who could animate corpses, and the vetala, spirits that animated the bodies of the dead. In addition, throughout India there were also numerous ghosts, demons, and evil entities who resided near cemeteries and had vampiric qualities. For example, the churels – women who had died an unnatural death who returned as ghosts to vampirize the blood of male family members.

Any outline of Indian vampires would be inadequate without mention of the fearsome and bloodthirsty goddess Kali, whose favorite places were the battlefield and burial grounds where she gorged herself on the blood of her victims.

See also: **PENANGGALAN**

Indonesia

In Indonesian legend the vampire can sometimes appear in the form of a woman with long hair and nails and a hollow in her back. She has been cursed and her soul rejected by God because she committed suicide after being raped. Seeking revenge she floats in a long white dress searching for male victims to drain the life blood out of. She appears at night near the asam tree or at bends of the road. In traditional accounts when she encounters a man she seduces him, bringing him to a sparkling place which turns out to be tomb in daylight. Similarly, at night she is beautiful but when her victim sees her in the morning she is hideous. Indonesian vampires can also appear in the form of the pontianak, believed to be a woman who died either a virgin or in childbirth. Out of jealousy it will attack infants or emasculate the men it seduces. They fly at night as birds, but in human form; there is also a hole in their backs.

Indonesia is a country rich with ancient mythology and in some areas belief in ghosts and vampires is still rife. As recently as 1984, according to the Jakarta *Sinar Harapan* newspaper and the *New York Times*, vampire-like attacks were reported by 21 young women in Sumatra who said a man had bitten their necks to suck blood. A local Member of Parliament told the paper that he had not believed the accounts at first but that after seeing the victims he was convinced a vampire was on the loose.

The Element Encyclopedia of Vampires

Infection

See: **VIRUS**

Inheritors

The term "inheritor vampire" or "inheritor" is sometimes used by those who believe in vampires to describe people who are born human but with the vampire trait dormant within them until they reach the age of 13 or so. According to this theory, which is unproven, when the inheritor's body reaches the late stages of puberty, a chemical is released which awakens the vampire within and triggers physical changes in the body. As a result of this most inheritors look around 20 years old their whole life. Most of the time the parents of the inheritor vampire will be human and vampire, or both vampires: there must be at least one vampire parent. Inheritor vampires supposedly live to be around 350 to 400 years old.

Sanguinarians (people who feel compelled to drink blood) are said to be the "mortal version" of these so-called inheritor vampires. They still require and crave blood, are sensitive to sunlight, and have many of the traits of the inheritor and traditional vampire. However, sanguinarians do not live much longer than the average human being.

Inovercy

"Inovercy" is a Russian word that refers to someone who follows a different creed or faith, and especially someone who does not follow the teachings of the Russian Orthodox Church. It was assumed that such people died in a state of sin. After death they were regarded as unclean and not entitled to a proper burial, and therefore doomed to become vampires. Their bodies would be dumped in large pits or charnel houses, called *ubogie doma*. The *ubogie doma* were banned in 1771 but the practice continued for many years after in some regions.

Intentional Psychic Vampire

See: **PSYCHIC VAMPIRE**

Internet

Among the first to establish websites and chat rooms on the Internet from the later 1980s onwards were people interested in vampires. Today there are literally thousands of vampire-related websites. A great deal of these websites contain a wealth of fascinating information, advice, and resources for all different kinds of vampire enthusiasts, from those interested in the vampire lifestyle and the science of vampires, to vampire tradition and legend, to vampire literature, comics, games, and films.

See the Vampire Directory for a selection of vampire websites.

Interview with the Vampire

The 1976 novel by Anne Rice, *Interview with the Vampire*, has often been described as the most popular vampire novel of the late twentieth century. In this first novel of what was to become a series of novels, the Vampire Chronicles, Rice created a compelling world in which vampires exist alongside humans.

According to Rice the inspiration came one day when she wondered what it would like to interview a vampire, and as she began to write she found herself identifying more and more with the vampire's point of view.

The novel

The central character in the novel is Louis de Pointe du Lac, a relatively young vampire at the age of 200 who narrates his life story to a present-day journalist in San Francisco. The story then travels back in time to 1791 New Orleans where Louis, in the midst of a period of despair, is transformed into a vampire by the androgynous Lestat de Lioncourt, a bewitchingly beautiful but brutal vampire. Louis suffers tremendous guilt over his new-found evil nature and explains to the reporter how he finally surrendered to his blood lust by attacking a five-year-old orphan girl called Claudia and how Lestat saved the girl by transforming her into a vampire. Louis and Claudia form an intense bond and soon begin to resent Lestat for turning them into vampires. Claudia, especially bitter that she has been trapped forever in the body of a child, sets their house on fire and the two leave thinking they have destroyed Lestat. They travel to Europe in search of other vampires who can enlighten them about their origin and nature. Eventually they go to Paris where they meet the beautiful Armand who runs a vampire coven and a decadent theater of vampires.

Armand falls in love with Louis but the coven destroys Claudia, and Madeleine, the vampire Louis created for Claudia to look after her, by exposing them to sunlight when they discover that Claudia had attempted to kill Lestat. In anger Louis retaliates by burning down the coven's underground lair. He later leaves Armand and meets with a weakened and withered Lestat in New Orleans.

The novel ends with Louis alone in San Francisco telling his story to the reporter. Much to his disappointment the reporter begs Louis to make him a vampire. In frustration Louis attacks the reporter and vanishes. Recovering from the attack, the reporter notes the address of the house where Louis last saw Lestat in New Orleans, and then leaves to track down the vampire – and the "Dark Gift" – for himself.

The movie

In 1994 the film version of *Interview with the Vampire* was released. The critically acclaimed movie starred Tom Cruise as Lestat, Brad Pitt as Louis, Kirsten Dunst as Claudia, Antonio Banderas as Armand, and Christian Slater as the reporter. Rice did not initially approve of the choice of Cruise as Lestat but after seeing the film changed her mind and fully supported the decision. The film was a major success, and created a resurgence of interest in the book that sent *Interview with the Vampire* back onto the bestseller lists.

Anne Rice's vampires

The vampires in *Interview with the Vampire* do not live in graves, avoid garlic, or fear crucifixes and they can see their reflection in the mirror. According to Rice, in religious terms not seeing one's reflection in a mirror means the soul is in hell but she wanted her vampires to have no more assurance of God than humans do. Like in many of her novels that followed, Rice's vampires in *Interview* struggle with their own evil nature and bloodlust. What sets this novel apart from previous vampire novels is its confessional tone from the vampire's perspective, touching on existential despair and the sheer boredom of immortality. In addition the novel explored in a radical new way a number of themes relevant to the vampire myth, in particular sex and homosexuality.

Ireland

The legends and folklore of Ireland are rife with banshees, elves, fairies, leprechauns, and vampires. Ancient Celtic beliefs in blood ceremonies and blood lines left their imprint on the Irish but vampire beliefs in Ireland were a relatively late development, probably dating back to the first days of Celtic migrations. The best-known vampire species from Ireland are the marbh bheo – the night waking dead – the dearg-due or dearg-diulai – the "red bloodsucker" – and the leanhaum-shee. The leanhaum-shee is more a fairy than a vampire, but a fairy who, in true vampiric style, delights in sucking the blood of her lovers. In a tiny churchyard near Strongbow's Tower or Tree in Waterford, a dearg-diulai is said to be buried, although a place of that name near Waterford has yet to be discovered.

"The Blood-drawing Ghost"

The most well-known vampire tale from Irish folklore is probably that of the "Blood-drawing Ghost," written down and published by Jeremiah Curtin in 1882. In the story a young woman called Kate is one of three women a young man from County Cork is thinking of marrying. To test the women he sets them a challenge to find a cane he has placed in the tomb of a recently deceased person. Only Kate accepts the challenge. When she arrives at the tomb she encounters a dead man who forces her to take him into town. Once there he drinks the blood of three young men who subsequently die. He mixes their blood with some oatmeal and tells Kate that this blood cake could bring the men back to life. Kate hides some of the oatmeal. Before returning to his tomb the vampire also tells Kate about some gold buried in a nearby field.

The next day, when the bodies of the three young men are found, the resourceful Kate strikes a deal with their parents. She will bring the men back to life if she can marry the oldest one and the land, where the gold is buried, is deeded to her. She then feeds each of the men the oatmeal and brings all three back to life. She marries the oldest man, discovers the gold, and leads a long and happy life.

Similar stories of malignant corpses, who caught those who passed by their resting places, climbed on their backs, and were carried about in the darkness, are found across the country, from Limerick to Leitrim. Ireland was also home of two highly significant contributors to vampire literature and legend: Bram Stoker and Sheridan Le Fanu.

See also: **ABHARTACH; CARRICKAPHOUKA CASTLE**

Iron

Iron in folklore, like silver, is traditionally a protection against the forces of evil, including vampires and witches, perhaps because human blood smells of iron and blood in many traditions is equated with the life force.

In ancient Roman custom, iron nails were taken from coffins and used as charms against evil, and in ancient China the metal was placed in the suspected grave of the chiang-shih to trap it underground. In Eastern Europe iron scissors and small implements would be placed at bedsides to ward off vampire attacks. Iron objects placed in coffins and iron nails driven into coffins were also thought to prevent the dead from leaving their graves. One Romanian tradition is to stab iron forks into the heart, eyes, and breast of a corpse and in Bulgaria a red-hot iron is driven into the heart.

See also: **PROTECTION**

Isithfuntela

In parts of Western Africa it was thought that witches could raise the dead and capture a departed spirit, which they could then control to terrorize the dead person's family. The body controlled by the witch was called an isithfuntela. The witch would cut out the tongue and drive a peg into the brain so that it became zombie-like. The isithfuntela would then attack people by hypnotizing them and driving a nail through their heads.

See also: **ASANBOSAM; OBAYIFO**

Italy

Italy, once the heart of the ancient Roman Empire and later the heart of Christianity, was one of the places from which both belief in and opposition to belief in the undead originated.

The ancient Romans believed in a number of vampire-like entities, such as the empusa and the lamia (which they first encountered in the Hellenic world), and most significant of all, the strix, a night owl believed to be a kind of demon that sucked the blood out of children. These pagan beings passed into Christian lore but did not become as established as they did in the Balkans and elsewhere. The creature most like a vampire in Italian tradition is the striga, a witch who attacks children with curses that cause them to wither away.

It was Christianity, and especially the Catholic Church in Rome, that helped to give shape to many of the recognizable elements of vampire lore in Europe – from the evil, godforsaken nature of the undead to their fear of crosses and other Christian symbols. Italians also contributed to the animated international debate about the nature of vampires when a "vampire plague" hit Serbia and other Eastern European lands in the seventeenth century.

In his 1743 *Dissertazione sopra i vampiri*, Cardinal Giuseppe Davanzati was among the first to posit a modern view of vampirism when he pointed out that belief in vampires mostly occurred in rural and less populated areas where superstition was rife, rather than in urban areas, where people tended to be better educated. Davanzati's view that vampirism was a superstition generated by ignorance, although accepted by the then Pope Benedict XIV, did not prevent reports of vampirism and vampire traditions becoming a widespread phenomenon in the mid-eighteenth century throughout Central and Eastern Europe.

One such tradition widespread in Italy and Greece held that crying at a funeral is essential because if a person is not properly mourned they will come back to haunt their relatives in the form of a vampire. For those with a small family or few friends, professional mourners were hired to weep and wail at the funeral procession, ostensibly making the dead feel loved and wanted, a practice widespread during ancient Roman times.

Discovery of a "real" vampire in Italy

According to an Italian archeologist the remains of a medieval "vampire" were discovered in 2006 among the corpses of sixteenth-century plague victims in Venice. The skull of a woman was found in a mass grave on the Island of Lazzaretto Nuovo with a brick forced into her jaw. At the time it was commonly believed that placing a rock into a vampire's mouth would prevent them chewing their shrouds, infecting others with plague. In 1578 the plague killed an estimated 50,000 people in the city.

It appears that the woman, aged about 60, died of the plague and some time later a gravedigger reopened the grave and jammed the brick into her mouth. The research team point out that although shrouds are destroyed naturally by bacteria, at the time this would not have been understood and superstitions about "shroud eating" would have been a way for a terrified population to explain waves of plague epidemics that killed thousands in the Middle Ages.

See also: **ROME**

I … Vampire

I … Vampire was a popular series of vampire stories created by writer J. M. DeMatteis that appeared in *The House of Mystery*, a comic book published by DC Comics in the early 1980s. Originally a back-up story for *House of Mystery* it quickly became so popular that it took over from the title story on the cover.

I … Vampire tells the story of Andrew Bennett, a late sixteenth-century lord in Elizabethan England who in 1591 is bitten by a dearg-dul, a type of vampire from Ireland, and becomes a vampire himself. Bennett turns his lover, Mary Seward, into a vampire so she can spend eternity with him, but Mary soon becomes corrupted by her newfound power. She has a thirst for blood but Bennett has sworn himself off human blood and the story follows their conflict right into the 1980s. Mary builds an organization called The Blood Red Moon to take control of the planet, and it is Bennett's fate to kill the vampires that operate as her agents and to destroy Mary, the monster he created.

Andrew Bennett has all the powers of a vampire. He is immortal and can shape-shift into mist, a bat, and a wolf. He also has super-human strength and the ability to transform others into vampires. However, he also has all the weaknesses of a vampire. His image cannot be seen in a mirror and he can be killed by sunlight, silver, and crucifixes. He is cursed to drink the blood of the living, but unlike other vampires he does not want to harm humans and chooses to drink animal blood or bottled human blood (a subtext for alcoholism, perhaps). Unlike other vampires, he can also reconstitute himself some time after being killed.

See also: **COMICS**

Ivan the Terrible (1530–84)

Often called "The Russian Dracula" for his merciless and brutal behavior, Ivan the Terrible, the first ruler of Russia to adopt the title of Tsar, has often been compared to the blood-thirsty fifteenth-century Wallachian tyrant, Vlad the Impaler.

Ivan IV assumed power in 1547 at the age of 17 (although he succeeded his grandfather, Ivan III, to the throne in 1533) and immediately proclaimed himself Tsar instead of Grand Duke. He justly deserved his reputation as a tyrant and his reign was peppered with bloody battles against foreign invaders. It is not, however, his political actions that are most remembered but his personal conduct. In his passionate desire to establish a central Russian government he ruled by fear and brutality and swiftly punished, tortured, or executed anyone who opposed or disrespected him, taking great delight in publicly humiliat-

ing powerful figures in Russian society to prevent their return to office with dignity. He also manifested symptoms of paranoia and madness and had a violent temper. In 1581 he killed his own son in a fit of rage.

Ivan possessed a sadistic personality, fairly similar to that attributed to Vlad, and many of the stories concerning him may have been variations of those originally told about Vlad a century before. For example, there was a Romanian folktale concerning a Turkish envoy visiting Ivan who foolishly refused to remove his hat in Ivan's presence. Ivan had the man's hat nailed to the top of his head. Vlad reportedly did the same thing to an Italian or French ambassador (accounts differ) who similarly showed him disrespect by not removing his hat.

See also: **HISTORICAL VAMPIRES**

Ivan Vasilli

The *Ivan Vasilli* was the name of a Russian steamer built in 1897 that was said to be haunted by a vampire-like phantom. The supposedly true story of the ship bears similarities to that of the *Demeter* in the novel *Dracula*, published in 1897 – the same year the *Ivan Vasilli* was built.

According to an account of the story recorded by Vincent Gaddis in the now out of print *Invisible Horizons* (1965), the crew began to have strange experiences in 1903. They were gripped by a sudden cold sensation, inexplicable bouts of paralysis, and sensations of terror. Some of the crew allegedly saw a mist in the shape of a human being appear on the deck. Fear of the entity became so great that crew members committed suicide or abandoned ship. Ultimately, the crew decided that fire was the only way to destroy the evil entity that haunted the ship, and so in the winter of 1907, on a clear starry night, they set it aflame. Those who watched swore that before the ship went under, an eerie scream emanated from the hulk. No one ever knew what or who the evil entity was.

"*The vampire is the night-prowling symbol of man's hunger for – and fear of – everlasting life … The mixture of attraction and repulsion … is the essence of the vampire concept.*"

Margaret Carter, preface to *Varney the Vampyre*

Jack the Ripper

A few years before Bram Stoker began work on *Dracula* (1897), a series of savage murders in the East End of London caused widespread panic throughout the country. The murderer was nicknamed "Jack the Ripper." It would have been virtually impossible for Stoker not to have been influenced by the tales of Jack the Ripper's killing spree when he was writing his vampire novel.

In Whitechapel, a seedy area of London's East End populated mainly by poor immigrants and prostitutes, at least five women were murdered within two months of each other in 1888. The first murder victim was Mary Ann Nichols. She went out on Friday, August 31 just after 1 a.m. to earn some money. She was seen at 2.30 a.m. by a friend and at 3.30 a.m. her body was discovered. Her throat had been cut with a bladed knife and there were severe cuts on her abdomen.

A week or so later, on September 8 the body of Annie Chapman was discovered. Again her throat had been cut and her abdomen slashed deeply. Then on September 30, two women were killed an hour apart. Elizabeth Stride's throat was cut only a few moments before her body was found, while the mutilated and disemboweled body of Catherine Eddowes was found in another part of Whitechapel. Finally on November 8, Mary Kelly became the last victim. Her body was found in her room. Her throat had been slashed and her body severely mutilated. Doctors estimated that the killing frenzy may have lasted for around two hours.

On September 25, after the murder of Annie Chapman, a note was sent to the Central News Agency signed, "*Yours truly, Jack the Ripper.*" The note was probably a hoax but from that moment on, the name Jack the Ripper stuck.

The papers bestowed widespread and enduring notoriety on Jack the Ripper because of the savagery of the attacks and the failure of the police to capture him – they sometimes missed him at the crime scenes by mere minutes. Over the years many authors, historians, detectives, and amateur detectives have proposed theories about the identity of the killer but to this day the identity of Jack the Ripper has never been confirmed. Not surprisingly many vampirologists have linked the Ripper's bloodlust with vampires and/or clinical vampirism, but also interesting is the idea that Stoker may have taken elements of the Ripper's crimes and used them to create the persona of Dracula.

Like the Ripper, Dracula is nocturnal and driven by bloodlust. Also like the Ripper, Dracula manages to elude the police and commit vicious crimes without detection. Although there are no obvious allusions to the Ripper murders in the novel, Stoker would have been aware of them as he was living in London at the time. For example, Dracula stores his boxes of Transylvanian earth in Whitechapel. And Dracula is eventually killed with knives rather than a stake; knives were the Ripper's weapons of choice. Also worth noting is the fact that Stoker specifically mentions the Ripper in his own preface to the 1901 Icelandic edition of *Dracula*.

Jacula

Jacula was the leading female vampire character in a highly successful Italian adult comic book series of the same name that ran for 327 issues from 1968 to 1982. According to the series, in 1835 Jacula was bitten by another vampire in Transylvania. She eventually became a vampire queen and had a number of action-packed encounters with characters such as Frankenstein and Jack the Ripper. In the series, vampires are in league with the Devil and their aim is to discover Christ's tomb so they can prove to the world that he did not rise from the grave. Although the series was among the most successful comic books of all time, public protest against the pornographic nature of the drawings – Jacula is often pictured nude – forced the series to end.

Jakobsdorf Vampire

According to Dieter Sturm and Klaus Völker in *Von denen Vampiren oder Menschensaugern* (first published in 1968), sometime in the 1740s there were several deaths in the Wollschläger family somewhere in Western Prussia. One of the deceased buried inside the family crypt in the unidentified monastery of Jakobsdorf was suspected of being a vampire. A family member called Joseph volunteered to decapitate the suspected vampire. After cutting off the corpse's head he then collected some of its blood in a glass and all the surviving members of the family drank the blood in the hope that it would prevent them from being attacked by the vampire.

Historian Paul Barber, in *Vampires, Burial and Death* (1988), makes reference to an article about Jakobsdorf written by Leo Gerschke in 1962. The article is called "Vom Vampirglauben im alten West Preussen" and in it Gerschke says that in 1916 he made a visit to Jakobsdorf and saw the body and head of the Wollschläger vampire on display there. However when he returned in 1940 in the hope of taking a photograph of the corpse and head, he found that the people of Jakobsdorf had decided to bury the vampire just a few weeks previously.

James, M. R. (1862–1936)

Montague Rhodes James, who published under the name M. R. James, was a noted British medieval history scholar and academic. An ardent admirer of Sheridan Le Fanu he is best remembered for his ghost stories, which are widely regarded as among the finest in English literature. James also wrote a number of vampire tales: *Count Magnus* (1904); *Wailing Well* (1928); and *An Episode of Cathedral History* (1919), where evil from the past comes to life in the present in the vampiric haunting of a church in the fictional Southminster. M. R. James's introduction to his 1904 collection *Ghost Stories of an Antiquary* made clear reference to his literary aim when writing:

If any of [the stories] succeed in causing their readers to feel pleasantly uncomfortable when walking along a solitary road at nightfall, or sitting over a dying fire in the small hours, my purpose in writing them will have been attained.

The Element Encyclopedia of Vampires

Japan

The mythology and folklore of Japan is rich in creatures that are grotesque representations of evil. Chief among these are demons, such as oni, ghosts, such as oiwa, and other magical entities. Although there are no traditional vampires or animated corpses that return from the dead to suck the blood of the living, there are however a number of creatures with vampiric qualities. Among the most feared vampire-like beings were the hannya, a female baby-eater and the kappa, a terrible creature with webbed fingers and toes who lives in the water and pulls animals in to drink their blood.

The vampire cat

Apart from the hannya and the kappa, the Japanese have the interesting folktale entitled *The Vampire Cat of Nabeshima*, which tells the story of Prince Nabeshima and his lovely concubine, Otoyo. One night a vampire cat broke into Otoyo's room and killed her. It then disposed of her body and took her form. In the form of Otoyo the cat began to slowly vampirize the life out of the prince when he slept. Eventually one night guards saw the vampire appear in the form of Otoyo. The guards searched the girl's apartments but she escaped and fled to the hill country. The prince organized a vampire hunt and the vampire was finally killed.

With the permeation of Western culture into Japan it was inevitable that the more commonly recognized image of the vampire took form. Films, such as *Lake of Dracula* (1971), illustrate the Japanese acceptance of the European vampire.

Jaracaca

The jaracaca is an unusual species of vampire found in Brazil that typically appears in the shape of a snake that feeds on the breasts of nursing mothers. If there are any children sleeping with the mother they will be pushed out of the way and kept quiet by the snake's tail being shoved into their mouths. If the creature enjoys the taste it will return time and time again, thus depriving the child of milk and leaving it hungry and weak.

Occasionally, the jaracaca can drink blood from the upper arms of sleeping men and women, but it will do this only if breast milk is not available. When confronted it can spit the most terrible venom, which can produce almost instant madness from which there is no recovery. Not surprisingly, the jaracaca is regarded with great trepidation and every night prayers are said to protect against attack.

Destroying the jaracaca is believed to be virtually impossible, so the best course of action is to said to be avoidance and protection in the forms of incantations, spells, and blessings.

Java

There are several species of vampire bat on the Indonesian island of Java but the most fearsome vampire species in Javanese folklore is a creature known as the sundal bolong, meaning "hallowed bitch." The sundal bolong is a female vampire that has returned from the grave as a result of suicide following her rape and impregnation. Her victims are young men and, dressed in a flowing white gown, she lures them to their deaths, draining their blood. The Javanese share much of their mythology with Malaysia and Indonesia and included in that mythology was belief in the pontianak, a terrible creature who attacked babies and sucked their blood.

Jigarkhwar/Jigarkhor

The jigarkhwar is a vampire-like witch found in the mythology of the Sind region of the Indian subcontinent. She is most noted for her ability to extract a person's liver through her piercing stare, which paralyzes her victim rendering them helpless while the organ is removed. Once removed the liver is shrunk to the size of a pomegranate seed and hidden in the witch's calf until she decides to cook and eat it. Once she has eaten the liver, her victim dies. Rescue is possible only by finding the creature and ripping the seed out of its leg and returning it to the victim, who must swallow it. The witch's power can be broken by binding her head, filling her eyes with salt, and hanging her underground in a chamber for 40 days.

See also: **INDIA**

Jones, Ernest (1879-1958)

Ernest Jones was a leading psychoanalyst, a disciple of Sigmund Freud, and a member of the Royal College of Physicians in London. Jones's specialist interest was psychoanalyzing folklore and literature.

One noted work was "On the Nightmare," a detailed and insightful review of the folklore and psychological nature of frightening dreams. Included in this work was an exploration of the vampire. According to Jones, vampires were compelled by both love and hatred. Love compelled them to visit relatives and partners first, while guilt and the thirst for revenge prompted hatred. Jones also closely associated the vampire with nightmares and nightmare experiences, such as visitations by incubi and succubi.

Another interesting paper is "The Vampire," published in 1931. In this paper Jones viewed the sucking and biting of the vampire fantasy as an indication that the person had regressed to a primitive stage of developmental maturity, during which pleasure is focused on the mouth.

See also: **INCUBUS/SUCCUBUS; NIGHTMARE**

Journal of Vampirology, The

Eighteen issues of *The Journal of Vampirology* appeared between 1984 and 1990. The scholarly journal was edited by vampire expert John L. Vellutini of San Francisco and each issue contained a variety of researched articles on vampire folklore and history. Although the journal was read by serious students of the subject there was not enough interest to keep the journal in print.

Judas

One unproven theory for the origin of vampires is that they date back to Judas Iscariot, the man who, according to New Testament accounts, betrayed Jesus Christ to the chief priests and elders for 30 silver pieces. When Judas found out that Jesus was to be condemned he felt so full of regret that he attempted to return the money, but the chief priests and elders refused to accept them from him. Judas threw down the silver in the temple, left the place and hanged himself.

According to the Judas theory, following his suicide Judas returned from the grave as the first vampire. God cursed him and his family to walk the earth until the second coming of Christ, and until that time he would thirst for the blood of Jesus, which he could only receive through Christians. Another radical theory suggests that during the Last Supper Jesus was quite literal when he said to drink of his blood and eat of his flesh; some have even suggested that Jesus himself was a vampire or that he created Judas knowing he would betray him and become the first vampire

The Judas theory can be used to explain a number of elements of the vampire myth. For example, vampires can be killed by stakes, and more precisely a stake of aspen wood. Aspen is the wood that it is believed the cross upon which Jesus died was made of. So, as Judas had ultimately caused Jesus' death he would be repelled by the item of his demise. The Judas theory can also explain a vampire's fear of crucifixes and, of course, silver; anything that reminded Judas of his crime would have repelled him. In addition, throughout most vampire folklore those who commit suicide or die an untimely death are said to become vampires themselves. In Christianity those who commit suicide are believed to be damned to hell and so Judas was not only damned by his betrayal but for taking his own life.

In some cultures, a common folklore belief about vampires was the presence of red hair, perhaps because red hair was fairly uncommon. Judas was said to have been a "redhead" and this is perhaps where the idea that vampires were descendants of Judas came from, because of the hair color.

Today, the Judas theory is no longer taken seriously by vampire experts. However, it is easy to see how in medieval times (especially in Christian Europe) the Judas theory could be stretched to explain certain key elements of the vampire myth.

Jumping over a Corpse

In Slavic regions and in China there is a tradition that if an animal jumps over a corpse this may cause it to become a vampire. The idea probably originated with the belief that the spirit of a dead person hovers close to the body and can snatch the life of a moving creature and use it to reanimate the corpse in the grave. Generally any animal can be a corpse jumper, but most often cats, dogs, bats, birds, and insects were feared. The Romanians particularly feared the black hen. Preventing animals, birds, and insects from getting close to the corpse was an obvious precaution, but not always easy to accomplish. For instance, the Slavs would try to ensure that the windows and doors of the house a body was laid out in were kept open as long as the corpse was inside, to give the spirit an opportunity to depart. But this practice could also allow insects and other creatures to get in and transform a corpse into a vampire.

See also: **SOUL-RECALLING HAIR**

Jung, Carl (1875–1961)

Carl Jung was a Swiss psychologist whose impact on twentieth-century thought has been enormous. Jungian principles have been adapted to nearly all academic disciplines, from psychology to mythology to religion to quantum physics. He was the founder of the analytical school of psychology, known as Jungian psychology, and along with Sigmund Freud, the most influential author of psychoanalytical theory. Jung believed that dreams and fantasies drew on an ancient and universal symbolism that represented the common heritage, or collective unconscious, of humanity. In his view it was not sex that was the basic driver of human behavior, as Freud had suggested, but the need for self-realization through the collective unconscious.

Jungian interpretation of vampire myth

Followers of Jung might regard the vampire fantasy as part of an archetypal pattern of universal behavior and instinct. In psychology an archetype is a model of a person, behavior, or personality that is universal to all thanks to common developmental and reproductive biology. Archetypes include the hero, an expression of the universal human need to feel empowered; the mother, an expression of the universal human need to nurture; the child, an expression of the human need to be nurtured; and so on. For Jungians, the fact that the vampire myth developed in nearly every culture in the world is proof both of the vampire as the archetype and of Jung's concept of the collective unconscious.

The Jungian interpretation of the vampire therefore assumes that all humans have some aspects of the vampire inside of them. In other words, the vampire archetype is a concept we understand in some way, shape, or form, from the moment we come into this world. And people who choose to develop their personality through the vampire archetype may either be attempting to express their urge to defy social convention, or their compulsive need to survive at the expense of others, or their deep spiritual thirst and longing for renewal and transformation.

For Jung, the vampire was an archetype, a representation of an aspect of the personality he called the "shadow." The shadow is made up of those parts of our character or personality that we do not want to acknowledge or admit. It is our instinctive, primitive side, our anti-social impulses, our immoral fantasies, and anything we feel ashamed to admit to or express. In the words of Jung:

> The Shadow is a moral problem that challenges the whole ego-personality, for no one can become conscious of the shadow without considerable moral effort. To become conscious of it involves recognizing the dark aspects of the personality as present and real.

According to Jungians the vampire can become a scapegoat for society because it allows us to project negative or shadow aspects of ourselves onto something we can openly condemn and admire at the same time, without having to act out our desires and fantasies ourselves. In short, the vampire acts in a self-satisfying, erotic, predatory, anti-social way that people admire or aspire to but can't admit to because of social and moral constraints.

The Element Encyclopedia of Vampires

An interesting paper entitled "Vampirism: Historical perspective and underlying process in relation to a case of autovampirism" and published in the November 1964 issue of the *Journal of Nervous and Mental Disease*, illustrates a Jungian perspective on a medical case of auto-vampirism. In this paper Robert McCully from the Medical University of South Carolina reported on a case of auto-vampirism concerning a teenage boy, who experienced sexual excitement whenever he punctured his veins and drank his own blood. In an attempt to understand this behavior McCully researched vampire folklore from ancient cultures and came to the conclusion that the vampire image has been an archetype for humanity since the dawn of history. For McCully the boy was suffering from immature ego development and was compensating for this lack by identifying with the vampire archetype. McCully also suggested that part of the reason for our con-tinuing fascination with vampires is that they are a projection of those (shadow) aspects of our personality that we would like to deny or hide. In his words, *"The vampire is surely a vivid symbol of the sado-masochistic side of evil."*

See also: **PSYCHOLOGICAL EXPLANATIONS OF VAMPIRISM**

Juniper

In Slavic Gypsy folklore, juniper – a family of evergreen tree and shrub with berry-like fruits and needle-shaped leaves – was thought to protect against vampires. Sprigs of juniper would be kept in a house to prevent a vampire entering it, and a juniper stake could be used to restrain or destroy a vampire.

See also: **PROTECTION**

"The origins of the vampire myth lie in the mystery cults of oriental civilizations … the Nepalese Lord of Death, the Tibetan Devil, and the Mongolian God of Time."

Devendra P. Varma, *The Vampire in Legend, Lore, and Literature*

Ka

To the ancient Egyptians ka was the vital life force that infused everything – people, animals, and plants. The precise meaning and nature of ka is no longer clear as ancient Egyptian ideas concerning the soul and spirit refuse to fit into any traditional Western categories, but in Egyptian art ka is generally portrayed as a kind of spirit double or astral body that lingered on in the tomb after death, inhabiting the corpse. It was thought to be independent of the body and able to move, eat, and drink.

The tomb was believed to be the home of the ka and it was important for relatives to leave offerings of food and drink and to pay their respects so the dead would send benevolent energy to the living. If inadequate offerings were made the ka would be forced to leave the tomb and to wander the earth in ghost form looking for food and drink. This idea that the ka could leave the tomb in search of sustenance adds weight to the theory that vampires may have originated in ancient Egypt.

See also: **EGYPT**

Kali

The vampire-like bloodthirsty goddess Kali is a major figure in Indian mythology, representing both the creative and destructive aspects of nature. She is often regarded as the dark, black, and fierce goddess of death and disease, but to her worshippers she represents a multi-faceted Great Goddess, who is both fierce and nurturing, and who is responsible for all of life, from conception to death.

In early sixteenth-century texts Kali is described as having fangs, wearing a garland of corpses and living in cemeteries, and in most representations she is depicted as a blood-drenched creature with dark hair and four hands, holding a knife, a severed head, and a noose. A few centuries later in the *Bhagavat-purana* she is said to have decapitated a band of thieves and got drunk on their blood. Her most noted appearance is in the *Devi-mahatmya* where she battles against the demon Raktavija. Every time a drop of the demon's blood touches the ground Kali faces one thousand new versions of the demon. Kali manages to survive by vampirizing Raktavija and eating the duplicates.

Followers of Kali sacrificed goats at her temple, but the Thuggees (bands of assassins and bandits who were devoted to Kali), who were more extreme, would offer their victims as ritual sacrifices to the goddess. The Thuggees were eventually purged by the British in the nineteenth century. In Tantric Hinduism Kali became an influential deity and a potent symbol of the untamable aspects of life and the disorder that will always appear whenever attempts at order are made.

The Black Goddess

As Kali Sara, the Black Goddess, Kali survived among the Gypsies who migrated from India to Europe in the Middle Ages, but her vampiric qualities were modified by the addition of a Christian myth. According to this story the three Maries of the New Testament – Mary Magdalene, Mary Jacobe, and Mary Salome – traveled to France to escape persecution and were met and assisted by a Gypsy called Sara. The Maries baptized Sara and taught the gospel to her people. To this day on May 24 every year the Gypsies hold a celebration at a small French village called Saintes-Maries-de-la-Mer where the baptism is said to have taken place. A small statue of Saint Sara is carried to the crypt of the church, a ceremony which many experts believe closely parallels annual processions in honor of Kali in India.

See also: **GODS, VAMPIRE; INDIA**

Kapnick

According to German researcher Klaus Hamberger, in his book *Mortuus Non Mordet: Vampirismus 1689–1791* (published in 1992), in the town of Kapnick, Transylvania, during the last couple of months of 1752, records showed that more people were dying that usual at that time of the year. The victims, who all died within a few days, complained of burning sensations inside their body and blood in their saliva.

It was not long before rumors began to circulate that two dead women, Dorothea Pihsin and Anna Tonnerin, were the cause of the deaths. In February 1753, their graves were opened and their bodies examined by an official team of investigators. Anna's remains were found to be decomposing naturally. It was decided that she was innocent. Dorothea's corpse, however, looked largely well preserved. Incisions were made and fresh blood came out of the wounds. Dorothea was declared guilty of sorcery and blood-sucking. Her corpse was placed under the gallows and cremated. After this "execution," the number of deaths in Kapnick returned to their normal rate.

Kappa

In Japanese mythology the kappa is a vampire-like creature that lives in swampy areas, ponds, rivers, and lakes and likes to drink blood and eat entrails. It is described as an unattractive, fishy-smelling, monkey-looking child with yellow-green skin, webbed fingers and toes, and a concave head that held water. If the water was spilled it lost its power.

Named after the river god Kappa, whom it serves, the kappa lures its victims (most typically children) into treacherous or deep water so they drown. It attacks both animals and humans and after its victims are dead it drinks their blood through the anus and sucks out their entrails and livers. In this way the kappa offered a paranormal explanation for the bulging anus of victims of drowning. To appease the kappa, people would write their names on a cucumber and throw it into the water where the kappa lived.

In general kappas are evil, but not always. In some stories they can offer healing and in others they are presented as trustworthy when they make a promise. According to the story of the Kappa of Fukiura a kappa lost an arm trying to attack a horse. A farmer found the arm and that night the kappa asked the farmer to give it back. In return for the arm the kappa promised not to attack the local people anymore and to warn them when it had a guest kappa coming to visit, who obviously would not have made the same promise to leave humans alone. The creature kept its promise.

See also: **JAPAN**

Kasha

The kasha is a repulsive, nocturnal, corpse-eating ghoul from Japanese mythology. As corpses are typically cremated in Japan, the kasha must steal a corpse before it is burned. A guard is therefore often placed over the coffin at night to prevent the kasha running away with the dead.

See also: **JAPAN**

Kashubs

The Kashubs are a Christian sect of Slavs originally from Northern Europe and Poland, who from the mid to late nineteenth century migrated in large numbers to Ontario, Canada, where they preserved their language, traditions, customs, and vampire lore. There are two types of Kashubian vampire: the vjesci and the opji. The vjesci is born with a caul, or amniotic membrane, covering the head and the opji has a tooth or teeth already showing a birth.

According to Kashubian folklore, if the caul of the vjesci is dried and reduced to ashes and then fed to the child at the age of seven, the vjesci can lead a normal life. However, at death special attention must be paid to the burial procedures to ensure that the vjesci does not rise as a vampire. If the correct burial procedures are not followed, the corpse of a vjesci is believed to remain red, flexible, and warmer for longer than usual, and blood may also appear on the fingernails or face. The left eye may also remain open.

At midnight the vampire may then sit up in its grave with open eyes, naked because it has eaten its burial clothes. The head will move from side to side and it will make moaning noises before leaving its grave to drain the blood of its family and relatives, which will cause their death. The vjesci can wander around during the day as well as the night and if it manages to ring a church bell everyone who hears that bell will die; the only way to prevent people dying is to exhume the corpse at midnight and behead it. The blood from the vjesci should then be collected and given to those who have fallen ill to help them regain their strength. At reburial the head should be placed between the feet of the corpse.

The opji vampire is considered even more dangerous than the vjesci as it is thought that nothing can prevent it becoming a vampire during life. Like the vjesci, correct burial customs are all-important.

The Kashubs call someone who is angry or excited "as red as a vampire" because although both the vjesci and the opji can look and live normally, they are said to have ruddy or red faces. After death, paying attention to the correct burial procedures is considered by far the best method of protection for both types of vampire. Dying "vampires" should be given the Eucharist; earth from under the person's house should be placed in the coffin to prevent the corpse returning home; the sign of the cross should be made on the corpse's mouth; and a crucifix or coin placed on the tongue so that it will not eat its shroud. The corpse should be placed face down so that it can't make its way back to the surface. Netting or seeds may also be placed in the coffin to keep the vampire forever busy untying the knots or counting the seeds.

The work of Jan Perkowski

In the late 1960s, Ottawa's National Museum of Man (now the Canadian Museum of Civilization) commissioned Jan Perkowski, a professor of Slavic languages and literature from Texas, to study Kashubian folklore among the residents of the town of Wilno. His studies led to a 1972 publication entitled *Vampires, Dwarves, and Witches Among the Ontario Kashubs.* This 85-page report included a story by an unnamed informant about a vampire drawing blood and marrow from a girl's arm and later inspired articles by such diverse publications as *Psychology Today, Canadian Magazine,* and *National Enquirer.*

Perkowski conducted his study by interviewing the residents, whom he referred to as informants. He utilized questionnaires and transcribed notes from taped conversations. The following are examples taken from the report:

Informant: *Something came in the night and drew blood from her arm. It was a vampire. It came to my daughter at night and took marrow. There was a sign. A ring was visible. She was weak and had all her blood drawn out.*

Informant: *Mother said that I had a cap on the head and that it was burned. Such a person is supposed to be lucky, but I don't know.*

Perkowski: *Informant does not recall having ingested the ashes when she was seven, but this is something her mother would hardly announce to her. The ashes were probably hidden in a favorite food.*

These quotes certainly appear as strong evidence of the superstitious belief system in Wilno, however as the informants all remained confidential they are impossible to verify, and many experts suspected Perkowski of sensationalism when writing his report. The report upset the locals, and was subsequently denounced in the Canadian House of Commons.

See also: **POLAND**

Keats, John (1795–1821)

John Keats was an English poet who became one of major poets of the English Romantic movement. During his short life he penned some of the most memorable and sensuous poetry in the English language, including *Ode to a Nightingale* and *Ode on a Grecian Urn.* Two of his works – *Lamia,* based on the story about Menippus and a female vampire, and *La Belle Dame sans Merci* – are often listed among the great vampire writings.

La Belle Dame sans Merci (1819)
Oh what can ail thee, knight-at-arms,
Alone and palely loitering?
The sedge has withered from the lake,
And no birds sing.

Oh what can ail thee, knight-at-arms,
So haggard and so woe-begone?
The squirrel's granary is full,
And the harvest's done.

I see a lily on thy brow,
With anguish moist and fever-dew,
And on thy cheeks a fading rose
Fast withereth too.

I met a lady in the meads,
    Full beautiful – a faery's child,
Her hair was long, her foot was light,
    And her eyes were wild.

I made a garland for her head,
    And bracelets too, and fragrant zone;
She looked at me as she did love,
    And made sweet moan.

I set her on my pacing steed,
    And nothing else saw all day long,
For sidelong would she bend, and sing
    A faery's song.

She found me roots of relish sweet,
    And honey wild, and manna-dew,
And sure in language strange she said –
    "I love thee true."

She took me to her elfin grot,
    And there she wept and sighed full sore,
And there I shut her wild wild eyes
    With kisses four.

And there she lulled me asleep
    And there I dreamed – Ah! woe betide! –
The latest dream I ever dreamt
    On the cold hill side.

I saw pale kings and princes too,
    Pale warriors, death-pale were they all;
They cried – "La Belle Dame sans Merci
    Hath thee in thrall!"

I saw their starved lips in the gloam,
    With horrid warning gaped wide,
And I awoke and found me here,
    On the cold hill's side.

And this is why I sojourn here
    Alone and palely loitering,
Though the sedge is withered from the lake,
    And no birds sing.

As the figure of power in this poem, La Belle Dame destroys more men than just the knight. These other men are seen in the brief dream the knight has before awakening to his loneliness, and they include kings, princes, and warriors, all men of power and all plural, indicating their large number. That La Belle Dame could ruin the most powerful of men indicates that she is supernatural. Her vampiric power is one that surpasses the boundaries of death, for the pale kings, princes, and warriors continue to be tortured by the memory of her after their death – their "*starved lips*" eternally crave her kiss and her love.

See also: **LAMIA; LITERATURE; POETRY**

Kemp, Ursula

Ursula Kemp was an English woman who in the early 1580s was tried for witchcraft in a wave of witch hysteria that swept through the remote area of St. Osyth in Essex. Kemp was accused of using familiars to kill and bring sickness to her neighbors. She allegedly confessed to her crimes and was hanged in 1582. Her corpse was staked like that of a vampire.

Ursula Kemp made a meager living by midwifery and "unwitching" or removing bad spells that people believed had been cast against them. However, the uneven results of the cures she offered resulted in accusations of witchcraft. Members of her own family were made to testify against her and the presiding judge claimed to have received her confession in private.

The remains of Kemp were exhumed in 1921 and later placed on display at the Boscastle Museum of Witchcraft. Researchers discovered that Kemp's body had been staked with iron spikes, suggesting that it was feared she would return as a vampire after her death. In 2007, Essex historian Alison Rowlands said that according to her research, the skeleton exhumed may not in fact belong to Ursula Kemp but could belong to any one of ten women that died in the sixteenth and seventeenth centuries in the area.

Killing Vampires

The classic, well-tested method in European vampire lore to kill a vampire is to drive a stake through its heart. In Russia and throughout the Baltic area the appropriate wood for such a stake was ash, for its magical properties. In Silesia, on the other hand, such stakes were carved from oak and in Serbia from hawthorn because of its thorny shrub properties – vampires were thought to be allergic to thorns.

The bloating of the corpse in the grave, which was once seen as proof of vampirism, would have led to blood rushing out when it was pierced by a stake and a groaning sound. Today this groaning sound can be explained by the pressure in the body built up by gases involved in the process of decomposition, and air and gas being forced rather explosively through the trachea by the staking producing a shriek not unlike that of a living person, but in medieval times it was considered to be the vampire's last cry of terror. It may also have been regarded as a groan of pleasure indicating that the vampire's soul was finally given peace, since it was generally believed that the soul of the vampire was suffering and unable to extricate itself from earth. The destruction of the corpse was therefore a much-longed-for liberation for the vampire's soul.

In the absence of a stake, a silver knife or bullet was also thought to be able to kill a vampire. A number of additional steps would then need to be taken after staking, knifing, and/or shooting. The heart could be cut out, burned, and its ashes scattered. In 1874 a Romanian prince allegedly settled in Paris after being forced into exile because members of his family were believed by their compatriots to turn into vampires at death. It was said that the prince cut open his heart as he was dying to prevent himself from turning into a vampire. Decapitation was another favored method of destruction.

It was sometimes the case that all or several of these remedies were undertaken together, resulting in a terrible and gory mess. The corpses of suspected vampires were often covered with a shroud, hide, or piece of cloth before doing anything to it as it was thought that vampire blood could drive a person insane if it spurted onto them, or turn them into a vampire.

After being decapitated and disfigured, the vampire's body might then be reburied at a crossroads and the coffin filled with poppy seeds, thorns, and holy objects. For extra safety, however, cremation was considered to be the ultimate way to kill a vampire; only when the vampire's ashes had been scattered was there was no possibility of a resurrection.

Vampire-killing kits

Vampire-killing kits – typically wooden boxes containing such items as silver bullets, crosses, and various herbs believed to ward off vampires – some dating back to the early

1800s have been preserved and survive intact to this day. And according to the auctioneers Sotheby's, similar vampire-killing kits were probably sold in the early twentieth century to capitalize on interest in vampires sparked by the publication of *Dracula* in 1897. These might have been bought by fans of the book or by those who genuinely believed in vampires.

One such kit was sold the day before Halloween in 2003 by Sotheby's for $12,000. It consisted of a wooden box that held a pistol, silver bullet, and a large bottle of holy water. Two small bottles were also included, one filled with garlic juice (which was used to coat the bullets) and the other containing a special anti-vampire serum. There was also a small bottle of sulfur powder or flour of brimstone, as it was thought that the odor would repel the vampire. Other items included a crucifix made of wood and copper, a small bottle of smelling salts to revive those who fainted during the vampire killing, and a copy of the 1819 book, *History of Phantoms and Demons* by Gabrielle de Paban. The label on the kit read as follows: "*This box contains the items considered necessary for persons who travel into certain little known countries of Eastern Europe where the populace are plagued with a manifestation of evil known as vampires.*"

In November 2008 another similar vampire kit, containing stakes, mirrors, a gun with silver bullets, crosses, a Bible, holy water, candles, and even garlic, all housed in an American walnut case with a carved cross on top, was sold at an estate auction for $14,850.

With such kits appearing on the Internet and selling for large amounts of money at auction, it was not long before anonymous sellers keen to cash in on the interest in vampires were offering their own updated versions for modern-day vampire hunters. Although the merits of twenty-first-century vampire-killing kits are highly dubious, their existence once again indicates how interest in (and fear of) vampires remain strong.

See also: CORPSE; DESTRUCTION; PREVENTION; PROTECTION; VAMPIRE HUNTERS

King, Stephen (1947–)

American writer Stephen King is considered by many to be the most prolific and highly successful horror writer of the twentieth century. As well as being the author of popular novels such as *Carrie* (1974) and *The Shining* (1977), he has also explored the vampire theme in his work.

King's most effective and critically acclaimed vampire novel, *Salem's Lot* (1975), is about the slow takeover of an insular hamlet called Jerusalem's Lot in Maine by a European vampire named Kurt Barlow. Other notable vampire stories or novels by King include: *Christine* (1983); "Jerusalem's Lot" (1978); "One for the Road" (1977); *Pet Sematary* (1983); *The Tommyknockers* (1987), and "The Night Flier" (1988).

See also: LITERATURE

King Vikram and the Vampire

King Vikram and the Vampire is a collection of ancient Hindu tales and legends about the adventures of King Vikram and a baital or vampire. It was originally written in Sanskrit as *Baital Pachisi* or *Vetala Panchvimshati* (Twenty-five tales of Baital) and was translated into English in 1870. Like *The Arabian Nights*, for which it established the literary foundations, *King Vikram* is a set of tales within a frame story.

The plot centers on the legendary King Vikram, identified as the first-century BC Vikramāditya, and his promise to a tantric sorcerer (Vamachara) to bring him the Baital, a mischievous rather than bloodthirsty vampire who hangs on a tree and inhabits and animates dead bodies. A series of Hindu fairy tales are strung on this frame, which typically include the following elements.

The Baital says he will go with Vikram, provided Vikram does not speak. The Baital tells Vikram a tale and some of the characters in that tale are typically awkward or unjust. The Baital ends each tale with a question about the character's behavior, which is often a well-disguised puzzle about righteousness and/or politics. Vikram answers and succeeds in justifying the character's behavior, but because he has spoken he has violated their agreement and the Baital flies back to the tree.

After telling 25 witty and entertaining stories, the Baital finally allows himself to be carried to the sorcerer. The Baital then reveals the sorcerer's plan to sacrifice a person who has 32 virtues (Vikram himself) by having him bow and then beheading him in front of the goddess, which would allow the sorcerer to gain control over the Baital. The Baital tells the king to instead ask the sorcerer how to perform his obeisance, and to use that opportunity to behead him. The king does exactly as he is told by the Baital and manages to cut off the sorcerer's head. The god Indra appears and grants Vikram a boon or gift, whereupon the king asks for his history to become famous all over the world.

Kiss

In European vampire folklore, vampires that are revenants or reanimated corpses were thought to suck blood from living humans or animals to keep their own dead bodies from decomposing. They were said to do this by biting or punching holes in their victims with their tongues, a process modern writers sometimes refer to as the "kiss" of a vampire. The victim typically experienced a slow wasting disease that often ended in death. After death the corpses of vampire victims then transformed into other revenants and created a vampire epidemic.

In vampire fiction, the kiss or bite of a vampire tends to be more subtle and sensual and although it can lead to immediate death as the vampire drains the victim of blood, more often than not it refers to the process whereby a vampire transforms a victim into a vampire. This process begins when a vampire attacks its victim, but instead of draining all their blood and killing him or her, the vampire at that time chooses to leave the victim close to death. The next day the bloodsucker returns and the victim, now weakened, is easily hypnotized by the vampire's charm and power and is willing to choose to live eternally. With the consent of the victim the vampire completes the process, paralyzing him or her with a kiss and drinking his or her blood. After this the vampire then bites its own wrist and allows the victim to drink blood for the first time. This is said to be an intense and profound experience for the new vampire, akin to falling in love, but the euphoria tends to wear off and the new vampire begins to feel despair and remorse for the death of his or her human body and his or her birth as a vampire.

See also: **BIRTH OF A VAMPIRE; BITE; TRANSFORMATION**

Kiss, Béla (c.1877– ?)

A Hungarian who allegedly murdered his victims and drunk their blood in the early twentieth century.

Béla Kiss began his career as a blood-drinking vampire, or serial killer inspired by the vampire legend, relatively late in life, in his mid to late thirties. In 1912 he married a pretty woman called Marie. Marie was 15 years his junior and within weeks of the marriage she allegedly had an affair with a neighbor. She disappeared along with her lover. Then in Budapest a number of other women went missing.

In 1916 Kiss went missing himself. He had been drafted into the army and army officers confiscated a number of metal drums he had bought to store gas in. The drums were opened by the officers and in each one they found the alcohol-preserved body of a naked woman. The women had not only been strangled, they also had puncture marks on their necks and their bodies were drained of blood. A search was ordered. Between 17 and 24 more barrels were found – reports detailing the exact number vary – but all the accounts agree that the bodies of Kiss's wife and her lover were found in these other barrels.

The case was closed as the authorities were convinced that Kiss had been killed on the battle-front, but everything changed when they heard from the nurse who had attended the wounded Kiss. Her description did not match the known appearance of Kiss. Reports about Kiss continued to surface in Budapest for many years after, but each time the authorities followed up on the rumors, Kiss had disappeared. He was never found and his eventual fate is not known.

See also: **HISTORICAL VAMPIRES**

Kithnos Vampire

The short but humorous story of Andilaveris the vampire or vrykolakas of Kithnos, a small Aegean island, survived well into the nineteenth century, even though other vampires on the island were believed to have been destroyed by the placing of wax crosses over the mouths of corpses. Andilaveris, however, the last of the vampires, was still said to wander the streets of the village of Messaria, eating the villagers' food and smashing their plates and glasses. Many occupants feared going outdoors after dusk. More mischievous than bloodthirsty, one of Andilaveris's more annoying habits was to climb the church roof and urinate on passers-by. Being a vrykolakas, he was unable to leave his grave on a Saturday and so the priest, a sexton, and several others opened his tomb on a Saturday, removed his body, and ferried it to the then virtually uninhabited island of Daskalio, where they left it, trapped and unable to do any more harm.

Kitsune

In Japanese and Chinese folklore, a kitsune is a wild fox demon that can appear in the form of a beautiful woman who vampirizes her victims. At their core, kitsune are vampires. All of them feed on intangibles: words, knowledge, writing, music, the land, and the people around them. The most common way for a kitsune to feed, however, is through sex.

The kitsune are said to hide in forests and to use human voices to bewitch and lure their victims. They especially like to prey on gluttons and drunkards. As well as sexually ravaging their victims they also like to cut women's hair and shave men's heads for pranks.

Kitsune-tsuki is a form of possession in which a woman (and occasionally a man) is taken over by a wild fox spirit. Symptoms of kitsune-tsuki, a "condition" recorded in Japan since the twelfth century, include cravings for red beans and rice, restlessness, insomnia, and erratic behavior. Some cases of kitsune-tsuki are said to be revenge for offences against the huli jing. The possessing fox spirit enters the body under the fingernails or through the breasts and it resides in either the stomach or the left side of the body. The possessed will hear the fox spirit speak to them inside their head.

See also: **CHINA; HULI JING; JAPAN**

Knots

In European vampire lore vampires were thought to have an obsessive urge to untie knots. Therefore knots, nets, and stockings were often placed in coffins and graves in the belief that when the revenant woke it would begin working, and would be able to untie only one knot a year. Although knotted ropes and nets have been used as a defense against evil spirits in many ancient cultures, in Romania knots were removed or cut before burial, as it was thought they would prevent the spirit of the dead departing to the next world. The Kashubs in northern Germany were also reluctant to provide the corpse with a net, and in areas under the influence of the Greek Orthodox Church there were also prohibitions against burying knots with a corpse.

Kosci

In Croatia a male vampire is called a koscima and a female vampire a koscama and the plural term for vampire is kosci. These vile creatures were said to enter houses at night, especially the houses of people they had had a disagreement with in their life. Once inside they would drink the blood of the inhabitants and feed on their hearts and entrails. Stakes made of blackthorn were believed to be the most effective weapons against kosci. Stabbing with pointed objects and decapitation were also favored methods of destruction.

In the early eighteenth century a villager of Lastovo Island stated that kosci can:

> designate the dead who have revived and who, residing in their graves, especially people who drowned during their lives, kill and destroy people and all too frequently go to their homes and have sexual intercourse with their wives, when they were men, as they did before death.

See also: **LASTOVO ISLAND VAMPIRES**

Kozlak

In Dalmatian folklore "kozlak" is a term for a kind of poltergeist vampire that likes to enter houses at night and torment the occupants by throwing items around and making noises. Little is known about this vampire species, but some experts believe its name may be derived in some way from the Croatian term for vampire, "vukodlak." If it is suspected that a corpse has become a vampire the room that the person died in must remain untouched and not cleaned or swept. If this preventative measure does not work a priest must go to the grave of the vampire and say prayers to summon it. When the vampire appears the priest then has to stake it with a thorn grown high on a mountain. If this is done it is said the kozlak will longer bother the living.

Kresnik/Krsnik

In Slavic countries a kresnik or krsnik is a person who is a kind of vampire hunter or shaman-like figure and the bitter enemy of the local vampire, the kudlak. The kresnik has Christian associations (the word *kresnik* comes from the root *krst* meaning "cross") and is often described as dressing in white and aided by the forces of light, in contrast to the kudlak who is associated with darkness and evil. Every town or community had both a kresnik and a kudlak, and they were said to fight ferociously. Luckily for the communities, the kresnik would always win, as the agents of God were always stronger than the agents of darkness. During the struggle the combatants would transform into animal forms. Variations on this vampire fighter can be found in different regions of Slavic lands. For example, in Hungary they were called *talbos*.

See also: **DHAMPIR**

Krvoijac

In Bulgarian, krvoijac was a name occasionally used for a vampire, alongside the more common vampir or ubour. The krvoijac was very similar to the vampir and ubour, typically staying in its grave for 40 days to acquire its supernatural powers and while its skeleton formed; it was thought that the bones remained in a jelly-like state during this time. It was said to have a pointed tongue and one nostril. Wild roses strewn around the grave or planted in the earth on the grave were thought to confine it to the ground.

Kuang-Shi

See: **CHIANG-SHIH**

Kudlak

The kudlak was a Slavic vampire believed to be active during both life and death, and reported in Istria and Czechoslovakia. Many experts believe it was a shortened term for the Croatian word for vampire, "vukodlak."

A symbol of evil and darkness that attacked the innocent at midnight and spread pestilence and misfortune, the kudlak was the bitter enemy and exact opposite of the kresnik, a representation of the forces of good. Each village had both a kresnik and a kudlak and the two would be locked in constant battle, assuming animal shapes such as an ox, a pig, or a horse. The kudlak, identified by its black color, could be a living person possessed by spirits. However, it was believed to be most dangerous after death, and to prevent its return the corpse would be impaled with a hawthorn stake or the tendons slashed at the knee to prevent it walking.

K'uei

"K'uei" is a Chinese term for the evil undead, who were said to be persons who had lived sinfully and therefore did not deserve to find peace and happiness in the afterlife. Angry and resentful at their inability to find peace after death, they took out their frustrations on sinners and other people who reminded them of themselves. The k'uei undead are typically described as skeletons with demonic faces. They must move in a straight line and an effective way to protect against them is to place screens and barriers inside a doorway so that they cannot move around them.

See also: **CHINA**

Kukudhi

In the vampire folklore of some regions of Albania, "kukudhi" is the term used to describe the final stage of a vampire's transformation. In Albania it was believed that the undead took time to develop the powers of a vampire and the longer they survived the stronger they became. Once it reached the final kukudhi stage it was at its strongest and able to leave its grave during both night and day. In some instances, it was so strong it no longer needed to return to its grave at all, and could travel in disguise as a merchant to other lands.

See also: **LIFE OF A VAMPIRE**

Kürten, Peter (1883-1931)

Peter Kürten, the so-called "Vampire of Düsseldorf," was a German serial killer who is often cited as a real-life or historical vampire. Kürten was certainly not a real-life vampire or a vampire of folklore or fiction, but his obsession with blood did have vampiric associations.

The son of an alcoholic, brutal father, Kürten was born in Mülheim in 1883 and lived part of his childhood with the town dog catcher, often killing unclaimed dogs. He later claimed to have committed his first murders at the age of nine when he pushed two children into the water. At the age 17 he was sent to jail for four years for the attempted rape and murder of a young woman. In 1913 he murdered a 10-year-old girl on the streets of Düsseldorf. It was not until February 1929, 16 years later, when he stabbed to death two children that he began in earnest to earn the name the Düsseldorf Vampire. In August the same year he killed nine people and continued his killing sprees throughout the winter of 1929–30. He was eventually arrested in May 1930, after a victim he had for some inexplicable reason stopped strangling and let go identified him to the police.

Kürten was described as an ordinary looking bespectacled man with a moustache and neat-looking clothes, but beneath his ordinariness lurked a merciless killer. After strangling his victims he would slit their throats and drink their blood, but during his reign of terror he liked to confuse the police by using a number of different weapons and methods of killing. It was only when he finally confessed to the police that his guilt was proved beyond doubt.

Throughout his trial Kürten showed no remorse and candidly recounted details of his crimes to the celebrated psychologist Karl Berg, whose book *The Sadist* (1932) became a classic of criminological literature. According to Berg, Kürten was a sexual psychopath and his crimes represented a perfect example of *Lustmord*, or murder for pleasure – in Kürten's case, sexual pleasure. The Vampire of Düsseldorf was eventually convicted for murdering or assaulting 29 people and was executed by decapitation on July 2, 1931. His last words reportedly were, *"Tell me, after my head has been chopped off, will I still be able to hear, at least for a moment, the sound of my own blood gushing from the stump of my neck? That would be the pleasure to end all pleasures."*

"Whether we read books and watch films about vampires for psychological reasons or simply for entertainment, each of us keeps the vampire myth alive. While we may be able to understand rationally that vampires do not exist, who among us does not start at the shadow at the window, the squeak in the dark?"

Daniel C. Scavone, *Vampires*

Là-Bas

This novel by French writer J. K. Huysmans (1848–1907), translated as "Down There" or "The Damned," has been described as *the great classic of Satanism.* It tells the story of a young writer in Paris who descends into a world of madness while researching the history of several cases of blood lust and vampirism, including the infamous Gilles de Rais and Sergeant Bertrand cases. The novel charts a terrifying journey into the heart of darkness. It is a masterwork of the so-called "decadent" movement of literature and a harrowing examination of the eternal struggle between darkness and light.

The book was first published in serial form in the newspaper *L'Écho de Paris*, with the first installment appearing on February 15, 1891. The subject matter shocked conservative readers and the editor was urged to halt the serialization. However the serialization continued, and the story appeared in book form in April of the same year. Sales of the book were, however, prohibited at French railway stations.

The most compelling vampire case in the book, which brilliantly captures the dread and threat of the predatory vampire without spilling a drop of blood, is that of Madame Chantelouve, a woman with the capacity to feed on the very life force of those around her, increasing her energy while her victims sink into depression and exhaustion.

See also: **LITERATURE**

La Llorona

Also called "The Weeping Woman" (*llorona* is Spanish for "weeper"), in Mexican folklore and in some parts of the United States La Llorona is a ghostly weeping woman who is said to float around at night. This vampiric seductress lures men to their deaths, in perpetual revenge against all males for the tragedy of her life.

There are several versions of the La Llorona story. In one La Llorona is looking for her lost children. In another she had many children but fell in love with a man who didn't want any children. To please her lover she murdered her children, but was subsequently executed. Her former lover was overcome with remorse and killed himself.

Whatever version of the tale is told, what is striking about this story and makes it similar to other vampire seductress tales, such as that of the lamia, is the breaking of a taboo – in this case a mother murdering her children. Folklorists believe that the story may have drawn its inspiration from Aztec mythology. The goddess Cihuacoatl dressed in white and carried an empty cradle. It was said she walked among Aztec women screaming and crying for her lost child. It's also possible that the story has a historical basis.

One of the earliest references to the La Llorona myth dates back to the sixteenth century and tells of an Indian princess who fell in love with an Italian nobleman and bore him twins. The nobleman, despite promising to marry the princess, married someone else. Consumed with rage the princess killed her children with a dagger and wandered the streets in torn and bloody clothes wailing for her children. She was found guilty of murder and executed. It is said that her ghost is cursed and must forever wander the earth looking for her children.

Over the years this story developed into the more well-known *Weisse Frau* or White Lady story centered around Cologne. In this story a tanner's daughter fell in love with a knight and bore his children. The knight refused to marry her and mocked her and her child. In anger she threw the child under the knight's horse and stabbed the knight to death. When in prison she hanged herself and her body was buried without ceremony. From that time onwards between the hours of midnight and 1 a.m. she would appear dressed in white at the scene of the murder, and anyone who saw or spoke to her died soon after, victims of her curse.

Typically La Lorona is described as shapely and dressed in white. She has long hair and long fingernails but no face. She is usually seen by riverbanks and deserted places at midnight with her back turned, but sometimes she appears during daylight asking for her missing children. She is also said to wait by the roadside and if unsuspecting motorists pick her up they are told her sad story. Sometimes she will appear out of nowhere in a car and disappear a few minutes later. Some say she will entice and kill men if they are drunk and stumble across her in lonely areas. Whether she appears in the back seat of a car or in a lonely deserted spot, seeing La Llorona or the White Lady is thought to be a bad omen; bad luck or death are said to follow within a year.

Lamia

The lamiae (plural) are a type of legendary female vampire believed to be extremely beautiful but also extremely dangerous for men and young children.

They are named after Lamia, a Libyan queen who was the mistress of the Greek god Zeus. When Hera, Zeus' wife, discovered her husband's affair she murdered Lamia's children by Zeus. In revenge and torment, Lamia swore to avenge herself on all children and men by sucking their blood. Her actions led to her transformation into a hideous blood-sucking beast. Other traditions suggest that the lamiae are a class of demon with deformed, serpent-like lower limbs that had the power to transform themselves into beautiful young women in order to attract, seduce, and kill young men. In Hebrew lore, lamiae are represented by Lilith, Adam's first wife.

In chapter 25 of his *Life of Apollonius of Tyana*, Philostratus (*c.*170–245) included a lengthy story concerning the lamia. In the account Menippus, one of Apollonius' students, fell in love with a beautiful woman he had first seen in an apparition. When Menippus told Apollonius his story the latter informed him that he was being seduced by a vampire. Despite protests from Menippus, Apollonius confronted the lamia who eventually admitted to her intention to *"feed upon young and beautiful bodies because their blood is pure and strong."*

The lamiae were sometimes confused with the empusa by the ancient Greeks and were typically invoked by nannies to frighten unruly children. When a child mysteriously died, a saying, still used today, suggests that it may have been strangled by a lamia.

Inspiration

The lamiae have been the inspiration for the female vampire in fiction and poetry for hundreds of years. In 1492 Angelo Poliziano published a poem entitled "Lamia." These creatures were also the inspiration for the English Romantic poet John Keats's immortal poem *Lamia* (1819). Keats's poem is derived from the account narrated by Philostratus in his *Life of*

Apollonius but the story changes considerably, in that the lamia theme is taken one step further by using it as a metaphor for the interchange of energies that takes place in human relationships – in other words it becomes an account of psychic vampirism. In Keats's version, in her need for love the lamia does not appear in her serpent-like form but moves into the mortal Lucius' world; Lucius in turn attempts to become a vampire, willing to drain the lamia to gain her powers. At this point Apollonius intervenes and drives the lamia away. Without the lamia, Lucius dies.

Lampir

A Bosnian term for a vampire that typically manifested during severe epidemics. Disease appeared to be the main cause for the appearance of a lampir; if disease swept the community it was often attributed to lampirs if no other cause could be found. The first person to die of the disease was labeled a vampire, and those who died afterwards were said to be victims infected by the vampire, and regarded as equally dangerous because they could pass the vampirism on. In 1879 when the Austrians took control of Bosnia, officials noted numerous cases of people exhuming corpses and burning

them as lampirs. The Austrians later banned such practices.

In a 1923 article M. Edith Durham, an English anthropologist who performed field work in Bosnia, reported her experiences in a feature for the journal *Man*:

> *A recent case was when there was an outbreak of typhus [in 1906] … A young man was first to die. His wife sickened and swore that her husband returned in the night and sucked her blood and said, "He is a lampir." The neighbours, filled with fear, begged the authorities to permit them to dig up and burn his body. Permission was refused, and a panic ensued. The lampir was seen and heard by many people and there were fifteen deaths.*

Langsuir

Sometimes used interchangeably with "pontianak," the term for a still-born child who becomes a vampire, the "langsuir" is a term used for a beautiful, flying vampire woman from Malaysian folklore who flies into trees and attacks children at night. She is typically described as wearing green clothes and having long nails and long black hair that reaches to her ankles. Her hair is supposedly so long because it covers a hole in the back of her neck from which she drinks the blood of children.

It was said that a woman transformed into a langsuir if she died in childbirth or died from the shock of delivering a still-born baby. It would take 40 days for a corpse to emerge as a langsuir, but it was possible to prevent the transformation by putting beads of glass into the corpse's mouth, or by putting needles in the palms of the hands and a hen's egg under each armpit. These preventative measures were thought to stop the creature opening its mouth to let out a terrible scream (called a *ngilai*), and to stop it opening its hands and waving its arms about so it could not fly.

Only a particularly powerful magician could drive away or tame a langsuir with specific incantations. The way to tame a langsuir was to capture her, cut off her nails, and stuff her hair into the hole in her neck. In this captured state she could then marry and have children and lead a normal life, but care had to be taken not to allow her to dance and make merry, as this could trigger a transformation back into her feverish vampiric state.

Larvae

In ancient Roman folklore "larvae" was the term used interchangeably with "lamia" – a type of female vampire found throughout the ancient world. Often associated with lemures, the term was also used to describe evil spirits who returned from the dead to torment the living.

Lastovo Island Vampires

Between 1737 and 1738 a series of vampire outbreaks were reported on the Croatian island of Lastovo. Belief in vampires was strong among some but not all residents of the island, and local vampire hunters were charged with grave desecration and the staking of corpses with blackthorn. A ban was placed on exhuming corpses by the archbishop but it was not entirely successful.

In 1737 and 1738 Lastovo residents testified in the archbishop's court in Dubrovnik. They claimed that over a number of years vampires – kosci – had been blamed whenever illness occurred and they were being blamed again for a recent bout of often fatal diarrhea-causing sickness. It was also said that victims who had died of the sickness were becoming vampires themselves. A group of islanders formed a vampire-hunting gang. The first grave they opened was that of a man who had died a year before by drowning (a death that was associated with the Devil) but his corpse was skeletal and therefore declared to be innocent. Other graves were opened and inspected. Some were revealed not to be vampires, but those that were believed to be vampires – often because of the strange sounds they made – were staked and mutilated with knives and axes.

The local priest, Dom Marin Pavlovic, was among those called to testify to the court. He recalled at least two occasions in the past that clearly demonstrated the firm belief in vampires that existed on the island. In one of these cases, that Pavlovic claimed to have witnessed 17 years previously, a plague was devastating the island and he accidentally came across a group of people digging up the grave of a priest. He urged them to show respect and cursed them when they did not, but the group insisted that the priest had become a vampire because when they stabbed his corpse blood had spurted out.

At the end of the inquest 17 islanders were found guilty of corpse and grave desecration. The sentence given to them by the archbishop was to wear a stone around their neck and to visit three churches to hear Holy Mass and beg mercy for their crimes. Some of those found guilty were expected to perform this penance for up to four years. If they refused to obey they were threatened with excommunication.

The Element Encyclopedia of Vampires

Latent Vampire

For those who believe in vampires a latent vampire is someone who is already naturally a vampire, but whose vampiric tendencies have not yet manifested. Apparently, some latent vampires who are not aware of their true nature may need to be "turned on" or "awakened," by a ritual awakening or significant life experience, while others may have their tendencies "activated" by indeterminate causes. Latent vampires can sometimes stand out to other already established vampires through a phenomenon known as the "beacon." The beacon is a particular feeling or energy signature generated by vampires in general, and by latent or potential vampires in particular. The beacon seems to exist to attract other vampires to the potential vampire so that they may instigate the awakening process.

See also: **LIVING VAMPIRES**

Lavater, Ludwig

Ludwig Lavater was a late sixteenth-century Protestant theologian and expert on all matters concerning the undead and vampires. His most notable treatise, a classic study of vampire species from the ancient world, such as lamia and larvae, was *De spectris, lemuribus, et magnis atque insolitis fragoribus*, which was translated into English in 1572 as *Of Ghosts and Spirits Walking by Night*.

Lavater believed that people were too influenced by any sudden movement that occurred in the night and too quick to ascribe supernatural causes to natural events. In his view the belief that unexplained noises were the "*souls of dead men, which crave help for them that are living,*"

was wrong. According to Lavater, if a vampire existed it was not the soul of a dead person but "*either good or evil angels, or some secret and hid operations by God.*" This belief was very much a reflection of late medieval belief that divine intervention was a fact of everyday life.

Lead

In Indian folklore, amulets made of the metal lead were believed to have magical properties to protect against night-flying demons.

See also: **APOTROPAICS; IRON; PROTECTION; SILVER**

Leanhaum-shee

Also known as *leanan sidhe*, the leanhaum-shee is a blood-drinking fairy with vampiric qualities from Irish folklore. The leanhaum-shee was said to be a beautiful woman who used her loveliness and charm to bewitch men and lure them away into mountains and caves. Once they were captured, the leanhaum-shee would then drain the blood and life of her victims. The only way to break the spell was to find a substitute, someone else who would become her prey.

See also: **DEARG-DIULAI; IRELAND**

Leap Castle

Leap Castle is an Irish castle with a sinister reputation in County Offaly, Ireland, once owned by Tadhg O'Carroll, whose bloodthirsty and brutal reign could well earn him a place alongside other well-known historical vampires such as Vlad the Impaler. The castle was built sometime in the thirteenth century by the O'Bannon family and was originally called *Léim Uí Bhanáin*, or "Leap of the O'Bannons." The O'Bannons were the secondary chieftains of the territory, and were subject to the ruling O'Carroll clan.

By the early 1500s, the O'Carroll clan had seized possession of the castle but following the death of Mulrooney O'Carroll in 1532, family struggles plagued the clan. A fierce rivalry for the clan leadership erupted within the family and brother turned against brother. One of the brothers, Thaddeus Macfir was a priest; one day when Thaddeus was holding Mass for a group of his family (in what is now called the Bloody Chapel) another brother, Tadhg, burst into the chapel, plunged his sword into his brother, and fatally wounded him. The priest fell across the altar and died in front of his family. This was not only an act of murder, it was an act of blasphemy, so the chapel was no longer used as a place of worship and became a banqueting hall instead. In this banqueting hall Tadhg had an oubliette installed – a small, dark cell with a terrifying drop down into it – into which his enemies were thrown and then bricked in and left to die. On one occasion Tadhg was said to have thrown around 40 of the O'Mahon clan – a clan he had invited to a banquet on the pretext of peace – into the oubliette. In 1552, Tadhg accepted a knighthood from the English and was promptly murdered by his other brothers, thus ending his brutal reign.

It was not long after that Leap Castle was said to be haunted by the ghost of Tadhg O'Carroll. Because Tadhg had committed blasphemy by killing his brother when he was talking to God, his soul was said to be eternally damned and the doors of heaven were not open to him. Rumors circulated that his restless soul was therefore confined to the Bloody Chapel, and some believe that he feeds on the blood of those foolish enough to enter it.

Much of Leap Castle was burned during the Irish Civil War and the chapel is little more than a blackened chamber today, but many people who have visited it report that it has an eerie feel about it. Even more disturbing was the discovery of the oubliette at the beginning of the twentieth century. When workers were cleaning out the bottom of the shaft they discovered three cartloads of human bones at the bottom. A somewhat chilling report indicates that these workmen also found a pocket-watch dated to the 1840s amongst the bones.

See also: **CARRICKAPHOUKA CASTLE**

Lee, Christopher (1922-)

The son of an Italian countess and a colonel in the King's Royal Rifle Corps, Christopher Lee is an English actor best known for his portrayal of Count Dracula in the horror movies by Hammer Films. In 1957, Lee played the part of Frankenstein in the monster movie hit, *The Curse of Frankenstein*, and the following year starred as Dracula in the equally successful, *The Horror of Dracula*.

Throughout the 1960s and into the 1970s Lee appeared in numerous other horror and vampire films. His last appearance as Dracula with Hammer Films was in *Satanic Rites of Dracula* (1974), and to many people the six foot four inch Lee remains the definitive on-screen Dracula. Even though Lee's commanding, sexually charged and charismatic Dracula has no resemblance to original vampire beliefs, the enduring interest and mass appeal of the persona he created serves to show that, even today, the image of the vampire still lies at the heart of the human psyche.

Lee, Tanith (1947–)

Tanith Lee is a British writer of science fiction, dark horror, and fantasy, whose compelling writing is noted for its elegance and evocative imagery. Her first vampire story, "Red as Blood" (which introduced the vampire theme into the Snow White story) appeared in 1979 as a short story in *Fantasy and Science Fiction* magazine. In 1980 her most well-known vampire work, *Sabella or Blood Stone* – a novel about an extraterrestrial who comes to earth to seduce men with her otherworldly beauty and to suck their blood – appeared. Her other significant vampire writings include: *Bite Me Not* (1984), a fantasy about a girl who falls in love with a vampire prince of the air; *Kill the Dead* (1980); *Nunc Dimitis* (1983); *The Vampire Lover* (1984); *Dark Dance* (1992); and *Vivia* (1995).

See also: LITERATURE

Le Fanu, Sheridan (1814–73)

Joseph Sheridan Le Fanu was an Irish poet and author of stories in the horror genre. His most famous works were *Carmilla* and *Green Tea* (both 1872). *Carmilla*, a short story about a female vampire published in the noted collection *In a Glass Darkly*, became a major influence on the development of the vampire in literature. Le Fanu's writing career began at Trinity College, Dublin, when in 1838 his short story "The Ghost and the Bone Setter" was published in

the *Dublin University Magazine*. In the years that followed, many of his stories and novels were judged to be mediocre but critics agree that *Carmilla*, the third English vampire story, is one of his finest. *Carmilla* narrates the story of Laura, the daughter of an Austrian civil servant called Karnstein, who is attacked by a female vampire named Carmilla, but who also takes the names of Mircalla and Millarca. The story begins with Laura recalling a visit from Carmilla in her childhood and then goes on to tell how the vampire reappears when Laura is a teenager. Eventually, Carmilla is followed to her resting place and killed.

Married in 1844, Le Fanu became something of a recluse, writing ghost stories in his bed after his wife died in 1858. After his death in Dublin in 1873 Le Fanu's work faded into obscurity for close on a hundred years. However, when Gothic fiction became popular again in the 1960s Le Fanu's stories, and in particular *Carmilla*, were critically reappraised and given the respect they deserve. Le Fanu's work also became extremely popular among vampire fans; *Carmilla* stands alongside *Dracula* as the vampire story most often adapted for the screen.

I had a dream that night that was the beginning of a very strange agony.

I cannot call it a nightmare, for I was quite conscious of being asleep. But I was equally conscious of being in my room, and lying in bed, precisely as I actually was. I saw, or fancied I saw, the room and its furniture just as I had seen it last, except that it was very dark, and I saw something moving round the foot of the bed, which at first I could not accurately distinguish. But I soon saw that it was a sooty-black animal that resembled a monstrous cat. It appeared to me about four or five feet long for it measured

*fully the length of the hearthrug as it passed
over it; and it continued to-ing and fro-ing
with the lithe, sinister restlessness of a beast in a
cage. I could not cry out, although as you may
suppose, I was terrified. Its pace was growing
faster, and the room rapidly darker and darker,
and at length so dark that I could no longer see
anything of it but its eyes. I felt it spring lightly
on the bed. The two broad eyes approached my
face, and suddenly I felt a stinging pain as if
two large needles darted, an inch or two apart,
deep into my breast. I waked with a scream.
The room was lighted by the candle that
burnt there all through the night, and I saw a
female figure standing at the foot of the bed, a
little at the right side. It was in a dark loose
dress, and its hair was down and covered its
shoulders. A block of stone could not have been
more still. There was not the slightest stir of
respiration. As I stared at it, the figure appeared
to have changed its place, and was now nearer
the door; then, close to it, the door opened, and
it passed out.*

(Sheridan Le Fanu, *Carmilla*)
See also: **LITERATURE**

Legend, Vampire

Legends, myths, superstitions, and traditions
about vampires can be found all over the world
and are as old as terror itself. Almost every culture has legends of ghosts, witches, demons,
fairies, and other evil entities who like to suck
human blood. Today, blood-sucking creatures
are called vampires, regardless of where they
came from and regardless of whether they are
actually witches or demons with a thirst for
blood, rather than pure vampires. Originally,

however, the word "vampire" and words similar
to it, like "vampir" and "upir," originated among
the Slavic people in the countries of Eastern
Europe.

Although a creature fairly similar to the
Slavic vampire, called the vrykolakas, can be
found in the traditions of ancient Greece, and an
undead menace called the chiang-shih can be
found in classic Chinese traditions, most experts
believe that it was in Eastern Europe that the
image of the traditional vampire originated.
Experts are less sure about the origins of the
Slavic vampire legend as there could be many
sources. Some researchers have suggested that
the Slavic vampire can be traced back to ancient
Egypt or India and that legends from those
countries were brought to Europe by traveling
Gypsies. Whatever their origin, it was in Eastern Europe that the vampire legend took shape
and over the centuries went on to capture the
imagination of the rest of the world.

Léger, Antoine (d.1824)

Antoine Léger, often classed as a so-called
historical vampire, was a French mass murderer accused of blood-drinking and cannibalism. In 1824, at the age of 29 he went to
live in the woods by himself, but apparently
he was not content to just live off animals.
He lured a girl into a cave and killed her.
Apprehended, he was tried by the district
court of Versailles, at which time it came out
that he'd eaten parts of his victim and drunk
her blood because he was "thirsty." He was
guillotined.

According to an 1873 report entitled *Insanity and its relation to crime; a text and commentary,*
the following transcript of the trial survives:

Q. At what o'clock did you go out of your cave, on the 10th of August?

A. I was not regular in the hour of going out. About half-past three.

Q. What did you do that day at about four o'clock?

A. I went to get some apples. I saw, at the end of the wood, a little girl who was seated on the ground with her back turned toward me; I determined to carry her off; I wound my handkerchief around her neck and threw her on my back; she only uttered a slight cry; I went through the wood to the place I have shown; I was thirsty, hungry, and hot; I waited perhaps half an hour unconscious; then my thirst and hunger overcame me, and I proceeded to devour her.

Q. In what state then was the girl?

A. Motionless; she was dead. I only tried to eat her; that is all.

Lemon

Perhaps because of its sharp, bitter, stinging taste, in Saxony, Germany, lemons were sometimes used to protect against evil and, if placed in the mouth of a corpse, were a way to dispose of the Saxon vampire species neuntöter. The use of the fruit appears to be unique to Germany.

See also: **APOTROPAICS; PROTECTION**

Lemures

In ancient Roman folklore, lemures were the restless ghosts of people who had died without a family member surviving to bury them. The Romans believed it was a curse to die without surviving family members. People who were sinners in life or who had died prematurely or by murder, violence, or execution were also prime candidates for becoming lemures after their death. The lemures were said to rise from their graves and transform into hideous creatures to attack the living. One way to prevent this was to burn black beans around the tomb, or to bang on drums, as the body was buried.

Lemuria was a four-day Roman festival of the dead held every May. During these four days it was thought that the wandering dead, all grouped together as the larvae, walked the earth and because some of them were terrifying and terrible in nature, according to Roman poet Ovid, they needed to be appeased by ceremonies and rituals.

Lenora

See: **POETRY**

Lesbian Vampires

Some of the earliest vampires, such as the Greek lamiae, were female but their victims were typically young men and children. It was in literature and poetry, and later in film, that lesbian vampiric relationships were eventually to establish themselves and to serve as yet another illustration of the essentially erotic nature of the vampire's relationship to its victim. Sometimes this relationship was mutual but more often than not, especially in nineteenth-century literature, the female vampire is presented as a powerful, intellectually superior character, attacking and seducing against her will a younger, more naïve woman.

Hints of lesbianism can clearly be seen in Samuel Taylor Coleridge's poem entitled *Christabel* (1816), where the *"lovely lady Geraldine"* mysteriously appears in the woods near the castle of Christabel's father. Taking pity on Geraldine's plight, the naïve Christabel invites Geraldine to take shelter in the castle. The two women drink wine together and then get undressed and go to bed. Although it is not directly stated, something clearly passed between the women overnight as Geraldine awakes refreshed but Christabel awakes feeling uneasy and if she has committed some kind of sin.

Carmilla

Towards the end of the nineteenth century perhaps the most famous lesbian vampire story was written by Irish writer, Sheridan Le Fanu. *Carmilla* tells the story of Carmilla Karnstein, also known as Mircalla and Millarca, who seduces and then attacks 19-year-old Laura to suck her blood. Some literary experts have suggested that *Carmilla* was an attempt by Le Fanu to rewrite *Christabel* in prose form. To get Laura's attention Carmilla uses seductive techniques such as touching, hand holding, and sensual kisses, and after finally offering the girl an unprecedented degree of attention she finally wins Laura's adoration. At night she goes into Laura's bedroom as a dark cat-like creature to suck her blood, leaving her with nightmares, sharp pain, and a small wound.

Although lesbian vampirism is now firmly established in vampire literature, with works such as Pam Keesey's collection of lesbian vampire stories *Dark Angels* (1995) leading the way, it is on screen that the portrayal of lesbian relationships has perhaps been expressed most realistically in recent years. Films such as *Vampire Lovers* (1970) − an adaptation of the *Carmilla* story − *Vampyres* (1974) − in which a lesbian vampire couple work together to attack male victims − and *The Hunger* (1983) − in which a female vampire seduces a doctor in the hope that she will find a cure for her lover's swift aging − skillfully use the metaphor of vampirism as a means for exploring the ways women relate to each other.

Elizabeth Báthory

The historical inspiration for vampire lesbianism may perhaps be the so-called seventeenth-century "Blood Countess," Elizabeth Báthory. Báthory's story was known by Bram Stoker and could have suggested ways for him to develop the character of Dracula in that whenever Dracula drinks blood he appears to grow younger. This element of the Dracula story cannot be traced back to the story of the fifteenth-century Wallachian prince Vlad the Impaler, often believed to be the inspiration for *Dracula*, but to Báthory who allegedly drank only the blood of young girls, believing it would restore her youth.

See also: **Gay Culture; Homosexuality; Sex**

Lestat de Lioncourt

Lestat de Lioncourt is the literary vampire created by writer Anne Rice in her Vampire Chronicles. Lestat first appeared in Rice's *Interview with the Vampire* (1976) and then went on to play the major role in the following Vampire Chronicles novels: *The Vampire Lestat* (1985), *The Queen of the Damned* (1988), *The Tale of the Body Thief* (1992), *Memnoch the Devil* (1995), and *Blood Canticle* (2003).

The son of a French marquis who became a vampire in seventeenth-century France, when he was bitten by a powerful alchemist vampire called Magnus, Lestat describes himself as six feet tall with thick blond hair, grey eyes, a short nose, and a large mouth. His character is outrageous and unapologetic but he has his own moral code in that he will not drink innocent blood. Lestat established a model for contemporary vampire-themed fiction by being more human than Dracula and by reinventing the vampire as an alluring, sensual, and sophisticated but determined and, if need be, deadly creature that can live undetected among humans and see his own face in a mirror.

According to Rice, the character of Lestat was largely based on her husband, the poet and artist Stan Rice, who shared his blond hair and birth date of November 7. Although he is painted as an anti-hero in *Interview with the Vampire*, Lestat spends much of the other books telling readers he is not the monster people often assume him to be. His character proved so popular with readers that in 1988 the Anne Rice Vampire Lestat Fan Club was formed. The club dissolved in 2000, despite having several thousand members all over the world, but in true Lestat style resurrected and reformed itself in 2006.

Lestat appears as a major character in both motion picture adaptations of the Vampire Chronicles novels. In the 1994 film adaptation of *Interview with the Vampire* he is portrayed by Tom Cruise. In the 2002 film *Queen of the Damned*, he is played by Stuart Townsend.

Liebava Vampire

The story of the Liebava vampire is included in Dom Augustin Calmet's *Dissertation sur les Revenants en Corps, les Excommuniés, Les Oupirs ou Vampires, Brucolaques, etc.* It's clear that Calmet found this story ridiculous and it does read a bit like a fairy tale, but this does not rule out the possibility that it was based on some element of truth.

According to the story a priest was invited by Mr. Jeanin, the Canon of the Cathedral of Olmuz, to accompany him to his village, called Liebava, where he had been sent by the Council of the Bishop to investigate the case of a suspected vampire attack. Witnesses told the priest that about three years previously an important man was regularly leaving his grave and disturbing the villagers of Liebava at night. Fortunately, these distressing visits were eventually brought to an end by a Hungarian stranger who was passing through the village. The Hungarian allegedly climbed to the top of the church tower and waited for the moment when the vampire left its grave. Then when the vampire had gone he quickly climbed down the tower, grabbed the vampire's shroud, and took it back with him to the top of the tower. When the vampire came back and could not find his shroud he shouted at the Hungarian, who signaled that if he wanted his shroud back, he should come and get it. The vampire started climbing up the tower, giving the Hungarian an opportunity to throw the creature off the ladder and cut its head off with a spade.

The priest who told Calmet this story admitted he had not witnessed any of the events, and that he had only heard the report from local villagers, *"who were very ignorant, very superstitious, very gullible and prejudiced on the subject of vampirism."*

Life Force / Source

Humans need blood to survive. A loss of blood can lead to fatigue and weakness and, if the loss is excessive, to death, so in ancient times blood was often described as the sacred life force or source. The traditional undead blood-sucking vampire was also thought to need blood to survive; without a ready supply of blood the vampire's reanimated body was thought to be unable to sustain itself. So blood is the vampire's life source or life force and the means through which they are energized.

The blood as life force theory doesn't only apply to the idea that the vampire is a corpse that somehow feeds on the blood of living humans to survive. According to the theory that a vampire is a demonically animated corpse, the demon also uses the energy of blood to animate the new vampire body.

The blood as life force theory does not apply to psychic vampires. The medium they use to acquire the life force from another person is "life energy." Life energy is known as chi or *prana* in some cultures, and it is manifested by everyone and everything. Psychic vampires believe that they can manipulate chi and feed upon it to sate their hunger. It is believed by some that, to a certain extent, blood-drinking vampires also feed upon chi, for a great deal of this subtle energy is believed to be concentrated in the blood.

Life of a Vampire

The "life" of a vampire is the amount of time the undead can spend wandering on earth. Contrary to popular belief that vampires can live forever, spending eternity feeding on humans, the vampires of folklore do not necessarily live forever. For example, some Gypsies believe that vampires can only live for 40 days, while others extend this "lifespan" to several months. In Albanian folklore, if the undead can wander the earth for 30 years they will become human and extremely hard to detect. In fiction the vampire's lifespan tends to be far longer and typically the older a vampire is the stronger, more intelligent, more deadly, but also more despondent and world-weary they become.

Although descriptions of the life of the fictional vampire vary from author to author, the following outline is fairly typical. If the vampire decides to live like a human, rather than wander in woods and deserted places, there are a few problems he or she must face. First of all, vampires do not eat and generally they cannot expose themselves to sunlight. The vampire must therefore pretend to eat and create a number of sicknesses and indispositions that prevent him or her seeing people during the day. Also the vampire must find a resting place of absolute security, as generally he or she is most vulnerable when resting. This aspect of the vampire's existence reminds us that he or she is most at home in death and yet most prone to danger.

Sometimes the vampire will have as a servant a revenant that is kept perpetually hypnotized to ensure that the conditions of life necessary to its master are maintained. This revenant will probably be the only close relationship the vampire has; the vampire is a lonely, isolated figure, notwithstanding this relationship, that must commit horrendous acts of inhuman behavior and yet still possesses human feelings. Living with another vampire is a dangerous proposition because their need to kill would soon exhaust the local supply of fresh blood and their lust for blood would bring them constantly into conflict with each other.

See also: **AGING, OF VAMPIRES; BIOLOGY OF VAMPIRES; TRANSFORMATION**

Lilith

Lilith is among the oldest known vampire demons in world folklore. She is often portrayed in Hebrew folklore and legend as the first woman, created to be the wife of Adam. She became known as the Queen of the Night because she had an evil nature and left Adam to join the forces of darkness.

Background

According to the Talmud (sixth century AD), Lilith disagreed with Adam over who should be in the dominant position during sexual intercourse. Adam insisted on being on top so Lilith used her magical knowledge to escape to the demon-infested Red Sea. Here she had many lovers and bore children called the Lilum. Three angels sent by God eventually worked out a truce with her; Lilith was granted vampiric powers over babies but agreed to leave alone those who wore an amulet bearing the names of the three angels. Still in love with Adam, Lilith returned to haunt him and his second wife, Eve, in the form of a succubus when they had been expelled from the Garden of Eden.

Also known as Lili or Lilitu, Lilith appeared in the Babylonian *Epic of Gilgamesh* as a beautiful vampire woman who had owl's feet (suggesting her nocturnal life) and was one of seven Babylonian evil spirits incorporated into Hebrew lore. In Islamic folklore, she is the mother of the *djinn*, a type of demon. Her story was well established in the Jewish community during the early Christian era but it was not until the tenth century that her biography was expanded and elaborated on in contradictory detail in the writings of the early Hasidic fathers. In the *Zohar*, perhaps the most influential Hasidic text, Lilith is not a vampire but a succubus, who attacks and steals the souls of human babies, especially those who laughed in their sleep. She is accompanied by a horde of succubi demons and her powers are greatest during the waning moon.

During the Middle Ages variations on the Lilith story multiplied. In some versions she is the queen of the succubi or night demons who prey on the blood and fluid of men as they sleep. In others she is Eve, who after being expelled from Eden escapes into the air to prey on children, or she is one of the two women who asked King Solomon to decide who was the mother of a child they both claimed was their own. Another version of the story tells that Lilith became the bride of the angel Samael, who is equated to Satan.

Characteristics

Whatever version of the story is told, Lilith typically hates children, perhaps because her own are always portrayed as twisted, deformed, and wicked. She is also particularly hateful of normal sexual relations between men and women and takes her anger out on the children born of this mating by sucking their blood and killing them. Lilith was also said to curse women with barrenness and miscarriages and as such became a vampiric being that was typically blamed for any problems or deaths associated with childbirth. Those who believed in Lilith developed elaborate rituals and incantations to banish her from their home.

Belief in the presence or influence of Lilith lasted well into the nineteenth century and remnants of that belief still exist today. The fact that Lilith and other ancient vampire-like beings pre-date Christianity is often offered as an explanation why crosses and other Christian objects do not deter all vampires. Clearly vampire lore encompasses both Christian and non-Christian influences, some of which pre-date Christianity.

In recent years Lilith has been recognized by modern mythologists as a symbol of independence and equality between the sexes, and as a potent symbol of primal lust and the mystery and power of darkness by occultists. She also appeared as a character in the Marvel Comics series *The Tomb of Dracula* and became a part of the mythology in the role-playing game *Vampire: The Masquerade*.

See also: **DEMONS; INCUBUS/SUCCUBUS; LAMIA**

Linen Seeds

In many European countries seeds of linen flax were sprinkled along paths or on graves of suspected vampires. It was thought that if a revenant rose from the dead they would be distracted from attacking and killing humans by the seeds and would be compelled to pick up each one first – sometimes at a rate of one seed per year.

See also: **APOTROPAICS; PROTECTION**

Literature

Ever since the concept of vampirism entered the media in the eighteenth century, when large numbers of "vampire epidemics" were reported in Eastern Europe, the vampire has played an influential role in literature. During that time the vampire has evolved from the revolting monster of folklore bringing death and disease, into an immoral deviant, and then into an anti-hero and even a romantic lead.

Early literature

Since ancient times vampire characters have appeared in stories, often as dead lovers returning from the grave. Vampire-like creatures also appeared in sagas such as *Beowulf* and the Babylonian *Epic of Gilgamesh*. However, it was in 1742, when an Austrian medical officer, Johann Flückinger, wrote a report about vampire beliefs and superstitions in Eastern Europe that the vampire emerged as an easily recognizable figure. One of the first works to touch upon the subject of blood, sex, and death shortly after was the short German poem "The Vampire" (1748) by Heinrich August Ossenfelder, which caused a scandal when it was published because it featured the nocturnal visitation of a vampire lover. The next influential tale about a dead person returning from the grave to visit his/her beloved or spouse was the narrative poem *Lenora* (1773) by Gottfried August Bürger. Another slightly later German poem with a vampiric theme was *The Bride of Corinth* (1797) by Goethe, a story about a young woman who returns from the grave to seek her betrothed … "*And the lifeblood of his heart to drink.*"

The Bride of the Grave, also known as *Wake not the Dead* (1800) usually attributed to German writer Johann Ludwig Tieck and frequently mentioned as the first story in which the familiar figure of the Western vampire appears, tells the story of Walter, a nobleman who with the aid of a necromancer raises his dead wife, Brunhilda, from the grave. At first Walter is delighted to have his wife back, but Brunhilda soon craves human blood and destroys his household. Eventually Walter overcomes her but not in time to save the lives of the children he has fathered with his second wife.

The nineteenth century

The first piece of work to clearly identify the vampire as its main character was John Polidori's *The Vampyre* (1819), one of the most important but also one of the least recognized vampire stories ever written. Polidori's rakish anti-hero Lord Ruthven established the prototype of the modern vampire as a deadly evil but also highly intelligent and seductive aristocratic individual. Another significant work was Théophile Gautier's 1836 *La Morte Amoureuse* ("The Dead Woman Lover"), the story of a young priest called Romauld who falls madly in love with a vampire but eventually loses her. The tale was one of the first where the previously clearly defined boundaries between good and evil begin to blur. Although good does eventually triumph over evil, Romauld is miserable at the end and regrets the loss of his vampire lover for the rest of his life.

An important later example of nineteenth-century vampire fiction was the penny dreadful epic *Varney the Vampire* (1847), a serialized tale that eventually became an unwieldy 800-page book. The story features Sir Francis Varney as the vampire and contains endlessly gory and sensational descriptions of his nocturnal feeding habits, as illustrated by the extract below:

The glassy, horrible eyes of the figure ran over that angelic form with a hideous satisfaction – horrible profanation. He drags her head to the bed's edge. He forces it back by the long hair still entwined in his grasp. With a lunge he seizes her neck in his fang like teeth – a gush of blood and a hideous sucking noise follows. The girl has swooned and the vampire is at his hideous repast!

Erotic thrills are also evident in Sheridan Le Fanu's classic novella *Carmilla* (1872), which features a female vampire who seduces the young heroine. Next to *Dracula*, *Carmilla* is the best-known Victorian vampire story. Another significant nineteenth-century author for the evolution of vampire fiction was Paul Féval, the author of *Le Chevalier Ténèbre* (1860), *La Vampire* (1865), and *La Ville Vampire* (1874). And one of the first, if not the first novels in the English language to feature psychic vampires was Charles Wilkin Webber's *Spiritual Vampirism* (1853). Other significant nineteenth-century novels about energy-draining vampires include James MacLaren Cobban's *Master of His Fate* (1890) and Florence Marryat's *The Blood of the Vampire* (1897).

Dracula

Bram Stoker's *Dracula*, published in 1897, became the touchstone for all future vampire fiction. The novel's undertones of disease, sex, blood, and death struck a chord in an age where tuberculosis and syphilis were common and where memories of Jack the Ripper's brutal and bloody murders of several prostitutes in London in 1888 remained vivid. Stoker carefully researched vampire legends and tradition before writing the novel but his Count differs greatly from the vampire of folklore. True to his roots, Dracula has hairy palms, bushy eyebrows, and foul breath and can shape-shift, but in a deviation from Stoker's sources his reflection will not show in a mirror, he has telepathic powers, the ability to travel the world as long as he has his box of earth to sleep in, and the ability to reinvigorate himself with the blood of his victims, instead of merely sustaining his corpse.

Stoker's vampire hunter Van Helsing – the archetype of all subsequent such characters in vampire literature – constantly insists throughout the novel that vampires are evil, sadistic,

and cruel. Due to Victorian moral codes Dracula's sexuality is not well developed. His feedings indicate rape rather than seduction and there is no hint yet of the seductive, often sympathetic hero that the vampire was destined to evolve into a century or so later.

Twentieth-century fiction

Although *The Transfer* (1912) by Algernon Blackwood and "Mrs. Amsworth" by E. F. Benson (1923) successfully feature psychic vampirism, and Sydney Horler's *The Vampire* (1935) was a significant vampire novel, the most notable vampire fiction to appear in the decades following the publication of *Dracula* appeared in American pulp magazines, notably *Weird Tales*, published from 1923 to 1954. *Weird Tales* presented such classic tales as "Four Wooden Stakes" by Victor Rowan (1925) and "The Traveller" by Ray Bradbury (1943). One of the most famous contributors to *Weird Tales* was H. P. Lovecraft. Vampirism played a significant part in some of his novels, most notably *The Hound* (1924) about an undead sorcerer who extracts revenge upon grave robbers.

In the 1950s vampire fiction began to move away from traditional Gothic horror to explore new genres, such as science fiction, crime, western, fantasy and romance. One of the finest examples of vampire science fiction was *I Am Legend* by author Richard Matheson (1954). In the novel one man is the sole survivor of an infection that is causing vampirism. Vampire detective fiction is well represented by *The Dracula Tape* by Fred Saberhagen (1975) and P. N. Elrod's *Vampire Files* (1990). A popular vampire western novel about a cowboy called Tucker who finds himself involved with the queen of the vampires is *The Cowboy and The Vampire* by Clark Hays and Kathleen McFall (1999). Fine examples of vampire fantasy include *Dark Spawn* by Lois Tilton (2000) and the Darkangel Trilogy by Meredith Anne Pierce. As they can live for centuries, vampires are well suited to historical novels that span generations. A well-known specialist in vampire historical fiction is Chelsea Quinn Yarbro, creator of the Saint-Germain series, based on the historical figure of the Comte de Saint-Germain, who lived in Europe in the eighteenth century.

In 1968 the copyright on *Dracula* expired, triggering a rush of novels about the Count as well as novels that attempted to rework *Dracula* in original ways. Stephen King described his 1975 vampire novel as *"a form of literary homage"* to the Count. Other interesting novels to successfully rework *Dracula* were *The Light at the End* (1986) by John Skipp and Craig Spector, and *Dracula Unborn* (1997), known in the US as *Bloodright: Memoirs of Mircea, son to Dracula* by Peter Tremayne. In the 1990s popular fictional descendants of Dracula included Poppy Brite's *Lost Souls* (1992) and Kim Newman's *Anno Draculina* (1992).

The 1981 novel *The Hunger* examined the biology of vampires, suggesting that they were a member of a species of predators that had evolved separately from humans. Other successful novels, such as Brian Lumley's *Necroscope* (1986) and Nancy Collins's *Sunglasses after Dark* (1989) also constructed intricate explanations for the origin of the vampire. *Carrion Comfort* by Dan Simmons (1989) deserves special mention as a novel about psychic vampirism, rather than bloodsucking.

Towards the end of the twentieth century multi-volume vampire epics began to appear, where the vampire evolved from a traditional embodiment of evil into a poetic tragic hero. This formula was followed with bestselling success in the popular Vampire Chronicles (1976–2003) series of novels by Anne Rice. In *Interview with the Vampire* (1976) the concept of vampirism as an enviable state first came to the public's attention. Rice's novels capture the romance and the sensuality of the vampire and give readers an idea of what it might feel like to be a vampire. Many literary experts agree that Rice has written the most influential vampire fiction since *Dracula*.

The twenty-first century

One of the most prominent twenty-first-century examples of the vampire-as-romance genre is Christine Feehan's bestselling Dark series, launched in 1999. Laurell K. Hamilton's Anita Blake: Vampire Hunter series shifted the genre boundaries from romance back toward the territory of erotica but the pendulum has swung again with Stephenie Meyer's wildly popular fantasy series about a teenager named Bella Swan and her vampire boyfriend, Edward Cullen, beginning with *Twilight* (2005) and ending with *Breaking Dawn* (2008).

The occult detective sub-genre of vampire fiction is explored skillfully in Jim Butcher's Harry Dresden fantasy series (2000–) and Charlaine Harris's *Southern Vampire Mysteries* (2001). The field of juvenile and young adult literature is represented by Darren Shan, who wrote a series of books about a boy who becomes a vampire's assistant, beginning with *Cirque Du Freak* (2000) and ending with *Sons of Destiny* (2004).

Elizabeth Kostova wrote a detailed historical horror book connecting Vlad the Impaler to Dracula, called *The Historian* (2005).

Swedish author John Ajvide Lindqvist's critically praised vampire story *Låt Den Rätte Komma In* (2004) about the relationship of a 12-year-boy with a 200-year-old vampire child was translated into English in 2007 as *Let the Right One In*. Also in 2007 the most recent incarnation of the Count features in John Marks's update of Bram Stoker's novel, *Fangland*.

Traits of the vampire in fiction

Over the centuries the literary vampire has evolved from the one-dimensional vicious animated corpses of folklore and the restless dead of myth and legend. Fictional vampires can be ruthlessly evil, as in Brian Lumley's *Necroscope* vampires, or victims as in Richard Matheson's *I Am Legend*, or good hearted as in *Fevre Dream* by George R. R. Martin, or exotic and seductive as in Anne Rice's novels, or outsiders as in Suzy McKee Charnas's 1980 *Vampire Tapestry*, or elegant and sensitive lovers as in Stephenie Meyer's Twilight Saga. However literary vampires are still sustained by either human or animal blood or the life force of living animals or people. They do not need other food, water, or even oxygen and often have a pale appearance with a skin that is cold to the touch. Beyond that it is impossible to generalize about the traits of the contemporary fictional vampire as they differ from book to book and from author to author.

And just as the traits of the fictional vampire are hard to classify, vampire literature in general, although it embraces horror, is also difficult to categorize because over the centuries it has transcended the Gothic horror to become a genre of its own. Increasingly vampire novels cannot be classed as "horror" because they fall into other genres or sub-genres, such as science fiction, mystery, romance, action, and erotica. In fact, vampires – or vampirism as a metaphor for oppression, terrorism, disease, and numerous other misfortunes suffered by society – have appeared in all the major genres of fiction in recent years.

Major works in vampire literature since 1748

Listed below is a time line of major works in vampire literature since 1748.

(*Note:* In a subject as vast as vampire literature, there are bound to be omissions in the list.)

- The Vampire *by Heinrich August Ossenfelder (1748)*

- Wake Not the Dead *by Johann Ludwig Tieck (1800)*

- The Marquise of O *by Heinrich von Kleist (1805)*

- Giaour *by Lord Byron (1813)*

- Christabel *by Samuel Taylor Coleridge (1816)*

- The Serapion Brethren *by E. T. S. Hoffman (1818–21)*

- The Vampyre *by John Polidori (1819)*

- Lord Ruthven ou Les Vampires *by Cyprien Berard (1820)*

The Element Encyclopedia of Vampires

Smarra, ou les Demons de la Nuit *by Charles Nodier (1820)*

La Guzla *by Prosper Mérimée (1827)*

Viy *by Nikolai Gogol (1833)*

La Morte Amoureuse *by Théophile Gautier (1836)*

Ligeia *by Edgar Allan Poe (1838)*

Varney the Vampire or The Feast of Blood *by James Malcolm Rymer / Thomas Peckett Prest (1847)*

Family of the Vourdalak *by Aleksey Tolstoy (1847)*

"The Pale-faced Lady" *by Alexandre Dumas (1848)*

Spiritual Vampirism *by Charles Wilkin Webber (1853)*

The Mysterious Stranger *by Anonymous (1860)*

La Vampire (The Vampire Countess) *by Paul Féval (1865)*

Vikram and the Vampire *by Sir Richard F. Burton (1870)*

Carmilla (1872) *by Sheridan Le Fanu*

The Vampire City *by Paul Féval (1875)*

The Fate of Madame Cabanel *by Eliza Lynn Linton (1880)*

The Man-Eating Tree *by Philip Robinson (1881)*

The Sad Story of a Vampire *by Count Stenbock (1884)*

Good Lady Ducayne *by Mary Elizabeth Braddon (1886)*

The Horla *by Guy de Maupassant (1887)*

The Parasite *by Sir Arthur Conan Doyle (1894)*

Kiss of Judas *by X.L. (1894)*

The True Story of the Vampire *by Count Stenbock (1894)*

The Blood of the Vampire *by Florence Marryat (1897)*

Dracula *by Bram Stoker (1897)*

The Tomb of Sarah *by F. G. Loring (1900)*

Count Magnus *by M. R. James (1904)*

A Vampire *by Luigi Capuana (1907)*

For the Blood is the Life *by Marion Crawford (1911)*

Alraune *by Hans Heinz Ewers (1911)*

"The Room in the Tower" *by E. F. Benson (1912)*

"The Transfer" *by Algernon Blackwood (1912)*

The Vampire *by Reginald Hodder* (1912)

An Episode in Cathedral History *by M. R. James (1919)*

"Mrs. Amsworth" *by E. F. Benson (1919)*

Vampire *by Hans Heinz Ewers (1922)*

The Hound *by H. P. Lovecraft (1924)*

"Four Wooden Stakes" *by Victor Rowan (1925)*

The Demon Lover *by Dion Fortune (1927)*

Bewitched *by Edith Wharton (1927)*

Shambaleu *by C. L. Moore (1933)*

Revelations in Black *by Carl Jacobi (1933)*

The Cloak *by Robert Bloch (1939)*

Over the River *by P. Schuyler Miller (1941)*

The Girl with the Hungry Eyes *by Fritz Leiber (1949)*

I Am Legend *by Richard Matheson (1954)*

The Living Dead *by Robert Bloch (1957)*

Some of Your Blood *by Theodore Sturgeon (1961)*

The Dracula Archives *by Raymond Rudorff (1972)*

An Enquiry into the Existence of Vampires *by Marc Lovell (1974)*

Salem's Lot *by Stephen King (1975)*

The Dracula Tape *by Fred Saberhagen (1975)*

Interview with the Vampire *by Anne Rice (1976)*

The Vampire Chronicles *by Anne Rice (1976–2003)*

Bloodright *by Peter Tremayne (1977)*

Hôtel Transylvania *by Chelsea Quinn Yarbro (1978)*

The Bunnicula Series (children's books) *by Deborah and James Howe (1979)*

The Vampire Tapestry *by Suzy McKee Charnas (1980)*

Sabella or the Bloodstone *by Tanith Lee (1980)*

The Keep *by F. Paul Wilson (1981)*

They Thirst *by Robert McCammon (1981)*

The Hunger *by Whitley Strieber (1981)*

Vampires of Nightworld *by David Bischoff (1981)*

The Delicate Dependency *by Michael Talbot (1982)*

Darkangel *by Meredith Ann Pierce (1982)*

Castle Dubrava *by Yuri Kapralov (1982)*

The Curse of the Vampire *by Karl Alexander (1982)*

Fevre Dream *by George R. R. Martin (1982)*

The Dragon Waiting *by John M. Ford (1983)*

I, Vampire *by Jody Scott (1984)*

Vampire Junction *by S. P. Somtow (1984)*

The Light at the End of the Tunnel *by John Skipp (1986)*

Necroscope series *by Brian Lumley (1986–)*

Little Dracula series *by Martin Waddell and Joseph Wright (1986–2001)*

The Penguin Book of Vampire Stories edited *by Alan Ryan (1988)*

Sonja Blue series *by Nancy A. Collins (1989–)*

Out of the House of Life *by Chelsea Quinn Yarbro (1990)*

Vampire Files series *by P. N. Elrod (1990–)*

The Silver Kiss *by Annette Curtis Klause (1991)*

The Gilda Stories *by Jewelle Gomez (1991)*

Under the Fang edited *by Robert McCammon (1991)*

The Ultimate Dracula Collection edited *by Leonard Wolf (1992)*

Anno Dracula series *by Kim Newman (1992–)*

Lost Souls *by Poppy Z. Brite (1992)*

Suckers *by Anne Billson (1993)*

Darkness on the Ice *by Lois Tilton (1993)*

Daughters of Darkness edited *by Pam Keesey (an anthology of lesbian vampire stories (1993))*

Anita Blake Vampire Hunter series *by Laurell K. Hamilton (1993–)*

The Hunger and Ecstasy of Vampires *by Brian Stableford (1996)*

The Kiss (1996) *by Kathryn Reines*

Night Bites: Vampire Stories by Women edited *by Victoria Brownsworth (1996)*

Dracula the Undead *by Freda Warrington (1997)*

Carpe Jugulum *by Terry Pratchett (1998)*

Dark Angel series *by Meredith A. Pierce (1998–)*

Dark Series *by Christine Feehan (1999–)*

Dark Spawn *by Lou Tilton (2000)*

- The Cowboy and the Vampire *by Clark Hays (1999)*

- Cirque Du Freak Series *by Darren Shan (2000–6)*

- Vampire Academy Series *by Richelle Mead (2006)*

- Harry Dresden fantasy series *by Jim Butcher (2000–)*

- Sookie Stackhouse Series (Southern Vampire series) *by Charlaine Harris (2001–)*

- Sunshine *by Robin McKinley (2003)*

- Argegneau series *by Lyndsay Sands (2003)*

- The Hollows series *by Kim Harrison (2004)*

- What Big Teeth You Have: A Vampire Tale *by Jimmy Aubrey (2004)*

- Undead series *by Mary Janice Davidson (2004)*

- Twilight Saga series *by Stephenie Meyer (2005–8)*

- Let the Right One In (Låt Den Rätte Komma In) *by John Ajvide Lindqvist (2004) (translated into English 2007)*

- The Historian *by Elizabeth Kostova (2005)*

- Fledgling *by Octavia Butler (2005)*

- The Black Dagger Brotherhood series *by J. R. Ward (2005–)*

- The Nymphos of Rocky Flats *by Mario Acevedo (2006)*

- The Circle Trilogy *by Nora Roberts (2006)*

- Fangland *by John Marks (2007)*

- Asetian Bible *by Luis Marques (2007)*

- The Year of Disappearances *by Susan Hubbard (2008)*

- Death by the Drop *by Timothy W. Massie (2008)*

See also: COMICS; FEMALE VAMPIRES; FILMS; POETRY; STAGE; TELEVISION

Lithuania

Lithuania is one of three small countries (the other two being Estonia and Latvia) located on the south-eastern shore of the Baltic Sea. The Lithuanians are descendants of the ancient Balts, and from the thirteenth century onward the dominant religion has been Roman Catholicism. Although the Baltic States did not have a strong vampire tradition they did share a belief in revenants with their neighbors, Russia and Poland.

One of the most well-known cases of vampirism from Lithuania was originally reported by a Captain Pokrovsky, a Russian-Lithuanian guards officer in 1905 and included by vampire historian Montague Summers in his 1929 book: *The Vampire in Europe*. The case refers to events that took place in a village near the family estate of Captain Pokrovsky.

The Captain heard about a peasant who had recently married and was growing pale and weak. The villagers believed he was being attacked by a vampire so Pokrovsky sent a doctor to examine the man. The doctor discovered puncture wounds in the man's neck and loss of blood. There was no inflammation as might be expected from an insect or animal bite, and the doctor could find no cause for the man's illness. Despite various medications administered by the doctor the wound grew larger and the man died. After his death, the man's widow left the community fearing that she would be attacked by villagers as the vampire who had killed her husband. Another explanation given was vampiric possession.

Liver

One of the most interesting aspects of eighteenth-century reports from Eastern Europe of the exhumation of suspected vampire corpses concerns the appearance of the corpse's liver, which was said to be white in color, instead of the normal reddish brown. White livers were also reported in both Slavic and German vampires, as well as in witches and in the wives of husbands who died suspiciously.

There is a natural explanation for this phenomenon. The human liver can lighten in color in the early stages of decomposition, when cirrhosis clogs the veins and prevents blood circulation. Exposure to fresh water could also turn the liver white because red blood cells take in water until they burst.

The connection between liver color and vampirism may have originated from the Slavic custom of throwing bodies in the river where it was feared they might become revenants, but

the body would have had to have been cut open before being thrown in the water for the liver to turn white. In addition, the livers of alcoholics, often believed to become vampires after death, would have turned yellow and it is possible that through the course of oral transmission of the tales, variations of shade between white and yellow blurred. Interestingly, in English being "white livered" or "lily livered" is a term used to describe cowardly behavior – a personality flaw often ascribed to people during their lives who were subsequently suspected of becoming vampires.

Liverpool Vampire

In the latter part of the twentieth century there were a number of sporadic and unconfirmed reports of a vampire attacking victims in Liverpool, England.

In a case widely reported in the press in 1983, 27-year-old Maureen Burns, who described herself as *"not the superstitious or paranoid type,"* was awakened by the sensation of an intruder biting into her neck and drawing off blood. Ms. Burns claimed to have been confronted by the vampire assailant at 2 a.m. at her home in the Lodge Lane area of the city. She passed out after the foreign-looking intruder allegedly sucked the blood from her neck.

Ms. Burns reported the incident to the police and officers were sent round to investigate. When they entered the flat next door they found the walls painted black and adorned with pentagrams. There was an empty coffin in the middle of the floor and next to it a milk bottle with clotted blood in the bottom. On hearing what the police had found, Ms. Burns became so scared that she immediately moved away.

There were other reports of a vampire-like being at large in the Lodge Lane area in the late 1990s. In June 1997, a man whose bedsit was directly under the black-walled flat of Ms. Burns's neighbor, claimed to have woken up at 2 a.m. one morning to see a bloodshot eye looking down at him from a hole in the ceiling. That same week, children playing in nearby Toxteth Park Cemetery were allegedly chased by a tall eerie man in a long black overcoat. Then in early May 2001 another incident was reported in Lodge Lane. A student was awakened at 3.30 a.m. by someone frantically pressing the buzzer of her door intercom. When she looked at the security monitor she saw the grotesque and distorted face of a pale, bald man. The student was so terrified she called the police, but when they turned up there was no sign of the unearthly caller, other than the eerie image on the monitor.

The Liverpool vampire sightings have been dismissed by many as an elaborate hoax, but a small group of vampire experts believe that the witness statements are credible and a vampire may well have been, and could be still, wandering the streets of Liverpool.

Living Vampires

"Living vampire" is a term used to describe people who are said to transform into vampires during their lifetime, or who are born as vampires.

Folklore

In folklore certain people, frequently but not always women, are said to be born as vampires and they are often those born with deformities or with bad signs such as a caul, red hair, or teeth. Children born out of wedlock were also considered to be candidates for vampirism, as were babies born from suspected intercourse with a vampire (although in some traditions such babies could become powerful vampire hunters). Various folk remedies, such as burning the caul to ashes and then feeding the ashes to the child at age seven, were used to prevent the person attacking other people in their lifetime with the evil eye, or through psychic attack or through magic. When that person died precautions were also taken to prevent them becoming a vampire after death.

In Romanian lore there was belief in a class of female vampires who were not born as vampires but could become them when they were taught by other vampires. However, generally in folklore living vampires were male and born and not "made" (unlike in modern fiction).

Modern vampires

The allure and power of the fictional vampire has inspired many fans to want to model their lifestyles on that of the vampire. Today, there are countless definitions and types of "living vampire," and many spell the word vampire with a y – vampyre – to distinguish themselves from the vampires of folklore. Some of these vampyres, such as the sanguinarians, drink blood from willing donors; many more do not feel the need to drink blood and say that they are simply "vampire like" in that they have attributes of the vampyre in their personality. Even though they are not immortal or the undead, vampyres often feel as if they are outsiders who have never fitted into mainstream society; the vampire myth offers them an opportunity to express themselves and create a persona. Others "feed" on the psychic energy of others while others join underground cultures such as the Goth movement. There are also those who assume the vampyre lifestyle simply because they are fans of certain vampire books, authors, films, comics, or games.

Once convinced that they are a vampyre, the more extreme modern vampires may experience sensitivity to sunlight or an allergy to garlic, or they may even become convinced that their DNA has changed to that of a vampyre and they are no longer human. These "symptoms" are probably induced by autosuggestion but to the person involved they feel authentic. Most modern vampires, however, are not as extreme in their personality and lifestyle changes, and simply enjoy the exotic mystery and dark allure of identifying with the vampyre image and associating with other like-minded individuals.

Historical vampires

The term "living vampire" may sometimes be used interchangeably with so-called historical vampires or notorious murders, such as Elizabeth Báthory, the "Blood Countess" who drank the blood of young virgins hoping it would restore her youth. The sadistic bloodthirsty lifestyles of these individuals have earned them the nickname "vampire," even though they are not vampires in the undead sense of the word but seriously disturbed humans.

In occult terminology the term "living vampire" is used to refer to corpses who have been animated by the astral body of a living person.

See also: **BURIAL CUSTOMS; CLINICAL VAMPIRISM; LATENT VAMPIRE; PSYCHIC VAMPIRE; TRANSFORMATION; VAMPIRE WITCHES**

Lobishomen

In Brazilian lore the lobishomen is a vampire species, resembling a tiny, furry, bald-headed monkey. It is similar to another Brazilian vampire, the jaracaca, in that it preys on vulnerable women during their sleep. However, instead of killing its victims it likes to draw out their blood gradually. The women who survive its attack become addicted to sex and in many communities this made the lobishomen a fairly popular vampire for male inhabitants and no attempt was typically made to destroy it. The origins of the lobishomen point to Portugal where there is also a belief in lobishomen, but in this case they are a kind of werewolf.

Locust

Locusts are winged insects frequently associated with plague, illness, death, and destruction. In vampire lore, the undead were believed to have control over plagues of locusts and to have the ability to transform themselves into a locust or grasshopper, if they desired. It is not difficult to see why vampires and locusts were often linked. Swarms of locusts can destroy crops and bring disease and they are virtually unstoppable, spreading like an epidemic. Like locusts, vampires were also thought to be plague carriers, bringing misery and destroying village crops and life wherever they went.

See also: **ANIMAL VAMPIRES; KUDLAK; SHAPE-SHIFTING**

London After Midnight

An MGM silent film released in 1927 and staring Lon Chaney, *London After Midnight* was the first American vampire film. Only stills survive of the original production but it was a detective story in which a police officer (Chaney) pursues a killer through the city. At the same time London is swept up in a wave of vampire hysteria as there are reports of a vampire stalking the dark streets of the city. The film climaxes with the capture of the murderer and the revelation that there was no vampire on the loose, only the police officer disguised as one. In 1935 the film was remade with sound as *Mark of the Vampire*, starring Béla Lugosi.

Longinus

Longinus is the name given in Christian traditions to the Roman soldier who pierced Jesus' side while he was on the Cross. Longinus' legend grew over the years to the point where he was said to have converted to Christianity after the Crucifixion, and he is traditionally venerated as a saint in various Christian denominations. In some occult traditions the act of piercing Jesus in the side turned Longinus into a vampire.

See also: **ORIGINS, OF VAMPIRES**

Loogaroo

In West Indian folklore, the loogaroo (also known as the *ligaroo*), are a species of witch-vampire, closely associated with the sucoyan and probably of African origin, although the name also bears resemblance to the French term for a werewolf, *loup-garou*.

The term typically refers to an old woman who has made a pact with the Devil. If she offers the Devil the warm blood she receives from her victims she will be granted magical powers by him. At night the loogaroo goes to the so-called Jumbie or Devil tree, removes its skin, and flies into the night in the form of a sulfurous ball. Closed doors and windows cannot stop it entering a house to suck the blood of the people inside. Scattering sand and rice outside the house can, however, prevent an attack as the loogaroo will be compelled to stop and pick up each grain. This task will keep them occupied until dawn. If a person finds the skin of the loogaroo, sprinkling salt on it will force the creature to cry out and when dawn approaches it will become visible to everyone. And, should the loogaroo be injured while in her shape-shifted form, that injury will show when she returns to her human appearance.

Lorca, "Count"

An alleged living vampire from Germany. On October 25, 1974, a man known as "Count" Lorca was arrested for a vampire-like attack on a drunkard he had lured to his house, promising him food and drink. Once home he bit the man in the neck and the man fainted. Lorca thought he was dead and went to sleep in his coffin, but his victim revived, escaped, and reported the incident to the police. When the police arrived Lorca was still asleep in his coffin with blood on his lips. According to local news reports Lorca was described as a strange man who insisted on being called Count. He only ate raw meat and slept by day in a coffin. At night he would read occult books.

See also: **HISTORICAL VAMPIRES**

Lord Ruthven

Lord Ruthven is the vampire anti-hero of *The Vampyre* by John Polidori, which appeared in 1819 in *New Monthly Magazine.* The first vampire story to be published in English, *The Vampyre* set the standard for future vampire fiction.

Polidori modeled the character on his charismatic employer, friend, and rival, Lord Byron and on elements of European vampire folklore. In his introduction to *The Vampyre,* Polidori refers to the Arnold Paole case and to the treatise on vampirism written by Dom Augustin Calmet and managed to transform this crude folklore into the first modern vampire. Lord Ruthven is no longer a mindless, demonic entity but a real person capable of moving unnoticed among humans and picking his victim.

Ruthven is presented as a handsome, self-absorbed rake, a moral degenerate and gambler with a chilling appearance that fascinates and curses all he encounters, especially women. He is immortal and sadistic and does not care about the consequences of his actions. There is also something of the psychic vampire about him as people feel drained after spending time with him, and lose their energy or their wealth or respectability while he grows in strength and vigor. Ruthven's traveling companion is Aubrey. He initially feels inferior to Ruthven, but as Aubrey becomes better acquainted with the vampire he becomes repelled by him. Many literary critics have suggested that the relationship between Aubrey and Ruthven mirrored the real-life relationship between Polidori and Byron. In the story Aubrey breaks away from Ruthven – a course of action Polidori may have wished he had taken. The story ends with Aubrey going insane after unwittingly resurrecting Ruthven by setting his corpse on fire under the rays of the moon.

Lord Ruthven Assembly

The Lord Ruthven Assembly was founded in 1988 and consists of scholars and writers who maintain an active interest in the presence of vampires in literature, myth, and folklore. According to the group's website, *"The group derives its name from the title character of John Polidori's* The Vampyre, *an 1819 work that has given us one of the most imitated conceptions of the vampire in literature."* The Lord Ruthven Assembly holds an annual meeting and each year presents the Lord Ruthven Award, recognizing a deserving work in vampire fiction or scholarship.

Lost Boys, The

The Lost Boys, a 1987 horror comedy film directed by Joel Schumacher, is set in the mythical town of Santa Carla and follows the activities of a group of teenage vampires who prey on unsuspecting victims. The plot focuses on the jealousy of the group's leader David (played by actor Kiefer Sutherland) toward a newcomer called Michael (played by Jason Patric) to the group. The film has often been criticized by vampire experts for its disregard of vampire customs and traditions, but the core premise of creating an undead vampire brat pack is considered by many others to be inspired.

See also: **FILMS**

Louis

Memorable for his bewitching innocence despite centuries of killing, Louis is the main character in Anne Rice's 1976 novel, *Interview with the Vampire*. In the novel he tells his 200-year-long story to a reporter in San Francisco, explaining how he began life as a mortal man and was transformed into the brutality of vampirism by the vampire Lestat. He is the protagonist and anti-hero of *Interview with the Vampire*, the first of The Vampire Chronicles, but also features in other books in the series.

Love

See: **SEX**

Lublov Vampire

According to vampire expert Klaus Hamberger in *Mortuus Non Mordet* (1992), the story of the Lublov vampire can be found in *Der Europäischen Niemand* vol. XI, Leipzig, 1719.

The story of what supposedly happened goes as follows:

In the town of Lublov (in north-east Slovakia, near the Polish border) a man named Michael Caspareck died. He was buried on February 20, 1718, but soon afterwards there were reports of him wandering about and talking to people. On one occasion he allegedly turned up at a wedding demanding to eat fish. The guests would not let him in and locked the doors, but he threatened to do horrible things to them so they let him in. Only when he had been given a drink and some fish to eat did he leave. It was also said that he visited his widow and got her pregnant, along with four other women. On April 26, his grave was opened and his corpse decapitated and cremated, but that did not stop him. He returned again and set fire to a house. His widow asked him why he would not stay in his grave and he reported that he was not welcome in heaven or hell because at his cremation they had burned someone else's heart and not his. He therefore had to wander the world for seven years.

Ludverc

Although belief in the malevolent undead was rife in the country, Hungary has practically no legends about blood-sucking vampires, which rather undermines the theory about the origin of the vampire as being Hungarian. The closest thing to a vampire in Hungarian folklore is the ludverc – a burning star or light shaft that can fly and enter people's homes through the chimney. Once inside, it can shape-shift into the form of a marriage partner – wife or husband – and sleep with the spouse, causing him or her to lose blood and become ill. The ludverc may have originated from the vampire lore of Transylvania.

Lugat

The lugat, also known as the kukudhi, is a species of vampire from Albanian folklore. It was similar in appearance to other types of undead in the Balkans and the way to destroy it was by hamstringing (cutting the tendons behind the knees), staking, or burning it. According to some sources the lugat grows stronger with time and after 30 years is virtually indestructible. Some northern Albanian communities believed that the only creature capable of defeating a lugat was a wolf. The wolf could attack it and bite off its leg. The vampire would then retreat to its cave and never be seen again.

See also: **ALBANIA**

Lugosi, Béla (1882–1956)

Béla Lugosi was a Hungarian actor who played the character of Count Dracula in the 1931 film version of *Dracula*. Alongside British actor Christopher Lee, he is the actor most closely identified with the image of the vampire in the public mind.

In 1927 Lugosi was cast in the title role of a stage version of *Dracula* in the United States and his life changed forever. His eyes, his hand movements, and his Hungarian accent were perfect for the part. However, despite his success in the stage play Lugosi was not director Tod Browning's first choice for the title role in the Universal Pictures film version of *Dracula* – he wanted Lon Chaney. However, when Chaney died during filming the part went to Lugosi. *Dracula* opened on February 14, 1931, and was an immediate hit. The film went on to influence every vampire movie that followed, with Lugosi firmly establishing the Hollywood prototype of the vampire.

Lugosi was an accomplished actor but his virtuoso performance as the Count stereotyped him, and in the years that followed he found it increasingly hard to escape being typecast as a monster, vampire, or mad scientist. He died in 1956, and at his request he was buried in the long black cape he wore as Dracula. Sadly, Lugosi never lived to see the acclaim of a new generation of horror movie fans who can understand and fully appreciate his significant contribution to the vampire movie genre.

Lumley, Brian (1937–)

Brian Lumley is an English fantasy and horror novelist and the creator of the Necroscope series of vampire books, set in a parallel world.

The series started in 1986 with *Necroscope* and concluded in 2002 with *Necroscope: Avengers*. The hero – or anti-hero as the story unfolds – is Harry Keogh, the Necroscope, a person who can speak to and hear the dead. Keogh is also able to teleport anywhere in the world via the mathematics of the Möbius continuum and is recruited by the British Secret Service to E Branch, a paranormal unit. He becomes involved in the parallel world of Sunside/Starside, a planet divided into two sides and inhabited by shape-shifting vampire lords called *wamphyri* as well as other supernatural creatures. Keogh becomes a vampire hunter but eventually is defeated by the vampires and becomes a *wamphyri* himself. The mantle of the Necroscope is passed on to Jake Cutter. Keogh establishes telepathic communication with Cutter and the 13 novels in the series concern themselves with various subplots. In 2003 Lumley resurrected the

Necroscope series with a new novel, *The Touch*, in which the enemies are aliens rather than *wamphyri*. This was followed by *Harry and the Pirates* in 2009.

See also: **LITERATURE**

Lycanthropy

In medical terminology lycanthropy, from *lycanthrope*, the Greek term for "man-wolf," is a psychiatric disorder in which a person believes he or she has transformed into a wolf, and so behaves like a wolf. Lycanthropy is responsible for many werewolf legends and there is a close connection between lycanthropy and vampirism, in particular the widely held belief that any person who died under the curse of the werewolf was bound to return from death as a vampire. In addition, many names originally used for the werewolf in Slavic territories, such as vrykolakas, were later applied to the undead.

The oldest known myths of lycanthropy date from classical times when mention is made in several works of people or whole tribes turning into wolves or wolf clans. These ancient records illustrate how lycanthropy was deeply intertwined with magic, sorcery, and witchcraft and a number of magical methods of taking on wolf form or spells for managing the transformation have also survived in medieval Russian, Norse, and Slavic sources. Although there were myths about magical shape-shifting into the form of a wolf, as early as the second century AD it was described by the Greek physician Galen as a melancholic medical condition with symptoms of delirium. The words *lycanthropia* and *lycanthropus* first appeared in the English language in 1584 in an anti witch-hunting manual, *The Discoverie of Witchcraft* by Reginald Scot. An upsurge of lycanthropus belief occurred during the wave of hysteria about Satanism and witchcraft that swept through Europe from about 1450 to 1700, and in the sixteenth century notorious werewolves were placed on trial and executed by French and German ecclesiastical courts.

During this period werewolvism and lycanthropy were often used interchangeably but today lycanthropy generally refers to the medical condition and not to any magical shape-shifting into a werewolf. It is linked to clinical vampirism, necrophilia, and other serious personality disorders. Symptoms include wolf-like behavior, including howling, going down on all fours, gnawing objects, and attacking animals and people with the intention to bite and tear their flesh and drink their blood. Hypersexual activity as well as profound feelings of alienation from society, frequenting of cemeteries, graveyards, and other lonely places, and a misguided belief that one can actually grow fur, fangs, and paws are also common features of this disorder.

Ancient remedies for the condition included blood letting to the point of fainting, and purging the body of the patient with various herbs. Rubbing the nostrils with opium was also prescribed although this probably did more harm than good. Today a combination of medication and intensive psychiatric assessment are typically prescribed.

The Beast within

Despite the strongly held belief in the Middle Ages that lycanthropy was linked to demonic possession, during the sixteenth and seventeenth centuries some authorities, including

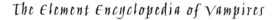

the French physician Jean Nynauld, the Oxford cleric Robert Burton, and the English skeptic Reginald Scot, came forward to suggest that lycanthropy was a form of insanity and not associated with the work of the Devil. This rational view of the condition became more widely accepted and lycanthropy was considered to be madness, insanity, hysteria, melancholia, and delusion well into the nineteenth century.

As the field of psychology developed in the twentieth century, cases of lycanthropy and zooanthropy (referring to animals in general) began to be diagnosed and treated as other conditions, notably schizophrenia, multiple personality disorder, bipolar disorder, paranoia, or hysteria. For psychologists lycanthropy is typically related to the concept of the "beast within" or the part of the human psyche that separates humans from their baser instincts. For Jungian psychiatrists, lycanthropy may be an expression of the shadow, the hidden, primitive part of the self which is repressed by the demands and conventions of society.

"Throughout the shadowy world of ghosts and demons there is no figure so terrible, no figure so dreaded and abhorred, yet dight with such fearful fascination, as the vampire, who is himself neither ghost nor demon, but yet who partakes the dark natures and possesses the mysterious and terrible qualities of both."

Montague Summers

Macedonia

Vampire traditions in Macedonia, a region in the Balkans, are a combination of both Slavonic and Greek concepts about the undead. Words used for a vampire include vrykolakas and vampyras. The Macedonian vampire was often thought to be a corpse animated by a demon and described as hideous, bloated with blood, and with eyes that looked like red-hot coals. When it fed on sheep and cattle it was said to ride on their back and shoulders, feasting on their blood.

One clearly defined superstition was the belief that if a cat jumped over a corpse a person could become a vampire, so family members would take it in turns to watch over a corpse prior to burial. If a cat did jump over the corpse, the body would need to be stabbed immediately with two large sack needles to prevent it turning into a vampire. If exhumation revealed that a corpse had become a vampire, a nail would be struck through its belly and it would then be burned in boiling oil. Mustard seeds would also be thrown onto roof tiles as it was thought that a vampire on the rampage would be compelled to stop and count them one by one until dawn. Although such preventative measures could give some protection against the undead, it was thought that people born on a Saturday, who possessed special powers against vampires, were best able to fight and destroy vampires, because they had the power to see a vampire when others could not.

Magia Posthuma

One of the first well-thought-out treatises on the vampire phenomenon was *Magia Posthuma*, written in 1706 by Charles Ferdinand de Schertz and published in the town of Olmutz in Moravia. De Schertz dedicated the short treatise to Prince Charles Joseph of Lorraine, Bishop of Olmutz and Osnabrück and, being an eminent lawyer, de Schertz argued his case from a legalistic viewpoint. In the treatise de Schertz examined a large number of vampire cases and discussed the decapitation and burning of the body of a suspected vampire. The conclusion he came to was that there had been so many reports of vampires, many from trustworthy people, that it was not unfeasible to assume that these creatures really did exist and that the decapitation and burning of the vampire's corpse to prevent it killing the living was therefore justified.

The Blow Vampire

One of the cases reported by de Schertz concerned the ghost of a dead herder from the village of Blow or Blau in Bohemia that could drain the life energy of people simply by calling their name, suggesting that even a vampire's voice could be vampiric. All the people the herdsmen called on died within eight days. The inhabitants of Blow dug up the herdsman's body and drove a stake through it, fixing it to the ground. But the herdsman laughed at them while they were doing this and that same night extricated himself from the stake and killed other people. Eventually, the specter was caught and handed to the hangman, who put the corpse into a cart in order to burn it outside the town. As the cart moved along the corpse shrieked and threw itself around, and when it was staked fresh, florid blood issued from the wound. Then the body was burned to ashes putting a stop to the herdsmen appearing and infecting the village.

De Schertz goes on to say that the same method was practiced in other places where these apparitions were seen. Whenever the bodies of vampires were exhumed they seemed fresh and florid with limbs that were pliant and flexible, without any worms or putrefaction, but not without a great stench.

Magic

Magic has existed in all cultures since ancient times. The word is derived from the Greek *megas*, which means "great." Magic is about power and control, the ability to create change in accordance with will, and this change is effected through ritual acts, spells, and incantations in which supernatural forces are invoked and made subservient to the will of the witch or magician. Will is understood by magical practitioners as the focusing of desire to achieve goals. Magic is often divided into two types, black and white, or left and right, or more simply evil and good, but magic itself is neither good nor bad – it is the magician's will that determines whether the magic serves good or evil.

Every culture has different names for practitioners of the magical arts – witch doctor, wizard, wise woman, witch, magician, sorcerer, shaman, and so on. The ability to practice the magical arts is typically considered to be hereditary, passed down through family lines. Like the use of blood in spells and rituals, the association of magic with vampires is an ancient one.

A brief history of magic

The earliest form of magic was probably mechanical sorcery, in which an act is performed to achieve a particular result. Paleolithic cave paintings at the Trois Frères caves in France, for instance, reveal images of magical rituals for a successful hunt. It is thought that the systems of "low" and "high" magic were first developed by the ancient Greeks. High magic, which involved working with supernatural forces, was considered to be akin to religion but low magic, providing spells and potions for a fee, had developed an unsavory reputation for attracting charlatans by the beginning of the sixth century BC.

In the centuries that followed, as Christianity spread throughout Europe, low magic became the folk magic and witchcraft of rural peoples, while high magic became intellectual, spiritual, and ceremonial. High magic thrived in the Renaissance as a reaction to the Church's denial of all magic outside that of religious miracles. It was nurtured by secret societies such as Freemasonry and the Rosicrucians. During the scientific revolution of the seventeenth and eighteenth centuries magic fell out of favor, but interest was revived in the nineteenth century by the Hermetic Order of the Golden Dawn and occultists such as Eliphas Lévi, whose *Dogma and Ritual of High Magic* (1856) was very influential.

The second half of the twentieth century saw the emergence of Wicca, a neo-pagan religion of nature and goddess worship, which advises against the use of magic for anything other than good and against blood sacrifice. Effectiveness at magic is believed to be the result of study and practice. Often magic is presented as an ongoing discipline, the cornerstone of which is self-knowledge. Neo-pagan magical training begins with knowing oneself and training one's will. This is not to say that spells are not expected to work in the material world. They are, but according to neo-pagan magic, changing the external world is not all that magic does. Magic changes the internal landscape as well, and is an elaborate dramatic metaphor for the individual's relationship with him or herself and the universe.

Magic and vampires

Throughout Europe during the Middle Ages it was thought that witches and evil magicians or sorcerers were doomed to eternal damnation and therefore the ideal candidates for returning from the grave as vampires. It was also thought that some evil magicians and witches made pacts with the Devil that allowed them to outwit death and return from the grave as a vampire. Vampire magicians are found in Russia, the Balkans, India, Asia, and other parts of the world, and magic is also sometimes used as a method of defeating the vampire. Bulgarian sorcerers, for example, could bottle vampires.

In Bram Stoker's *Dracula* (1897), the Count appears to be skilled in black magic and occult arts. Professor Van Helsing suggests that Dracula has probably made a pact with the Devil when he describes the Count as a member of a once *"great and noble race, though now and again were scions who were held to be coevals to have dealings with the Evil One."*

See also: **ALCHEMY; BLOOD; MAGICIAN; NECROMANCY; SHAMAN; SORCERER; WITCHCRAFT; VOODOO**

Magician

A magician is a person who practices magic and is skilled in spell-casting and the magical arts. Someone who practices magic for the good of others is thought of as a white magician whereas someone who uses magic with evil intent may be thought of as a black magician or sorcerer. During the Middle Ages it was accepted through much of Europe that sorcerers and black magicians were likely to return from the grave as vampires, a suitable punishment for turning from God. It was also thought that some sorcerers made pacts with the Devil which enabled them to rise from the grave and spread evil in the form of vampirism; others were skilled in the art of necromancy, the power to conjure up and control revenants.

Malawi

In 2002 rumors that the government of Malawi in southern Africa was colluding with vampires to collect human blood in exchange for food sent terrified villagers fleeing from their work and leaving their fields unattended for fear of being the next victims of the mysterious blood-suckers. President Bakili Muluzi joined with other officials to try to calm fears, stating that the rumors were unfounded and a plot to undermine the government.

The BBC reported that residents were taking the law into their own hands, as more people came forward to say that they were victims of the blood-stealers. One woman had a mark on her arm where she said blood had been drawn via a needle. Strangers were becoming victims of vigilantes and one man was stoned to death for being a suspected vampire; three others were badly injured. The alleged attacks took place in Blantyre, Malawi's commercial capital, as well as in the districts of Thyolo, Mulanje, and Chiradzulu.

According to an insightful feature written by journalist Ralph Blumenthal for the *New York Times* on December 29, 2002, it was no accident that the vampire myth spread like wildfire in Malawi, just as it was no accident that it spread during the seventeenth and eighteenth centuries when the peasantry was cruelly persecuted. In 2002 Malawi faced widespread starvation and a severe AIDS epidemic, and there was public outrage over attempts by Bakili Muluzi, the country's first and only democratically elected president, to override a two-term limit to remain in office until after 2004. The vampire myth often expresses a society's deepest fears and, in the words of Blumenthal, the 2002 Malawi vampire panic was a timely reminder that *"among desperate people, who with reason feel their life's blood, or that of their children, is being sucked away, the vampire myth still resonates uncannily with human experience."*

See also: **MODERN VAMPIRES**

Malaysia

In Malyasian folklore, belief in a number of vampire-like beings, fairly similar to the lamia of Greece, remains strong. The most clearly defined of these vampire-like creatures are the langsuir, the pontianak and the penanggalan.

Langsuir

The langsuir is said to be a woman of extraordinary beauty with long fingernails and ankle-length dark hair who was transformed into a vampire by the shock of giving birth to a still-born baby. According to tradition when she saw her dead baby she clapped her hands and flew to a nearby tree. Her hair concealed an opening in the back of her head from which she sucked the blood of children. Women who died in childbirth or within 40 days of giving birth were said to become langsuir. To stop this happening her family would place glass beads in the corpse's mouth to stifle its screaming, eggs under the arms to stop the creature flying, and needles in its hands. It was possible to tame a langsuir by cutting off her hair and nails and stuffing them in the hole in the back of her neck. In this subdued state a langsuir could marry and have children, but care had to be taken to stop her dancing, as this could trigger a transformation back into her vampire-like state.

Pontianak

There has sometimes been confusion between the langsuir and the pontianak, but the latter was said to be the deceased unborn child of the langsuir, which took the form of a night owl. To prevent it attacking the living, similar precautions would be taken with the corpse as with the mother's, placing needles in its hands and eggs under its armpits.

Penanggalan

According to tradition, during a religious ceremony a woman emerged from the sap of a palm tree. When confronted by a man her head detached from her body and flew away to a nearby tree where it became an evil bloodsucking spirit that appeared on the rooftops of homes when children were born.

Other blood-drinking entities

Two other blood-drinking entities in Malaysian folklore are the polong and the pelesit. The polong appeared in the form of a small female creature and the pelesit as a house cricket. The polong could be captured with a bottle containing blood from a murder victim. A ritual would be performed over a period of several days and the sound of birds singing would be the signal that the polong had settled in the bottle. Once in a bottle the polong could be fed on blood from a cut finger, and in return for this sustenance the polong would attack its owner's enemies. The only way to remove a polong was by exorcism.

The pelesit was generally a front runner for the polong, accompanying it on journeys and entering the body of its victim first to prepare the way for the polong.

Generally, in Malaysian folklore vampirism and the drinking of blood are strongly associated with witchcraft. It is believed that sorcerers can raise bodies from among the dead and command them to drink the blood of the living and spread disease. In many parts of Malaysia the distinction between vampires and demons is rather blurred. For example, it is sometimes thought that pelesit can possess people, making them do things at the command of a sorcerer. They could, for example, make them vomit green bile or drink blood; a sure sign of vampirism.

Throughout Malaysia vampire-like invisible spirits and demons are said to lurk everywhere waiting for victims to attack. The differences between these creatures are a reflection of the difference in beliefs among the many peoples of Malaysia. For example, to this day the belief in a vampire called the maneden remains strong for the Chewong. The maneden is said to live in the leaves of a plant and will only attack humans or animals that injure the plant in some way. It is a tiny, virtually invisible creature that can attach itself to either the elbow of a man or the nipple of a woman to drink their blood and drain their life energy. The best way to stop this is to give it an oily nut from the hodj tree or a sweet to suck on instead. Another interesting vampire species among the Chewong is the eng banka, the dangerous and deadly ghost of a dead dog that lives in swamp areas and in a form of psychic attack could be used by magicians to spread illness and insanity.

See also: **Bajang; Bottling a Vampire; Zombie**

Malleus Maleficarum

The *Malleus Maleficarum* or "The Hammer against Witches" was a comprehensive theological treatise devoted to the discovery and eradication of witches in Europe. It was written by two Dominican Inquisitors named Jacob Sprenger and Heinrich Kramer and was published in Germany in 1487. For the next two centuries it was so well regarded that it was adopted by both Catholic and Protestant witch-finders and was a major source of the witch hysteria that gripped Europe. Thousands of innocent people suffered because of its insistence that clerics were empowered by the Pope to become witch-finders and, according to the Bible, witchcraft was punishable by death.

The *Malleus Maleficarum* is divided into three parts: how the Devil harms others through his followers, how witches cast spells, and what legal procedures should be used for interrogating and torturing suspected witches. The work was influential in establishing vampirism as one of the most deadly manifestations of the Devil and contains some accounts of vampire activity.

Manananggal

The manananggal – the word means "self remover" or "separate" – is a vampire species from Philippine folklore that looks like an older but very beautiful woman. It is said that at night she divides her torso in two at the waist, leaves her lower body behind and flies away with huge bat-like wings to seek her prey. Her favorite victims are pregnant women and she uses her elongated tongue to suck the heart of the fetus or an unborn child or the blood of the pregnant woman. When she flies away the lower half of the manananggal's body is left standing. If the creature cannot rejoin her body by daylight she will be destroyed, so there are folk remedies to prevent the two halves from reattaching. These include sprinkling the lower torso with salt or smearing it with garlic.

Manducation

In the seventeenth and eighteenth centuries manducation was a term used to refer to a corpse eating or chewing its own shroud and then its own flesh. Although we know today that shroud disintegration is caused by bacteria, and that blood expelled to from a corpse's mouth can cause the shroud to shrink inwards into the jaw, in centuries past this was frequently held up as proof that a corpse had transformed into a vampire and was believed to be caused by either the Devil or by a demon.

Manducating corpses or "shroud eaters" were somehow thought to have a deathly effect on the living relatives and friends of the corpse, and became a subject of heated debate among theologians, philosophers, and scientists. For example, the subject of manducation was explored comprehensively in *De Masticatione Mortuorum* (translated literally as "on the chewing dead"), a 1679 treatise by German theologian Philip Rohr. According to Michaël Ranft's *De Masticatione Mortuorum in Tumulis*, published in Leipzig in 1728, it is during times of plague that corpses are most likely to devour their own shrouds, noisily chewing on them and grunting like pigs. And as long as they are chewing in their graves and making noises, through some kind of mysterious vampirism they spread infection and their surviving relatives mysteriously grow weaker and die.

Manducating corpses are different from the classic European vampire in that they do not need to leave their graves to vampirize their victims. However, they are still corpses accused of preying upon the living.

See also: **DECOMPOSITION**

Mandurugo

The mandurugo ("blood-sucker") is a species of vampire from the folklore of the Tagalog people, who are from a number of regions in the main island of Luzon in the Philippines. They are said to appear as a flying fiend at night and a beautiful woman during the day. Though the woman appears to be alive, she is in fact dead. Her body is animated and her beauty preserved by an evil spirit. The mandurugo uses her loveliness to attract and wed young men so she is never without a constant supply of blood. At night she transforms into a flying creature to hunt for her prey until the crow of the cock at dawn forces her to return home and transform back into a woman.

In 1922 there was an alleged sighting of a mandurugo during the country's presidential election.

See also: ASWANG

"Man Eating Tree, The"

This curious story by Philip Robinson was originally published in *Under the Punkah* in 1881. It is unusual in that it was the first story written about a vampire tree in Africa. The leaves of the tree are described as being like fingerless hands that try to grab any living thing that comes near them. Other stories of vampire plants include: *The Strange Orchid* (1895) by H. G. Wells; "The Transfer" by Algernon Blackwood (1912), and, more recently, *The Day of the Triffids* by John Wyndham (1951).

See also: LITERATURE

Mara

Known in the Slavic as *mora*, a mara is a malignant female entity from Scandinavian mythology that appears as early as the thirteenth century in the Old Norse sagas, but the belief itself is probably of older date.

The mara was thought of as an immaterial entity, capable of moving through a keyhole, seating itself on the chest of a sleeping person, and glaring at them with terrible red eyes, "riding" him or her and thus causing terrible nightmares and exhaustion the next day. In Norwegian, the word for nightmare is *mareritt* or *mareridt*, meaning "mare dream" or "mare ride." The weight of the mara could result in the victim suffering breathing difficulties or a feeling of suffocation. The entity was also believed to "ride" horses, which left them exhausted and covered in sweat by the morning. Even trees could be ridden by the mara, resulting in branches being entangled. The undersized, twisted pine-trees growing on coastal rocks and on wet grounds are known in Sweden as *martallar* or "mare pines."

Vampiric tendencies

Like the alp and other vampire species such as the langsuir, the mara has vampiric tendencies in that the creature is nocturnal and in some traditions has a fondness for human blood. According to the southern Slavs, once a mara drinks a man's blood she will fall in love with him and forever torment his sleep. She may also suck the breasts of his children. Among the Kashubs of Ontario the mara is a wandering spirit of a dead or sleeping girl who has not been baptized that tries to suffocate its victims. The mara is typically female but in some Slavic lore a man can be a mara; if so it will typically have black, bushy eyebrows that meet in the middle.

The word "mara" comes from the Anglo-Saxon verb *merran* meaning "to crush" and which also provides the root for the word "nightmare." In English folklore, hags and witches later took on many of the roles of the mara. In Germany the activities of the mara were shifted to the elves ("nightmare" in German is *alptraum* or "elf dream"). Similar mythical creatures are the succubus/incubus, although the mara lacks the fundamental sexual element of these beings.

See also: **NIGHTMARE**

Marks of a Vampire

See: **BAD SIGNS/OMENS**

Marquise of O, the

The Marquise of O is an influential novel in the creation of the vampire character in Gothic literature. It was written in 1805 by the German playwright and poet Heinrich von Kleist (1777–1811). The story begins with an arrestingly mysterious one-sentence paragraph:

In M…, an important city in upper Italy, the widowed Marquise von O…, a lady of excellent reputation and the mother of several well-raised children, let it be known through the newspapers that without her knowledge she had become expectant, that the father of the child to whom she would give birth should declare himself and that she, out of family considerations, was resolved to marry him.

The man who turns out to be the father of the child is no angel – as the Marquise previously thought – because he ravished her when she was unconscious. She throws holy water on him believing him to be evil, but in time the two are united by love.

See also: **LITERATURE**

Marryat, Florence (1837-99)

In 1897, the same year that Bram Stoker published his immortal *Dracula*, British author and spiritualist Florence Marryat published *The Blood of a Vampire*, a lengthy novel about a psychic vampire called Harriett Brandt. Marryat's inspiration for this novel was the British colony of Jamaica. In the story, Harriett's father has moved to Jamaica from Switzerland after being thrown out of medical school. Jamaican natives become victims of his experiments. Harriett's mother is a witch and as evil as her husband, and at one point in the story she develops a thirst for human blood after being bitten by a vampire bat. Not surprisingly, the natives rise up and kill Harriett's parents when she is still a child and she is raised in a convent school. When she is old enough she inherits her father's estate and

travels to Europe where she marries. It is only after she is married that she discovers she has vampiric tendencies, but not in time to save her husband, who wastes away and dies. After his death and with her vampirism out of control, Harriett kills herself.

Unlike Stoker's *Dracula*, Marryat's vampire is portrayed very much as a victim and the unwitting cause of the death of those close to her. The novel is interesting because of its exploration of the theme of psychic vampirism, but it loses much of its tension with a slow-moving plot.

See also: **LITERATURE**

Marschner, Heinrich August (1795–1861)

German-born musician Heinrich August Marschner was the author of *Der Vampyr*, the first vampire opera, which opened in Leipzig in March 1829. The opera was a great success and played for six months to packed houses. It has rarely been revived since but is still occasionally performed, most recently by the BBC in 1992 in an updated adaptation entitled *The Vampyr: a Soap Opera*.

Der Vampyr, based on John Polidori's *The Vampyre* (1819), opens with a gathering of witches. Lord Ruthven arrives and is told that he has to locate three victims. His first victim, Janthe, is killed but Janthe's father then kills Ruthven, who is in turn revived when his friend Aubrey places him in the moonlight. The complicated plot then moves to the home of Malwina, a young woman with whom Aubrey is in love, but Malwina's father has promised his daughter to Lord Ruthven. Unable to prevent the wedding, and Ruthven's killing spree, Aubrey finally breaks an oath he has made never to reveal Ruthven's vampiric condition. Ruthven is struck by lightning and cast down to the pits of hell and the opera closes with a hymn of praise to God.

See also: **STAGE**

"Marusia"

"Marusia" is a Russian folk story about a girl who gets involved with an upir, a vampire. The moral of the story is to be wary of strangers and to tell the truth and it is similar in many ways to the Slavic folktale *The Girl and the Vampire*.

The story typically goes as follows:

Marusia is the beautiful daughter of an old man and woman who lives in a "certain kingdom." One St. Andrew's Eve celebration she meets and dances with a handsome, well-dressed young man. The man proposes to her and the delighted Marusia returns home to tell her mother the good news. Her mother gives her a ball of thread and asks her to tie it around one of the man's buttons the next time she meets him. This way she will be able to follow the thread and find out who he really is. Marusia does as she is instructed and the ball of thread takes her to a church where she watches the man eat a corpse laid out for a funeral. In her haste to escape she makes a noise. Marusia does not tell her mother what she has seen.

The next day when Marusia sees the man he asks her if she saw him at the church but she denies it. He tells her that her father will die. The next day Marusia's father dies. In the evening the man asks Marusia the same question, she denies it again, and this time he tells her that her mother will die. As the man predicted, Marusia's mother is found dead in the morning. The story repeats itself the next day but this time the man tells Marusia that she herself will die the following night.

Marusia consults her blind grandmother and tells her what she saw at the church. The grandmother tells her to instruct the priest that, when she dies, he should dig a hole under the floor sill and carry out her corpse through the hole. She is also to be buried at a crossroads. Marusia dies and the priest follows her instructions.

Not long after her burial the son of a nobleman picks a beautiful flower from her grave and takes it home to plant in a pot. At night the flower transforms into a beautiful girl, Marusia. The man falls in love with Marusia and marries her on the condition that for four years they do not go to church. Two years later, when a baby boy is born, Marusia's husband decides that they should go to church. Once inside the church Marusia sees the vampire sitting on a windowsill; he is invisible to everyone else. The vampire asks her the same question and again she denies having seen anything. He tells her that her husband and son will die in the night. Marusia visits her grandmother again and the old woman gives her some holy water. The next day Marusia's husband and son are found dead. The vampire comes again to Marusia and asks her the same question. This time she tells the truth and casts holy water on the vampire, turning him to dust. Marusia sprinkles the dust on her husband and son and with the water they are restored to life and live happily.

Masan/Masani

The masan is a terrifying vampire-like demon from Indian folklore that is said to be the spirit of a low-caste person that likes to murder children. The victims can turn green, red, or yellow or simply waste away. The shadow of the masan is also said to be a curse. For reasons unknown the masan is attracted to fingers that have been rubbed on clothes after snuffing out a candle, to the dragging of a woman's gown on the floor, and to the water used to put out a cooking fire.

Hideous in appearance and black as the night she haunts, the masani is an equally terrifying female demon from Indian folklore. The masani emerges from a funeral pyre and attacks anyone passing a burial site at night.

See also: **INDIA**

Mau Mau

Some experts believe that Mau Mau was a name invented by European settlers and applied to native insurrectionists in Kenya, but others say that the name is shrouded in ancient African tribal mystery and covered in blood and that no one understands its real meaning other than a Kikuyu tribesperson of Kenya. Whatever its origin the name was first heard among the white population of Africa in 1948 when police officials heard rumors of strange ceremonies, involving flesh eating and blood drinking, taking place late at night in the jungle. There were also a number of reports of native people being beaten or maimed and forced to swear oaths of initiation to a secret society. In each case, their assailants were said to be members of a secret society called the Mau Mau who opposed British rule.

The so-called Kikuyu Central Association used the name Mau Mau to add a supernatural black magic element to their struggle, which claimed both African and European victims. The British waged war against these rebels between 1952 and 1956 and eventually suppressed the movement, killing 11,000 and placing another 20,000–50,000 in internment camps (estimates vary widely).

See also: AFRICA

Maupassant, Guy de (1850–93)

Nineteenth-century French writer Guy de Maupassant was the author of numerous short horror stories. Among his works was *The Horla* (1887), the morbid story of an invisible Brazilian vampire that attaches itself to the narrator of the story, eventually destroying both his sanity and his life. Some literary critics regard *The Horla* as a foreshadowing of Maupassant's own demise; in 1891 he went insane, and died in an asylum in 1893.

I sleep – a long time – two or three hours perhaps – then a dream – no – a nightmare lays hold on me. I feel that I am in bed and asleep – I feel it and I know it – and I feel also that somebody is coming close to me, is looking at me, touching me, is getting on to my bed, is kneeling on my chest, is taking my neck between his hands and squeezing it – squeezing it with all his might in order to strangle me.

I struggle, bound by that terrible powerlessness which paralyzes us in our dreams; I try to cry out – but I cannot; I want to move – I cannot; I try, with the most violent efforts and out of

breath, to turn over and throw off this being which is crushing and suffocating me – I cannot!

And then suddenly I wake up, shaken and bathed in perspiration; I light a candle and find that I am alone, and after that crisis, which occurs every night, I at length fall asleep and slumber tranquilly till morning.

(*The Horla*, Guy de Maupassant)

In 1963, actor Vincent Price starred in a movie version of *The Horla* entitled *Diary of a Madman*.

Mayo, Herbert (1796–1852)

Herbert Mayo was a respected mid-nineteenth-century English surgeon and professor of anatomy and physiology at King's College, London. He was also the author of *On the Truths Contained in Popular Superstitions* (1849), which contained an entire chapter on the subject of vampires. In this chapter Mayo attempted to bring logic and rationalism to the vampire frenzy sweeping parts of Europe by arguing that there were either medical or psychological explanations, such as anemia or sexual fantasies associated closely with the blood kiss, when kissing becomes biting, for the characteristics of vampire attacks.

See also: LITERATURE

McNally, Raymond T. (1931–2002)

Raymond T. McNally was a leading American scholar on vampires in folklore and fiction who wrote many books around the subject. He is best known for his work on the fifteenth-century "historical" Dracula, Vlad Tepes, better known as Vlad the Impaler.

In 1958 McNally went to Boston College and met Romanian scholar Radu Florescu, an expert on Vlad Tepes. The two men collaborated on several books together. In 1969 they investigated the ruins of Castle Poenari and wrote their first book together, *In Search of Dracula* (published in 1972). It was during his visit to Romania that McNally allegedly witnessed a genuine vampire staking when he passed through the village of Rodna near the Borgo Pass. A burial was taking place and McNally stopped to watch. During the burial the corpse of a girl who had committed suicide was staked to prevent her returning as a vampire.

In Search of Dracula was the first book to offer details about the previously obscure Vlad the Impaler and it went on to become a bestseller. The next year McNally and Florescu completed a more scholarly study, *Dracula: A Biography of Vlad the Impaler*, which also went on to become very influential among Dracula scholars. McNally and Florescu worked together on two more Dracula books: *The Essential Dracula: A Completely Illustrated and Annotated Edition of Bram Stoker's Classic Novel* (1979), and *Dracula, Prince of Many Faces: His Life and Times* (1989). On his own McNally also wrote a compilation of essays and stories entitled *A Clutch of Vampires: These Being Among the Best from History and Literature* (1974), and *Dracula Was a Woman: In Search of the Blood Countess of Transylvania* (1983), a biography of Elizabeth Báthory, the other historical personage strongly associated with Dracula.

Critics of McNally have argued that there is only a tenuous connection between the fictional Count Dracula and Vlad Tepes.

Although Tepes was a bloody and brutal tyrant he was not associated with the vampire myth, but he was known as Dracula or "son of the Dragon" or "son of the Devil", suggesting that Stoker simply borrowed the name.

See also: **CASTLE DRACULA**

Medical Vampirism

See: **ANEMIA; BLOOD; CATALEPSY; CLINICAL VAMPIRISM; PORPHYRIA**

Melrose Abbey Vampire

The case of the vampire of Melrose Abbey was recorded by the twelfth-century English chronicler William of Newburgh in his *Historia rerum Anglicarum*.

According to Newburgh's account the revenant ("vampire" was not yet a term in the English language) was the chaplain of a high-ranking lady who during his life had ignored his vows and had spent so much time hunting with horse and hound that he earned the nickname "Hundeprest," Dog Priest. After his death and burial the chaplain was said to have risen from his grave, but he could not enter the abbey cloister because the purity and goodness of the other monks were intolerable to him. Instead he was condemned to wander restlessly, and he started to appear by the bedside of the lady he had served during his life, terrifying her. The lady urged the senior monk to pray for her.

The monk went to the chaplain's grave with three other monks for an all-night vigil. During the night it became very cold and the three others went to warm themselves by the fire, leaving the senior monk alone at the graveside. At that moment the ghost of the chaplain appeared. In the words of William, *"as the horrible creature rushed at him with the most hideous yell, he firmly stood his ground, dealing it a terrible blow with a battle axe which he held in his hand."* The specter retreated again into the ground, which opened to receive him and closed again quickly, leaving the ground above undisturbed.

The following day the four monks exhumed the corpse and examined the wound made by the axe. Black blood had flowed out from the wound and so the monks carried the corpse to the boundaries of the monastery and burned it, scattering the ashes to the wind. There were no more reported sightings of the revenant.

See also: **ENGLAND**

Melton, J. Gordon (1942–)

A contemporary American author, lecturer, scholar, vampire expert, and head of the Transylvania Society of Dracula's American Chapter. Dr. Gordon Melton is best-known for his sometimes controversial work on religion and cults, and for his 1994 bestselling book, *The Vampire Book: The Encyclopedia of the Undead.*

Menstruation

Austrian psychiatrist Sigmund Freud made a link between menstruation and vampirism in his essay *The Taboo of Virginity* (1918), and according to some experts the vampire myth has an anti-menstrual subtext, which constructs female blood as polluted and male blood as pure.

Kinship with vampires

In some cultures menstruating women could be said to be associated with vampires because they upset the natural order of things – for both it is normal to survive and thrive with blood flowing outside the body. Both have also been condemned as unclean, agents of pollution, and instigators of corruption. Just as making love to a vampire was regarded as potentially lethal, some pre-industrial societies believed that a man could die from having contact, particularly intercourse, with a menstruating woman. In some cultures, after menarche or her first menstrual bleed, a young girl would be kept out of the sun lest she, vampire-like, shrivel up into a withered skeleton.

In their book *The Wise Wound: Menstruation and Everywoman* (1979), authors Penelope Shuttle and Peter Redgrove relate the significance of blood in vampire legend to the menstrual cycle. They go back to the creator of the modern vampire prototype, Bram Stoker, and theorize that his wife may have been uninterested in sex. They also suggest that women with unsatisfactory sex lives often have menstrual disturbances and ask if some image of menstrual disturbance gave Stoker the myth of the "frustrated, bleeding woman." To support this provocative theory (which has not been accepted by modern physicians, who point out that whether a woman is sexually fulfilled or not has no impact on her menstrual cycle), Shuttle and Redgrove point out that Dracula's title of Count could refer to the idea of women counting or keeping measure of their menstrual cycles. They also see a connection between the vampire's neck bites and the loss of menstrual blood through the neck of the womb, the cervix.

See also: **BLOOD**

Mercure Galant

Along with the *Gleaner* or the *Glaneur Hollandois*, the *Mercure Galant* was a late seventeenth-century French journal that helped to spread the vampire hysteria that swept across Europe in the later seventeenth century. In its 1693–4 edition many column inches were used to discuss vampires, describing in gory, sensational detail their characteristics and habits. Journalists declared that vampires made their appearance after lunch and remained hungry until midnight, first eating their shrouds and then drinking the blood of people and cattle through their nose, mouth, or ears.

Mermaids

Mermaids are legendary supernatural water creatures that have appeared in the mythology of different cultures around the world from ancient times. Though mermen also figure in some stories, in most cultures the mermaid is a powerful female presence that can be charming and gentle, but more often than not she is a malicious femme fatale with predatory, vampiric qualities.

Background

The earliest mermaid story comes from Assyria and dates back to around 1000 BC. In the story Atargatis, an Assyrian priestess, jumps into the sea to wash away the shame of an unwanted pregnancy and emerges as a fish-tailed goddess, and in the second century AD the Syrian historian Lucian reported that the statue of the goddess Atargatis at the temple of Hierapolis had a fishtail instead of legs. In other ancient Mediterranean cultures mermaids were regarded as semi-divine aspects of the goddess and revered for their connection to the sea from which life arises. Mermaids were described by Pliny the Elder in the first century AD as having bodies that were *"rough and scaled all over,"* but by the fifth century the bestiary *Physiologus* described them in terms that accord with the modern image of the mermaid – *"wonderfully shaped as a maid from the navel up and as a fish from the navel down."*

During the Middle Ages there were numerous reported sightings of mermaids and they figured strongly in the lore of sailors. In 1493 Christopher Columbus reported seeing three mermaids on his first voyage to the Americas. In some of these tales mermaids were gentle creatures but this was not always the case. Though known to be beautiful, in European folklore, seeing a mermaid was often a sign of coming misfortune or a bad omen. Mermaids were also said to have a taste for human flesh and blood. This is illustrated well by *The Laird of Lorntie*, a tale from Scottish folklore. In the story a lord returning to his castle with a servant hears a woman crying for help. He rushes toward the voice and sees a beautiful woman drowning in a nearby loch. Just before he jumps in to save her, his servant stops him and explains to his master that the girl is after his blood. The mermaid admits: *"Lorntie, Lorntie, Were it na fa your man, I had gart your heart's blood Skirl in my pan."*

There are also tales, most typically from French and British folklore, of mermaids causing shipwrecks by luring sailors into dangerous waters with their charm and beauty, and then devouring the sailors as they drowned. In these stories the mermaids typically take on the role of sirens singing to sailors from rocks.

Their enchanting song lures the sailors dangerously close to the rocks and when the ships crash and founder the mermaids carry the sailors down into the depths of the sea where they devour them. In other tales mermaids can shape-shift into humans, step ashore, marry, and even have children. The only telltale sign of their origins is that they never age.

Rusalka

There are also tales of mermaids in folklore that resemble revenants. One example of this is the rusalka from Ukrainian and Russian lore. The rusalka is said to be the ghostly soul of a young woman who died by drowning or that of an infant who was stillborn or who otherwise died unbaptized. The rusalka most typically appears to people as a beautiful young woman, but she can also appear as a bird, animal, or mermaid. She is said to haunt rivers, ponds, lakes, and bays and has a reputation for appearing to young men and luring them to the waterside and either drowning them or leading them to her castle under the water where she marries them. But even if the latter is the case the rusalka has a dark side, in that the soul of the seduced man is doomed to hell.

Mexico

Mexico has a rich vampire folklore tradition dating back to the ancient Aztec belief that human sacrifice, in which victims' hearts were torn out and offered to the gods, was essential for the world's survival. In this way numerous Aztec rituals have identified the Aztecs with brutality and a morbid fascination with blood.

Aztec deities

The elaborate mythology of the Aztecs had several vampire-like deities, including Tlaltecuhtli, the personification of the earth upon which humans lived but represented as a terrifying toad with blood coming out of her mouth, and the Cihuacoatl, the ancient goddess of Culhuacan. The appearance of Cihuacoatl was terrifying – a snake-like creature that sometimes carried spears – but she had the ability to shape-shift into a beautiful young woman who, like vampire demons in other cultures, could lure young men to their deaths. She would have intercourse with them and then they would wither away and die. The cihuateteo originated from women who died in childbirth and resembled other vampire-like figures such as the lamia of ancient Greece who attacked children during the night. Food offerings were left at crossroads for the cihuateteo so they would eat that and not gorge on children.

In addition to the Aztec mythology, accounts of vampires in Mexico can also be traced back to the Mayans of Guatemala, south of Mexico, who recognized a fierce and bloodthirsty god of the underworld known as Camazotz. Part man and part bat, Camazotz was said to live in caves like a bat and preside over the cycle of life and death.

Following the destruction of the Aztec empire in 1521 by the Spanish, various elements of European vampire folklore were imprinted upon Mexican folklore. For example, stories such as that of La Llorona that had their origins in Europe spread into Mexico and became interchangeable with stories of Cihuacoatl. Other Aztec goddesses transformed in popular imagination into blood-drinking witches with the power to shape-shift into animals that were called bruja by the Spanish, bruxsa by the Portuguese and tlahuelpuchi by descendants of the Aztecs.

Belief in vampiric creatures has resurfaced in Mexico in recent decades with reports of a mysterious creature called a chupacabra, or "goat-sucker," that preys on livestock by sucking their blood.

Meyer, Stephenie (1973-)

Stephenie Meyer is an American author, best known for her romantic vampire series The Twilight Saga, which is aimed primarily at young adult audiences. A film adaptation of *Twilight* was released on November 21, 2008.

The Twilight Saga is unusual in that it boils with romantic and sexual desire that goes painfully unconsummated. Meyer herself turns out to be a far from typical author, with a rise from obscurity that matches that of an author she is often compared to – J. K. Rowling, author of the Harry Potter novels.

Prior to the publication of her first novel *Twilight*, Meyer was a full-time mother of three small boys, living on the edge of the Arizona desert. Meyer is a devout Mormon who had never read a vampire book before she started writing. One night, much to her surprise, she had a dream about a teenage girl who met a surprisingly courteous vampire. The handsome young man explained to the girl that he really wanted to drink her blood, but couldn't bring himself to kill her.

Even though Meyer had never written a short story before, her dream was so vivid and frustrating – she woke up before discovering whether the vampire had succeeded in restraining himself – that she determined to write it down and make up an ending. In a matter of a few months she had transformed that vivid dream into a completed novel, and eventually signed a three-book deal with publishers Little, Brown. The book was released in 2005.

Twilight quickly gained recognition and won numerous honors. Following its huge success Meyer expanded the story into a series with three more bestselling books: *New Moon* (2006), *Eclipse* (2007), and *Breaking Dawn* (2008). Meyer, an avid reader, has said that each book in the series was inspired specifically by a different literary classic: *Twilight* by Jane Austen's *Pride and Prejudice*; *New Moon* by Shakespeare's *Romeo and Juliet*; *Eclipse* by Emily Brontë's *Wuthering Heights*; and *Breaking Dawn* by Shakespeare's *A Midsummer Night's Dream*.

Even though Meyer makes no attempt to present her work as having literary merit, her writing style has been heavily criticized for its galloping melodrama. A random page from *Breaking Dawn* starts: "*I blinked the tears out of my eyes, torn. 'Oh Edward' … 'Tell me Bella,' he pleaded, eyes wild with worry at the pain in my voice.*" To her devoted fans, however, Meyer's novels are pure genius and have generated innumerable Internet websites and fan clubs.

Mikonos

Mikonos, an island in the Aegean, south of Andros, was the location for an appearance by a vrykolakas, a Greek vampire species, which was reported by Joseph Pitton de Tournefort, a French botanist who traveled in Greece in the early 1700s.

According to Tournefort, who reported the incident in his *Relations d'un Voyage du Levant*, in life the vampire had been a peasant of Mikonos who had been a bully and had been murdered by unknown assailants. Just two days after his burial he was seen in the streets attacking people. The local priest decided to wait nine days to see if the vampire would disappear. On the tenth day a Mass was held and the corpse exhumed and its heart cut out. Large amounts of incense were burned to mask the putrid smell of the corpse and the burning heart. According to de Tournefort, it must have been the lack of fresh air that caused many of the people to think they saw vampirical signs on the corpse. Despite the mutilation of the corpse the attacks continued. People panicked and some made preparations to leave the island. Others put swords in the grave and conducted religious ceremonies. An Albanian man advised against the use of swords with cross handles and recommended they use curved Turkish scimitars instead, but they proved just as ineffective.

Eventually, some people took the corpse to the small island of St. George where on January 1, 1701, they prepared the corpse with tar and set the body alight on a large pyre. This act finally ended the plague, causing locals to write ballads and songs that mocked the Devil's futile attempt to unleash evil on the island.

See also: **GREECE**

Miller, Elizabeth (1939–)

Elizabeth Miller was born in 1939 in St. John's, Newfoundland. She earned a doctorate at Memorial University in Newfoundland and went on to become one of the world's leading experts on Bram Stoker's *Dracula*. Miller is the author of several books, the best known of which is *Dracula: Sense and Nonsense* (2000), which highlights errors in previous books and research about Dracula. She also founded the Canadian chapter of the Romanian-based Transylvanian Society of Dracula and served as president of the Lord Ruthven Assembly, a scholarly organization devoted to the study of vampires in literature.

Miller's vampire research is devoted to vampires in folklore, literature, and popular culture. She does not support belief in supernatural creatures, suggesting instead that vampires should be read as a projection of a particular society's fears and anxieties.

Millet

Millet is thought to be one of the first grains cultivated by man. The first evidence for the cultivation of millet dates back to around 5500 BC in China and since ancient times, millet seeds and cereals have been used as a form of vampire prevention in Europe, not so much for any magical properties ascribed to millet but because of the belief that vampires were obsessive counters of the small grains. In Bulgaria millet was thought to be as effective as garlic in repelling vampires and was rubbed on the face of the corpse. In other regions millet was scattered around graves and cemeteries or paths because it was thought that the vampire would be compelled to stop and collect each seed one by one at a rate of one a year.

See also: **APOTROPAICS; PREVENTION; SEEDS**

Milos Vampire

According to a story reported by Dom Augustin Calmet in his 1751 *Dissertation*, a man died on the Greek island of Milos and returned from the grave. This man had been excommunicated and was buried without ceremony in an unconsecrated place outside of his village. It was not long before rumors of the dead man leaving his grave at night began to appear. In the roughly translated words of Calmet:

> They opened the grave and found his body intact, with veins that were full of blood. After some discussion, the monks were of the opinion that the corpse should be dismembered, cut into pieces and then boiled in wine, for that was their usual way of treating with revenants. But the parents of the dead man begged them not to touch the corpse. While they travelled to Constantinople to ask the Patriarch absolution for their son, the corpse was put in the church, where daily masses were celebrated, and where prayers were said for the dead man's soul. One day, during the mass, a loud noise came from the coffin. When the coffin was opened it was found that the dead man's corpse had corrupted as if it had been dead for seven years. It turned out that this had happened at the precise moment when the Patriarch had signed the dead man's absolution.

No date is given for this story but it must have taken place before Calmet wrote his *Dissertation*. The story is interesting because it contains the notion that excommunication from the Greek Orthodox Church could create vampires, and absolution could destroy them.

Milošović, Slobodan (1941-2006)

See: **BUTCHER OF THE BALKANS**

Mirrors

Although there is a great deal of folklore about mirrors, the idea that vampires cast no reflection in a mirror seems to have been put forward by Bram Stoker in his 1897 novel, *Dracula*.

Background

In some tribal societies a person's reflection is thought to be the soul, and exposing the soul in a mirror makes it vulnerable to misfortune or death. In the Greek myth Narcissus fell in love with his own reflection in a pool and then wasted away and died. This mirror-as-a-soul-stealer theme is echoed in many other cultures in the common belief that if a person sees their own reflection they will soon die. A widespread folk custom is the removal of mirrors from sick rooms in case the mirror draws out the soul. In Bulgarian lore mirrors are turned toward the wall after someone dies to prevent another death in the house should the image of the corpse be reflected back into the room. In Romania not only mirrors but containers of

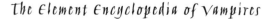

water are covered as they too can reflect an image. This could explain a practice reported from Macedonia and Bulgaria of leaving a container of water in the empty grave after an exhumation. Perhaps the water is intended to capture the soul, keeping it in the grave? In Serbia the graves of those who died young may also be decorated with mirrors for the same reason; and before the burial, house mirrors are covered because the soul should not remain in the house but in the grave where it belongs.

Eyes

Just as mirrors and water are traditionally covered because they have the potential to capture the soul, so too are the eyes of the deceased closed and covered as they can also reflect an image and have the potential for soul capture. It is therefore extremely important to avoid the gaze of a dead man, for death is reflected in his eyes and will consequently bring death to the observer. Herein may also be the origin of the belief in the vampire's hypnotic stare, reflecting death upon the victim and therefore hypnotizing him to death. In modern funeral practice the eyes of the deceased are still closed, although now it is to give rest to the dead.

Superstitions

In other superstitions, if one looks long enough into a mirror at night or by candlelight one will see the Devil (hence it is advised to cover up mirrors at night). Breaking one is thought to damage the soul and bring bad luck for seven years and perhaps a death in the family. A mirror that falls of its own accord is a death omen.

On the other hand mirrors can also be used to protect against evil, reflecting it away.

Folklore aversions to mirrors stem from the concept that a mirror reflects the soul and evil creatures have no soul. Some experts have also argued that the undead exist in two worlds, the living and the dead, and as they exist in neither world completely they cannot be seen in a mirror.

Vampires and mirrors

It appears that the inability of vampires to see their reflection in a mirror was an idea created by Bram Stoker. When he arrives at the Count's castle Jonathan Harker notices that there are no mirrors, and later in the novel Dracula recoils when Van Helsing pushes a mirror into his face and he is forced to confront the nature of his undead existence. Stoker was probably aware of mirror superstitions and adapted them for his novel. Dracula, as a soulless creature also casts no shadow, and he cannot be photographed, or painted, or captured in any way either. (Stoker did not use this information in his novel but it is in his original notes.) On a psychological level it could be argued that the vampire's traditional failure to reflect in mirrors is a matter of psychological denial – we block out the vampire's reflection to avoid seeing aspects of ourselves we wish to deny.

The idea that vampires cast no reflection in a mirror or are repelled by mirrors remained strong in vampire literature until the 1970s and Anne Rice's influential *Interview with the Vampire*. Rice's vampires live among humans and therefore have reflections, because without them it would be hard for the creatures to remain in society undetected.

Mists

In parts of Hungary and China vampires have the ability to transform themselves into mist that floats through the night in search of victims and slides under the doors of its victims, although in most vampire folklore mist is not a common characteristic. There is, however, a logical link between mist and the way that vampires leave their graves, as it was thought that misty forms escaped through multiple holes around the vampire's grave.

The image of the vampire transforming into mist is a powerful one and has been developed in both fiction and film. In Bram Stoker's novel the Count can disguise himself as mist but can only travel short distances in this form. In Mina's record of her first attack she notices a thin white mist move through her door. The mist concentrates into a cloud out of which Dracula emerges. Not surprisingly, the idea of the vampire transforming into mist has been developed more in film than in fiction because of the spectacular opportunity it offers for special effects, demonstrated most notably in *Bram Stoker's Dracula* of 1992.

Miyu

Vampire Princess Miyu is a Japanese horror series by Narumi Kakinouchi and Toshiki Hirano. An animated adaptation was released on video in 1988, and later adapted into a 26-episode television series licensed by Tokyopop and released in 1997. After the success of the video Miyu became the subject of many comic books, the first of which was translated into English in 1995.

Miyu, a vampire girl and the last of her kind, is the central character in the animation and her task is to hunt down the *shinma*, gods and demons, and return them to the spirit world. To accomplish this task Miyu's aging has been halted and she is not affected by garlic or sunlight or holy objects. She moves among humans as a beautiful girl and although she must pick people who will serve as her food source she also helps mortals fulfill their dreams. Most locations in the series are evocative of traditional Japan.

Modern Vampires

Despite the general belief that vampires are creatures of fiction, occasional sightings of vampires continue to be reported.

In early 1970 local and national newspapers ran a series of features on reports that an alleged vampire was haunting Highgate Cemetery in London. In January 2005, there were rumors that a number of people had been bitten by a mystery attacker in Birmingham, England, fueling concerns about a vampire roaming the streets. One of the most recent cases of modern vampirism is that of the chupacabra ("goat-sucker") of Puerto Rico and Mexico, a creature said to feed on the flesh and drink the blood of domesticated animals — as recently as 2008 there were reports of the creature attacking livestock in Texas. In Europe in some small communities belief in vampires is still rife. In February 2004 in Romania relatives of a man called Toma Petre feared that he had become a vampire after his death, so they dug up his corpse, tore out his heart, burned it and mixed the ashes with water so that they could be drunk.

Vampire-hunting societies continue to exist, even if most of these are for social reasons only. However, in 2007 the corpse of the ex-Serbian President Slobodan Milošević was staked by a so-called vampire hunter, and in 2002 mobs stoned one person to death and injured several others when fears of vampire attacks swept through the African country of Malawi during that year.

Vampire subculture

Today, vampirism is an integral part of the modern-day occult movement because the predatory, magical, and alluring vampire archetype expresses a strong symbolism that can be used in ritual and energy work. The mysterious, morbid, and subversive vampire image is also one that many people or groups of people, such as the Goth movement or the Sanguinarium movement, feel they can identify with and model their lifestyles around. There are many different kinds of "vampire lifestylers," from those who drink the blood of willing donors, to those who "feed" on the energy of others, to those who simply want to express themselves and forge social ties by drawing on the vampire myth in folklore and/or fiction.

See also: **FAN CLUBS; LIVING VAMPIRES; PSYCHIC VAMPIRE; SANGUINARIANS; SANGUINARIUM**

Mongolia

Mongolia is a country in East and Central Asia. The Mongols once had the most extensive empire in the world, and in their primitive era ritual cannibalism, in which they ate the flesh of fallen warriors hoping to gain some of their bravery and courage, was common practice. The ancient Mongolians also had among their array of fearsome, war-like deities a vampire known as the god of time, often depicted with fangs and the bones and rotting corpses of his enemies strewn around him.

See also: **INDIA**

Montenegro

Montenegro is in the Balkan region of southeastern Europe. The vampire in the folklore of Montenegro is traditionally called the tenatz and could be either a living vampire or an animated corpse that returned from the grave to torment the living. A corpse could become a tenatz in ways similar to those that led to the creation of vampires in other Balkan countries – for example, if an animal jumped over a corpse. The methods of destruction – staking, burning, hamstringing – were similar too.

Moon

The moon is an age-old symbol of the feminine and the deep layers of the unconscious, and for centuries has been associated with magic, witchcraft, the supernatural, illusion, and insanity.

The moon's phases correspond to the seasons of nature and because it waxes, wanes, and reappears in fullness each month, it also became associated with life, death, and rebirth. The ancient Greeks believed the moon to be a midway point for souls making their transition to and from earth. The moon governs the night and therefore it was thought to govern the creatures of the night, including supernatural entities such as werewolves, vampires, ghosts, spirits, fairies, and ghouls.

The moon and madness

In ancient lore moonlight can cause insanity, giving rise to the terms "lunatic" and "moonstruck." According to the sixteenth-century physician Paracelsus, the moon was most dangerous when it was full and had the *"power to tear reason out of man's head."* This link between the moon and madness took such firm hold that in 1842 a British Lunacy Act held that a lunatic was someone who appeared normal in the two weeks prior to a full moon but who acted strangely during the following days. Modern science can find no link between insanity and the phases of the moon but in folklore this belief still lingers on, as does the belief that epileptic seizures can be intensified by phases of the moon. Popular belief also holds that crime, accidents, and violence increase during the time of the full moon, but although some researchers have collected evidence to suggest that violent human behavior and an increase in suicides may be linked to lunar phases, as yet not enough research has been done to prove or disprove the theory.

The moon and vampires

The supernatural creature most influenced by the moon is the werewolf, a human being who is said to undergo a kind of moon madness and shape-shifts into a werewolf whenever the moon is full. (Medical science describes symptoms of this condition as lycanthropy.) The vampire is, however, another supernatural creature strongly influenced by the moon. The vampire does not need moonlight to see (its vision is better than that of an owl) but the rays of the moon do seem to have an energizing effect. Eastern European vampire lore holds that the powers of vampires are often strongest at night, when they are under the influence of the moon. The vukodlak, meaning "wolf's hair," is a Slavic vampire; the Romanian varcolac is a vampiric eclipse demon; and in some European traditions vampires can shape-shift into wolves, while werewolves are said to become vampires when they die.

In John Polidori's *The Vampyre* (1819), the first vampire story in English, the rays of the moon allow the vampire anti-hero Lord Ruthven to resurrect himself, and the same capacities of the moon were used to great effect by James Malcolm Rymer in his famous 1847 epic, *Varney the Vampire*. Varney is mortally wounded. However, when moonbeams *"came to touch the figure that lay extended on the rising ground, a perceptible movement took place in it. The limbs appeared to tremble and although it did not rise up, the whole body gave signs of vitality."* Not long after, Varney is fully revived and escapes from his "murderers."

It is almost certain that Bram Stoker utilized moon folklore when he wrote *Dracula* in 1897, but instead of endowing the moon with energy-giving qualities he used it to provide a sense of atmosphere and an eerie backdrop to the action. For instance, in the very first chapter as Harker travels by coach to Dracula's castle,

the moonlight emphasizes the chilling atmosphere and Dracula's command over the night:

*All at once the wolves began to howl as though
the moonlight had some peculiar effect on them.
The horses jumped around and reared, and
looked helplessly round with eyes that rolled in a
painful way to see; but the living ring of terror
encompassed them on every side.*

Mora

See: MARA

Morbius, Michael

Michael Morbius, a Marvel Comics vampire
villain, was the first vampire to be introduced
after a revision of the Comics Code, which
banned the depiction of vampires in 1954,
allowed vampires to appear in comic books
again. Morbius is presented in the comics as a
living man who is given vampiric abilities via
scientific means, not supernatural ones.

Created by Roy Thomas and Gil Kane,
Morbius first appeared in *Amazing Spider-
Man #101* in October 1971 as a Nobel Prize-
winning biochemist with a rare blood disease.
In the search for a cure Morbius turned himself into a living vampire. He originated as a
villain in the Spider-Man stories and continued throughout the 1980s with appearances
in varied Marvel comics. In 1992 Marvel
gave Morbius his own comic book – *Morbius:
The Living Vampire* – and updated his appearance and his powers, which now included the
ability to fly and hypnotize others. Solo stories starring Morbius also appeared in the

pages of *Marvel Comics Presents* #144 (1993),
Midnight Sons Unlimited #2 (1993), *Strange
Tales: Dark Corners* #1 (1998), and *Amazing
Fantasy, Vol.2* #18 (2005). *Legion of Monsters:
Morbius*, a one-issue special, was released in
May 2007.

Morbius may appear in an up-coming
Spider-Man movie, scheduled for release
sometime after 2010. Sam Raimi, director of
the *Spider-Man* films, expressed interest in
putting Morbius in film, citing the *"combination of superhero plus supernatural."*

More, Henry (1614-1687)

Henry More was an English poet, philosopher, and humanist who became a fellow of
Cambridge University in 1639. He was the
author of many well-known treatises and the
author of a collection of stories about vampires, ghosts, and witches entitled *An Antidote
Against Atheism: or An Appeal to the Natural Fac-
ulties of the Mind of Men, Where there be not a
God* (1652). This collection included tales such
as that of the Breslau Vampire and the Pentsch
Vampire, and was the first collection of such
stories to be recorded by an English writer
since the twelfth century.

See also: LITERATURE

Morieve, Viscount de

According to Jess Adelaide the Middleton in
Another Grey Ghost Book (1912), the Viscount
de Morieve was an aristocrat who allegedly
returned from the grave as a vampire to haunt
his ancestral grounds for many years after the
French Revolution.

During the Revolution Morieve managed to hide and escape execution, but he never forgot the leaders of the local peasantry who had humiliated him and his peers. So after the Revolution he summoned the peasants to his estate and had their heads chopped off. He was eventually assassinated but not long after his burial children began to disappear. When their corpses were discovered their throats had been cut and their bodies were drained of blood.

The terror and the killings continued for 72 years and only ended when a grandson of the Viscount with the help of a local priest investigated the case and exhumed his grandfather's corpse. The corpse was described as well preserved with soft skin and protruding teeth, and when it was removed and impaled with a stake, blood spurted out everywhere and terrible screams issued from it. A search of the family archives revealed that the Viscount had originally come from Persia, and it was concluded that he had the vampiric taint in his blood. It was not said whether the grandson had inherited this too.

See also: **FRANCE**

Morlacchi

Beliefs about vampires among the Morlacchi or Morlachs, a people living in Dalmatia, were preserved by naturalist Giovanni Battista "Alberto" Fortis (1740–1803) in his *Viaggio in Dalmazia* or "Travels in Dalmatia." The Morlacchi believed in the vukodlak, evil entities that sucked the blood of children. The most common method of destruction was sticking pins into and hamstringing the corpse of a suspected vampire. Morlacchi who feared they would return from the grave as a vampire left careful instructions to their relatives to do all they could to their corpses to keep them in the earth where they belonged.

Mormo

In Greek mythology, the mormo or mormon was said to be a hideous female entity, similar to the lamia and a companion of the goddess Hecate. The name was often used to signify a female vampire-like creature in stories told to Greek children by their nurses to keep them from misbehaving. In *De Spectris* (1575) the mormo are included by Ludwig Lavater in his investigation of vampire species from around the world.

Moroi

In Romanian folklore, "moroi" is a name for a living vampire. If the moroi was a male it was said to be bald and if it was female it was said to be red in the face. The term for an undead or dead vampire was *strigoi*.

See also: **LIVING VAMPIRES; ROMANIA; STRIGOI**

Morris, Quincey P.

One of the leading characters in Bram Stoker's *Dracula* (1897), Quincey P. Morris is the only American character in the novel, appearing first in chapter five as a suitor of Lucy Westenra, who describes him as *"such a nice fellow, an*

American from Texas, and he looks so young and fresh, that it seems impossible that he has been so many places and has had such adventures." She also describes him as *"well educated"* with *"exquisite manners"* and is delighted that he *"doesn't always speak slang."*

Quincey's passion for Lucy makes him concerned for her ailing health and a willing blood donor. After her death and descent into vampirism his commitment to Lucy is demonstrated by his determination to join the group of men who set out to destroy Dracula. Working with the coalition he tracks Dracula to Transylvania and kills the Count by driving a knife into his heart. Unfortunately, in the battle to reach Dracula's box Quincey is wounded and dies. Jonathan and Mina Harker name their son after him.

In the years following the publication of *Dracula* the character of Quincey in stage and screen adaptations suffered and either took a back seat or was eliminated entirely. The situation was eventually rectified by film director Francis Ford Coppola in *Bram Stoker's Dracula* (1992), where the character appears as he appeared in the book, but in recognition of the slight a group of Dracula enthusiasts formed the now defunct Quincey P. Morris Dracula Society.

Mosquitoes

Mosquitoes are flying insects that can be found all over the world. They feed by sucking blood from humans and animals. As they feed they pierce the skin, inject saliva, and then withdraw blood. As both creatures are bloodsuckers it is not difficult to see how the association between vampires and mosquitoes originated, especially when one considers that they are also associated with the spread of disease. In some areas of Europe it was thought that vampires could shape-shift into mosquitoes to spread disease or to enter a house to feed on victims.

Mothman

In the mid 1960s sightings of a mysterious creature that looked human with moth-like wings were reported in the Charleston and Point Pleasant areas of West Virginia. Vampiric activity has been associated with these sightings although no blood-drinking has been reported. The creature has been called "Mothman" by the media.

Sightings

The first sighting of Mothman occurred on November 12, 1966, when five men saw something that looked like a brown man with wings fly to nearby trees at a gravesite near Clendenin. On November 14 glowing red eyes were reported in Salem in West Virginia, and on November 15 two married couples saw a huge creature with hypnotic red eyes and wings folded on its back at an old abandoned TNT plant near Point Pleasant. Terrified they sped off in their cars but the creature pursued them a while before vanishing.

Other similar sightings occurred, and there were several discoveries of mutilated wild animals and reports of strange lights or UFOs appearing in the sky. Local wildlife authorities suggested that what people were seeing was an owl but witnesses insisted that this was a creature with moth-like wings and hypnotic red eyes that shuffled on human legs and could take off into the air and glide, rather than flapping its wings. The creature was sometimes reported as having no head with its eyes set into its chest, and the descriptions were fairly similar to other human bat-like creatures that have been reported in other countries, such as the Coventry Street Vampire in England.

On December 15, 1967, there were sightings of Mothman before the collapse of a bridge that crossed the Ohio River at Point Pleasant. The accident killed 46 people. In the decades that followed there have been other Mothman sightings at ill-famed incidents around the world, such as the 1986 Chernobyl accident and the 1985 Mexico City earthquake. This has led some paranormal experts to suggest that Mothman appearances seem to foretell disastrous events.

The Mothman Prophecies

In his book *The Mothman Prophecies* (1975), UFO and anomaly expert John A. Keel stated that there have been at least 100 sightings of Mothman, including one incident when a UFO chased down a Red Cross van carrying hospital blood supplies. According to Keel, Point Pleasant was a "window" area, meaning an area where another reality could seep through into ours and manifest as supernatural phenomena.

Other explanations put forward for the Mothman sightings include chemical experiments by the military; a 200-year-old Native American curse on the area; mutant strains of owls or cranes; chemical spills; and creatures summoned by occult activity. Skeptics suggest that Mothman is a cleverly constructed hoax

or a simple case of misidentification, and that Mothman's glowing eyes are actually red-eye caused by the reflection of light from flashlights or other light sources that witnesses may have had with them.

In 2002 Sony Pictures released *The Mothman Prophecies*, based on Keel's book and starring actor Richard Gere as John Klein, a character based on John Keel. An annual Mothman Festival was launched in 2002 in Point Pleasant and to this day alleged Mothman sightings – often before some kind of disaster – continue to be reported.

Moths

See: **BUTTERFLY; DEATH'S HEAD MOTH; MOTHMAN**

Movies

See: **FILMS**

Mullo

The mullo, also known as *mulo* and *muli*, means the "living dead" and in Gypsy lore the mullo are spirits of the dead. They rise from their graves at midnight filled with hatred to take revenge on those who have wronged them in life or failed to give them a proper burial. As with Indian vampirism, suicides and murder victims were also prone to becoming mullos.

The mullo can appear in human form, but it is a very pliable, soft form as the mullo are said by some Slavic and German Gypsies to leave their bones in their graves. They typically have very long hair. In other cases the mullo have the appearance of a monster with huge fangs, missing fingers, tangled hair, and skin the color of blood. In India they are described as having yellow or flaming hair. Still others believe that a mullo is invisible and can appear only to its victims. The mullo can also shape-shift into a cat or dog or wolf. Swedish Gypsies believe it can transform into a horse or a bird.

As well as strangling animals and feeding on the blood of humans, the mullo are said to have an insatiable desire for sex. They can have sex with their spouses or any man or women they choose and can be invisible to everyone except their lovers. In fact, their lust for sex is so great that they can exhaust their partners. It is possible for a woman to become pregnant by her mullo husband, and among the Slavic Gypsies the child that is born of this supernatural union is called a "dhampir." Unlike other vampire species with lengthy lives sometimes spanning centuries, the mullo are believed to have limited life-spans, emerging 40 days after burial and sinking back into their graves after three to five years, after which they no longer bother the living.

According to tradition a mullo can be destroyed by thrusting an iron needle doused with holy water in its stomach. It can also be killed by a knife or bullet, preferably one that is fired by a dhampir. Black dogs, black cocks, and white wolves can also destroy a mullo, as can shouting the Romanian curse, *"God send you to bust."* Another tradition involves the mullo's left sock. If it is found it must be filled with rocks and then tossed into a river so that the mullo goes in search of it and drowns. In addition, the mullo can be destroyed by the traditional method of exhuming and then staking, decapitating, or burning the corpse.

See also: GYPSIES; INDIA

Munsters, The

Similar in many ways to *The Addams Family*, *The Munsters* was an American sitcom about a family of supernatural characters attempting to live a normal life that aired from 1964 to 1966 on CBS.

The Munsters, a Transylvanian immigrant family, live in an eerie mansion at 1313 Mockingbird Lane. Members of the family included Herman, a monster-like man who works at a funeral parlor; Lily, his vampiric wife; Grandpa, the "real" Count Dracula; Edward Wolfgang, their werewolf son; and Marilyn, their horribly normal and unlucky niece because she has been born mortal.

The plot revolves around the family's bizarre relatives and strange habits. With eclectic housing and furniture, to strange habits among themselves, the Munster family consists of several generations of monsters trying to fit in with modern American society.

Like the ABC *The Addams Family*, which *The Munsters* originally ran opposite, *The*

Munsters had a devoted fan base and numerous spin-offs in the form of movies, comic books, and other paraphernalia. In 1988 MCA resurrected the series featuring the same characters but with a different cast. In spite of bad reviews by fans of the original, *The Munsters Today* ran for 72 episodes.

See also: **TELEVISION**

Murony

Also known as *muroni*, the murony are a much-feared vampire species from the southern Romanian region of Wallachia. The murony were fairly similar to the Romanian strigoii but were noted for their ability to shape-shift into a variety of animal and insect forms. In these forms the murony could kill in disguise. It left no puncture marks and the only clue was that its victims would be drained of blood. Anyone killed by a murony was destined to become a vampire. Pounding a long nail through the corpse and staking it through the heart were believed to be the only way to "kill" a murony.

Music

In Eastern European folklore, vampires are creatures known to love music. In Serbia, for example, it was said that vampires could only be slain by professional vampire hunters with almost magical powers. These slayers could play music that would enthrall a vampire. The songs would cause the creature to let down its guard, allowing the slayer easily to shoot it or stab it through the heart with a wooden stake.

Fast-forwarding to the present day, vampire imagery looms large in the music of the Goth counter-culture movement that first appeared in most urban centers in the West during the 1980s. Vampiric names that bands have selected for themselves include Vampire Slaves, Liquid Blood, Nosferatu, Astro Vampes, Type O Negative, Blood Flag, and Vampire Weekend. Performers' names include Eva Van Helsing of the Shroud, Vlad of Nosferatu, and Tony Lestat of Wreckage. Album names include Merciful Fate's *Return of the Vampire* (1992), Paralyzed Age's *Empire of the Vampire* (1999), Cradle of Filth's *Vampire* (2000), Gypsies Maladon's *Vampire Music* (2005), Vampire Weekend's *Vampire Weekend* (2008), and Dead Vampire's *Day After Halloween* (2009). In 2005 Nox Arcana released the album *Transylvania* based on Bram Stoker's *Dracula*.

For Bauhaus fans the classic Bauhaus track "Bela Lugosi's Dead" can be heard in the soundtrack from the vampire film *The Hunger* (1983).

See also: **ART**

Mustard Seeds

In Eastern Europe, mustard seeds have been used in the same way as millet, linen, and other seeds as a preventative measure against vampires. According to tradition they should be sprinkled around graves or thrown onto paths leading to graveyards. The vampire would then be compelled to stop and count or eat the seeds at a rate of one seed per year. Mustard seeds are odorless but have a pungent taste and their use as a form of protection against vampires may be related to the traditional medicinal uses of mustard.

See also: **APOTROPAICS**

Myiciura, Demetrius (1905-73)

Demetrius Myiciura was a Polish immigrant who lived in England for 25 years before dying at the age of 68 in 1973. According to the landlady of his apartment in Stoke-on-Trent he was a retired pottery worker with a terrible fear of vampires, convinced they were living in his neighborhood. He tried to protect himself and his room from possible vampire attack with folk charms and crucifixes as well as bowls of salt and garlic, mixed with his urine. He stuffed garlic in his keyhole, sprinkled salt and pepper on his furniture and bedclothes, and slept with a clove of garlic in his mouth, a bag of salt to the left of his head, and a bag of salt between his legs. One night he swallowed a garlic clove in his sleep and choked to death. The investigating police officer consulted *The Natural History of the Vampire* by Anthony Masters (1972) and his death was ruled accidental. There is also a report that another Polish man, Jan Dbworski, died in similar circumstances in Stoke-on-Trent in 1966.

See also: **POLAND**

"Mysterious Stranger, The"

Written in 1860 by an anonymous German author and then translated into English and published in *Odds and Ends* magazine, "The Mysterious Stranger" is a short story set in the Carpathian Mountains that bears a strong resemblance to Bram Stoker's *Dracula* (1897). Some experts believe that Stoker may have used the story as a prototype because the plot (which includes a destruction scene in a castle) foreshadows the novel closely. The main character, known in full as Count Azzo von Klatka, bears remarkable similarities to Dracula: he chooses young women as his victims, lives in the Carpathian Mountains, has power over wolves, and is described as *"tall and extremely thin"* with *"cold grey eyes"* that ooze sarcasm and contempt.

When I came a little to my senses I felt a sort of superstitious fear creeping over me — how great you may imagine when I tell you that, with my eyes open and awake, it appeared to me as if Azzo's figure were still by my bed, and then disappearing gradually into the mist vanished at the door!

"You must have dreamed very heavily, my poor friend," began Bertha, but suddenly paused. She gazed with surprise at Franzista's throat. "Why, what is that?" she cried. "Just look, how extraordinary — a red streak on your throat!"

("The Mysterious Stranger")

Myth, Vampire

Myths, superstitions, and traditions about vampires can be found all over the world and are as old as terror itself. Almost every culture has stories of ghosts, witches, demons, fairies, and other evil entities who rise from the dead to feed on animal or human blood. Today, blood-sucking creatures are typically called vampires, regardless of where they came from and regardless of whether they are actually witches or demons with a thirst for blood, rather than pure vampires. Originally, however, the word "vampire," and words similar to it like "vampir" and "upir," originated among the Slavic people in the countries of Eastern Europe.

Although a creature fairly similar to the Slavic vampire, called the vrykolakas, can be found in the legends of ancient Greece, and an undead menace called the chiang-shih can be found in classic Chinese traditions, most experts believe that it was in Eastern Europe that the myth of the traditional vampire originated. Experts are less sure about the origins of the Slavic vampire as there could be many sources. Some researchers have suggested that the Slavic vampire can be traced back to ancient Egypt or India and that legends from India or Egypt were brought to Eastern Europe by traveling Gypsies. Whatever their origin, it was in Eastern Europe that the vampire myth took shape and over the centuries, with the help of Bram Stoker in his 1897 novel *Dracula*, went on to capture the imagination of the rest of the world.

Rational perspectives

Although the vampire can be described as a creature of myth (in that a myth is often regarded as an untrue symbolic story), it is a creature that cannot be viewed entirely from a mythological perspective and should also be viewed from a scientific, psychological one. The actions of certain perverted individuals or people who possess an unnatural craving for blood must be taken into account in the evolution of vampire stories, as must the infancy of medical science. At the time when vampires were truly feared, people in coma or shock were often buried alive; those who managed to escape their premature graves were therefore regarded as vampires.

Another facet of the story is the coincidence of plagues and the onset of vampire attacks. The vampire attacks were always considered an epidemic because anyone killed by a vampire became one and the numbers increased in a rapid mathematical progression, as did the victims of a plague. The vampire, then, is at least partially scientifically explainable.

From a psychological point of view, the concept of the so-called psychic vampire – a person who somehow drains the energy, health, wealth, or youth of another – adds a fascinating layer of insight to the vampire myth. The process of evolution should also be taken into account in that even though people have grown intellectually over the centuries, dark fears about what happens after death and the nature of evil can never quite be explained away. The vampire grew out of these dark fantasies and has remained with humankind just like an unexplained childhood fear can stay with a person for the rest of his or her life.

Basis in historical fact

There are people who cite the vast number of eyewitness accounts of vampiric activity that have been reported over the centuries as evidence that vampires are not a myth but a legend with basis in historical fact. And as vampire stories continue to be reported to this day, there is also the chilling possibility that vampires are a reality. One person who asserts the reality of vampires is Hugo Pecos who oversees an organization called the Federal Vampire and Zombie Agency, which, although not taken seriously by most vampire experts, claims responsibility for monitoring America's vampire population while overseeing scientific research into the undead.

The Element Encyclopedia of Vampires

According to Pecos, a number of myths about vampires are simply untrue because they grew up during times when people looked to religion or superstition to interpret the world around them. In the words of Pecos, *"While many vampire myths have their basis in Christian orthodoxy, others represent imaginative interpretations of actual vampire behavior."* Pecos then goes on to dispel what he calls The Top Ten Vampire myths:

1. Vampires sleep in coffins: vampires will sleep wherever they feel safe.
2. Garlic repels vampires: vampires have sensitive noses but will not be distracted for long by garlic.
3. Crosses repel vampires: crosses have no effect on vampires.
4. Vampires can be killed by a stake through the heart: vampires can survive such injuries because their blood is circulated by skeletal muscles.
5. Vampires prey on virginal women: vampires prefer young blood but have no preference which gender that blood comes from.
6. Vampires can fly: vampires can leap very high but they cannot fly.
7. Vampires can turn into bats: vampires are associated with bats but cannot turn into bats.
8. Vampires can't see their reflection in the mirror: Christian interpretation is that evil creatures cannot see their souls in a mirror, but vampires are visible in mirrors.
9. Holy water burns the flesh of vampires: although vampires can be drowned, water, whether holy or not, has no effect on vampires.
10. Vampires are destroyed by sunlight: vampires are rendered blind by sunlight but are not destroyed by it.

But first, on earth as Vampire sent,
Thy corpse shall from its tomb be rent:
Then ghastly haunt thy native place,
And suck the blood of all thy race;
There from thy daughter, sister, wife,
At midnight drain the stream of life;
Yet loathe the banquet which perforce
Must feed thy livid living corpse.

Lord Byron, *Giaour*

Nabeshima Cat

See: CAT; JAPAN

Nachzehrer

The nachzehrer, also nachtzehrer, is a revenant found in parts of Germany, Silesia, and Bavaria, and among the Kashubs of northern Europe. Like the Slavic vampire, the nachzehrer was believed to originate from a person who had died suddenly from suicide or an accident. A child born with a caul was also said to become a nachzehrer, especially if that caul was red.

The nachzehrer was associated with epidemic disease. If one person died of a disease and others followed, the first person to die was identified as a nachzehrer and the cause of the disease. The creature was also thought to have the ability to kill the living while still in its grave. As it devoured its shroud, and then its own flesh, living relatives would start to waste away and die. In some traditions, once it had killed its relatives the nachzehrer could leave its grave, coffin, or tomb to eat the corpses of others in the graveyard, sometimes taking the shape of a pig. It could also climb church towers and ring the bells; anyone who heard the bell ring would die. People would also die if the shadow of the nachzehrer fell on them.

The corpse of a nachzehrer could be identified by its contorted expression, ripped shroud and rotting flesh – beliefs likely derived from finding bodies buried in shallow graves that had been subject to predator damage. If the corpse was found lying in pools of blood or holding the thumb of one hand in the other with its left eye open, these were other signs that it had become a nachzehrer. Those hunting the creature in the graveyard needed to listen for sucking, munching sounds, while the creature feasted on its own shroud and flesh. In Bavaria placing a coin or stone in the corpse's mouth, removing names from the deceased's clothing, and cutting off its head with an ax were thought to destroy the creature. Other preventative measures included tying a handkerchief tightly around the corpse's neck and pinning the head to the ground with a spike.

See also: GERMANY; MANDUCATION; VRYKOLAKAS

Nadilla

See: GHOUL

Name of a Vampire

The first vampires were not called "vampires." They may have been called something like "upir" or "obur." The English word "vampire" probably comes from a German rendering of the Serbian word *vampir*, although *vampir* was only one of many different words for vampire-like creatures.

The following terms used to identify vampires are all related linguistically: *Upir* is Russian; *vampir* and *upirnina* Serbian; *upior* and *upierz* Polish; *lampir* Bosnian and Croatian; and *vepir*, *vapir*, and *ubour* are Bulgarian. Another linguistically related set of terms used to describe vampires include the Greek *vrykolalas*, the Serbian *vukodlak*, the Croatian *volkodlak*, the Romanian *varcolac*, and the Turkish *vurkolak*.

There are also all the other names used to identify the creatures we know as vampires, such as *nachzehrer* and *doppelsauger* in Germany, *moroi* and *strigo* in Romania, and *vjesji* in Poland, to name but a few. All these different names illustrate just how many different species of vampires there are, depending on region, context, local religion, and local superstitions.

Acula

In vampire literature, author Sheridan Le Fanu in his 1872 story *Carmilla* suggested that vampires must choose a name that, if not their real one, comprised without omission or addition of a single letter, the letters which compose their name. Therefore Carmilla was originally known as Millarca and then Mircalla. Although few writers have followed Le Fanu's stipulation concerning the name of the vampire, in some sequels to *Dracula* (1897) the leading character would sometimes call himself Alucard, which is simply Dracula spelled backwards, as in *Son of Dracula* (1943). Other name variations include Dr. Acula, in *Night of the Ghouls* (1959) and the fictional screenplay and home video written by the character J.D. in the TV series *Scrubs*.

Native Americans

The Native American peoples have a vast number of beliefs concerning the dead, ghosts, and revenants. For example, the Ojibwa Indians believe that if a soul was denied entry to the afterlife for some reason, it could return to its corpse and bring it back to life.

There are also a number of vampire-like beings, such as the Ojibwa ghostly man-eater and the Cherokee liver-eater – a vengeful and bloodthirsty ogress who slaughters people and eats their livers. Known as the U`tlûñ'ta, or spear-finger, this she-creature can adopt any shape or appearance to suit her purpose. In her right form she looks very much like an old woman, except that her whole body is covered with a skin as hard as a rock that no weapon can penetrate. On her right hand she has a long, stony forefinger made from hard bone, shaped like an awl or the head of a spear. She uses this ghastly weapon to stab whoever she encounters.

Such evil spirits were believed to gather around the bedside of an ill tribe member to torment him or her. They may even remove that person from the bed, lift them up, and beat them on the ground until they are dead. After burial these vicious spirits would dig up the body and feed upon it to avoid death and lengthen their own "lives."

See also: **America; Bell Witch, The; New England; Ray Family Vampires; Rhode Island Vampires; Shaman; Shape-Shifting; Voodoo; Werewolf**

Native Soil

In Eastern European folklore vampires were thought to be the reanimated bodies of the recently deceased. Although they resided in their local graveyard there is, however, no special mention of native soil in either vampire folklore or early vampire fiction.

The idea that Dracula needed to rest during the day in a box filled with his native Transylvanian earth was introduced by Bram Stoker in his 1897 novel. In the story, attacking this resting place becomes the most effective means of destroying the Count. Of the 50 boxes of earth Dracula transports to England the vampire hunter coalition led by Van Helsing manages to locate 49. They fill them with Eucharist wafers, leaving just one so Dracula is forced to return to his native Transylvania to gather more soil. For some literary critics the transportation of native soil to England is a metaphor for the fear that existed in Victorian England of "uncivilized" cultures invading home soil. Whatever the meaning, later writers of vampire fiction tended to abandon the idea of the vampire needing to rest on his native soil, because it limited the vampire's movement (and plotlines) too much.

See also: DUST; EARTH

Necromancy

Necromancy is the occult art of conjuring up and commanding spirits of the dead. In Bram Stoker's *Dracula*, Van Helsing points out that Dracula is skilled in the occult arts and can use necromancy. Although the Count never actually conjures up a spirit or exhumes a body, the implication is that the undead have the ability to command the spirits of the dead, presumably because they are closer to death than mortals.

Ancient practice

Often considered dangerous and unwholesome, necromancy (from the Greek *nekros*, "corpse" and *manteia*, "divination") is a universal and ancient practice based on the belief that the dead, unrestricted by human limitations, are able to see into the past, present, and future and, if conjured and questioned, can tell what lies ahead. Necromancy therefore assumes that not only does a soul or spirit survive death but that disembodied spirits of the dead possess knowledge about the life of mortals.

Some form of necromancy was practiced in every ancient culture, sometimes for good and sometimes for evil purposes. Typically the practice would involve animal or human sacrifice. Bodies might be opened to read the message in their entrails. A classic case of necromancy is that of the Old Testament Witch of Endor. The witch was hired by King Saul to conjure up the dead prophet Samuel, who foretold Saul's downfall (1 Samuel 28).

In the Middle Ages necromancy was widely practiced by magicians, sorcerers, and witches. Necromantic rituals aimed to raise a corpse back to life or, more typically, to summon the spirit of the corpse, forced by the skill of the necromancer to obey. There are many different techniques recorded but rites usually took place in cemeteries or graveyards. For example, one medieval ritual involved going to a graveyard and, as the hour of midnight struck, scattering graveyard earth about and loudly proclaiming: *"Ego te peto et videre queto!"* ("I seek you and demand to see you!"). Elaborate preparations lasting days required fasting, meditation, and dressing in clothes taken from the corpse. Some felt it necessary to eat dog's flesh and black bread and drink unfermented grape juice – items all associated with the underworld and the dead – and in some cases necromancers may even have eaten the flesh of the corpse itself.

Rituals

In other rituals, those who wished to invoke the spirits of the dead would draw circles near or around a sarcophagus and speak the dead person's name to call him or her forth. If the dead did not appear the corpse would be exhumed. If the corpse had been a long time dead the necromancer would attempt to summon an apparition of the soul. If the corpse was only a few days old, however, the necromancer might attempt to force the soul back into the body to reanimate it to speak. After the ritual it was usual to burn or rebury the corpse to reduce the risk of vampirism by a demon or troublesome spirit. The appropriate time for performing such a summoning ritual was within a year of the death, as this was how long it was thought a spirit remained close to the body.

Necromancy was also supposedly employed in Haiti by voodoo magicians who, according to belief, become the incarnation of the god of death. The rites aimed to raise corpses from the dead in order to create a zombie.

The Church condemned necromancy as the work of "evil spirits" and "demons" and a path the Devil took to enter a human soul. In England it was outlawed by the Witchcraft Act of 1604. During the middle of the nineteenth century in the United States and much of Europe, a movement called spiritualism, built around the practice of mediumship or communication with spirits of the dead, gathered momentum. Spiritualism is several steps removed from necromancy, however, many of its critics labeled spiritualists necromancers, and in Stoker's time this misidentification was still common.

See also: **ALCHEMY; MAGIC; SHAMAN;
WITCHCRAFT**

Necrophagism

Necrophagism, also known as necrophagy, is a psychological term for the frenzied consumption of pieces of dead or decaying animal or human flesh. The word is derived from Greek *nekros*, meaning "corpse" and *phagos*, meaning "glutton." This taboo act can be differentiated from cannibalism, which may be a culturally sanctioned act or a desperate act of survival, in that it is often directed to a specific body part or to a victim that has recently been murdered.

Necrophilia

Necrophilia is a serious mental and sexual disorder in which a person, usually male, has an uncontrollable erotic urge to engage in sexual activity with a corpse. This deviant behavior has been recorded throughout history and evidence dates back to the time of the tyrant of Corinth, Periander (d. 585 BC) and the writings of Herodotus in the fifth century BC. Herodotus writes in *The Histories* that, to discourage intercourse with a corpse, ancient Egyptians left deceased beautiful women to decay for *"three or four days"* before giving their bodies to the embalmers. Necrophilia is often mentioned in European criminal history alongside murderers, and in particular in the cases of so-called historical vampires or living vampires who killed people and then raped their victims and drank their blood.

Often accompanying necrophilia is necrosadism and necrostuprum. "Necrosadism" is a term for a mental disorder involving an uncontrollable sexual and/or psychological desire to mutilate a corpse. One of the most well-known necrosadists was Sergeant Bertrand, a corpse-loving "vampire" who spread terror through Paris in the 1840s. "Necrostuprum" is a term used to describe the act of stealing a corpse for the purposes of necrosadism or necrophilia.

In the twentieth century vampiric behavior was recognized as a clinical psychiatric disorder, also called Renfield's syndrome, after a character in Bram Stoker's novel. Alongside vampiric fantasies and blood-drinking, symptoms include necrostuprum, necrophilia, necrophagia, and necrosadism. A number of cases have been described in psychiatric literature.

See also: **CLINICAL VAMPIRISM**

Need Fire

Across Europe during times of plague, the need fire, also known as wild fire, was a well-known method of protection, kindled as a form of ritual purification to save dying livestock against the spread of disease and vampirism. In times of epidemic, such as the cattle plague of 1598 at Neustadt, near Marburg or the 1792 sickness at Sternberg, huge bonfires were constructed and set alight. References to their use can be found as far back as the year AD 750 but the practice probably dates much further back than that and may represent a lingering element of the pagan belief that evil can be repelled by driving a herd of animals between roaring flames. In the ceremony all fires in the village must be put out before the need fire is lit – a serious step to take in earlier times when people didn't normally ever let fires go out. When the fire is ignited it must be done naturally by friction.

In times of epidemics it was common to find such fires blazing and, despite being banned by the Christian Church in the Middle Ages, the practice survived in pastoral regions and continued well into the nineteenth century. Often bodies of those thought to be vampires were exhumed and also burned, to stop them spreading disease and death. Regions where the need fire was used include Germany, England, Bulgaria, Russia, the Carpathian mountains, and Switzerland.

See also: **CREMATION; FIRE; USTREL**

Needle

Among the ancient Slavs, sharp objects such as nails, knives, and needles have been found in urn burials containing cremated remains. It has often been suggested that their function was to prevent the return of the dead. Even at the end of the nineteenth century there were cases in which people drove a needle, thorn, or sharp nail into the heart, the abdomen, or the navel of a corpse to prevent it from walking or leaving the grave or being reanimated by the Devil.

See also: **APOTROPAICS; PREVENTION**

Nelapsi

"Nelapsi" is little-known local term for a Slovakian vampire in the Zemplin district of that country. This creature was said to have two hearts and two souls and it could destroy entire herds and villages by suffocating victims and draining them of blood. It can also kill with the evil eye.

If a corpse had not become stiff after burial, had two curls in its hair, eyes that were open, and a flushed face it was said to be a nelapsi. Fresh blood would also flow from its heart when it was staked. To prevent the corpse transforming into a nelapsi it had to be carried out of the house head first and care taken to ensure it did not hit the threshold. Once the corpse was in its grave it had to be stabbed in the head or heart with an iron wedge or a stake made of hawthorn or oak. The corpse's clothes, hair, and limbs must also be nailed to the coffin and poppy seeds or millet poured into its nose and mouth and also into the coffin, grave, the ground near the grave, and on the road into the cemetery. Holy objects could also be placed in the coffin alongside herbs, over which spells have been cast. After the burial family members would wash and purify their hands.

If the nelapsi did manage to return from the grave the corpse had to be exhumed and the preventative measures repeated.

See also: **Burial Customs; Slovakia**

Neo-vampire

The modern vampire culture is unique in its diversity. There are pagan vampires, psychic vampires, blood-drinking vampires, Goth vampires, and those that call themselves neo-vampires. A neo-vampire is not someone who was born with the innate vampiric nature, or someone like a sanguinarian who drinks blood from willing donors; they are individuals who feel drawn to the vampire archetype for personal spirituality or as a means of self-expression. In other words neo-vampires "adopt" the vampire archetype but are not themselves vampires.

Nets

In parts of northern Germany it was once thought that revenants were obsessed with untying knots, so nets were often buried with corpses to provide them – at a rate of one knot a year – with years of what was apparently a riveting occupation. Most important for the living, it was an occupation which was harmless to them. The Kashubs of northern Germany, however, did not provide corpses with nets, since they believed that this was too torturous an occupation for the corpse. The Greeks also would not leave nets in a grave as it would prevent the corpse from decomposing and the soul leaving to take its rightful place in the afterlife.

See also: **Apotropaics; Burial Customs; Prevention**

Neuntöter

The "neuntöter" is local term for a species of vampire found in Saxony. The creature was believed to be the cause of disease and was usually seen during times of serious epidemics. Placing a lemon in the mouth of the corpse was thought to "kill" the neuntöter. Neuntöter actually means "nine killer" and refers to the nine days it was thought that it took for the vampire to be formed in his or her grave.

See also: GERMANY

Newburgh, William of (c.1136-c.1198)

William of Newburgh or Newbury was an English historian and monk at Newburgh Priory, Yorkshire. His major work was *Historia rerum Anglicarum* (History of English Affairs), a history of England from 1066 to 1198, written between 1196 and 1198. His *Historia* contains fascinating stories and insights into twelfth-century life and is a major source for stories of medieval revenants, those souls who return from the dead as walking corpses.

Newburgh's account of the Squire of Alnwick is remarkable in that it presages in many ways tales of vampirism that were to be related during the vampire frenzy that swept Europe in the seventeenth and eighteenth centuries. The description of the state of the body is uncannily like those contained in later accounts: the swollen body and puffed cheeks and torn shroud; similarly, the feeling of suffocation at the revenant's visits.

Even more chilling is Newburgh's account of the revenant of Melrose Abbey. In this account Newburgh introduces other elements that can be found in later "historical" accounts of vampires, namely that the story is about a man who has sinned during his life. A Christian element is introduced too, in that there is a holy threshold which the restless priest cannot pass. There is also a wound on the revenant's body, suggesting that this is no ghost that has come back from the grave but a physical resurrection.

See also: ALNWICK CASTLE VAMPIRE; ENGLAND; LITERATURE

New England

During the eighteenth and nineteenth centuries a number of alleged vampire cases took place in all states of New England – Connecticut, Rhode Island, Vermont, New Hampshire, Massachusetts, and Maine. Amid fears that the undead were spreading tuberculosis, corpses were dug up and mutilated; body parts were burned and consumed as ashes. In many of the cases a number of deaths in one family were blamed on the family member who had died first.

Epidemics of consumption (TB) were common in New England in the seventeenth and eighteenth centuries. If someone had died of consumption it was thought that the corpse fed off the living so that the living wasted away. It was also thought that the condition could be cured or prevented by exhuming the body, removing the heart or other organs, burning them and then drinking the ashes mixed with water.

The fact that vampirism is not used in early accounts to describe the corpse mutilation has led some researchers to speculate that the subject of vampirism was added into accounts by later writers to explain what may in fact have originally been a ritual associated with witchcraft and the occult, or a belief in psychic vampirism. According to this theory, no belief in vampires, or the reanimated corpses of Eastern Europe, was actually present in New

England. However, by the time of the Mercy Brown case in 1892, "vampirism" was used as a label by journalists and researchers to describe such incidents.

Likely origins for these superstitions were European folklore and English traditions about vampires that had been imported into the New World. Accounts of European vampires were published in contemporary New England newspapers. Toward the end of the nineteenth century the number of alleged vampire cases reported in New England fell as public understanding of contagious diseases advanced, when the tubercle bacillus was identified in 1882. The last significant vampire case of New England was the 1892 Mercy Brown case in Exeter, Rhode Island. However, periodically over the years, accounts of New England "vampire" cases have reappeared. For instance, in 1993 Paul Skedzik, a researcher at the National Museum of Health and Medicine, reported on the mutilation of corpses that showed signs of tuberculosis at a cemetery near Griswold, Connecticut.

See also: **Corwin Vampire, The; Harris, Rachel; Ray Family Vampires; Ransom, Frederick; Rhode Island Vampires; Spaulding Family Vampires; Tillinghurst, Sarah; Walton Family Cemetery; Young, Nancy**

New Guinea

Among the peoples who inhabit New Guinea, an island to the north of Australia, there are a number of beliefs and traditions concerning the power of blood, which was thought to contain magical properties of a person's spirit or soul.

Villagers would take great care to ensure that not a drop of blood fell into the hands of evil sorcerers and all bandages were burned or thrown into the sea. Even a few drops of spilled blood could attract evil spirits who could gain power over humans by drinking it. If a sorcerer did obtain some blood it was thought that he could summon a restless, evil spirit and use the blood to give it a human form.

See also: **Magic**

Newly Weds

According to Romanian lore, newly married couples are a favorite target for vampires who will render them infertile. Preventative measures include sprinkling the bed sheets with holy water, as this was thought to repulse vampires; dropping poppy seeds on paths in front of doorways in the hope that vampires would be compelled to count the seeds before crossing the threshold; or leaving a ball of tangled wool in the path, as any vampires would be compelled to untangle it before attacking the couple.

New Moon

New Moon is the second book in the international bestselling young adult, fantasy romance series of novels, Twilight Saga, written by American author Stephenie Meyer.

According to Meyer, this book is about losing true love and the title refers to the darkest and most mysterious phase of the lunar cycle, suggesting that it is also the darkest time of the protagonist Bella Swan's life. *New Moon* remained at number 1 on the *New York Times* bestseller list for children's books for 12 weeks.

A film adaptation is tentatively set for release in late 2009 or in 2010.

New Orleans

For many fans of vampire literature New Orleans has emerged as a true vampire city. Although there are vampire figures, such as the feu-follet and the loogaroo in the folklore of Louisiana, the association between vampires and New Orleans is not based on folklore. And although there were two serial killers in the 1930s who drunk the blood of their victims before killing them, the association is not based on any so-called historical vampire cases either. The association between vampires and New Orleans can be found in vampire literature in the writings of Anne Rice, and particularly in *Interview with the Vampire* (1976), which is partly set in New Orleans.

New Orleans is a fitting place for the vampire for a number of reasons. First it is the American home of voodoo, a secret magic brought by slaves to the region. Second, the French quarter within New Orleans with its unique Old European heritage provides a suitably Gothic backdrop for vampire enthusiasts. Today, the reputation of New Orleans as the vampire capital of America is maintained by fans who continue to visit the city and enjoy the many tours of locations fea-

tured in Anne Rice's novels. Fortunately for the tourism industry in New Orleans, the French quarter was relatively lightly affected by Hurricane Katrina in 2005, compared with other areas of the city and the region as a whole.

See also: **AMERICA**

Night

Night is the time between dusk and dawn when the powers of darkness and evil are believed to be at their most powerful. In medieval Christian homes it was customary to say prayers to protect oneself during the hours of darkness:

> *And now I lay me down to sleep*
> *I pray the Lord my soul shall keep*
> *If I should die before I wake*
> *I pray the Lord my soul to take.*

The real fear of the night was not dying but that a person might lose their soul to the Devil. The night was a time when witches appeared, when nightmares took a grip on the soul and when visitations from incubi took place. To wake to a new dawn was considered a blessing.

It is often thought that vampires are purely nocturnal creatures, but there are some species of vampire, such as those found in Russia and Romania, who can go out during the day. Although the most horrible activities of the undead tended to be reserved for the dead of the night, there are many accounts in European folklore of the undead attacking during the day and the night. In fact, the association between the dark of night and vampiric activity was not so much a product of folklore but of fiction. For example, the powers of Bram Stoker's Count Dracula are notoriously enhanced during darkness, and more than half the novel, and especially the most significant moments, take place at night.

See also: NIGHTMARE

Nightmare

Nightmares are a distinct type of dream, distinguished from other dreams by their vividness and terrifying images and powerful emotional content. In ancient times, nightmares were thought to be caused by evil spirits. The word derives from a Scandinavian legend in which a *nachtmara* – a mara being a female demon – came and sat on the sleeper's chest at night, leaving him or her with a heavy, suffocating sensation of being awake but paralyzed. Nightmares are also closely associated with the attack of the incubus or succubus. In addition, many reports of eighteenth-century vampire attacks, such as those of Arnold Paole, state that vampires appeared during the night to attack when their victims were asleep.

Rational explanations

Toward the end of the nineteenth century supernatural explanations for nightmares started to be replaced with more rational ones, such as indigestion. During the twentieth century the psychological explanation took precedence. Sigmund Freud tried to explain nightmares as part of his thesis that dreams are the expression of unfulfilled wishes. Later, Carl Jung described them as part of humankind's "collective unconscious" and said the helplessness we feel in nightmares is a memory of the fears experienced by our primitive ancestors.

Nightmares, like most dreams, occur during REM or rapid eye movement stages of sleep, and they generally cause the dreamer to wake up. They are often characterized by the following symptoms:

- *A sense of fear and dread that lingers for hours or days after the dream upon awakening*

- *The ability to recall all or part of a dream scene; in most cases the dreamer is threatened or actually harmed in some way*

- *A recurrence of powerful images in the dream or the repetition of the dream itself for months or even years after*

- *A physical paralysis or lack of muscle tone called atonia, which signifies REM sleep*

Drugs, alcohol, lack of sleep, spicy food, and stress can alter the quality and quantity of REM sleep and perhaps trigger nightmares, but there is no hard evidence to support this.

While these things can increase the risk of nightmares, most dream experts today believe that it is often the struggles of daily life that can bring on dreams.

Modern-day dream therapists believe that nightmares may be a way for the unconscious to draw attention to a situation or problem that is being avoided or is creating problems in waking life for the dreamer. From this perspective nightmares are seen as arising from a person's deepest fears, frustrations, and repressions, and therefore present an opportunity for the dreamer to discover what part of themselves or their life is threatening to destroy their happiness and sense of well-being.

Night terrors

Like nightmares, over the centuries night terrors have often been misinterpreted as evidence of a so-called vampire attack. Night terrors are also often confused with nightmares but they are not the same. In fact they are not even dreams. Also known as sleep terrors, night terrors occur during non-REM, rather than REM sleep. They typically occur within the first few hours of going to sleep. The person may wake up for about 20 seconds and in most cases settle back to sleep. Typically there is an increase in heart rate, blood pressure, and respiration. There will also be a classic physiological response to fear with dilated pupils, confusion or panic, and sweat. Subjects may scream or yell during an episode and flail their arms and legs around or sit upright in bed. If the terror wakes the sleeper up they may recall a single image of terror, but if they fall back to sleep there is unlikely to be any recall of the feeling. In adults, alcohol, stress, fever, or lack of sleep may trigger night terrors, and they are believed to have their basis in a purely biological function rather than psychological or supernatural explanation.

See also: **Dream Sending; Dreams, about Vampires; Hag Attack; Incubus/Succubus; Old Hag**

Nodier, Charles (1780–1844)

Jean Charles Emmanuel Nodier was a French writer and playwright who introduced one of the earliest vampire dramas to the stage and therefore played a significant part in the evolution of the European vampire in literature. A prominent Romantic literary figure in Paris, Nodier wrote a theatrical adaptation of John Polidori's *The Vampyre* (1819) – *Le Vampire, mélodrama en trois actes avec un prologue* – which opened at the Theatre de la Porte-Saint-Martin in Paris on June 13, 1820. Despite mixed reviews the play was a huge success and encouraged a host of similar plays and productions. Nodier returned to the theme of nightmares and vampires in his 1821 opium-inspired story *Smarra, ou les démons de la nuit*.

See also: **Literature; Stage**

Nosferatu

The nosferatu are often said to be a Romanian species of the undead but it was not a Romanian word. Bram Stoker used the word twice in *Dracula* (1897). The first reference is in chapter 16, when Van Helsing explains what the undead are, and the second reference is in chapter 18 when he says: "*The nosferatu do not die like the bee when he sting once. He is only stronger and being* stronger, have yet more power to work evil." It seems that Stoker picked up the word from Emily Gerard's *The Land Beyond the Forest* (1885), where she writes: *"More decidedly evil is the nosferatu, or vampire, in which every Roumanian peasant believes as he does in heaven or hell."*

However, many linguistic experts argue that Gerard simply garbled the term when she was living in Transylvania and that it was a combination of some or all of the following words: *necuratul* – a Romanian term for the Devil; *nesuferit* – a Romanian term meaning unbearable; *nesophorus* – a Greek term meaning plague carrier; and *nesufuratu* – an Old Slavic word also meaning disease carrier. Therefore the nosferatu is associated with the idea of spreading infection and evil, and by association the disease of vampirism.

In Romanian lore the nosferatu is said to be the illegitimate child of parents who are also illegitimate. Soon after burial the creature leaves its grave to suck the blood of the living. It particularly resents married couples and will make the male infertile and the woman barren. The male nosferatu is able to impregnate women and the resulting children are destined to become living vampires (moroi) or witches. The way to destroy this creature is to shoot into its grave or to impale it on a stake.

The term "nosferatu" did not become part of popular language about vampires, however, until a film by F. W. Murnau, *Nosferatu, eine Symphonie des Grauens*, was released in 1922. The silent film was a thinly disguised version of *Dracula* for the screen and in the decades since it has often appeared in novels and films as a term synonymous with the vampire.

Nosferatu

Nosferatu, a Symphony of Horror (in German: *Nosferatu, eine Symphonie des Grauens*) is a classic silent film made in 1922 starring actor Max Schreck. It was directed by F. W. Murnau and released by the German company Prana-film. The film was based on Bram Stoker's novel *Dracula* (1897) but with certain changes to avoid copyright violation. Count Dracula is therefore Graf Orlok, a vile, rodent-like creature with a bald head, fangs, and long claw-like fingernails – much closer to the foul vampire of Eastern European lore than Dracula. The location for the latter part of the film is also changed from England to Germany. In addition, Graf Orlok is destroyed by exposure to sunlight whereas in Stoker's *Dracula* the Count is stabbed. Destruction by sunlight went on to become a much-copied theme in later vampire films and books.

Art house film

Nosferatu was conceived as an art-house film, using the vampire as a metaphor for the plague-like destruction of Germany in World War I. On its first release, the film was elaborately color-tinted and accompanied by a lush score from composer Hans Erdmann.

Florence Stoker, Bram Stoker's widow, learned about the film soon after its release. She was in dire financial straits and dependent on the royalty income from *Dracula*. *Nosferatu* was a clear copyright violation in her mind as she had not yet attempted to sell the film rights. She launched a campaign to have the film banned and in 1925 the courts ordered the destruction of all negatives and prints of the film. Despite this, in true vampire style *Nosferatu* refused to die, and much to Stoker's frustration kept resurfacing in private screenings and in pirate copies. After Florence Stoker's death in 1937, *Nosferatu* circulated more freely but there was little critical acclaim until the film was transmitted in condensed form on television in the 1960s. In 1972 it was re-released as a collectors' item under the title *Nosferatu the Vampire.* With its indelibly haunting images of death, decay, and disease, *Nosferatu* is now hailed as one of the greatest vampire films ever made.

In 1979 the film was remade, as *Nosferatu: Phantom der Nacht.* This time it starred Klaus Kinski and was directed by Werner Herzog. The film was produced as homage to *Dracula* rather than to the original movie, and was widely regarded as inferior to the original by film critics, who disliked its less sinister vampire.

See also: **FILMS**

Nuckelavee

One of the most fearsome and gruesomely described vampiric creatures in Scottish folklore, the nuckelavee inhabited parts of northern Scotland. The creature lived mainly in the sea, but was also held responsible for ruined crops, epidemics, and drought. When the creature moved on land it rode a horse as terrible in aspect as itself.

The nuckelavee was believed to be a spirit in flesh and said to be the size of a small human, albeit one that is several feet wide, with a skinless human upper body on a skinless horse-like torso. Its enormous head, ten times larger than a human's, sported a pig-like nose that snorted steam, and a gigantic bloodshot eye. Vampire-like, its breath drained the life force of crops, animals, and people.

Burning seaweed to make kelp was thought to offend the creature. Despite living in the sea the creature was also said to have an aversion to fresh water, rain, and running water. In one tale a man called Tammy escapes the beast by jumping over running water, leaving his bonnet in the monster's clutches.

"It takes us back to primitive times when we worshipped dark gods as well as light gods. And it's a powerful metaphor for the outcast – and monster in all of us."

Anne Rice

Obayifo

The obayifo is a species of living vampire or vampiric witch traditionally found among the Ashanti people on the Gold Coast in West Africa. The name is derived from the Ashanti word *bayi* which means "sorcery." The obayifo can take the form of a male or female human and has the ability to leave its body at night and fly with phosphorescent light coming from its shoulders. It can blight crops – cacao crops mostly – and drink the blood of children, causing their slow and painful death. It is not easy to identify an obayifo as anyone could be one, but shifty eyes and a compulsion to eat meat can be warning signs.

See also: **LOOGAROO**

Obour

The obour is a Bulgarian vampiric spirit and a revenant that according to folklore is created when the spirit of a murdered person escapes from the grave in the form of a corpse candle nine days after its burial. For 40 days it will remain in this state, before transforming into an animated corpse with one nostril missing. It is said to drink the blood of animals and to commit acts of vandalism. The way to destroy it is to indulge its gluttonous nature and offer it large quantities of food. Once distracted by the food a witch must be hired to destroy the obour.

See also: **BULGARIA**

Obur

In the traditions of the Karachay people of Turkey the obur is a shape-shifting witch or wizard. During the day they appear as normal elderly people but at night they take off all their clothing, smear their bodies with ointment, and then wallow in the ashes on the edge of their fires. Then they mount brooms and run around the room until they have generated enough energy to fly up the chimney in the form of cats. They enter the houses of their victims through the chimneys and drink the blood of those inside, especially children, leaving a dark bruise on their necks. At dawn they return to their homes and resume their everyday activities. The obur can also shape-shift into wolves and dogs and drink the blood of livestock too.

See also: **ANIMAL VAMPIRES; UBOUR**

Occult

The word "occult" means "secret" or "hidden" and is used to describe practices involving secret or hidden magical or mystical knowledge. The existence of psychic vampires has often been theorized on from an occult perspective because of the abundance of information, both ancient and modern, that can be analyzed. This, however, is not the case with immortal blood-drinking vampires, largely because they do not seem to be as active today as they were in the seventeenth and eighteenth centuries. As a result occult theories regarding the tangible existence of immortal blood drinkers are dated and few in number.

Frequently cited occult theories to explain the existence of undead blood-drinking vampires include:

- Demonic possession: *One of the most incredible occult theories is the view that immortal blood drinkers are corpses possessed by demons or evil entities. To maintain their host corpses these entities need the energy of human blood. This theory of demonic possession after death explains why the reanimated corpse often finds it so easy to kill family members, because the spirit of the once-living person would no longer be controlling it. It could also explain why vampires are repelled by religious or holy objects. The problem with this theory is that it is difficult to prove demonic possession exists in a living person, let alone a corpse. However, the power of blood to sustain a corpse theory could apply to another theory that does not involve demons, the Devil, or religion: the idea that the vampire is a corpse that somehow becomes animated and feeds off others to survive.*

- Transmission: *Another cause of vampirism that is often cited in fiction is that when a person is bitten (sometimes referred to as a kiss) by a vampire, or drinks the blood of another vampire, he or she becomes one. According to this theory the blood or life force of the vampire becomes fused with the blood or life force of a human, thus creating a vampire. The problem with this theory is that if this is how vampires are created, who created the first vampire? One possible explanation is that the first vampire was demonically created and from then on the giving of blood created a line of vampires.*

- Strong will: *In folklore, vampires are created when people commit suicide or die a violent death. The occult explanation of this is that after death the soul has memories of its death and cannot find peace in the afterlife. The soul can also cling to the earth because it fears moving on to the afterlife because it has led a life of sin. In both cases – violent death or sinful life – if the will of a soul is strong enough, it might be able to reanimate the corpse and then hunt down humans to maintain its existence and create more vampires.*

- Magic: *Another occult explanation is the theory that an evil magician or sorcerer can become a vampire after death. The magician would either make a pact with the Devil or learn some technique for animating his or her body after death. The occult power of excommunication must also be considered. When a person is excommunicated the curse pronounced upon them basically states that they can never find peace in the afterlife. An excommunicated soul who believed in the potency of that curse might therefore be able to reanimate its own corpse in some way with the energy of its hatred.*

All the above occult theories for the existence of immortal blood drinkers are unproven and impossible to disprove. Not surprisingly such theories are no longer taken seriously today by most vampire experts, but centuries ago those who claimed they had experienced the onslaught of a vampire attack honestly believed they had experienced something unearthly, malevolent, ferocious, and tangible.

See also: **ASTRAL BODY; ORIGINS, OF VAMPIRES; PSYCHIC ATTACK**

Ogoljen

"Ogoljen" is a term for a Czech vampire. It was said to hunt for victims with dirt from its burial site in its navel. It must be buried at a crossroads to prevent it leaving its grave.

Ohyn

"Ohyn" is a term for a Polish vampire, the creation of which was said to be proved by the presence at birth of teeth and a caul. After the person died, the vampire was said to awaken and chew its own flesh before killing its relatives. To prevent the baby from becoming an ohyn the birth teeth would need to be removed.

See also: **POLAND**

Oil

In vampire folklore, boiling oil is said to help destroy vampires, especially the vrykolalas from Greece. Vampire hunters would often douse a corpse in hot oil before staking it. Boiling oil would also be poured around a grave to prevent vampires from leaving the earth. Although holy water was the preferred liquid used by vampire hunters (because it could be easily obtained in large quantities), holy oil – oil that had been consecrated by a Christian priest for use in ceremonies – was also believed to be a potent weapon in the fight against vampires. Holy oil could be thrown on vampires or used to anoint stakes and daggers to be used against the creatures.

Oils, ointments, and salves feature in many records of European witchcraft trials and werewolf cases. Witches claimed that magical ointments or oils enabled them to fly or shape-shift, and those who claimed to change into wolf form said they could do so when they rubbed magical ointment on their bodies. Obviously the majority, if not all, of these claims would have been obtained through torture.

Oldenburg

In the nineteenth century, people in Oldenburg, a district in northern Germany, believed that corpses had to be buried very deep in the ground. If a corpse was not buried deeply or placed in a shallow grave then it was thought that it could easily rise from the earth and become a revenant.

Old Hag

From ancient times, ugly, shriveled, old women, also known as hags or crones, have been associated with witchcraft and the forces of evil. This fear of old hags inevitably blended into the vampire myth in both folklore and fiction (E. F. Benson's "The Room with a Tower" (1912) portrays a fine example of an older vampiric woman).

Old hag syndrome has been recorded since the earliest times and involves nightmares, fears of suffocation, and paralysis. In folklore it has often been blamed on vampires or witches and sorcerers who can travel out of their bodies to attack human beings in spirit form. From a psychological standpoint the term "old hag" has been used to describe a malevolent presence that torments sleepers at night, "riding their chests," and is fairly similar to the mara, a demon that sexually assaults humans at night. ("Hag" often refers to a witch and to be "hagged" or "hag ridden" means to be assaulted by a witch in your sleep.)

Terror in the night

According to folklorist David Hufford, in *The Terror that Comes in the Night* (1982), up to 15 percent of the general population may suffer at least one old hag attack in their life. Sufferers typically say that they are lying down sleeping or napping and wake up suddenly to feel an invisible presence crushing down on them. They also experience paralysis and feelings of terror. Sleep disorders, stress, indigestion, and psychological disorders have been put forward as possible explanations but although some or all of these are often a factor in the great majority of cases, they cannot explain them all. In his *On the Nightmare* (1931), Freudian analyst Ernest Jones suggested that sexual repression was the cause – he also argued that vampires were expressions of sexual repression as well – but once again, although sexual repression may play a part in some cases it cannot explain them all.

Supernatural causes for such attacks are unlikely but they cannot be entirely discounted. Famous cases of vampire attacks recorded in Eastern Europe, for example, the Breslau Vampire, certainly suggest old hag symptoms. It's also highly likely that Bram

Stoker was familiar with the syndrome when he wrote *Dracula* in 1897. Mina Harker's description of a nocturnal visitation by Dracula established forever in the public's imagination the image of the paralyzing vampire appearing by its victim's bedside:

I felt the same vague terror which had come to me before and the same sense of some presence ... For an instant my heart stood still and I would have screamed out, only I was paralysed.

See also: **HAG ATTACK**

Opji

Among the Kashubs of northern Poland, the opji is more deadly than the other type of Kashubian vampire – the vjesci – because in the case of the opji it is impossible to prevent the onset of vampirism. The opji can be recognized by the presence of one or two teeth at birth.

Origins of Vampires

Assuming that vampires do actually exist, the question of how they may have originated comes to mind. The answer has differed widely over the centuries. The vampire has appeared in the folklore of virtually every culture and numerous writers have speculated on the nature of vampirism. What follows is a snapshot of some of these different points of view.

Scientific explanations

Generally, the scientific viewpoint is one of denial: vampires cannot, never did, and do not exist. In 2005, Costas Efthimiou, a physics professor from University of Central Florida, made the headlines by claiming that vampires are a mathematical impossibility in that if vampires created other vampires by biting them even at a slow rate of one vampire a month, the human population would disappear within a matter of years.

Other scientists speculate that the reason certain individuals have been accused of vampirism over the centuries is due to the fact that their physical characteristics or symptoms resembled the symptoms of a vampire attack. The medical conditions that may have been mistaken for vampirism include anemia, porphyria, sleep paralysis, and Renfield's syndrome. In addition, catalepsy is a dysfunction of the nervous system that causes a slowing down of the body's regulatory functions, so much so that to the untrained eye the sufferer appears dead. That person may then have been buried prematurely and then woken up in their coffin. If they managed to escape they would have been considered vampires. If they didn't manage to escape, however, their desperate attempts to do so might easily have been misinterpreted as the attempt of a revenant to leave its grave.

Some experts argue that ignorance about the decomposition process of the corpse after death may have led people to believe that a vampire was leaving its grave and returning to feed on the blood of the living. The re-emergence of limbs or whole corpses buried in shallow graves after flooding, the attack of wild animals, and the actions of body snatchers may also have generated fears that the dead were leaving their graves to stalk the living.

Also worth noting in this section is the theory often put forward by those who study the "science" of vampires, namely that vampires originate from some strange virus that alters the DNA of humans so they can then transform into vampires. It has been long theorized that the vampire's bite deposits a kind of enzyme found in the vampire's saliva into the bloodstream of its victim. This enzyme triggers a metabolic change in the victim's body, beginning with the production of a strange, dark-green liquid called ichor within the victim's bloodstream.

Such theories have no scientific basis and have generally been invented by writers and novelists. Equally improbable is the theory that vampires are a race of nanobots, or genetic experiments gone wrong, created by renegade scientists who introduced them into human bodies in order to repair damaged cells. These nanobots performed so well that they took control of their hosts and replicated themselves by utilizing the iron from the hemoglobin in the host's red blood cells. Unable to keep up with the demand, the host has no choice but to seek out blood from others.

Mythological explanations

Though the term "vampire" does not appear until early modern times in Europe, from the earliest times people have feared predators that come in the dark to kill the living. The first vampiric figures date back at least 4,000 years, to the ancient Assyrians and Babylonians of Mesopotamia. Mesopotamians feared Lamastu (also spelled Lamashtu), a vicious demon goddess, often depicted with wings and bird-like talons and the head of a lion, that preyed on humans. In Assyrian legend, Lamastu, the daughter of the sky god Anu, would creep into a house at night and steal or kill babies, either in their cribs or in the womb. She would also suck blood from young men and bring disease, sterility, and nightmares. Lamastu is closely associated with Lilith, a prominent figure in some Jewish texts.

According to the sixth-century AD Talmud, Lilith was the first wife created for Adam but when he refused to treat her as an equal she left him. She became a witch, the mother of all demons, and was allowed to kill children until their naming day (seven days after birth) unless they had a charm with the names of three angels on it. Cain, the first-born son of Adam and Eve who was banished with a mark on his head for killing his brother Abel, met Lilith by the Red Sea and from their union came a host of demons and vampires. Little is heard of the children of Cain and Lilith until they resurfaced some centuries later in the epic poem *Beowulf*, which originated sometime between the eighth and eleventh centuries in England.

> *... Cain had killed his only*
> *Brother, slain his father's son*
> *With an angry sword, God drove him off,*
> *Outlawed him to the dry and barren desert,*
> *And branded him with a murder's mark.*
> *And he bore*
> *A race of fiends accursed like their father ...*
>
> (Ll. 1261–1266)

The ancient Greeks feared similar creatures, notably Lamia, a demon with the head and torso of a woman and the lower body of a snake. The Greeks also feared the empusai, the malicious daughters of Hecate, the goddess of witchcraft. Vampire-like figures also have a long history in the mythology of Asia. Indian folklore describes a number of nightmarish characters, including rakshasa, gargoyle-like shape-shifters who preyed on children, and vetala, demons who would take possession of recently dead bodies to wreak havoc on the living. In Chinese folklore, corpses could sometimes rise from the grave and walk again. Nomadic tribes, Gypsies, and traveling traders spread different vampire legends throughout Asia, Europe, and the Middle East. As these stories traveled, their various elements combined to form new vampire myths.

In ancient mythology once the first vampire was created, a community of vampires generally followed. And when a particular figure with vampiric qualities took its place in the mythology of a people as a demon or deity, they would multiply into other sets of similar beings. For example, in Greek mythology there are several demonic entities classed as lamia. The assumption was that vampiric entities were simply a part of the supernatural universe and therefore there was no need to consider what their origins were. In addition, these vampiric entities did not create new vampires by attacking humans or feeding on their blood. In this way they were unlike the vampires of Eastern Europe who were typically former members of a community who contaminated other members of that community by their presence or by biting them.

Vampires as scapegoats

As bringers of disease and death and the personification of evil, in folklore vampires can all too often be seen to be scapegoats to explain the unexplainable. Death is one of the most mysterious aspects of life and one way to come to terms with it is to personify it to give it some tangible form. At their root, Lilith and similar early vampires are explanations for a terrifying mystery – the sudden death of young children and fetuses in the womb. The strigoi and other animated corpses are the ultimate symbols of death; they are the actual remains of the deceased.

The vampires of European folklore have typically been associated with outbreaks of specific diseases such as tuberculosis and plague. This epidemic pattern is obvious in the classic cases of Peter Plogojowitz and Arnold Paole. Once it became clear that the disease was spread by contact with the sick and the dead, the vampire therefore became the explanation for the plague.

The earliest vampires, such as the langsuir from Malaysia and the Greek lamia, also seem to have originated thanks to the dangers associated with pregnancy and childbirth. Vampire lore also sprang from unusual circumstances during birth, and children who were different in some way when they were born were often considered likely candidates for vampirism. For example, among the Kashubs of Poland children born with teeth were thought to become vampires when they grew up.

Other vampire stories surrounded the death of a loved one. In Eastern Europe symptoms of vampire attack included weakness and nightmares but these may actually have been a product of the grieving process. In his book, *De Masticatione Mortuorum in Tumulis* (1725), Michaël Ranft makes an early attempt to explain folklore belief in vampires in a natural way when he gives the following explanation of the case of Peter Plogojowitz:

This brave man perished by a sudden or violent death. This death, whatever it is, can provoke in the survivors the visions they had after his death. Sudden death gives rise to inquietude in the familiar circle. Inquietude has sorrow as a companion. Sorrow brings melancholy. Melancholy engenders restless nights and tormenting dreams. These dreams enfeeble body and spirit until illness overcomes and, eventually, death.

The belief that vampires originated when the family did not pay attention to correct burial customs may indicate hidden tensions within a family. Vampirism that was caused by unexpected or sudden death again points to unfinished emotional business on the part of grieving relatives.

Vampires as social and moral control

Suicide was considered to be a cause of vampirism within many Eastern European communities, as was leading a sinful life or dabbling with witchcraft. In these cases vampirism served as methods of social and moral control for leaders of the community. In much the same way, anyone guilty of heresy or who died in a state of excommunication from the Christian Church was said to become a vampire after death.

Another occurrence believed to cause vampirism in folklore was an animal jumping over the body of a dead person prior to burial. It was thought that before burial the soul of a dead person remained close to their body and it might be tempted to escape via the animal. However, the superstition could also have a lot to do with the need to protect the corpse from being torn apart by animals.

Psychological explanations

Vampires personify the dark side of humanity. Lilith, like other early vampire demons, is the opposite of the good wife and mother. Instead of caring for children and honoring her husband, she destroys babies and seduces men. Similarly, undead vampires feed on their family, rather than supporting it. By defining evil through the image of the vampire, people can understand their own evil tendencies better by externalizing them.

According to some psychologists, the vampire archetype originated and took such firm hold in society because it became a mental scapegoat for all sorts of evils, hidden tensions, and frustrations. The personality of the vampire is predatory, sexual, erotic, anti-social, rebellious, and parasitic and it allows us to project the negative aspects of ourselves onto something we can openly revile and admire at the same time, without actually acting out the desires and impulses ourselves.

One modern variation on the origin of the vampire legend is the psychic vampire. These vampires claim that they crave psychic energy from others and have the power to drain it without the person's knowledge. According to some believers, this sort of vampire has been around for thousands of years and may have inspired the undead vampires of folklore.

Fantastical explanations

Another vampire origin myth is inspired by the Hebrew Book of Enoch, which claims that vampires are the offspring of the union between the Watchers (fallen angels) and humans. In an adjunct, vampires are the result of a union between the daughters of Eve (female humans) and the Angel of Death sent by God, and their mission is to destroy the demonic offspring of the fallen angels.

Yet another myth suggests that vampires were first created by the people of Atlantis, who, in their quest to prolong life, conducted biological and genetic experiments that resulted in a new human that could live for centuries but had to drink the blood of ordinary humans in order to survive. These vampires somehow managed to escape the Great Flood.

A somewhat obscure myth holds that Judas Iscariot became the first vampire after he committed suicide for betraying Jesus. Another interesting origin of the vampire myth is its association with the negative image of the Christ, or the Antichrist, as a series of oppositions can be found. Blood in Christianity is a symbol of the life-giving force of Christ. In the vampire myth the vampire drinks in blood that Christ gave away. Christ is the source and an energy that radiates, whereas the vampire sucks in energy like a black hole. Christ gave his life to save humanity, the vampire takes it away. Some scholars have also noticed a parallel between the use of the spear that pierced Christ on the cross and the staking of the vampire.

Satanic explanations

The Antichrist theory closely links in with the idea that vampirism is associated with Satan and Satanism. In medieval Europe vampires were thought to originate from witches (worshippers of Satan) or those who had been excommunicated from the Church and were therefore thought to be dealing with the Devil. Unacceptable to God and in league with Satan, the vampire was therefore repelled by holy objects, such as the crucifix, and stayed away from Church. In this way the doctrine of excommunication could have directly contributed to the development of the vampire myth.

Explanations in fiction

Bram Stoker does not deal directly with the origins of the vampire in his 1897 book *Dracula*, merely suggesting the idea that vampire bats might explain the origin of vampires, or that the Count *"had dealings with the evil one."* For Stoker, it seems that what mattered most was not an explanation for vampirism but Dracula's power to transform others into his own kind. Although some novelists have attempted to create a myth to explain the origin of the vampire, in most books and movies the issue is not dealt with directly, except through the idea that vampires can pass their condition on to others through their bite.

The origin of vampires has been explored more thoroughly in the science fiction genre. In his 1942 short story "Asylum," author A. E. van Vogt suggested that vampires were an alien race. However, the idea that vampires were from another dimension was first explored in 1894 by H. G. Wells in *The Flowering of the Strange Orchid*. Science fiction has also suggested that disease is the cause of vampirism and this disease can be spread to humans by the vampire's bite. The idea is explored most successfully in Richard Matheson's *I Am Legend* (1954).

See also: **BECOMING A VAMPIRE; BIRTH OF A VAMPIRE; BIOLOGY OF VAMPIRES; CHRISTIANITY; SEX; SHADOW; SYMBOLS; TRANSFORMATION**

Orlok, Graf

The vampire Graf (Count) Orlok appeared in the 1922 German silent film *Nosferatu, eine Symphonie des Grauens*. When creating the character, director F. W. Murnau drew on the tradition of Eastern European folklore rather than the vampire created by Bram Stoker in *Dracula* (1897), who wore formal evening clothes and revealed few effects of death. Graf Orlok, played with great skill by actor Max Schreck, clearly revealed the effects of death and was given a rat-like distorted appearance, with fangs placed together at the front of his mouth rather than elongated canine fangs. He was also bald with claw-like fingers.

Unlike Stoker's Dracula, Orlok can cast a shadow and see his reflection in a glass, and whereas Dracula could move around in the day Orlok cannot be exposed to sunlight at all. In a stunning climax to the film, sunlight proves to be Orlok's destruction when he lingers too long in the room of a virtuous woman and the sun disintegrates him.

See also: **NOSFERATU**

Ossenfelder, Heinrich August

Heinrich August Ossenfelder was an eighteenth-century German poet and the author of one of the earliest poems about vampires, *Der Vampir*, which was published in Leipzig in May 1748 in *Der Naturforscher*. A translation of *Der Vampir* appeared in *The Vampire in Verse* in 1985, edited by Stephen Moore.

The poem caused a sensation when it was published because of its erotic overtones. It tells of a man whose love is rejected by a pious maiden and who then threatens to pay her a nightly visit and drink her blood by giving her the seductive kiss of the vampire, thus proving to her that his teaching is better than her mother's Christianity.

My dear young maiden clingeth
Unbending, fast and firm
To all the long-held teaching
Of a mother ever true;
As in vampires unmortal
Folk on the Theyse's portal
Heyduck-like do believe.
But my Christine thou dost dally,
And wilt my loving parry
Till I myself avenging
To a vampire's health a-drinking
Him toast in pale tockay.
And as softly thou art sleeping
To thee shall I come creeping
And thy life's blood drain away.

And so shalt thou be trembling
For thus shall I be kissing
And death's threshold thou' it be crossing
With fear, in my cold arms.
And last shall I thee question
Compared to such instruction
What are a mother's charms?

Der Vampir has been hailed as the first modern vampire poem, not because of its erotic overtones but because of the suggestion that there is far more to vampirism than a simplistic battle between good and evil.

See also: **LITERATURE**

Outsider

Social historians have long noted the value of the vampire as a scapegoat for society's misfortunes, fears, and evils. But another reason why people have identified with the vampire story for so long is because vampires are perceived as different. They are creatures that don't fit in, which is how almost everyone feels at some stage in their lives. Twentieth-century vampire author Anne Rice interprets the vampire as a metaphor for the outsider and the alienated, or those who feel like "a monster inside." She sees the vampire as an elegant but doomed individual because his or her appearance, behavior, and sensitivity make him or her different from ordinary people.

An anthropological analysis also interprets the vampire as an outsider who arouses hate, suspicion, and fear rather than sympathy. The vampire's strange habits, unconventional sexuality, and transgressing of boundaries and convention arouse feelings of distrust, disgust, and even xenophobia, among ordinary people.

See also: **GAY CULTURE; ORIGINS,**
OF VAMPIRES; SYMBOLS

Ovid (43 BC–AD 18)

One of the early Latin poets of Imperial Rome, Ovid wrote about love, seduction, and mythological transformation. Considered a master of the elegiac couplet, he is traditionally ranked alongside Virgil and Horace as one of the three canonic poets of Latin literature and his poetry, much imitated during the Middle Ages, decisively influenced European art and literature. Ovid's most direct reference to vampirism comes in his *Amores* (111, XIV, 34) when, in Dryden's translation, he writes:

> *Why do your locks and rumpled*
> *head-clothes show*
> *'Tis more than usual sleep that made*
> *them so?*
> *Why are the kisses which he gave betray'd*
> *By the impression that his teeth have made?*

In Ovid's *Fasti* the poet suggests that the demonic strix could assume the form of ravenous birds (shape-shifting is a timeless characteristic of vampires) that suck the blood of children and eat them.

See also: **LITERATURE**

Owenga

In the folklore of African Guinea the owenga are vengeful ancestors, evil spirits, or dead magicians who are as tall as trees and attack the living for their blood. Spilled blood must be cleared up immediately so as not to tempt the owenga and anything stained with blood, such as clothing, must be burned or thrown into the sea.

Owl

A nocturnal bird of prey, the owl is found in many countries around the world. The association between the owl and the powers of darkness is one of the oldest known to man. A Sumerian clay tablet dating back to around 2000 BC depicts two owls flanking a goddess, believed to be the goddess of death. Roman writers such as Ovid described the owl as a harbinger of doom, and the ancient Roman strix was a spectral screech owl that fed off the blood of children. In Persia too the bird is regarded as the angel of death and in many African countries the owl is associated with witchcraft. In North America many Native American peoples regarded it as an evil spirit, and in Malaysia the owl is believed to be the embodiment of the langsuir and the pontianak.

In parts of Eastern Europe the owl was compared to the vampire because of its nocturnal nature, superb vision, and the sinister, predatory way it patrols the night hours looking for prey, in much the same ways that vampires were believed to search for their victims and suddenly pounce on them. Peasants would rarely address the owl by name but used other words to describe it, because they feared that the owl was a shape-shifting vampire.

In vampire poetry and fiction, the fear and repulsion that the owl could spread by its mere presence and the omen of death it could bring as a messenger of the other world, all helped to create a perfect backdrop to the vampire's story. The following is from *Christabel* by Samuel Taylor Coleridge.

> *Tis the middle of night by the castle clock,*
> *And the owls have awakened the crowing*
> *cock;*
> *Tu – whit ! – – Tu – whoo !*
> *And hark, again ! the crowing cock,*
> *How drowsily it crew.*

See also: **ANIMAL VAMPIRES; BATS; BIRDS**

*"There are reasons for talking mummies and roaming vampires — psychological ones.
Psychologists tell us that nearly every one of us has a hidden fear of being buried alive."*

Thomas Aylesworth, *Vampires and Other Ghosts*

Pacu Pati

The pacu pati is a fierce Indian vampire whose name means "master of the herd." Said to be the lord of ghouls, ghosts, and vampires, and other flesh-eaters created by the vices of humankind, this demonic creature haunts cemeteries and places of execution with his revolting followers. Also known as mmbyu ("embodiment of death") the pacu pati is considered to be the chief of all malevolent creatures in Indian folklore.

See also: **INDIA**

"Pale-faced Lady, The"

Translated into English as "The Pale-faced Lady," this short story by French writer Alexandre Dumas was published in 1848 as a subplot in his multi-volume work *Thousand and One Phantoms*, in a section called *Une Journée à Fontenay-aux-Roses*. The work was published in England as a stand-alone story in *In the Moonlight* (1848) and reprinted as "The Carpathian Vampire" in *The Horror at Fontenay* (1975). The story, about a Moldavian nobleman vampire called Kostaki who is destroyed by a blessed sword, is of note because it may be the first vampire story to be set in the Carpathian Mountains.

See also: **LITERATURE**

Palis

Palis, which means "foot-licker" is a vampiric demon in Persian Islamic lore who attacks victims at night and kills them by licking the soles of their feet and draining their blood. Salt is an effective repellent but fortunately, as one popular folktale told in many different versions suggests, the creature can be easily outwitted. In the story two camel drivers lie down to sleep with the soles of their feet touching each other. When the palis arrives it is confused because there are no soles to lick and because it has never seen a "man with two heads" before. There are no known descriptions of the physical attributes of this creature but it does seem to bear some similarities to modern vampire myths, such as that of the chupacabra.

Palm Hair

Palm hair is a characteristic of the vampire mentioned by Bram Stoker in his 1897 novel, *Dracula*, and it appears to be largely his invention. There is no folk tradition of hairs on hands or palms but once Stoker mentioned it, twentieth-century vampire writers such as Montague Summers accepted it as fact.

See also: **APPEARANCE OF VAMPIRES**

Paole, Arnold

The case of Arnold Paole, the so-called vampire of Medvegia, Serbia, carefully documented by Johann Flückinger, became one of the most famous cases of vampirism in eighteenth-century Europe. It came in the middle of the wave of vampire cases reported in Central Europe from the late seventeenth century onward and received a wide press in Europe.

Paole was born sometime in the early 1700s in Medvegia, north of Belgrade in a part of Serbia that was then in the Austrian Empire. While serving in the army he was stationed in Greece where he learned that his company was staying near a site allegedly haunted by vampires. One night he believed he was attacked by a vampire so he went the next day to its grave and destroyed it. To protect himself against future attacks he also smeared vampire blood on himself and ate some of the earth of the grave.

In the spring of 1727 Paole returned to his homeland, purchased some land and settled down. Although he was considered good natured and honest by the townspeople they did notice a certain gloom about him. Paole told his wife, the daughter of a neighboring farmer, about the vampire attack and that he felt he had been cursed forever.

Soon after his confession Paole fell off a hay wagon and broke his neck. About 20 to 30 days after his burial, rumors and reports began to surface of appearances by Paole. Four of the people who reported sightings died and panic soon spread around the community. It was feared that Paole had turned into a vampire and was attacking and killing livestock and people.

Forty days after Paole's burial his grave was opened. Two military surgeons were present as the lid was taken off his coffin. They examined the body and declared it to be as if Paole had recently died. The body had moved to its side in the coffin and the jaw was open, with blood trickling from the mouth. There was also new skin present under the old skin and

nails that were growing longer. The body was pierced and blood flowed out. Convinced that Paole had transformed into a vampire his body was staked and, according to witnesses, was said to utter a loud groan (probably caused by gases being forced up the throat by the violent compression of the chest). Paole's head was cut off and his body burned. As an extra precaution the bodies of the four people who had also died were treated in a similar way.

In the same area three to four years later, in 1731, around 17 people died of suspected vampirism within a matter of months. A local girl complained that she was attacked in the middle of the night by a man called Milo who had recently died. Word of this new outbreak of vampirism reached the Austrian Emperor who ordered an inquiry to be conducted by Flückinger, a regimental field surgeon. On December 12 he departed for Medvegia and started to gather accounts. Milo's body was disinterred, and because it was found to be preserved like Arnold Paole's had been, it was staked and burned. Locals theorized that the vampirism must have been caused by eating the meat of cows that Paole had vampirized before his destruction. Forty bodies of those who had died in recent months were also dug up. Seventeen of these were found to be in the same preserved state of that of Paole and Milo. These bodies were all staked and burned.

Flückinger presented a full report of his observations in Medvegia, entitled *Visum et Repertum* ("Seen and Discovered"), to the Emperor in early 1732. His report was published and by March 1732 accounts of Paole and the Medvegia vampires were circulated in French and English periodicals. The report was so well documented that it became the

The Element Encyclopedia of Vampires

focus of future vampire studies and was discussed at all social levels, turning Arnold Paole into the most famous "vampire" of the eighteenth century.

"Seen and Discovered"

The following is a translated excerpt from *Visum et Repertum*, published in Nuremberg in 1732.

> After it had been reported that in the village of Medvegia the so-called vampires had killed some people by drinking their blood, I was, by high degree of a local Honorable Supreme Command, sent there to investigate the matter thoroughly along with officers detailed for that purpose and two subordinate medical officers, and therefore carried out and heard the present inquiry in the company of the captain of the Stallath Company of haiduks [a type of soldier], Gorschiz Hadnack, the standard-bearer and the oldest haiduk of the village, as follows: who unanimously recounted that about five years ago a local haiduk by the name of Arnold Paole broke his neck in a fall from a haywagon. This man had during his lifetime often revealed that, near Gossowa in Turkish Serbia, he had been troubled by a vampire, wherefore he had eaten from the earth of the vampire's grave and had smeared himself with the vampire's blood, in order to be free from the vexation he had suffered. In 20 or 30 days after his death some people complained that they were being bothered by this same Arnold Paole; and in fact four people were killed by him.
>
> In order to end this evil, they dug up this Arnold Paole 40 days after his death – this on the advice of Hadnack, who had been present at such events before; and they found that he was quite complete and undecayed, and that fresh blood had flowed from his eyes, nose, mouth, and ears; that the shirt, the covering, and the coffin were completely bloody; that the old nails on his hands and feet, along with the skin, had fallen off, and that new ones had grown; and since they saw from this that he was a true vampire, they drove a stake through his heart, according to their custom, whereby he gave an audible groan and bled copiously.
>
> Thereupon they burned the body the same day to ashes and threw these into the grave. These people say further that all those who were tormented and killed by the vampire must themselves become vampires. Therefore they disinterred the above-mentioned four people in the same way. Then they also add that this Arnold Paole attacked not only the people but also the cattle, and drank their blood. And since the people used the flesh of such cattle, it appears that some vampires are again present here, inasmuch as, in a period of three months, 17 young and old people died, among them some who, with no previous illness, died in two or at the most three days. In addition, the haiduk Jowiza reports that his step-daughter, by name of Stanacka, lay down to sleep 15 days ago, fresh and healthy, but at midnight she started up out of her sleep with a terrible cry, fearful and trembling, and complained that she had been throttled by the son of a haiduk by the name of Milloe, who had died nine weeks earlier, whereupon she had experienced a great pain in the chest and became worse hour by hour, until finally she died on the third day…

The report, written in language that would not be out of place in the pages of a horror comic, and other reports like it, were taken very seriously. It was signed and witnessed by local and city officials and doctors and formed the very real basis for vampire beliefs in the eighteenth century and beyond. The following points are of note as far as the characteristics of eighteenth-century vampirism are concerned:

- *The situation clearly causes great distress in the whole local community and is not simply a matter involving one or two households.*

- *People complain that the dead Paole terrorizes them at night.*

- *In two instances, one of which is Paole, people are said to have used the blood of a vampire as an antidote to vampirism, and in both cases the "remedy" seems to have failed.*

- *The exhumation takes place 40 days after Paole's death. According to Serbian beliefs it was impossible for the body to be intact at this stage, but Paole's body is found undecayed; his blood is fresh and his hair and nails have continued to grow.*

- *Paole's body is staked and then cremated. The corpse groans and then bleeds. Officials do not witness this directly but it is noted as hearsay evidence.*

- *The victims of the vampire are said to become vampires themselves.*

- *The vampire also attacks cattle, and those who eat the flesh of the cattle become vampires themselves.*

- *To provide proof that the undecayed bodies are unusual, it is noted by contrast that the other bodies have decayed naturally.*

- *It is noted that one body has been dug up by animals. This is interesting as the use of coffins may have been brought about through fears of vampirism. If a body was dug up by animals it would become vulnerable to vampirism.*

- *One vampire had a mark on its ear, and according to Flückinger this was sure-fire evidence of "throttling." It was customary to look for such marks on the corpses of suspected witches and vampires as it was believed that this was "evidence" of unnatural processes taking place within the corpse.*

It is difficult to dismiss Flückinger's report, especially as it was signed by no fewer than five army officers, three of whom were doctors and all of whom would have been extremely familiar with corpses. It must not be forgotten however, that the details pertaining to Arnold Paole in this account are not first-hand accounts, as the report was written five years after his death following investigation of a fresh outbreak of vampirism in Medvegia.

See also: **AGING, OF VAMPIRES; BIOLOGY OF VAMPIRES; BITE; DECOMPOSITION; EPIDEMIC; PREMATURE BURIAL; PORPHYRIA; RABIES; SCIENCE BEHIND VAMPIRES; STANA; TRANSFORMATION**

Pecos, Hugo (1925-)

Born in Texas in 1925, American vampirologist Hugo Pecos oversees an organization and website (www.fvza.org) he calls the Federal Vampire and Zombie Agency (FVZA), which claims responsibility for controlling America's vampire and zombie population while overseeing scientific research into the undead. According to Pecos, from the late 1800s to 1975 the now defunct FVZA kept America safe from vampires and zombies. Although Pecos's knowledge of vampire lore, and the science of real vampires, is extensive he remains a controversial figure, and the FVZA has frequently been dismissed by historians and researchers as a fictional organization.

Pelesit

The pelesit is a vampire spirit from Malaysia that is typically described as a house cricket or fly that is the pet of the polong. The pelesit is said to be made by magic from the tongue of a still-born baby. In a sense it was a forerunner or scout of the polong and its mission was to invade the body of a victim, causing illness and insanity in preparation for the attack of the polong. It drank blood from open cuts and wounds but its primary purpose was to cause illness and unhappiness.

Victims scream about cats while they are under attack, a sure sign of the presence of a polong. A charm can compel a pelesit to leave its victim, or a magician can force the controlling agent to reveal its name through the voice of the victim. However, without the help of the magician who created it, there is no real way to destroy the pelesit, although it could be trapped in a bottle and fed by blood drawn from the fourth finger of a person's hand.

See also: **MALAYSIA**

Penanggalan

One of the most common and ghastly forms of the undead in Malaysian folklore was the penanggalan or penanggal. This creature was little more than a floating head with dried blood around its mouth and a neck, with trailing entrails and a still-beating heart that flew through the air during the night in search of the blood of women and children. It made loud screaming noises as it flew. After feeding on the blood of its victims, it was thought that the creature reconnected to the rest of its body and would rest until it needed to feed again. It is most commonly said to be the head of a woman who had died in childbirth, who now (out of spite and jealousy) drank the blood of children while they were still in the womb or just after they had been born. Another version states that the creature was a woman surprised by a man during a religious penance. In shock she tore off her head and flew away.

In his 1834 book entitled *The Malayan Peninsula*, P. J. Begbie states that the penanggalan is an evil spirit that can take possession of a woman and turn her into a sorcerer or witch. He tells how the creature can detach its head and drink the blood of both the living and the dead. Begbie also records the tale of a man with two wives, one with light skin and one with dark skin. Suspecting that they might be possessed by penanggalan he watched them one night in secret and witnessed them leaving to feed. He switched their bodies round so in the morning they attached themselves to the wrong bodies. When the king saw the women with the wrong heads on, this was taken as proof of their possession and they were both executed.

Destruction

The penanggalan could be destroyed by catching its entrails to prevent the head reconnecting with the body. As the penanggalan fed only at night it was assumed that it could not exist for long in the sunlight and would shrivel and die. Because of such beliefs women in childbirth were enclosed in houses decorated with the leaves of the jeruju or sea holly, with their sharp spines that could snare the intestines of the creature, and trap her until dawn when she was vulnerable.

Another way to destroy the penanggalan was to stop its beating heart. Destroying the penanggalan was, of course, very dangerous as the creature was said to be extremely vicious, with long sharp teeth and eyes that shot fire. Blood and other juices dripped from its dangling intestines and should any such drops fall on anyone they would immediately fall ill. In some areas it was said that the creature could spit deadly venom that could paralyze its victim. Its scream could also stun those who heard it, allowing the creature to feed on the victim while he or she was still alive.

A less risky way to kill the penanggalan was to find the lower half of its body and to trap it in a box or container. This method wasn't thought to be entirely effective, however, as the penanggalan might be able to turn itself into smoke and enter the container that way.

Pentsch Vampire

See: CUNTIUS, JOHANNES

Petronius (c.27–66)

Gaius Petronius Arbiter was a Roman courtier during the reign of Emperor Nero. He was known for his self-indulgent lifestyle and is speculated to be the author of the *Satyricon*, a satirical novel. Fragments of the *Satyricon* still survive including the "Dinner of Trimalchio," which recounts the tale of a vampire and a werewolf. The story is a fiction but interesting in that it offers a glimpse into beliefs about the Roman vampire witch, known as the strix.

Philinnion

Philinnion was a female revenant whose story was told by the second-century AD Greek writer, Phlegon of Tralles in his *Book of Marvels*. Philinnion's story was well known during the period of the Roman Empire and forms the basis for Goethe's ballad *The Bride of Corinth* (1797).

The story of Philinnion is set in fourth-century BC Macedonia (the king referred to by Phlegon being Philip II of Macedon). Most of the early portions of the tale are not extant but it begins with a nurse in the household discovering Machates, a handsome young man staying with Philinnion's parents, in bed with a female who looks like the recently deceased and buried Philinnion. The parents of Philinnion are alerted and they see the same but say nothing until morning. When asked the next day, Machates claims ignorance about the death of their daughter and says his lover's name is Philinnion. He tells them that she gave him a ring and a ribbon – the same as those on the hand and tied onto Philinnion's corpse in the tomb. Machates is convinced that his lover is alive but agrees to help the girl's parents the following night. When Philinnion visits him again, he gives a signal and her parents come in to greet their returned daughter. The shock of seeing them again causes the girl to collapse back into death.

> *You will grieve sorely for your curiosity for I must now return to the place that is appointed to me. It was against the will of god that I came here.*

Rumors of the episode spread through the town. The tomb of Philinnion is opened but found to be empty. Her body is eventually found in the house and burned by terrified townsfolk beyond the town boundaries.

Philinnion's appearance in the story appears to be relatively benign, but the reaction of the townsfolk suggests something more malevolent. Presumably if Philinnion's affair had continued she would have drained Machates' blood, as ghosts in Greek legend were believed to crave blood. The story is therefore regarded as among the earliest vampire-myths, especially when read in conjunction with the story of the lamia of Corinth.

See also: **LITERATURE; POETRY**

Philippines

The folklore among the people of the Philippines is complex and confusing, with a vast array of demons, ghouls, witches, ghosts, and vampire-like beings, mainly due to the fact that there are many different ethnic groups scattered through the island chain and each has its own belief system. There are numerous different types of Filipino vampire and their names are often interchangeable with one another and applicable for both the living and the dead. Integral to Filipino belief is the concept of the vampire witch. This is not an undead witch but a living woman or man who can shape-shift into other forms to drink their victims' blood.

The aswang

Of all the vampire-like beings in Filipino lore, the aswang is the most well known. As early as the sixteenth century Spanish colonizers noted that the aswang was the most feared among the mythical creatures of the Philippines. The term actually means "dog" but it can have a variety of different meanings from island to island, and can be applied to sorcerers both living and dead, as evil is not thought to end with a person's death.

Generally the aswang are young, beautiful females by day who attack males and young children by night. Some of these women have an ointment that they rub on their body prior to their supernatural activity. They travel in the form of large birds seeking the weak and vulnerable. The creature hides in trees or on the roof of a house waiting for the moment when its victim is alone and it can attack. When that moment comes a large sharp-tipped, hollow tongue emerges from its beak and lowers into the room where the individual is lying. The creature then proceeds to draw and drink blood, semen, or sweat through its tongue from a spot of the base of the neck, upper arm, or ankle. As the victim grows weaker the aswang swells and stores blood in its breasts which grow enormous. The creature then flies home and returns to its witch form. Her breasts and belly, however, remain bloated, which meant that any well-built woman was treated with suspicion. The aswang then feeds her own children with the blood she has collected.

The aswang are most likely to be women and when they shape-shift they do so in the form of birds or small animals like dogs or pigs, but there are also male aswang and when they shape-shift they tend to do so into the form of a fly or small dragon-like creature with wings. These creatures hide in the shadows of a victim's house before again piercing the skin of their victim with their tongue and drawing up semen, blood, or sweat. The victim will wake the next morning feeling weak and irritable but unable to explain why. If this continues on a regular basis the victim will eventually die and flies are therefore constantly being driven from the house in case they are aswang, or vampires in fly form.

Salt is said to be a form of protection against the aswang and in some remote areas a bowl of salt is still left beside cots or cribs to protect sleeping infants. Bags of salt may also be tied around the necks of the weak and vulnerable.

Sometimes this salt is mixed with human urine, which in some areas is believed to have protective qualities, and sometimes protective herbs are burned in the room. The aswang against which salt is thought to be most helpful is known as *mannannagel*, which is similar to the Malaysian word for vampire – *pennangal* – suggesting a connection between the two.

See also: **DANAG; FLYING VAMPIRES; MANDURUGO**

Pick

A pick is a double-headed tool used for digging and in Eastern Europe it was often used for the destruction of vampires. Along with stakes, nails, and a sexton's spade it was one of the weapons of choice for vampire hunters. The pick had an advantage over other weapons in that it was extremely heavy and could be used to dig the soil of the grave, crush the coffin, and impale the corpse with one single blow. It also had the advantage of achieving all this from a little distance and therefore minimizing the risk of coming into contact with the vampire's blood; according to some traditions this was thought to cause madness.

Piérart, Z.-J. (d. 1878)

Z.-J. Piérart was a French psychical researcher whose theories of astral body projection became prominent during the 1850s when spiritualism swept across Europe.

According to Piérart vampires were the astral bodies (ghostly doubles) of the dead ejected from the body of a person buried alive.

This astral body then vampirized the living to nourish the body in the tomb. Piérart's theory of psychic vampirism ranks among the first to suggest that a person's energy could be drained by a supernatural force. Later it would be taken up and developed by Theosophist Franz Hartmann.

See also: **PSYCHIC VAMPIRE**

Piercing

In many regions, especially in northern Europe, the Balkans, and in Greece, a corpse would be pierced, impaled, or mutilated in some way to prevent it returning from the dead as a revenant or vampire.

Corpse piercing differs from using a stake to impale a corpse or a sexton's spade to decapitate it – acts typically performed by vampire hunters after a transformation was thought to have taken place – in that it was performed as a preventative act to ensure a transformation did not take place at all. When a corpse was pierced, nails or stakes would be hammered into the chest, hair, limbs, or head to ensure that it remained in the earth where it belonged. The practice is similar to corpse binding, where the arms or legs of a corpse were tied to prevent it leaving its coffin, but differs in that flesh was pierced.

See also: **PREVENTION**

Pig

In ancient Wallachian folklore vampires can shape-shift into the form of pigs. To prevent this happening, corpses would be smeared with pig lard. Moreover, on the feast of St. Ignatius (October 17) killing a pig and smearing the lard on a living person's body was also thought to prevent vampire attack.

Pijavica

The pijavica is a Slovenian vampire found in parts of north-western Yugoslavia that is said to be created as a result of evils committed by the deceased during his or her life, especially incest. The creature can be destroyed by decapitation and the head should then be placed between the corpse's legs. The word *pijavica* comes from the root *pit*, meaning "to drink." In Eastern Europe alcoholism is associated with vampirism. The Croatian variation is the *pijawica*.

Pisacha

The pisacha or pisaca is an Indian demon with vampiric qualities that is often associated with the rakshasa or the spirits of murderers, liars, and those who died insane. In Hindu mythology the pisacha ("flesh-eater") was a personification of the god Brahma's anger at the immorality and vices that had developed in humanity. Created by Brahma from stray drops of water used to create humans, this creature lives in water supplies and infects people with a fatal illness when they drink the water. It also likes to lurk in cemeteries and eat corpses. The pisacha can, however, cure diseases if approached in a respectful manner. In appearance the pisacha is tall and skeletal, with its ribs sticking out and with hair that stands on end as if perpetually in a state of shock.

See also: **INDIA**

Pishtaco

Although native to Peru and so not strictly a Brazilian vampire, the pishtaco is one of the most feared vampire-like creatures in Brazilian folklore. There are few descriptions of it but it does like to operate at night when its victims are asleep. This creature is interesting in that it does not initially drink blood, preferring to feed first on the fat and the semen of the sleeper. It sometimes takes the guise of the bat and in this form it can enter houses and attack sleepers, both men and women, by attaching itself to the soles of their feet and drawing off fat and then blood, which leaves the victim feeling weak the following morning.

Pitt, Ingrid (1937-)

Ingrid Pitt, an actress famous for her roles in Hammer Film productions, most notably *Vampire Lovers* (1970) and *Countess Dracula* (1971), was born on November 21, 1937, in Poland. Her first vampire movie was *The Vampire Lovers*, based on Sheridan Le Fanu's *Carmilla*. The movie required a degree of nudity from the glamorous Pitt and a number of same-sex scenes described as lesbian, although Pitt did not see things this way, suggesting that vampires had no gender or sexual preference. Nicknamed the "Queen of Horror," Pitt performed in numerous other film and television roles and is also an author. Her non-fiction works include *The Bedside Companion for Vampire Lovers* (2000) and *The Bedside Companion for Ghost Hunters* (2003). The Ingrid Pitt Fan Club is well represented internationally and has an annual reunion in London each November.

Plague

See: EPIDEMIC

Pliny the Elder (23-79)

Gaius Plinius Secundus, better known as Pliny the Elder, was a famed Roman author and natural philosopher who wrote *Naturalis Historia* (Natural History), a collection of 37 books containing information about the world that he collected from a variety of sources. He is known for his saying *"True glory consists in doing what deserves to be written; in writing what deserves to be read."* Among his writings Pliny appears to subscribe to the premature burial theory concerning the return of the dead, suggesting that in many cases people who were thought dead were actually alive and revived in their tombs. In later times in parts of Eastern Europe the practice of cremation was used to ensure that the person really was dead.

Plogojowitz, Peter (d. 1725)

Along with the case of Arnold Paole, the case of Peter Plogojowitz is one of the most well-known vampire cases of the eighteenth century. Like Paole's case, the story is of note because of the completeness of the official documents involved in recording aspects of vampirism. The story was reported in *Lettres Juives* by the Marquis d'Argens, which was quickly translated into English and published in London in 1729, under the title *The Jewish Spy*.

Peter Plogojowitz was a farmer from the village of Kisolava in Serbia who died in

September 1725 at the age of 62. Three days later he returned from the grave and appeared before his son, demanding food. He returned the next night but the son refused this time. Plogojowitz gave his son a threatening look and left. The next morning the son had died. Within the next few days nine other people had also died, all having previously complained of exhaustion and blood loss. They also claimed to have been visited by Plogojowitz in a dream during the night. In the dream Plogojowitz glided into their rooms, bit them, and sucked their blood. His wife said that he came to her in her dreams and demanded his shoes be placed beside his coffin because his bare feet were sore from walking on the cobbled streets every night.

As panic spread through the community, the parish priest wrote to a local magistrate who contacted a nearby commander of the imperial troops. The commander arrived with two offices and an executioner, and the corpses of all who had died were exhumed. Plogojowitz's corpse was said to be perfectly preserved and his mouth was stained with blood. When his body was staked blood gushed everywhere. After this the body was burned to ashes on a pyre and the other bodies were reburied with garlic and whitethorn placed in their graves.

Comment

Unfortunately, the lengthy official report recorded in 1725 tells us nothing about the personality of Peter Plogojowitz or his physical characteristics before he died, but it is clear that he was certainly not from aristocratic stock. The account illustrates quite clearly the difference between the fictional and the folklore vampire. The former tends to be eccentric with the deadly aspect of his nature only just visible beneath his or her elegant exterior. The latter is perhaps more treacherous for he or she is very much an ordinary person.

Also significant about this report is that vampirism occurs as an epidemic. Within a week of Plogojowitz's death nine others die, suggesting that in contrast to fiction where vampirism causes a lingering death, in folklore death is sudden. Peter is held responsible for these deaths, just as the victim of an epidemic illness, such as the plague, might have been held responsible for the deaths of other villagers. To ordinary peasants in the eighteenth century, vampirism itself was an epidemic and if action wasn't swiftly taken the whole village would be populated as the walking dead. The villagers' fear is palpable in the official report. They beg the commander to allow them to proceed with the exhumation of Plogojowitz:

And although I at first disapproved, telling them that the praiseworthy administration should first be dutifully and humbly informed, and its exalted opinion about this should be heard, they didn't want to accommodate themselves to this at all, but rather gave this short answer: I could do what I wanted, but [if] I didn't accord them the viewing and the legal recognition to deal with the body according to their custom, they would have to leave the house and home, because by the time a gracious resolution was received from Belgrade, perhaps the entire village – and this was already to have happened in Turkish times – could be destroyed by such an evil spirit, and they did not want to wait for this.

The vampire in this account is what vampirologists call an ambulatory type, in that it leaves its grave at night, appears before its victims, and either strangles them or sucks their blood. The body is also said to be *"completely fresh"* with signs of rejuvenation in that new skin has formed under the old and nails have grown. The strongest proof that the corpse was a vampire, however, seemed to be the fresh blood trickling around the corpse's mouth and that when it is staked it bleeds profusely after several weeks in the grave.

In many folklore vampire cases the vampires tended to be rather difficult or devious people when they were alive. If something terrible happened in the community soon after they died, suspicion quickly arose that they might have had something to do with it. No mention is made of Peter Plogojowitz being a difficult or deviant person in this account. He was simply the first person in his village to "catch" vampirism, and by "infecting" others he became one of the most famous vampires in the history of folklore.

Pniewo Vampire

The case of the vampire of Pniewo in the West Prussian district of Schwetz, mostly populated by Kashubs, was reported in 1989 by Jan Perkowski in *The Darkling: A Treatise on Slavic Vampirism*.

According to Perkowski, in 1870, the wife of a Mr. Gehrke, the forest keeper at Pniewo died and soon after her death her husband and children fell ill. It was suspected that their illness was due to the dead woman having become a vampire, and four weeks after her burial Mr. Gehrke, accompanied by a Mr. Jahnke, opened her grave. They discovered a corpse that had a red face and were convinced she had become a vampire. Flaxseeds and nets were put in her grave in the belief that she would become obsessed with counting the seeds and untying the knots. Mrs. Jahnke arrived on the scene and convinced the two men that it was too late for seeds and nets, so the men cut off the corpse's head and placed it under one of its arms. As a result of their actions all three were brought to the local district court and convicted for the crime of desecrating a grave.

Po

"Po" is the name given by the Chinese to the second of two souls that are said to belong to a person, and it plays an important part in Chinese lore concerning the creation of the undead. The hun, the superior soul, partakes in the characteristics of goodness but the po is considered the inferior soul, and is characterized by evils spirits and malevolence. If any part of the corpse remains intact it is said that the po can use this to leave the grave and become a blood-drinking vampire, so cremation was considered the ultimate form of destruction and protection It was also thought to be disastrous if a body part was exposed to sun- or moonlight as this could energize the po.

See also: CHINA

Poe, Edgar Allan (1809–49)

Edgar Allan Poe was a nineteenth-century American poet, short-story writer, editor, and literary critic. Best known for his tales of mystery and the macabre, Poe was one of the earliest American practitioners of the short story. He reinvented the horror tale with stories such as "The Pit and the Pendulum" and a number of his stories, for example "Morella" (1835), "Berenice" (1835), "The Fall of the House of Usher" (1839), and "The Oblong Box" (1844), use the vampiric theme to highlight a form of relationship between lovers or family members. Poe's fascination with women who are lead or dying has clear echoes with classic vampirism. In "Ligeia" (1838) a husband absorbs the very life essence of his wife into his unconscious, and in "The Oval Portrait" (1842) an artist transfers the life essence of a model into his painting of her. "The Premature Burial" (1844) is a horror short story on the theme of being buried alive. Fear of being buried alive was common in that time and Poe exploited that fear.

See also: LITERATURE

Poenari Castle

See: CASTLE DRACULA

Poetry

The transformation of vampires from stumbling revenants (walking corpses) into Gothic anti-heroes is first evidenced not in literature but in poetry. Poems that explored the vampiric theme appeared first in mid-eighteenth-century Germany but they did not take long to travel across Europe and to the New World.

Eighteenth-century poetry

Der Vampir (1748) by German Heinrich August Ossenfelder is the first example of vampire poetry and at two stanzas, an extremely short poem. More significant, was *Lenora* (1773), written by Gottfried August Bürger, a poem that plays along the themes of love and death. *Lenora* tells the story of William, a young man who dies but comes back to take his bride, Lenora, to claim her soul.

> *Loud snorted the horse as he plunged and*
> *   reared,*
> *And the sparks were scattered round: –*
> *What man shall say if he vanished away,*
> *Or sank in the gaping ground?*
> *Groans from the earth and shrieks in the*
> *   air!*
> *Howling and wailing everywhere!*
> *Half dead, half living, the soul of Lenora*
> *Fought as it never had fought before.*

Lenora was initially derided by literary critics, but in the 1790s it was translated into English by William Taylor and found an enthusiastic following in the years that followed. It was also the inspiration for what has traditionally been called the first vampire poem – *Die Braut von Korinth* (The Bride of Corinth) by Goethe. This 1797 poem features the official arrival of the female vampire into Romantic poetry. Goethe was said to have based his poem on the ancient Greek story of the encounter between the philosopher Apollonius with a lamia but it is actually rather more similar to the story of Philinnion.

In Goethe's version a young man travels to Athens to claim his bride, the daughter of his father's friend. When he arrives and is shown to his guest room a beautiful pale woman appears at his door. He invites her in and offers her a drink but she will not drink until midnight when she suddenly grows in energy. As dawn approaches the lady of the house hears the two lovers in the guest room and bursts into the room. She is shocked to discover that the girl is none other than her recently deceased daughter, returned from the grave to claim the love denied her. Before she departs the apparition tells her mother that she had been given an ineffective burial and was now roaming the land in search of peace. She also tells her lover that he will soon join her in death and asks her mother to make sure their bodies are burned together.

Gods, though, hearken ne'er,
Should a mother swear
To deny her daughter's plighted troth.
From my grave to wander I am forc'd,
Still to seek The Good's long-sever'd link,
Still to love the bridegroom I have lost,
And the life-blood of his heart to drink;

When his race is run,
I must hasten on,
And the young must 'neath my vengeance sink,

"Beauteous youth! no longer mayst thou
  live;
Here must shrivel up thy form so fair;
Did not I to thee a token give,
Taking in return this lock of hair?

View it to thy sorrow!
Grey thoult be to-morrow,
Only to grow brown again when there.
Mother, to this final prayer give ear!
Let a funeral pile be straightway dress'd;
Open then my cell so sad and drear,
That the flames may give the lovers rest!

When ascends the fire
From the glowing pyre,
To the gods of old we'll hasten, blest."

Lenora and the *Bride of Corinth* were a source of inspiration for the first vampire poems in English: Samuel Taylor Coleridge's *Christabel* (1797) and Robert Southey's *Thalaba the Destroyer* (1801). The mysterious creature Geraldine in *Christabel* has many vampire-like characteristics but was never directly identified as a vampire. Southey's poem on the other hand was the first to directly introduce a traditional vampire as a character. In the poem, the protagonist Thalaba is forced to "kill" his recently deceased wife by thrusting a lance through her. When writing the poem Southey was influenced by accounts of Eastern European vampires, and in its representation of the heartless vampire, Gothic storms, and abandoned cemeteries this vampire poem set the stage for the later versions that appear.

The Element Encyclopedia of Vampires

A night of darkness and of storms!
Into the Chamber of the Tomb
Thalaba led the Old Man,
To roof him from the rain.
A night of storms! the wind
Swept through the moonless sky,
And moan'd among the pillar'd sepulchres;
And in the pauses of its sweep
They heard the heavy rain
Beat on the monument above.
In silence on Oneiza's grave
Her Father and her husband sate.

Nineteenth-century verse

Once firmly established in British and German poetry the vampiric theme made other appearances in the early nineteenth century. John Stagg's *The Vampyre* (1810) was a significant and unique piece of a work in that it was perhaps the first poem dedicated to vampires and because it was a blend of prose and poetry. It begins with a prose argument section, which shows that it is derived from reading Eastern European vampire reports, and is then followed by an extended rhymed poem. The poem tells the story of an attack on Herman, a young husband of Gertrude, by his recently deceased friend Sigismund. Herman dies but Gertrude sees Sigismund. The next day Sigismund's tomb is opened and his corpse found to be warm and undecayed. The townspeople drive a stake through the corpses of both Sigismund and Herman.

The choir then burst the fun'ral dome
Where Sigismund was lately laid,
And found him, tho' within the tomb,
Still warm as life, and undecay'd.

With blood his visage was distain'd,
Ensanguin'd were his frightful eyes,
Each sign of former life remain'd,
Save that all motionless he lies.

The corpse of Herman they contrive
To the same sepulchre to take,
And thro' both carcases they drive,
Deep in the earth, a sharpen'd stake!

By this was finish'd their career,
Thro' this no longer they can roam;
From them their friends have nought to fear,
Both quiet keep the slumb'ring tomb.

Lord Byron's *Giaour* (1813) has a section that deals with a Christian vampire in Muslim Turkey. The Christian becomes a vampire after being slain in battle, only because he is a Christian. Byron was followed by John Keats's *Lamia* (1820), a poem about a vampiric relationship between the lamia and Lucius that once again drew inspiration from the ancient account of Apollonius and the lamia. Another significant poem by Keats to explore the vampiric theme was *La Belle Dame sans Merci* (1819), which features a supernatural female predator who is pale and appears to weaken males with whom she comes into contact.

After Keats, there was a lull in the appearance of the vampire in English poetry. Among the rare contributors were Henry Thomas Liddell, who wrote *The Vampire Bride* (1833) and James Clerk Maxwell, author of *The Vampyre* (1845).

In French poetry few poets made reference to the vampire, with the notable exception of Théophile Gautier, author of *La Morte Amoureuse* (1836) and Charles Baudelaire, author of *Le Vampire* and *Les Métamorphoses du Vampire*, which appeared in his 1857 collection *Les Fleurs du Mal*. Baudelaire's vampire-themed poems were considered outrageous and earned him a trial for obscenity. *Les Métamorphoses*, for example, features a seductive female vampire. The detailed physical description of her represents the temptation toward sin — with her *"red mouth," "husky tones," "serpent-like tones,"* and *"white breasts falling from imprisonment."* She plays the typical demonic role, showing the woman in her age-old role of temptress, and demonstrating her coaxing the non-sinner toward sin by calling the rules against the desired sin an *"antique demon."*

Poetry from the twentieth century onward

From the twentieth century onward the vampire or vampiric themes have made a number of appearances in poetry in Europe and the United States. One of the most influential early twentieth-century vampire poems draws on the legend of the *Flying Dutchman* — a ghostly ship manned by the undead — and can be found in James Joyce's 1922 novel *Ulysses*. Fellow Irishman William Butler Yeats also wrote a brief but evocative vampire poem in 1929 entitled *Oil and Blood*.

*In tombs of gold and lapis lazuli
Bodies of holy men and women exude
Miraculous oil, odour of violet.
But under heavy loads of trampled clay
Lie bodies of the vampires full of blood;
Their shrouds are bloody and their lips are
    wet.*

American poets began to fully embrace the vampire in the twentieth century and over the decades they have become the largest community to explore it. One of the first to make use of the theme was Conrad Aiken with his *La Belle Morte* and, more significantly, his *The Vampire*, published in 1914, a poem about an extraordinarily beautiful female vampire.

*She rose among us where we lay.
She wept, we put our work away.
She chilled our laughter, stilled our play;
And spread a silence there.
And darkness shot across the sky,
And once, and twice, we heard her cry;
And saw her lift white hands on high
And toss her troubled hair.*

*What shape was this who came to us,
With basilisk eyes so ominous,
With mouth so sweet, so poisonous,
And tortured hands so pale?
We saw her wavering to and fro,
Through dark and wind we saw her go;
Yet what her name was did not know;
And felt our spirits fail.*

We tried to turn away; but still
Above we heard her sorrow thrill;
And those that slept, they dreamed of ill
And dreadful things:
Of skies grown red with rending flames
And shuddering hills that cracked their
frames;
Of twilights foul with wings; …

As the decades marched on and the popularity of vampire short stories, novels, and comics increased, the popularity of vampire poems also increased significantly. From the late 1970s onward, with the development of vampire and Goth subcultures, countless poems have been produced by poets who identify with the vampire archetype or find inspiration from the characteristics of the vampire.

It was perhaps inevitable that with the twenty-first-century revival of interest in vampires a number of websites have provided focus and space for vampire poetry and for vampire poets to express their feelings. Contemporary vampire poems differ from the epic verse or ballad form of early vampire poetry in that they tend to be shorter and to focus on the subjective feelings of the poet, rather than telling a story. They also tend to focus more on forms of psychic vampirism rather than the traditional blood-drinking vampire, with vampirism providing a metaphor for the power play that takes place within human relationships and within society.

See also: LITERATURE

Poland

The vampires of Slavic Poland are notorious for their seemingly insatiable desire for blood and are known as *upior* (*upier* if male and *upierzyca* if female), a variation on the root Slavic word *opyrbi*. Another more obscure species of vampire in Poland is the *vjiesce*.

Much of the knowledge we have of the Polish vampires derives from research undertaken by Jan Perkowski among the Kashubs, northern Polish immigrants to Canada, where to this day belief in vampires remains present, although Perkowski acknowledges that it is declining due to the depersonalization of the processes of birth and death in hospitals. Among the Kashubs it was a common belief that a baby born with a caul or with two teeth would be a future vampire. Removing the caul, drying it, grinding it to a powder, and feeding this powder to the child at age seven would prevent this transformation. Those destined to become vampires were noted to have red faces and high energy levels, but otherwise they could lead normal lives. However, when they died their bodies had to be watched carefully and a number of preventative measures (see below) taken because it was thought they did not really die.

The upior

A description of the upior is given in the 1753 edition of the *Treatise on Vampires and Revenants* by the French Dominican monk and scholar Dom Augustin Calmet. Calmet's source for his description was an article published in the 1693/94 edition of the French journal *Mercure Gallant*. According to Calmet, the upior was characterized by its habit of eating its linen shroud when it revived from death, and the hours it kept – the upior can appear from noon to midnight. At night the upior attacks its friends and relatives, embracing them before sucking their blood. The way to destroy an upior is to exhume the corpse and then either decapitate it or *"open its heart."* Once opened up, the blood that gushed from the upior must then be mixed with flour to make dough and this dough should be baked into a bread that would cure those suffering from the after-affects of the vampire's bite.

Calmet records an incidence of suspected vampirism among the Polish in his treatise. No date is given but it would have to be sometime before 1753 when his treatise was written. The account concerns the intendant of Count Simon Labienski, Staroste of Posnan, who had died. The Countess Dowager Labienski decided that the dead man should be buried in the family crypt in recognition of his service and loyalty to the family. However, some time later the verger in charge of the crypt noticed that the position of the intendant's coffin had changed. He informed the Countess, and, as was the custom in Poland, the coffin was opened and the dead man decapitated. This was done in the presence of several people. When the body was lifted out of the coffin by the verger it was noticed that the dead man appeared to be grinning. And when his head was cut off the blood looked fresh. Some of this blood was collected on a white handkerchief and everyone drank some of it to ensure the house would not be haunted anymore.

Another early source on the Polish vampire is the manuscript *Everio Atheism* (The Destruction of Atheism) written by a Jesuit priest. This was reprinted in 1721 in a natural history of Poland, *Historia Naturalis Curiosa* *Regni Poloniae* by another Jesuit priest, Gabriel Rzaczynski. In this the upior rises from its grave and wanders past crossroads and houses, appearing here and there to various people. It often attacks the person who sees it and suffocates him. When the corpse of the vampire is exhumed, it is often found that not only is the flesh undecayed and flexible, but also the head, eyes, mouth, and the tongue sometimes move.

Prevention

The Poles developed a number of preventative measures against possible vampirism, such as prone burial (burial face down), placing a willow cross under the armpits, chin, and chest, and burying the body very deep within the ground. Seeds and nets would also be placed in the coffin in the belief that the vampire would be forced to count or untie at a rate of one seed or one knot a year. Staking and decapitation were also recommended, with the vampire's head placed between the corpse's feet to ensure that it could not return from the grave again to attack the living.

See also: **POMERANIA**

Polidori, John (1795–1821)

John George Polidori was an Italian-Scottish writer and poet, and physician to the charismatic poet Lord Byron. He was also the author of what has often been called the first modern vampire story – *The Vampyre* (1819) – which launched a new wave of interest in vampires and remained a dominant influence on vampire stage productions and literature until *Dracula* was written by Bram Stoker in 1897.

The Element Encyclopedia of Vampires

Polidori and Lord Byron

Polidori joined literary society after he had gained a medical degree from the University of Edinburgh at the age of 19. He was chosen by Byron's publisher to become Byron's physician and traveled with the poet on a trip to Europe in 1816. Soon the relationship between the two men became strained with Polidori, who had aspirations to become a writer himself, seesawing between admiration and resentment of Byron's treatment of him. On May 27 the two men reached Geneva and stayed at the Villa Diodati on Lake Geneva, where they were joined by the poet Percy Bysshe Shelley and his soon-to-be-wife, Mary Godwin.

Polidori immediately took a dislike to Shelley and Mary and the feeling appears to have been mutual. Relations within the group were strained when during a bout of bad weather a competition took place where each member of the party wrote a ghost story. Byron's story, which had vampiric elements, concerned two friends traveling to Greece, where one of them died. Before his death, however, he made his friend swear that he would not reveal the conditions of his death. Upon his return to England the surviving traveler discovered that his dead friend was not dead but having an affair with his sister.

The relationship between Polidori and Byron went from bad to worse and Polidori, hungry for money and for the fame he felt he deserved more than Byron, was dismissed from Byron's employment after September 1816.

The Vampyre

Byron had not seen any potential in his oral ghost story and abandoned it, but Polidori had kept a journal of his experiences in Europe and took the framework of the tale and wrote *The Vampyre*, part of a *"letter from Geneva, with anecdotes of Lord Byron."* The story appeared in *New Monthly* magazine in April 1819, prefaced with a description of the story-telling evening. The title character of the story, Lord Ruthven, bore strong similarities to Byron and the article implied that the author of *The Vampyre* was Byron himself, which caused it to receive more attention than it might have done had it appeared under Polidori's name.

Byron was outraged and declared: *"I have a personal dislike to vampires and the little acquaintance I have with them would by no means induce me to reveal their secrets."* Though Polidori was soon revealed as the true author, the tale remained strongly associated with Byron. The German poet Goethe announced that *The Vampyre* was *"the best thing Byron had written."* The story was soon translated into French, Spanish, German, and Swedish and turned into a three-act play.

To this day the controversy over the authorship of *The Vampyre* continues, even though Polidori tried to claim credit. Sadly, he never lived to see the far-reaching success of his efforts and continued to lead a troubled life. He incurred heavy gambling debts and committed suicide in 1821 at the age of 26.

See also: **LITERATURE**

Political Vampires

In May 1732 an article entitled "Political Vampires" was reprinted in the London *Gentleman's Magazine*. Thought to be one of the earliest uses of the word "vampire" in the English language, the article – which closely followed the March 1732 publication in the *London Journal* of an English translation of the Arnold Paole investigation – is a satire comparing the evils of the undead to the more terrifyingly real evils of living vampires.

Vampirism as a metaphor

The 1732 article makes it clear how easy it is to use vampirism as a metaphor for the blood-sucking and life-draining evils of government. The article states that vampires are said to *"torment and kill the living by sucking their blood"* and that in the real world a *"ravenous Minister"* can be compared to a *"leech or a bloodsucker"* who *"carries his oppression beyond the grave, by anticipating the publick revenues, and entailing a perpetuity of taxes, which must gradually drain the body politick of its blood and spirits."*

Vampirism as a political/economic metaphor was recognized by Voltaire in 1764 in his *Philosophical Dictionary*, in which he sarcastically noted that when compared to the vampire hysteria reported in Eastern Europe, *"we never heard a word of vampires in London, nor even Paris."* He goes on to explain that in both these cities there were brokers and men of business who *"sucked the blood out of people in broad daylight; but they were not dead, though corrupted ... These true suckers lived not in cemeteries but in very agreeable palaces."*

Vampirarchy

In the nineteenth century the German political theorist Karl Marx used the vampire metaphor to condemn the capitalist bourgeoisie. For Marx capitalism and industry sucked the life out of the worker. In *Das Kapital* he famously wrote: *"Capital is dead labor, which vampire-like lives only sucking living labor and lives the more the more labor it sucks."* In a similar fashion political humorists of the nineteenth century sometimes referred to the ruling classes as a "vampirarchy" rather than as a "hierarchy."

Some literary critics have emphasized the social comment hidden within Bram Stoker's 1897 novel *Dracula*, suggesting that the tale expressed fears about the decline of the British Empire and the civilized world. In the person of Dracula the uncivilized unknown of the East and racial strife attempt to corrupt and conquer London. In other words Dracula represents Victorian racism. After Mina is bitten by the Count she becomes "unclean."

More recently, vampirism has been strongly associated with Communist regimes, in particular that of the Romanian dictator Nicolae Ceauşescu. *Mad Forest* (1990), a play by Caryl Churchill that includes a dialog between a vampire and a dog, is set in Romania in the wake of the Ceauşescu regime. In the play vampirism is associated with political corruption and economic and social exploitation.

The metaphor's continuing resonance

During the twentieth century and beyond the vampire has remained a stock metaphor for political, economic, and social corruption. War, fascism, atheism, and consumerism have all been labeled vampiric. Vampire stories have been especially prominent in the political tensions and fears created by colonization, from the point of view of smaller, less complex cultures being taken over by cultures that are larger and more complicated. In East and Central Africa rumors have spread in the form of "vampire" stories about workers suspected of conspiring with white men to drain the blood of Africans. Not surprisingly, with such stories circulating and many Africans believing them, drives to encourage blood donation for medical purposes have proved ineffective.

Another less valid and dramatic example is the formation of "Operation Vampire Killer 2000," a step-by-step program allegedly launched to inform police, the military, and law enforcement units about the formation of a so-called New World Order. This refers to a conspiracy theory in which a powerful order of wealthy individuals has supposedly created a secret plan to eventually rule the world via a unitary world government.

See also: **SYMBOLS**

Polong

In Malaysian folklore the polong is a vampiric imp or spirit the shape of a thumb, usually female, with the ability to fly. The polong is created when a magician or sorcerer places the blood of a murder victim in a bottle and says certain incantations over it. Within two weeks the sound of chirping birds is heard and the polong will emerge from the bottle. Its human creator then cuts a finger daily for the polong to suck. The polong can be dispatched by its creator to attack his or her enemies and burrow

into them, making them sick and mad until they eventually die. The polong has a pet or plaything called a pelesit, a cricket-like demon spirit that burrows with its sharp tail into the polong's victim first and prepares a tunnel for the polong to enter and suck the victim's blood.

Murder by a polong can be detected when large amounts of blood issue from the mouth of a corpse and also from extensive bruising. Aside from keeping the creature in its bottle, reciting charms, or forcing its creator to remove it from the victim, there are few remedies against its attacks.

See also: **MALAYSIA**

Poltergeist

From the German words *poltern*, "to crash" and *geist*, "spirit," "poltergeist" is the term used to describe a ghost or energy form which specializes in making sounds and moving things about a house or building, often resulting in breakages. These spirits can be malevolent but on the whole are thought to be mischievous nuisances. The attacks of poltergeists have long been associated with the characteristics of vampire attacks – for example, the so-called Belgrade Vampire.

The earliest reports of poltergeist activity date back to ancient Rome, and they continue to be reported to this day. Characteristics of a poltergeist attack typically include flying objects, especially dirt and rocks, extremely loud noises, terrible smells, raps, strange lights and apparitions, and the opening and shutting of doors and windows. Modern manifestations include light bulbs exploding or spinning in their sockets and telephone malfunctions. In a tiny percentage of cases physical assaults, such as scratching, biting, spitting, and sexual molestation are reported. In most cases poltergeist activity starts and stops suddenly and lasts from a few hours to a few years, although most often carries on for a few months. Activity usually occurs when a particular individual is present and that individual is most often female and under 20 years of age.

Explanations

Since the late nineteenth century poltergeists have been the subject of serious study by psychical researchers and a number of theories have been put forward to explain the phenomenon. Until the nineteenth century poltergeist activity was blamed on demons, vampires, witches, ghosts, or the Devil. Such cases resembled possession and clergy were often called in for exorcisms. In the 1930s, however, psychical researcher Nandor Fodor came to the conclusion that is still widely held today – that poltergeists are a type of unconscious psychokinesis on the part of the living, the so-called agent. In other words, unconscious thought processes somehow produce the phenomena. At first attention focused on repressed sexual tension as a cause or factor but due to the frequency of poltergeist activity in households with disturbed adolescents experiencing frustration and emotional tension, later researchers theorized that poltergeists were projections of repressed anger and hostility. Psychokinesis is therefore an unconscious way for a child to express that anger and distress within the family without the fear of punishment, and in most cases the child has no idea they are causing the disturbances.

Other poltergeist investigators disagree with the psychokinesis theory and point out that in numerous cases the agent is emotionally stable. Some believe the idea that poltergeists are spirits of the dead has been too often overlooked. Still others suggest that poltergeist activity is a form of conscious or unconscious psychic attack activated by a stressful situation, and the activity is a projection of some element of the agent's personality into an apparition-like form or astral body, which can somehow separate from the agent's body and be the cause of the disturbances.

Polycrites

Polycrites, also known as Philocrites, was a vampire of the ancient world whose story was recounted by the early nineteenth-century writer Jacques Collin de Plancy in his *Dictionnaire Infernal* (1818).

Polycrites was a respected citizen and governor of Aetolia in ancient Greece. After serving in office for three years he died, just four days after his marriage to a woman from Locris. His widow went on to give birth to a hermaphrodite, a sexless baby, regarded as an omen of forthcoming war between Aetolia and Locris. The augurs believed that the only way to prevent this happening was to burn both mother and child. When the fires were lit Polycrites appeared, looking pale and terrifying in a robe that was stained with blood. He threatened great misfortune if his family were killed, and when the crowd didn't take him seriously he ate his own child. The crowd threw stones at him but this did not harm Polycrites in any way, and a delegation was sent to the oracle at Delphi to seek advice. Polycrites eventually disappeared, but he left behind the head of his child (the only part that remained uneaten), which prophesized terrible calamities for everyone.

Polynesia

Throughout Polynesia, which includes the Hawaiian Islands, Samoa, Tonga, Easter Island, and New Zealand, tales concerning bloodthirsty revenants and vampire species sometimes known as *tu* are fairly common and typically handed down orally from generation to generation. In most cases the revenant will return from the dead to attack a family or village for a specific reason. In Hawaii, for example, often that reason is to complain about improper burial rites or to reveal or take revenge for some evil that has or is being committed among the living.

Pomerania

Pomerania is an historic region on the southern edge of the Baltic Sea, split today between Poland and northern Germany, with a strong vampire tradition. One unique vampire custom among the Pomeranians was to place a song book in the coffin of the deceased to provide the corpse with entertainment and to distract it from chewing its shroud. Another custom involved taking a part of the shroud of the revenant, dipping it in the revenant's blood, squeezing the blood out of the shroud into a glass of brandy and drinking it, to protect against future attacks.

As late as 1870 in Neustatt-an-der-Rheda (today's Wejherowo) in Pomerania there was a suspected outbreak of vampirism, when a citizen by the name of Franz von Poblocki died of consumption. Within days his son, Anton, died and other relatives complained of fatigue and nightmares. Family members hired Johan Dzigielski, a vampire hunter, to decapitate the corpses of Franz and Anton and place the heads between the corpses' legs. The local priest complained to the authorities and Dzigielski was arrested, tried, and sentenced to jail for four months. He never served his full term though, and was released early when his family appealed the decision.

Pontianak

The pontianak, also known as the *mati-anak* from the term *matiberanak* meaning "still born," is a type of vampire found in Malaysia and Indonesia that is said to be the still-born child of a female vampire, the langsuir. This child is likely to become a vampire and so special care must be taken at its burial. To prevent the creature leaving its grave, eggs must be placed under each armpit; a needle must be stabbed into the palm of the hand and glass beads must be put in the mouth. As a vampire the pontianak was said to appear as a night owl that, banshee-like, could be heard wailing as it flew about in the night. It would attack babies and suck their blood out of jealousy over the death of its mother, the langsuir, in childbirth. It would also attack young men. The only way for the young man to escape death was to grab the pontianak's long hair – which covered a hole in their back – and pull out a single strand.

The pontianak was featured in a number of Malaysian films, beginning in 1956 with *Pontianak*, the story of a woman who is made beautiful by magic. When her husband is bitten by a snake she sucks out the venom and in the process becomes a vampire. She attempts to vampirize her daughter but is killed before she can do so. Other pontianak-themed films followed. However they were seen by few in the West prior to their release in the United States on video, and had little effect on the developing image of the vampire in Hollywood.

Poppy Seeds

Due to the narcotic nature of the plant, poppy seeds are associated with rest. Strewn on the ground around graves they have been used for centuries to distract revenants or help the dead rest peacefully in their graves.

See also: **PREVENTION; SEEDS**

Porphyria

Porphyria, often incorrectly called vampire disease, is the medical term given to a rare congenital blood disease with symptoms that are similar to what we now perceive as the classic characteristics of a vampire. The disease is due to a recessive gene and affects more men than women.

The term "porphyria" is derived from the Greek word for purple, because purple urine is one of the symptoms of the disorder, the urine turning dark red after exposure to sunlight and fluorescent under ultraviolet light. It is also known as "King George III's disease" after the English king who suffered from it. People with porphyria have problems producing heme, an essential component of red blood cells. This means they often suffer from photosensitivity (sensitivity to sunlight), lack of pigmentation, chemical imbalances, and poor wound healing. They also become allergic to garlic (the herb stimulates heme production and can turn a mild case of porphryia into a severe and painful one) and often have tightened skin around the lips and gums, thus making the incisors more conspicuous. The disease is a serious medical disorder but is extremely rare and has often been misdiagnosed, as certain forms of porphyria are also associated with neurological symptoms, which can create nervous or psychiatric disorders.

Until the mid twentieth century porphyria was relatively unknown. Then in 1985 Professor David Dolphin made headlines when in a presentation to the American Association for the Advancement of Science he suggested that symptoms of porphyria might be responsible for reports of vampirism. Dolphin noted that one treatment was injections of heme, and suggested that people suffering from the condition in previous centuries might have tried to drink the blood of others in an attempt to alleviate the symptoms.

Dophin's theory received a lot of attention at the time but his suggestion that porphyria sufferers crave the heme in human blood, or that the consumption of blood might ease the

The Element Encyclopedia of Vampires

symptoms of porphyria, is based on a severe misunderstanding of the disease. There is no real evidence to suggest that drinking blood will alleviate the disease or that porphyria had anything to do with the development of the original vampire folklore. The reports do not describe people who had symptoms of porphyria and typically related to descriptions of corpses, not living persons. In addition, porphyria is rare so it is unlikely to provide an explanation for many cases of clinical vampirism or lycanthropy.

In recent years some porphyria patients have felt embarrassed by the speculative link between the disease and vampirism, but there is no evidence to suggest that porphyria patients are, or ever were, vampires.

See also: **DISEASE; DOLPHIN HYPOTHESIS**

Portugal

Portugal does not have an extensive tradition of vampires, but there is a strong belief in a female species of the undead known as bruxsa.

Although the country only has a limited vampire tradition it does have at least one so-called living vampire. On September 17, 1910, near the town of Galazanna, Portugal, a child was found dead in a field. The corpse was bloodless. The child had been seen last with a man named Salvarrey. He was arrested, and confessed that he was a vampire, although he was probably just a disturbed individual suffering from clinical vampirism.

See also: **SPAIN**

Possega Vampire

According to vampirologist Klaus Hamberger in his *Mortuus Non Mordet* (1992), at the beginning of 1730 a vampire in the shape of a snake killed and drained the blood of a sheep. A man found the sheep and took it home to feed his wife and children. They all got sick and died. People in the nearby village of Possega (which may be Pozjega in Croatia) heard about the case and sent some doctors to investigate. The investigators learned that in 1721 something similar had occurred when people had been sucked and killed by vampires in the shape of snakes. The graves of the victims who had recently died were opened and it was found that the most recent victim – a man who had died three weeks previously – looked fresh and uncorrupted, so a stake was placed through the corpse's heart. To be on the safe side all the corpses were decapitated and cremated.

Possession

Possession is a form of psychic attack, or a condition in which a person feels they have been taken over or controlled mentally, physically, and emotionally by an outside spirit entity or separate personality.

Some possessions are benign, for example voluntary and temporary ones that take place during séances or religious services, but more often than not it is a malevolent or evil spirit or demon that attempts to take over the body and mind of an unwilling subject. Unwilling possession is not always viewed as demonic. It is sometimes held that possessing spirits are souls of the dead who do not realize they are dead and try to return to a body, or that they are spirits who have a message they want to communicate to someone. In either case, victims of unwanted possession hear voices and experience extreme mood disorders, poltergeist phenomena, and, in some cases, bouts of insanity.

In both folklore traditions and literature the bite of a vampire can lead to symptoms of possession; the victim either slowly dies or transforms into a vampire. In Bram Stoker's *Dracula* (1897), for example, once bitten by Dracula Mina Harker displays many of the violent and uncontrolled malevolent characteristics of possession by an evil entity. The cure for unwanted possession is exorcism, performed according to a specific ritual. Except for possession by the Holy Spirit, Christianity regards possession as the work of the Devil and cases of demonic possession and exorcisms to remove the spirits continue to be reported to this day.

The belief that mental illnesses, such as multiple personality disorder and clinical vampirism, may be caused by spirit possession is an ancient one. In the nineteenth century, spiritism, a European offshoot of spiritualism founded by French physician Allan Kardec, holds that mental illnesses have a spiritual cause and can be treated by communicating with spirit guides. Kardec's theories did not catch on in Europe but they did find an enthusiastic response in Brazil, where to this day Brazilians practice spiritual healing. In the early part of the twentieth century, James Hyslop, President of the American Society of Psychical Research, suggested that many people suffering from personality disorders could be showing signs of spirit possession. This view has the support of a few psychiatrists but it is not endorsed by the wider medical and scientific community.

It is not just the living that can be possessed by evil entities. From ancient times the notion that corpses can be reanimated by evil spirits has been widespread. In medieval times preserved bodies, corpses that did not decay as expected, or individuals that had been excommunicated from the Church were thought to be the perfect vehicle for possession by evil spirits and demons. It was thought that a demon animated the corpse, which emerged from the grave as a revenant or vampire and wandered the earth in search of nourishment: the blood of the living.

See also: **EXCOMMUNICATION; EXORCISM; PSYCHIC VAMPIRE**

Potsherd

In parts of Europe a potsherd, or piece of broken earthenware, was used as a way to prevent the dead returning from their graves. For example, among the Kashubs in Prussia, a piece of pot was put into the mouth of a corpse so that it could chew on that instead of itself or surviving family members. And in Chios in the Greek islands, during a funeral service the priest would put a potsherd bearing the legend "Jesus Christ conquers" on the lips of the body.

See also: **PREVENTION**

Powers, of Vampires

Confusion and misunderstandings are commonplace when the powers of vampires are discussed, as it is often very hard to distinguish between what is real and documented and what is fantasy. The folklore vampire certainly does not have as many supernatural powers as the vampire of fiction. Indeed, many documented cases of "real" vampires indicate that they simply sucked the blood of their victims and then ran away.

Listed below are the most common attributes of the physical vampire of folklore, but it is important to note that not all species of the undead possess the powers listed, and that fictional vampires in literature and film will have variations of these powers.

Primary powers

🩸 The ability to live off the blood of humans.

🩸 Great strength. In most documented cases of vampire attack, victims report not being able to defend themselves against the vampire when it feeds. Later in fiction and film this power would be developed into superhuman strength that increases with age.

🩸 The ability to create other vampires by biting them at least three times.

🩸 Invulnerability. Vampires have remarkable recuperative powers and cannot be harmed by conventional weapons. They are also immune to all forms of human diseases and illnesses. Only when moving about during the day or when resting in its coffin is the vampire vulnerable.

Secondary powers

The secondary powers of the vampire vary from species to species, but here are some of the most commonly reported.

🩸 Sexual relations with the living. The vampire's ability to do that is similar to the powers of the incubus/succubus.

🩸 Sire children.

🩸 Live life again as a mortal. Another attribute of the physical vampire in some regions is the ability at some point to live a mortal life again. For instance, the langsuir, the female vampire of Malaysia, can be captured and cured of her vampirism to the extent that she can rejoin the human race and lead a normal life.

🩸 Shape-shift. The ability to turn into bats, cats, dogs and wolves, butterflies, insects, rats, birds, mice, snakes, and locusts.

🩸 Flying. Some vampire species, such as the langsuir and aswang, can fly or levitate. Other vampires change shape to fly.

🩸 Misting. The ability to vaporize themselves into mist so they can enter rooms through chimneys, keyholes, etc.

🩸 Agility. The ability to scale walls or escape from impossible situations.

🩸 Acute hearing and sight. Some vampires possess acute hearing (equivalent to that of a wolf) and night vision, enabling them to see with better than 20/20 vision in total darkness.

🩸 The ability to control the direction of the wind, rain, and other natural forces.

🩸 Power of control over many creatures including rats, bats, and flies.

- *Longevity, although this varies in length; not all vampires are immortal.*

- *The ability to cause crop failures and the deaths of livestock.*

- *The ability to cause plagues and epidemics.*

- *The ability to cause impotence.*

- *Some vampires can control the will of humans through a form of hypnotism, even to the point of inducing a catatonic state and amnesia. This power explains why victims often have no memory of being attacked. This hypnotic control can be conveyed either verbally or telepathically, depending on the power of the vampire.*

- *The ability to project an astral form to attack a victim or to somehow drain the vitality, beauty, strength, and sanity of its victim.*

The fictional vampires of today have dropped many of the limitations imposed by superstition and have acquired more supernatural powers than their previous incarnations. As well as the powers listed above, a list of vampire traits today could also include:

- *The ability to command demons or communicate with the Devil.*

- *The ability to project their voice to ear-shattering levels.*

- *The ability to move with great speed.*

- *The ability to jump great heights.*

- *The ability to read minds.*

- *The ability to heal their own wounds and the wounds of others.*

- *The ability to re-grow hair that has been cut.*

- *The ability to mimic speech.*

- *The ability to read with hyper speed.*

- *The ability to move objects at will.*

- *The ability to endure the sun.*

- *The weeping of blood tears.*

- *The ability to feel more vividly than they did as humans.*

- *The ability to raise the dead, who will come to the vampire to be commanded like zombies.*

In her landmark book *American Vampires: Fans, Victims, Practitioners* (1990), vampire researcher Norine Dresser suggests that along with the allure of immortality and forbidden sex, it is the power (or powers) of the vampire that explains their enduring appeal in American society, where winners and powerful people are highly valued.

See also: **AGING, OF VAMPIRES; PSYCHIC ATTACK; WEAKNESSES, OF VAMPIRES**

Predisposition/Predestination

See: **BAD SIGNS/OMENS**

Pregnant Women

Pregnant women are frequent victims of vampire attacks in vampire lore. They can also give birth to future vampires and, like the Malaysian langsuir, become vampires themselves should they die during or just after childbirth. In Romanian lore there are a number of traditions about vampires and pregnant women. For example, should a vampire look at a pregnant woman after her sixth month it is held that she is destined to give birth to a vampire; the only way to prevent this happening is to receive a church blessing.

The process of decomposition may account for why pregnant women were often viewed as especially apt to become revenants during the seventeenth- and eighteenth-century vampire crazes that swept through Europe. When the body of a pregnant woman decomposed the fetus can be expelled from the uterus. It would have appeared to the exhumers of the body that the woman's corpse had given birth in the grave.

Premature Burial

Premature burial, when an individual is buried alive, has frequently been suggested by experts as contributing significantly to the spread of vampire fears in eighteenth-century Europe. In earlier times, those who woke in the grave or tomb and managed to escape would have been regarded with terror and hysteria by those who had buried them. Fears that they had returned from the grave as vampires to feed on the living would have been enormous. Those who did not manage to escape from their graves and died of suffoca-

tion may also have been regarded as vampires if their bodies were exhumed. Their frantic and desperate struggle to escape would have changed their body position in the grave and resulted in torn fingernails and wounds – all signs that could have been misinterpreted as vampirism or evidence of life beyond death. In his 1896 book *Premature Burial*, Franz Hartmann analyzed premature burial in morbid detail.

Eighteenth-century physicians would simply not have been able to determine whether a person was actually dead or in a coma or cataleptic state, so the incidence of premature burial may have been fairly high. The Roman naturalist Pliny the Elder was convinced that many of those who were buried were actually alive. In Eastern Europe corpse mutilation and cremation were used to guarantee death. The Bavarians adopted a waiting period before burial, placing corpses in a hut for a while to determine if they were really dead.

"The Premature Burial" (1844) and "Berenice" (1835), two short stories by American poet and writer Edgar Allan Poe, superbly capture what must have been the grotesque and terrifyingly claustrophobic nature of premature burial.

See also: **CATALEPSY**

Pret

In Indian mythology the pret, also known as the paret or pretni, is held to be the ghost of a deformed child or one that died at birth. After its burial the pret, said to be the size of a man's thumb, wanders the earth weak and sad for a period of 12 months. It cannot drink water because it has been banned from water by Varuna, the deity of water, but villagers will leave it offerings of food and drink. Milk is poured into vessels with small holes cut into them so the liquid seeps out, which allows the pret to drink in midair, as the creature cannot touch the ground. The creature was feared because if it was not placated with offerings it was likely to become a bhut, a malevolent vampire-like creature.

Prevention

European peasants developed many rites and customs to keep the dead from rising from the grave. The choice of method depended on the people, region, and dominant religion, but whatever procedures were chosen, they were typically performed immediately after death or during burial.

Common steps to ensure a vampire did not rise from the grave included the following.

Pre-burial steps:

- *Closing all windows to prevent the soul of the deceased escaping. (In some areas, however, windows were opened.)*

- *Stopping any clocks at the time of death to put the corpse in a state of suspended animation, to prevent demonic forces entering the body.*

- *Covering all mirrors (and standing water) because the reflective surfaces were believed to reveal the soul, and because if a corpse is seen in the mirror by the living, the soul can have no rest and is at risk of becoming a vampire. For the same reason the eyes of the corpse were closed.*

- *Placing a glowing candle near to the body to provide it with light to find its way to the underworld. Without this guidance it was thought the soul might get lost and become a vampire.*

- *Preventing animals from jumping over the corpse, as this was a sure sign of impending vampirism.*

- *Preventing moonlight from falling on the corpse and energizing it.*

- *To prevent a vampire from chewing its way out of the grave, people would stuff the corpse's mouth with coins or dirt or garlic, or prop the mouth shut.*

- *Painting doors with tar to prevent evil entering.*

- *Weeping at the funeral. In Italy and Greece especially, crying is required at a funeral because it is said that if a person is not mourned properly they will return in the form of a vampire.*

- *Watching over the corpse continuously to check for signs of supernatural activity.*

- *Removing the corpse though a hole cut into wall of house.*

- *Mutilating the corpse by hamstringing it, removing the heart, placing thorns in the* mouth, pounding a stake into the chest or nails into various body parts. By wounding the body in this way it was thought to make it impossible for the Devil to "inflate" the corpse.

🩸 Placing a songbook or cross or brick under the chin to distract the corpse with music or prevent it chewing.

🩸 Burying the corpse with food to eliminate a possible need for it to leave the grave and feed on humans. A Romanian tradition was to carry bread and wine to the gravesite within a few days of burial.

🩸 In Bulgaria, the nostrils, eyes, and ears of a corpse were stuffed with millet to prevent vampirism.

🩸 Binding the corpse by tying the mouth shut, and tying the feet and legs together to prevent it moving.

🩸 Decapitating the corpse and placing the head under the arm or between the legs of the body, or burying it in a separate grave.

Preventative steps taken at the burial included:

🩸 Placing the body face down so that it cannot crawl back to earth after burial.

🩸 In Romania, people buried a candle, a coin, and a towel in with the corpse to prevent vampirism.

🩸 The corpse may be weighed down with rocks or wrapped in a net to confine it in its coffin for centuries (according to German tradition, a revenant could only untie one knot per year).

🩸 Sharp objects, such as knives, daggers, nails, and thorns, were placed on the corpse to prevent it rising. In Romania a sickle was often placed across the neck so that if a corpse tried to move it would decapitate itself. A sickle can also be used to pierce the heart.

🩸 Filling the coffin with poppy, mustard, or carrot seeds or millet grain, and strewing the path around the graveyard with seeds to distract the vampire (Eastern Europeans believed that the corpse would be compelled to eat each seed, at a rate of one seed a year, before leaving its grave).

🩸 Placing stakes around the coffin so if the vampire tried to rise from the grave, its heart would be pierced.

🩸 Burying the corpse at a crossroads.

🩸 Headstones were originally used not as a memorial to the person buried in the grave, but as a weight to prevent a vampire from escaping.

🩸 Cremating the corpse.

See also: **APOTROPAICS; BURIAL CUSTOMS; CREMATION; PROTECTION**

Price, Vincent (1911–93)

Although American actor Vincent Price was an immensely successful horror film actor in his day, he never got to play the big screen role that he might have been perfect for: Dracula. He did, however, star in several films featuring vampires, which included *The Last Man on Earth* (1964), *The Oblong Box* (1969), *The*

Monster Club (1975), and *Diary of a Madman* (1963). Price was also the host of *Dracula: The Great Undead*, a 1982 TV documentary.

See also: **Films**

Prone Burial

"Prone burial" is the term used to describe the Eastern European custom of burying a corpse face down. The origins of this tradition are obscure but may date back to the ancient Celts and ideas about widdershins – the reversal of direction of something about to enter the world of the dead. It was held that burying a corpse face down either confuses a rising vampire as to which direction is up, or makes it impossible to get out of the coffin. According to cultural historian Paul Barber, a corpse buried face down cannot become a vampire because it will not be able to perform the destructive task of chewing its burial shroud or limbs while in the grave. If the corpse was allowed to chew, it was believed that through that action it would spread death (in the form of disease) to the living. And even if a corpse did become a vampire, burying it face down would prevent the vampire from ever finding the surface and escaping its grave. In addition, the Silesians believed that the gaze of a vampire was deadly, and turning the body toward the earth would prevent it gazing on anyone disinterring it.

Some reports leave it unclear as to whether the vampire lies prone because he or she was buried that way or because he or she chose to. If the latter was the case, a vampire might actually be recognized by its prone position rather than having been placed thus to prevent it from rising from its grave.

See also: **Burial Customs**

Prostitution

The persona of the vampire can sometimes blend in with that of the prostitute, as both are said to be predatory "creatures of the night." In Victorian times, prostitutes were dreaded carriers of syphilis, an incurable disease, which like AIDS today fed the notion that vampirism is a sexual contagion.

See also: **Female Vampires**

Protection

There are a number of folklore precautions that are said to protect animals, homes, and people from vampire attacks. Methods of protection differ from region to region and country to country, but some of the most common means of securing safety are listed below:

- Garlic: *This is the most common protective herb, rubbed on windows, doors, hung around the neck, or rubbed on the body.*

- Magic or witchcraft: *The earliest protection known to have been used against vampires was magical words and acts. In the first century AD, Ovid records an ancient child-protection ritual that included sprinkling the entrance of the house with water, touching the door of the infant's room with a plant, and sacrificing a pig to the strix.*

- Thorns: *Considered to be magical barriers against vampires and witches.*

- Turning objects upside down: *In Romanian lore, on St. Andrew's Eve – when vampires were believed to be most active – all objects in*

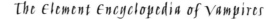

the home were turned upside down. On St. George's Eve – another day closely associated with vampires – people traditionally turned their shirts inside out and slept reversed in bed, with their feet where their head should be, to confuse the vampire.

🖌 Calling three times: *In Romanian lore it was believed that you should never answer someone unless they call three times, because it was said that vampires can only ask a question twice. If someone answers a vampire the vampire has the power to kill them.*

🖌 Bullet: *In Romania as recently as the nineteenth century, the precaution of shooting a bullet through a person's coffin was taken.*

🖌 Drinking ashes: *For suspected cases of vampirism, the body of the vampire was dismembered and the pieces burned, mixed with water, and drunk by family members as a cure.*

🖌 Lemon: *In Saxony in Germany, a lemon was placed in the mouth of suspected vampires.*

🖌 Crosses or crucifixes: *Holy objects are believed to ward off vampires. Crosses painted with tar on doors and windows are also protective, as are objects and icons that have been blessed.*

🖌 Holy water: *Vials of blessed water can be poured on graves, thrown on vampires, or sprinkled around a house.*

🖌 Incense: *Burned for cleaning and protection.*

🖌 Bells: *The constant ringing of bells will drive away vampires.*

🖌 Candles: *Light deters vampires.*

🖌 Eating blood bread: *This method, where the blood of a suspected vampire was gathered and mixed in with dough to make bread, was used in Poland; in Pomerania a blood and brandy mix was drunk. In both cases, it was said to provide protection against further vampire attack.*

🖌 Seeds and grain: *Seeds, such as mustard, and grains like oats or millet, were scattered on yards and walkways to distract vampires, who were regarded as obsessive about counting.*

🖌 Fire: *A major element in destroying vampires, fire could also be used to drive them away.*

🖌 Fishing nets: *These were placed on windows and doors where vampires were thought to be obsessed with untying knots.*

🖌 Knives: *Along with needles and scissors, knives were placed near the bed to be used as protection.*

🖌 Iron: *Metal, typically pieces of iron or silver, was thought to keep vampires away.*

🖌 Bread and cheese: *Among some Slavic Gypsies, offerings of bread and cheese were made to appease vampires. In Transylvania wine was buried with bodies for the same purpose.*

🖌 Holly, hawthorn, *and wild rose are all said to harm vampires.*

🖌 Mirrors: *Although not traditionally regarded as an apotropaic, mirrors have been used to ward off vampires when placed facing outwards on a door.*

🖌 Prayer: *Always considered useful.*

With the secularization of the vampire myth and the increasing strength and power of the modern vampire in literature, most of the protective attributes of the traditional items used against vampires have been lost, with the possible exception of garlic. Modern vampires are not typically affected by holy objects, seeds, or grains. They can even overcome fire. The only form of protection left to humans appears to be the vampire's own moral or ethical code or resolution not to kill.

See also: **APOTROPAICS; BURIAL CUSTOMS; DESTRUCTION; PREVENTION**

Psychic Attack

The term "psychic attack" refers to an alleged supernatural or magical attack that drains the energy and life force of a person, animal, or crop. It is typically caused by non-physical agents, such as spirits and demons, which attack a person, mentally and/or physically. In some cases these agents are sent to vampirize another person by a witch, magician, sorcerer, or vampire. Vampires are capable of psychic attack, as numerous accounts of attacks in Eastern European vampire literature testify.

Almost every culture has its techniques of psychic attack, from the Huna death prayer to the voodoo dolls of Haiti. In sorcery the equivalent of psychic attack is the curse. Symptoms of psychic attack resemble old hag syndrome and include extreme fatigue, depression, and nightmares.

Negative energy

The nineteenth-century German physician and psychical researcher Franz Hartmann described the experience of a psychic attack.

[They] *vampirize every sensitive person with whom they come in contact, and they instinctively seek out such persons and invite them to stay in their houses. I know of an old lady, a vampire, who thus ruined the health of a lot of robust servant girls, whom she took into her service and made them sleep in her room. They were all in good health when they entered, but soon they began to sicken, they became emaciated and consumptive and had to leave the service.*

Such attacks may leave the victim feeling extremely depressed, confused, and even suicidal. After experiencing such an attack it is said that the victims themselves may start to suck up the life force or energy of others.

Occultists believe that psychic attacks are the manipulation of supernatural energies and forces. They occur when dark and negative energetic vibrations are sent from one individual to another or to a place, creating disturbances in the energetic and physical bodies of that person or place. This negative energy can be called a spirit, an entity, a thought form, or a dark negative energy.

Whatever it is called, negative energy when sent is believed to create harmful effects within the person who is the recipient of that energy. Sometimes dark energies are sent unconsciously, for example when a person thinks negative things about someone else. At other times, however, negative energy is sent intentionally by the deliberate

The Element Encyclopedia of Vampires

sending of powerful thought forms and/or through ritualistic techniques or ceremonies, typically performed when the moon is either new or waning. (The moon is said to govern psychic forces and these lunar phases rule the so-called left hand or evil path of magic.) This is also why psychic attack typically occurs at night when the victim is sleeping, because these are the times when psychic resistance is believed to be at its lowest.

According to occultists, most people are immune to psychic attack because their energy fields are vital and strong. However, the strength of their energy fields can be weakened by depression and negative thinking, dabbling in the occult, extreme sensitivity, or falling victim to a person who is adept at handling and directing negative energy.

Dion Fortune

In her classic 1930 text *Psychic Self-Defence* (1930), English occultist Dion Fortune maintained that psychic attack was much more common than usually believed. She gave an account of her own experience of psychic attack when aged 20. She believed she was psychically attacked by her employer, which depleted her energy field, or aura, to such an extent that she suffered a nervous breakdown. On one occasion Fortune reported waking up in the morning with dried blood on her pillow from a small puncture wound on her jaw. She believed that this puncture wound had been caused by a psychic vampire.

Fortune asserted that there were two kinds of psychic attack: by non-physical entities, and by human beings. The non-physical entities are demons or thought forms created by magic that may be acting on their own or be directed by a human being. Psychic attacks by human beings are perpetrated by traveling out of the body in an astral form.

According to Fortune, the purpose of psychic attack is to weaken and destroy, to make the victim obey the attacker, or simply to draw off energy. Symptoms include overwhelming feelings of dread and fear, nervous exhaustion, mental breakdown, bruises on the body, poor health, and in extreme cases death. The weight on the chest of a sleeper, a symptom of hag attack, is another primary symptom. In all cases the victim feels psychically drained or vampirized of their life force.

Fortune's prescribed defenses against psychic attack are to sever all contact with the suspected people and places; to avoid going to the sea, for water is the element of psychic forces; to keep the stomach full, as this shuts down the psychic points of entry; to get plenty of sunshine; to avoid being alone; and to undertake certain protective and banishing rituals, such as picturing an ovoid shell of white mist surrounding one's body, which becomes stronger and denser with each breath whenever entering crowds or encountering undesirable or threatening individuals or situations.

Power of suggestion

Most psychical researchers today assume that if psychic attack works it is through the power of suggestion, and that superstitious, poorly educated people are likely to be the most gullible and therefore the most vulnerable. It seems, however, that well-educated, non-superstitious people are not immune to psychic attack, and that even domestic animals, not normally expected to react to suggestion, are affected.

Although they admit that in certain circumstancs suggestion plays a part, occultists generally assert that psychic attack is real and that this real technique operates via the projection of the astral body. They also hold that not all cases of psychic vampirism are perpetrated by calculating and malevolent people or intentional psychic vampires.

Psychic Vampire

The term "psychic vampire" refers to the disembodied spirit or astral body of a living person when this body is sent out to menace others. It can also refer to living people who drain others emotionally. Psychic vampires are said to feed upon the life force or energy field that surrounds people and "psychic vampirism" is the term used to describe the act of preying on the life force or energy of others. Unlike blood-drinking vampires, psychic vampires drain the energy of unwilling victims through psychic attack.

The life force

The traditional vampire needs blood to survive but there is a type of vampire in folklore, literature, and (if the many accounts of alleged psychic attacks are to believed) in real life that supports his or her life by vampirizing or draining the energy or vitality of others. In the words of vampirologist Montague Summers in *The Vampire: His Kith and Kin* (1928): "*He may be called a spiritual vampire, or as he has been dubbed a 'psychic sponge'.*"

Today, this type of vampire has become known as a psychic vampire, although they can also be referred to as energy vampires, psychological vampires or PSI vampires – PSI referring to the life force.

Occult explanation

Some experts believe that the universality and immortality of the vampire myth can be explained by the idea of psychic vampirism. Psychic vampirism originated with the earliest vampire-like beings, which were described as demons, such as the lamia, or with folktales that depicted the vampire as a life-draining, disease-bringing ghost or spirit rather than as a physical body.

In centuries past, doctors warned against letting small children sleep in the same room as old people, as it was thought that old people could prolong their lives by draining the energy of the young. The nineteenth-century doctor Laurence Oliphant wrote about this belief in *Scientific Religion*: "*Many persons are so constituted that they have the extraordinary faculty for sucking the life principle from others who are constitutionally incapable of retaining their vitality.*"

Although vampires have been part of human culture for thousands of years it was not until the nineteenth century that psychic explanations of vampirism began to emerge. Among the psychical researchers and Theosophists of the late nineteenth and early twentieth centuries vampirism was explained as due to an astral body. Every person had this second, invisible body that separated from the physical body at death, and it was this that accounted for phenomena such as ghosts and spirits. According to American Henry Steel Olcott, the first president of the Theosophical Society, victims of premature burial could send their astral body to suck the blood or life force from the living and transfer it to the body in the grave. Olcott's theories were expanded on by the German Franz Hartmann, who developed his own theory of astral vampirism in the early twentieth century. Hartmann spoke of individuals who unconsciously vampirize every sensitive person they come into contact with. He believed that such people were possessed themselves by a vampiric entity that drained not just them but other people as well.

Some contemporary occult experts, referencing the work of influential twentieth century English occultist Dion Fortune, author of *Psychic Self-Defence*, a book about the prevention of psychic attack, believe that astral vampirism may account for many reports of vampire attacks, past and present. Others assert that the most common form of psychic vampirism may not involve an astral body but the sapping of the life force from a person simply by being in the presence of certain people.

Fact or fiction?

In folklore, psychic vampires were shadowy, supernatural beings who leeched the energy of others and left them as empty shells. Many unexplained diseases were thought to have been caused by this type of psychic attack from an ethereal creature. With advances in medical science some of these stories can be dispelled as fantasy, but occultists hold that this does not necessarily mean that psychic vampires didn't exist in the past, or that they don't exist today.

According to Michelle Belanger, an author and self-confessed modern-day psychic vampire, psychic vampires are as much a part of our past as well as of our present. Like sanguinarians (blood-drinking vampires), psychic vampires often believe they are born

that way and that their souls originated in a different dimension from other humans. Their souls therefore operate at a much higher energy frequency, which creates a higher energetic metabolism than normal. This increased energy metabolism creates within them a hunger for energy that they obtain by draining energy from people.

In *Piercing the Darkness* (1998), vampire expert Katherine Ramsland describes some of the familiar characteristics of psychic vampires and the destructive methods they employ to feed on the energy of others. She cites the fascinating case of Carly and her unwilling victim – her husband – and explains how Carly's erratic moods, childish fits, and attention-seeking, manipulative behavior drove her husband into a mental hospital. Ramsland then details how, when Carly's husband was finally back on his feet again, Carly's vampirism began all over again.

She drains her husband again and again and nearly destroys him. Most of us know someone like this and we've experienced this vampire's charms, as well as the inevitable destruction that follows from their needs, lies, manipulation and demanding moods. They tease, provoke and exploit high drama to create an impact. No one is safe from such people.

Types of psychic vampire

Occultists distinguish between two different types of psychic vampire: intentional and unintentional. Unintentional psychic vampires are people who feed on the psychic energy of others unconsciously, because they need the energy of others to survive. Although vampires of this type can be any age, they tend to be much older than their victims because with age often comes energy-depleting illnesses; these vampires need to feed off younger people to stay vital.

Unintentional vampires are dangerous, but even more dangerous and vicious are intentional vampires, or individuals who drain the energy of others on purpose. They might do this by projecting negative thoughts or, like the Romanian strigoi, by astrally projecting themselves and feeding off the energy of sleeping victims.

According to Michelle Belanger there are two types of intentional psychic vampire: Darwinian and sustainable. The Darwinian vampire is someone who steals energy without permission and values their own survival above all else. If this type of vampire did not drain the energy of others it would become tired and ill. This Darwinian vampirism is considered unethical by other psychic vampires who describe themselves as ethical, "sustainable" vampires who feed off willing donors. When donors are not available, sustainable vampires drain the free-floating energy given off by crowds. This kind of energy, however, is not very sustaining. If sustainable vampires reach a state of extreme hunger they are in danger of becoming Darwinian vampires or black holes that unintentionally drain the energy from those around them.

Psychic self-defense

Some experts believe that anyone who leaves you feeling tried and drained every time you meet them, and you feel a sense of relief when they leave the room, could be a psychic vampire. These feelings might be coupled with guilt because in most cases psychic vampires are fun to have around. They are often said to be bubbly and over-excitable, because they are drawing in your energy. They can do this through physical contact – a handshake, a touch, a hug – but it can also be done without any physical contact at all. For unintentional vampires this is not a conscious choice: they simply take what they need, leaving a person feeling depleted or suffering from headaches.

Occultists claim that the best form of protection against psychic vampires is self-defense. You need to be on your guard and mindful of your energy levels when spending time with them. This doesn't mean cutting off all contact but being aware of the time you spend with them and employing protection techniques. One of the most effective forms of protection is said to be visualizing your entire body cocooned in a protective golden egg with a shell that is hard but flexible so you can move around. If you feel drained after spending time with a psychic vampire, visualizing a protective beam of light can help, as can surrounding yourself with mood-lifting yellow and orange colors and carrying a piece of citrine crystal. Citrine is said to be good for general energy because allegedly it can revitalize and motivate people.

Finally, and because the majority of psychic vampires are believed to be the unintentional type, while it may be relatively easy to spot the traits of psychic vampirism in others, it may not be so easy to spot vampiric traits in yourself. These traits include erratic energy levels, a need to be with others, an inability to feel comfortable when alone, and a desire to be the center of attention. It's a chilling thought but psychologists agree that within every person there is a deep-seated need to be the center of attention, suggesting that there might be something of the psychic vampire in us all.

Psychological Explanations of Vampirism

The vampire myth is an archetype that can be found in all cultures around the world. With its focus on images of the undead, its metaphor of the life-giving power of blood, its hidden sexuality, the power of darkness and evil, and its ability to spread like a contagious disease, the vampire myth has been an endless source of fascination for psychologists.

Long before Sigmund Freud and Carl Jung developed their theories of human psychology at the turn of the twentieth century, people were forced to rely on supernatural or demonic explanations for deviant behavior. Today, bizarre acts that were once explained by the influence of evil spirits, and treated by inquisitors and exorcists, have become the province of psychologists, therapists, and psychiatrists.

An influential leader in psychotherapy was a German doctor called Richard von Krafft-Ebing. In his *Psychopathia Sexualis* (1886) Krafft-Ebing collected evidence to support his belief that the blood-hungry acts committed by psychopaths were frequently sexual. It appeared to him that blood, violence, and the taking of life heightened erotic pleasure for these individuals. Krafft-Ebing's work had a powerful impact on Sigmund Freud and some experts believe it may well have influenced Bram Stoker when he wrote *Dracula* in 1897. The twin themes of sexuality and blood lust are strong in the novel, and in many vampire novels since. In addition, some psychoanalysts have used the vampire myth to describe actual cases where blood-drinking is involved; "clinical vampirism" and "Renfield's syndrome" (named after the bug-eating insane man in Stoker's novel) are both terms used to describe real-life psychopathic killers, and certain killers (such as Peter Kürten) have been described as "vampires" by the media.

Freud and Jung

Many psychological explanations for vampirism have drawn on Freudian or Jungian theories, although neither Freud nor Jung spoke much about vampirism. Their ideas have, however, been applied to vampirism by other psychologists and thinkers.

From a Freudian perspective the vampire myth is grounded in archaic images of repressed sexual longings and fears. The innate sexuality of blood-sucking can be seen in its intrinsic connection with cannibalism and incubus-like behavior. Many legends report various beings draining fluids other than blood from victims, an association with semen being obvious. According to Freudians the vampire myth is linked to incestuous feelings of guilt and hate and to infantile oral fixation. When vampires return from the grave they typically attack their own relatives, suggesting that when people feel a combination of hatred and erotic desire for members of their own family these feelings (in a form of denial) express themselves in the vampire myth.

Jungians, on the other hand, regard the vampire myth as a symbolic expression of primal instincts. For Jungians, the vampire myth should be understood as an expression of what Jung called the "shadow," or the aspects of a person's personality that the ego — the conscious self — does not want to acknowledge. This analysis yields great insight into both the universality and widespread appeal of the vampire myth since ancient times, as it indicates that the vampire archetype lives within each one of us but more often than not we tend to project it onto others. What we fail to fully comprehend, however, is that this projection is not something "out there" but is something inside us – an expression of our inner reality that is predatory and threatening not just to ourselves but to others as well.

The vampire and narcissism

In addition to projecting vampiric traits onto others, Jungians also observe that certain narcissistic, autistic, erotic, and predatory personality traits can result in a personality that, like the psychic vampire, is parasitic on the energy and life of those around it. In contemporary psychology this is called "narcissistic personality disorder."

Although Jungians have not tended to explore fully the parallel between the vampire image and narcissistic self-indulgence, other psychoanalysts and researchers have. One influential commentator in the 1970s and 80s was an American theology professor, Peter Homans, who suggested that in the modern culture of narcissistic self-indulgence the vampire image was a perfect icon to express the psychological character configuration underlying it. It was, however, psychoanalyst Heinz Kohut who became the chief interpreter of narcissistic personalities. His work on self-psychology offers what many experts believe to be one of the most far-reaching insights into the psychology behind the vampire myth. According to Kohut, vampiric psychological illness draws attention to the significance of inner emptiness, the drive for emotional nutrients or affirmation from others, and the resulting envy that sees such "good" things in others, which manifests in a desire to take these things away from them.

The vampire as explanation

The psychological significance of the vampire image does not just relate to interpersonal interactions or individual response but to whole communities. Death is one of the most mysterious aspects of life, and all cultures are preoccupied with it to some degree. One way to come to terms with death is to personify it, to give it some tangible form. Vampires also personify the dark side of humanity, so as representations of death and evil, vampires were a way for humans to explain the unexplainable. The appearance of so many vampire-like monsters throughout history, as well as our continued fascination with vampires, demonstrates that it's simply human nature to cast our fears as monsters.

In the psychological dynamics of scapegoating, someone or something is used as a focus for the projection of the vampire image. In this way the "vampire" can be blamed, cast out, or persecuted by the community. The scapegoating mechanism can be seen working alongside the vampire-as-explanation-for-the-unexplainable theme in the eighteenth-century vampire frenzy that swept through Europe. The vampires of folklore are typically associated with a series of deaths, usually within a community or village, by an illness that the community cannot understand or explain. The epidemic pattern is clearly demonstrated in the classic cases of Peter Plogojowitz and Arnold Paole, where a disease, plague, or outbreak of consumption (tuberculosis) can be identified alongside fears of vampirism. Once it was established that dead bodies – as opposed to spirits of the dead – were the cause of death, the vampire, as the walking undead, became both the scapegoat and the explanation for the plague.

See also: **ORIGINS, OF VAMPIRES; POLITICAL VAMPIRES; SEX**

Pulp Magazines

Pulp magazines, widely circulated American periodicals printed on cheap pulpwood paper, were important for the spread of the vampire myth in the early twentieth century. In the days before television they gave readers a variety of different genres of fiction, ranging from detective to action adventure to horror. During the 1920s and 1930s the periodical *Weird Tales* dominated the market. Pulp magazines were eventually supplanted by the growing market for comic books, with their evocative artwork conferring visible reality to vampires.

The vampire theme first began to emerge in the February 1924 issue of *Weird Tales* in a story called "The Hound," written by influential horror writer H. P. Lovecraft. It was, however, "The Vampire of Oakdale Ridge" by Robert W. Sneddon in the December 1926 issue of the periodical *Ghost Stories* that is often said to be the first true vampire story to appear in a periodical. From 1927 onwards, with the publication of "The Man who Cast no Shadow" (by Seabury Quinn, one of the most prolific contributors of short stories to *Weird Tales*), a number of vampire stories began to appear regularly in *Weird Tales*. In 1931, alongside the release of Universal Pictures' *Dracula*, staring Béla Lugosi, what have often been regarded as two of the best vampire pulp stories appeared in *Weird Tales*: "Placide's Wife" by Kirk Mashburn and "A Rendezvous in Averoigne" by Clark Ashton Smith.

The decade following the 1931 release of *Dracula* witnessed the publication of many vampire pulp stories. These stories continued during World War II but toward the end of the 1940s there was a noticeable decline. *Weird Tales* went bankrupt in 1954.

See also: **COMICS; LITERATURE**

Pumpkin

Among the Gypsies of the Balkans the pumpkin (along with the watermelon) is held to be a fruit capable of transforming into a vampire, albeit not a very frightening or deadly one. According to tradition, pumpkins with the appearance of a drop of blood on them that have been kept for more than ten days, or that are kept after Christmas will come alive and start rolling on the ground and wailing. In this state, the pumpkin-vampire can harass people and cattle, but it doesn't do much harm.

"If there is in this world a well-attested account, it is that of vampires. Nothing is lacking: official reports, affidavits of well-known people, of surgeons, of priests, of magistrates; the judicial proof is most complete. And with all that, who is there who believes in vampires?"

Jean-Jacques Rousseau

Quantum Theory and Vampires

Quantum theory is the theoretical basis of modern physics that explains the nature and behavior of matter and energy on the atomic and sub-atomic level. In itself it does not postulate the existence of a soul or spirit but it does provide a mechanism in which the mind can affect matter, and a mechanism in which non-physical or supernatural entities, such as ghosts, demons, and spirits, could exert their influence on the physical universe.

The first presentation of quantum theory was given in 1900 by physicist Max Planck to the German Physical Society. While attempting to discover why radiation from a glowing black body changes in color as the temperature rises, he made the assumption that energy exists in individual units, rather than just as a constant electromagnetic wave as had been formerly assumed. Planck called these individual units of energy quanta and so began a completely new and fundamental understanding of the laws of nature. Over the next 30 years a number of scientists made their own significant contributions to our modern understanding of quantum theory.

Quantum physics revolutionized the scientific thinking of the nineteenth century by challenging the fundamental principle of a cause preceding an effect, and by assigning as much importance to the observer as to his or her observations. It gave reasons to suppose that the universe was more than just a complex arrangement of physical matter but rather that it consisted of dynamic packages of unpredictable energy. By so doing it opened up the possibility of the interconnectedness of mind and matter. It also opened up the possibility that ghosts, spirits, and other supernatural phenomena, perhaps even vampires, could exist by slightly shifting the probability distribution associated with individual quantum events. From a logical or rational perspective supernatural creatures can't exist; from a quantum perspective they are things humans have yet to understand well enough.

A deeper understanding of the myth

According to vampire expert Katherine Ramsland in her 2002 book *The Science of Vampires*, quantum theory can also deepen our understanding of the ever-evolving but always contemporary vampire myth. Ramsland believes that the vampire tale should not be defined as something without the ability to shift and change, because this will prevent it from corresponding to an individual's changing inner reality. It is only the vampire archetype that remains intact – the rest changes to meet the differing needs of individuals and the culture and time they live in.

To quote Ramsland:

Because the vampire tale is a monster story that mirrors aspects of ourselves, watching how the vampire tale evolves opens a window into our shifting perceptions about what we experience as truth.

For example, just as the early perception of the vampire was based on the "truth" that good and evil were two separate and opposite forces, so today our perception of the vampire shows a willingness to see the boundaries between good and evil blur, making the modern vampire something of a paradox.

In short, the vampire myth is constantly changing and evolving and although, like quantum theory, this makes it impossible to pin down or define, this is how, again like quantum theory, it probably works best. Attempting to recreate or resurrect the vampire myth as it was comprehended in times past, or even in the era of Bram Stoker, will result in the myth losing its potency in a modern society that has a new set of anxieties and fears and a new perception of what constitutes good and evil.

"The vampires have always been metaphors for me. They've always been vehicles through which I can express things I have felt very, very deeply."

Anne Rice

Rabies

Some experts have found parallels between outbreaks of rabies in certain regions and an increase in vampire folklore. This could be related to the fact that rabies is caused by the bite of an animal and can trigger the following vampire-like symptoms:

- *Hypersensitivity to light and odor, including the scent of garlic*

- *Increased sex drive*

- *Extreme thirst*

- *Inability to see own reflection in mirror*

- *Muscle spasms that cause bared teeth*

- *Froth bloody fluid at mouth*

- *Ferocious, aggressive behavior*

- *Others infected through a bite, because the virus is transmitted through saliva*

A report in the September 1998 issue of the journal *Neurology*, authored by Dr. Juan Gomez-Alonso a neurologist at Hospital Xeral in Vigo, Spain, suggested that eighteenth-century European rabies victims may have been the inspiration for the vampire legend. Not only do people with rabies have symptoms strikingly similar to the traits ascribed to vampires, but the vampire legend originated in Eastern Europe at this time, where there was a major rabies outbreak in the 1720s.

Gomez-Alonso decided to investigate the rabies–vampirism connection after watching a vampire movie in 1981, and came to the conclusion that rabies, a virus usually transmitted via the bite of an infected animal, does bear strong similarities to what was described in vampire reports. Symptoms usually do not appear for at least a couple of weeks, and by then the bite has healed. Once symptoms have appeared, anti-rabies treatment is ineffective, and the infection is most often fatal.

In addition to medical evidence, Gomez-Alonso discovered historical support for his theory when he found records of a rabies epidemic among dogs, wolves, and other animals in Hungary between 1721 and 1728 – the time people first began to report sightings of vampires. Gomez-Alonso also found accounts of exhumed bodies that appeared lifelike, and were filled with still-liquid blood. This again fits in with his rabies theory because when people die of collapse, shock, or asphyxiation, as is often the case in rabies, their blood is often slow to clot. In addition, the regions of Hungary where the outbreaks occurred is damp and cold for many months of the year, and corpses take longer to decompose in the cold.

Gomez-Alonso concluded that:

Much evidence supports that rabies could have played a key role in the generation of the vampire legend. This would be in accordance with the anthropologic theory that assumes that many popular legends have been prompted by facts. Under this approach, saying that the vampire is "mere fiction" may be somewhat inappropriate.

Vampire bats

Wolves and bats, which are often associated with vampires, can be carriers of rabies. Outbreaks of rabies spread by vampire bats are a problem in various tropical areas of South America, including Brazil and Peru. According to medical experts, between June 2007 and August 2008 at least 38 Venezuelans died as a result of a suspected outbreak of rabies spread by bites from vampire bats. The common vampire bat, which feeds on mammals' blood, swoops down and generally approaches its sleeping prey on the ground. The bat then makes a small incision with its teeth, and an anticoagulant in its saliva keeps the blood flowing while it drinks.

See also: **DISEASE; EPIDEMIC**

Raković, Miloš

Miloš Raković was a Serbian man who died in 1836. Suspected of being a vampire, his body was dug up several times. The case is intriguing because it shows how in some instances, when Christian methods of preventing vampire attacks failed, in desperation people would turn to traditional methods to dispatch the undead.

Raković died shortly after Easter in 1836 in Svojdurg, a Serbian village. By August the same year he was suspected of having transformed into a vampire. A group of villagers exhumed and examined his corpse, and then reburied the body without informing the priest. When the priest found out, he returned with the villagers to the grave and the body was dug up a second time. The priest poured holy water on it and the body was reburied. Neither exhu-

mation prevented the vampire attacks so the villagers dug up the body for the third time. This time the corpse was shot through and decapitated before being reburied. Reports of vampire attacks stopped.

Rakshasa

The rakshasa, or rakshasi (female), is a species of nocturnal vampire demon in Indian folklore. The name means "destroyer" and these evil creatures typically attack women at weddings and children, but they can also enter the bodies of men while they eat and drink and drive them mad. It is also believed that the rakshasa might have been a king or leader called Ravana, the lord of the undead.

The rakshasa is often represented as a grotesque human with fiery eyes, a huge, lolling tongue, and yellow or red matted hair and beard. They also have coarse body hair, potbellies, slits for eyes, horns, and an odd number of limbs such as one arm and three legs. They may only have one eye and can also wear a wreath of back, green, yellow, or blue entrails. On occasion they can have animal heads.

These foul creatures can become invisible, and may also shape-shift into dogs, eagles, vultures, owls, cuckoos, dwarves, husbands, and lovers. Their habits, such as drinking human blood from the skull, eating corpses, and eating food that has been sneezed or walked upon, are revolting. Their hunger for human and animal flesh is insatiable and they are said to roam restlessly around jungles, woods, forests, and places of worship in search of prey. Their power increases at night, and they can also reanimate corpses.

In modern folklore the rakshasa lives in trees and can induce vomiting and indigestion in all who trespass on its territory at night. It is still common in India to call someone rakshasa or rakshasi if they do something bad.

Limitations

The rakshasa has incredible power but limited intelligence, and in Indian myth and lore there are a number of stories which show how the creature can be outwitted. For example, one story in the *Panchatantra* – the much-loved collection of Indian folktales and fables – concerns a rakshasa that jumps on the shoulders of a Brahmin and demands to be carried. The Brahmin notices as he carries the creature that it has very delicate feet. He asks the rakshasa why this is so and the rakshasa tells him that he has made a vow to never walk on or touch the earth. When they reach a pond the rakshasa orders the Brahmin to wait while it bathes. As soon as the rakshasa starts to bathe the Brahmin runs away, aware that the rakshasa cannot follow him because of the vow it had taken.

Dispelling the rakshasa

The rakshasa can be driven away by purifying fire but this remedy can be difficult if the creature goes about invisibly. Prayer and meditation can upset them, but the most effective way to dispel the rakshasa is through a special exorcism known only to holy men, which involves the burning of certain sacred herbs and chanting holy names.

When a community suffered from rakshasa attacks on livestock and humans the sites of recent burials were visited. If the ground around the grave showed signs of disturbance it was thought this was due to the activity of the rakshasa and the grave would be opened. If the body looked well preserved this was a clear sign that the corpse had become a rakshasa. The corpse would then be cremated but even though this destroyed the physical vehicle for the spirit, it was thought that the rakshasa was still at large and still dangerous. Those who witnessed the cremation needed to be careful that they did not breathe in any smoke as this could lead to them being possessed by the rakshasa. Animals were also believed to be vulnerable, so they were kept well away from the cremation. When the body was burned to ashes, the remains needed to be buried deep in the ground and the spot avoided forever, in case the essence of the rakshasa still lingered there, waiting for unwary victims to inhabit.

See also: **INDIA**

Ramanga

The ramanga is a species of living vampire who served royalty in Madagascan folklore. This person lived outside the normal boundaries of society and served the chief of the tribe. They would eat the fingernail clippings and drink the spilled blood from medical treatments of their noble masters and mistresses so that these precious things did not fall into the hands of evil sorcerers.

Ramsland, Katherine (1953-)

Born in Michigan in 1953, author and vampire expert Katherine Ramsland holds graduate degrees in forensic psychology, clinical psychology, and philosophy. She is the author of bestselling books on the works of vampire novelist Anne Rice, and is widely considered to be one of the foremost experts of the science of vampires. In her *The Science of Vampires* (2002), Ramsland offers a comprehensive investigation of vampire myths and realities, exploring the dark force that has played host to centuries of fears concerning human infection, depletion, and disease.

See also: **LITERATURE; SCIENCE BEHIND VAMPIRES**

Ranft, Michaël

Michaël Ranft was an eighteenth-century German theologian and academic who wrote a number of influential treatises on vampires, including *De Masticatione Mortuorum in Tumulis* (On the Chewing Dead) which was published in 1728 in Leipzig. In this treatise Ranft discussed the subject of manducation, corpses that chew their shrouds and then eat themselves.

Ransom, Frederick

Frederick Ransom of South Woodstock, Vermont, was a student at Dartmouth College when he died from tuberculosis on February 14, 1817, at the age of 20. Within his family there was a belief that dying of tuberculosis before the age of 30 was an inherited tendency, so after his death, Frederick's father, in the hope of preventing other family members dying, exhumed his corpse, cut out his heart, and burned it in a blacksmith's forge. Despite taking this precaution Frederick's mother died of tuberculosis in 1821, followed by his sister in 1828 and two of his brothers in 1830 and 1832.

Another brother, Daniel, did not contract the disease and survived until his 80s. It was Daniel who left a written account of his family's activities.

Rasputin, Grigori Yefimovich (1869–1916)

Some people have argued that Rasputin, a non-ordained Russian mystic who helped discredit the tsarist government, leading to the fall of the Romanov dynasty in the Bolshevik Revolution of 1917, was a vampire.

There is much uncertainty concerning the life of Rasputin. Accounts of his life have often been based on hearsay and contemporary opinions variously saw him as a saintly mystic, a visionary, a healer, a prophet, or a debauched religious charlatan. There is no doubt that he exerted a powerful influence over the royal family but if his life was bizarre the circumstances of his death were even more so. Confronted with death, Rasputin appears to have demonstrated the superhuman strength typically associated with vampires.

The murder

The murder of Rasputin has become the stuff of legend. It is generally agreed that on December 16, 1916, having decided that Rasputin's influence over the Tsarina made him too dangerous to the Empire, a group of noblemen lured Rasputin to Moika Palace in St. Petersburg, where they served him cakes and red wine laced with a large amount of cyanide. Although there was enough poison to kill ten men, Rasputin was said to have exhibited a remarkable immunity to the poison. It had no impact on him.

Determined to finish the job, one conspirator shot Rasputin in the back with a revolver. This still wasn't enough to kill him, as Rasputin got up and ran away. More shots were fired and he was hit three more times. When the conspirators neared his fallen body they found he was still trying to get up, so they clubbed him into submission. Then, after wrapping his body in a sheet, they threw him into the icy Neva River.

Three days later Rasputin's body – poisoned, shot four times, and badly beaten – was recovered from the river and examined. It was determined that the cause of his death was drowning but it was also determined that he had been poisoned and that the poison alone should have killed him. The Tsarina had Rasputin's body buried in the grounds of Tsarskoe Selo, one of the royal residencies a few miles outside St. Petersburg. After the February Revolution, a group of workers from the city uncovered Rasputin's body, carried it into a nearby wood, and burned it.

See also: **HISTORICAL VAMPIRES**

Rat

The brown common rat (*Rattus norvegicus*) and the black ship or house rat (*Rattus rattus*) are the most common species of rodent. By carrying disease with their fleas, such rodents are often associated with the spread of epidemics, such as rabies and bubonic plague. As unclean animals who reside in dark places and feed on the waste of the living, it is no surprise that rats have long been associated with disease, death, and vampires.

In folklore, vampires are said to be able to transform into rats and this image was elaborated on by Bram Stoker in his novel *Dracula* (1897), where rats are part of the Count's plague of evil. The Count's castle is alive with rats and rats also figure strongly in Renfield's vision of a new order of evil, where "*I could see there were thousand of rats with eyes blazing red – like his, only smaller.*" In the classic vampire film *Nosferatu* (1922), rats are used to represent the vampire's pestilence.

See also: **ANIMAL VAMPIRES**

Raven

The raven is a member of the crow family found in North America and North Europe. While the crow is honored in folklore for its ability to fight vampires, the raven's dark wings, sharp eyesight, ferocious beak, and predisposition to feed on the blood and flesh of the dying or dead, means that it has often been considered to be a preferred form for the vampire to shape-shift into. Ravens are also thought to serve as familiars to witches and sorcerers.

See also: **BIRDS**

Ray Family Vampires

The story of the Ray family of Connecticut was originally reported in an 1854 article in the *Norwich Weekly Courier*. The article quotes the father's name as Horace but there are no records of a Horace Ray in Jewett City where the family were reported to be from. The case details do, however, match the circumstances of the Henry B. Ray family.

Between 1847 and 1854 vampirism was suspected after several deaths from tuberculosis among the Henry B. Ray family of Jowett City. The vampire was supposed to be the unquiet revenant of Horace (Henry) who died in 1847 and was said to be preying on two of his surviving sons. When they too died, a number of people around Jowett City dreamed of them and awoke feeling exhausted. The remaining family members suspected vampirism and decided to dig up the body of Horace and the two dead brothers and burn them to prevent more loss of life. The dreams and exhaustion stopped.

Over a century later in October 1991 in nearby Griswold, Connecticut, archeologists investigated a local building site after three young boys found a human skull. Excavations soon uncovered human remains and traces of graves from the late 1700s into the early 1800s that had obviously been treated for vampirism. Evidence of tuberculosis was found in the remains. In one grave the skull had been placed among the bones of the chest, and the arms and legs had been broken. Anthropologists have suggested that this method of burial was not native to Connecticut but more common in Eastern Europe.

See also: **AMERICA; NEW ENGLAND**

Real Vampires

For many people today "real vampire" is a contradiction in terms, as vampires are creatures of myth, folklore, and fiction. For others the word "vampire" applies to notorious murderers and serial killers with a lust for blood. Yet others refer to cases of clinical vampirism or diseases associated with vampirism, such as porphyria, for evidence of so-called real vampires. There are, however, some people today who not only believe that vampires were, and are, real but that they themselves might be vampires.

According to Hugo Pecos, who oversees an organization he calls the Federal Vampire and Zombie Agency (FVZA), vampires are not only real but a threat to national security. Pecos claims that from the late 1800s to 1975 the now defunct FVZA kept America safe from this threat.

Sanguinarians are a group of modern-day blood drinkers who describe themselves as vampires, and the Temple of the Vampire is a religious organization that practices the religion of vampirism. According to the Temple, not only are vampires real but with the correct training it is possible to become one. There are also people who may not necessarily be blood drinkers but believe they have been infected by a vampire virus or were born with certain vampiric abnormalities, like sensitivity to sunlight, heightened psychic abilities, and an aversion to garlic. Others believe real vampires are mortal humans with immortal souls, subject to reincarnation.

In addition, some people believe that real vampires are not the blood drinkers of history and folklore but psychic vampires, or people who feed on the life force or energy of others. Finally there are so-called "lifestyle vampires," who associate themselves with the vampire archetype and way of life.

Lifestyle vampires

The novel *Dracula* has spawned countless books, films, TV shows, and comics dedicated to vampires. However, it wasn't until the 1980s that people began living as if they were real vampires. These voluntary vampires are not murderers or necessarily blood drinkers; they are just people so intrigued by vampire lore that they attempt to live in the manner of a vampire. This vampire lifestyle phenomenon can be traced to the vampirification of Europe and the United States by the Vampire Chronicles of Anne Rice in the 1970s. Rice's fictional vampires are not ugly revenants or the menacing undead but exquisitely beautiful and intelligent creations.

Energized by numerous websites and Internet chatrooms, lifestyle vampires have grown rapidly in numbers since the 1990s. These modern-day vampire lovers are inspired by a number of influences – from ancient Roman vampires to Vlad the Impaler to Rice's fictional Lestat – and have skillfully managed to combine fantasy, fiction, and folklore into a thriving subculture. These lifestyle vampires do not commit violence, worship the Devil or even drink blood; they are simply inspired by the vampire archetype. Sometimes they appear perfectly normal; sometimes they dress in black or paint their faces white with blood-red lips, the choice is an individual one. Rather than calling themselves "vampires," they prefer to be called

"vampyres" with a "y" or "dark angels" or "the kindred," to distinguish themselves from vampire stereotypes.

See also: **BIOLOGY OF VAMPIRES; HISTORICAL VAMPIRES; LIVING VAMPIRES; PSYCHIC VAMPIRE; REINCARNATION; SANGUINARIUM; SCIENCE BEHIND VAMPIRES; TEMPLE OF THE VAMPIRE; TRANSFORMATION**

Reanimation

Reanimation is a term used to refer to the alleged return to life of a corpse. It is more commonly associated with zombies, Mary Shelley's novel *Frankenstein* (1818), and the practices of voodoo but it also played a part in theological debates and treatises concerning vampires that appeared in the eighteenth century. Satan was believed to the cause of reanimation, as were demons, sorcery, and the inhabitation of a corpse by the soul of the deceased or the soul of another person.

See also: **ASTRAL BODY; TRANSFORMATION**

Red

Although in folklore red is a color believed to protect against vampires and demons – red ribbons and amulets are worn to protect against the evil eye – red is also the color of the vampire, most likely because it is the color of blood. A sure-fire sign of vampirism was the red appearance of a corpse, suggesting that the vampire had been feeding on blood. Among the Slavs the expression "*he was as red* as a vampire" refers to someone who is very angry. In vampire fiction too, the color red is closely associated with the vampire. In the 1897 novel *Dracula*, the Count's eyes and lips are described as blood red.

In addition, red hair was said to be a telltale sign of a vampire. Among the Greeks, Serbs, Bulgarians, and Romanians red was the hair color that signified vampires, especially if combined with blue eyes. Judas Iscariot was said to have had red hair; it was believed that from Judas came the vampire clan known as the Children of Judas.

See also: **APPEARANCE OF VAMPIRES; REDCAP**

Redcap

The redcap is a type of malevolent spirit from Scottish folklore. They were said to haunt abandoned places, especially where violent acts had been committed. These creatures delighted in attacking unwitting passers-by. Lord Soulis of Hermitage Castle in Scotland was said to have had a redcap as a familiar.

The spirits were called redcaps because they were said to carry a cap that had been dyed red with human blood and this is where their association with vampirism probably comes from – along with the fact that they could be repelled by making the sign of the cross or reciting verses from the Bible.

See also: **BAD LORD SOULIS**

Reflection

See: **MIRRORS**

Reincarnation

Reincarnation is the doctrine that the soul returns after death to a new physical body to live another life. It is a central belief in Buddhism and Hinduism but it is not limited to the East and is also common in the West. There is a modern-day school of thought that believes that real vampires are mortal humans with immortal reincarnated souls.

According to this school of thought vampiric souls are not Satanic in nature but are from a spiritual realm, one which is not hell or heaven, purgatory or earth but simply another spiritual realm. In each lifetime a vampire has an awakening through dreams, visions, out-of-body experiences, near-death experiences, and astral projection that leads the vampire to believe that he or she has lived before in a past life.

Most people's ideas about reincarnation derive from Hinduism or Buddhism. These religions grew out of a set of animistic soul beliefs characteristic to the indigenous tribal peoples of India. One common characteristic of animistic beliefs about reincarnation is that the spirit of the dead person divides after death: one part travels to the land of the dead where it becomes a spirit, while the other part returns to earth to be reborn. Of the several ways animistic reincarnation beliefs differ from those typical of Hinduism and Buddhism, the most important is the concept of karma – the idea that the circumstances of a person's present life are molded by their actions, good or bad, in previous lives. The theory of karma is absent from animistic beliefs about reincarnation.

Scientific investigations of reincarnation support the animistic idea of reincarnation better than the Hindu and Buddhist view. Scientific studies of reincarnation have also shown how important beliefs about reincarnation are to the alleged recall of past lives. For example, children who claim memories of past lives are common in Eastern cultures where this belief is considered acceptable, but less common in cultures when it is not taken seriously by parents.

For many believers the idea that a person can be reincarnated is substantiated by stories of past-life recall that can be backed up with corroborating evidence. However, for scientists, just as the jury is still out on whether vampirism is a genuine phenomenon or not, the jury is also undecided as to whether reincarnation is a genuine phenomenon. Efforts have been made to investigate reincarnation scientifically and validate claims of past lives. Most notable is the research conducted by Ian Stevenson, Professor of Psychiatry at the University of Virginia, who began investigating the reincarnation memories of children all over the world in the 1960s with impressive results. The main problem, however, is that science does not recognize the existence of an essence that survives the brain after bodily death, and reincarnation by its very nature implies survival after death.

Religious Objects

See: **HOLY OBJECTS**

Renfield, R. M.

R. M. Renfield is a memorable character in Bram Stoker's novel *Dracula* (1897), who thinks that in order to survive he must consume blood.

First mentioned in chapter 8 in Dr. Seward's journal, Renfield is presented as a 59-year-old mental patient in the London-based asylum of Dr. Seward, who describes him as suffering from *"homicidal and religious mania"* and *"monomania"* or hysteria. As Dracula approaches England, Renfield deteriorates mentally and his appetite for blood increases. He eats insects and sparrows and asks for but does not receive a kitten. Mystified but intrigued by his patient, Seward coins a new term to describe him: "zoophagous" or life-eating.

Renfield manages to escape at one point but is caught trying to get to Carfax Abbey where Dracula has stored his boxes of earth. On another occasion he attacks Seward with a knife, slashing Seward's left wrist. When attendants rush in Seward writes that they find Renfield *"lying on his belly on the floor, licking up like a dog, the blood which had fallen from my wounded wrist."*

Promised the souls and blood of thousands of rats and animals by Dracula, Renfield becomes enraged when the Count does not keep his promise. He also senses that Dracula has been drinking the blood of Mina Harker and is determined to stop the vampire. The next time Dracula comes to him, in the form of mist, Renfield tries to kill the Count, only to have his back broken and his skull crushed. Found by attendants, Renfield is able to relate what happen to Professor Van Helsing before he dies.

The presence of Renfield, the *"mad man,"* adds greatly to the evil atmosphere of the novel. He represents not just victims of vampiric manipulation but the nineteenth-century belief that the mentally ill were susceptible to evil or were human counterparts to the vampire.

Renfield's Syndrome

See: **CLINICAL VAMPIRISM**

Reproduction

According to the majority of accounts, vampires cannot reproduce biologically, but there do appear to be certain circumstances where this can occur. In Gypsy lore, for example, a dhampir is a mortal child who results from the coupling of a human mother and a vampire father, typically a dead man returning from the grave to have intercourse with his widow. Although the offspring are mortal, some of the vampire's nature gets transferred to them. Often they become skilled in hunting down and killing vampires.

Those who study the science of vampires suggest that if vampires existed and a vampire male somehow mated with a human female, then the vampire must pass on a chromosome that codes for certain vampiric characteristics but fails to override certain human traits. (It is interesting to note that in some folklore, vam-

pires who mate with humans produce children with no bones.) The dhampir, or half-breed vampire, therefore is mortal and does not drink blood, but he or she does have supernatural senses and powers.

There are stories in folklore of female vampires mating with human males and conceiving a child. The "explanation" for how this can be possible is that when female vampires mate with humans they do so by becoming temporarily human. Whether or not they return to their vampiric state when pregnant, and what the biological status of the child conceived is, remain unclear.

See also: **SEX**

Revenant

The term "revenant," from the French *revenir* meaning "to come back," is a broad one used to describe a being who has returned from the dead, including spirits, ghosts, zombies, and vampires. However, it is often used to differentiate between the restless or wandering undead and vampires – a vampire is a revenant in that he or she has returned from the dead, but a revenant is not necessarily always a vampire.

Originally the word meant a restless ghost or spirit who could not find peace in the afterlife. There were a number of reasons why revenants would leave their graves, including:

- *Their corpses had not been given the proper burial rites.*

- *An animal had jumped over their corpse before burial.*

- *Their soul was not at rest due to jealousy of the living or because they led a sinful life, or because they had unfinished business on earth.*

- *They had been cursed by a witch or sorcerer.*

- *They had died suddenly or violently or by suicide.*

- *They had been excommunicated from the Church.*

Decaying corpses

Revenants could not only appear as spirits and ghosts but in forms that were solid and alive, and sometimes as the reanimated body of a loved one. The revenants of the Middle Ages that appeared in solid form were often described as decaying corpses. In other words, they didn't look like living humans but like decomposing corpses with rotting flesh. This is again where vampires tend to differ from revenants. When vampires die the process of decomposition stops and he or she tends to look intact, however pale or old they may appear. A revenant, on the other hand, has no means to prevent his or her body decomposing after death, and therefore he or she looks far more hideous and repelling.

Not all revenants were violent or blood-thirsty. Many reports of vampirism, from the Middle Ages to the early eighteenth century, feature revenants that were considered unthreatening. It was only when the Church decreed that the corpses of those who had been excommunicated could be inhabited by evil spirits that revenants became more sinister and dangerous, and it became easier to

confuse them with blood- or energy-drinking vampires.

See also: **CUNTIUS, JOHANNES**

Reverse Vampirism

In both Eastern European and New England vampire lore there are instances when the blood of a vampire was used to "cure" a victim of vampirism or to protect the vulnerable against a vampire attack. Even though there was no evidence to suggest that this remedy ever worked, the belief that vampires were repelled by the blood of their own kind was strong. It was also thought that eating the ashes of a cremated vampire, or the ashes from the cremated organs of a vampire, was a form of protection.

Once gathered from the corpse, the vampire blood was baked into bread called blood bread, or smeared onto a potential victim, or simply drunk. In both Romania and Rhode Island, there was a related practice: fumigation by the smoke from the vampire's burning heart or corpse.

Rhode Island Vampires

Beginning in 1799 and ending in 1893 there were a number of vampire attacks reported on Rhode Island. Historians believe that the deaths attributed to vampires and demonic forces were most likely the result of deaths from consumption.

Some of the records of these attacks are very detailed, although with others there is only a simple short statement to be found. All these stories have one thing in common; the Rhode

Island Vampires tended to be young women and they are all gruesome accounts of family tragedies and brutal mutilations in often failed attempts to stop and kill the vampires.

The vampires

🩸 Perhaps the first record is a short cryptic request made by a Mr. Stephen Staples to the Cumberland Town Council in 1796 to "try an experiment" in an attempt to save one daughter's life by digging up his other daughter who had recently died.

🩸 The next notable vampire case – that of Sarah Tillinghurst of Exeter – was recorded in 1799. Reports of vampires then moved to Foster in 1827 when the body of the 19-year-old daughter of Captain Levi Young was exhumed after others in the family became ill. The remains of Nancy Young were burned and the fumes inhaled by the family members as a cure and to provide protection.

🩸 The next significant case comes from almost 50 years later. According to an 1874 news report, William G. Rose, a resident of Placedale, Rhode Island, dug up his daughter's corpse and burned the heart because he was convinced that she had transformed into a vampire and was attacking her living relatives. Some reports state that the name of the daughter was Ruth Ellen who was born in 1859 and died on May 12, 1874, most likely from consumption.

🩸 The vampires and the gruesome solutions to them marched next to West Greenwich, where to this day in Historical Cemetery No. 2 the grave of suspected vampire Nellie Vaughn, who died at the age of 19 in 1889, can be found, inscribed with the strange and haunting words, "I am waiting and watching you." Legends hold that nothing will grow on her grave and it is cursed.

🩸 A similar report was recounted in 1892 when George Brown, a resident of Exeter whose wife died, again probably from consumption. Brown's daughters fell ill and died. His son also fell ill before visiting Colorado Springs, where he recovered. On returning to Rhode Island, however, he fell ill again so Brown exhumed his wife and daughters and allegedly found that one of the bodies was well preserved with a heart and liver that dripped blood. These organs were cremated. Accounts in the Providence Journal at the time documented the story.

Interestingly, clippings from the *Providence Journal* about the Mercy Brown case were discovered among the papers of Bram Stoker after his death. This has lead many to speculate that he based many items in his novel *Dracula* on the Rhode Island vampire stories.

See also: **NEW ENGLAND**

Rice, Anne (1941-)

Anne Rice is an American writer whose monumentally bestselling Vampire Chronicles, a series of novels that revolve around the fictional character Lestat de Lioncourt, contributed significantly to the increase in interest in vampires in the late twentieth century. Her writing singles her out as the foremost practitioner of Gothic fiction in the modern age.

Born as Howard Allan O'Brien in New Orleans, Rice changed her name to Anne shortly after starting school. She graduated from San Francisco State University and published her first novel, *Interview with the Vampire*, in 1976. This novel became the most popular and successful vampire story of the twentieth century. It was followed by other vampire-themed novels: *The Vampire Lestat* (1985), *The Queen of the Damned* (1988), *The Tale of the Body Thief* (1992), *Memnoch the Devil* (1995), *Pandora* (1998), *The Vampire Armand* (1998), *Vittorio the Vampire* (1999), *Merrick* (2000), *Blood and Gold* (2001), and *Blood Canticle* (2003).

In 1991 Katherine Ramsland finished her biography of Anne Rice, entitled *Prism of the Night*. Ramsland also compiled a reference volume entitled *The Vampire Companion: The Official Guide to Anne Rice's Vampire Chronicles*. In 1988 a group of women in New Orleans founded an Anne Rice Fan Club. Rice suggested that the name be changed to the Anne Rice Vampire Lestat Fan Club in honor of her major character, Lestat de Lioncourt, a French nobleman made into a vampire in the eighteenth century. In 1994 the movie version of *Interview with the Vampire*, produced by Geffen Pictures, became the eighth highest grossing movie in the USA that year.

Rice's vampires

The vampires created by Anne Rice differ from those of Bram Stoker in that although they can be killed by fire and sunlight they are not affected by the usual weapons used against classic vampires: garlic, crosses, and stakes. They can see their reflection in a mirror. They need blood and prefer human blood because it is more nutritious, but they can feed on animal blood. They do not physically age; instead they become more statuesque and smooth with time. They can have the power to fly and most have the power to read the minds of mortals and weaker, younger vampires. They possess superhuman strength, eyesight, and agility and may also have artistic talents such as singing, painting, and acting.

As they lose all natural bodily fluids, they are unable to have children. If their hair or nails are cut they grow back as they were when they "died." They also have pale and reflective skin and luminous eyes. Perhaps the main characteristics of Rice's vampires are that they are usually attractive, even beautiful, and excessively sensual and sensitive.

Richard, Father François

Father François Richard was a mid-seventeenth-century Jesuit priest who lived on the Greek island of Santorini (Thera) for many years. While on the island he wrote a treatise about the island and its vampires: *Relating what occurred on the island of Santorini in the Archipelago* (1657, published in Paris). According to the priest, Santorini was the most vampire-infested place on earth. In his opinion vampires were created by Satan and demons that animated bodies in order to spread their evil.

Richmond Vampire

The story of the Richmond Vampire is an urban legend that tells of a blood-covered creature with jagged teeth and skin hanging from its muscular body. It began to circulate soon after a collapse in the Chesapeake and Ohio Railroad's Church Hill Tunnel at Church Hill, a district of Richmond, Virginia. The tunnel collapse buried several workers alive on October 2, 1925.

According to the story this creature emerged from the cave-in and started to race toward James River. When pursued it took refuge in Hollywood Cemetery, where it disappeared into a mausoleum built into the hillside bearing the name W. W. Pool. Experts who have analyzed the story have discovered that after the tunnel collapsed someone did escape: 28-year-old railroad fireman Benjamin F. Mosby, who had been loading coal into the steam tank of a train with no shirt on when the cave-in occurred. According to witness reports, Mosby's upper body was horribly scalded and several of his teeth were broken before he made his way through the opening of the tunnel. He died later at Grace Hospital. It was from there that the story probably took on a life of its own through numerous retellings over the decades.

Riva, James P. (1958–)

On April 10, 1980, 22-year-old James P. Riva stabbed and then shot his handicapped grandmother twice in the heart as she sat in her wheelchair. The gun was loaded with golden bullets. He drank the warm blood gushing from the wounds before trying to cover his tracks by burning her body and her home. Later Riva said that "*the vampire voices*" had instructed him to murder his grandmother.

Jimmy Riva was a troubled youngster who developed a blood lust in his early years. By the time he was a teenager he was fascinated with vampires and became obsessed with the notion that his infirm grandmother was a vampire predator. He had a history of mental illness and schizophrenia dating back to 1975, when he spent time in a mental institution. He began by drawing horrific pictures and slowly moved to killing and drinking the blood of animals. Finally, he snapped completely and killed his grandmother.

Riva gave two separate stories when confronted about his crime. He told his mother that he was a vampire who would gain strength from drinking his grandmother's blood, and he also told psychiatrists he thought his grandmother was a vampire who came to feed on him as he slept. At the conclusion of his lengthy trial in 1981, a jury found him guilty of second degree murder and he was sentenced to life imprisonment in Walpole State Prison.

See also: **CRIME**

Roberts, Sarah Ellen

Shortly before midnight on June 8, 1993, over a thousand people turned up at a cemetery in Pisco, Peru, in the hope of witnessing the resurrection of an alleged vampire named Sarah Ellen Roberts. The story is an illustration of how, even in relatively modern times, stories of vampires continue to be reported, especially in remote areas.

The corpse of Sarah Roberts had allegedly been brought to Pisco from Blackburn,

England, by her husband, John, in 1913, because British authorities refused to let him bury his wife in England as they believed her to be a vampire. Shortly after her burial, so the story goes, John Roberts boarded a ship for England and was never heard of again. Soon afterward news reached Pisco from England that Sarah Roberts had been bound in chains and shut up in the lead-lined coffin after being found guilty of witchcraft, murder, and vampirism.

Eighty years later in June 1993, people visiting a grave in the Pisco cemetery noticed a crack appearing in the headstone marking Sarah Roberts's grave. Later that night a thousand spectators descended on the graveyard when word went round that the vampire would rise from her grave at midnight. Local women hung garlic and crucifixes around their doors to prevent the vampire attacking their children. When midnight arrived, the police had to be called in to control the hysterical crowds. Shots were fired in the air, and slowly the crowds gradually dispersed.

A small group of local witch doctors were apparently allowed to stay at the grave. They splashed the cracked headstone with holy water and sprinkled white rose petals around it. Sarah Roberts did not rise from the grave and the witch doctors celebrated their success at helping the undead woman find rest.

Rodna

In his 1974 book *A Clutch of Vampires*, Professor Raymond T. McNally reported that in 1969, when he was passing through Rodna, a village near to the Borgo Pass made famous in Bram Stoker's 1897 novel *Dracula*, McNally noticed a funeral going on in the village graveyard and went to have a look. He talked to some locals and was told that they were burying a girl who had committed suicide. The locals feared that she would become a vampire and so, to quote McNally, *"They did what had to be done and what I have read about for many years. They plunged a stake through the heart of the corpse."*

Although McNally's story seems to suggest that he actually witnessed the alleged staking, he does not directly say so. This has led some experts to suggest that he may have made it up.

Rohl, Johann Christopher

Johann Christopher Rohl was an early eighteenth-century German theologian, who along with Johann Hertel, authored a lengthy vampire treatise translated as *Dissertation on the Bloodsucking Dead*, which was published in Leipzig in 1732. The work compares favorably with that of Philip Rohr.

Rohr, Philip

Philip Rohr was a late-seventeenth-century German expert on the undead who wrote the influential pseudoscientific treatise *De Masticatione Mortuorum* (On the Chewing Dead), which was published in Leipzig in 1679. The treatise made a significant contribution to belief in manducation, where a corpse is believed to eat its shroud and itself in the grave.

Romania

Romania is a south-eastern European nation historically once divided into Transylvania, Moldavia, and Wallachia. Rich in folklore and with traditions that differ from district to district and village to village, this country faced numerous foreign invasions and occupations from the Romans (who named it Dacia), Hungarians, and Turks. Some experts believe that it was this rich folklore – which extended to vampires and traditions to prevent the return of the dead – that kept communities stable and maintained social order during times of crisis and invasion.

When gathering material for *Dracula*, Bram Stoker drew on the goldmine of Romanian folklore so skillfully that to this day no other country in the world is more associated with vampires than Romania.

Romanian vampires

Romania is surrounded by Slavic countries, so it is not surprising that Romanian vampires share similarities with Slavic vampires.

In Romanian lore, the term used to describe vampires of all types was "strigoi" (female strigoaica; plural strigoii). The Romanians also distinguished between the strigoi *vii* or live vampire and the strigoi *mort* or dead vampire. The word "strigoi" was closely related to the Romanian word *striga*, "witch," a term derived from the Latin *strix*, meaning "screech owl" and also used to refer to demons that attacked children at night. Therefore the strigoii *vii* were witches who were destined to become vampires at death and who could send out their souls at night to drain the life force of the living by a process of psychic vampirism. The strigoii *mort* were reanimated bodies of the dead who returned to life to suck the blood of the living, typically starting with their family.

Another Romanian term for a living vampire was "moroi" (female moroaica), also spelled murony or muroni in some older sources. Other terms include the varcolaci, the pricolici, and the nosferatu. The varcolaci and the pricolici tended to be much closer to the popular concept of werewolves than vampires. Nosferatu has often, mistakenly, been cited as a Romanian word meaning "undead" or the "devil." No matter where the name comes from, the nosferatu is associated with a blood-drinking vampire that possesses the ability to have sexual relations with the living.

Traits

The traits and characteristics of Romanian vampires differed from village to village but there were some common themes. There were a number of ways for a corpse to become a vampire, including being a seventh son, being born out of wedlock, being born with a caul, or having an extra nipple. Pregnant women who did not eat enough salt or who allowed themselves to be stared at by a vampire could give birth to a vampire. In addition to conditions of irregular birth, leading a sinful life, dabbling with witchcraft, dying unbaptized or unmarried, committing suicide, having a cat jump over the corpse, or being bitten by a vampire could all predispose a person to vampirism.

Vampires, like witches, were said to be most prevalent on St. George's Eve (April 22, according to the Gregorian calendar, May 4 on the Julian calendar). St. George's Eve, still celebrated today in Europe, was the night when all manner of evil was said to manifest on earth. The presence of vampires in a community would first be noticed by a number of poltergeist-like disturbances in a house, for example, food disappearing or objects flying around. A number of illnesses and deaths in a family (and/or among livestock) would typically follow the death of a family member or someone thought to be a vampire. Then other deaths would follow in the village.

Detection and prevention

A vampire in the grave could be discerned by holes in the earth surrounding the grave, by which the vampire could enter and exit. Once the coffin was opened, a corpse with a red face, with fresh blood on its mouth or with one foot in the corner of the coffin would be declared vampiric. Graves were often opened three years after the death of a child, five years after the death of a young person, or seven years after the death of an adult to check for signs of vampirism. Living vampires were identified by distributing garlic in church and seeing who did not eat it.

To prevent a person becoming a vampire any caul would be removed from a newborn and destroyed before the baby could eat it. Careful preparation of the recently deceased was also considered vital. This would include preventing animals, especially black cats, from jumping over the corpse, placing a thorny branch of wild rose in the grave, and placing garlic on windows and rubbing it on cattle, especially on St. George's Eve (and St. Andrew's Eve). Once in the grave, stakes might be driven into the ground above the grave so that if the corpse should re-emerge it would impale itself. Millet seeds might also be placed in the coffin or on pathways leading to the grave to distract the vampire, as it was thought that they would be compelled to eat the seeds, at a rate of one seed a year.

Destruction

Once a vampire began to attack a family and/or community and the identity of its grave had been discovered, the vampire would have to be destroyed. This was done by either driving a stake through the heart or navel, followed by decapitation and the placing of garlic in the mouth. A bullet might also be fired into the coffin. In addition the body could be replaced face down and reversed in the coffin. If it was suspected that a vampire might be the cause of a plague or the slow, wasting death of a number of people, then sometimes the heart and liver of an exhumed corpse would be burned and the ashes mixed with water. This mixture would then be drunk by those suffering from the disease in the hope it would cure them. It would also be drunk by those not yet ill as a form of prevention. (Quite the same practice occurred in Poland and New England.) The people might also fumigate themselves by standing in the smoke of the burning heart.

In the Romanian journal of folklore and folk art, *Ion Creanga*, vol. vii (1914), there is an article by the Romanian folklorist N. I. Dumitrascu that contains accounts he recorded concerning the detection, destruction, and disposal of vampires. In three of these cases, the heart (and the liver too, in two instances) of the vampire was cremated, the resulting ashes mixed with water, and the mixture drunk by the vampire's victims. One of these cases concerned the village of Amarasti in the north of the Dolj district, in the south-east of the country.

In around 1899 an old woman in the village of Amarasti died. She was soon followed by the children of her eldest son, Dinu Gheorgita, and the children of her youngest son. In an attempt to prevent more deaths within the family, Dinu and his brother exhumed their dead mother, cut her corpse in half and reburied it. The deaths still continued. So, they dug up their mother a second time and allegedly found that her body had become whole again. This time, they disemboweled her and cut out her heart, from which blood was flowing. The heart was cut into four pieces and burned into ashes that they mixed with water and gave to their children to drink. The remaining parts of their mother's corpse were burned and scattered as ashes. Finally, the deaths ceased.

Contemporary note

In some rural parts of Romania fear of the dead returning from the grave to attack the living is still strong. In 2004, forensic scientists were called to a cemetery in the Romanian village of Marotinul de Sus, to examine a mutilated corpse.

Plagued by nightmares and illness since the death of their elderly relative, six members of the same family exhumed the corpse of the 76-year-old retired schoolteacher and drove a pitchfork into his chest. His heart was removed and burned and the ashes mixed with peppermint schnapps and drunk by the family. The corpse was also stabbed with wooden stakes, and covered with garlic. According to one member of the vampire-slaying gang the corpse had blood around his mouth, and had moaned when they stabbed him.

The six family members were all eventually caught and jailed by local police, but their imprisonment greatly angered the local villagers, who believed that they had performed a great service for the village.

See also: **BURIAL CUSTOMS; GIRL AND THE VAMPIRE, THE; PRONE BURIAL; TRANSYLVANIA; VLAD THE IMPALER**

Rome

The vampire myth in ancient Rome was not as clearly defined as the vampire myth in ancient Greece. In general, vampirism was a characteristic of living witches and not revenants or the returning dead. The most vampire-like entity was the strix, a night demon associated with the screech owl that attacked and drained the blood of babies. Language experts believe that the term survived in Romania as "strigoi" and from the strix the concept of the strega, a shape-shifting female witch, also developed.

See also: **ITALY; LEMURES**

The Element Encyclopedia of Vampires

Ropes

In many regions ropes were used to bind or tie corpses to prevent them leaving the grave. Often these ropes would be tied into knots in the belief that the vampire would be distracted and compelled to untie the knots instead of attacking the living. However, the Saxons of Transylvania removed the knots and ropes prior to burial, as they thought they might prevent the passage of the dead to the afterlife.

See also: **BINDING A CORPSE**

Rosary

The rosary is a string of beads used by Catholics and members of the Eastern Churches to aid in the recitation of prayers. A rosary is held to work like a cross or crucifix to keep vampires away.

See also: **HOLY OBJECTS**

Roses

As a symbol of Christ, blood, beauty, and love, roses in both fiction and folklore have long been considered repellent to all evil entities, including vampires. Their sweet aroma repels, their thorns destroy, and their flowers can burn vampires like acid.

In Muslim Slavic Gypsy lore a vampire can be killed by thrusting a sharp stake of wild rosewood through its belly at dusk. In Transylvania, a branch of the wild rose was placed upon a corpse prior to burial, or upon the grave of a suspected vampire, to prevent its return as a vampire. In the third chapter of *Dracula* Jonathan Harker asks *"What meant the giving of the crucifix, of the garlic of the wild rose of the mountain rose?"* and readers have come to know these items as protective devices against vampires.

See also: **APOTROPAICS; PREVENTION**

Roslasin

In 1870 reports of vampire attacks centered round a churchyard at Roslasin, which was part of German territory but is now (renamed Rozlazino) part of Poland.

According to local records discovered by author Hermann Schreiber for his book *Es spukt in Deutschland* (1975), on February 5, 1870, in the town of Kantrzyno, a man called Franz von Poblocki died of consumption and was buried in the churchyard of Roslasin. On February 18, 1870, von Poblocki's son Anton also died and other family members started to suffer from nightmares and poor health. Before Anton's burial, the family decided that Franz had become a vampire and was causing the illnesses so they hired local vampire-hunting expert, Johann Dzigielski, to help them destroy the vampire. Dzigielski urged them to decapitate both bodies.

After decapitating the corpse of Anton, Johann tied to bribe the undertaker to let him dig up Franz's corpse. The undertaker was concerned and went to the local priest, who wrote a letter to the Poblocki family, warning them that vampire hunting was forbidden in his churchyard. The Poblocki family decided to ignore the priest's letter and take matters into their own hands. They dug up Franz and decapitated his corpse.

When the priest discovered what the family had done he notified the authorities and the family went on trial. Dzigielski, the vampire hunter, received a four-month sentence, but the Poblocki family (who were clearly influential in the area) appealed to a higher court, stating that they had only acted out of self-defense because they feared their lives were in danger. As a result of this, all charges against the vampire hunters were dropped on May 15, 1872.

Rowan

Also known as mountain ash, rowan is a member of the *Sorbus* genus of small trees and shrubs found in parts of Europe and Britain, and is said to have powers to protect against evil. A rowan tree was often planted in churchyards and outside homesteads to prevent evil spirits entering. In Scotland women would wear a necklace of protective rowan berries.

Russia

Russia has an ancient vampire cult and folklore and a genuine dread of the returning undead that dates back centuries. Many experts believe Russia to be the homeland of the Slavic vampire.

A number of sources suggest an early belief in blood-drinking spirits and demons but the Russian word for vampire, upur or upir, first appeared in a text written for a medieval Novgorodian prince which may date back to 1047. The text calls a priest *upir lichy*, which means "wicked vampire." Upir appeared consistently over the centuries and even though it was joined over time by, among others, the vieszcy of the Kashubs, the upar of Belarus, and the upior of Ukraine, it gradually established itself as the name for the undead.

Like the Romanians, the Russians believed in a number of causes for vampirism, including witchcraft, suicide, and birth irregularities that produced a predisposition to vampirism. More unique causes included leaving a corpse exposed to the strong winds of the Steppes and being a heretic. Vampires that were heretics before their death were known as eretica or eretik. In Russian thought, heresy and vampirism were virtually identical concepts. Another vampire in Russian lore, the erestun, was an ordinary person – most likely a robber, villain, or someone depraved – who while alive or after death had his or her body invaded by evil. The victim would appear normal but would start to feed on members of the family in the form of a psychic vampire.

Methods of vampire destruction in Russia were similar to those in other Slavic countries. The body of the suspected vampire would be exhumed and a stake driven through the heart. Sometimes the body would be burned.

Russian folktales and literature

Through the centuries Russian folktales have kept the myth of the vampire alive. In the 1860s Russian scholar Alexander Afanasiev collected and preserved these folktales, and they were also collected by W. R. S. Ralston in *Russian Folktales* (1873). Vampire tales in this collection include "The Shroud," "The Coffin Lid," "The Two Corpses," and "The Soldier and the Vampire."

"The Coffin Lid" illustrates the belief in vampires in tzarist times.

A moujik [peasant] was driving along one night with a load of pots. His horse grew tired, and all of a sudden it came to a stand-still alongside a graveyard. The moujik unharnessed his horse and set it free to graze; meanwhile he laid himself down on one of the graves. But somehow he didn't go to sleep.

He remained lying there some time. Suddenly the grave began to open beneath him: he felt the movement and sprang to his feet. The grave opened, and out of it came a corpse, wrapped in a white shroud, and holding a coffin lid. It came out and ran to the church, laid the coffin-lid at the door, and then set off for the village.

The moujik was a daring fellow. He picked up the coffin-lid and remained standing beside his cart, waiting to see what would happen. After a short delay the dead man came back, but couldn't find his coffin-lid. Then the corpse began to track it down. It traced it to the moujik, and said:

"Give me my lid: if you don't, I'll tear you to bits!"

"And my hatchet, how about that?" answers the moujik. "Why, it's I who'll be chopping you into small pieces!"

"Do give it back to me, good man!" begs the corpse.

"I'll give it when you tell me where you've been and what you've done."

"Well, I've been in the village, and there I've killed a couple of youngsters."

"Well then, now tell me how they can be brought back to life."

The corpse reluctantly made answer:

"Cut off the left skirt of my shroud, and take it with you. When you come into the house

where the youngsters were killed, pour some live coals into a pot and put the piece of the shroud in with them, and then lock the door. The lads will be revived by the smoke immediately."

The moujik cut off the left skirt of the shroud, and gave up the coffin-lid. The corpse went to its grave – the grave opened. But just as the dead man was descending into it, all of a sudden the cocks began to crow, and he hadn't time to get properly covered over. One end of the coffin-lid remained sticking out of the ground.

The moujik saw all this and made a note of it. The day began to dawn; he harnessed his horse and drove into the village. In one of the houses he heard cries and wailing. In he went – there lay two dead lads.

"Don't cry," says he, "I can bring them to life!"

"Do bring them to life, kinsman," say their relatives. "We'll give you half of all we possess."

The moujik did everything as the corpse had instructed him, and the lads came back to life. Their relatives were delighted, but they immediately seized the moujik and bound him with cords, saying:

"No, no, trickster! We'll hand you over to the authorities. Since you knew how to bring them back to life, maybe it was you who killed them!"

"What are you thinking about, true believers! Have the fear of God before your eyes!" cried the moujik.

Then he told them everything that had happened during the night. Well, they spread the news through the village; the whole population assembled and swarmed into the graveyard. They found the grave from which the dead man had come out, they tore it open, and they drove an aspen stake right into the heart of the corpse, so that it might no more rise up and slay. But they rewarded the moujik richly, and sent him away home with great honor.

During the nineteenth century the vampire made its appearance in Russian literature, and in the 1840s Aleksey Tolstoy (1817–75) combined the Russian vampire myth with the vampire myth that had emerged in Germany and France. Tolstoy's *Upyr* and *The Family of the Vourdalak* became classics of both Russian and vampire literature.

Some people believe that the first-ever vampire film, *The Secret House No. 5*, was made in Russia in 1912, and ever since the vampire theme has appeared frequently in Russian movies.

Chupacabra

In recent years Russia has also been one of the countries where alleged sightings have been made of the so-called chupacabra or "goatsucker," a mysterious creature said to attack and drain the blood of animals, in particular goats. In April 2006, *MosNews* reported that the chupacabra was spotted in Russia for the first time. Reports from Central Russia from March 2005 tell of a beast that kills animals and sucks out their blood. Thirty-two turkeys were killed and drained overnight. Reports later came from neighboring villages when 30 sheep were killed. In most cases puncture wounds were found on the animals and they had all had their blood drained.

Ruthven, Lord

See: **LORD RUTHVEN**

Rymer, James Malcolm (1804-84)

James Malcolm Rymer was the author of the 1847 penny dreadful *Varney the Vampire, or The Feast of Blood*, which was sold as a serial in 109 weekly installments.

In 1842 Rymer, a civil engineer, switched career and became editor of the respected *Queen's Magazine* and a year later the editor of *Lloyd's Penny Weekly Miscellany*. While working at *Queen's* he wrote an article that ridiculed penny dreadfuls – serial novels that sold for a penny an installment – and characterized the readership as ignorant. However, he later discovered that he was good at writing the fiction he detested and wrote penny dreadfuls himself for *Lloyd's* under pseudonyms.

As Rymer wrote under pseudonyms it is not easy to know when he began writing, but the most popular book written largely by him was *Varney the Vampire*. It appeared in the mid 1840s and ran to 220 chapters and 868 pages. In 1847 the chapters were then collected into a single volume which continued to sell well for the next decade. The inspiration for Varney seems to have come from a reprinting in 1840 in a penny dreadful format of Polidori's *The Vampyre*.

For many decades authorship of *Varney* was attributed to Thomas Preskett Prest, author of *Sweeney Todd*, another very successful penny dreadful. However, in 1963, Louis Jones, who had inherited many of Rymer's notebooks, found conclusive evidence that it was Rymer – and not Prest – who was the author, even though it is possible that other writers worked on certain chapters. Collective authorship was common practice for penny dreadfuls and may account for their uneven style and plot contradictions.

The chapter that started it all:

…The figure has paused again, and half on the bed and half out of it that young girl lies trembling. Her long hair streams across the entire width of the bed. As she has slowly moved along she has left it streaming across the pillows. The pause lasted about a minute – oh, what an age of agony. That minute was, indeed, enough for madness to do its full work in.

With a sudden rush that could not be foreseen – with a strange howling cry that was enough to awaken terror in every breast, the figure seized the long tresses of her hair, and twining them round his bony hands he held her to the bed. Then she screamed – Heaven granted her then power to scream. Shriek followed shriek in rapid succession. The bed-clothes fell in a heap by the side of the bed – she was dragged by her long silken hair completely on to it again. Her beautifully rounded limbs quivered with the agony of her soul. The glassy, horrible eyes of the figure ran over that angelic form with a hideous satisfaction – horrible profanation. He drags her head to the bed's edge. He forces it back by the long hair still entwined in his grasp. With a plunge he seizes her neck in his fang-like teeth – a gush of blood, and a hideous sucking noise follows. The girl has swooned, and the vampyre is at his hideous repast!

Next Time: The Alarm. – The Pistol Shot. – The Pursuit and Its Consequences.

(Extracted from the final paragraphs of the first chapter of *Varney the Vampire*)
See also: **LITERATURE**

"There are such beings as vampires, some of us have evidence that they exist. Even had we not the proof of our own unhappy experience, the teachings and the records of the past give proof enough for sane peoples."

Bram Stoker

Sabbatarians

In vampire lore the definition for Sabbatarian differs from the common dictionary definition of a person who either advocates the strict religious observance of Sunday or observes Saturday as the Sabbath, in that the name is applied to someone who is born on a Saturday and who is said to possess special powers to see ghosts and vampires, during both day and nighttime. Male and female twins born on a Saturday were believed to be extremely powerful and were thought to protect Gypsy villagers if they wore their underwear inside out. In Greece and Macedonia, Sabbatarians were said to hunt and capture the vrykolakas.

Sabbatarians acted as vampire hunters and were often aided in this task by a spectral vampire-hunting hound, a kind of familiar. One Greek case describes how a Sabbatarian lured a vrykolakas into a barn where millet seeds had been scattered. While the vrykolakas was distracted by the seeds the Sabbatarian nailed it to the wall.

See also: **DHAMPIR**

Saberhagen, Fred (1930–2007)

Fred Saberhagen was a much-respected American author of science fiction and fantasy novels that skillfully combined mythology and science. He was the author of a series of novels about Dracula that expanded the Dracula theme and transformed the Count into a hero. In the novels Dracula is placed in a number of different historical settings, meeting historical, fictional, and mythological characters as diverse as Leonardo da Vinci, Sherlock Holmes, and Merlin.

The first book in the series was *The Dracula Tape* (1975) and the series continued into the mid 1990s with *Seance for a Vampire* (1994) and *A Sharpness on the Neck* (1996). Film director Francis Ford Coppola chose Saberhagen to co-author (with screenwriter James V. Hart), the novelization of Coppola's film, *Bram Stoker's Dracula* (1992). In 2002 Saberhagen contributed his last book in the Dracula series, entitled *A Coldness in the Blood*.

See also: **LITERATURE**

Sade, Marquis de (1740–1814)

The term "sadism" is derived from the infamous lifestyle and writings of Donatien Alphonse François, Marquis de Sade. A French aristocrat, revolutionary, and novelist, de Sade had an insatiable appetite for pornography and sexual perversion, which led to his imprisonment in Milan, Vincennes, the Bastille, and eventually a lunatic asylum at Charenton.

De Sade was a proponent of extreme freedom (or at least licentiousness), unrestrained by morality, religion, or law, with the pursuit of personal pleasure being the highest principle, and he lived a scandalously libertine existence. While in prison, he wrote novels that expressed and explored such controversial subjects as rape, necrophilia, and bestiality. Among them were *Justine, ou les Malheurs de la Vertu* (Justine, or the Misfortunes of Virtue) and *Juliette*, both of which contained scenes of vampirism. In *Juliette*, characters include a cannibal and a necrophiliac and in *Justine*, the Comte de Gernade enjoys watching his victims bleed.

De Sade's perverted, twisted lifestyle and literature has encouraged many vampirologists to describe him as a living vampire.

After his death in 1814, de Sade's will was found to contain detailed instructions forbidding that his body be opened up upon any pretext whatsoever, and that it be left untouched for 48 hours in the chamber in which he died, and then placed in a coffin and buried on his property, located in Malmaison near Epernon. His skull was later removed from the grave for scientific examination or, as has been suggested by some over the years, to prevent his corpse rising from the grave as a vampire.

See also: **HISTORICAL VAMPIRES**

Saint-Germain, Comte de

Saint-Germain is a fictional character created by author Chelsea Quinn Yarbro based on the historical figure of the eighteenth-century Comte de Saint-Germain.

The real Saint-Germain

The historical Saint-Germain was said to be the third son of Prince Ferenc II Rákóczy of Transylvania (or, variously, the son of Charles II of Spain, or of John V of Portugal). When Saint-Germain first appeared in Europe in 1743 he was said to be in his mid forties. Although he was an astute politician who traveled Europe on behalf of both Louis XV of France and Frederick the Great of Prussia, he was also an elusive and mysterious figure. He was described as not particularly handsome and of medium height with small hands and feet, but he had hypnotic eyes and dressed extremely well, often wearing diamonds on every finger.

He had strange habits, such as never eating or drinking in public, and was fluent in at least 10 languages. He collected fine art and jewels, painted, and played violin and harpsichord.

Many believed that the Comte was a spy and it is likely that he was giving information to the King of Prussia when he was working for Louis XV. In 1762 he was said to have helped put Catherine the Great on the Russian throne, and through prophecy he was said to have tried to warn Louis XVI of the coming revolution. After his death in 1785 or 1786 he was said to have appeared to members of the French royal family to warn them of their destruction.

The Comte was alleged to be a student of the occult and of alchemy, and he led others to believe that he had discovered the secret of transforming base metal into gold. He also reportedly had the elixir of life and told people he had lived for thousands of years. According to some occultists, before his incarnation as the historical Saint-Germain, he had already had numerous illustrious incarnations including as Joseph, the father of Jesus, Merlin the Wizard, and Christopher Columbus.

The fictional Saint-Germain

An intriguing combination of Count Dracula, the Count of Monte Cristo, and the historical Saint-Germain, the fictional Comte de Saint-Germain first appeared in the novel *Hôtel Transylvania* (1978). Over the many novels that followed Yarbro gradually leaked details about his life. Born 4,000 years ago in Transylvania in a society that worshipped a vampire god, Saint-Germain was kidnapped and beheaded by a rival clan, but they failed to burn his body and he survived to travel through time and history. He is presented as a mysterious, cultured, sophisticated man able to move with ease among the very highest circles of society. He is learned, seductive, passionate, and compassionate to a degree, and he is able to walk in sunlight because of small amounts of native soil that fill the hollow heels of his shoes. He feeds by drinking small amounts of blood from women who provide it in return for his romantic attentions.

Salem's Lot

Salem's Lot is the bestselling 1975 vampire novel by horror author Stephen King. The title King originally chose for his book was "Second Coming." He later decided on "Jerusalem's Lot" but the publishers shortened it to the current title, thinking the author's choice sounded too religious.

The novel, consciously modeled on Bram Stoker's *Dracula*, supposedly attempts to answer the question of what would happen if a vampire lived in a small American town. Like Dracula, the vampire Barlow has a terrifying presence, and red eyes that are *"like the furnace doors to hell."* Barlow's blood-drinking also makes him appear younger and again, like Dracula, Barlow appears only a few times in the novel, fueling the atmosphere of foreboding and mystery around him. King felt that the

sexual undercurrent that was so powerful in *Dracula* would not work as well in modern times, so King's vampire is pure evil. Whereas Dracula preys on young women, Barlow preys on everyone, especially children.

The plot

Ben Mears, a writer, returns to his hometown, the small New England town of Jerusalem's Lot to research a house that has lingered in his mind because of a terrible childhood memory. He notices that two strangers have moved into the house that haunts him and that townspeople are dying at a rapid rate. Mears is convinced that vampires have moved into the house and organizes a hunt to destroy the blood-sucking Barlow, but is prevented from killing Barlow by Barlow's servant. Barlow transforms citizens into vampires, creating an army of the undead that slowly begin to take over the town and kill the hunters one by one, until only Mears and a young friend, Mark, are left to face the vampire.

The vampire hunters turn to the novel *Dracula* to find out how to fight vampires, and they make crosses and stakes out of firewood. They also learn to battle their own evil within and rediscover the importance of faith. Eventually Mears stakes Barlow, who dies dramatically in his coffin with his skin and flesh disappearing rapidly. The story does not end here because even though the master vampire has been destroyed his vampire creatures have not. Eventually, after taking a year to recover psychologically from their ordeal, Ben and Mark go back to Jerusalem's Lot and light a fire of purification to burn the town and the vampires, suggesting that now it is possible for something new and pure to rise from the ashes.

For many fans of King's writing *Salem's Lot* is one of his finest and most gruesome tales, with its chilling theme of absolute evil introduced into the lives of ordinary folks. In 1979, the novel was presented as a television movie, staring David Soul as Mears and Reggie Nalder as Barlow. A further television adaptation aired in 2004, staring Rob Lowe as Mears and Rutger Hauer as Barlow.

Salic Law

Salic law, the so-called *Lex Salica* in Latin, was an important body of traditional law codified for governing the Salian Franks who conquered Gaul in the fifth century AD. Although Salic law reflects very ancient usage and practices, the earliest codification of the law was probably made by King Clovis between 507 and 511, and was twice reissued by his successors, including a proclamation of the law by Charlemagne (747–814)

The best-known tenet of Salic law is agnatic succession, the rule excluding females from inheriting a throne or fief. But the importance of Salic law extends beyond the rules of inheritance, as it is a direct ancestor of the systems of law in many parts of Europe today. In addition to civic law, the *Lex Salica* contained a long list of crimes and punishments, including severe pronouncements against vampirism, a reaction to the fear concerning vampires in early medieval Europe. When he reissued the Salic laws, Charlemagne was particularly concerned that Christian rites and pagan rites had become mixed, and pronounced a death sentence on anyone burning a suspected vampire, termed a "striges."

Salt

In folklore, salt is often a protective agent that can be used against witches, vampires, and other evil spirits. Salt is thought to be able to repel evil because it is a symbol of purity and goodness (whiteness), and also because it has the ability to preserve and is of vital importance for life and health.

In some traditions, people would carry salt at night to protect them against vampires and evil spirits, or it would be thrown over the left shoulder to blind whatever evil might be lurking there. For the same protective reason salt would also be sprinkled in a baby's cradle or around a person's bed or in a coffin. In Romanian lore, if a woman did not eat salt during her pregnancy some believed that her child would become a vampire.

See also: **APOTROPAICS; PROTECTION**

Sampiro

In the folklore of Albania the sampiro, also known in some regions as liugat, is an unusual and incredible vampiric entity. In ancient times it was believed that anyone born to Turkish parents would become a sampiro within days of their burial. There is a tradition of animosity between the Albanians and the Turks and sampiro folklore demonstrates how the notion of difference, tied in with fear and suspicions of strangers, can play a large part in the creation of the vampire myth.

Descriptions of the sampiro differ from region to region but some common features remain. Typically the creature is swathed in its grave shroud or in flowing garments and follows victims on foggy nights making kissing sounds, which are said to be the creature antici-pating the drinking of blood. It wears incredibly high heels and has enormous eyes. This descrip-tion of the sampiro verges on the ridiculous but in Albania the creature is greatly feared.

It is not just Turks who were believed to become sampiro when they die. Liars and thieves, as well as people who have had sex with animals, or who have had sex with Turks, or frequented prostitutes, or eaten meat han-dled by a Turk, or attended a Muslim service can all become sampiro. According to vampire lore expert Bob Curran, it is possible that the idea of the sampiro has been used over the cen-turies to help maintain the purity of the Alban-ian people and also as a form of moral control. In this way fear of the undead can be seen to serve as a powerful form of social control for the Albanians, and as a means of keeping the ethnic grouping free of outside influences.

In many cases, the sampiro first attacks its own family. Not only does it drink blood from individual family members, it can also spread disease and sickness through a whole commu-nity. In some regions the sampiro have been blamed for plagues and epidemics and in others just the gaze of a sampiro, as it stops at the win-dow of a house to gaze within, can induce sick-ness. In this way whole villages can fall ill and die.

Destruction

The most effective way to kill the sampiro is said to be by staking it, but it is considered unwise to attempt to do this while the vampire is out of its grave. The sampiro must be destroyed in its grave. To identify the grave, vampire hunters need to look for a faint blue candle-light flame or will-o'-the-wisp hovering over it. The soil around the grave will also be porous and easily disturbed. This is because it is said that the vampire needs air to breathe when it "sleeps." When the grave is identified the corpse must be removed with the recitation of prayers and rituals and then staked through the heart.

Sanguinarians

Sanguinarians are a group of people who feel they need to drink blood like traditional vampires. They call themselves sanguinari-ans after the Latin word for bloodthirsty – *sanguinarius*.

According to the Nocturnus website (http://www.nocturnusonline.net/), dedicated to "real" vampires,

Sanguinarians are mortals who have a need to feed on the blood of others to maintain a state of good health. Sanguinarians do not produce a sufficient amount of pranic or "life" energy, and therefore need to replace this energy by drinking blood, which is a high source of pranic energy.

Sanguinarians believe that they are born as vampires but do not become aware of their true nature until their late teens. This increasing awareness of their true vampiric nature is called "awakening" and when they learn to sat-isfy their urgent need for blood they undergo a vampiric transformation. Their bodies grow stronger, their reflexes faster, and their minds become telepathic; they also develop a painful sensitivity to sunlight that means they tend to sleep during the day and feed and socialize at night. Sanguinarians do not believe they are immortal but they do believe that they are ageless, in other words they do not age. They will die eventually but some sanguinarians claim to be able to achieve a state called "torpor," a very deep sleep that lengthens their life for tens or hundreds of years.

Some sanguinarians are very open about their lifestyle and blood-drinking habits but many refuse to reveal their true identity to "mundanes," the sanguinarian term for humans, as they feel that the centuries of hatred against vampires has produced a prejudice against blood drinkers. They fear that people might threaten or harm them in some way.

Feeding

Sanguinarians believe that having the traits of a vampire does not necessarily make one a vampire. It is the need to feed on blood and energy which defines a vampire. Sanguinarians do not kill people for blood but rely on willing donors who volunteer to give them small amounts of blood. Donors are carefully screened to ensure feeding is safe, with blood tests conducted at medical clinics to ensure diseases are not transmitted through the exchange of blood. (Donors do not become vampires after being bitten by a sanguinarian.)

Sanguinarians believe they grow in strength after each feed and when in need of blood they experience a condition called the Thirst, the Hunger, or the Need. This intense feeling can't be sated with food or drink but only by human blood. Again, to quote the Nocturnus website: *"Sanguinarians have a NEED to feed. Without regular feeding, they will become very sick, and experience stomach cramps, headaches, muscle cramps, irritability, nausea and lethargy."* According to the sanguinarius website (www.sanguinarius.org), blood drinking is a *"very driving need and takes a great deal of resistance to overcome the desire / craving / urge / lust / need / pull / demand / thirst / hunger / addiction / want."*

See also: **MODERN VAMPIRES**

Sanguinarium

The Sanguinarium (not to be confused with sanguinarians) is a modern vampire movement that purports to be an international association of vampire lifestylers: people who fashion themselves and their lifestyles around vampires and vampirism.

Founded in 1995 in New York's underground club scene, the Sanguinarium was designed to be a network, community, and resource for the vampyre subculture and scene. Over the years it has expanded to include organizations, businesses, havens, and individual members who are united under a code of ethics and morality known as The Black Veil. Although officially disbanded as an actual organization sometime around 2002, the Sanguinarium continues to exist in practice.

Inspired by the collection of vampire bars, nightclubs and safehouses founded in Anne Rice's Vampire Chronicles, the Sanguinarium serves to bring this vision to life as a real vampire community. However, many vampire enthusiasts are not attracted to the Sanguinarium because of the non-vampiric lifestylers it attracts and the hierarchy it endorses.

Types of vampire lifestylers

Within the Sanguinarium movement there are a number of different types of vampire lifestylers and different ways to transform into or become a vampire:

- *Born vampires are those who realize they are vampires and have always known it.*

- *Made vampires become vampires through a ritual initiation.*

- *Sanguinarians, who actually drink blood.*

- *Pranic vampires, who feed on spiritual energy known as* prana.

- *Sexual vampires, also called incubae and succubae, pursue erotic gratification.*

- *Fashion vampires, who enjoy dressing up as vampires.*

Strigoii vii

Sanguinarium members call the codes and practices of the movement the *Strigoi vii*, which in Romanian means "living vampire." The *Strigoi vii* is not a set of rules but a series of guidelines and suggestions for vampire lifestylers that draws on a variety of sources, including Eastern philosophy and shamanism, in developing the vampire myth.

The *Strigoi vii* suggests that the vampire lifestyle is one of self-discovery in which a per-

son discovers their true nature and discards conventional ways of thinking. The first step is to identify the vampire within and then to join a like-minded community; typically there would be some kind of initiation ritual involved when joining an organization. Once an initiate has become a member there are several different levels within an organization – Courts where procedure is discussed; Qabals for ceremonies and conferences; Temples for spiritually minded lifestylers; and Households.

Sanguinarium households are surrogate families made up of vampire lifestylers who provide support and recognition for each other. There are surrogate fathers, mothers, and siblings, and special roles within the household, such as elders, concubines, and guardians. In addition, there are classes of people affiliated with the vampire community who do not actually lead vampire lifestyles themselves, such as black swans – supportive non-vampires; white swans – members of the Goth scene; and invisibles – former vampire lifestylers who have been exiled from the community.

See also: **COVICA; LIVING VAMPIRES; MODERN VAMPIRES; REAL VAMPIRES**

Sanguisuga

Sanguisuga means "bloodsucker," from the Latin *sanguis*, "blood" and *sugere*, "to suck." The term was used in the Latin Vulgate Bible to offer insight on a passage in the Book of Proverbs (30:15) that referred to the algua, a bloodsucking demon. Sanguisuga was also used in several eighteenth-century treatises on vampires, for example the 1732 *Dissertation de hominibus post mortem sanguisua* (Treatise on the Bloodsucking Undead) by Johann Christopher Rohl.

Santorini

Santorini, a Greek island in the Aegean Sea, also known as Thera, has traditionally been known as the most vampire-infested place on earth. The phrase "vampires to Santorini" was equivalent to "cars to Detroit" or "coals to Newcastle."

Numerous accounts of travelers to Santorini, for example, Paul Lucas in *Voyage au Levant* (1705), mention its vampire reputation. In his *The Vampire in Europe* (1929), Montague Summers reports that he has found the following passage about Santorini in *Murray's Handbook for Travellers in Greece*:

> *The antiseptic nature of the soil, and the frequent discovery of undecayed bodies have given rise to many wild superstitions among the peasantry of the island. It is supposed to be the favourite abode of the Vrukolakas, a species of Ghoul or Vampire, which, according to a belief once popular in Greece, has the power of resuscitating the dead from their graves, and sending them forth to banquet on the living.*

Summers goes on to say that he visited Santorini in 1906–07, and heard *"many a gruesome legend of vampire events which were said to have taken place there quite recently."* He also reports that there had been two recent incidents where vampires had been sent over from Mykonos and Crete to be taken care of in Santorini.

The reason for Santorini's reputation is, as *Murray's Handbook* stated, probably associated with the antiseptic quality of the soil there, which prevents corpses from decomposing quickly. Since Santorini is formed from the remains of a volcanic crater its soil is very new and corpses that were exhumed there were often found remarkably preserved and held to be vampires by the locals. In ancient times, Santorini was notable for preferring cremation to burial to dispose of the dead, even though cremation was a more expensive and time-consuming procedure. With such a reputation for a thriving vampire community, it is not surprising that residents of Santorini became recognized as skilled experts in dealing with the undead and the corpses of suspected vampires were often brought there from other Greek islands.

Sarbanovac Vampires

The case of the Sarbanovac Vampires, which took place in 1839–40, is an illustration of how the Christian Church in Europe made great efforts to discourage vampire beliefs and superstitions. In some areas priests were sympathetic and would pray over bodies as they were dug up and sprinkle holy water over them, but in many cases the punishments were fines, whipping, imprisonment, or compulsory attendance at church.

In 1839 villagers in the Serbian community of Sarbanovac came to the conclusion that nine people who had recently died had transformed into vampires and were strangling people and animals. They applied to the local priest for permission to dig up their bodies but were forbidden to undertake any pagan or folklore remedies. When the priest left town on business the villagers ignored his warning and, led by a vampire hunter called Novak Mikov, who agreed to lead the hunt for a fee, they dug up eight bodies, cut out the hearts, boiled them in wine, and reburied the corpses. A ninth body was also exhumed but found not to be in a vampiric condition and so was reburied intact.

It was not long before the grave desecrations were discovered by Church officials and the matter was turned over to the secular court. Mikov and a man called Radovan Petrov were found guilty of corpse mutilation and were sentenced to a week in jail and 30 strikes of the cane.

Satan/Satanism

Satan, translated from the Hebrew, means "an adversary" or "enemy." Considered to be the embodiment of evil in Jewish, Christian, and Islamic religions, Satan has many aliases – the Devil, the Prince of Darkness, and Beelzebub being among the most common. There are those who revere Satan as a deity, as a source of black magic, and rituals are performed to him. Although many vampire experts and authors seem to suggest that vampires are created by the bite of another vampire, there is also a school of thought that believes that the origin of vampires and vampirism is directly related to Satan and Satanism.

The link between vampires and Satanism

In Emily Gerard's 1885 newspaper articles "Transylvania Superstitions," mention is made of a school in the Carpathian Mountains called Scholomance where the Devil himself taught the secrets of magic. Picking up on Gerard's research, Bram Stoker in his novel *Dracula* (1897) seems to suggest that vampirism is directly linked to Satanism, when

Van Helsing states that Dracula *"learned his secrets in the Scholomance … where the devil claims the tenth scholar as his due."*

However, long before *Dracula* was written there were stronger and more ancient traditions connecting the vampire with Satan. For example, in medieval Russia the vampire was called eretik, meaning a heretic or someone who was outside the realm of God and the one true faith. People outside the Church were thought to be servants of the Devil. Among the Slavs it was thought that the vampire originated from people who were witches or Satan worshippers, people who had killed themselves, or people who had been excommunicated from the Church and were therefore no longer acceptable to God.

Excommunicated from the Church, condemned to live in darkness, and thought to be dealing with the Devil, it was logical therefore that the vampire would be repelled by holy objects, such as crosses or holy water, and could not enter churches or sacred places. In this way it could be said that the Christian practice of excommunication had a lot to do with both the development of the vampire myth and the link between vampirism and Satanism.

It is also interesting to note that Dracul, the name of the historical Dracula, Vlad the Impaler, can be translated both as "dragon" and as "devil" and this has led some scholars to suggest a link between Vlad, Satanism, and vampirism. Occult theories concerning the origin of vampires also focus on possible links between vampires and Satan, the so-called Antichrist.

Modern attitudes

In modern-day pluralistic and secular cultures, vampire authors such as Anne Rice and Stephenie Meyer have tended to move away from the ancient connection between vampires and Satan and Satanism. Vampirism is typically presented in a secular way, either as a disease or as a superhuman potential that the vampire must learn to harness and control, and then choose whether to direct this potential in a positive or a negative way. Alternatively, supernatural myths not based on Christian assumptions may be put forward.

It could be argued that vampirism is a form of Satanism in that vampires attempt to survive on the energy or life blood of others, but many modern vampires, or individuals who model their lives and their lifestyles around vampires, do not believe they are evil or that vampirism is linked to Satanism in any way. The media goes into overdrive when disturbed individuals commit crimes in the name of vampirism but modern vampires do not identify themselves with these individuals or condone the crimes they commit. To them vampirism is simply a philosophy of energy. Everybody has a day side and a night side, but most people tend to repress or ignore the darkness inside. The goal of the modern vampire is to recognize and to understand the darker, hidden side of their nature so that a state of "twilight" or balance and control can be found.

See also: **CHRISTIANITY; ORIGINS, OF VAMPIRES**

Saturday

Saturday is the day of the week traditionally said to be holy because it was sacred to the Virgin Mary and therefore a day when vampires had little power. Saturday is the day when vampires must sleep in their graves, and the best day, therefore, for finding and destroying them.

In European folklore, babies born on a Saturday were called Sabbatarians and thought be born with the ability to see vampires and ghosts and to have powers against them.

Saxo Grammaticus

Saxo Grammaticus was a late twelfth-century historian whose early history of the Danes, *Gesta Danorum*, is thought to contain one of the earliest medieval reports of vampires.

Gesta Danorum contains a number of legends about the Danish kings but there are also two accounts of the returning dead, and in both cases the undead are destroyed in a way later vampire hunters would be familiar with. One of these accounts, from Book Two, is the tale of Aswid and Asmund. Both men died but Aswid was buried with his dog and horse and Asmund was buried with food. Asmund appeared after his death and stated that the spirit of Aswid had returned to the corpse and had eaten both his horse and dog and, still hungry, was now trying to eat Asmund, starting with his ears.

Scandinavia

Scandinavia consists of the three Northern European countries of Norway, Sweden, and Finland. Historically it could also be said to include Denmark and Iceland. The vampire was present in Scandinavian folklore although it was not a prominent tradition.

In old Scandinavian literature, such as the *Grettis Saga*, dated to around 1320, there was a tradition of fear of the dead who appeared as revenant-like ghosts. They were typically dispatched by stake and decapitation, practices similar to those carried out against the vampire in Eastern Europe. More characteristic of Scandinavian belief, especially in Denmark, was the mara, the nightmare. The mara was a female spirit, dangerous because of her ability to function on several different levels of consciousness and unconsciousness, which attacked people when they slept. She adopted human form during the day, often strangling unsuspecting males. Preventative steps against the mara included turning shoes to face the wrong way by the side of the bed and spreading seeds around the house. A knife was the most effective way to destroy the mara.

See also: **Draugr; Haugbui; Iceland**

Schertz, Charles Ferdinand de

Charles Ferdinand de Schertz was an early eighteenth-century lawyer and author of *Magia Posthuma*, a short 1706 treatise on the vampire published at Olmutz and Osnabrück. In *Magia* de Schertz related several stories of apparitions and the mischief done by them. One of the most well known was the Blow Vampire.

Dom Augustin Calmet stated in his 1748 treatise *Dissertation sur les Apparitions, des Anges … et sur les revenants, et Vampires* that de Schertz related a story about a woman who died in a certain village, after having received all the sacraments, and who was buried with the usual ceremonies in the churchyard. About four days after her death and for several months afterward, the inhabitants of the village were terrified by unusual noises and

many saw a specter, sometimes shaped like a dog and sometimes like a man, who tried to choke or suffocate them. Several victims were bruised all over and were left utterly weak, pale, lean, and disfigured. The specter took his fury out even on the animals; cows were frequently found beaten on the earth, half dead, at other times with their tails tied to one another, lowing hideously. Horses were found foaming with sweat and out of breath, as if they had been running a long and tiresome race. The fact that Calmet reviewed *Magia* shows how experts on the undead were beginning to use each other's work to spread stories and theories.

De Schertz was a lawyer so it is not surprising that he examined the subject from the perspective of a lawyer. In his opinion, if a person had returned from the dead as a vampire and was found guilty of crimes against the living, then cremation of the corpse was justified and acceptable.

Scholomance

In Bram Stoker's *Dracula* (1897), Scholomance is mentioned as an academy or school where the Count was trained to be an apprentice of the Devil. There are indications that Stoker got the idea for this so-called school of Satanism from Emily Gerard's 1885 newspaper articles, "Transylvanian Superstitions." Gerard was an Englishwoman who lived in Transylvania and wrote about the folklore and superstitions she discovered there. According to Gerard, Scholomance could be found in the mountains south of Hermannstadt (now Sibiu) where thunderstorms were common. Only 10 students were accepted at a time to learn the *"secrets of nature,* the language of animals and all imaginable spells and charms." When their studies were completed the Devil would choose one of the students to be his apprentice.

Solomonari

In Romanian folklore there is no mention of Scholomance and it is likely that Gerard confused it with the term "Solomanari," or "wise ones," considered to be the successors of the biblical King Solomon. In essence the Solomonari were wizards who rode dragons and controlled the elements. According to Romanian tradition Solomonari were recognized at birth by certain signs, such as a caul or membrane cap, that are curiously similar to traditional signs that point to future vampirism. As the child grows older it is said he will have red eyes, a wrinkled forehead, and red hair. He will wear white clothes and lead the life of a wandering beggar. Around his neck he'll carry a bag in which he keeps his magical instruments, including his magical book which he must concentrate on to discern what to do in any given situation.

The Solomonari were said to learn the secrets of nature and the language of animals, and the ability to shape-shift at a secret school hidden in the center of the earth. At around the age of 13 they were kidnapped by an older wizard and taken to the school for anything between 7 and 20 years. They would undergo a series of initiations at the school, where there could be no more than 10 pupils, and the teacher was the dragon or the Devil. At the end of their training they would receive their "book," described as a stone talisman with letters on it.

Science Fiction

The vampire is a supernatural being of mysterious origin that defies explanation, and it is therefore ideally suited to the imaginative genre of science fiction writing. Some science fiction writers have suggested that vampirism is a disease passed on through feedings. Others have explored the theory that vampires are actually extraterrestrials or aliens visiting earth and taking over bodies to feed on life energies, while still others suggest that vampires are from earth but are an entirely new species. The possibilities are endless as there is no limit to the imagination.

One of the most well-known science fiction vampire novels is Richard Matheson's *I Am Legend* (1954) that presents a grim, apocalyptic view of the world's future in which plague has wiped out most people, the survivors turned into vampires. Other influential science fiction vampire novels include: H. G. Wells's *The Flowering of the Strange Orchid* (1894), which first explored the concept of a space alien taking over a human body to live off the energies of others; *Vampires of Space* (1932) by Sewell Wright; *Pillar of Fire* (1948) by Ray Bradbury; *Vampires from Outer Space* (1959) by Richard Watson; *The Blood Stone* (1980) by Tanith Lee; Colin Wilson's *The Space Vampire* (1976); Meredith Ann Pierce's *The Dark Angel* (1982); and Brian Aldiss's *Dracula Unbound* (1992), to name but a few.

Comics and movies

The most well-known vampire to appear in comic book format during the 1960s was Vampirella, the first space vampire to be the heroine of the story rather than the villain. Vampirella tried not to kill for blood, and if she had to kill she felt remorse.

Vampires, both as earth-bound vampires and as space aliens, have appeared in numerous science fiction films, such as *The Thing* (1951), *Planet of the Vampires* (1965), *Life Force* (1985), and, more recently, the *Underworld* movies (2003–9).

Science behind Vampires

The science behind vampires attempts to explain the different aspects of a vampire's existence within the physical universe. It is not necessarily an attempt to prove that vampires are real but rather an attempt to prove that the vampire myth can be explained rationally. In other words, the question is not do vampires exist but could they exist? And if they could, what would the rules of their existence be?

A scientific impossibility?

Most supernatural aspects of the vampire's existence can be explained by science. It might seem strange to apply scientific rationale to a shape-shifting creature like the vampire but several authors have written books that attempt to combine forensic science with biology and folklore to describe vampirism. These include *Five Books on the Structure of the Vampire Body*, written in the sixteenth century by the Flemish physician Andreas Vesalius and, more recently, *Clinical Vampirism: Blending Myth and Reality* by Philip D. Jaffe, and *The Science of Vampires* (2002) by Katherine Ramsland.

According to these sources the transformation into a vampire can begin when the human brain secretes a "feel-good" chemical called dopamine. This "feel-good" chemical is also produced every time a vampire feeds on its victims. Other changes typically occur within the new vampire's sense organs. Perhaps the most noticeable is that their eyes become super-dilated, which means they have excellent night vision but find it hard to see clearly during the day. The eyes also become inflamed, which in turn makes the whites of their eyes glow red. Extra receptor cells in the nose and throat give vampires exceptional hearing and sense of smell, and the most obvious change is the growth of upper and lower canine teeth, which give the vampire the appearance of having fangs. These changes may be due to high levels of a substance called ectodysplasin A. In elevated amounts, this substance is capable of inducing tissue dysplasia, or morphological change, and could account for all the visible changes.

Other physiological changes may be a result of the vampire's blood diet or the fact that they live so long. Researchers say vampires have pale skin, which becomes translucent and blueish as they age and the veins under their skin become visible. The vampire's body temperature is also much lower than the normal human body temperature, with the temperature of a 200-year-old vampire as low as 65°F (18°C) compared with a human's of 98°F (37°C). It is also said that vampire blood lacks a protein in the red blood cells called hemoglobin and this makes blood black. This black blood is pumped not by a heart but by contractions in the skeletal muscles in the chest. Over the years the skeletal bones and muscles in the vampire's chest are said to grow stronger, allowing vampires to move at extraordinary speed. Another aspect of their extraordinary power and speed is the high amount of adrenaline in the vampire's blood. Adrenaline is the "fight or flight" hormone released when humans are stressed.

As for the question of how it is possible for vampires to exist on a diet of blood, the problem is the excess amount of iron in blood. Vampires have enzymes that can filter excess iron and a more finely developed network of capillaries to absorb it from the gut. In addition, vampires, like vampire, blood-drinking bats, are equipped with a chemical called draculin. Draculin is an anti-coagulant, which prevents blood from clotting and allows for the continuous flow of blood.

Immortality?

According to Katherine Ramsland, the incredible endurance and vitality of vampires is attributed to what she calls *"immortalized cells,"* or microscopic cells within the body that resist aging when fed on a diet of blood. If, however, a vampire is deprived of blood they will become weak and eventually die if the starvation continues. In this way fresh blood acts as a tonic enabling the vampire to regain his focus and vitality. It has also been suggested that an increase in white blood cell production, a component of which is responsible for wound healing, is perfectly feasible, and can explain not only the rapid wound healing but also the complete resistance to disease and aging.

The major player in immortality, at least cellular immortality, is telomerase. Telomerase is an enzyme that maintains telomere length. Telomeres are the ends of chromosomes that contain the DNA coding for chromosome (and therefore cell) replication, and so for keeping cells alive and healthy. Telomerase is normally inactivated very soon after embryonic development and birth, so that with each cell division, telomeres become shorter and shorter. When they reach a critical length, the cell will no longer divide, and will eventually die. The telomeres of old people are much shorter than those of 30-year-olds. If telomerase is reactivated, however, the cell will regain its telomeres and will divide again. Those who study the science of vampires believe that vampires are somehow able to reactivate telomerase so cells can regain their telomeres and divide again. Whatever happens, their enhanced immune systems are enough to prevent cancer-development and premature aging, and to maintain cellular immortality. Vampires are thus cancer-free, disease-free, and immortal.

The paradox

From a scientific and even a medical perspective, vampires can certainly be explained without any need to delve into supernatural or occult territories or theories. In short, vampirism is scientifically possible. However, as Ramsland states in her conclusion to *The Science of Vampires*, the vampire is a shapeshifter, a paradox who works best when he is impossible to define. *"That means he can never be trapped inside clear cut concepts, rituals or rigorous analysis … in many ways a science of vampires reveals more about us, than them."*

See also: AGING, OF VAMPIRES; SEX; TRANSFORMATION

Scotland

See: BAOBHAN-SITH; LEANHAUM-SHEE; REDCAP; SCOTT, SIR WALTER

Scott, Sir Walter (1771–1832)

Sir Walter Scott was a Scottish author often credited as being the inventor of the historical novel. His works include *Waverley* (1814), *Old Mortality* (1816), and *The Heart of Midlothian* (1818). In 1794 he made a significant contribution to vampire literature when he translated into English Gottfried Bürger's 1773 ballad *Lenora*. He also translated the Icelandic *Eyrbyggja Saga*, which includes an account of a vampire killing 20 servants in a household in the year 1000.

Season of the Dead

In Europe the term "season of the dead" is used to describe the days of the year in which the dead are said to leave their graves and mingle with the living. This season typically fell in November and was closely associated with the feast of All Souls' Day (November 2 or 3). A number of traditions would be observed during the season including the eating of soul cakes, and everything possible was done to ensure the dead would not be offended. Graves were decorated with flowers, offerings of food would be left, and empty chairs would be placed by the fireside or at the table.

Seeds

Seeds or grains, such as oat, rice, linen, carrot, poppy, flax, and (more commonly) mustard and millet, were used throughout Europe as a form of protection against vampires. The seeds would be scattered across thresholds or around beds to prevent vampires entering homes and attacking the living. They were also poured into coffins and sprinkled around graves to prevent the dead leaving their tombs. It was believed that before a vampire could leave its grave and attack the living it would be compelled to pick up or eat each seed one by one, so each seed represented a delaying unit of time. And if the vampire did manage to leave its grave, encountering seeds on a threshold or around someone's bed would play on the vampire's obsessive need to count the seeds one by one.

The Kashubs believed that vampires could only pick up or eat one seed a year. Therefore, according to this logic, a handful of seeds could delay or distract them for a very, very long time.

See also: **APOTROPAICS; PREVENTION**

Sekhmet

In ancient Egyptian mythology, Sekhmet (also spelled Sachmet, Sakhet, and Sakhmet), was originally the blood-drinking war goddess of Upper Egypt, although when the first Pharaoh of the Twelfth Dynasty moved the capital of Egypt from Thebes to Memphis, her cult center moved as well. The name Sekhmet means "(One who is) powerful," but she was also given titles such as "(One) before whom evil trembles," "She who dances on blood," and

"Lady of slaughter." Sekhmet was pictured as a lioness, a serpent, or as a woman with the head of a lioness, dressed in red. She was believed to protect the pharaoh in battle, stalking the land and destroying his enemies with arrows of fire. It was Sekhmet who was seen as the avenger of wrongs. As the goddess with blood lust, she was also seen as ruling over menstruation.

In one myth about Sekhmet Ra, the sun god (of Upper Egypt) created her from his fiery eye to destroy mortals who had conspired against him (Lower Egypt). Then Sekhmet walked among men and destroyed them and drank their blood. Night after night Sekhmet waded in blood, slaughtering humans, tearing and rending their bodies, and drinking their blood. The other gods decided that the slaughter was enough and should stop, but they could find no way to stop Sekhmet, who was by now drunk on human blood. At this point Ra intervened and tricked her into drinking blood-colored beer, making her so drunk that she gave up slaughter and became the gentle Hathor.

See also: **EGYPT**

Senses

In vampire fiction there is a long tradition that once a mortal has transformed into a vampire they acquire extra powers. One of these powers is that of heightened senses. The vampire is a creature of the night so it stands to reason that its senses should be suited to a life of darkness. Dracula and other vampires can see in the dark, probably along the infrared spectrum, and they also appear to be better than mortals at sniffing things out. Biologists theo-

rize that over the course of evolution, as humans rely more on their eyes than their sense of smell, up to 60 percent of our odor receptors have become non-functional. They are still there but we don't use them. It could be that the condition of vampirism wakes up these receptors and helps the vampire become a more efficient predator. The smell of living blood tantalizes vampires and they appear to have the ability to distinguish different persons by their different blood scents.

The taste of a vampire is centered on blood. Their sense of touch is also highly acute, as is their hearing. The beating of a human heart can be heard from a distance of many miles. In addition, vampires also seem to acquire the ability to sense the presence of good and evil or strength and weakness, knowing what areas and what people to avoid and what areas and people to focus their energies on.

Heightened sense of reality

In Anne Rice's novel *Interview with the Vampire* (1976), when Louis's transformation from mortal to vampire is complete he describes vividly the magnification of his senses and how he starts to see the world around him for the first time through the eyes and ears of a vampire.

> *I saw as a vampire ... It was as if I had only just been able to see colors and shapes for the first time. I was so enthralled with the buttons on Lestat's black coat that I looked at nothing else for a long time. Then Lestat began to laugh and I heard his laughter as I had never heard anything before. His heart I still heard like the beating of a drum, and now came this metallic laughter. It was confusing each sound running*

The Element Encyclopedia of Vampires

into the next sound, like the mingling reverberations of bells, until I had learned to separate the sounds, and then they overlapped, each soft and distinct, increasing but discrete peals of laughter.

This passage shows how, by having trespassed through the curtain of death, the vampire is endowed with a heightened sense of reality. He has become a supernatural being, and as such he possesses powers and senses that go far beyond the human capacities for survival.

See also: **POWERS, OF VAMPIRES; TRANSFORMATION; VISION**

Serbia

Serbia, long regarded as the cradle of vampirism in Europe, was the region of Eastern Europe in which several vampire epidemics took place in the seventeenth and eighteenth centuries, including the cases of Arnold Paole and Peter Plogojowitz.

The vampire tradition in Serbia is a longstanding one. During the Middle Ages the Serbian ruler Stephen Dušan (1331–51) issued decrees to limit vampire hunting, which suggests how widespread the tradition already was at the time. Serbian vampire species are called vampir and vudkolak. The vampir was said to lie perfectly preserved in its grave and at night it would set out to attack and drink the blood of the living. Staking with whitethorn, decapitation, and cremation were the preferred methods of destruction for the vampir. "Vudkolak" was a term that originally meant werewolf but was later used to refer to

vampires. In Bosnia, Croatia, and Montenegro another name for vampire was lampir. In documented testimony from a 1737 trial for grave desecration in the then independent Croatian city-state of Dubrovnik, not far north from Montenegro, the names given for vampire include *kosak*, *pricosak*, and *tenjac*, as well as vukodlak.

Serbian traditions were spread to other areas in Europe by the Slavic and Gypsy peoples. These traditions included the idea that the undead must be destroyed within 30 years lest it become mortal, change its name, and travel to a different county where it might marry and have children; the painting of a tar cross on doors to prevent vampires entering; and the vampiric transformation into a butterfly. Some Serbians also believed that vampires were invisible to most people.

Serial Killers

The depraved acts of notorious serial killers such as Peter Kürten and Fritz Haarmann have been linked to vampires and vampirism for centuries.

Some experts believe that before people knew much about criminology, the blood-drained state in which mutilated victims of serial killers have often been discovered may have helped to create the vampire and werewolf myths. The fact that serial killers tended to operate at night, combined with the inability of a community to accept that someone within their midst could be capable of the kind of evil seen, would have helped to create the idea of supernatural nocturnal monsters draining the blood of the living.

See also: **CRIME; HISTORICAL VAMPIRES**

Seventh Sons

In English folklore, the seventh son of a seventh son is believed to be born with psychic and healing gifts. However in Romanian lore, if a family has seven children of the same sex, especially if they are all boys, the seventh child will be born with a tail and is destined to become a vampire after death. It seems that for the Romanians, the seventh child's psychic gifts have an affinity with vampirism.

Seward, Dr. John

Dr. John Seward is a fictional character in Bram Stoker's novel *Dracula*. He is in charge of a lunatic asylum where one of his patients is R. M. Renfield. In the novel Seward's scientific mind and medical expertise are constantly challenged by the supernatural events taking place around him.

Sex (and Love)

Combing the allure of death, the temptation of the nocturnal demonic lover, and the casting away of inhibitions, in both fiction and folklore the vampire possesses the ability to conjure a sexual response.

Myth and folklore

An understanding of the erotic spirituality of vampirism has been recognized since ancient times in figures such as Lilith and the incubus/succubus, nightmare creatures whose appetite for sex exhausts and kills their victims. In vampire myth, mortals attacked by vampires experience an eroticism that is physical and spiritual; physical in that it involves the draining of bodily fluid – blood – and spiritual in that it involves intimacy with the ultimate mystery of death and dying.

The folklore of vampires can be seen to originate from this sensual mythology as vampire species all over the world have used the promise of sex as a trap for their victims. The mullo of Gypsy folklore has a huge appetite for sex, and in many other traditions vampires are lustful and capable of fathering children. The langsuir of Malaysia was a sexual female creature. In addition, corpses dug up as suspected vampires during the eighteenth-century vampire frenzy in Eastern Europe occasionally were reported to have erections, indicating belief in their sexual potency.

Although this tradition is not as strongly developed, the vampires of folklore also seem to be capable of love. There are reports of medieval revenants returning from their graves to take care of family business or, in the case of the shoemaker in Constantinople, returning to make shoes for his children. There were also reports of vampires returning to declare their love for someone with whom they had never consummated their relationship.

Fiction

Sex may have been a potent theme in vampire folklore but the vampire of folklore was not typically a sexy figure; he or she was a corpse, who fed on blood. In fiction, however, the vampire developed into a more "attractive" prospect.

A sexual theme is present in *The Bride of Corinth*, the original vampire poem written by Goethe in 1797. It is also present in Samuel Taylor Coleridge's *Christabel* and Sheridan Le Fanu's *Carmilla*. Although the sexuality in Bram Stoker's *Dracula* (1897) was hidden from literary censors, the sexual nature of *Dracula* is an underlying theme that the author may not even have been aware of himself. This sexual theme manifests itself early on in the novel when Jonathan Harker is attacked by the Count's three vampire brides, who describe their bites as "kisses." Then the novel moves on to present sex as something dangerous, when the Count transforms "good" women into seductively beautiful sirens and the very opposite of the Victorian view of chaste womanhood. Throughout the novel the penetration of skin by sharp teeth evokes images of both violence and eroticism, even though when in distress or danger the vampire still reveals its ugly, corpse-like side. In the blood transfusion scene when Van Helsing is attempting to save the life of Lucy, Stoker's presentation of the sexual nature of vampirism becomes even clearer when he appears to suggest that the sharing of blood creates a "bond" in the eyes of God that is equivalent to marriage.

Since the publication of *Dracula*, no doubt spurred on by the sexual liberation that occurred in the twentieth century, the sexual nature of vampirism has expressed itself openly in vampire-themed literature and films. Vampires, whether presented as overt symbols of the erotic sexual predator or covert metaphors for the dark sexual urges within, are seductive creatures that elicit sexual responses from enemies and victims alike.

Love between vampires, or between a vampire and a human, has also been well rep-resented in contemporary novels, from Armand and Daniel in the Vampire Chronicles to Bella and Edward in The Twilight Saga. In fact, the transformation of the vampire into a lover was an important element of the reintegration and revitalization of the vampire myth into contemporary culture.

How do vampires have sex?

Male and females vampires in folklore and fiction are sexualized creatures but there is a tradition that they cannot engage in "normal" penetrative sex because of certain erectile dysfunctions. This, of course, does not apply to vampires that can father dhampirs and to female vampires, although a body that has died will obviously not function as well as it did when alive. According to Katherine Ramsland in *The Science of Vampires* (2002), vampires may have trouble with "normal" sex *"because their need for oral gratification is so much stronger than their need for genital gratification."*

Vampires are erotic because the presence of death provokes the need for an intense affirmation of life, but the issue of how vampires actually have sex is a controversial one. The general consensus among vampire experts and authors appears to be that vampires invoke sexual ecstasy through their bite. In *Interview with the Vampire* (1976) Louis states that sex *"is a pale shadow of killing,"* suggesting that sucking blood is far more erotic and intimate an experience than human orgasm. Both Louis and Lestat do not know how a human can survive the profound intimacy of the vampire's bite.

See also: **GAY CULTURE; PSYCHOLOGICAL EXPLANATIONS OF VAMPIRISM; REPRODUCTION**

Shadow

For the ancient Greeks, the shadow was one of the metaphors for the *psyche*, the soul. A dead person's soul was compared to a shadow, and Hades was the land of shadows, the land of death. In the lore of Slavic Muslim Gypsies, vampires are the shadows of dead people. In Romanian folklore a corpse will transform into a vampire if the shadow of a living male falls over it. For occultists the shadow is an astral projection or thought form.

There is hardly any tradition in folklore suggesting that the undead can cast no shadow. This concept can be credited to Bram Stoker's *Dracula*. In the novel the Count is a soulless creature who cannot cast a shadow; he cannot cast reflections in mirrors, nor can he be painted or photographed. In folklore, vampires can cast shadows; the nachzehrer, for instance, can cause death to anyone who falls within their shadow.

Jung's shadow

According to Swiss psychologist Carl Jung, the vampire was a representation of a psychological aspect he called "the shadow." The shadow is the hidden or unconscious aspect of a person that the conscious self (the ego) has either repressed or ignored. The shadow is mostly composed of those elements of themselves a person finds distasteful, such as taboo urges, resentments, and animal instincts. These repressed elements, however, can still find a way to be heard by the projection of these qualities onto someone else. In other words, someone or something else is blamed or made a scapegoat for a person's own weaknesses. Despite, the negative associations of the shadow, acknowledging and assimilating it into the ego is, according to Jung, a sign of a healthy person.

Shaman

A shaman is a magician-priest-healer wise person who serves tribal peoples of the Americas, India, Australia, Siberia, and Mongolia, as well as occurring in some Northern European traditions. In other traditions shamans are also known as witch doctors, or medicine men. In these societies, much of the shaman's power is said to stem from his experience with altered states of consciousness, during which he travels spiritually and learns from the spirits and demons of other words. The shaman can send his spirit out into the world, sometimes in the form of an animal. Shape-shifting into animal form is also part of the shaman's mystical power. There is no traditional association between vampires and shamans, although lore surrounding shamans who shape-shift may lie behind the legend of the werewolf.

The shaman is a follower of a visionary tradition that reaches right back to prehistory and is based on animistic ideas about the world. They are often well versed in herbalism and spiritual healing and can enter altered states of consciousness to tap into the elemental powers of nature and the spirit world for the health and well-being of their people. They will typically use rhythmic drumming, dancing, chanting, fasting, drugs, and visualization (vision quests) to induce trance states. These states allow the shaman's soul to enter the spirit world in order to heal, divine the future, communicate with spirits of the dead, and perform other supernatural feats. Shamans also consult spirit guides in the form of animal guardians called totems. They guide their people to awareness and maturity by helping them to contact their own totem guides, or sometimes through the use of psychogenic or psychedelic substances.

The shaman lives in two worlds: ordinary reality and a non-ordinary reality called the "shamanic state of consciousness." Non-ordinary reality is believed to be a unique altered state of consciousness in which the shaman has access to three cosmologies: earth, sky, and underworld. The shaman remains lucid throughout his altered state, controls it and recalls afterward what transpired during it. In this state he has access to information that is closed off during ordinary reality.

This ability to enter the shamanic state at will is essential to a shaman. The shaman also has the clairvoyant skills to see spirits and souls and the mediumistic ability to communicate with them. He is able to take magical flights to the heavens where he serves as an intermediary between the gods and his people; he can also descend to the underworld to the land of the dead. The flights are achieved through shape-shifting.

The shaman's primary function is to heal and restore the connectedness of his people to the universe. No distinctions are made between body, mind, and spirit: all are seen as part of a great whole. Shamanic healing differs from Western medicine in that it is not so much concerned with extension of life but rather in protecting the soul and preventing it from eternal wandering. The kidnapping of lost souls of the living is believed to be responsible for many kinds of illnesses and only by retrieving the soul can a shaman effect a cure. Other cures are effected by sucking out the disease or illness with the help of spirits. Dream interpretation is another important function of shamans. They also perform various religious rites, divine the future, control the weather, identify thieves, and protect their community against evil spirits.

Some vampire experts believe that there may be a parallel between blood-drinking rituals and shamanic rituals in which an initiate is exposed to intense pain or hardship in order to bring about an altered mental state.

See also: **MAGICIAN; SHAMANISM; VOODOO; WITCHCRAFT**

Shamanism

"Shamanism" is the term used to refer to the spiritual practices of a shaman, a person who can access altered states of consciousness through the use of spirit guides and through invoking a trance-like state using rhythmic drumming, chanting, or dance. Once in a deep state of trance the shaman is said to be able to access his or her guardian spirit, known as a totem, for healing, guidance, and advice.

Shamanism has been described as the "world's oldest profession"; archeological evidence suggests shamanic techniques are at least 20,000 years old. Shamans were probably the first healers, priests, and magicians who helped people make sense of the world they lived in. Until recently the shamanic tradition was regarded simply as a precursor to modern religion, but now a new breed of urban shaman is attempting to adapt this ancient system to Western life in an effort to regain an understanding of the interconnection of all life.

Today, shamanism is commonly associated with a life devoted to mystic self-discovery, and because many vampire lifestylers are also spiritual seekers, shamanism has become tied in with modern vampire orders, such as the Sanguinarium.

Shan, Darren (1972–)

Darren O'Shaughnessy, who commonly writes under the pen name Darren Shan, is an Irish writer and author of *The Saga of Darren Shan*, known as *Cirque Du Freak: The Saga of Darren Shan* in the United States, an international bestselling young adult 12-book series about the struggles of a boy who has become involved in the world of vampires. A movie based on the first three books in the series is currently in production by Universal Studios.

Shan's vampires

The vampires in *The Saga of Darren Shan* (2000–05) can't turn into bats, don't die only with a stake in the heart or when exposed to sunlight, and aren't necessarily evil. They have sharp nails that they use to cut a vein so they can drink small amounts of blood before healing the wound with their saliva. They can run at very fast speeds (an action called "flitting") and don't believe in using firearms or crossbows, as they consider using projectile weapons dishonorable. They do, however, believe in hand-to-hand combat using swords. They cannot reproduce, but they can create half-vampires when blood-to-blood contact is made with humans. They also don't live forever, and age at one-tenth the human rate. Half-vampires age at one-fifth the rate. Vampires can't be photographed, however, because the flash bounces off of the vampire's atoms.

The sworn enemies to the vampires in the *Saga* are their cousin vampires, the vampaneze. These vampires broke away from the clan because of different beliefs; for example, the vampaneze have no problems draining the blood of humans and killing them. The vampaneze have purple skin and red hair, eyes, lips, and fingernails, a side-effect of drinking a lot of blood.

See also: **LITERATURE**

Shape-shifting

A common theme in myth and folklore, shape-shifting is a supernatural change in the physical form or shape of a person or animal. It involves the transformation from one body into another, such as humans into animals. A human who transforms into an animal becomes a were-animal: in the case of a wolf, a werewolf. In mythology demons and gods often have the power to shape-shift. Shamans, witches, vampires and sorcerers are believed to use this supernatural power at will.

Shape-shifting powers

In folklore and fiction the animals that vampires are most often thought to change into are bats, but vampires can transform not only into a number of other animals – cats, rats, and dogs for example – but also into birds, insects, frogs, and butterflies. Moreover, while they are in their shape-shifted form they manage to retain their vampire intelligence and instincts. In the lore of Wallachia in Romania the murony is a shape-shifting vampire that can assume many shapes, including those of cats, dogs, mice, and even fleas.

In both folklore and fiction, vampires can disperse into elemental vapors, dust clouds, or mists, thus allowing them to slip through door slits or narrow cracks. For example, the West Indian vampire species of loogaroo has the ability to shape-shift into a blob of light, and in the novel *Dracula* the Count enters rooms as a mist.

It was also thought that the vampire can alter his size within certain limits, becoming either larger or smaller so that he can easily go out from his grave or coffin. Vampires could also climb walls like a large insect. In addition, according to Romanian lore, vampires could, if they so desired, take away a person's voice, strength, and beauty and transfer them either to themselves or others. In *The Vampire in Europe* (1929), Montague Summers wrote that the Romanian vampire could

> gather the "power" of beauty, which he sold for money, and here in fact we have the regular love charms. These female vampires are generally of a dry burning skin and a notably florid complexion. The men are

bald and distinguished by peculiarly piercing eyes.

See also: **ANIMAL VAMPIRES; BATS; POWERS, OF VAMPIRES; WEREWOLF**

Shroud

Shrouds typically comprised a piece of white cloth, and were in previous centuries the customary wrapping used for corpses and therefore the most common attire for the vampires of folklore. In some regions of Europe, such as in and around Mecklenburg in Germany, it was important not to allow the shroud to touch the corpse's face, to prevent the corpse chewing on it, before chewing on its own flesh and cursing living relatives.

See also: **BURIAL CUSTOMS; MANDUCATION**

Shroud-eater

See: **MANDUCATION**

Sickle

A sickle is a tool with a curved blade on a short handle that was traditionally used for reaping. From as early as the tenth century in Romania and the Balkans, suspected vampires were buried with sickles as it was thought that the tool had the power to prevent the dead from rising. In Hungary it was thought that if the corpse tried to move it would be injured by the sickle. In Transylvania sickles were tied around the neck in the belief that the vampire would behead itself. The Romanians would also plunge a sickle into the heart of a corpse suspected of becoming a vampire.

See also: **PREVENTION**

Silesia

Silesia, a region that historically stretches across south-eastern Germany and south-western Poland, was the site of two well-known vampire cases, those of the Breslau Vampire (sometimes referred to as the Shoemaker of Silesia) and Johannes Cuntius.

Silver

Since ancient times, silver has traditionally been regarded as a precious metal that has protective powers against the forces of evil, because it is a symbol of the moon and is considered to be pure. In Eastern European folklore silver nails were used in coffins to prevent the vampire from leaving its grave. Crosses made of silver were said to be more powerful than other crosses. Silver was also said to protect against the evil eye.

Silver bullets were thought to have the power to kill vampires both in and out of their coffins, but they were more commonly used against werewolves than vampires.

See also: **PROTECTION**

Skal, David (1952-)

David J. Skal is an American cultural historian best known for his writings on horror films and literature. He has also turned his attention to Dracula research and vampires in general in a major publication entitled: *V is for Vampire: The A to Z to Everything Undead* (1996).

Slavic Vampire, The

Vampires appear in the mythology of almost all cultures but they are perhaps most prominent among the Slavs of Eastern and Central Europe, from Russia to Bulgaria and from Serbia to Poland. Romania and Hungary are non-Slavic lands but each share language and folklore with the Slavs. The Slavs experienced vampire outbreaks in the seventeenth and eighteenth centuries and, although not as common as often thought due to the institution of legal penalties for vampire hunting, it was these outbreaks and the grave desecrations that accompanied them that brought the vampire myth to the attention of the West.

Origin of vampire belief

Many experts believe that the roots of vampire belief in Slavic culture are based in the spiritual beliefs and practices of the pre-Christianized Slavic peoples. Demons and spirits and the concept of a soul that was not perishable were important parts of pre-Christian Slavic beliefs

The Slavs believed that after burial the soul left the body and wandered the earth for 40 days before moving onto the eternal afterlife. Windows and doors were left open in a house where a death had occurred to help the soul leave. During this 40-day transition period the soul was believed to have the ability to re-enter its corpse and either bless or attack its family and neighbors. Great attention was paid to correct burial rites to ensure that the soul remained pure when it left the body. The death of an unbaptized person, or a sinner, or a violent death was ground for the soul to become unclean and vengeful after death.

From these deeply held pagan beliefs concerning death and the soul the Slavic concept of the vampir may have originated. A vampir is an unclean soul that can animate a corpse. It is vengeful and jealous toward the living and in need of their blood to survive. As a symbol of evil, in the pre-scientific world of village life the role of the vampir was to explain various forms of unpredicted and undeserved bad events.

The Slavic vampire may also have developed as a result of the confrontation between paganism and Christianity. Indeed it was probably the introduction of Christianity into Slavic territories that played a significant part in the development of the vampire myth. Throughout the ninth and tenth centuries the Eastern Orthodox Church and the Western Roman Church disputed each other's authority, and in 1054 they broke with and excommunicated each other. The Bulgarians, Russians, and Serbians adhered to the Eastern Church while the Poles, Czechs, and Croatians stayed with the Roman Church. The two Churches could not come to agreement over the incorruptibility of the body. In the West this was seen as a sign of sanctity but in the East it was seen as a sign of vampirism.

Slavic vampires

The vampires from Slavic folklore take many forms and because they come from different regions, sources, and religions they exhibit a number of different traits and characteristics.

There are, however, some common elements that unite them.

In Slavic beliefs, the victims of vampires did not always become vampires themselves. There were other causes and although these causes differed they were often to do with the way an individual was born, died, or was buried.

- *Being born with a caul, teeth, red hair or a red birthmark, or being born illegitimate or on certain unfortunate days of the year could predispose a person to becoming a vampire after death.*

- *Dying unbaptized, committing suicide, leaving unfinished business, dying violently or unexpectedly or unattended, or dying excommunicated were all considered to be dangerous signs.*

- *Improper burial rites, being buried at a crossroads, being buried with the shroud touching the mouth or if a cat jumped over the corpse before burial could indicate that the deceased would come back as a vampire.*

Preventive measures included the use of garlic, as vampires were thought to be repelled by it, placing a crucifix in the coffin, placing blocks under the chin to prevent the body from eating its shroud, nailing clothes to coffin walls for the same reason, putting sawdust or seeds in the coffin for the vampire to count should he or she wake up, or pinning the body down with thorns or stakes.

Evidence that a vampire was at work in the neighborhood included: the death of cattle, sheep, relatives, or neighbors, or the sudden illness or death of a person, especially a relative or friend of the deceased within 40 days of the original death. Once the work of a vampire was suspected, the body of a person who had recently died might then be exhumed and examined for characteristic signs of vampirism, which included being in a lifelike state with new growth of the fingernails or hair, a body swelled up like a drum, or blood on the mouth coupled with a ruddy complexion. Once located, the "vampire" could then be destroyed by any or all of the following: staking, decapitation (the Kashubs placed the severed head between the corpse's feet), burning, repeating the funeral service, sprinkling holy water on the body, or exorcism.

The Slavic vampire today

Despite generations of hostile governments denouncing belief in vampires and vampire hunting, stories about vampires continue to circulate and to persist. In 1993 in Serbia during the era of violence that followed the break-up of the former Yugoslavia, a man made a number of bizarre appearances on Serbian television. He argued that an army of vampires would arise from the cemeteries to defeat Serbia's enemies and urged everyone to keep a ready supply of garlic.

However, despite the persistence of vampire folklore in the twenty-first century, it is mainly among the more isolated rural Slavic communities that belief in vampires is kept alive. In the more densely populated and industrialized areas vampire beliefs do not appear to be as strong. It is not just the secularization and modernization of society that has caused this loss of belief but the distancing from death which results when burials are organized by undertakers, rather than by families directly.

Sleep

The period between dawn and dusk is traditionally the time when vampires are said to rest or to be at their most vulnerable to attack. However, the idea that vampires need to return to their coffins and graves during the day appears more in literature and films than it does in traditional folklore. Their powers may be somewhat weakened but the vampires of folklore can not only leave their graves during the day, they can also attack and kill during the day.

As with many vampiric characteristics that are today taken for granted, the vampire's need for sleep or rest by day was a fictional development that owed a great deal to Bram Stoker's 1897 novel, *Dracula*. In the novel, the Count must sleep during the day to restore his energies and also to avoid the potentially damaging rays of the sun.

Sleep Paralysis

Sleep paralysis is a condition thought by some to account for hallucinations, nightmares, and supernatural experiences that occur during the night, such as out-of-body travel, hag attack, attacks from an incubus or succubus and the attack of a demon, vampire or witch. It is estimated that between 25 and 30 percent of the population have experienced at least a mild form of sleep paralysis at least once, and 20–30 percent of these have had the experience on several occasions.

Sleep paralysis is a condition that occurs in the state just before dropping off to sleep or just before fully awakening from sleep. A person, who is typically lying down, realizes that they are unable to move, speak, or cry out, and he or she senses a terrifying presence that is evil or threatening. This feeling of a malevolent presence, which may only last a few moments but leaves sufferers with lingering feelings of anxiety afterwards, is often said to involve the presence watching the person or standing over them. On some occasions the presence may crush down on the person's chest. People frequently try, unsuccessfully, to cry out or to move.

Causes

In folklore the condition has long been associated with the attack of a vampire, witch, or demon. In African culture, sleep paralysis is commonly referred to as "the witch riding your back." In Icelandic folk culture sleep paralysis is generally called having a mara, an Icelandic word for a mare but which has taken on the meaning of a sort of a devil that sits on a person's chest at night, trying to suffocate the victim. In many parts of the United States, the phenomenon is known as a hag and the event is often said to be a sign of an approaching tragedy or accident. *The Nightmare*, a well-known eighteenth-century painting by Henry Fuseli, is thought to be one of the classic depictions of sleep paralysis perceived as a demonic visitation, and to this day there are those who believe that sleep paralysis has a supernatural explanation.

Physiologically, sleep paralysis may be related to the normal paralysis that occurs during REM (rapid eye movement) sleep. In this way it may be a natural part of the sleep cycle that occurs when the brain is awakened

from REM into a fully awake state but the bodily paralysis of sleep has not yet worn off. This results in the person being fully aware but unable to move.

Some researchers believe that sleep paralysis occurs to prevent the body from acting out the sleeper's dreams. There is also a significant positive correlation between those experiencing this disorder frequently and those suffering from stress and from chronic sleep disorders.

See also: **NIGHTMARE**

Sleepwalking

Sleepwalking, a phenomenon also referred to as "somnambulism," occurs when a person moves about and acts out their dreams while still asleep.

Some experts believe that sleepwalkers may be a possible source of the vampire legend. R. E. L. Masters, mythology scholar and author of *Eros and Evil* (1962), has defined the Slavic vampire as: *"Somnambules (occasionally regarded as possessed by demons) who ravish young girls and drink their hot nourishing blood. While in trance the Voukodlaks are exceedingly dangerous and attack with tooth and nail any living creature they may meet."*

According to this theory, if someone died and they had a living relative who sleepwalked then the sleepwalker became a symbol of the walking dead. And among those who claimed to have experienced the savagery of a vampire attack, it is possible that they had encounters with individuals who were not in their normal waking minds but were sleepwalking and acting out their dark dreams. In this way, it could be said that vampires may in fact be the stuff that dreams are made of.

See also: **NIGHTMARE; SLEEP PARALYSIS**

Slovakia

In Central Europe the Slovakian and Czech vampire is called either a nelapsi or, more commonly, upir and bears strong similarities to the Slavic vampire.

According to Slovak scholar Jan Mjartan, who investigated Slovakian beliefs concerning vampires in the Zempline district of East Slovakia, publishing his findings in 1953 in the Slovak academic journal *Slovensky nardopis*, the nelapsi attacks cattle and people. This creature suffocates its victims and sucks their blood. They can also kill by a single glance and by bringing plague to a community they can kill a whole village or entire herd. The ways to prevent a person from becoming a nelapsi after death include:

- *Striking the coffin against the threshold of the house when carrying the coffin out for burial.*

- *Carrying the body head first to the grave.*

- *Placing magical herbs, poppy seeds, or millet in the corpse's mouth and nose and in the coffin, scattering the seeds along the road to the cemetery and around the grave.*

- *Nailing the clothes, hair, or arms and legs of the corpse to the coffin.*

- *Piercing the heart or head with a hat-pin, or an iron wedge, or a stake made of hawthorn, blackthorn, or oak.*

- *After the burial, taking precautionary measures, such as washing hands or holding on to the stove, was regarded as important.*

- *Lighting need fires to keep the vampire away.*

Both the upir and the nelapsi were thought to have two hearts and hence two souls. (This belief also occurred in a few parts of Romania.) If a corpse was discovered well preserved or had a ruddy complexion and open eyes it was thought that the second soul was still present in the body and that the corpse had transformed into a vampire.

Although folklorist Jan Mjartan's research suggested that belief in vampires was very much alive and well in the twentieth century, today belief in vampires has receded to the more rural corners of the Czech Republic and Slovakia.

Snake

Although strong connections between snakes or serpents, as symbols of evil and sin in Judeo-Christian traditions, and vampires seem likely, because of the ability of snakes to shed their skins (symbol of rebirth and immortality) and kill their victims with a single bite, there are only limited connections between the two. In Yugoslavia snakes were included in the list of creatures that vampires could transform into, however, and the union between the two was greatly feared.

See also: **ANIMAL VAMPIRES; POSSEGA VAMPIRE**

Sneezing

There are numerous widespread folk beliefs that the soul temporarily leaves the body through the mouth during a sneeze and is therefore vulnerable to the forces of evil. Sneezing creates an opportunity for evil entities to enter the body through the mouth and take possession of it. In the folklore of Romania, sneezing can attract or empower a vampire unless a blessing is given immediately after. Villagers would always try to say "good health," "bless you," or "long life" to prevent bewitchment by vampire-witches or sorcerers.

The two folktales below are quoted from the Romanian periodical of peasant art and literature, *Ion Creanga*, and both warn of the danger of sneezing.

The Thief and the Vampire

There were once two partners, a thief and a vampire. "Where are you going this evening?" said the thief to the vampire. "I am going to bewitch the son of Ion," said the vampire. "Don't go there. It is there that I want to go this evening to steal oxen. You can go somewhere else." "Go somewhere else yourself," said the vampire. "Why should you go to Ion's house of all places? He has only one son, and there are heaps of other houses you could go to," said the thief. "No, I'm going to Ion's," said the vampire. "Well, I'm going there too," said the thief. Both of them went. The vampire went to the door, and the thief to the window. Ion's son inside sneezed, and the thief said quickly, "Long life." This took away the vampire's power. He was able to make the boy's nose bleed, but he did not die. The thief then went in and told the parents what had
happened, and they gave him some oxen as a reward. It is always well to say "Long life" when anyone sneezes.

The Noble and the Horse

A young noble was about to start on a journey, and his horse was waiting saddled and bridled. There was a thief creeping up to steal the horse. As he came near he saw a vampire just under the window, waiting for an opportunity to put a spell on the noble. The noble sneezed, and quickly the thief said, "Good health," for if he had not done so the vampire would have seized the occasion to bewitch the noble, and he would have died. It was, however, the vampire who burst with anger at missing his chance. People came out to see what was the matter. The thief showed them the burst body of the vampire, and explained what had happened. The parents were so glad that their son had escaped that they gave the horse to the thief as a reward. This shows us that we must always say "Good health" when anyone sneezes.

Sociology of Vampires

According to contemporary vampire expert Hugo Pecos, who oversees an organization he called the Federal Vampire and Zombie Agency (FVZA), by conducting interviews with real vampires and observing vampires in the wild, scientists have been able to study their behavior patterns.

The following information is based not on fictional or folklore accounts of vampires but on the unproven assumption made by Pecos that vampires are real. In other words, it is pure conjecture.

🩸 Demographics: *According to Pecos the great majority — around 80 percent — of vampires are men aged between 18 and 35 upon transformation, with 10 percent being females of similar age on transformation and the remaining 10 percent made up of males and females slightly outside the 18 to 35 age range upon transformation.* "The racial and ethnic makeup of a pack will generally mirror that of the local populace."

🩸 The first few days: *After transformation the first few days are the toughest for newborn vampires, as they awaken disorientated and confused by their fierce desire for blood. This desire eventually brings them focus however, as they set about to find ways to satisfy it. Once the vampire begins feeding, the blood acts as a tonic and helps him or her grow in strength.*

🩸 Fledglings: *Vampires under 200 years old possess three times the strength of humans but are still apprentices who need training and lessons from older vampires in how to survive. The fledglings also need older vampires to help them hunt. Without being guided by their elders they are vulnerable and more easily detected. Despite this vulnerability fledglings possess powers far beyond ordinary humans. They can communicate telepathically, move objects without touching them, and at six months they can control the weather. Around two years of age they can control animals. Within ten years they can hypnotize their victims, become invisible and climb walls like an insect, and around their 15th year after*

transformation they can shape-shift and even fly.

🩸 Alpha vampires: *A vampire over the age of 200 is called an "alpha vampire" by Pecos, who describes them as the strongest and most intelligent vampires of the pack. Alphas lead packs of younger vampires on hunts. When the younger vampire catches a victim, the alpha vampire drinks first.*

🩸 Living conditions: *The dwelling place of a vampire is crude and utilitarian, its main functions being to keep the vampire safe and undetected and out of the sunlight during waking hours. Caves, abandoned mines, barns, houses, and tunnels under piers are ideal, according to Pecos. Again, according to Pecos, hygiene is of no importance for vampires but if they need to blend into the world of humans they will have no choice but to wash and put on new clothes — often those of their victims.*

See also: **AGING, OF VAMPIRES; BIOLOGY OF VAMPIRES**

Sock

According to the lore of Gypsies from Eastern Europe, the left sock of a vampire can be used to drive it away or even kill it. Vampire hunters steal the sock from the grave, fill it with rocks, and throw it outside the village, preferably into a river or running water. The vampire will then wake up, miss its sock, and start searching for it, even if that means entering water and drowning in an attempt to retrieve it. Like the use of seeds and grains to distract the vampire into counting for

The Element Encyclopedia of Vampires

centuries, this is based on the widespread belief that vampires are obsessive creatures.

See also: **DESTROYING VAMPIRES; KILLING VAMPIRES**

Solis, Magdalena

Magdalena Solis was a serial killer who participated in a blood-drinking sex cult in Mexico. She somehow managed to convince villagers in Yerba Buena that she was a goddess and orchestrated rituals that involved murder and blood-drinking. When the remains of the human sacrifices were discovered outside the village, police came in and rounded up the cult. The Solis high priests and 12 followers were brought to trial on 13 June, 1963. Each of them received a prison sentence of 30 years.

See also: **CRIME; HISTORICAL VAMPIRES**

Sorcerer/Sorcery

Sorcery is a form of magic that uses spells, charms, and incantations to summon up supernatural power, demons or spirits, mostly, but not always, for evil purposes or to gain power. It is typically associated with black magic or the left-hand path. Someone who practices sorcery is called a sorcerer or wizard if they are a male and sorceress or witch if they are a female. In the late Middle Ages it was accepted through much of Europe that evil sorcerers were doomed to eternal damnation and would return from the grave as vampires. Some sorcerers made pacts with the Devil to allow them to live beyond the grave by spreading the evil of vampirism. Sorcery is also a powerful weapon in defeating vampires and the undead. Bulgarian sorcerers could bottle a vampire.

See also: **BOTTLING A VAMPIRE; MAGIC; MAGICIANS; WITCH**

Soul Cake

A soul cake is a small round cake, bun, or loaf made of the finest white flour, which was traditionally baked on November 1 and eaten the following day, All Souls' Day, in Bohemia, the Netherlands, southern Germany, Austria, and parts of England (where they were called dirge-loafs and baked on or around the feast of St. Jude or St. Simeon at the end of October). The cakes were made to honor the dead, probably as a way of giving food to the dead so they could join in family life for one night a year. Often simply referred to as "souls," the cakes, which were shaped in human form with currants for eyes, were given out to soulers (mainly children and the poor), who would go from door to door singing and saying prayers for the dead. Each cake eaten would represent a soul being freed from Purgatory. The practice of giving and eating soul cakes is often seen as the origin of modern trick-or-treating.

Soul-Recalling Hair

Belief in soul-recalling hair originates in China where it was held that a cat, especially a big cat such as a tiger, had the ability to bring back the souls of the dead because it had a magical hair on its tail. When the tiger dragged its victim into a mountain cave it would wave its tail over the dying person.

Once the victim had died the soul would return to the body, which meant that the victim would suffer death twice. Thus the Chinese were careful not to let any cats or felines jump over corpses and this tradition spread to Europe.

South, American

The American South was the recipient of vampire traditions from both Africa and Europe. The slave population brought the folklore traditions of voodoo and African vampires, such as the West Indian loogaroo, into the New World. Tales of vampires were not, however, restricted to the slave population; among the white population there were many tales of blood-sucking creatures lurking in the swamps, waiting to pounce on unsuspecting victims.

See also: **BELL WITCH, THE; NEW ENGLAND; MEXICO**

Southern Slavs

See: **ALBANIA; YUGOSLAVIA**

Southey, Robert (1774–1843)

Often considered one of England's finest writers, British poet Robert Southey is often credited alongside Samuel Taylor Coleridge as being among the first to introduce the vampire theme into literature.

In July 1799 Southey started work on the Gothic vampire ballad *Thalaba the Destroyer*.

The work was eventually completed in 1800 and from the notes of his own edition (1837) it is clear that Southey researched vampirism to write *Thalaba* and that he was familiar with the case of Arnold Paole and with outbreaks of vampirism in Greece.

In *Thalaba* Southey took the Greek view that a vampire was a corpse inhabited by an evil spirit. The vampire is presented as the recently deceased bride of Thalaba, who had died on their wedding day. Her body has been reanimated by demons.

"This is not she!" the Old Man exclaim'd;
"A Fiend; a manifest Fiend!"
And to the youth he held his lance;
"Strike and deliver thyself!"
"Strike HER!" cried Thalaba,
And, palsied of all power,
Gazed fixedly upon the dreadful form.
"Yea, strike her!" cried a voice, whose tones
Flow'd with such sudden healing through
*   his soul,*
As when the desert shower
From death deliver'd him;
But, unobedient to that well-known voice,
His eye was seeking it,
When Moath, firm of heart,
Perform'd the bidding: through the vampire
*   corpse*
He thrust his lance; it fell,
And, howling with the wound,
Its fiendish tenant fled.
A sapphire light fell on them,
And garmented with glory, in their sight
Oneiza's Spirit stood.

Spain

There is not a strong tradition of vampirism in the folklore of Spain as there is for much of the rest of Europe and Spain did not contribute greatly to the vampire debates of the eighteenth century. There is, however, a tradition of witchcraft and evil witches with vampiric qualities, similar in many respects to the Portuguese bruxsa and the Italian striges, who lurk on the roofs of houses and try to get into the rooms of babies and children so they can suck their blood.

From the 1960s onwards, beginning with *El parque de juegos* (The Park of Games, 1963) Spanish cinema has distinguished itself with its treatment of the vampire theme.

Spaulding Family Vampires

The case of the Spaulding family vampires was described in the *Vermont Historical Magazine* in 1884.

Beginning in 1782 and continuing for a period of 16 years, a number of tuberculosis deaths occurred in the family of Lieutenant Leonard Spaulding of Dummerston, Vermont. The first death was of his daughter Mary in 1782, aged 20. She was followed by her father Leonard in 1788; Leonard Jr. in 1792; twins Timothy and John in 1793 and then Josiah in 1798. Only three daughters survived.

According to the *Vermont Historical Magazine*, after six deaths an unnamed daughter fell ill with consumption and was believed to be close to death. Family and friends suspected vampirism and exhumed a body, although no mention is made of which body was exhumed, and burned the corpse's organs. After the exhumation the unnamed daughter recovered and survived.

Accordingly the body of the last one buried was dug up and the vitals taken out and burned, and the daughter it is affirmed got well and lived many years. The act doubtless raised her mind from a state of despondency to happiness.

Prior to discussing the exhumation the magazine mentions the growth of grave plants and vines between each coffin. There is not a strong association between the growth of grave plants and vampires but in folklore there are traditions which suggest that certain plants can indicate the state of the dead, because some of the essence of the dead is transferred into them.

See also: **NEW ENGLAND**

Spider

There are obvious comparisons between the predatory vampire and the predatory spider in their method of luring their victim, trapping it, and then draining the life out of it leaving only an empty shell. Vampires are also said to be able to crawl up and down walls and cliffs with the agility of a spider, and in some traditions they have the ability to shape-shift into a spider.

The East African spider *Evarcha culicivora* — sometimes referred to as a "vampire spider" — cannot pierce skin and sip blood, but it can pick up the scent of blood and feeds indirectly on blood by eating female mosquitoes that have just engorged themselves with a victim's blood.

See also: **ANIMAL VAMPIRES**

Spike

Spikes were often used to prevent vampires from rising from their graves. It was thought that if the vampire tried to leave it would impale itself on the spikes, which were typically made of iron or hawthorn. Spikes differ from stakes in that they are not intended to be driven into the heart of a vampire but into the ground.

In TV's *Buffy the Vampire Slayer*, Spike is an evil vampire made docile by the implantation of a chip in his brain.

See also: **PREVENTION**

Spiritualism

Spiritualism is a religious and social movement that began in the United States in 1848 and quickly spread to Britain and Europe. Interest peaked in the early twentieth century and then subsided, although today it still remains a vigorous religion around the world, especially in Britain and America. Its appeal originally derived from the evidence it purported to provide of survival after death, manifested through mediums who could allegedly communicate with spirits and perform paranormal feats.

Spiritualists believe that the soul survives death and makes a transition to the spirit world. Communication with these souls is made possible through purposeful contact with the departed – a séance – via a medium. The medium goes into a trance and through his or her psychic ability allegedly establishes a link between this world and the world of spirit. The spirits then speak through the medium, who is temporarily possessed by these entities. This contact is taken as proof by believers that there is indeed life after death.

The official start date of Spiritualism is considered to be 1848, as it was then that the Fox sisters of New York became well known for their rapping communication (the spirits supposedly knock on a table to send messages). The idea behind techniques like rapping was that spirits and ghosts lacked the physical means to communicate with the living by word of mouth so they needed mechanical help.

Following in the footsteps of the Fox sisters, numerous other mediums sprang up, claiming to be able to communicate with the dead. Séances were extremely popular. Early séances were mostly table rappings or table turning but in time they became highly entertaining affairs with huge audiences witnessing incredible paranormal feats such as levitation and even full-blown materializations. Fraud was commonplace but even this did nothing to dampen the public's enthusiasm. Private home séances were also conducted and by 1855 Spiritualism claimed around two million followers on both sides of the Atlantic.

Some spiritualists believed that vampires could communicate as spirits. Others believed in psychic vampirism, in which spirits of the living and the dead could prey on living people. Spiritualism was an extremely popular interest among middle- and upper-class Europeans and Americans from the mid nineteenth century until the early twentieth century, and there is no doubt that Bram Stoker would have been aware of its popularity and influence when he wrote *Dracula* in 1897.

Spirit Vampires

Spirit vampires are vampires without physical bodies. They can't be killed with a stake through the heart. If they can be killed at all, it is typically through the use of magic.

A spirit is a discarnate entity or the animating essence within our physical bodies; it is sometimes referred to as soul but is not precisely the same as the soul. The term is often used to describe all non-physical entities, including ghosts, but a spirit is not strictly speaking the same as a ghost even though the distinction between the two is sometimes vague. To attempt a definition: Spirit is the divine essence of who we are, an indivisible part of the three aspects of human existence: mind, body, and spirit. In many belief systems the spirit survives death.

Spirits are commonplace in the religions and folklores of the world and come in a multitude of shapes and forms, such as fairies, elves, demons, and angels. They are believed to exist in an invisible realm but can be seen by persons with clairvoyance. They are believed to intervene at times in the affairs of humanity, for better or for worse. A spirit is also often thought capable of passing through material barriers, appearing and disappearing at will and floating or flying through the air. They are considered immortal and indestructible. Some can appear in various forms and others can take possession of a human body.

Vampiric spirits

Spirit vampires are typically blood-sucking human spirits, of people living or dead, or blood-sucking demonic powers.

The belief that all human beings have a soul or a spirit is common to many cultures, as is the belief that the spirit separates from the body at death. Typically the spirit leaves the body to inhabit the spirit realm but sometimes it remains on earth as a ghost or becomes a vampire spirit that attacks the living. As well as separating from the body at death, vampiric spirits can also separate from the body before death. Living people who send out their spirits or astral bodies to do evil are often called shamans or witches. Occultist Franz Hartmann put forward the theory that living people could become vampire spirits. He called these spirits astral vampires, the disembodied spirits of living people who send them out to prey on others. According to Hartmann the Slavic vampire phenomenon could be explained by the astral bodies of people who had been buried alive. To survive in the grave these people sent out their astral bodies to obtain nourishment from living people.

In world folklore demonic spirits are more ancient than vampires, but a number of these spirits are so similar to vampires that lore concerning them often merged with that of vampires. Prominent examples are the incubus and succubus – demon spirits who stole in upon sleeping people at night to drain the life force of their victims. In Eastern Europe these demon spirits were more commonly known as mara or mora.

See also: **Astral Body; Psychic Vampire; Spiritualism**

Spit

Spit or spittle has been considered a protective force against the evil eye and vampires for centuries. This may be because in some regions it is associated with the soul and therefore to spit it out is to invoke the forces of goodness. When evil is sensed spitting should therefore be done immediately.

See also: **APOTROPAICS; PREVENTION**

Stage

Vampire characters have become an established feature in numerous English, French, and American plays. They have appeared and continue to appear in hundreds of stage productions all over the world, including opera and ballet. The vampire character first appeared on stage in the nineteenth century during a time when attitudes toward sex, death, women, disease, and foreigners were rapidly changing. As a personification of dark anxieties and fantasies about sex, the vampire proved an ideal stage character because it could seduce and violate without involving the genitals.

Many early vampire plays originated in France and were then imported to England and America. French writer Charles Nodier was the first to adapt for the stage *The Vampyre*, a story written in 1819 by John Polidori. He altered the ending of Polidori's story to assure his audience that the forces of good triumphed over the lead vampire anti-hero, Lord Ruthven, who in Nodier's version was killed. His three-act play, *Le Vampire, mélodrame en trois actes avec un prologue*, opened on June 13, 1820, at the Théâtre de la Porte-Saint-Martin in Paris. It was an immediate and somewhat unexpected success and inspired several imitations, with the last noteworthy effort, Alexandre Dumas's *Le Vampire*, opening at the Théâtre de l'Ambigu-Comique in Paris in 1851. In 1828 the opera *Der Vampyr* by Heinrich Marschner opened in Leipzig and London.

Dracula on stage

It is certainly probable that Bram Stoker had the theater in mind when he wrote *Dracula* in 1897. He organized a stage reading a few months after its publication hoping that his employer, the well-known actor Henry Irving, would play the Count. Unfortunately, Irving was not impressed and Stoker never saw his work translated to the stage in his lifetime.

It was not until 1924, over a decade after Stoker's death, that *Dracula* was adapted for the British stage by Hamilton Deane. Deane transformed the Count from an evil, loathsome villain into a well-dressed, tragic, even romantic figure and this reinvention had a significant impact on all later stage productions of the novel. When the production came to America in 1927, after American writer John L. Balderston had streamlined the plot, it played to packed houses and riveted audiences, despite coming with a warning that it would be wise for people to have their hearts examined before watching it due to the thrills and shocks that awaited the audience.

During the twentieth century, the overwhelming majority of new vampire plays and dramatic productions were based on *Dracula*, and the character of Lord Ruthven from *Der Vampyr*, who dominated the stage in the nineteenth century, disappeared. Plays based on Sheridan Le Fanu's *Carmilla* also appeared but in nowhere near as large a number as *Dracula* productions. Hamilton Deane's play, with Balderston's adaptations, was revived with great success in the 1970s, with Frank Langella as a contemporary and seductive Count.

From the 1980s onward the number of vampire-themed productions has steadily increased and, given the heightened interest in vampires at the beginning of the twenty-first century, there is every reason to believe that new plays will continue to be written and new productions staged. In recent years vampires have also been the subject of musicals, operas, and ballets. For example in the United States the Houston Ballet produced *Dracula* in 1997, choreographed by Ben Stevenson and featuring music by Franz Liszt.

See also: **ART; FILMS; POETRY; TELEVISION**

Stagg, John (1770-1823)

English poet John Stagg was the author of a balled entitled *The Vampyre* (1810). The ballad, which included a discussion of vampirism in the prologue, was written nine years before John Polidori's influential *The Vampyre.*

Written in the Gothic style reminiscent Bürger's *Lenora* (1773), Stagg's ballad tells the story of Gertrude who is concerned about her husband, Herman, and the deadly paleness of his face. Herman tells her that every night blood is being drained from him by his friend Sigismund, who has recently been buried. He tells Gertrude that he think he will die that night but Gertrude keeps watch and sees the specter of Sigismund, whose corpse is mutilated the next day after being discovered warm and undecayed.

See also: **POETRY**

Stake

A wooden stake was the preferred means of containing and destroying vampires in European folklore. The stake was typically made from a thorn wood, such as hawthorn; other wood considered sacred and pure, such as oak, aspen, or juniper might also be used. In other areas an iron stake or long spike might be used.

The practice of staking suspected revenants was an ancient one and originated in a time before coffins were used. Corpses were staked as a way of keeping them attached into the ground. The stake would be plunged through the vampire's belly, which was easier to penetrate than the heart. The corpse might also be turned face down and the stake plunged through the back. Stakes might also be driven into the ground over the grave to prevent the vampire from rising.

When the use of coffins became more widespread the purpose of staking changed from fixing the body to the ground to the mutilation of the corpse. Stakes were plunged into the heart, the organ that circulated blood, to kill the vampire. In Russian lore the stake had to be driven in with one blow as a second stroke was thought to reanimate the vampire. The recommended length of the stake was about two or three feet with a sharp point and a smooth flat top, and a hammer or mallet might be used to pound the stake into the chest of the corpse.

During staking great care would be taken to ensure that none of the vampire's blood was splattered onto onlookers, as it was thought that touching the blood of a vampire could drive a person insane. Sometimes an animal hide or cloth would be placed over the corpse.

Witness accounts report that vampire corpses would shriek and gasp when staked. This was taken as evidence of vampirism but it was probably due to the forced expulsion of natural gases. Among some Serbs, staking could only contain the vampire in its grave, but it could not destroy it; burning or cremation was the only way to destroy a vampire.

In fiction and film, staking is often enough to destroy vampires, who typically scream and disintegrate once staked. In *Dracula* Lucy Westenra is destroyed by a stake but the Count himself requires decapitation and a knife through his chest. In some comics, novels, and films, however, the stake is a more temporary measure and removing it is a means of reviving the vampire.

See also: **Burial Customs; Destruction; Killing Vampires**

Stana

In the Serbian village of Medvegia in the 1730s, medical officers researching and reporting on the Arnold Paole vampire case made reference to the case of a woman named Stana, or Stanacka or Stanicka. According to the investigators, before her death Stana com-

plained that *"she had been throttled by the son of a Haiduk [a soldier] by the name of Milloe who had died nine weeks earlier, whereupon she had experienced great pain in the chest and became worse by the hour, until she died."*

In *The Vampire in Europe* (1929) Montague Summers states that on her death bed Stana confessed that she had been anointed by the blood of a vampire. When Stana's body was dug up it was found to be untouched by decomposition. The body of Milloe was also dug up and, in the words of Summers, it *"was rosy and flabber, wholly in the vampire condition."* Stana's baby had died too, but when the body was dug up it had been so savaged by wolves that it was impossible to tell if it was in a state of vampirism.

Stoker, Bram (1847-1912)

Abraham "Bram" Stoker was the author of *Dracula* (1897), a novel that was integral to the development of the modern vampire myth.

Stoker was born in Dublin, Ireland, in 1847. A frail child he was not expected to live for long and spent much of his childhood confined to bed. His long convalescence contributed to his shyness around people and his preference to read, study, and to write rather than socialize. It also exposed him to his mother's stories of Irish folktales and details about a cholera epidemic that hit County Sligo in 1832.

By the age of 16 Stoker regained his health and energy and entered Trinity College, Dublin. He graduated with a science degree in 1870 and, like his father before him, went to work as a civil servant at Dublin Castle. He did continue his studies part time, and was awarded a Master's in 1875. During his college years he attended a performance at the Theatre Royal by the charismatic actor Henry Irving, and this led him in 1871 to offer his services to the Dublin *Evening Mail* as a drama critic, without pay. As his reviews began to circulate in various papers he was welcomed into social circles and in 1873 was offered the editorship of a new newspaper the *Irish Echo*, later renamed *Halfpenny*. The paper failed and Stoker resigned in 1874. Around the same time he began writing the so-called penny dreadfuls: his first novel, *The Primrose Path* (1875) and his first horror story, *The Chain of Destiny* (1875) were serialized in the periodical *Shamrock*.

In 1876 Stoker met Irving and probably used the actor's Mephistophelian stage appearance as one of the models for the character of Dracula. When Irving took over management of the London Lyceum Theatre in 1878 he invited Stoker to London to work for him. While working in the theater Stoker continued to write, producing a collection of children's stories – *Under the Sunset* – in 1882 and a novel, *The People*, in 1889. Many of his works have been largely forgotten today but some of his short stories, for example "The Squaw," which involves the impaling of an American tourist at Nuremberg Castle, still circulate among fans of horror writing. In 1890 Stoker began work on *Dracula*, inspired perhaps by a nightmare he had had of a vampire rising from a tomb.

Dracula

Dracula was published in 1897. It was once thought that the novel was written quickly and hastily, beginning in August 1895 while Stoker was on holiday at Cruden Bay in Scotland. However, recent research on Stoker's notes for the novel has indicated that his research began at least seven years before its publication, in 1890.

Stoker's decision to begin work on *Dracula* may have been triggered by a nightmare he had after reading Sheridan Le Fanu's *Carmilla*, which had been published in 1872. To this he added his own research on medicine, the supernatural, Transylvania, and folklore. In 1890 Stoker met Arminius Vámbéry, an expert on folklore, and he conducted research at the British Museum and London Zoo. He read the *Account of the Principalities of Wallachia and Moldavia* by William Wilkinson in 1890, and in this work he may have been introduced for the first time to the fifteenth-century Wallachian prince Vlad Tepes, known as Vlad the Impaler, who was also called "son of Dracul." In 1892 there are clear references to Vlad in Stoker's notes.

Although he never traveled to Transylvania Stoker did travel to other locations in the book, such as Whitby Harbour, where a number of shipwrecks had occurred, most notably the Russian schooner *Dimitry* in 1885, which strongly echoes the *Demeter* shipwreck in *Dracula*. Originally, Stoker wanted to set the book in Styria, but his research led him to the decision to set the book in Transylvania, "the land beyond the forest" in literal translation. Echoing most probably the style of Victorian crime and mystery author Wilkie Collins in *The Moonstone*, Stoker also made the decision to tell the story through the eyes of several characters in a series of diary extracts, letters, and news clippings.

Reviews

Dracula was published in 1897 to mixed reviews from critics and readers. Some loved its exotic gloom, others condemned it for its crudeness; few realized its importance or significance. Just after its publication, Stoker led a four-hour reading of the novel by members of the Lyceum Company, which was to be the only stage presentation of *Dracula* during his lifetime. Unfortunately, it was not well received by either Henry Irving or the watching audience.

Stoker produced a series of novels after *Dracula*, including *The Mystery of the Sea* (1902); *The Jewel of Seven Stars* (1903); *The Lady of the Shroud* (1909); and *The Lair of the White Worm* (1911), his last work. With all his literary output Stoker achieved little fame and even less money in his lifetime. In his final years his book royalties were around £80 a year and his letters to his friends are full of comments on worries concerning his health and his finances. In 1905 Stoker suffered a stroke and his health never fully recovered. He died on April 12, 1912, of what might have been tertiary syphilis, although some biographers have refuted this as the cause of his death, citing exhaustion and kidney failure as recorded on his death certificate. The obituary that appeared in *The Times* commented on his work with Irving and briefly mentioned that he wrote lurid and creepy fiction. He was cremated and buried at Golders Green in North London.

Florence Stoker

In 1914, Stoker's widow, Florence, published a collection of Stoker's short stories entitled *Dracula's Guest and Other Weird Stories*. She claimed that "Dracula's Guest" was actually a chapter that had been deleted from the book by the publishers.

Although Florence inherited Stoker's copyright and had some income from book sales, Stoker never earned a great deal from his writing and he left his widow often hard pressed for money. In 1921 German director F. W. Murnau decided to make a film version of *Dracula* entitled *Nosferatu*. To avoid copyright issues he altered the plot, setting it in Germany and naming the Count Graf Orlok, but Florence sued for breach of copyright and eventually won. A German court ordered that all copies of *Nosferatu* be destroyed.

Hamilton Deane did manage to obtain Florence Stoker's permission to adapt *Dracula* for the stage. His play opened in 1924 in Ireland and after playing to packed houses eventually moved to London in 1927. The stage adaptation was a great success and through it Florence Stoker, who died in 1937, was able to witness at least some of the success and popularity of *Dracula*, a novel which went on to inspire an entire industry of vampire fiction, film, drama, and lifestyles.

See also: **Dracula; Films; Literature**

Strength, of Vampires

In folklore the extent of the vampire's strength is unknown. Many vampires of folklore are unable to resist a group of vampire hunters and vampires tend to attack vulnerable, weaker members of a community, such as animals and children. Despite this, however, many people still greatly feared the supernatural powers of vampires.

In fiction the superior physical strength of the vampire when compared with humans is a prominent theme. In *Dracula* Van Helsing describes the vampire as having the strength of 20 men. In modern fiction other supernatural qualities such as the ability to shape-shift may have been stripped from the vampire, but generally they are said to retain this supernatural strength that is equivalent to the strength of many humans. It does appear, however, that the conduit of their strength is blood; if deprived of blood their strength and energy diminish to the extent that the vampire becomes weak and thin.

See also: **POWERS, OF VAMPIRES**

Striges/Strix

In Greco-Roman folklore, "striges" (singular strix) is the term for female witch-vampires who were said to be able to transform at night into birds that drank the blood of humans, especially children. They also had poisonous breath. The striges are ranked as living vampires by some, as they are clearly alive when they hunt their human prey.

The name "striges" originated from the Latin *strix*, a kind of screech owl known to the Romans who attributed to it the ability to drink the blood of children. Over time the term became associated with vampirism and probably survived and evolved in Greece as *striges*, in Romania as *strigoi*, and in Italy as *strega*.

In the first century AD the Roman poet Ovid mentions striges in the fourth book of his work *Fasti*:

They fly by night and look for children without nurses, snatch them from their cradles and defile their bodies. They are said to lacerate the entrails of infants with their beaks and they have their throats full of the blood they have drunk. They are called striges.

Ovid also mentions rituals used to protect an infant against a strix, which include the placing of whitethorn branches in the windows of a house, sprinkling the entrance with water, and offering the bloody entrails of a pig to appease the creature. Belief in the striges continued through the old and new Roman Empire. In the ninth century Charlemagne, who established the new Holy Roman Empire, decreed capital punishment for anyone who attacked or burned a person because they believed they were a strix.

Witchcraft

After the fall of the Roman Empire, striges became low Latin for "witch" and as Christianity spread the striges became firmly associated with demons and the Devil. During the fifteenth century striges were said to be female servants of Satan who could practice sorcery and turn themselves into blood-drinking birds at night to prey upon unprotected sleeping men and women. People believed to be vampire witches were arrested, tried, and executed throughout Europe during the notorious witch hunts of the seventeenth and eighteenth centuries. By the end of the nineteenth century most of Europe began to doubt the existence of witches and vampires but remnants of belief in both creatures do continue to this day.

See also: **WITCHCRAFT**

Strigoi

In Romanian lore "strigoi," or "strigoii," is a term for a male vampire. The strigoi were either dead vampires (*strigoii mort*) – quite literally walking corpses – or *strigoii vii* or moroi – the living varieties. The word comes from the Latin word *strix*, or screech owl.

The strigoii could drink blood but more often than not they preferred to eat normal food. However, rather than drinking blood or other vital fluids, they could draw energy from a person by a kind of osmosis, leaving them weak and helpless. As well as attacking people they could spread disease. A corpse transforming into a strigoi could be identified by its left eye being open and staring. Distinguishing features also included red hair, blue eyes, and the presence of two hearts, the second heart apparently credited with the mechanism whereby the creature remained alive after death.

The location of the tomb or grave of a strigoi could be identified by a blue flame, like a candle, which hovered close by and burned brightly at night. It was also believed that small holes around the grave were identifying features. Once exhumed the body would typically be found in an uncorrupted state with hair and nails that continued to grow after death and a ruddy complexion.

Prevention/Protection

People who died unmarried were considered to be at great risk of becoming strigoii after death. To prevent family members being attacked their corpses needed to be stabbed through the heart with a sickle. Corpses that had been walked over by a cat were also in danger. To prevent the risk of the corpse becoming a strigoi it would need to be buried with a bottle of wine. After six weeks the bottle should be dug up and the wine drunk with relatives as a form of protection.

Other people thought to be in danger of turning into strigoii after death included people who died unforgiven by their parents; people who committed suicide; criminals; those who died unbaptized; those born with a membrane cap or caul, or those who had been stared at in the womb by a vampire. In addition, the ropes used to tie the feet of the corpse had to be cut and buried close to the body; however, if they are stolen and used in black magic the body was thought to become a strigoi.

Other preventative/protective measures used against the threat of the strigoi included: placing a candle, a coin, and a towel in the corpse's hand; removing the heart and cutting it in two; driving a nail into the forehead; placing a clove of garlic under the tongue; turning the body face down in the grave; piercing the corpse with a needle; scattering poppy seeds around the grave to appeal to the vampire's obsessive need to count them one by one; or burying the body with a bottle of whiskey in the belief that the corpse would drink it and be too drunk to find its way home. In extreme cases, the body would be exhumed and cremated and the ashes thrown to the wind.

"The girl and the strigoi"

In an article entitled "The Romanian Folkloric Vampire" by Jan Perkowski, published in the September 1982 issue of the journal *East Europe Quarterly*, the following tale is recorded as heard by Romanian linguist

Professor Emil Petrovici in the Romanian town of Ohaba, in south-western Transylvania, on June 21, 1936:

Once a strigoi turned into a handsome young man and a young girl fell in love with him. They were married, but the girl also wanted a religious wedding. He rejected this idea. Her parents insisted, so he agreed to go to the church, but when they emerged from the church he looked at his wife in a strange way, baring his teeth. She became afraid and told her mother about it. Her mother said, "Don't be afraid. He loves you. So that's why he bared his teeth." When their parents came to visit them, they couldn't find them. They had locked themselves in, but the people could see them through the window. He was sucking her blood. When the people saw it, they shot him through the window.

Strigoica is the Romanian term for a female vampire, either living or dead. While alive the strigoica drains energy and power from people and animals and after death transforms into a blood-sucking vampire.

See also: **ROMANIA; STRIGES**

Styria

A region in Austria known for its mountains, Styria was the original setting for Bram Stoker's novel *Dracula*. In notes dated 1890, perhaps influenced by Sheridan Le Fanu's *Carmilla*, which is set in Styria, Stoker places Dracula's castle in Styria. Instead of traveling to Transylvania, Jonathan Harker travels from England to Munich and then on to Styria. Later, probably after researching and reading about Romanian folklore, Stoker changed the setting to Transylvania.

Succubus

See: **INCUBUS/SUCCUBUS; NIGHTMARE**

Suicide

In European, African, and Chinese folklore a person who took their own life was considered to be at risk of becoming a vampire. Suicide was considered a sin against God, for in the act a person assumed the powers of deciding upon their life and death. It was also regarded as a statement of complete disregard for the community and its traditions and rituals. In return that community would register its disapproval by denying the victim a proper burial. Suicides were traditionally not buried in hallowed ground, but at a distance from the village or at crossroads. In England suicide victims were buried at crossroads and a stake was impaled into their chest to prevent evil spirits animating their body. Such practices against suicides continued until the reign of King George IV in the early nineteenth century, when private burial was allowed.

Suicide left unfinished business and unresolved grief with relatives and family members, and this may well have played a part in accounts of suicides returning to the living in nightmares or during the night as a vision. The exhumation and mutilation of corpses therefore also served the function of breaking the connection with the deceased.

See also: **BRESLAU VAMPIRE**

Sumerians

For the ancient Sumerians, like many ancient peoples, the distinction between vampires and demons was blurred. Demons were said to feed on human blood and were drawn to battlefields and scenes of murder or violence. The spilling of blood was an invitation to the forces of evil. It was also thought that demons were associated with disease and infection, something that vampires were also associated with later. Although it is often difficult to distinguish between demon and vampire in Sumerian mythology, three basic types of vampire can be found: the ekimmu, the uruku (utukku), and the seven demons.

- *The ekimmu was said to be created when death happened violently or the burial was not handled properly. The person could only be released by an exorcism performed by a priest or priestess.*

- *The uruku is referred to as a "vampyre which attacks man" in a cuneiform inscription.*

- *The seven demons are mentioned in many texts and incantations of the Mesopotamian*

cultures. One Sumerian banishing rite describes them as immortal blood-drinkers.

See also: **EKIMMU; UTUKKU**

Summers, Montague (1880–1948)

English cleric, scholar, and writer, Montague Summers was celebrated as the world's foremost authority on occult matters in the 1920s and 30s. Summers achieved notoriety within the field for writing several books on supernatural subjects, which have become classics. His titles include: *The History of Witchcraft and Demonology* (1926); *The Vampire: His Kith and Kin* (1928); *The Vampire in Europe* (1929); and the first English translation of the fifteenth-century witch-hunting manual, *Malleus Maleficarum.* In 1934 he published a study of the werewolf.

Summers' life remains obscure, but he was ordained a deacon in the Church of England in 1908 and was well known in London's literary circles. To the skeptic Summers' research seems a little naïve and overtrusting of his sources, but he is known to have gone to great lengths to gather evidence of vampires and ghosts, particularly in the latter part of his life when he was able to explore Europe at leisure, and with a reputation that allowed him ready access to many alleged haunted locations.

Still in print today, *The Vampire: His Kith and Kin* and *The Vampire in Europe* are two of the most famous research studies on vampires ever to be written. The two books complement each other but *Kith and Kin*, the longer of the two, is perhaps less popular because it contains extensive footnotes in Greek, Latin, French, and German. In both books Summers attempts to trace the origin of and examine the folklore surrounding vampire traditions and his compilations of numerous accounts of alleged vampire activity make his work of great interest to vampire scholars. Also of great interest for modern readers is his total conviction that vampires do exist.

Sunlight

In contemporary opinion, largely derived from a mixture of fiction and folklore, vampires are creatures of the night that must avoid the rays of the sun because being exposed to them will bring about their destruction. The unwillingness of a person to go out into sunlight is often taken as a sign of vampirism. Vampire hunters typically fear sunset as this is the time of day that heralds the coming of darkness and the moment when vampires stir in their graves. Conversely, the approach of dawn creates moments of tension for vampires as they must rush back to their resting places.

In vampire folklore, although vampires are usually night creatures who rise from their graves under cover of darkness to attack the living, there is no precedence for them being destroyed by sunlight; this is a theme that has been popularized by film and fiction. Generally in folklore the powers of vampires are at their strongest during the night but they can also appear during the day to cause trouble. Some vampires, for example those from Poland and Russia, can hunt victims from noon until midnight.

In the novel *Dracula*, the Count's powers are weakened during the day but he can appear in daylight without any ill effects. It was the film *Nosferatu* (1922) that first used sunlight as the most potent weapon against the vampire. In Anne Rice's Vampire Chronicles sunlight is equally lethal to vampires, but the pendulum swung back again in Stephenie Meyer's Twilight Saga series of 2005–8. Meyer's vampires are not destroyed by sunlight; they grow more beautiful in it.

Supernatural

The term "supernatural" describes any experience, occurrence, manifestation, or object that is beyond the laws of nature and science and whose understanding may be said to lie with religion, magic, or the mystical. (The term is often used interchangeably with "paranormal," which is a term also used to describe events or phenomena that cannot be explained by rational or scientific means or by the laws of nature as currently understood by science.)

Vampires are typically classified as a supernatural phenomenon because their existence cannot be explained within the laws of nature and because they seem to derive their evil characteristics chiefly through their opposition to the natural order of things. In this way they can be distinguished from diabolical creatures, like demons and witches, who traditionally derive their evil powers from their opposition to God. Supernatural beings can be diabolical as well, as God and nature are often thought to be one and the same, and the vampire myth did grow out of legends of demons and witches. However, in general, at least from the intellectual turning point in history that took place in the eighteenth century (the Age of Reason), supernatural beings are regarded as more closely related to human beings and less directly concerned with heaven and hell.

The most popular view of the supernatural contrasts it with the term "natural," i.e. the assumption that some events occur according to natural laws and others do not, because they are caused by forces external to nature. In essence, the world is seen as operating according to natural law normally until a higher force external to nature, for example God, interferes. Others deny any distinction between the natural and supernatural. According to this view, because God is sovereign, all events, even seemingly supernatural ones, are directly caused by God and not by impersonal powers of any kind. Another view asserts that events that appear to be supernatural occur according to natural laws which we do not yet understand. Those who believe that vampires are real might subscribe to this point of view.

Some believe the supernatural is a form of magic but others, particularly among the skeptical academic community, believe that all events have natural and only natural causes. They believe that human beings ascribe supernatural attributes to purely natural events in an attempt to cope with fear and ignorance. For example, in earlier times before scientific and medical understanding revolutionized our lives, belief in vampires arose as an attempt by people to explain disease, misfortune, evil, and death.

Swan, Bella

Isabella (Bella) Swan is a fictional character and the protagonist of Stephenie Meyer's Twilight Saga (2005–8), which consists of the novels *Twilight, New Moon, Eclipse,* and *Break-*

ing Dawn. The Twilight series is primarily narrated from Bella's point of view.

Bella is presented in the first novel as a 17-year-old girl who is pale-skinned with brown hair and eyes, and a heart-shaped face. Beyond this, a detailed description of her appearance is never given in the series. Meyer explained that she deliberately left out a detailed description of Bella in the book so that the reader could more easily step into her shoes. In the 2008 movie *Twilight* the part of Bella Swan was played by American actress Kristen Stewart.

Sweden, Unsolved Murder

On May 4, 1932, a 32-year-old prostitute was found murdered in her small apartment in the Atlas area of Stockholm. She had been dead for a couple of days, her skull had been crushed, and the investigating detectives discovered that someone had been drinking her blood.

Almost immediately panic about a vampire on the loose spread, and the newspapers kept this idea alive with numerous stories concerning the details and investigation of this crime. The woman was known as a prostitute so the investigation never really got the police attention that other murders received. As a result there is very little known about the murder suspect and the case has remained unsolved – a cold case sometimes referred to as "the Atlas Vampire Murder."

Symbols

A symbol is something such as an object, image, picture, written word, sound, or idea that represents something else by association, resemblance, or convention. For example, for many people a cross is a symbol of Christianity.

In mythology and folklore vampires symbolically expressed the problems of evil, disease, death, and the issue of unresolved grief concerning the loss of a loved one. More recently, the vampire myth has come to represent a host of different things, from the challenges of everyday life and relationships to parasitic relationships, from taboo sexuality to a wide range of social and political problems.

Dangerous sexuality

During the Victorian era vampirism symbolized sexual taboos. *Dracula* was written in 1897 at a time when sex was not a topic of polite conversation and sexual fantasies were repressed. Few scenes in fiction would have seemed as disturbingly erotic as the nocturnal visits of Dracula to his female victims and the staking of the vampirized Lucy Westenra by her fiancé, Arthur Holmwood, on what should have been their wedding night. In the sexually liberated twentieth century vampirism came to symbolize homosexuality and other forms of sexuality frowned on by mainstream society. It also resonated strongly with all kinds of problems related to love and sex: unrequited love, parasitic love, taboo love, and bereaved love. In recent years, however, instead of representing repressed sexuality or sexual taboos, vampires have come to represent an emergence beyond sexual stereotypes. The vampires of today are comfortable with all forms of sexual and personal expression.

Sex, power, and immortality

In times past, vampires were symbols of disease, evil, and death but their functions in the society of today are fundamentally different from what they were originally. Whereas in the past the vampire was a scapegoat for unexplainable calamity, this no longer appears to be the case today.

Despite a fundamental shift in symbolic meaning, the appeal of the vampire remains strong. Many experts have attempted to explain the vampire's continuing appeal in psychological terms. One school of thought suggests that the vampire retains its appeal because it symbolizes the problems and challenges of growing up. Adolescents must deal with their first-time feelings of sexual energy and hostility, and the vampire acts out these feelings. Others maintain that vampires are appealing simply because they are horrifying symbols of evil and in this way they become a focus of fascination for secret and forbidden desires.

According to Norine Dresser in *American Vampires: Fans, Victims, Practitioners* (1989), vampires are an endless source of fascination for American culture because they have come to symbolize sex, power, and immortality – interests often attributed to wider American society. Vampires are potent symbols of power over others, which can be very attractive to people who feel they don't have any power of their own. Vampires also symbolize sex and sexuality, a powerful drive within us all, and last but by no means least, vampires have the appeal of immortality, which has been a goal of humankind for centuries.

Dark rebel

The vampire today is a symbol of the dark side of humans – lust, greed, and desire – but on another level it also has the appeal of the dark rebel, the outcast who challenges the establishment. Doomed to spend eternity in a universe neither living nor dead, the vampire is a potent symbol of the outsider who – even when he appears to blend in unnoticed – does not fit in, a situation many people feel they can identify with at some point in their lives.

Today the vampire is no longer tied to its limiting negative associations with disease, decay, and death and has become a true archetype, symbolizing not just the "shadow" but many different aspects of the human psyche. Whether real or symbol, one thing remains certain – the image of the vampire has stood the test of time and in this sense it has achieved immortality.

See also: **BLOOD; GAY CULTURE; POLITICAL VAMPIRES; SEX**

Syphilis

Syphilis, a venereal disease, was rife during Victorian times and like the AIDS epidemic today it could have fueled much of the era's fascination with vampires and dangerous, fatal sexuality. To quote vampire expert David J. Skal from his book *V is for Vampire* (1996):

A story like Dracula can be read as an almost transparent, syphilis parable with its images of wanton women, blood contamination, skin lesions and pseudoscientific "cures" resonating powerfully with widespread panic about sexual contagion, demonization of prostitutes and the attendant rise of blood purifying quacks.

The Element Encyclopedia of Vampires

"So you faint at the sight of blood?"

Edward Cullen, in *Twilight* by Stephenie Meyer

Tail

In Slavic folklore a baby born with a bony protuberance at the end of the spine – a tail – was thought destined to become a vampire after death.

See also: **BAD SIGNS/OMENS**

Talamaur

"Talamaur" is the name given to a species of living vampire, male or female, found in the Bank Islands in the South Pacific. The talamaur was thought to be able to make the soul or *tarunga* of a deceased person his or her familiar who could then be ordered to attack others. If someone was suspected of being a talamaur because people felt apprehensive or threatened in some way by them, they would be forced to endure the smell of burning leaves until they gave up the name of the deceased person whose soul they were controlling. Another species of talamaur was a person who could send out his or her soul to drain any remaining life essence out of a recently deceased corpse.

Tar

In many regions in Europe tar applied to doors or posts in the shape of a cross was used as a form of protection against vampires. Like garlic, its anti-vampire qualities are no doubt associated with its strong odor.

See also: **APOTROPAICS**

Tarrant Gunville

In *The Vampire's Bedside Companion* (1975), British paranormal expert Peter Underwood mentions the story of William Doggett, the steward of Eastbury house, a magnificent mansion in Tarrant Gunville, Dorset. Doggett shot himself when he was unable to pay back money he had borrowed from his master. His suicide was said to have left a bloodstain on the floor that could not be washed away or removed.

According to Underwood, soon after his death poltergeist activity was reported in the house with doors opening by themselves and noises being heard. There were even reports of the bloody face of Doggett being seen by terrified witnesses. In 1845, during renovation of the church and churchyard, Doggett's corpse was exhumed. When the coffin was opened the legs were found tied together with yellow ribbon but the body was not decomposed and the face had a rosy complexion. To quote Underwood, "*Now the secret was out and after the 'vampire' was dealt with in the accepted way, there was no further trouble and there were no more reports of Doggett's blood-stained ghost.*"

Other reports of the story can be found in *Tales of the supernatural, with some accounts of hereditary curses and family legends* (1907) by Charles G. Harper, and *The haunted homes and family traditions of Great Britain* (1897) by John H. Ingram.

Taxim

In parts of Eastern Europe, "taxim" is a term used to refer to a type of revenant or reanimated body that is unable to find eternal release until it has satisfied its need for revenge. What distinguishes the taxim from other vampires and revenants is that it is a rotting corpse in a state of decomposition and it exists for one reason and one reason only – to make others pay for the sins committed against it while it lived.

Teeth

In fiction the vampire's teeth, which often become fangs when they need to feed, are an essential characteristic that distinguishes them from other monsters. In folklore, however, there are only infrequent comments to the effect that a body's teeth had grown when a corpse had become a vampire. Some vampires did not even use teeth to draw blood – for instance the Russian vampire has a pointed tongue, which is used to pierce the skin of victims. When teeth are mentioned it is usually as an observation that a newborn is destined to become a vampire. Among the Kashubs and the Poles of Upper Silesia, a child born with teeth was identified as a potential revenant.

In *The Vampire: His Kith and Kin*, Montague Summers demonstrates how easily scholars can slip into fictional mode when describing the appearance of the vampire when he writes: *"the lips will be markedly full and red and drawn back from the teeth which gleam long, sharp as razors and ivory white."*

Tehran Vampire

Gholamreza Kordieh was dubbed the "Vampire of Tehran" because he preyed on girls and women at night while working as a taxi driver. There are few vampires in Islamic culture but Kordieh was similar to other vampire criminals in that he was a serial killer. He did not drink the blood of his victims but he killed them by staking.

The 28-year-old began his killing spree in March 1997 and was caught a few months later after he had killed at least nine women. He raped his victims and then killed them and staked them before attempting to burn them. He was finally caught when identified from sketches drawn by two women who had managed to escape from him. He was executed on August 13, 1997.

See also: **CRIME**

Television

The first formal appearance of the vampire on television took place in 1954 with the appearance of horror actor Béla Lugosi in a live television show, *You Asked for It*. On November 23, 1956, the first made-for-television program featuring vampires was a live performance of *Dracula* broadcast from New York and starting John Carradine as the Count. After these appearances by Lugosi and Carradine, vampires appeared in comic roles in series such as *The Addams Family* and *The Munsters*.

In 1966 Dan Curtis's *Dark Shadows* soap opera debuted on daytime television. It was not a success until a vampire character, Barnabas Collins, was introduced in 1967. The series went on to become a popular and lasting one, and even though it ended in 1971 it demonstrated that the character of the vampire had potentially huge audience appeal and could be a convincing television drama lead or theme. In the decades that followed, vampire characters went on to feature prominently in numerous dramas, films, and series, most notably the hit TV series, *Buffy the Vampire Slayer*.

More recently, the series *Blood Ties* premiered on Lifetime Television in 2007. Set in modern-day Toronto it features a vampire character called Henry Fitzroy, who is an illegitimate son of Henry VIII of England. In 2008 a new series from HBO, entitled *True Blood*, gives a Southern take on the vampire theme.

The continuing popularity of the vampire theme on television over the decades has often been ascribed to a combination of two factors: the representation of sexuality, which in the Internet age has become more overt, and the perennial longing for immortality.

See also: COMICS; FILMS; STAGE

Temple of the Vampire

The Temple of the Vampire is an organization that claims to practice the religion of vampirism. To quote the organization's website (www.vampiretemple.com):

The Temple of the Vampire is an international organization that can enable you to acquire authentic power over others, build real wealth, achieve vibrant health, and even live beyond the usual human lifespan.

This is part of what it means to become a real Vampire.

The Temple believes vampirism is an ancient religion that has been known over the centuries by different names, including the Order of the Dragon and the Temple of the Dragon, and its aim is to locate those people who might be of "the Blood." In other words, those people who recognize themselves as different from others, who are predators of the night, and who understand that there is something more to life.

According to the Temple website, vampires are the next stage of human evolution and they exist as predators of humans. During the day their daytime self is a skeptic, but during the night they learn how to master the traditional powers of the vampire, such as hypnosis and shape-shifting. Through rituals their night-side self is strengthened so that it can connect to the cosmic powers of darkness.

Temple membership is international and there are several different levels of membership. Once accepted into membership, after making a commitment and a donation to the Temple, a person becomes a "lifetime member" and gains access to instruction, meetings, and support. After success in rituals designed to advance vampiric powers, a lifetime member can advance to become an "active member," then to a "vampire predator" and finally to become a "vampire priest" or priestess.

The Temple describes itself as a secret organization but it does not tolerate criminal activity or blood-drinking in any form. It publishes *The Vampire Bible*, which is a manual of fundamental instruction and vampire lore issued to lifetime members. Often criticized as a sales gimmick, the Temple defends itself by stating that it expects all members to first be true skeptics and then to test the Temple teachings to move from non-belief to authenticated knowledge.

See also: **REAL VAMPIRES**

Tepes, Vlad

See: **VLAD THE IMPALER**

Thailand

In Thai folklore the phi were spirits fairly similar to the ghosts and fairies of Western Europe. Among the phi, however, there were said to be the ghosts of people killed by animals, women who died in childbirth, people who had not been given proper funeral rites and those who had died suddenly and violently, and it was these ghosts that could sometimes demonstrate vampiric qualities. The phi song nang, for instance, were analogous to the pontianak of Indonesia in that they appeared as beautiful young women who vampirized men. If someone had been attacked by a phi, sorcerers would be called in to use charms, spells, and incantations to remove the spirit.

Theater

See: **STAGE**

thorns

Since ancient times whenever traditions concerned corpse mutilation, thorns, the sharp spines from trees such as hawthorn, have been used as a form of protection against vampires. In Romania, the head and feet of a corpse would be wrapped in thorns. The Slavs pierced the tongues of corpses with thorns to prevent them chewing and sucking. Thorns could also be put in coffins or around graves to catch the shroud of the vampire should it attempt to rise from the ground and so hinder its attempts to walk.

See also: **DESTROYING VAMPIRES;**
PROTECTION

Thornton Heath Poltergeist

The Thornton Health Poltergeist case involved a house in South London that was allegedly haunted by a poltergeist with vampiric qualities in 1938.

The poltergeist activity seemed to center round Pat Forbes, a 35-year old woman who was the owner of the house at the time. Objects flew around the house or materialized from thin air. Glasses shattered and there was the smell of rotting flesh in the air. The phenomena increased in intensity until Mrs. Forbes reported that she had been visited and attacked by an invisible vampire at night.

It wasn't long before the media was drawn to the case. It also attracted the attention of Hungarian psychical researcher Nandor Fodor, who, after detailed observation and research, described the case as one of "poltergeist psychosis." By this he meant that

The Element Encyclopedia of Vampires

Mrs. Forbes's unconscious mind was responsible for the activities. He believed that the cause was sexual trauma that she had suffered as a child and which had been repressed.

The vampire attack

The vampire allegedly came to visit Mrs. Forbes on the night of May 18, 1938. On the morning of May 19, Fodor phoned Mrs. Forbes and found her so shaken that she said she feared for her sanity. Her experience, said Fodor, *"read like a page from Bram Stoker's Dracula"* but seemed to be nevertheless real and terrifying. He went on to state that *"She awoke feeling something like a human body lying beside her on top of the cover; something cold and hard which she took to be a head was touching her neck. She was unable to move."*

When a doctor examined Mrs. Forbes's neck he found two irregular and fairly deep punctures. Asked to elaborate on what had happened, Mrs. Forbes said that around midnight she had felt something bite her and that there was a smell of rotten meat in the air. When she recovered from her paralysis she felt the thing leave her, swishing through the air with a flapping noise like beating wings. When she awoke she tasted blood on her mouth and noticed that her neck was sore. She also felt extremely cold and looked pale.

Fodor's conclusion

Almost from the very first day that Fodor investigated the case he suspected that Mrs. Forbes might be causing the poltergeist activity by normal means, despite her obvious distress in reaction to the activities and his lack of proof. He believed that the vampire attack was a fantasy carried to extremes with self-mutilation. He also examined her psychological background and discovered that her past clearly showed a history of hysteria and dissociated personality disorder, which included hearing voices. He became convinced that Mrs. Forbes was a neurotic with a disorganized personality and that she was somehow hiding objects in her clothing to produce the poltergeist phenomena. Searches revealed nothing but an X-ray proved Fodor to be correct. Two small objects seemed to be hidden under Mrs. Forbes's left breast and they both appeared after she allegedly collapsed.

This event convinced Fodor that Mrs. Forbes was fabricating the phenomena. He did, however, believe that the case was important because it suggested a new direction for psychical research – one that attempted to understand the mental patterns that accompany such occurrences, even if these occurrences are fraudulent.

The full story of Thornton Heath did not reach the public until 1945, when Fodor finally published it in the *Journal of Clinical Psychopathology*. The reason for the delay was the criticism that had been directed at him from other psychical researchers for his emphasis on tracing psychic phenomena to a sexual neurosis. Eventually, though, Fodor won recognition for his theory. The case has become a classic in psychical research and psychological reasons are now routinely considered in cases of paranormal phenomena.

Thought Form

In occultism a thought form is a non-physical shape, pattern, or vibration that is created by thoughts and emotions, which allegedly can be perceived visibly by clairvoyants or sensed intuitively by others. Psychic vampires can allegedly create thought forms and use them against others for the purpose of psychic attack.

The idea behind thought forms is that every thought generates an energy pattern or wave. Once created, thought forms radiate outwards and attract similar essences, which is the theory that forms the basis of the occult law of attraction or "like seeks like." Thought forms that are dark in nature (such as hate, jealousy, and rage) are dense in color and in form, whereas thought forms that are more pure, such as love and happiness, are lighter. According to occultists, thought forms can be consciously directed against others without the targets even knowing what is happening. Vampire thought forms are those that drain others' energy, causing tiredness, poor health, and depression.

Threshold

The threshold is an entrance to a dwelling place that vampires cannot step across unless given permission to do so by the person inside. The concept probably arose from the Christian idea that the Devil cannot go where he is not welcome. In other words, people can stay safe if they do not invite the vampire in or show him or her hospitality, because once inside the vampire is free to attack. The problem of course is that it is often hard to recognize the true nature of the vampire.

Tibet

Given the number of blood-drinking spirits, demons, gods, and vampire-like entities in Tibetan mythology, folklore, and religious art, some of which may date to even before the days of Hindu and Buddhist religious expansion, it is not surprising that Tibet has been suggested by some experts as the place where vampires may have originated. The Tibetans cremated their dead in part because they believed that a corpse was an invitation for the soul to return to earth as a blood-drinking vampire. Blood offerings were also made in many temples to fearsome deities, such as bhayankara, known as the "awful one."

Some of the most highly visible vampire entities were the Wrathful Deities, also known as the 58 blood-drinking deities, who appear in *The Tibetan Book of the Dead*. These deities, who had the heads of different animals and engaged in vampiric activities, were thought to appear on the eighth day after a person had died. Another significant vampiric deity was the green-faced Yama, the Tibetan Lord of the Dead, who drank the blood of sleeping people.

The Sikkim vampire

In Tibet's neighbor state, Sikkim, a case of vampirism was recorded in a fresco in a monastery in Sinon near Mt. Kangchenjunga. According to the fresco, in the early eighteenth century Princess Pedi Wangmo, the half-sister of the monarch, Chador Namgyral, plotted to kill her half-brother. With the assistance of a doctor she bled Chador to death and drank his blood. She and her accomplice were eventually caught and killed, and some believed that after her death she became a vampire.

Tikoloshe

The tikoloshe, or tokoloshe, is vampire-demon found among the Xhosa people of Lesotho and the southernmost African plains. The creature also has strong associations with witchcraft. In many of the legends the tikoloshe is a demon that resembles a baboon but it can take on numerous forms and can shape-shift into a friendly (perhaps overly friendly) person or a black bird with a skull-like head. The tikoloshe is male and most of its victims tend to be local village women, although children and men can also be attacked. The tikoloshe feeds on the energy or life force of its victims rather than their blood, leaving them feeling fatigued and weak. The creature can also be used by a sorcerer or witch to attack his or her enemies.

The services of a professional witch doctor may be required to imprison and destroy the tikoloshe, but generally among the Xhosa people prevention is often better than a cure. Because the tikoloshe is thought to be small and because it only attacks its victims at night, the bed will be raised on stacks of bricks so the tikoloshe cannot reach the occupant. The sleeper may also rest with an iron knife across his or her breast.

See also: **AFRICA**

Tillinghurst, Sarah

Sarah Tillinghurst was an alleged vampire of South County, Rhode Island, and the oldest child of Stuckely Tillinghurst, a wealthy orchard farmer who was nicknamed "Snuffy" because of the tobacco color of his coat.

Stuckely had 14 children with his wife, Honor, and most of them worked for him in the orchards. One night during the harvest season of 1796 he began to have a series of recurring nightmares in which his daughter Sarah was calling to him; when he turned to look at her the fruit in his orchard had withered and died and the smell of decay made him feel ill. He was so concerned about this vision that he consulted his pastor, who told him he was only worried about his harvest.

The harvest was plentiful but later that year Sarah fell ill and died from what the doctor thought was tuberculosis. After her death five more of Stuckely's children died of the same wasting illness. Stuckely was convinced his dream had been prophetic and the dream became even more ominous when his children complained that the dead Sarah visited them at night causing great pain. He discussed his concerns with his neighbors, who told him about the returning dead and how to put them to rest.

The six children were dug up; five of the bodies were found to be in a state of decomposition but Sarah's body was found incorrupt and intact in her wooden casket. Her eyes were open and fixed, her hair and nails seemed to have grown, and her body appeared bloated with blood. Stuckely cut out her heart and burned it. After the exhumations one more child died but another recovered and no longer complained of nocturnal visits by

Sarah. The rest of the family remained untouched by death.

The Tillinghurst family cemetery can be found in the township of Exeter today. Sarah's reburial may be one of the several unmarked graves close by.

See also: NEW ENGLAND; RHODE ISLAND VAMPIRES

Tlahuelpuchi

In the lore of rural Tlaxcala, Mexico, the vampire-witches known as tlahuelpuchi are much feared as they personify everything that is evil and hateful.

The tlahuelpuchi was a person believed to possess magical powers, including the power to transform themselves into one of several animals and in that form attack and suck the blood of humans. Although they can be male, they are typically female and in their female form they are believed to be at their most deadly. Elements found in tlahuelpuchi tradition can be traced to ancient Aztec goddesses, and they provided a supernatural explanation for unexplained infant deaths.

Origin and traits

A tlahuelpuchi is born, not made, and they cannot infect others with their condition. They work independently as agents of evil but can also make pacts with the Devil. When a tlahuelpuchi is born, there are no identifying signs. Differences from other children only emerge at puberty when supernatural powers such as shape-shifting suddenly manifest. For females, this often occurs with the onset of menstruation. When their powers manifest, both male and female tlahuelpuchis are gripped by an insatiable and lifelong desire to feed on human blood, their preference being for the blood of infants aged three to six months old, but not younger as the blood of younger infants is not so palatable to them. They hunt at night, particularly between the hours of midnight and four in the morning, but can also hunt during the day if their blood craving is extreme. Tlahuelpuchis do not hunt every night, only when their blood cravings are extreme, which is usually one to four times a month. They are more active during rainy and cold weather.

The tlahuelpuchis can shape-shift into many different animal forms but fowl and turkey are their favored incarnations. When they have transformed into their animal form they are restricted to the limitations of that animal and cannot use their magical powers; the only exception being that they can make turkeys fly. They also give off a phosphorescent glow that is a sign of their true identity.

Tlahuelpuchis can enter a home at night in a mist that seeps under doors and windowsills, or through keyholes, or they crawl in as an insect. Once inside, they shape-shift into a turkey and hypnotize their victims into a deep sleep before carrying out their attacks. Blood is sucked from the back of an infant's neck or from its cheeks and neck. The dead infants are usually discovered in their cribs or on the floor; a tell-tale sign of Tlahuelpuchi attack being a door left ajar. The bodies will have bruises and purple and yellow spots. There may also be dried blood on the infant's mouth.

In addition to sucking the blood of infants, tlahuelpuchis can use their hypnotic powers to make adults jump to their death in their sleep. They can also kill or injure domestic animals and ruin crops. Thus many types of misfortune over the centuries have been attributed to the work of these vampiric witches.

For obvious reasons tlahuelpuchi lived incognito in their communities.

Tlahuelpuchis cannot kill members of their own family. Although they cannot transmit their powers to others, when they are killed their powers transfer to the killer. For this reason family members are often reluctant to expose them for what they are and will go to great lengths to keep their shame a secret to avoid being stigmatized by the community.

Protection and remedies

The corpse of the victim of a tlahuelpuchi attack must be cleaned immediately and placed in a small, wooden coffin on top of a table in the main room, with lighted candles at the head and feet to ward off attacks on other children in the community. There must also be a cross made of pinewood placed underneath the table as pinewood was said to have the power to ward off evil. Neighbors must undertake these cleansing tasks as families should not handle their own dead.

A *tezitlazc* – a sorcerer and healer – may also be called in to perform a number of cleansing rituals over the corpse and for family members. The *tezitlazc* will also be needed to deal with the symptoms of grieving and stress, such as weeping and depression, which are also blamed on the tlahuelpuchi. Funeral rites must be conducted in complete silence and after the funeral the dead infant must be forgotten as though he or she never existed.

Other preventative measures against the tlahuelpuchi include the use of garlic, onions, metal, and the scattering of pieces of tortilla, which protect in a similar way to seeds. Infants can be protected with silver, metal crosses, and mirrors, and by placing an open pair of scissors near the crib. Adults can protect themselves by wearing raw garlic in their undergarments, pinning underclothes with safety pins in the form of a cross, attaching a pin to the inside of a hat, or by wearing a blessed cross.

Killing the tlahuelpuchi

The most effective way to kill tlahuelpuchis is when they are in their more easy-to-identify animal form and unable to use their magic powers. Encounters in their human form are rare.

Tlahuelpuchis can be paralyzed by throwing a pair of pants with one leg turned inside out at them, or by knotting three corners of a white handkerchief, wrapping it around a stone and throwing it at them, or by taking off one's hat, throwing it to the ground, and driving a knife through it. Once paralyzed the creature can then be clubbed or stoned to death. Touching a tlahuelpuchi is considered unclean and vampire killers must be ritually cleansed with a brushing of capulin leaves. If killed in human form the corpse of a tlahuelpuchi will be symbolically killed again by tearing the eyes out of the sockets and cutting off the ears, nose, tongue, lips, and fingers.

In rural areas of Mexico belief in tlahuelpuchis remains widespread to this day. Accusations of blood-sucking and witchcraft that have resulted in trial and execution have declined greatly since the late nineteenth century, but as recently as 1954 the state of Tlaxcala passed a law requiring that cases concerning infants allegedly killed by witchcraft had to be referred to the medical authorities.

See also: **MEXICO**

Tolstoy, Aleksey (1817–75)

Count Aleksey Konstantinovich Tolstoy was a nineteenth-century Russian nobleman who introduced the vampire into Russian literature. His novel, *Upyr* (*The Vampire*, 1841) showcased his keen knowledge of Slavic and Russian folklore.

Tolstoy also wrote three vampire-themed novels in French, of which the best known is *The Family of the Vourdalak* (1839). It tells the story of the aristocratic Marquis d'Urfe who while traveling through Serbia stops for the night with a family whose father had left to fight the Turks. Before he went on his way, d'Urfe tells the family to beware if the father comes back within ten days because this was a sign he had become a vourdalak (a vampire of the southern Slavs) and should be impaled with an aspen stake. As predicted the father returns. His oldest son wants to kill him but the family refuse, even though the father is acting strangely and refusing food and drink. The father then attacks and kills the family. D'Urfe returns to the village a few months later and is told that the entire family has become vampires, including a daughter he had been attracted to. D'Urfe barely escapes from the family with his life.

See also: **RUSSIA**

Toma Family, The

In early 2004, Romanian police were called to investigate the desecration of a grave in Marotinu de Sus, a remote village in the south of the country.

According to media reports, after 76-year-old Toma Petre died in a farming accident in December 2003, his relatives complained that he was to blame for a child's illness as some neighbors claimed they had seen him posthumously walking in his yard. Six local men then volunteered to enact the ancient Romanian ritual for dealing with a strigoi. Just before midnight, they crept into the cemetery on the edge of the village and gathered around Toma's grave. But rather than drive a stake through the corpse's heart, the six men dug Toma up, split his ribcage with a pitchfork, removed his heart, put stakes through the rest of his body, and sprinkled it with garlic. Then they burned the heart, put the embers in water, and shared the grim cocktail with the sick child.

The Element Encyclopedia of Vampires

Eventually, the sick girl got better again. Toma's daughter called in the police – not because her father's grave had been desecrated but because she had not been invited to the ritual. Local police arrested the men and charged them with illegally exhuming the corpse. They were jailed for six months but did not serve their sentences.

The police investigation and subsequent media interest highlighted not only local fears of the undead but a startling willingness to act on them. On April 12, 2004, another local farmer, 68-year-old Tita Musca, told a *Sunday Times* correspondent in Bucharest: *"For centuries we have had to protect ourselves against these creatures by finding the graves of the undead and risking our lives by ripping out their hearts."*

See also: **ROMANIA**

Tomb of Dracula, The

Along with *Vampirella, The Tomb of Dracula* was one of the most successful vampire comic books. Billed as "Comicdoms Number 1 Fear Magazine," it debuted in Marvel Comics in 1972 and enjoyed huge sales for a total of 70 issues. It was eventually discontinued in 1979.

After a few issues the comic was taken over by Marv Wolfman, who employed a strategy similar to the one used by Bram Stoker in his novel *Dracula*, in that the Count was a constant, menacing presence but his appearances were cleverly rationed. In this way the narrative gained a lot of momentum from the human characters struggling to deal with the threat of evil looming over them. Wolfman's heroes also included descendants of Stoker's characters, notably Quincey Harker – the baby born to Jonathan

and Mina at the end of *Dracula*. In the comic Quincey survives as an elderly vampire hunter confined to a wheelchair.

"Tomb of Sarah, The"

"The Tomb of Sarah" is a short story by F. G. Loring which was published in December 1900 in *Pall Mall* magazine. The plot is conventional but the story has become a favorite among readers because of the stylish and riveting way it presents its female vampire, Sarah. Gothic scholar Montague Summers identified "The Tomb of Sarah" as *"one of the best vampire stories I know."*

The story begins with this memorable inscription.

> *SARAH. 1630. FOR THE SAKE OF THE DEAD AND THE WELFARE OF THE LIVING, LET THIS SEPULCHRE REMAIN UNTOUCHED AND ITS OCCUPANT UNDISTURBED TILL THE COMING OF CHRIST.*

The chilling warning is, of course, ignored and the vampire is accidentally unearthed by a workman and goes on to drain the blood of the inhabitants of a nearby English village.

See also: **LITERATURE**

Tomić, Paja

In 1923 in the village of Tupanari, Bosnia, Paja Tomić, an old peasant, died. Within a few days his wife, Cvija, complained that her recently deceased husband had become a vampire and was appearing during the night in her house. Eventually Cvija's sons, Stevo and Kršto, called the entire village together and everyone agreed that the vampire should be destroyed. Led by the sons, villagers went to the cemetery and dug up Tomić's corpse. They pierced it with a stake made of hawthorn and burned the body to ashes that were then scattered.

Tools

Among the Gypsies, and most especially the Muslim Gypsies of Yugoslavia, agricultural tools could become empowered by vampiric spirits if they were not used for a period of three years. The most common vampire tools were the knots used with wooden yokes and the rods for tying sheaves of wheat, although no vampire tool was considered to be extremely dangerous.

Totenlaut

Totenlaut, translated from the German as "death cry," is the term used to describe the moaning sound that was heard from a corpse when it was staked. Such moaning, often accompanied by thrashing about, is often mentioned in eighteenth-century reports of vampire killings. The sound is actually caused by the stake forcing the air out of a corpse. The sound can also be heard when the corpse was moved and in previous centuries this led to speculation that the vampire was vocalizing its discomfort and terror at being discovered in its grave.

See also: **DESTRUCTION**

"Transfer, The"

"The Transfer" is a famous short story written by Algernon Blackwood and published in 1912 in *Pan's Garden*. It features two vampires; the first is a psychic sponge called Mr. Frene who is described as:

> *A man who dropped alone, but grew vital in a crowd. He vampired, unknowingly, no doubt, everyone with whom he came in contact; left them exhausted, tired, listless … he took your ideas, your strength, your very own words and later used them for his own benefit and aggrandizement. Not evilly, of course, the man was good enough; but you felt he was dangerous owing to the facile way he absorbed into himself all loose vitality that was to be had. His eyes and voice and presence devitalised you. Life, it seemed, not highly organised enough to resist, must shrink from his too near approach and hide away for fear of being appropriated, for fear, that is – of death.*

The second vampire is the "Forbidden corner" – a barren patch of earth in a rose garden that is hungry for new life. When Mr. Frene stands too close to the starved earth it devours him and transforms him into a plot that is strong and *"bursting thick with life."* "The Transfer" stands out in vampire literature because of its skillful presentation of psychic vampirism alongside the larger, devouring image of Mother Nature.

See also: LITERATURE; PSYCHIC VAMPIRE

Transformation

Also known as "turning," transformation is the process of becoming a vampire. It is not the same as awakening, as those who are transformed are not born as vampires, but become vampires after death or the bite of another vampire. Through it a corpse becomes an undead creature with fangs or a barbed tongue, sharp nails, glowing red eyes, enhanced vision, superhuman strength, and an insatiable thirst for living blood.

The process of transformation is completed when the vampire tastes its first blood, hence the emphasis in some cultures of preventing this ever happening by mutilating the corpse or placing weapons and sharp objects in the coffin. Should the vampire manage to escape from its grave its insatiable desire for blood would compel it to hunt, attack, and kill humans and animals, as generally vampires can only feed on living blood rather than the blood of corpses.

Causes

There appears to be no agreement in folklore or fiction on how a vampire is made, nor what causes the transformation. Sometimes it is through a single bite of another vampire, sometimes it is through drinking the blood of another vampire, and sometimes a vampire is made through a supernatural curse. In the case of the bite of another vampire triggering a transformation, there seems to be some

degree of intentionality and choice on the vampire's part, in that from all his prey he can decide which humans to kill and which humans can join him in his vampiric state. In short, some humans are food but others are potential companions.

In folklore the attack of a vampire may have caused the victim to transform into a vampire but more generally the victim's vampiric state did not occur until after death. Fear of vampire infection did not lead to persecution of the living but to mutilation of corpses at the local graveyard. In some cultures all it took to become a vampire was to die unbaptized, in an accident, a state of sin, through suicide, from a wasting disease, or to be drowned or exiled from the community. Sometimes becoming a vampire was the result of something as simple as an animal jumping over a corpse or lack of attention paid to the correct funeral rites.

Medieval theologians held that the process of transformation from corpse to vampire was caused by demonic infestation, which then spreads like a disease or infection from corpse to corpse. Modern occult theories tend to agree that vampiric transformation is caused by some type of negative energy that needs blood or the life energy of others to sustain itself. Another more recent theory suggests that vampirism is caused not by demons or negative energy but by a virus.

Louis's transformation

The process of transformation offers unrivalled imaginative opportunities for writers, and arguably one of the best accounts of the transformation of a vampire is given in Anne

Rice's *Interview with the Vampire* (1975). Rice's story gives readers a sound account of the physical process that might occur in the body during transformation.

In the novel the vampire Louis tells the tale of his transformation to a young journalist in modern-day America. He tells him that he became a vampire at the age of 25 in the year 1791. At that point in time he was suffering from suicidal depression caused by the loss of his family to a terrible tragedy for which he felt responsible. In this vulnerable state the vampire Lestat attacks him and drains him of blood, eventually almost to the point of death. The creature returns over several nights. Louis is weakened more with each visit and hypnotized by the vampire, who promises him eternal life and supernatural power away from the mundane preoccupations of daily life.

Lestat eventually attacks and paralyzes Louis to complete the ritual transformation of a human into a vampire. Lestat sucks Louis's blood and then bites his own wrist and gives it to Louis to drink, for him to savor a vampire's delight for the first time.

I drank, sucking the blood out of holes, experiencing for the first time since infancy the special pleasure of sucking nourishment, the body focused with the mind upon one vital source.

After this Louis hears a powerful and intense sound like the pounding of drums, which seems to reverberate around his whole body and in his mind. His temples throb, matching the beat of the drums. When Lestat breaks free from Louis's bite, Louis realizes that the sound he heard was the beating of their hearts,

and that their two hearts have merged together. At this point Louis has passed the threshold from humanity into the supernatural world and sees the world around him through the eyes of a vampire. He is outside the time frame of ordinary existence and can see, feel, hear, and sense every event, every detail of life as detached from time and physical deterioration, and therefore is able to fully perceive and savor its uniqueness. *"I saw as a vampire … It was as if I had only just been able to see colors and shapes for the first time."*

See also: BECOMING A VAMPIRE; BIRTH OF A VAMPIRE

Transformations

In folklore the vampire can transform itself into various animals. The most well-known transformation is that of vampire to bat, but vampires can also transform into birds, rats, cats, flies, locusts, dogs, mice, wolves, and fleas. In addition, they can transform themselves into mist, dust, or even dancing lights and on rare occasions into plants and tools.

In fiction, the ability of vampires to transform into animals and different forms was utilized by Bram Stoker in *Dracula* (1897). The Count can change himself into a bat, a wolf, and a dust-like mist, but he can only change at will during the night. By day he can only change form at noon, or at sunrise and sunset. It's possible that Stoker borrowed this idea from Emily Gerard, who in her study of Transylvanian folklore suggested that Romanians believed that evil spirits were more active at specific times of the day.

The Element Encyclopedia of Vampires

This idea of special powers tied to certain times of day, and indeed the idea of vampires transforming into animals and other forms, has often been dropped by subsequent vampire writers, who tend to focus more on their great strength and long life.

See also: **ANIMAL VAMPIRES;**
SHAPE-SHIFTING

Transylvania

Transylvania, one of the main areas in Romania in South-eastern Europe, means "the land beyond the forest." Most of Transylvania was part of Hungary from the eleventh century until 1920. Hungarian descendants of Attila the Hun settled in Transylvania along with the Saxons and for centuries the area was a war zone between the Christian West and Muslim East. Romanian, German, and Hungarian influences remain strong in Transylvania and to this day medieval towns and cities retain much of their historic atmosphere alongside the modern cosmopolitan cities. Among the hills and forests and Carpathian Mountains, folklore about vampires lives on. Today, Transylvania has become a major tourist attraction, drawing people not only for the stunning scenery but as the home of the fictional Count Dracula.

Bram Stoker and Transylvania

And then away for home! away to the quickest and nearest train! away from this cursed spot, from this cursed land, where the devil and his children still walk with earthly feet!

Although the stereotyping of Transylvania as a wild and desolate place had begun in Gothic literature, the area was relatively unknown until the beginning of the twentieth century when Bram Stoker used it as the homeland of the vampire in his novel, *Dracula*. In spite of the fact that only a small amount of the action takes place in Transylvania, it leaves an indelible impression on the reader. As a world of dark and dreadful things and a land beyond scientific understanding it represents a descent into primitive darkness. But most significantly, from Transylvania comes Count Dracula, who embodies late-Victorian England's worst fears about degeneration, atavism, and devolution. The Count poses a threat to the pure bloodlines of England and must be driven away and destroyed on his native soil.

Even though Stoker never visited Transylvania he did visit Austria and Switzerland, which has led many people to believe that his descriptions of the Carpathian Mountains must have been inspired by these countries. On one occasion, when an American journalist criticized Stoker for not having visited Transylvania, he replied *"Trees are trees, mountains are generally mountains, no matter what country you find them and one description may be made to answer for all — thus reinforcing the old adage among novelists: Never let the facts stand in the way of a good story."*

Stoker originally intended to set Dracula in Styria, Austria, but according to notes he made in 1890 he changed the setting to Transylvania. The reason behind this change may have been to do with research that his notes show he had done on the following books and articles concerning Transylvanian history, geography, and folklore.

- Round About the Carpathians *(1878) by Andrew F. Cross*

- On the Track of the Crescent *(1885) by Major E. C. Johnson*

- An Account of the Principalities of Wallachia and Moldavia *(1820) by William Wilkinson*

- Transylvania *(1865) by Charles Boner*

- "Transylvanian Superstitions" *(1885) by Emily Gerald*

Gerard's collected articles, in particular, provided a wealth of information about Transylvanian superstitions and folk customs. The following is a brief excerpt:

> *There are two sorts of vampires — living and dead. The living vampire is, in general, the illegitimate offspring of two illegitimate persons, but even a flawless pedigree will not ensure anyone against the intrusion of a vampire into his family vault, since every person killed by a nosferatu becomes likewise a vampire after death, and will continue to suck the blood of other innocent people till the spirit has been exorcised, either by opening the grave of the*

> *person suspected and driving a stake through the corpse, or firing a pistol shot into the coffin. In very obstinate cases it is further recommended to cut off the head and replace it in the coffin with the mouth filled with garlic, or to extract the heart and burn it, strewing the ashes over the grave.*

> *That such remedies are often resorted to, even in our enlightened days, is a well-attested fact, and there are probably few Roumenian villages where such has not taken place within the memory of the inhabitants.*

Count Dracula never lived, but it is important to point out that Transylvania was home to bloody historical figures, such as the fifteenth-century Wallachian prince Vlad Tepes (Vlad the Impaler) and Countess Elizabeth Báthory, whose legendary evil exploits have also strengthened the association of vampirism with the area.

Vampire tourism

Although Romanians had beliefs in the undead or strigoi, contrary to popular belief vampires never figured as prominently in Romanian folklore as in other European counties. The word "vampire" is of Serbian, not Romanian origin and most early accounts of vampires are linked to the areas of Hungary, Poland, and Serbia rather than Transylvania. In fact to this day there is a widespread tendency among Romanians to deny the existence of vampire figures in their folk beliefs.

For Romanians today, the word "vampire" typically refers either to an evil blood-sucking entity from Western mythology or to blood-hungry murderers. During Communist rule in the twentieth century, vampire fiction (including *Dracula*) was banned in Romania, because it represented the decadent West and because there was justified anger that the world's most notorious vampire bore the nickname of one of Romania's national heroes, Vlad Tepes. The ban was lifted, however, when Romanian officials realized that the Count was a major draw for foreign visitors and a vital ingredient for a thriving tourist industry.

See also: **ROMANIA**

Transylvanian Society of Dracula

The Transylvanian Society of Dracula is a non-profit-making Romanian organization with established chapters in other countries including Canada, Russia, and Germany that was founded in the early 1990s to encourage and promote the study and interpretation of Romanian history, myth, and folklore, especially as it related to Vlad Tepes. The society aims to provide a clearing house for information pertaining to the serious study of Dracula and related topics. Its members comprise historians, folklorists, literary critics, researchers, students, and film enthusiasts: anyone with a serious interest in Dracula.

In May 1995, the Society in Romania organized the first World Dracula Congress. This event attracted scholars and vampire researchers and enthusiasts from many countries, including some of the leading experts in the field. The congress provided the first opportunity for Romanian folklorists to share their knowledge and research on both the vampire legend and the history of Vlad Tepes with their counterparts in the West.

See also: **VLAD THE IMPALER**

Tremayne, Peter (1943–)

Peter Tremayne is the pseudonym of English-born writer Peter Berresford Ellis when writing horror and fantasy works. He is the author of a number of short stories and novels featuring Count Dracula or his fictional ancestors. His first book, *Dracula Unborn* (1977) (known as *Blood Right: Memoirs of Mircea, Son to Dracula* in the United States) features Vlad Tepes's son who attempts to escape his vampiric fate. *The Revenge of Dracula* (1978) and *Dracula, My Love* (1980) completed the "Dracula Lives" trilogy.

See also: **LITERATURE**

True Blood

Produced by Alan Ball, *True Blood* is a critically acclaimed, award-winning HBO American television drama series based on *The Southern Vampire Mysteries* by Charlaine Harris that premiered on September 7, 2008.

True Blood is set in a fictional small north Louisiana town called Bon Temps where vampires and human co-exist. The series centers on Sookie Stackhouse (played by Anna Paquin), a telepathic bar waitress who falls in love with a vampire, Bill Compton (Stephen Moyer).

In the drama, the invention of a Japanese scientist has led to vampires evolving from monsters to citizens. Many humans remain uneasy about these creatures "coming out of the coffin," and in Bon Temps, the jury is still out on the question.

The action in the first series revolves around the murder of young women in Bon Temps and the search for the perpetrator; Sookie uses her telepathic gifts to solve the mystery. Among the suspects are Sookie's brother, Jason, Bill, Sookie's vampire love interest and her other love interest, her boss Sam, who is a shape-shifter.

See also: **TELEVISION**

Tuberculosis

During the 1800s, pulmonary tuberculosis, or consumption, was credited with one out of every four deaths in Europe. Consumption could kill a person slowly over many years, or end life quickly in a matter of weeks. The symptoms of consumption are the gradual loss of strength and skin tone and difficulty breathing as the body is gradually starved of oxygen. The victim becomes pale, stops eating, and literally wastes away. At night, the condition worsens because the patient is lying down and fluid and blood may collect in the lungs. During later stages, a person might wake up to find blood on their face, neck, and nightclothes.

Some experts believe there may be a direct connection between vampire cases reported in Eastern Europe during the eighteenth and nineteenth centuries and consumption. A person in the later stages of consumption would look the way vampires have always been portrayed in folklore – emaciated, like a walking corpse – and the symptoms were also quite similar to those believed to denote a vampire attack. In fact, there are a number of documented cases in both Europe and the United States, in which a family or town viewed a person who had died from consumption as a vampire. For example, the epidemic allusion and vampire/tuberculosis link is obvious in the 1892 case of North American vampire Mercy Brown and also in the vampire outbreaks of New England.

See also: **CONTAGION; DISEASE**

The Element Encyclopedia of Vampires

Twilight Saga

The Twilight Saga is a bestselling series of four vampire-based young adult fantasy/romance novels by the American author Stephenie Meyer. The series follows the story of Isabella "Bella" Swan, a teenager who moves to Forks, Washington, and falls in love with a vampire named Edward Cullen. An unorthodox love triangle is later introduced between Edward, Bella, and Jacob, a werewolf.

Meyer has stated that the idea for the first book of the series, *Twilight*, came to her in a dream on June 2, 2003. In her dream a human girl was in love with a vampire who wanted to suck her blood. Inspired, Meyer wrote a version of what is now chapter 13 of the book. *Twilight* was a huge success and it was followed by three more books: *New Moon* (2006), *Eclipse* (2007), and *Breaking Dawn* (2008). The Twilight series has sold over 42 million copies worldwide with translations into numerous different languages around the globe.

Structure, genre, and themes

The series falls into the genre of young adult fantasy and horror but the author has stated that she considers her books more *"romance than anything else"* and therefore avoids provocative sex scenes, drugs, swearing, and dark horror. The books are written in first-person narrative, primarily through Bella's eyes with the epilogue of the third book and a part of the last book being from Jacob's point of view. Although based on the vampire myth, Twilight vampires are different from the vampires of folklore. For example,

they don't have fangs but strong, piercing teeth instead; sunlight makes them glitter instead of burn; they sleep in bedrooms rather than coffins; and they can drink animal instead of human blood.

According to Meyer the series is about life and love not death and lust, and each book was inspired by a different literary classic: *Twilight* on Jane Austen's *Pride and Prejudice*; *New Moon* on Shakespeare's *Romeo and Juliet*; *Eclipse* on Emily Brontë's *Wuthering Heights*; and *Breaking Dawn* on a second Shakespeare play, *A Midsummer Night's Dream*. Choice and free will are two other main themes in the books – Bella's choice to lead her own life, Edward's decision to exercise restraint in his relationship with Bella (consummating the relationship could compel him to drain her blood and kill her), and the choice of the Cullens to not follow their temptation to drink the blood of humans.

Plot overviews

 Twilight: *The story begins with teenager Bella Swan moving from Phoenix, Arizona, to live with her father in Forks, Washington, so that her mother can travel with her new husband. Bella is portrayed as a perpetually clumsy "danger magnet" with dark brown hair and brown eyes. She finds herself drawn to a mysterious, handsome boy, Edward Cullen. The attraction is mutual and Edward and Bella fall in love. Edward has the power to read anyone's thoughts within a few miles but Bella is immune to his power. She eventually learns that Edward is a member of a vampire family who drink animal blood rather than human. Edward introduces Bella*

to his vampire family who help defend her when James, a sadistic vampire from another coven, is drawn to drink Bella's blood. Bella escapes to Phoenix, Arizona, but finds James waiting for her. He tries to kill her and she is seriously wounded but Edward rescues her and kills James. Edward and Bella return to Forks.

New Moon: *Edward and his family decide to leave Forks because he feels that he is putting Bella's life in danger. Bella becomes deeply depressed but her depression begins to lift when she develops a friendship with werewolf Jacob Black. Jacob and the other wolves in his tribe help protect Bella from Victoria, a vampire seeking to avenge the death of her mate James. Misunderstandings occur and Edward believes that Bella is dead. In Volterra, Italy, he decides to kill himself but is stopped by Bella and Alice, his sister. Before they leave Italy the Voluri, a powerful coven of vampires, tell them that Bella, a human who knows of the existence of vampires, must either be killed or transformed into a vampire. When they return to Forks, Edward tells Bella that he only left to protect her and she forgives him. Much against Edward's will the book ends with the Cullens voting to transform Bella after her graduation.*

Eclipse: *The vampire Victoria creates an army of "newborn" vampires to battle the Cullens and kill Bella. In the meantime Bella is forced to choose between her relationship with Edward and her strong friendship with Jacob. The Cullens and Jacob's werewolf pack make their peace and join together to destroy Victoria and her vampire army. Bella eventually chooses Edward and agrees to marry him.*

Breaking Dawn: *Bella and Edward get married and consummate their relationship. Bella's pregnancy makes her weak and she nearly dies giving birth to her and Edward's half-vampire-half-human daughter, Renesmee. To save her life Edward injects Bella with his blood thus finally transforming her into a vampire. A vampire from another coven mistakes Renesmee for an "immortal child" whose existence violates vampire laws and informs the Volturi. Eventually the Cullens manage to convince the Volturi that Renesmee poses no threat to vampires and their secret, and they are left to live their lives in peace.*

The huge popularity of the Twilight series and enthusiastic fan following it has created have been dubbed "The Twilight Phenomenon" and parallels have been drawn between Meyer and the Harry Potter phenomenon created by author J. K. Rowling. Tourism has significantly improved the town of Forks, Washington, the setting for the series.

Literary critics have been less enthusiastic about the series and it has received generally mixed reviews. Despite this the series, like *Dracula* (another novel heavily criticized for its poor literary quality when it was first published), has become a literary phenomenon that has captured the imagination of millions all over the world. On November 21, 2008, a movie version of *Twilight* was released by Summit Entertainment, On November 22, 2008, following the box office record-breaking success of *Twilight*, Summit Entertainment confirmed a sequel of the second book in the series, *New Moon*, is to be released in 2009.

Twins

In Gypsy lore twins are often honored for their power over vampires but to have this power the twins must be born on a Saturday and be brother and sister rather than same-sex twins. If they meet these requirements their village will be safe. Among the Muslim Gypsies of Yugoslavia, twins were also believed to be able to see vampires in their invisible form, although they have to wear their underclothes inside out. This would seem to be another example of ritualistic reversing – turning widdershins – to protect against the forces of evil.

"Sic Gorgiamus Allos Subjectatos Nunc."
"We gladly feast on those who would subdue us."

Addams Family motto

Ubour

In Bulgarian folklore, the ubour is a common vampire species, alongside the vapir and the vurkolak. An ubour is created when a cat jumps over a corpse, when a spirit refuses to leave its body, or when a person dies a violent or sudden death. After death for 40 days the corpse is bloated and fills with a gelatinous substance until a new skeleton forms. The ubour is a blood drinker but generally only drinks blood as a last resort when ordinary food and manure are not available. It has one nostril, a barbed tongue, and after nightfall will emit sparks. The ubour can be destroyed by a sorcerer, known as a *vampirdzhija* – a vampire hunter with the ability to detect an ubour before it forms and to destroy it after it has risen, using the bottling a vampire technique.

See also: BOTTLING A VAMPIRE; BULGARIA

Undead

Most vampires are undead. This means they have died but have broken the laws of existence by returning from the grave to attack the living. For many people today the undead are creatures of folklore and fiction. However, in the first literature that makes mention of the undead, they were in every way considered real by those who wrote; indeed many early treatises about vampires were written by respected scholars of the day. Another common misconception is that the Romanian word "nosferatu" means "not dead" or the "undead." The word actually means "plague carrier."

Revenants

Mystics, occultists, and religious people from all times and cultures have commonly regarded death as not the end of existence but the beginning of a new kind of existence. Death is a transition, the end of one stage and the beginning of another – the afterlife.

Belief in the afterlife not only helps people deal with the fear of death, which comes to us all; it also offers comfort to the living who are left behind and helps them deal with their sense of grief and loss. In this way belief in an afterlife created important connections between the living and the dead; for example, the notion that how you choose to live your life will determine what happens to you when you die, and the idea that the dead are watching over us. Many myths and legends and folktales tell of living people who visit the world of the dead, for example the Greek myth of Orpheus, but more common are stories about the dead visiting the world of the living. There are many names for the various beings that can return from the dead and the term that is often used to cover them all is "revenant." A revenant is a being that comes back from the grave to mix with the living.

Many cultures had burial rites and rituals that they believed would prevent the dead returning as revenants and help them take their place in the afterlife with their ancestors. If, however, something went wrong with a burial rite it was thought that something might also go wrong with the transition to the world of the dead. In ancient Greek and Slavic lore this belief can be seen in many old legends where the transition to the next world is derailed and the dead come back as revenants/vampires to haunt the living.

Undeath

Undeath, or the undead state, is a physical state that science simply cannot explain. Therefore in the pre-scientific age when life and death were interpreted from a spiritual perspective, no one could really conceptualize it. The fact that belief in vampires goes back to at least the Middle Ages has tended to obscure the relatively recent concept of undeath, which has its origins in the nineteenth century. It was then that people began to question the existence of God, and when the Romantic period in literature also began to make people feel distant from science.

Some undead monsters, especially vampires and zombies, probably started out as revenants. (Zombies are similar in many ways to vampires in that they are dead people who have been reanimated.) The shift from revenant to undead monster probably began when communities came into contact with Christianity and that religion's concept of the afterlife, which was very different from the view that the dead reside with their ancestors.

For Christians people either go to heaven or to hell, and revenants are damned human souls destined for hell. Semi-Christian Slavic communities may have attempted to reconcile the Christian view with their traditional burial customs, resulting in confusion over burial rites and an increase in potential revenants.

The next stage in the evolution of the undead vampire took place when Christianity began to lose its hold on Western society during the eighteenth-century Enlightenment. Vampires became monsters who opposed the natural order of things, rather than damned souls or demons. They were more closely related to human beings and less directly concerned with God. They were no longer inhabitants of hell or even the afterlife, but of the grave.

One of the most influential embodiments of undeath is contained in Mary Shelley's novel, *Frankenstein*, published in 1818. The monster is put together from the parts of newly dead corpses dug up from the cemetery. He appears normal but does not fit in, being misunderstood, feared, and despised. The scientific process that gave him life is simply not enough for him. He wants to be human. He wants to belong, but cannot. In this way, undeath becomes a metaphor for many spiritual problems, including the problem of not believing in spirituality.

See also: AFTERLIFE BELIEFS

Underwood, Peter (1923–)

Peter Underwood is a respected British investigator of the paranormal who has investigated hundreds of alleged hauntings and several reports of vampire attacks, including the infamous Highgate Vampire case. His aim has been to establish some kind of middle ground between skepticism and belief. Although he has acknowledged that the majority of hauntings and attacks can be explained naturally, he believes that there are some types of ghost certain people can see and that such things as vampires could exist. As well as lecturing internationally, Underwood is the author of numerous books on the paranormal, ghost hunting, vampires, and other subjects. His best-known titles include *Into the Occult* (1982), *The Vampire's Bedside Companion* (1975), *The Ghost Hunter's Guide* (1985), *Dictionary of the Supernatural* (1978), and *Exorcism!* (1990).

Underworld Film Series

The Underworld series is a series of films about vampires and a type of werewolf known as lycan (abbreviated from lycanthrope) directed by Len Wiseman. The first film, *Underworld*, was released in 2003, and the second, *Underworld: Evolution*, in 2006. A prequel, *Underworld: Rise of the Lycans*, was released in 2009.

In the Underworld universe vampires and werewolves are not supernatural creatures but rather the product of a virus. Alexander Corvinus (played by actor Derek Jacobi) was the only survivor of a plague that wiped out his community. Somehow his body has mutated the virus so that he becomes immortal. Later he has three sons, two of whom were bitten, one by a bat and one by a wolf, creating the vampire and lycan species. The third son does not inherit immortality and is human, but he carries within his genetic code the mutated virus, which is passed to his human descendants through the centuries.

The main plot of the film series revolves around an internecine war between the vampires and the lycans and the character of Selene (Kate Beckinsale), a death-dealing vampire

whose brief is to hunt and kill lycans. She finds herself attracted to a human, Michael Corvin (Scott Speedman), who is being targeted by the lycans. After Michael is bitten by a lycan, Selene must decide whether to do her duty to her vampire elder Viktor (Bill Nighy) and kill him or go against her clan and save him.

Although the Underworld series remains popular with film-goers and has developed a cult following, reviewers have been less than enthusiastic, although some have praised the films' stylish Gothic visuals and the extensively worked out *Romeo and Juliet*-like vampire-werewolf mythology that serves as the back-story.

See also: **FILMS**

Unintentional Psychic Vampire

See: **PSYCHIC VAMPIRE**

United States

See: **AMERICA; NEW ENGLAND**

Upior/Upier

"Upior" or "upier" is the name most commonly used for a vampire in Poland by the eastern Slavs. It is different from other Eastern European vampire species, with the exception of the upyr, in that it sleeps during the night and rises only between noon and midnight, and has a barbed tongue instead of fangs which it uses to drink blood from its victims. Among the blood-drinking undead, the upior appears to have the greatest obsession with blood in that it drinks it, sleeps in it, and, when it is staked, blood bursts out of it. The upior is sometimes seen riding a horse.

To prevent a person becoming an upior he or she must be buried face down with a cross of willow placed under the chin, armpits, and chest. The creature can be destroyed by staking or decapitation, but burning is the safest option. When burned, the body of the creature bursts and hundreds of maggots and rats crawl out. These creatures must not be allowed to escape because if they do the upior's spirit will escape with them and return to seek revenge. Immunity to an upior attack can be obtained by mixing vampire blood with flour, baking it, and eating it as baked blood bread.

Upier is a Polish variation of the name, given to a male vampire. The upier lies incorrupt in its grave with a ruddy face and it also has eyes and a tongue and sometimes a head that may move. It can eat its burial clothes and sometimes itself for sustenance. The female version is called upierzyca, meaning "feathered one," because the corpse is typically covered with down or feathers. Such a creature is much lighter and more agile than the male upier. When the upier/upierzyca rises from the grave and attacks people, it tries to suffocate them.

See also: **PRONE BURIAL**

Upir

Generally similar to the Russian upyr, the upir (also opir) is a species of vampire in Ukrainian folklore and is also found in some Czech and Slovak regions. What makes it unique is its preference for eating huge amounts of fish. In the history of Russia the term "upir" was associated with gods who were spirits of the restless dead, but from the eleventh century onward the term is used to refer to vampires. In time the term "upir" was replaced by that of eretik, which mutated from heretics to vampires.

Upor

Upor is a Belorussian vampire species whose name is a variant of the Russian upyr. It is noted for its ability to shape-shift and to ride horses.

Upyr

In Russian folklore, "upyr" is the most common name for a vampire. Traditions surrounding this creature differ greatly from region to region but there are some common features. The upyr has incredibly strong teeth that they use to chew their way through virtually anything. Like the Polish upior, the upyr wanders during the day, typically from noon until midnight. It hunts for the blood and hearts of children first and will then drain the blood of their parents and devour their hearts too. The way to destroy an upyr is to attach a thread to one of its buttons and then use that thread to trace the creature back to its resting place. Once identified, the creature should be staked in the chest and holy water should be sprinkled around the grave. It is extremely important, however, that the creature be killed with one blow, as it is thought that two strikes will bring it back to life. Therefore decapitation and cremation are the safer methods of destruction.

See also: **RUSSIA**

Ustrel

In Bulgarian folklore the ustrel is a species of vampire that only preys on cattle, leaving behind bloated carcasses. It is said to be the restless spirit of a dead child who was born on a Saturday and died before being baptized. Nine days or so after burial the child escapes from its grave and goes in search of a herd of cattle. After feeding on the cattle for ten days, typically targeting the healthiest, fattest animals first, the ustrel will have grown in strength and confidence and will reside between the horns of a bull or between the hind legs of a cow. The creature can be removed with a need fire, moving the cattle through the purifying flames. No living person must go near the remains of the fire for it is said that the ustrel will latch on to that person and follow them home. If, however, the creature is left alone it will be devoured by wolves.

See also: **BULGARIA**

Utukku

The utukku is the Babylonian spirit of a dead person who has returned from the grave for a reason, typically because they died a violent or premature death. Although it has vampiric qualities, the ekimmu spirit is much more feared. According to vampire expert Montague Summers, "utukku" was the collective name for a kind of transparent and rather feeble ghost that drifted about in the wind and was not particularly hostile.

No one holds command over me.
No man. No god. No prince.
What is a claim of age for ones who are immortal?
What is a claim of power for ones who defy death?

Gunter Dorn, Das Ungeheuer Darin. *Vampire: The Masquerade*

Vámbéry, Arminius (1832–1913)

Hungarian historian, linguist, explorer/traveler and writer, Arminius Vámbéry may have been the inspiration or model for the fictional character of Van Helsing in Bram Stoker's novel *Dracula* (1897).

Stoker met Vámbéry at the Beefsteak Club Room at the Lyceum Theatre after a performance by Henry Irving in the play *Dead Heart* on April 30, 1890. The two men met again two years later when Vámbéry received an honorary degree at Trinity College, Dublin. It is possible that through conversations and through his research and writings on Hungary that Vámbéry influenced Stoker, although the extent of that influence is uncertain as no correspondence between the two has survived.

Some experts believe that Vámbéry provided Stoker with information about Vlad the Impaler, who became a possible model for the Count, and encouraged him to switch the focus of his research from Austria to Transylvania. Other *Dracula* scholars believe that while there is no documented evidence to suggest that Vámbéry gave Stoker information, it is possible to argue that Vámbéry was a model for the character of Abraham Van Helsing. In the novel itself a compliment was paid to Vámbéry from Stoker when Van Helsing mentions his *"friend Arminius, of Buda-Pesh University."*

See also: **STOKER, BRAM**

Vamp

"Vamp" is an American slang word for an alluring, hypnotic, and seductive woman whose charms ensnare her lovers in bonds of irresistible desire, typically leading them into compromising, dangerous, and deadly situations or leaching their vitality until they are shells of themselves. The vamp is a popular archetypal character of modern literature, film, and art and she developed from the *femme fatale* or "deadly female" vampire myth, represented by figures such as the lamia, into the realm of relationships between men and women.

The vamp persona may have been established by *The Vampire*, a short poem written by Rudyard Kipling in 1897, inspired by a famous painting by Philip Burne-Jones which depicts a woman mounting a sleeping/unconscious man. Purportedly a portrait of Mrs. Patrick Campbell, a stage actress and the artist's ex-lover, the image shows the woman casting a shadow upon the bed curtains, which might suggest a supernatural theme. Like much of Kipling's verse, *The Vampire* was incredibly popular, and its refrain: *"A fool there was …,"* describing a good man seduced and brought down by a bad woman, became the title of the popular 1915 film *A Fool There Was* that made Theda Bara a star.

The Vampire

A fool there was and he made his prayer
(Even as you and I!)
To a rag and a bone and a hank of hair
(We called her the woman who did not care),
But the fool he called her his lady fair
(Even as you and I!)

Oh the years we waste and the tears we waste
And the work of our head and hand,
Belong to the woman who did not know
(And now we know that she never could
* know)*
And did not understand.

A fool there was and his goods he spent
(Even as you and I!)
Honour and faith and a sure intent
But a fool must follow his natural bent
(And it wasn't the least what the lady meant),
(Even as you and I!)

Oh the toil we lost and the spoil we lost
And the excellent things we planned,
Belong to the woman who didn't know why
(And now we know she never knew why)
And did not understand.

The fool we stripped to his foolish hide
(Even as you and I!)
Which she might have seen when she threw
* him aside –*
(But it isn't on record the lady tried)
So some of him lived but the most of him
* died –*
(Even as you and I!)

And it isn't the shame and it isn't the blame
That stings like a white hot brand.
It's coming to know that she never knew why
(Seeing at last she could never know why)
And never could understand.

The source of the vamp's dark powers is her ability to trigger strong sexual reactions or urges in men – urges that typically are hidden by the conventions of polite society. She draws men to her and feeds on their vitality. Once established and popularized by Kipling, the vamp persona proved to be a figure of continuing interest in literature, art, and film, although the role of the temptress has now become less one dimensional and more complex and human.

Vampir/Vampyr

"Vampir" is the European spelling for vampire. It can be found in many countries, including Hungary, Serbia, and Bulgaria, and other areas where there has been a strong Slavic influence. According to vampire historian Montague Summers, the word is a Hungarian word of Slavic origin. In Sweden and Denmark and other countries the term "vampyr" is found.

Vampire

A vampire is a creature or creation that has existed for millions of years by feeding on the living blood, vitality, or imagination of humans to ensure its immortality or to create more of its own kind. The vampire has evolved over the centuries from a primitive, decaying corpse into a sophisticated, charismatic creature, but despite this remarkable metamorphosis at the hands of writers and filmmakers it has still managed to retain its folklore inheritance.

The word

Researchers don't agree on the etymological origins of the word and Turkish, Hungarian, Greek, and Slavic roots have all been put forward. Suggested roots include the Greek word meaning "to drink" and the Turkish term for "witch," *uber*. However, most scholars are of the opinion that the word "vampire" has a Slavic origin. The Serbian word *bami-iup*; the Serbo-Croat verb *pirati* ("to blow") and the Lithuanian term *wempti* ("to drink") have all been suggested. The Magyar (Hungarian) name *vampir*, an eastern Slavic word indicates that the origin of the term may be Hungarian, but *vampir* post-dates the first appearance of the word "vampire" in the West by more than a hundred years. Cognate forms include the Russian *upyr*, the Polish *upior*, and *upir* in Belorussian.

The word "vampire" (or vampyre) was known in late seventeenth-century England and was used in *Observations of the Revolution of 1688* to describe extortionate business practices. It also appeared in an anonymous work, *Travels of Three English Gentlemen from Venice to Hamburg, Being the Grand Tour of Germany in the year 1734*, which was published in 1810. *Travels* gave the first English explanation of vampires, and also quoted a paragraph from Johann Heinrich Zopfius's *Disseratatio de Vampiris* (1733). From the beginning of the nineteenth century the term "vampire" was firmly established in English literature and in the popular press, and, in the decades that followed, vampire lore was imported to the American colonies, where it became especially noticeable in the area of New England.

Definition

In early editions of the *Oxford English Dictionary* the definition of a vampire was given as:

A preternatural being of a malignant nature (in the original unusual form of the belief, an animated corpse) supposed to seek nourishment and do harm by sucking the blood of sleeping persons; a man or woman abnormally endowed with similar habits.

In the early twentieth century, vampirologist Montague Summers gave the following description of a vampire:

The vampire has a body, and it is his own body. He is neither dead nor alive; but living in death. He is an abnormality; the androgyne in the phantom world; a pariah among friends.

These classic definitions of the vampire as a revenant (returning dead) or a blood-sucking supernatural entity do not include psychic vampires, astral vampires, living vampires, or clinical vampirism. A more broad definition might be that the vampire is a self-seeking, often malevolent force or being who needs to derive physical or emotional sustenance from a victim who is drained or weakened in some way by the experience. Therefore there can be said to be a number of different types of vampire:

- *The vampire of folklore*

- *Living vampires*

- *Literary vampires*

🕴 *Psychic vampires*

🕴 *Psychotic vampires*

Background

It wasn't until the eighteenth century that Western writers, theologians, and scholars first began to debate the existence of vampires and whether or not they were just creatures of folklore and superstition. This scholarly debate was ignited by the vampire hysteria that took place in Eastern Europe and found expression in a number of well-documented cases, including that of Arnold Paole. Although many scholars defended the existence of vampires, the majority concluded that there was not enough evidence to suggest they were real.

From the middle of the eighteenth century until the end of the nineteenth, no serious attempts were made to prove that vampires existed in their folklore form, although a new theory for vampires began to emerge – psychic vampirism. Accounts of vampire crime also began to appear. In the 1920s two German serial killers with vampiric tendencies, Fritz Haarmann and Peter Kürten, sent shock waves throughout Europe. During the 1960s and 1970s public interest in vampires grew noticeably, due in part to Hammer Films and the writings of Anne Rice, and a number of vampire fan clubs, research groups, and vampire lifestyle movements were founded, setting the scene for the emergence of a Goth subculture across Europe and America in the decades that followed.

Homeland

A number of regions and countries have been suggested as the homeland or place of origin of vampires, including Egypt, India, China, Greece, Russia, Mesopotamia, Hungary, Romania, and Ireland. The idea that Transylvania in Romania is the homeland of the vampire is largely due to its being the setting for Bram Stoker's novel *Dracula*, even though the evidence to support this idea is lacking.

Blood-drinking gods or undead monsters were a part of ancient cults and religions where blood and earth as givers of life and food were revered, and vampires probably survived because of these ancient associations with death, blood, and the earth. The creatures emerged from their earthy grave and could defy death by drinking the life blood of others. They were associated with contagious illness, unexpected deaths, crop blights, and droughts. They embodied fears about death and lives of sin, witchcraft, and crime. Over the centuries vampires became contaminated with witchcraft and the lore of evil wasting entities, such as the nightmare demons mara and the Old Hag, and continued to be an established part of the fears and superstitions not just of peasants and villagers but also of Church leaders and men of learning and influence.

Vampires were not released from their rural associations until the eighteenth and nineteenth centuries, when they became a popular motif for Romantic writers. They have since proven to be extremely adaptable to the needs of new generations of writers who each see in them something identifiable and compelling. Today the vampire is no longer a simple embodiment of the existence of evil but a metaphor for the rebel and the outsider, who has managed to achieve immortality without moral or religious limitations or personal responsibility for its deeds and actions. One of the most compelling creatures of the world, vampires today are seductive, charismatic, and immune to the most terrible aspects of life – disease, violence, drugs, war, famine, and financial chaos.

See also: **AGING, OF VAMPIRES; BECOMING A VAMPIRE; BIOLOGY OF VAMPIRES; BLOOD; CLASSIFICATIONS OF VAMPIRES; CHILDREN OF VAMPIRES; CREATING A VAMPIRE; ORIGINS, OF VAMPIRES; SEX; SOCIOLOGY OF VAMPIRES; TRANSFORMATION**

Vampire, Le

Le Vampire was a play written by Charles Nodier in 1820, based on John Polidori's *The Vampyre* (1819).

"Vampire, The"

"The Vampire" is a short story written by Czech writer Jan Neruda, first published in English in 1920 in *Czechoslovakian Stories*. It tells the story of a young artist who earns the nickname "vampire" because his subjects, chosen because they are ill or weak, soon die after he paints them.

See also: **LITERATURE**

Vampire Bats

Vampire bats are bats that subsist on the blood of animals and humans. These bats can drink a wine glass of blood within 20 minutes and are found throughout Central and South America and the Caribbean. They are carriers of rabies and earned their vampiric association from Europeans who discovered these night creatures feeding on the blood of the living. Charles Darwin was the first European to witness a vampire bat drawing blood.

Vampire bats roost in caves, trees, and buildings. When they sense danger they run up vertical walls and, like rodents, hide in crevices. This characteristic may well have influenced Bram Stoker's description of Count Dracula climbing down the vertical walls of his castle in his 1897 novel, *Dracula*. Indeed it has been in vampire fiction and film rather than in folklore that the vampire bat has played a prominent role.

Vampire Chronicles, The

The Vampire Chronicles is the name given to the vampire novels of Anne Rice. In 1969 Rice wrote a short story she called "Interview with the Vampire" and in 1973 it was turned into a novel which would eventually become the first of The Vampire Chronicles. Following a number of rejections, Alfred A. Knopf bought *Interview with the Vampire* and it was published in 1976. It was an instant success and has never been out of print.

It would be nine years before a sequel appeared, with the publication of *The Vampire*

Lestat in 1985. This novel further developed the character of Lestat introduced in the first volume. He emerged as a minor French aristocrat from the eighteenth century who defied the vampire establishment in Paris and decided to forge his own path in the world. A deadly predator and man of action, Lestat is also sensitive and emotional and entranced by poetry and music. Rice once described him as her *"androgynous ideal."* Like Rice herself, Lestat rejected his Catholic upbringing, and justifies his need for blood by only selecting those he feels have done wrong in their lives.

Only in 1988, when Rice's third vampire volume, *The Queen of the Damned*, appeared did the series become known as The Vampire Chronicles. Like the previous two books *The Queen of the Damned* was a bestseller and firmly established Rice as the reigning queen of popular vampire fiction. Two further volumes – *The Tale of the Body Thief* (1992) and *Memnoch the Devil* (1995) – appeared. In *Memnoch* Rice took Lestat into the philosophical realms of heaven and hell but it was not as well received as her previous books. After *Memnoch*, Rice announced that there would be no more novels featuring Lestat but she returned to the theme of vampirism with *Pandora* (1998) and *The Vampire Armand* (1998), the first in a series of vampire-themed novels that followed other characters in the Chronicles. In 2003 with the publication of *Blood Canticle* Rice announced that it marked the end of The Vampire Chronicles.

Vampire Empire

The Vampire Empire is one of the largest horror organizations in the world dedicated to Bram Stoker and his literary creation Count Dracula, and to the fifteenth-century Wallachian prince Vlad Tepes, or Vlad the Impaler, as well as other horror subjects and characters. It is based in New York and was founded by Dr. Jeanne Keyes Youngson as the Count Dracula Fan Club in 1965. The Club's name changed to the Vampire Empire in 2000. The aim of the Vampire Empire is to encourage the study and research of vampires and related subject matter.

Vampire Fraud

Documented cases of vampire impersonation for personal gain reveal how powerful superstitious fears of the vampire were in Europe.

In the former Yugoslavia, during times of hunger people would dress as vampires with burial shrouds over their shoulders and loiter around mills and granaries. Terrified employees fled the buildings, leaving the "vampires" free to help themselves to food. A more recent case of vampire fraud occurred among Slavic Muslim Gypsies after World War I. The "vampires" climbed onto rooftops and hurled stones down at people, so that they left their homes. When the homeowners returned food, clothes, and personal items had literally vanished. The thieves moved from village to village to escape the police but were eventually caught when the abbot of the monastery of Decani climbed on top of a roof and caught the men in the act of throwing stones. The police were called and the "vampire" thefts ended.

Perhaps the most common vampire fraud was to cover up extramarital affairs. Married women who had affairs or women who got pregnant with married men would pass off their children as the offspring of vampire sleeping partners. It was widely believed, especially among Gypsies, that vampires known as mullo were sexually insatiable and would return from their graves to have sex with their partners or other women.

In *The Encyclopedia of Vampires, Werewolves, and Other Monsters* (2004), Rosemary Ellen Guiley cites the curious case of a man from Baja in Serbia who visited a recently widowed woman at night, wearing a white shroud threaded with bells, a white cap, and white socks. After three or so months of the "vampire's" nocturnal visits, three young men started to have their suspicions and decided to spy on the widow. With the permission of the widow's in-laws (but without the knowledge of the widow) they hid behind the kitchen door. When the "vampire" arrived at midnight they grabbed him and his true identity – a living man – was revealed. Later at a village court, the case took an even more disturbing turn when it was discovered that the "vampire" and the widow had actually poisoned the husband so they could have their affair. Both the "vampire" and the widow were sentenced to death.

Vampire-hunting fraud

Another major cause of vampire fraud was the so-called professional vampire hunter hired by many communities to hunt and kill vampires.

Among the Romany these vampire hunters, called dhampirs, were believed to be the half-human offspring of vampires. Although feared, dhampirs were often hired by villagers and paid handsomely with money, food, livestock, and goods for their services. Not surprisingly, many exploited the fears of people about the undead.

Often the fraudsters would work in pairs; one of them would visit a village secretly after a funeral and kill livestock or perform other vampire-like stunts. Once news spread among terrified villagers that a vampire was on the rampage, the partner would arrive in the village claiming to be a dhampir. For an arranged fee the fraud would then continue with staged screams and a victorious battle with an invisible blood sucker.

Vampire Hunters

Wherever there have been vampires there have typically been vampire hunters. In some countries vampire hunters were just a group of villagers who joined together with the purpose of detecting and destroying vampires attacking their community. However, in Eastern Europe the task of hunting and destroying vampires was assigned to professional vampire hunters. The Romany people called their vampire hunters "dhampirs," the half-human sons of vampires. The dhampir figures prominently in Gypsy lore as male vampires were thought to be sexually insatiable and to produce many children. Therefore in times past a number of Eastern European men were said to be dhampirs, born with heightened senses and supernatural abilities that allowed them to see vampires when they were invisible or disguised as animals. Among the most notable and more recent dhampirs was a man called Murat who operated in the 1950s in the Kosovo-Metohija district of Serbia.

Vampire hunters were also called Sabbatarians in Greek and Gypsy lore, as tradition held that those born on a Saturday made the best vampire hunters. In Bulgaria vampire hunters were referred to as *glot* or *vampirar*. They tended to operate in a more traditional manner than the dhampir. Their main task seems to have been to identify the grave of a vampire; after locating the vampire the villagers would mutilate or destroy it.

Hunting techniques

European vampire hunters were often summoned when a village was experiencing a series of wasting deaths, crop failures, or other misfortunes, all of which were thought to be caused by a vampire. More often than not the vampire hunter would put on an incredible show using bizarre hunting techniques, such as removing his shirt and holding one of the long sleeves up to his eye like a telescope. Spotting the invisible vampire he would then command the creature to leave the village. If it refused to leave, he would then try to kill the (still-invisible) creature in vicious hand-to-hand combat or by shooting it with a silver bullet blessed by a priest.

In some regions of Serbia vampire hunters would be skilled musicians, and their music would enchant vampires so that they were distracted and could be easily destroyed by a gun shot or run through with a stake. Other slaying techniques included stealing a vampire's shroud or clothing and throwing it into a river, so the vampire would try to recover it and drown, or placing the item on a high cliff so that the vampire could be pushed off, dying as it hit the ground.

If the identity of the vampire's corpse was not known, the vampire hunter would use a number of techniques to identify it. These techniques, which were typically used on a Saturday, the day of the week vampires were said to remain in their grave, included:

- *Scattering ash and salt around graves for the vampire to leave footprints in*

- *Leading black or white horses around graveyards in the belief that the horse would not step over the grave of a vampire*

- *Looking for a blueish light or flame in a cemetery at night. In European folklore the blue glow was said to be a wandering soul*

- *Inspecting graves for holes over them, which were believed to be the exit and entrance to the grave for the vampire*

The Element Encyclopedia of Vampires

Once exhumed the vampire hunter would look for specific signs of vampirism in the corpse, such as a swollen or bloated body, a red face, fresh blood, hair or nails, and evidence of movement. (Today there are scientific explanations for these supposed signs of vampirism, which are caused by the natural process of decomposition.)

The vampire hunter's task was made easier once the vampire's corpse had been identified. In such cases the corpse would be exhumed, staked and decapitated and then reburied face down. The severed head of the corpse might have its mouth filled with coins or stones so the vampire could not bite anyone, and be buried under an arm, or under the buttocks, knees or feet. The head and torso might also be buried in separate locations. At all times during the corpse mutilation the hunter would cover the corpse to ensure blood wasn't sprayed on anyone; vampire blood was thought to cause insanity and death. The vampire might also be reburied at a crossroads or outside consecrated grounds. If all these measures failed and the vampire still returned, the corpse would be cremated and the ashes scattered.

The vampire hunters of fiction

The character of Professor Abraham Van Helsing in Bram Stoker's 1897 novel *Dracula* became the fictional model for vampire hunters. Van Helsing is an intelligent, mature, well-traveled and well-read man who tells the other characters in the novel how to destroy vampires. Van Helsing's determined and passionate crucifix-and-garlic vampire-hunting method emerged as a strong theme in vampire literature and even spilled out into real life in vampire scares, such as that of the Highgate Vampire in the 1970s. More recently vampire hunters in fiction and film have been less reluctant than Van Helsing to assume their role, either destined by birth to become vampire hunters as is the case for Blade or Buffy the Vampire Slayer, or forced by circumstances to do so, as is the case for Ben Mears in Stephen King's *Salem's Lot*.

See also: **DESTRUCTION;**
KILLING VAMPIRES;
PREVENTION; PROTECTION

Vampire Personality Disorder

See: **CLINICAL VAMPIRISM; CRIME**

Vampire Rapist

In 1985 John Crutchley kidnapped a 19-year-old hitchhiker and became known as the "vampire rapist." He raped his victim; then he tied her to his kitchen counter and used needles and tubing to drain her blood into a jar, which he then drank. The woman escaped through a bathroom window, handcuffed and naked, and was hospitalized for the loss of about half of her blood.

Crutchley pleaded guilty to kidnapping and sexual battery. He was released to a halfway house in Orlando, Florida, in 1996 after serving 10 years of his 25-year prison sentence, prompting outrage among residents who did not want him in the community. He was sent back to prison for life one day later, however, when a drug test showed he had used marijuana. In 2002 at the age of 55 he committed suicide in prison.

The term has also been used to refer to Wayne Boden and other deranged murderers who drink their victim's blood or bite their victims. In June 2006 40-year-old Andrew Wild was jailed for life for biting off parts of a women's face on a barge in Uppermill, Manchester, England. The woman described her attacker as *"a wild dog and a vampire."*

See also: **CRIME**

Vampire Research Center

The Vampire Research Center was founded in 1972 by American parapsychologist Stephen Kaplan. In Kaplan's first book, *Pursuit of Premature Gods and Contemporary Vampires* (1976), he suggested that some reality might lie behind the vampire myth. Nine years later, in his controversial 1984 book *Vampires Are*, Kaplan described his decade-long research on people who defined themselves as real vampires. These people were individuals who adopted vampire-like habits, for example, drinking blood, sleeping in coffins, working at night, shunning daylight, and so on.

Kaplan's research led him to the conclusion that vampires were not the undead who returned from the grave to drink the blood of the living. For Kaplan the vampires he had interviewed were ordinary people with an extraordinary urge to drink blood every day, and if they were unable to obtain their daily supply they would get withdrawal symptoms. These "vampires" believed that drinking blood kept them looking youthful and extended their lifespan. Using a series of questionnaires and censuses, Kaplan estimated that there were approximately 150 to 200 actual "vampires" in North America, of which 40 lived in California, and approximately 850 worldwide. The response to Kaplan's book and research was largely negative. As a result he distanced himself from his vampire studies and concentrated on other areas of research.

Vampire Research Society

The Vampire Research Society was founded in 1970 by Highgate Vampire investigator Sean Manchester as the official United Kingdom advisory service for all matters pertaining to vampires and vampirism. For the first two decades the society had an open membership policy, with around 300 members, but in 1990 it decided to restrict membership and distance itself from the vampire subculture – people who model their lives and personalities around vampires – by concentrating only on practical research into reports of vampiric and paranormal activity.

Vampire: The Masquerade

Vampire: The Masquerade is a role-playing game introduced in 1991 by White Wolf Game Studio and created by Mark Rein-Hagen. It soon became extremely popular and established itself as the top role-playing game about vampires, with an international community of players.

In The Masquerade a fantasy world called the World of Darkness is created with its own rules, mythology, and characters. The origin of vampires is traced back to the biblical character Cain, eternally cursed to drink blood for killing his brother, Abel. In this way the Kindred – a race of vampires – was born. Vampires created more vampires but with each generation their powers become weaker. Then in 1435 the Inquisition turned on vampires as well as witches, making vampire extinction a real possibility. In response a global organization of vampires established the Camarilla, a secret underground network that established The Masquerade. All vampires were to live in secret and efforts had to be made to convince humans that vampires no longer existed.

The game features a number of vampire clans each with their own history and characteristics. These include the Nosferatu, deformed monsters but with excellent survival skills; the Toreador, passionate artists; the Malkavian, clever but unpredictable creatures; the Brujah, rebels; the Tremere, warlocks; the Lasombra, murderers; the Ventrue, aristocrats; the Tzimisce, scientists; and the Gangrel, nomad warriors. In addition the Camarilla clans are opposed by a huge barbaric sect that believes vampires to be superior to humans, called The Sabbat. There are also a number of independent clans as well as social distinctions or castes within each vampire clan.

Players in The Masquerade create a character and then interact with other characters in a game created and judged by the storyteller or game master. In the game the worldwide vampire society exists very much as a parallel society to that of mortals, with each vampire clan organized into territorial clans ruled by a prince. The aim of the game is not only to remind vampires to pose as ordinary humans but to persuade humans that the vampires have all been wiped out, or never existed. Vampires within the Camarilla must vie among themselves for power, compete against non-Camarilla clans, and hunt for human prey while keeping their identity secret.

The success of *Vampire: The Masquerade* helped it evolve in 1993 into a live action game, where the delays caused by the use of dice were replaced by a series of hand signals, allowing players to remain in character throughout the game. *Vampire: The Masquerade* had its own fan club, fittingly called Camarilla, with its own hierarchy made up of the game's most skilled players and storytellers.

In August 2004, *Vampire: The Masquerade* was discontinued by White Wolf and replaced by *Vampire: The Requiem*. Although it is an entirely new game, rather than a continuation of the old one, it is still set in the World of Darkness and uses many elements of the old game, including certain clans and disciplines. The game's title is a metaphor for the way vampires within the game view their life. According to the White Wolf Requiem website, Requiem is a *"modern, gothic story-telling game"* that allows players to create stories that explore the metaphor of vampirism. *"In Vampire, you play the monster, and what you do as that monster both makes for an interesting story and might even teach you a little about your own values and those of your fellows."*

See also: GAMES, VAMPIRE

Vampire Tapestry, The

Published in 1980, *The Vampire Tapestry* is a collection of five related novellas featuring the clever and ironic vampire predator Edward Lewis Weyward. Written by American-born feminist writer Suzy McKee Charnas the work strips the vampire tale of its Gothic and sadomasochistic elements and has been praised by literary critics for the stylish way it looks at prey–predator relations as a metaphor for what goes on between men and women, between those with power and those without, and between the outlaw and the society that both feeds and hunts him. Two of Charnas's best-known stories are among the tales included: *The Ancient Mind at Work* (1979) and *Unicorn Tapestry* (1980).

See also: LITERATURE

Vampire Witches

Vampire witches are people who are evil witches, wizards, or sorcerers who practice vampirism and therefore are a kind of living vampire. When they die they become vampires and leave their graves to suck the blood of the living.

In Eastern European folklore, vampire witches can shape-shift into dogs, cats, and horses. They can cast the evil eye and evil spells on others. In Romanian lore female vampire witches are red in the face before and after death, while the male versions are bald and after death grow a tail and hooves. In Russian lore, living vampire witches can take over the body of someone who is dying or who has died and turn them into a vampire species called an erestun.

Vampire witches can come out during the day, but their power is strongest when the moon is full and weakest during new moon. They are especially active on St. Andrew's Eve and St. George's Eve, before Easter, and on the last day of the year. During such periods garlic should be placed at entrances to prevent them from coming into homes. Vampire witches also practice a form of psychic vampirism by walking around the edges of villages and taking energy from animals and bread so they do not perform their functions. For example, cows do not give milk, hens do not lay eggs, and bread loses its taste. In addition, for a fee they can take beauty, love, or power from others for a third party.

Vampirella

Vampirella is the sexy female vampire character in a comic book series of the same name from Warren Publications that made its debut in 1969. It was the first comic book series to be named after a vampire.

The comic series was inspired by Jean-Claude Forest's *Barbarella*, a sexy French science fiction comic strip; Jane Fonda played the title role in a 1968 film. Warren wanted an attractive female character to lead the comic series and the end result was a scantily clad voluptuous vampire named Vampirella. In the first issue she was presented as an inhabitant of Drakulon, a world where she drinks and bathes in blood. When Drakulon begins to wither and die she escapes on a spaceship and vampirizes the crew to nourish herself before arriving on earth. In the issues that followed, the comic series emphasized Vampirella's basically virtuous character as she battles against the forces of evil. She only kills and drinks the blood of those who deserve it.

With her sexy red outfit, magical powers, feisty attitude, and sensational battles against demons, ghouls, and human injustice and evil, Vampirella earned supernatural heroine status and her comic book series ran for an extraordinary 112 issues from 1969 to 1983.

Vampiri, I

I Vampiri was an Italian opera by Neapolitan composer Silvestro di Palma performed at Teatro San Carlo in 1800. The opera is interesting because it was inspired by Giuseppe Davanzati's vampire treatise *Dissertazione sopra i vampir* (1744), and also because it appeared almost 20 years before John Polidori's landmark story *The Vampyre*.

I Vampiri should not be confused with *Il Vampiro*, a ballet with music by Paolo Giorza that was performed in Milan in 1861, a few years after another less obscure vampire ballet *Morgano* debuted on May 25, 1857, in Berlin. *Morgano*, which was set in Hungary, tells the story of Elsa, a young woman who is taken by a group of vampires led by Morgano. After dancing with them in the castle she is saved by her lover Retzki, who kills Morgano with a consecrated sword.

See also: **STAGE**

Vampirism

The term "vampirism" is used to describe the action of a vampire that involves taking the blood, fluid, or physical vitality or energy, or some other power of others, such as youth or beauty, in order to survive and increase personal vitality. Most people associate vampirism with blood-taking but there are many different types of vampirism. Psychic vampirism refers to the draining of physical, psychic, spiritual, mental, or life energy from others, leaving victims weakened or dead. Sexual vampirism refers to the insatiable need for sexual gratification, conquest, and abuse. (Perhaps the most common form of vampirism today concerns those people who drink blood for sexual satisfaction.) Political or financial vampirism is a form of vampirism in which a person or a group of people feed off society.

See also: **CLINICAL VAMPIRISM;**
POLITICAL VAMPIRES;
PSYCHIC VAMPIRE; VAMPIRE

Vampirologist

A vampirologist is a person who researches, studies, and discusses vampires, both the fictional and real world vampires, and the trends that follow them; in short, a vampire expert. One of the most well-known vampirologists of the early twentieth century was Montague Summers.

Vampyr

The unconventional 1932 French film *Vampyr*, directed by Danish-born Carl Dreyer and known in England as *The Strange Adventure of David Gray*, is regarded by some horror movie critics and fans as a masterpiece of psychological depth that ranks among the best vampire movies ever made. Based loosely on *Carmilla*, the film's disturbing imagery and contemplative pace was way ahead of its time and failed to attract a significant audience.

See also: FILMS

Vampyre

Vampyre is a variant spelling of the word "vampire" that is closely connected to the Latin *vampyrus*. For some vampire enthusiasts "vampyre" is a more suitable word than "vampire" as it was the word used by Johann Heinrich Zopfius, Philip Rohr, and other vampire experts of previous centuries and therefore is a reminder of the word's ancient, mysterious, and dark origins. It was also the word used by John Polidori as the title for his 1819 story, *The Vampyre*. Vampyre was

gradually replaced by vampire in the eighteenth and nineteenth centuries when Eastern European words for the vampire, such as upior, upyr, and vampir, were translated into English.

Some vampire novelists prefer to use the word "vampyre" or "vampyr" for their fictional creations as a way of distinguishing them from the vampires of film and folklore. In much the same way some modern vampires – people who model their lives and their lifestyles on vampires – prefer to call themselves vampyres to differentiate themselves from the bloodsucking corpses or revenants of Eastern European lore.

See also: LIVING VAMPIRES

Vampyre, The

The Vampyre: A Tale by John Polidori, physician to Lord Byron, published in England's *New Monthly Magazine* in April 1819, was the first vampire story to be published in English.

When writing the tale Polidori borrowed heavily from a story he had heard Byron tell one night in 1816 when he had accompanied him on a trip to Europe and stayed at the Villa Diodati on the banks of Lake Geneva. When first published it was hinted that Byron was the author and it therefore got more attention than it probably would have if Polidori had submitted it under his own name. The story was a huge success and was translated swiftly into French and German.

The vampire anti-hero of the novel is the seductive but deadly Lord Ruthven (pronounced *rivven*), *"a man entirely absorbed in himself,"* and it is clear that Polidori modeled this character on Lord Byron. It is also likely that Polidori modeled the character of Ruthven's naïve and trusting friend, Aubrey, upon himself.

The story

The story begins with the introduction of Lord Ruthven to the genteel society of London and the arrival of the orphan Aubrey, a naïve and imaginative young man who attracts the interest of Ruthven. Aubrey refuses to recognize the evil within Ruthven and by so doing curses himself and causes the death of his lover, Ianthe, at the hands of Ruthven. Aubrey is almost killed too but Ruthven nursed him back to health and the two men travel into the Greek countryside, where Ruthven is attacked and mortally wounded by robbers. He is revived by the rays of the moon.

Aubrey discovers that Ruthven is implicated in Ianthe's murder and returns to England knowing that Ruthven is a vampire. Ruthven also returns to England and becomes engaged to Aubrey's sister. Aubrey begs his sister not to marry him but everyone thinks he is mad to object; overwrought, he bursts a blood vessel. On his deathbed he begs his guardians to save his sister. They rush to her rescue but find her already dead and Ruthven, his thirst "glutted," has disappeared.

Impact

The sensational impact of *The Vampyre* on literature and drama was not matched until the publication of Bram Stoker's *Dracula* in 1897. Soon after publication a flood of stories, novels, and plays about Lord Ruthven or other vampires appeared on a regular basis.

The Vampyre established a number of elements of vampire fiction that were later incorporated by other notable vampire authors, including Stoker and Sheridan Le Fanu. In *The Vampyre* Polidori drew on folklore beliefs that a vampire is a reanimated corpse of someone who has led a sinful life, but unlike the vampires of folklore he is able to live undetected in human society. He can be revived by the rays of the moon. In addition, the vampire is no longer a peasant or villager but a wealthy aristocrat who is seductive, dark, and completely amoral. He attacks others for sustenance but there is also an erotic element and a form of psychic vampirism between him and his victim.

See also: LITERATURE

Vampyre of the Fens

Considered by some vampirologists to be the first vampire poem in European literature, *The Vampyre of the Fens* is an eleventh-century Anglo-Saxon poem whose title was probably added at a later date in the eighteenth century when the word "vampyre" started to be used.

Vampyroteuthis infernalis

Vampyroteuthis infernalis, literally "vampire squid from hell," is the name for a deep ocean cephalopod that measures only a few inches long. Little is known about the creature's life cycle and it is not supernatural, but it does resemble the vampire it is named after in some ways with its red eyes, black body, and mouth ringed with white teeth.

Van Helsing, Professor Abraham

Professor Abraham Van Helsing is the fictional vampire expert and chief vampire hunter in Bram Stoker's *Dracula* (1897). The character became the classic model for all future fictional vampire hunters with his sharp mind, determination, and compassion. He was probably named after Stoker's father, Abraham, and modeled on the scholar Arminius Vámbéry. Other possibilities suggested are the fictional narrator Dr. Hesselius of Sheridan Le Fanu's *Carmilla* (1872) and Van Helmont, an alchemist mentioned in a text Stoker consulted in his research, *On Superstitions connected with the history and nature of Medicine and Surgery* (1844), by T. J. Pettigrew.

Van Helsing is presented in the novel as a famous Dutch physician from Amsterdam who specializes in *"obscure diseases."* He is summoned to England by Dr. Seward to help save Lucy Westenra. Although he does not manage to save Lucy from death, as the novel progresses he becomes the leader of the forces against Count Dracula using a variety of vampire-hunting weapons, which include garlic and the consecrated Host, and his methods combine Christianity with science and psychology.

When Van Helsing first examines Lucy he does not immediately share his knowledge of vampirism with the other characters. He offers no explanation why he orders her to wear garlic at night and even after she dies he is still reluctant to offer information. It is not until the others actually see Lucy as a vampire in her tomb that he finally delivers a long lecture on vampires and organizes the hunt for the Count.

Among Van Helsing's many wise comments about so-called real vampires, one of the most insightful is when he remarks that *"The power of the vampire is that people do not believe he exists."* This disbelief allows the vampire to remain hidden until the time he decides to emerge and plunge his victims into shock, fear, and terror as disbelief is turned into belief.

Van Helsing the movie

In 2004 Universal Studios released a movie in which a nineteenth-century monster hunter by the name of Gabriel Van Helsing takes on some of the most well-known supernatural monsters. The inspiration for the character of Gabriel (played by Hugh Jackman) was Bram Stoker's Professor Van Helsing, but much to the disappointment of *Dracula* fans and to movie critics – who heavily criticized the film – he was reinvented as an Indiana Jones action hero, demon hunter, and warrior against evil. Despite this criticism the film went on to be a major box office success.

The Element Encyclopedia of Vampires

Varcolac / Varcoli / Vircolac

In Romanian mythology a varcolac, also known as *priculics*, is a demon vampire species that has the ability to "eat" the sun and the moon and cause an eclipse. Their appearance is described in a number of different ways including as dogs (always two in number), dragons, and animals with many mouths. During an eclipse people would ring church bells and fire guns to frighten away the varcolaci but in the end the moon, being stronger, would always win. According to one belief, God orders the varcolac to eat the moon to encourage people to repent.

Origin and traits

🩸 *They are the souls of those cursed by God.*

🩸 *They are the souls of children of unmarried persons.*

🩸 *They are the souls of unbaptized children.*

🩸 *They can be created when women spin at midnight without a candle, as the varcolaci will fasten themselves to the thread and go up to eat the moon and the sun.*

🩸 *They can be created when a porridge stick is placed in a fire.*

🩸 *They can be created when a person sweeps the house at sunset and directs the dust towards the sun.*

🩸 *They can appear as humans with pale faces and dry skin.*

🩸 *They can be recognized by their death-like sleep when they send their spirits out of their mouths to eat the sun or moon. If they are moved during this deep sleep they die because their spirit will not be able to find the mouth to re-enter the body.*

Varney the Vampyre

Varney the Vampyre, or The Feast of Blood was an immensely popular serialized novel, the first in the English language, published in 109 weekly installments over the years 1847–8. Varney was presented anonymously and its authorship remained uncertain for many years until the name of Thomas Preskett Prest, author of *Sweeney Todd*, was suggested by early twentieth-century vampiriologist Montague Summers. More recent research has now shown that the author was probably James Malcolm Rymer, but more than one writer probably worked on the project.

The novel is massive and runs to 868 pages with 220 chapters. It is labored and repetitive and not an easy read for a modern audience, but it is fairly representative of the penny dreadful – stories serialized as cheap entertainment in newspapers and magazines in the nineteenth century. Some vampire fiction enthusiasts, for example Summers, prefer it to Bram Stoker's *Dracula* but this opinion tends to be a minority one.

Francis Varney

The title character, the evil but complicated Francis Varney, remains one of the most influential vampires in literature. It is certainly possible that *Varney* had an influence on Bram Stoker when he created Count Dracula. Like his precursor, Lord Ruthven in Polidori's *The Vampyre* (1819), Varney is an aristocrat who can walk freely in sunlight, but unlike Ruthven he is neither charming nor seductive. He is described as ugly, tall, and hideous-looking with huge eyes like tin, a white, bloodless face, long fangs and a body as *"cold and clammy like a corpse."* There are inconsistencies in the story due to the length of the novel and its chaotic and poorly written nature but the most constant theme is that in life Varney had committed suicide and had returned from death as a vampire. He preys on the wealthy Bannermouth family and is not only after their blood but also their money and their property.

Throughout the novel Varney preys on vulnerable women and transforms them into vampires. He also tries to kill himself many times or is killed by others, but each time he is restored to life by the moon's rays. Eventually, when Edwin Lloyd, the publisher, decided that Varney had died and returned to life more than enough times, Rymer made his character, overcome with disgust at the horror of his life, leap into Mount Vesuvius.

See also: LITERATURE

Vaughn, Nellie

Nellie Vaughn was an alleged vampire of Rhode Island but recent research has suggested that stories about her may be a fiction. Nellie was the daughter of George B. and Ellie Vaughn of West Greenwich, Rhode Island. She died at the age of 19 on March 31, 1889, and was buried in the Plain Meeting House Baptist Church Cemetery. Her body was not exhumed; no other family members died around the same time and there are no written accounts of her being a vampire.

The message on Nellie's grave read "I am waiting and watching for you." This was probably used at the time to suggest that as she died young she was awaiting a reunion with her family in heaven. However, given that this was Rhode Island and given the history of vampirism in that state, close to a century later the words were interpreted in a very different way. In 1977 the first published reference to Nellie appeared in the *Westerly Sun* newspaper in Rhode Island. The article spoke of her sunken grave (in European folklore the sign of a vampire) and a myth in the area that no vegetation grew on the grave. It was not long before the gravesite generated a massive amount of interest. There were also reports that Nellie still haunted her grave and scratched the faces of those who disturbed it.

Urban legend

The source of the vampire story was said at the time to be an unnamed school teacher who, in 1967, told his students that there was a vampire buried in the cemetery, a girl who had died at the age of 19. It's possible that the teacher was talking about Mercy Brown but his students went to the cemetery, found Nellie's grave, and assumed she was the vampire.

Eventually Nellie's grave became so desecrated with the number of visitors that in 1990 the headstone was removed to a safe place in an attempt to stop the vandalism. This did not completely stop vampire hunters from attempting to find her unmarked grave. In 1993 a coffin was dug up at the Plain Meeting House Cemetery by a vampire hunter looking for Nellie's grave and opened, exposing the recently buried corpse of a man with a can of beer in one hand and a pack of cigarettes in the other.

See also: BROWN, MERCY LEA; RHODE ISLAND VAMPIRES

Vetala

Known in some regions as the baital, the vetala is an evil vampire demon spirit in Indian lore that lingers around cemeteries to reanimate corpses. These corpses no longer decay once inhabited by a vetala. They make their displeasure known by attacking humans. They can drive people mad, kill children, and cause miscarriages. The vetala can also appear in human form with the hands and feet turned backwards or as an old hag sucking the blood of women, typically those who are drunk or insane.

The vetala inhabits a twilight zone between life and death and, being outside space and time, it has knowledge of past, present, and future. Therefore sorcerers seek to capture them and use them to serve their own end. Some traditions hold that the vetala is not a malevolent force. The creature is best known from a collection of Indian folktales called the *Vetala Panchvimshati* or *Baital Pachisi* told by a vetala to King Vikram.

In the *Baital Pachisi* a sorcerer asks King Vikram to capture a vetala who lived in a tree that stood in the middle of a crematorium.

The only way to do that was by keeping silent but each time Vikram caught the vetala, the vetala would enchant the king with a story that ended with a question and Vikram would not be able to resist answering. This would enable the vetala to escape and return to his tree. The stories told by the vetala in the *Baital Pachisi* were adapted for the West as *King Vikram and the Vampire* by Richard Burton in 1870.

See also: INDIA

Victims

There are significant differences between the victims of the folklore vampire and the victims of vampires of fiction. In folklore victims are restricted to a grave site or to the home, people, and village among whom the vampire lived before death. In contrast the vampires of fiction can travel the world and choose victims from any location. Dracula was perhaps more limited by his need to be close by his boxes of native soil.

There are also differences between the fate of the folklore and fiction victims of vampires. With the exception of babies and infants, who would often be found dead in their cribs after a vampire attack at night, victims of the folklore vampire did not generally die straight away; instead they would be cursed with a lingering illness or wasting disease, such as tuberculosis (consumption). The vampires of fiction, on the other hand, often immediately killed their victims to feast on their blood, although there were exceptions: Dracula and Carmilla preferred to feed on their victims over a prolonged period as they gradually got weaker and weaker.

Virgins

The vampires of traditional folklore generally tend to be indiscriminate in the choice of victim; men, women, children, babies, and animals are all potential victims. However, over time vampires in folklore and, most noticeably, in fiction tended to have a real preference for virgins as victims. This may have something to do with the creatures' long association with sexuality and sexual awakening – the act of feeding on living blood is itself penetrative and involves bodily fluid exchange. It may also have something to do with the idea that the loss of virginity depletes a person of their life force and the blood of a virgin is therefore somehow purer and more potent than the blood of a non-virgin.

In medieval times the Church was obsessed with Satan's carnality, warning that demons, such as the incubus or succubus, would prey on young innocents in their sleep and commit savage sexual acts with them. There are similarities here with the vampire's nocturnal visits, as in both cases the victim awakes feeling drained, weakened, and somehow corrupted. Sex was a taboo in earlier times, particularly for nuns and monks sworn to a life of celibacy, so any visions of a sexual nature were thought to be from Satan. Sexual repression therefore found expression in stories of vampires ritually deflowering young virgins. This close connection between vampirism and the loss of sexual innocence which threatens the immortal soul proved especially captivating to Victorian audiences brought up to deny their sexual impulses. In *Dracula*, Lucy Westenra, a virgin, returns from the grave as a lustful seducer.

One modern theory on the vampire's supposed preference for virgin blood is that virgin blood simply tastes the best.

Transformation

On some occasions in folklore the attack of a vampire was said to have caused the victim to also become a vampire, but more often than not the victim did not transform into a vampire until after death. Fear of vampire attacks led not to a persecution of the living but to the mutilation of corpses.

In nineteenth-century literature vampire victims typically fell ill or died when attacked and did not become vampires. However, in *Dracula*, although it is never specifically stated there is the implication when the Count attacks Mina that drinking his blood will transform her into a vampire. Lucy Westenra certainly survives as a vampire after her vampire attack. This shared-blood method of transformation was deemed too shocking for adaptations of *Dracula* on stage or screen and over the decades it was replaced by the idea that all that was needed for the vampiric transformation was the bite of a vampire.

As the vampire tradition has evolved in the twenty-first century and the vampire has acquired the status of hero rather than villain in literature and film, his or her victims have tended to be animals or willing donors or people who are so reprehensible that they clearly deserve to be attacked. These "victims" rarely transform into vampires themselves unless the vampire consciously decides to transform them. Modern vampires may also seek blood from blood banks.

See also: **BECOMING A VAMPIRE;** *CARMILLA*

Virus

According to a recent school of thought, real vampires are just sufferers of a viral disease, not unlike AIDS. In this way the vampire is still human but an infected human, and, as some believe, they represent the next stage of human evolution.

The vampire virus theory is totally speculative and may be science fiction inspired by books such as *I Am Legend* by Richard Matheson, but for some vampirologists it is plausible enough to be looked into. Some people even believe that the virus is currently being researched by secret commercial labs, where it goes under the name of RV K-17.

The speculation

An unproven medical explanation for the physiological differences between vampires and humans, suggested by those who believe in real vampires, comes in the form of a virus called V5. Viral vampires experience anemia, improved night vision or sensitivity to light, a stronger immune system or slowed aging process, and in some cases, more acute psychic capabilities. V5 can be passed on to a child via its mother or from an exchange with an infected person, much like HIV or the flu. The virus alters the recipient's DNA to allow for greater speed, strength, psychic ability, and so on, but theoretically, he or she must have an ideal blood chemistry and relatively weak immune system to allow the change.

According to Hugo Pecos, who oversees an organization and website he calls the Federal Vampire and Zombie Agency, the source of vampirism is not V5 but the Human Vampiric Virus (HVV). The natural host of HVV is allegedly a flea commonly found on cave-dwelling bats, especially the vampire bat. In this way a bat bitten by the flea passes the HVV virus on to animals and humans through a bite and the virus is passed on in turn to someone else through the bite of an infected person. Within hours of being bitten, the victim develops a headache, fever, chills, and other flu-like symptoms as the body attempts to kill off the infection. These symptoms are often confused with those of common viral infections, but the diagnosis can be confirmed by the identification of bite marks. This stage typically lasts between six and twelve hours and during this time vaccines and medications may be effective in reversing the condition. Twenty-four hours after being bitten, however, the victim will slip into a coma and during this phase the pulse slows down, breathing is shallow, pupils are dilated, and medical intervention is generally ineffective. Only a small percentage of people survive vampiric comas and in most instances the old, the very young, and the frail die. A bite victim who survives the coma will awaken transformed into a blood-drinking vampire. An acclimatization period may follow, characterized by confusion, despondency, and paranoia.

See also: **DISEASE; TRANSFORMATION**

Vision

The eyes of vampires are often described as hellish and hypnotic and able to paralyze victims. They may also turn blood red when the vampire begins to feed. When describing the sight of vampires in *Dracula* the character Van Helsing states that they can see clearly in the dark. The superb night vision of vampires isn't explained or even mentioned in folklore but it is implied, as generally the vampire of folklore is a nocturnal creature. Some vampirologists have suggested that the vampire may be able to adjust their infrared spectrum, while others have suggested that their night vision is similar to that of bats with their sensitive radar system.

See also: **SENSES**

Vjesci

The "vjesci" is the name used for a vampire species found among the Kashubs of north-eastern Poland.

According to lore the vjesci could be identified at birth by the presence of a membrane cap or a caul. To prevent the child becoming a vjesci the caul had to be removed, dried, ground, and fed to the child on their seventh birthday. Apart from this, the vjesci appeared normal in every way and could live undetected within the community, although some vjesci could have a ruddy complexion and a restless nature. The term "vjesci" was often used interchangeably with the term "wupji" or "opji." The opji was fairly similar to the vjesci but instead of being born with a caul the opji had two teeth at birth. In addition, while there was

the possibility of avoiding the vampiric fate for the vjesci, there was thought to be no way of altering an opji's destiny.

Prevention and protection

It was after death that the vjesci was most feared as it was thought that he could awake in the grave and eat his burial clothes and some of his own flesh. He could then leave the grave and suck the blood of sleeping family members and neighbors at night. Victims would typically be found the next morning with a small wound over their heart.

To prevent the creature leaving its grave it was essential that the dying vjesci should receive the Eucharist. A coin or crucifix should also be placed under the vampire's tongue and a net placed in the coffin, in the belief that the vampire would untie the knots at a rate of one knot a year. Sand or seeds might be used in the same way. The body might also be laid face down. If the corpse of a vjesci was disinterred it would be found sitting in its coffin with its left eye open. It might also move its head and make noises. To destroy it the head had to be cut off or a nail placed in the forehead. Any blood that flowed from the corpse should be collected and given to those who had been attacked.

Vlad II Dracul (d. 1447)

Vlad Dracul was a fifteenth-century Wallachian warlord or prince (*voivode*) and the father of Vlad Tepes (Vlad the Impaler), the man most frequently identified as the so-called historical Dracula.

Vlad Dracul was born around 1390, the illegitimate son of Prince Mircea of Wallachia. His reign lasted from 1436 to 1442 and then again from 1443 to 1447. He was invited by Sigismund I of Hungary to become a member of the Order of the Dragon, which Sigismund founded in 1418. The Order of the Dragon had a number of aims, one of which was to fight the Muslim Turks. Vlad supported Christendom but during his reign his allegiance wavered between supporting the Hungarians and maintaining the status quo with the Turks. In 1447 Vlad Dracul was assassinated near Bucharest after the new Hungarian ruler János Hunyadi marched into Transylvania and laid siege to Tirgoviste, one of Dracul's cities.

A year after the death of Vlad Dracul, his son, Vlad Tepes tried unsuccessfully to regain his father's throne. He was not able to do so until 1456 when he avenged the death of his father.

Vlad the Impaler (1431–76?)

Vlad the Impaler was the nickname for Vlad Dracula, a fifteenth-century *voivode* (prince) of Wallachia, because of his policy of impaling his enemies on spikes. Vlad III Tepes ("Tepes" meaning "Impaler") was also the namesake of Bram Stoker's vampire in his 1897 novel, *Dracula*.

The principality of Wallachia

Vlad's principality of Wallachia, now part of Romania but then a province south of Transylvania, came into existence sometime in the late thirteenth century. Its society was based on a feudal system with a ruling class of landed aristocracy called *boyars* and a ruling prince or warlord, called the *voivode*. During the rule both of Vlad's father (Vlad II Dracul) and Vlad himself Wallachia was under constant threat of invasion by the Ottoman Turks.

In 1447 Vlad Dracul was killed and his sons were taken as hostages to the Ottoman court, perhaps learning from them first-hand lessons in terror and brutality. Less than a year later, with Ottoman support Vlad III invaded Wallachia to briefly seize control. He next returned to power in 1456, but details on how this return to power took place are not clear. During his second reign Vlad established his residence in Tirgoviste, making it the capital of Wallachia.

The second reign of Vlad III (1456–62)

When Vlad seized power for the second time the *boyars* were increasing their power and wealth. To keep them in check and establish his authority immediately, Vlad allegedly killed 20,000 men, women, and children in a short space of time. Stories of the atrocities he committed against them have become legendary. On one occasion he was said to have invited the *boyars* to a feast and when they failed to give him the right answer to the question of how many princes there were in Wallachia (the correct answer was seven), he impaled all 500 of them on stakes. On another occasion he invited citizens to a feast and at the end he impaled all the elderly and forced the children and young adults into servitude to build a castle at Poenari.

Anyone who was suspected of treason was tortured and impaled and the number of his victims over his six-year reign was conservatively totaled at 40,000. Vlad's method of torture and execution shocked his contemporaries. As well as impaling people on stakes it was also said that he forced people to dig their own graves before beheading them, or he boiled them alive in cauldrons and forced others to eat them. If reports are to be believed the atrocities did not stop with his enemies. He had the stomach of his mistress split open to prove her pregnancy. It was also said he nailed the turbans of visiting ambassadors to their heads and burned a whole group of beggars alive at a feast.

While many of these reports were probably embellished there is no doubt that Vlad's reputation for cruelty is justified. His brutal methods of terrorizing his enemies and the ruthless manner in which he punished people earned him the contemporary nickname of Impaler, the name by which he is known to this day.

Vlad's downfall and legacy

Vlad's brother Radu seized the throne in 1462 and Vlad was imprisoned in Hungary for 13 years. He was released in 1475 and attempted to take the throne for a third time in 1476. This time his reign only lasted about a month. The Turks invaded again and Vlad was killed.

Accounts differ concerning Vlad's death. Some say he was shot in battle. Others say he was assassinated by a Turk in the forest near Stagnov and his body decapitated and staked at Constantinople. The remains of his body were said to be buried at the monastery of Stagnov but if he was buried there his grave has never been found. Another legend says that Vlad and his wife were trapped at Castle Poenari when the Turks invaded. Vlad's wife threw herself off the castle wall into the river below. Vlad supposedly escaped through a secret tunnel and this legend was the opening storyline for Francis Ford Coppola's 1992 film, *Bram Stoker's Dracula*.

After death Vlad assumed a defining role in Romanian legends as stories of his cruelty and propaganda to discredit him spread around Europe. This was not the case in Romania where he was honored historically as a symbol of nationalism and a hero in the country's struggle for independence.

Vlad and folkloric vampirism

Despite popular opinion there is no association between Vlad and the vampire of folklore. Some recent accounts state he drank the blood of his enemies but there is no evidence to suggest this from more authentic accounts, and even if he did drink his enemies' blood the practice would have symbolized the absorption of the enemy's power by the conqueror and has no association with vampirism. There is a famous woodcut which shows him dining while surrounded by victims impaled on stakes, but although this suggests reprehensible cruelty, again it does not suggest blood drinking.

Vlad and Bram Stoker's Dracula

Just as there is no association between Vlad Tepes and the vampire of folklore, it is also wrong to assume that Vlad Tepes was the so-called historical inspiration for Bram Stoker's fictional vampire Count Dracula. It was most likely that Stoker used just the name, not the historical figure. Vlad's father was known as Dracul ("dragon" or "devil") and Dracula means "son of the dragon/devil."

Stoker was introduced to the name Dracula in *An Account of the Principalities of Wallachia and Moldavia* (1820) by William Wilkinson and possibly from information given him by the scholar Arminius Vámbéry. Originally he was going to call his vampire Count Wamphyr, an Eastern European name for vampire, but he liked the meaning of the word "Dracula" so much that he changed the name to Count Dracula. Although there is information about Wallachian lore and history in Wilkinson's account there is no evidence to suggest that Stoker ever had a detailed knowledge of Vlad's reign of terror.

The assumption that Dracula's character was built on the historical figure of Vlad has often been based on remarks made by the character of Van Helsing in the novel:

> He [Dracula] must, indeed, have been that voivode *Dracula who won his name against the Turk, over the great rivers on the very frontier of Turkey-land. If that be so, then was he no common man; for in that time, and for centuries after, he was spoken of as the cleverest and most cunning, as well as the bravest of the sons of the "land beyond the forest." That mighty brain and that iron resolution went with him to the grave, and are even now arrayed against us. The Draculas were, says Arminius, a great and noble race, though now and again were scions who were held by their coevals to have had dealings with the Evil One.*

The associations between vampirism and Vlad did not exist before Stoker put these words into the mouth of Van Helsing. Vlad was a brutal and ruthless nobleman who was accused of spilling the blood of innocent people, but now in the novel he was accused of blood drinking, and ever since then that accusation has stuck. Despite being weak the association between the fictional Dracula and the historical Vlad the Impaler continues to be promoted in fiction and film and was given a tremendous boost by the research of historians Raymond T. McNally and Radu Florescu in the early 1970s. In *Dracula: A Biography of Vlad the Impaler* McNally and Florescu indicated that Vlad was an integral part of the Dracula myth.

Despite the fact that in Romania Vlad remains a hero and a symbol of national pride and is not in any way associated with vampirism, a large portion of Romanian tourism continues to depend on Stoker's association between the fictional character and the historical figure.

See also: **CASTLE DRACULA; DRACULA; ROMANIA; TRANSYLVANIA**

Vlad Tepes

See: **VLAD THE IMPALER**

Volkodlak

In Slovenia "volkodlak" is a term for a vampire but in western Slavic lore it also refers to a werewolf, illustrating the close association that there was in some regions between these two creatures of the night. People who were dark or savage looking or who had misshapen limbs were sometimes called volkodlak.

Voltaire (1694–1778)

Voltaire was the pen name for French Enlightenment philosopher and writer François-Marie Arouet. Voltaire was a prolific writer and outspoken supporter of social reform. Among his many works and essays was the *Dictionnaire philosophique* (1764), in which he expresses amazement that in the eighteenth century people could still believe in vampires and that academics should give their time and enthusiasm to treatises about the undead.

Voodoo

Voodoo is a magical tradition practiced in Haitian and African communities in the Caribbean and Southern United States, which combines Roman Catholic religious traditions with African occult magical rites. Although voodoo is specific to Haiti and the Southern United States, offshoots and related cults appear all over the world. It is estimated that currently voodoo has around 50 million followers worldwide.

Voodoo, also known as voodun, is a product of the slave trade. African slaves transported to North and South America were forbidden to practice their religion and their masters baptized them as Catholics. As a result voodoo became a mixture of Catholicism superimposed upon secret native beliefs and rites and some say this is the reason for the ferocious anger at the heart of the religion. Tribal deities took on the form of Catholic saints, and fetishes were replaced by Catholic statues, candles, and holy relics. Animal sacrifices, spirit possession, black magic, sexual magic, and shamanic trances are common features of this religion, although some sects do practice white magic. Voodoo blood rituals connect voodoo to vampirism and voodoo sorcerers are said to have supernatural powers, including those of necromancy, spell casting, and the power to raise flesh-eating zombies from the dead to do their bidding.

One of the most terrifying and well-known voodoo magic spells is for the voodoo practitioner to make a small doll or puppet in the shape of the person they wish to curse. The doll is then tortured and abused with the intention of transferring that pain and harm to the person. As well as being the action of the powerless against those with power, it's likely that the voodoo doll is something slaves assimilated from their masters, rather than the other way round. Puppet magic has been practiced in European cultures for a long time.

Vourdalak

The "vourdalak" is the name for a vampire species found in Russian lore who is a beautiful but malevolent female spirit.

See also: **RUSSIA**

Vresket

"Vresket" is a Croatian term for the sound that only corpses suspected of being vampires made when they were disinterred and staked. The noise was probably made by gases escaping from the corpse, which would explain the shrieking, groaning, and even laughing sounds described in a number of cases when a vampire corpse was impaled.

See also: **DECOMPOSITION**

Vrykolakas

Also known as *vyrkolaka*, *vroukalakas*, and *brucolocas*, the vrykolakas were the main vampire species of Greece and Macedonia. The name was originally used in Slavic regions to refer to a werewolf and its association with vampires probably originated with the belief that after death werewolves were thought to rise as vampires. Until Slavic culture integrated into the Aegean the Greek revenant was a fairly placid creature, but the vrykolakas eventually took over and became the most common vampire species in the region.

In folklore belief, the vrykolakas is a person whose body and soul are taken over by a demon between death and burial so that the corpse is reanimated and rises from the grave to drink the blood of its relatives, causing a wasting disease that often led to death. The purpose of this demon was to lure people away from the path of righteousness and into evil and death. In some areas of Greece the vrykolakas reveals itself 40 days after death and a telltale sign of its presence is a grave with a hole. Once it has risen from the grave it will knock at doors calling out the name of a person inside; should that person answer, death will follow. In some regions it was believed that a knock or call should never be answered the first time as the vrykolakas is impatient and will never knock on a door twice.

Greek vampires were not restricted to darkness and the night; noon was considered just as dangerous as midnight and vampires could wander both by day and by night. They were also fairly hard to distinguish from humans although there were certain signs: they had a lost and vacant stare; they did not eat; their hair had a reddish tinge; and they cast no shadow.

A number of factors can create a vrykolakas, including:

- *Lack of proper burial*

- *Violent or sudden death, such as murder or drowning*

- *Death by suicide*

- *Excommunication from the Church*

- *Committing a sexual act with an animal*

- *Death from plague or unidentified disease — there was a belief that vampires were the cause of disease and that corpses had been in contact with the vrykolakas*

- *Those who had been prostitutes or who had committed a sexual act with a foreigner (once again xenophobia lies at the heart of this belief)*

- *A person who dies unbaptized*

- *A person who has led a sinful life, or practiced sorcery or evil*

- *A person who has eaten a sheep killed by a wolf*

- *Those whose bodies had been jumped over by animals*

- *A person whose body was left unattended between death and burial*

- *Those who were of Turkish extraction – this is no doubt associated with long-standing feuding between the Greeks and Turks*

Destruction

The best day to destroy the vrykolakas was on a Saturday, the one day vampires are supposed to sleep in the earth. If the body was swollen or bloated or gorged with fresh blood, it was judged to be a vrykolakas and a priest was called in to perform an exorcism while boiling vinegar and oil were poured over the body. If the trouble continued the exorcism was repeated or the corpse was decapitated or impaled on a spike. If these measures did not work the corpse had to be taken to a small, uninhabited island and buried there, as it was thought that vampires could not travel over water.

A related species, the *vrykolatios*, is a flesh-eating, blood-drinking vampire ghoul that was mentioned in the 1900 *Handbook for Travellers in Greece*. The vrykolatios were said to be found on the island of Santorini, an island believed by some vampire experts to be the most vampire-infested place on earth.

Vukodlak

The Serbian term for vampire, the word "vukodlak" originated from the word for werewolf because in Slavic folklore the werewolf is associated with vampires. After death werewolves were thought to return from the grave as vampires. Although in some parts of Yugoslavia the vukodlak remained a werewolf, in other areas the vampire associations eventually overtook the werewolf associations.

According to Serbian lore the vukodlak is created 40 days after death by the entry of a demonic spirit into the corpse of a murdered man. In other lore a child, typically a boy, who is born with teeth will become a vukodlak. After death the body is reanimated and will then rise from its grave to drink human blood and to have sex with former wives and girl-friends or young widows. If a child is born from such a union it is said to have no bones and a jelly-like body.

See also: SERBIA

Vulture

Vultures are scavengers, carrion birds that feast on the decaying flesh of dead animals. Their bald heads allow them to feed without fouling their feathers. They are found all over the world in areas where winters are mild.

Many cultures recognized their importance in clearing away the bodies of dead animals but vultures have also attracted negative superstition and myth. The ancient philosophers Aristotle and Pliny the Elder both thought that vultures were omens of misfortune and death. Although more often associated with the bat, the vampire has often been portrayed in fiction and in film as looking like a vulture, with a flowing black cape, wide stand-up collar, and a clean-shaven face.

Vultures have a number of sinister characteristics that make them obvious symbols for evil, death, and misfortune and that explain their association with the undead:

- *The classic vulture is a menacing dark brown or black with a bald head and a powerful hooked beak. Their bare skin is often pink or red, and wrinkled.*

- *Vultures are known to congregate in battlefields after a battle, and feast on both the dead and the wounded.*

- *Before descending to feed on a dying person or animal, some species gather ominously in nearby trees, as though waiting for the person or animal to die.*

- *Vultures have a disquieting ability to find a corpse very quickly – this has given rise to the belief that like the vampires of fiction, and in some cases folklore, they have excellent eyesight, an extraordinary sense of smell, and a prescience of death.*

"The lips which will be markedly full and red are drawn back from the teeth which gleam long, sharp as razors, and ivory white."

Montague Summers, *The Vampire: His Kith and Kin*

Wake Not the Dead

Wake Not the Dead is a vampire story rich in sexual symbolism written by German folklorist Johann Ludwig Tieck in 1800. It was published in English in 1823 in a three-volume anthology, *Popular Tales and Romances of the Northern Nations*. Tieck's presentation of Brunhilda, a dead woman who is brought back to life by a sorcerer paid by her husband, Walter, ranks among the first influential female vampires in literature. Brunhilda must seek nourishment and vitality from the blood of humans, taken *"whilst warm from the veins of youth."* Lamia-like, she feeds on children first and then turns on her *"spell enthralled"* husband.

See also: **LITERATURE**

Wales

Wales is home to both the vampire-like fairy creature called Gwrach y Rhibyn and one of the most unusual vampire species in folklore – a chair with a taste for blood. According to legend, a minister visiting a family that lived in a converted farmhouse sat on a chair and when he got up he discovered teeth marks on his hands and backside. A resident of the farmhouse told the minister that two other ministers had been attacked in the same way and that the farmer who had previously owned the chair had returned from the dead as a vampire. Some versions of the story state that the minister's horse also carried the same bite marks.

See also: **BRITISH ISLES, THE**

Wallachia

Along with Moldavia and Transylvania, Wallachia historically is one of the provinces of Romania. Like the rest of Romania, Wallachian folklore contains many stories of different vampire species including the nosferatu, moroi, varcolac, and zmeu, but the species it is most associated with is the murony. Some vampire experts believe that because the vampire tradition was so widespread in Wallachia, it, rather than Transylvania, may have been the Romanian home of the vampire.

In addition, toward the end of the thirteenth century a line of rulers bearing the name *voivode* ("warlord" or "prince") established themselves, becoming known to history as the Draculesti. This family produced two Wallachian princes who were vital to the development of the Dracula myth – Vlad II Dracul and Vlad III Tepes or Vlad the Impaler, also known as Dracula or "son of Dracul."

Walpurgis Night

Walpurgis Night (Walpurgisnacht) is a festival celebrated by Pagans as well as Roman Catholics, on the night of April 30 in large parts of Central and Northern Europe. It was originally held in honor of the eighth-century abbess and missionary St. Walburga, to celebrate the moving of the saint's relics to Eichstätt. However, over time Walburga was confused in folklore and legend with the pagan fertility goddess Waldbourg, and the festival became entwined with pagan spring rites where the arrival of spring was celebrated with bonfires. Witches and vampires were believed to be active on this night and Bohemians would place hawthorn and wild rose around stables to prevent vampires entering.

Walton Family Cemetery

In November 1990, near Griswold, Connecticut, an abandoned rural farm family cemetery was discovered that revealed evidence of the New England vampire superstitions related to deaths from tuberculosis.

The initial and accidental discovery was made by a sand and gravel company working at the site of the forgotten cemetery. Two human skulls were exposed but because of the instability of the sand and gravel knoll in which they were found, the burials could not be preserved where they were, and an archeological team had to remove them from the site. As Paul Sledzik and Nicholas Bellantoni reported in an article entitled "Bioarcheological and Biocultural Evidence for the New England Vampire Folk Belief" that appeared in *The American Journal of Physical Anthropology* in 1994:

> The skeletal remains of 29 individuals (15 subadults, 6 adult males, and 8 adult females) were excavated in the course of 1 year. Documentary evidence in land deeds indicated that the Walton family, who had emigrated to Griswold in 1690, had utilized the knoll as a family burial ground by the 1750s.

In 1690 Nathaniel and Margaret Walton had moved from Boston to Griswold to establish a farm and in 1757 the Walton family established a family cemetery on land they bought from a neighbor. The cemetery was used by the family until the early 1800s when they moved to Ohio. It was then used by an unidentified family until 1830, after which time it was abandoned.

Experts believe that some of the children buried in the cemetery may have died of smallpox or measles epidemics which hit the area in 1759 and then again in 1790. Only one set of remains indicated death from tuberculosis. The lid of this man's coffin was inscribed "J B, 55," probably his initials and the age he died. J B was buried sometime between 1800 and the late 1830s but his skull and two femora (thighbones) had been placed on top of his ribs, the femora in the sign of a cross, and his vertebrae were disordered, indicating to researchers that at some time after his burial another family member died of tuberculosis and J B's body was exhumed to stop the disease progressing. The traditional remedy was to remove the heart and liver, but with no internal organs to burn due to the corpse's decomposition an alternative remedy was used and J B's bones were rearranged to make sure he could not leave his grave.

See also: NEW ENGLAND

Ward, J. R.

J. R. Ward is the pen name American writer Jessica Rowley Pell Bird uses for her paranormal erotic romance series called the Black Dagger Brotherhood. Beginning with *Dark Lover* (2005), the *New York Times* bestselling series focuses on six vampire brothers and warriors who live together and defend their race against Lessers, de-souled humans who threaten their kind.

See also: LITERATURE

Washington, D.C.

Several years after the publication of Bram Stoker's *Dracula* in 1897, stories began to circulate that vampires were on the prowl in Washington, D.C., the capital of the United States.

One story concerned a girl from a well-to-do family who had fallen in love with a European prince in the 1850s. He met her at an embassy party and she fell for his handsome face and piercing black eyes. One night the prince drained her blood and her corpse was found the next morning with bite marks on the neck in a clearing a few miles from her home. The girl was buried in her family vault in a white lace dress that was to have been her wedding gown but she rose as a vampire. People began to talk about a girl dressed in white with fangs.

According to a 1923 report in the *Washington Post* written by writer Gorman Henricks, a woodcutter saw the girl float through the sealed vault door. He told others but no one

believed him and a few days later he was found dead, with his blood drained and fang marks on his neck. This caused a panic; people protected themselves with garlic, and guards were placed on the family vault. One night during a thunderstorm, the girl appeared, causing the guards to run off. The next morning, the slab at the entrance of the vault had been moved. The girl was found in her coffin with blood on her lips. The family became anxious and eventually moved away and the neglected vault fell into ruins.

Rumors about the girl in white began to surface soon after the publication of *Dracula*. The vault, the girl in the white dress, the nocturnal wanderings, the corpse with blood on its lips are all classic scenes from the novel, which has led many researchers to speculate that on this occasion the story was probably an urban fantasy inspired by the novel. However, this does not detract from the fascination such stories hold for researchers, illustrating the very real effect belief in vampires can have upon culture and society.

Water

In folklore, water, as a symbol of life, can be used to defeat vampires or protect against them. Evil entities and witches cannot swim in or cross running water. Water has ancient associations with purity, cleansing, and healing.

Although avoidance of water is characteristic of the Chinese chiang-shih and Bram Stoker's vampire (the Count cannot cross running water unless at flood or slack tides), in Eastern European lore fear of water is not a prominent characteristic, perhaps due to geographical limitations. In some regions, however, there are associations with vampires and water. For instance, in Russia there was a bizarre trial by water in which a dead body was placed in water; if it floated it had become a vampire because the water could not tolerate accepting it. And in parts of Germany water might be poured around a vampire's grave to prevent it leaving.

A potential source of the fictional Count's fear of water might have been old Greek accounts of troublesome revenants sent away to small islands surrounded by water to ensure they could not leave. Montague Summers gives an example in his book *The Vampire: His Kith and Kin*, first published in 1928, taken from *Travels and Discoveries in the Levant*, volume I, by Charles T. Newton (1866).

> *Newton … says that in Mitylene the bodies of those who will not lie quiet in their graves are transported to a small adjacent island, a mere eyeot without inhabitants where they are re-interred. This is an effectual bar to any future molestation for the vampire cannot cross salt water. Running water he too can only pass at the slack or flood of the tide.*

Holy water

Holy water is water blessed by a priest and therefore made sacred and powerful against the forces of evil. In European folklore it is often used to destroy vampires in their graves and, if sprinkled in an empty coffin, to protect that coffin against vampire habitation. It could also be sprinkled around houses to protect against vampires and evil forces. Although the Eucharist and holy wafer appear in *Dracula*, holy water does not. However, as a natural and easily acquired

extension of these two objects it was often included in vampire-hunting kits. If thrown at a vampire holy water was said to be able to burn them like acid and leave heavy scars, and if it was poured on the ground that a vampire had walked on it would boil.

See also: **PROTECTION**

Watermelons

Among the Muslim Gypsies of Yugoslavia watermelons, like pumpkins, could become vampires, especially if they had teeth and had been kept for more than ten days or for too long after Christmas. Stained with drops of blood, these not very deadly or threatening vampires roll around making growling sounds, for no other reason than to irritate the living.

Weaknesses of Vampires

In Eastern European vampire folklore, vampires are said to have limitations on their supernatural powers. These limitations vary from region to region but some common themes can be seen to emerge.

 An inability to enter unless invited: *In Romanian folklore vampires are unable to cross a threshold where humans dwell unless invited to do so, and a person must not be answered until they have been called three times, for vampires can only ask a question twice. In a text by Leo Allatius that was originally published in 1645, concerning the beliefs on his native Greek island of Chios, a possible origin for this belief may be found.*

For very often, inhabiting this body, he [the Devil] comes forth from the grave, and going abroad through villages and other places where men dwell, more especially at night, he makes his way to what so ever house he will, and knocking upon the door he calls aloud by name in a hoarse voice one who dwells within. If such a one answers he is lost; for assuredly he will die the next day. But if he does not answer he is safe. Wherefore in this island of Chios all the inhabitants, if during the night they are called by anyone, never make reply the first time. For, if a man be called the second time it is not the vrykolakis who is summoning him but somebody else.

🩸 They cannot enter holy places: *Even if they are invited in, vampires are not able to cross the thresholds of churches, temples, or other places that are sanctuaries for goodness. The only way they can gain access to such places is if the sanctuaries have been desecrated beforehand. (In addition, vampires cannot cross a thicket of wild rose or a line of salt, and are compelled to stop and count every grain or seed in a pile of grain or seed thrown in their path.)*

🩸 They are helpless when in their grave or coffin: *The vampire may only leave its resting place at sunrise, noon, or sunset and is at its most vulnerable when resting in its grave or coffin.*

🩸 They must rest upon their native earth: *There is no tradition in myth and folklore that supports this allegation, indicating that it was an invention of Bram Stoker in Dracula.*

Other weaknesses/vulnerabilities include the following:

🩸 *An inability to cross running water*

🩸 *Sunlight destroys them*

🩸 *Cannot see own reflection*

🩸 *Vulnerable to apotropaic objects*

See also: **APOTROPAICS; DESTRUCTION; MIRRORS; POWERS, OF VAMPIRES**

weather

According to Bram Stoker in *Dracula* (1897), vampires can to a limited extent control the weather. There is no evidence in vampire folklore that this is the case, however. In subsequent vampire movies and fiction the weather plays an important role in setting the atmosphere and scene but the vampire's powers in relation to the weather have not been developed.

Weird Tales

First published in March 1923, *Weird Tales* was the foremost and greatest of the so-called pulp magazines. Until it went out of business in 1954 it outlasted rivals such as *Horror Stories, Terror Tales, Uncanny Tales,* and *Strange Tales*. The magazine specialized in offering readers a huge variety of fantasy, horror, and strange stories featuring vampires, ghouls, werewolves, and other evil monsters. The magazine began with reprints of horror stories from great writers such as Edgar Allan Poe and Arthur Conan Doyle but over the years it attracted great horror story contributors such as Robert Bloch, H. P. Lovecraft, and Ray Bradbury. In July 1947 the magazine released a special illustrated vampire edition.

See also: COMICS

Werewolf

A werewolf is a human being who at various times, typically at the full moon, transforms voluntarily or involuntarily into a vicious wolf-like creature that attacks and eats victims before resuming human form again. There are close associations between vampires and werewolves but the key difference is that werewolves are *living* creatures. Unlike vampires they have not died and returned from the grave.

The characteristics of a werewolf include: savage attacks on humans and animals; a compulsion to eat animal flesh and drink blood; insatiable sexual lust; wolfish behavior such as howling and running on all fours; and exhaustion after a werewolf episode.

Lycanthropy is a condition closely linked with the werewolf myth, because it is a physical and mental disorder in which people believe they have changed into wolves when they have not.

Origins

Like vampires, werewolves are age-old figures that can be found in the mythology of many cultures all over the world. Perhaps the oldest myth of a man changing into a wolf can be found in the mythology of ancient Greece. Lycaon (from which the term "lycanthropy" came) angered Zeus and was transformed into a wolf. The wolf is also prominent in Norse, Scandinavian, Icelandic, and Teutonic lore. In some legends the werewolf (involuntary werewolf) is born under a curse, or is cursed because of a sinful life and cannot prevent the metamorphosis, which happens on nights when the moon is full. In other tales the werewolf (voluntary werewolf) is a witch or sorcerer who accomplishes the transformation with the use of magic.

Werewolf lore may have some basis in primitive cannibalism practices but werewolf legends were particularly strong in those parts of Europe, such as France, Spain, Germany, Switzerland, and the Baltic regions, where wolves were common and presented dangers to the community. Werewolf sightings continue into modern times and are often grouped together with reports of other mysterious and malevolent creatures such as the chupacabra and Bigfoot.

Vampires and werewolves

There has long been a close association between vampires and werewolves in Slavic and European folklore. In Greek and Serbian lore a werewolf was condemned to become a vampire after death. In some rural areas of Germany, Poland, and northern France, people who died sinners could come back to life as blood-drinking wolves. These vampiric werewolves would return to their human corpse form at daylight. They were dealt with by decapitation with a spade and exorcism by the parish priest. The vampire was also linked to the werewolf in Eastern European countries, particularly Bulgaria, Serbia, and Slovakia. In Serbia, the werewolf and vampire are known collectively as one creature – the volkodlak. The Serbian term for the vampire, "vlokoslak" and the Greek term "vrykolakas" are names that can be applied to both vampire and werewolf. In Hungarian and Balkan mythology, many werewolves were said to be vampiric witches who became wolves in order to suck the blood of men born under the full moon in order to preserve their vitality.

Belief in werewolves peaked in Europe in the late Middle Ages; between 1520 and 1630 many thousands of cases were reported. Werewolves, like witches, were seen as servants of the Devil and there were a number of witch-werewolf trials. Many of those accused of werewolf murders were clearly deranged individuals, in much the same way as many of those accused of vampire-like murders were and are mentally unstable. Many authors have therefore speculated that werewolf and vampire legends may have been used to explain serial killings in less rational ages.

See also: **LYCANTHROPY;**
            SHAPE-SHIFTING

Westenra, Lucy

One of the main characters in Bram Stoker's novel *Dracula*, Lucy Westenra first appears in chapter five of the novel where mention is made of her correspondence with her friend Mina Murray. Lucy is never described in great detail but she is an attractive Englishwoman in her twenties who lives with her mother and has secured the ardent affections of three suitors – Arthur Holmwood, to whom she becomes engaged, Dr. John Seward, and Quincey P. Morris.

As the novel progresses Lucy undergoes a series of attacks by the Count. In an attempt to save her life she receives blood transfusions from her suitors. The blood transfusions fail and Lucy dies and returns as a vampire, known to her child victims as the "Bloofer Lady." On what should have been their wedding night, Lucy the vampire is confronted in the family crypt by Holmwood. She is staked by her fiancé and then the vampire hunter Van Helsing cuts off her head and stuffs her mouth with garlic.

At one point in the novel Lucy regrets that she cannot marry all three of her suitors and many literary critics see her character as a personification of the repression of Victorian women. Lucy is a "new woman" whose secret longing for sexual freedom poses a threat to a society dominated by men. By introducing Lucy to his dark world, Dracula allows her to fully express her sexuality, and her final rejection of the traditional and socially accepted role of nurturing wife and mother is displayed when she feeds on the blood of children.

Whitby

Whitby, a small town in Yorkshire in the north of England, is the setting for three chapters of Bram Stoker's *Dracula*. In chapter five of the novel Mina Murray arrives at Whitby station to join her friend Lucy Westenra for a holiday. The two women join the Westenra family in rooms they have rented for the summer vacation. During the first days of their holiday, Lucy and Mina enjoy visits to local tourist spots, which include the ruins of Whitby Abbey. Meanwhile Dracula has traveled to England with his boxes of earth on board the ship *Demeter*. The ship crashes into Whitby's harbor. The captain is found dead, lashed to the wheel with a cross in his hands and a huge dog is seen leaping from the wreckage. The Count stays in Whitby for a week and a half and attacks Lucy twice. Shortly after the second attack Dracula, and the action of the novel, move to London.

Stoker and Whitby

Stoker first visited Whitby in 1890 after he had begun research for his novel. He went there on a family holiday with his wife and son and spent three weeks there at 6 Royal Crescent, on the West Cliff. Three ladies from Hertford – Isabel and Marjorie Smith and their friend Miss Stokes – also stayed at the guest house and some have speculated that the ladies became the models for Lucy and Mina.

Stoker relished the brooding atmosphere of Whitby and particularly enjoyed the majestic ancient ruins of Whitby Abbey on East Cliff, founded by St. Hilda in 657. He also found a book in the town library entitled *An Account of the Principalities of Wallachia and Moldavia* by William Wilkinson, published in 1820. This book mentions the historical figure of Vlad Tepes Dracula, also known as Vlad the Impaler.

The *Demeter* incident in the novel may have been inspired by a real event. In October 1885, a Russian schooner named *Dimitry* ran aground in the harbor in a strong gale, narrowly missing the rocks. Stoker made note of the incident in his research and he may have changed the name to *Demeter* out of respect to the crew of the *Dimitry*. He also made notes on other shipwrecks in the area told to him by local fishermen.

Today, tourists can visit all the sights mentioned in the novel by Stoker. "The Dracula Trail" is a self-guided tour available from the town's visitor center, developed with the help of the London-based Dracula Society. The tour's starting point is the Bram Stoker Memorial Seat, which was carefully placed to give the same view of Whitby, as Bram Stoker would have had when he wrote Whitby into his novel.

White Lady

See: La Llorona

Whitethorn

Whitethorn, also known as hawthorn, is a tree with white flowers that is believed to have special powers against vampires in Eastern European folklore. Its wood would be carved into a stake or placed in coffins with garlic to ensure the creature did not leave its grave. Whitethorn was used to give protection during the Peter Plogojowitz vampire epidemic of 1725.

Wilde, Oscar (1854–1900)

Oscar Wilde was an Irish writer and the author of many witty plays, poems, novels, and stories, perhaps the most famous of his plays being *The Importance of Being Earnest* (1895). He was also the author of a well-known horror story entitled *The Picture of Dorian Gray* (1890), which is a clever literary presentation of a vampire-like character who never grows old and brings suffering and misfortune to those around him, while growing in beauty and vitality. Dorian Gray makes a devilish pact with his own likeness captured perfectly in a portrait. He somehow manages to transfer his life force to the painting because his wickedness only reveals itself on the canvas, which over the years changes from depicting the face of a vibrant, healthy, and handsome man into a hideous, leering monstrosity. Dorian has sold his soul and by so doing has already died, so when he decides to destroy the painting and stabs it, he ages instantly in the manner of the traditional vampire whose animated corpse has been staked.

See also: **LITERATURE**

Will-o'-the-Wisp

See: **IGNIS FATUUS**

Wine

In Romania, wine was used to prevent attacks by the strigoi vampire species. A bottle of wine would be buried near the grave of a suspected vampire and then dug up six weeks later and drunk by relatives of the deceased as a form of vampire protection. In parts of Bulgaria wine would be boiled and then thrown onto a corpse to expel demons, and in Serbia the heart of a suspected vampire would be cut out and boiled in wine and then placed back into the chest of the corpse. In Russia, whiskey, known as rachia, would be buried with the corpse of a suspected vampire. It was thought that the vampire would be so distracted and satisfied by the alcohol that it would have no interest in rising from the grave to attack and kill.

Although in Bram Stoker's *Dracula* the Count never drinks wine or any liquid (with the exception, of course, of blood), with the emergence of Dracula-themed tourism in Romania several companies have created Dracula wine souvenirs.

See also: **KILLING VAMPIRES; PREVENTION**

Witch/Witchcraft

Witchcraft is the practice of magic or sorcery and someone who practices witchcraft is called a witch (female) or a warlock (male). In European folklore witchcraft and vampirism have a long and close association that dates back centuries to the blood-sucking lamia of ancient Greece and the *strix* of ancient Rome. The Romanian word "strigoi" that is used to refer to vampires comes from a term that is closely akin to the Italian word *strega* meaning "witch," making Slavic vampires hard to distinguish from Slavic witches. It was also thought that people who practiced magic or sorcery during their lives were a type of living vampire. These living vampire witches could cast the evil eye and bewitch people and animals with magic. Upon death they transformed into vampires and left their graves to suck the blood of the living.

Work of the Devil

Up until the end of the fifteenth century witchcraft was considered to be an imaginary belief system of ancient paganism by the Roman Catholic Church, but when Pope Innocent VIII issued his bull, *Summis desiderantes affectibus* in 1484, it was redefined as Satanism. In the middle of the sixteenth century the link between witchcraft and vampirism was further strengthened by the work of Father Leo Allatius and Father François Richard on the "vampire-infested" island of Santorini. Both men published treatises which suggested that vampirism was real and that the Devil had the power to reanimate corpses. Soon after, Philip Rohr's influential treatise *De Masticatione Mortuorum* was published in 1679 in Leipzig.

A similar close association can be found in the Orthodox Church of Russia. Here the vampire and the witch were identified with each other and the vampire designated as a heretic, *eretik* in Russian. Over time eretik was used to refer to vampires, witches, and all those who did not believe in one true God and who were associated with evil magic. This identification of vampires with witchcraft during the Middle Ages redefined vampirism as an evil, a work of the Devil or Satan, that could be fought with the symbols and weapons of the Church, such as the crucifix and holy water.

As the nineteenth century drew to a close belief in vampires, like belief in witches, declined significantly. Interestingly, however, a century or so later, both vampirism and witchcraft have started to attract a following again, despite the fact that modern culture tends to deny the existence of real vampires or real witches.

See also: **BAJANG**; **BELL WITCH, THE**; **BRUXSA**; **CHORDEWA**; **CIVATATEO**; **EMPUSA**; **FEMALE VAMPIRES**; **LAMIA**; **LOOGAROO**; **MAGIC**; **MOROI**; **OCCULT**; **OLD HAG**; **PELESIT**; **PENANGGALAN**; **POLONG**; **SCHOLOMANCE**; **SORCERY**; **TALAMAUR**

See also witch-related entries: **ALCHEMY**; **BLACK MASS**; **BOTTLING A VAMPIRE**; **FLYING VAMPIRES**; **GYPSIES**; **HERETICS**; *MALLEUS MALEFICARUM*; **NEED FIRE**; **NIGHTMARE**; **WALPURGIS NIGHT**

Witch doctor

See: **SHAMAN**

wolfsbane

Also known as wolfsbay or aconite, wolfsbane is a flowering plant and herb that contains a poisonous alkaloid used in medicine. Since ancient times it has been associated with anti-evil properties and used in a similar way as garlic against vampires in certain parts of Europe, notably Germany.

wolves

Wolves are dangerous carnivores that used to be found throughout Europe, Asia, and North America. In some regions wolves were closely associated with vampires but in Slavic and Gypsy folklore vampires and wolves are enemies. In Romania it was said that white wolves stood guard at cemeteries ready to attack vampires as they rose from the grave. In other Gypsy communities, wolves were used to attack vampires and tear them to pieces.

See also: **ANIMAL VAMPIRES;**
SHAPE-SHIFTING;
TRANSFORMATIONS; WEREWOLF

wood

See: **STAKE**

See also: **ASH; ASPEN; BLACKTHORN;**
CROSS; HAWTHORN; HOLLY;
JUNIPER; ROWAN; THORNS;
WHITETHORN

woodstock Vampire

See: **CORWIN VAMPIRE, THE**

wool

In much the same way as coins or garlic would be put into the mouth of a corpse to prevent it chewing or returning from the grave, in the Balkans among the Gypsy communities wool would be stuffed into a corpse's mouth.
See also: **PREVENTION**

women
See: **FEMALE VAMPIRES**

"Death is a mystery and burial is a secret."

Stephen King

Xenophobia

"Xenophobia" is a term used to describe the unwarranted fear of foreigners or strangers and it is a steady theme in vampire literature. Some literary critics have argued that Victorian vampire stories, in particular Bram Stoker's *Dracula* (1897), represent the ugly side of British imperialism. The fact that Dracula cannot see his reflection in a mirror is seen in effect as the inability of Britain to recognize the darker aspects of its expansionist policies during Queen Victoria's era. Dracula also represents fears of the parasitic alien, arriving from foreign shores to multiply his own kind and deplete the country he has invaded.

Xeroderma

Xeroderma pigmentosum is an extremely rare genetic defect that causes severe sensitivity to the sun's ultraviolet rays, and in times past when the condition was not understood it may have been misinterpreted as a sign of vampirism. Ultraviolet light disrupts normal cell functioning in people who have the disorder, causing cancerous cell changes. There are many different degrees of seriousness with this disorder but most people with xeroderma pigmentosum acquire severe sunburn after any sun exposure.

See also: **DISEASE; SUNLIGHT**

Xloptuny

This is the name used by Russians for the eretica vampire species.

Yara-ma

The yara-ma, or yara-ma-yha-who in full, is a vampiric creature from Australian Aboriginal folklore. It looks like a little red man, no more than four feet tall, with a large head and a mouth with no teeth. On the ends of its hands and feet are suckers which it uses to grip its victims and to suck their blood.

The yara-ma lives in fig trees and does not hunt for food, but waits until an unsuspecting traveler rests under the tree. Then it catches its victim and drains their blood with its suckers, leaving the victim weak. Later the creature comes back to eat its victim and take a nap. When it has woken from its nap, the yara-ma spits out the person, leaving them shorter and with skin that is redder than before. If the victim cannot escape and the process of being swallowed and vomited alive is repeated enough times, the victim becomes a yara-ma themselves.

Yarbro, Chelsea Quinn (1942–)

Chelsea Quinn Yarbro is an American novelist and creator of the fictional immortal character the Comte de Saint-Germain, first introduced in her 1978 novel *Hôtel Transylvania*. Saint-Germain is an alchemist-turned-vampire based upon an actual historical character of eighteenth-century France. He is presented as an accomplished, seductive, and compassionate vampire with a wide range of interests beyond blood-drinking. To adhere to the requirement stipulated by Bram Stoker in *Dracula* that a vampire must rest on his native soil, Saint-Germain lines his footwear with the earth so he can travel wherever he pleases. *Hôtel Transylvania* was followed by *The Palace*

(1978), *Blood Games* (1979), *Path of the Eclipse* (1981), *Tempting Fate* (1982), and a short story collection in 1985 – *The Saint-Germain Chronicles*.

Over the decades Yarbro has continued to expand her vampire contribution to literature with a series of spin-off books featuring Saint-Germain and set in colorful periods. They include *A Flame in Byzantium* (1987), *Out of the House of Life* (1990), *Come Twilight* (2000), *Borne in Blood* (2007), *Saint-Germain: Memoirs* (2007), and *A Dangerous Climate* (2008). Yarbro's extensively researched novels expertly combine horror with historical romance and by so doing have significantly increased general readership for vampire novels.

Young, Nancy (1807-27)

Nancy Young, an alleged vampire of Foster, Rhode Island, was the eldest daughter of Captain Levi Young. Young was not a native of Rhode Island but came from Sterling, Connecticut. Shortly after leaving the army he married Anna Perkins and bought a plot of land in the Foster district, settling there around 1807, the year of Nancy's birth. He became a prosperous farmer with a family of eight children. When Nancy grew up she assumed accounting duties on the farm.

In 1827, at the age of 19 Nancy fell ill with what appeared to be a cold. However, she died on April 6 of consumption. Just before she died her younger sister, Almira, fell ill with the same symptoms and other children also got sick. In a desperate attempt to save Almira and his family Captain Young exhumed Nancy's corpse and burned it on a pyre while family members stood around inhaling the smoke in the belief that it would cure those who were sick and prevent others getting sick. Although two sons and a daughter did survive, the "remedy" clearly failed. On August 19, 1828, aged 17, Almira died. Four other children also died of tuberculosis: Olney, on December 12, 1831, aged 29; Huldah, in August 1836, aged 23; Caleb on May 8, 1843, aged 26; and Hirman on February 17, 1854, aged 35.

Yugoslavia

Following World War I, the now former state of Yugoslavia was created in 1918 as a centralized nation by uniting the formerly independent Serbia, Bosnia and Herzegovina, Croatia and Montenegro, and parts of Macedonia and Slovenia. Slavic people first moved into this region and Albania sometime during the sixth century, and by the eighth century they had established themselves as the most dominant influence in the Balkan Peninsula. Their vampire beliefs had close associations with the Slavic vampire and many experts believe that the lands of the former Yugoslavia were a possible land of the origin of the vampire. In 2003 the name "Yugoslavia" was officially abolished and in 2006 the Yugoslav state ended when Montenegro declared its independence from Serbia.

Southern Slavic vampire

Among the Southern Slavs many different forms of the word for vampire evolved, including the Bosnian *lampir*, the Serbo-Croat *upirina* the Croatian *vukodlak*, and the Albanian *lugat* or *vurvulak* (which eventually became the *kudlack*). The term *tenatz* was also found in Montenegro where it was used interchangeably with *lampir*, a variation on the word *vampir*. The *tenatz* was said to be a blood-drinking corpse that wandered around at night and transformed itself into a mouse to enter and leave its burial place. A black horse (or a white one in Albania) would be used to identify the grave of a *tenatz*; if the horse refused to walk over the grave then the body would be disinterred and examined for signs of vampirism, and if these were found it would be staked and burned. The *strigon* (Slovenia) and *shtriga* (Albania) were blood-sucking witches with close connections to the Romanian strigoi.

In Croatia various names were used for the undead including *tenjac, kosac, prikosac,* and *vukodlak*. Croatian vampires were said to rise at night from the grave to attack people, especially those they had had an argument with in life. They would eat their hearts and drink their blood. They could be identified by the sounds they made at night, which were said to be similar to those made by a donkey or a dog. They also made a crying, shouting sound called *vresket*. Once disinterred the body of a vampire would be found turned face down and bloated. If only bones were discovered it was not considered a vampire. Blackthorn stakes were used to destroy the vampire and axes and sharp objects were used for decapitation. A priest would then say prayers and sprinkle holy water over the grave.

In general the vampire of the Southern Slavs was a revenant, a corpse that had returned from the grave to suck the blood of those it had strong emotional attachments to, such as family and friends or those it had argued with in life. Some believed the corpse had been taken over by an evil spirit. A sure sign of a vampire attack was an outbreak of contagious illness in a community and sickness and death from an unknown cause were often attributed to vampire activity. Livestock could be attacked in the same way. Vampirism was believed to be infectious – an attack by a vampire would lead to vampirism.

A person was said to become a vampire in several ways but a violent or sudden death, suicide, or a wasting disease were major causes. Irregularities concerning burial rites were also a danger sign. The corpse would need to be watched so that animals did not jump over the body and turn it into a vampire. Like the Gypsy vampire, the Southern Slavic vampire could have sex with a spouse or lover. The Serbians and Bosnians also shared a belief with the Gypsies in the dhampir, the son of a vampire, who was born with the power to see and destroy vampires.

It was common practice among the Southern Slavs to dig up bodies some years after they had been buried in order to clean the bones and rebury them. If the soft tissue had not completely decomposed this was said to be a sign of vampirism. Once identified the vampire would be staked and/or decapitated and in serious cases dismembered or burned. A priest would usually be present during the exhumation and reburial. In Serbia and Montenegro, in an attempt to stop the exhumation and mutilation of bodies, priests were threatened with excommunication if they attended these exhumations. In Croatia and Serbia a stake would also be driven into the ground over the grave to prevent the vampire from rising.

Misdirection

The beliefs and practices of the Southern Slavs concerning vampires were brought to the attention of Western Europe in the first half of the eighteenth century by the official inquiries into two cases by the Austrian authorities: the case of Peter Plogojowitz and the case of Arnold Paole. Both of these sensational and widely reported cases occurred in a region of Serbia that had recently been incorporated into the Austro-Hungarian Empire. As a result public attention focused not on the rich vampire mythology of Serbia and the Southern Slavic countries, as it should have done, but on Hungary, a country which had the least vampire mythology and folklore of all the Eastern European countries. This misdirection given to vampire mythology was later strengthened by Montague Summers and other vampire writers in the nineteenth and early twentieth centuries.

See also: **ALBANIA**; **GYPSIES**; **MACEDONIA**; **MONTENEGRO**; **SERBIA**; **SLAVIC VAMPIRE, THE**

Yuki-onna

In Japanese lore, Yuki-onna or "lady of the snow" is a demon with vampire breath that sucks the life force from her victims. The demon appears as a beautiful maiden dressed in white and with breath like frost. She can shape-shift into white mist to slip under doors and through cracks in walls to attack her victims. She kisses her victims and then breathes killing mist on them. Her preferred victims are travelers stuck in snow storms, and if seen she may look like a white mist hovering over a person. She can on rare occasions take a man she falls in love with as her husband, but he will always have the threat of death hanging over him.

See also: **BREATH, OF A VAMPIRE**; **JAPAN**

Zmeu

In Moldavia the zmeu is a ghost with vampire-like qualities that takes the form of a flame that can enter the rooms of young girls or widows. Once it has entered the room the flame will transform into a young man who seduces the occupant. The zmeu figures prominently in many Romanian folk tales as the manifestation of pagan evil and the destructive forces of greed and selfishness. In Transylvania the zmeu appears as a young girl who offers to lead shepherds and their sheep into green pastures if they will make love to her. To protect themselves from the zmeu, travelers were urged to carry a mixture of garlic, candle wax, and celandine, an herb.

Zombie

In Haitian and West African voodoo traditions, a zombie is a soulless, reanimated corpse resurrected from the dead by a voodoo priest, known as a Bocor, for the purposes of indentured servitude. Etymologists and anthropologists speculate that the term is derived from *zombi*, a West African snake deity.

A natural explanation may exist for the zombie phenomenon. The misdiagnosis of catalepsy as death may be an important feature in the development of the Caribbean zombie as well as the traditional European vampire. It has also been suggested that the zombie may have been a person who was buried alive and only seemed dead through the administration of a drug containing the poison of various plants and animals and various human remains. The poison puts the victim in a death-like state. Not all those who take the drug survive; those who do remain conscious and witness their own burial and funeral. After two days the Bocor raises the victim from the tomb and administers an hallucinogenic concoction that awakens the "zombie," who is now so psychologically traumatized that he or she is willing to answer to a new name and follow the Bocor into a new life, which is usually to work in the fields. (Not surprisingly zombification was once described as the African slave's ultimate nightmare, as not even death can release them from never-ending labor.)

Voodoo sorcerers are said to create zombies by capturing the souls of the deceased. If the sorcerer is able to capture the soul he can make a zombie ghost who wanders eternally in the astral plane at the command of the sorcerer. To prevent this happening, relatives of the deceased will often stab corpses in the heart or decapitate them.

Zombies and vampires

Popular understanding of the term "zombie" is of a mindless animated corpse that has somehow had life restored to it by magic, or a living person under the control of a magician. Some zombies have been portrayed as flesh-eaters in horror films, notably in the films of George Romero, beginning with *Night of the Living Dead* (1968), and this may explain some of the confusion between them and vampires. Zombies, however, are not the same as vampires as they do not need blood to survive, are mute, and derive their strength from magic alone.

In addition, unlike vampires zombies are held to have no will or consciousness of their own. The life-without-consciousness characteristic has led some philosophers to trace the roots of this back to the theories of French philosopher René Descartes (1596–1650), who suggested that animals lack consciousness, acting and reacting automatically on the basis of physical stimuli.

Zopfius, Johann Heinrich

Johann Heinrich Zopfius was an eighteenth-century German vampire expert who, with Francis von Dalen, wrote an authoritative and popular pseudoscientific treatise on vampires published at Halle in 1733, *Dissertatio de Vampyris*. The *Dissertatio* became widely read in English when translated excerpts were included in *The Travels of Three English Gentlemen*, which was published in London in 1745.

Zotz

"Zotz" is the Mayan word for "bat." The Mayans worshipped Camazotz, a vampire-like blood-drinking monster with the body of a human and the head of a bat. The zotzhila or bat house was a region of the underworld said to be inhabited by Camazotz. Zotz was also the name of one of the months of the Mayan calendar.

The cult of Camazotz, which worshipped the vampire god of bats, caves, and twilight, began around 100 BC among the Zapotec Indians in what is the modern-day Mexican state of Oaxaca. Camazotz was associated with night, death, and sacrifice and feared for his blood-drinking tendencies, fearsome appearance (which included large teeth and claws), and his tendency to dwell in caves, where he would presumably take people for their blood.

There is some evidence to support the idea that the Camazotz myth may have sprung from actual large, blood-drinking bats of the Mexican, Guatemalan, and Brazilian areas. Evidence is in the form of fossils of *Desmodus draculae*, the giant vampire bat. Some experts believe that worship of zotz-like creatures and/or gods lingers on. Researchers John E. Hill and James D. Smith in their 1984 book, *Bats: A Natural History*, make reference to a large cave in Veracruz where pregnant women hoping to secure a safe delivery of their children still make offerings to vampire bats.

See also: **BATS; VAMPIRE BATS**

THE
VAMPIRE
DIRECTORY

Vampire Timeline

Prehistory Vampire-like beliefs and myths take form in cultures all over the world.

1047	"Upir," an early form of the word that later became "vampire" appears in written form in a document referring to a Russian prince as a wicked vampire.	*1710*	Vampire hysteria appears in East Prussia.

1047 "Upir," an early form of the word that later became "vampire" appears in written form in a document referring to a Russian prince as a wicked vampire.

1196 William of Newburgh's *Historia rerum Anglicarum* records stories of vampire-like revenants in England.

1476 Vlad III, Prince of Wallachia, more commonly known as Vlad the Impaler, is assassinated.

1484 The *Malleus Maleficarum* (The Hammer against Witches), authored by Heinrich Kramer and Jacob Sprenger, discusses how to hunt and kill vampires.

1610 Elizabeth Báthory is arrested for killing several hundred people and bathing in their blood.

1645 Leo Allatius completes the first modern treatise on vampires, *De Graecorum hodie quorundam opinationibus.*

1679 *De Masticatione Mortuorum* (On the Chewing Dead) is written by Philip Rohr.

1710 Vampire hysteria appears in East Prussia.

1725-30 Vampire hysteria sweeps through Hungary.

1725-32 Austrian Serbian vampire hysteria produces the famous cases of Peter Plogojowitz and Arnold Paole.

1732-4 The word "vampyre" enters the English language in translations of accounts of European vampire hysteria.

1744 Cardinal Giuseppe Davanzati publishes his treatise on vampires, *Dissertazione sopre i vampiri.*

1746 Dom Augustin Calmet publishes his treatise on vampires, *Dissertations sur les Apparitions des Anges des Démons et des Esprits, et sur les Revenants, et Vampires de Hongrie, de Bohème, de Moravie, et de Silésie.*

1748 *Der Vampir* by Heinrich August Ossenfelder, perhaps the first modern vampire poem, is published.

1772 Vampire hysteria sweeps through Russia.

1793	First known New England vampire case reported in Manchester, Vermont.
1797	Goethe's *Bride of Corinth* (a poem about a vampire) is published.
1798-1800	Samuel Taylor Coleridge writes *Christabel*, often said to be the first poem concerning vampires in English.
1801	*Thalaba* by Robert Southey is the first poem to mention the vampire by name in English.
1810	Reports of sheep being killed and drained of blood appear in northern England.
1819	*The Vampyre* by John Polidori is published in the April issue of *New Monthly Magazine*. It is the first vampire story in English.
1819	John Keats writes *Lamia*, a poem built on ancient Greek legends about vampiric beings.
1820	*Le Vampire*, a play by Charles Nodier, opens at the Théâtre de la Porte-Saint-Martin in Paris.
1829	*Der Vampyr*, an opera based on Nodier's play, opens in Leipzig.
1841	Aleksey Tolstoy publishes *Upyr*, the first modern vampire story by a Russian.
1847	*Varney the Vampyre* serialized as a penny dreadful.
1854	The case of the Ray Family vampires in Connecticut is published in local newspapers.
1872	The poem *Carmilla*, by Sheridan Le Fanu, is published.
1872	Vincenzo Vierzeni is convicted in Italy of murdering two people and drinking their blood.
1874	Reports from Cavan, Ireland, appear about sheep being killed and having their blood drained.
1888	Emily Gerard's *Land Beyond the Forest* is published; this work later became a source of information about Transylvania for Bram Stoker.
1892	Body of Mercy Brown is exhumed in Exeter, Rhode Island, because members of the community suspected the vampire Mercy Brown was attacking her dying brother, Edwin.
1894	H. G. Wells's short story, *The Flowering of the Strange Orchid*, the first "vampire science fiction," is published.
1897	*Dracula* by Bram Stoker is published.
1897	*The Vampire*, a poem by Rudyard Kipling, is published.
1914	"Dracula's Guest" by Bram Stoker is published posthumously as a short story.
1922	Coventry Street vampire attacks in London, England.
1922	*Nosferatu*, a German-made silent film is released.
1924	Fritz Haarmann, the so-called vampire butcher of Hanover is convicted of murdering and drinking the blood of his victims.
1928	*The Vampire: His Kith and Kin* by Montague Summers is published in England.
1929	*The Vampire in Europe* by Montague Summers is published.
1931	*Dracula*, the American film version starring Béla Lugosi, opens at the Roxy Theatre in New York City.

1931	Peter Kürten of Düsseldorf, Germany is found guilty of vampiric murders and is executed.
1943	*Son of Dracula* (Universal Pictures), starring Lon Chaney Jr. as Dracula, is released.
1954	*I Am Legend*, a novel by Richard Matheson, presents vampirism as a disease.
1954	The Comics Code banishes vampires from comic books.
1958	Hammer Films releases *Dracula*, starring Christopher Lee. (It is released in the United States as *The Horror of Dracula*.)
1964	*The Munsters* and *The Addams Family*, both television horror comedies with vampire characters, debut.
1965	Jeanne Youngson founds The Count Dracula Fan Club.
1966	Vampire Barnabas Collins makes his debut on TV series *Dark Shadows*.
1969	First issue of *Vampirella*, the longest-running vampire comic book to date, is released.
1970	The British Vampire Research Society is founded by Sean Manchester.
1971	A young girl is attacked by a vampire-like figure close to Highgate Cemetery in London, England.
1971	*The Tomb of Dracula* from Marvel Comics appears and Morbius, the Living Vampire, is the first new vampire character to be introduced after the revision of the Comics Code allowed vampires to reappear in comic books.
1972	Researchers Raymond T. McNally and Radu Florescu link the fifteenth-century Wallachian prince Vlad the Impaler to Bram Stoker's character Dracula.
1975	In *The Dracula Tape* by Fred Saberhagen, Dracula is presented as a hero rather than a villain.
1975	Stephen King's *Salem's Lot* is published.
1976	First book of Anne Rice's international bestselling vampire series, *Interview with the Vampire*, is published.
1977	A new dramatic adaptation of *Dracula* opens on Broadway starring Frank Langella.
1979	Bauhaus records "Bela Lugosi's Dead" and the track marks the beginning of the Goth rock music movement.
1980	Richard Chase, the so-called vampire of Sacramento, commits suicide in prison.
1980	The Bram Stoker Society is founded in Dublin, Ireland.
1985	The movie *Fright Night* combines vampire horror with humor.
1989	Overthrow of Romanian dictator Nikolai Ceauşescu's regime opens Transylvania up to vampire tourists.
1991	The highly successful role-playing game *Vampire: The Masquerade* is released by White Wolf.
1992	*Bram Stoker's Dracula*, directed by Francis Ford Coppola, is released.
1994	The film version of *Interview with the Vampire* is released in cinemas.
1997	TV version of *Buffy the Vampire Slayer*, starring Sarah Michelle Geller, debuts.

1998	*Blade* the movie is released, starring Wesley Snipes as a vampire slayer.
2002	The movies *Blade II* and *Queen of the Damned* (based on the novel by Anne Rice) are released. (The movie *Blade: Trinity* follows in 2004.)
2002-3	Allegations of vampire attacks sweep through the African country of Malawi, with mobs stoning one individual to death and attacking at least four others, based on the belief that the government was colluding with vampires.
2004	In Romania relatives of the recently deceased Toma Petre fear that he had become a vampire. They dig up his corpse, tear out his heart, burn it, and mix the ashes with water in order to drink them.
2005	Rumors circulated in Birmingham, England, that an attacker had bitten a number of people, fueling concerns about a vampire roaming the streets.
2005	Sightings of chupacabra, the so-called goat-sucker vampire of Puerto Rico and Mexico, are reported in Central Russia.
2005	Publication of the first of the international bestselling Twilight Saga novels by Stephenie Meyer.
2006	Archeologists in Italy discover the remains of a female "vampire" with a brick forced into her jaw. Italian forensic archeologists report the find to *National Geographic* and other news outlets. When the discovery took place the archeologists were investigating a 1576 mass grave of medieval plague victims.
2007	Movie version of *I Am Legend* based on the novel by Richard Matheson released, starring Will Smith.
2007	Vampire hunters mutilate the corpse of the deceased Serbian dictator Slobodan Milošević.
2008	*Twilight*, the movie based on the novel by Stephenie Meyer, is released.
2008	Swedish film *Let the Right One In*, based on the vampire novel by John Lindqvist, is released.
2008	A blood-sucking vampire dog is blamed for the death of 30 chickens in a farm in Texas.
2009	*New Moon*, the movie based on the novel by Stephenie Meyer, is released.

Select Bibliography

Johannes van Aken, *Histoire Vraie du Vampirisme* (1984: Editions Famot, Geneva)

Robert Ambelain, *Le Vampirisme – de la légende au réel* (1977: Robert Laffont, Paris)

Miguel G. Aracil, *Vampiros: Mito y Realidad de los No-Muertos* (2002: Editorial EDAF, Madrid)

Francisco Javier Arries, *Vampiros: Bestiario de Ultratumba* (2007: Ediciones Minotauro, Barcelona)

Nina Auerbach, *Our Vampires, Ourselves* (1995: University of Chicago Press, Chicago)

Paul Barber, *Vampires, Burial, and Death* (1988: Yale University Press, New Haven & London)

Michael E. Bell, *Food for the Dead: On the Trail of New England's Vampires* (2001: Carroll & Graf Publishers, New York)

Norbert Borrmann, *Vampirismus – oder die Sehnsucht nach Unsterblichkeit* (1998: Diederichs, Munich)

Matthew Bunson, *The Vampire Encyclopedia* (1993: Crown Trade Paperbacks, New York)

Dom Augustin Calmet, *Dissertation sur les Revenants en Corps, les Excommuniés, Les Oupirs ou Vampires, Brucolaques, etc.* (1986: Reprint Éditions Jérôme Millon, Paris, first published 1751)

Dom Augustin Calmet, *The Phantom World: Concerning Apparitions and Vampires* (2001: Wordsworth Editions, Ware, Hertfordshire)

Matei Cazacu, *Dracula: la vera Storia di Vlad III l'Impalatore* (2004: Mondadori, Milan)

Daniel Cohen, *Real Vampires* (1995: Cobblehill Books, Dutton, NY)

Basil Copper, *The Vampire in Legend and Fact* (1973: Robert Hale & Company, London)

Scott Corrales, *Chupacabras and Other Mysteries* (1997: Greenleaf Publications, Murfreesboro, Tenn.)

Adrien Cremene, *La Mythologie du Vampire en Roumanie* (1981: Éditions du Rocher, Monaco)

Bob Curran, *Encyclopedia of the Undead. A Field Guide to the Creatures that Cannot Rest in Peace* (2006: The Career Press, Franklin Lakes, NJ)

Giuseppe Davanzati, *Dissertatione sopra i Vampiri* (1998: Besa, Bari, first published 1774)

David Dolphin, "Werewolves and Vampires." Abstract of paper presented at meeting of the American Association for Advancement of Science, 1985.

François Ribadeau Dumas, *A la recherche des Vampires* (1976: Marabout, Verviers)

Alan Dundes (ed.), *The Vampire: A Casebook* (1998: University of Wisconsin Press, Madison)

Manuela Dunn-Mascetti, *Chronicles of the Vampire* (1991: Bloomsbury Publishing, London)

Barbara Ehrenreich, *Blood Rites: origins and history of the passions of war* (1997: Henry Holt and Company, New York)

Frederick Thomas Elworthy, *The Evil Eye: An Account of This Ancient and Widespread Superstition* (1989: OBC, New York)

Tony Faivre, *Les Vampires* (1962: Le Terrain vague, Paris)

David Farrant, *Beyond the Highgate Vampire* (1992: B.P.O.S., London)

Daniel Farson, *Vampires, Zombies, and Monster Men* (1975: Aldus Books, London)

Alan Frank, *Monsters and Vampires* (1976: Octopus Books, London)

Christopher Frayling, *Vampyres: Lord Byron to Count Dracula* (1991: Faber and Faber, London)

Nancy Garden, *Vampires* (1973: J. P. Lippincott, Philadelphia & New York)

Ivanichka Georgieva, *Bulgarian Mythology* (1985: Svyat, Sofia)

Emily de Lastowski Gerard, *The Land Beyond the Forest: Facts, figures and fancies from Transylvania* (1888: William Blackwood and Sons, London)

Fabio Giovannini, *Il Libro dei Vampiri* (1997: Edizioni Dedalo, Bari)

Donald F. Glut, *True Vampires of History* (2004: Sense of Wonder, Rockville, Md.)

Juan Gomez-Alonso, *Los Vampiros a la Luz de la Medicina* (1995: Neuropress S.L., Vigo)

Tim Greaves, *Vampyres* (2003: Draculina Publishing, Glen Carbon, Ill.)

Constantine Gregory, *The Vampire Watcher's Handbook. A Guide for Slayers* (2003: Piatkus Publishers, London)

Rosemary Guiley, *The Complete Vampire Companion* (1994: Macmillan, New York)

Peter Haining, *A Dictionary of Vampires* (2000: Robert Hale, London)

Peter Haining, *The Dracula Centenary Book* (1987: Souvenir Press, London)

Peter Haining, *The Dracula Scrapbook* (1976: New English Library, London)

Clare Haworth-Maden, *The Essential Dracula: The Man, the Myths and the Movies* (1992: Magna Books, Wigston)

Vincent Hillyer, *Vampires* (1988: Loose Change Publications, Los Banos, Calif.)

Barbara E. Hort, *Unholy Hungers: Encountering the Psychic Vampire in Ourselves & Others* (1996: Shambhala, Boston & London)

Olga Hoyt, *Lust for Blood* (1984: Stein & Day, New York)

Bernhardt J. Hurwood, *Passport to the Supernatural* (1972: New American Library, New York)

Bernhardt J. Hurwood, *Terror by Night* (1963: Lancer Books, New York)

Bernhardt J. Hurwood, *The Vampire Papers* (1976: Pinnacle Books, New York)

Bernhardt J. Hurwood, *Vampires* (1981: Omnibus Press, New York)

Bernhardt J. Hurwood, *Vampires, Werewolves and Ghouls* (1968: Ace Books, New York)

Nigel Jackson, *Complete Vampyr: the Vampyre Shaman, Werewolves, Witchery & the Dark Mythology of the Undead* (1995: Capal Bann Publishing, Chieveley)

Martin Jenkins, *Informania: Vampires* (1998: Walker Books, London)

Ernest Jones, *On the Nightmare* (1951: Liveright Publishing, New York)

The Element Encyclopedia of Vampires

John Keel, *The Mothman Prophecies* (1975: E. P. Dutton, New York)

David Keyworth, *Troublesome Corpses – Vampires and Revenants from Antiquity to the Present* (2007: Desert Island Books Ltd., Southend-on-Sea)

Peter Kremer, *Draculas Vettern – Auf den Spuren des Vampirglaubens in Deutschland* (2006: PeKaDe Verlag, Düren)

Peter Mario Kreuter, *Der Vampirglaube in Südosteuropa – Studien zur Genese, Bedeutung und Funktion – Rumänien und der Balkanraum* (2001: Weidler Buchverlag, Berlin)

John Cuthbert Lawson, *Modern Greek Folklore and Ancient Greek Religion* (1910: Cambridge University Press, Cambridge)

Clive Leatherdale, *Dracula: The Novel & The Legend* (1985: The Leisure Circle, London)

Clive Leatherdale, *The Origins of Dracula* (1987: William Kimber, London)

Claude Lecouteux, *Dialogue avec un revenant* (1999: Presses de l'Université de Paris-Sorbonne, Paris)

Paul van Loon and Jack Didden, *Vampierhandboek* (1997: Elzenga, Amsterdam)

Sean Manchester, "The Highgate Vampire" in *The Vampire's Bedside Companion* edited by Peter Underwood (1975: Leslie Frewin, London)

Sean Manchester, *The Highgate Vampire* (1991 rev. edn.: Gothic Press, London)

Anthony Masters, *The Natural History of the Vampire* (1972: Granada Publishing, London)

Bruce A. McClelland, *Slayers and their Vampires: A Cultural History of Killing the Dead* (2006: University of Michigan Press, Ann Arbor)

Georgess McHargue, *Meet the Vampire* (1979: J. B. Lippincott, New York)

Raymond T. McNally, *A Clutch of Vampires* (1974: Warner Books, New York)

Raymond T. McNally, *Dracula Was a Woman* (1983: McGraw Hill, New York)

Raymond T. McNally and Radu Florescu, *In Search of Dracula* (1994: Houghton Mifflin, Boston)

Gordon Melton, *The Vampire Book: The Encyclopedia of the Undead* (1994: Visible Ink Press, Canton, Mich.)

Hans Meurer, *Vampire – Die Engel der Finsternis* (2001: Eulen Verlag, Munich)

Lynn Myring, *Vampires, Werewolves & Demons* (1979: Usborne Publishing, London)

Hugo G. Nutini and John M. Roberts, *Bloodsucking Witchcraft - an epistemological study of anthropomorphic supernaturalism in rural Tlaxcala* (1993: University of Arizona Press, Tucson)

Jan L. Perkowski, *The Darkling: A treatise on Slavic Vampirism* (1989: Slavica Publishers Inc., Columbus, Ohio)

Jan L. Perkowski (ed.), *Vampires of the Slavs* (1976: Slavica Publishers Inc., Cambridge, Mass.)

Franco Pezzini, *Cercando Carmilla – la leggenda della donna vampira* (2000: Ananke, Torino)

Michaël Ranft, *De la mastication des morts dans leur tombeaux* (1728: Jérôme Millon, Grenoble)

Laurence A. Rickels, *The Vampire Lectures* (1999: University of Minnesota Press, Minneapolis)

Philip Rohr, *De Masticatione Mortuorum* (1679: Leipzig)

Gabriel Ronay, *The Dracula Myth* (1972: Pan Books, London)

Jean-Paul Ronecker, *Vampires* (2001: Editions Pardès, Puiseaux)

Harry A. Senn, *Were-Wolf and Vampire in Romania* (1982: Columbia University Press, New York)

David J. Skal, *V Is for Vampire* (1996: Plume, New York)

David J. Skal, *Vampires: Encounters with the Undead* (2001: Black Dog, New York)

Otto Steiner, *Vampirleichen – Vampirprozesse in Preussen* (1959: Kriminalistik, Hamburg)

Petr Stepan, *Kniha Nosferatu – Vampyrska bible* (2003: Adonai, Prague)

Montague Summers, *The Vampire: His Kith and Kin* (1928: University Books, New York)

Montague Summers, *The Vampire in Europe* (1929: Kegan Paul, Trench, Trubner & Co., London)

Gerhard van Swieten, *Vampyrismus* (1988: S. E. Flaccovio, Palermo)

Tony Thorne, *Children of the Night – of Vampires and Vampirism* (1999: Victor Gollancz, London)

Travels of Three English Gentlemen from Venice to Hamburgh being the grand Tour of Germany in the Year 1734. Harleian Miscellany, vol. IV (1745: London)

Peter Underwood (ed.), *The Vampire's Bedside Companion* (1975: Leslie Frewin, London)

Rowan Wilson, *Vampires: Bloodsuckers from Beyond the Grave* (1997: Parragon, Bristol)

Leonard Wolf, *Dracula: The Connoisseur's Guide* (1997: Broadway Books, New York)

Dudley Wright, *Vampires and Vampirism* (1914: William Rider & Son, London)

Jeanne Keyes Youngson, *The Bizarre World of Vampires* (1996: Count Dracula Fan Club/Adams Press, Chicago)

Johann Heinrich Zopfius, *Dissertatio de vampyris serviensibus* (1733: Duisburg)

Connie Zweig and Jeremiah Abrams, *Meeting the Shadow: The Hidden Power of the Dark Side of Human Nature* (1991: Putnam Publishing Group, New York)

Vampire Organizations, Societies, Fan Clubs, and Websites

Anne Rice's Vampire Lestat Fan Club, P.O. Box 58277, New Orleans, LA 70158-8277, USA

The Count Dracula Fan Club (The Vampire Empire), 29 Washington Square West, Penthouse North, New York, NY 10011, USA

The Count Dracula Society, 334 West 54th Street, Los Angeles, CA 90037, USA

The Count Ken Fan Club, 12 Palmer Street, Salem, MA 01970, USA

Dark Shadows Festival, P.O. Box 92, Maplewood, NJ 07040, USA

The Miss Lucy Westenra Society of the Undead, 125 Taylor Street, Jackson, TN 38301, USA

The Quincey P. Morris Dracula Society, P.O. Box 381, Ocean Gate, NJ 08740, USA

Vampire Information Exchange, Box 328, Brooklyn, NY 11229-0328, USA

Realm of the Vampire, P.O. Box 517, Metairie, LA 70004-0517, USA

Vampire Studies (Society), P.O. Box 151, Berwyn, IL 60402-0151, USA

The Dracula Experience, 9 Marine Parade, Whitby, Yorkshire YO21 3PR, UK

The British Vampyre Society, 38 Westcroft, Chippenham, Wiltshire SN14 0LY, UK

Dracula Society, P.O. Box 3048, London W12 0GH, UK

The Vampire Register, 7 Cornwall Rd, Stourbridge, West Midlands DY8 4TE, UK

Vampire Research Society, c/o Rev. Sean Manchester, P.O. Box 542, Highgate, London N6 6BG, UK

Bram Stoker Society, 43 Castle Court, Killiney Hill Road, Killiney, Co. Dublin, Ireland

The Vampires Archives of Istanbul, Giovanni Scognamillo, PostacilarSokak 13/13, Beyoglu, Istanbul, Turkey

Transylvania Society of Dracula, c/o Nicolae Padararu, President, 47 Primaverii Blvd, Bucharest I, Romania

The Dracula Society: www.thedraculasociety.org.uk – website for lovers of vampires and their kind.

The Coven Organisation: www.thecovenorganisation.com – bills itself as an online vampire research and news portal.

London Vampyre Group, formerly the Vampire Information Exchange: www.londonvampyregroup.co.uk – a site for anyone with an interest in all things vampyric.

Vampire junction: www.afn.org/~vampires – dedicated to the promotion of vampires in fact, fiction, and art.

Les vampires: www.darksites.com/souls/vampires/lesvampires/lesv1.htm – website devoted to "real" vampires.

Real vampire website: www.realvampirewebsite.com – website devoted to "real" vampires.

Vampire church: www.vampire-church.com – information on energy vampires.

Twilight Poison: www.twilightpoison.com – website for fans of The Twilight Saga.

Vampiric studies: www.geocities.com/athens/Forum/7935/vampires.html – information and links on vampires.

Psychic vampire resource: www.psychicvampire.org – site dedicated to psychic vampirism.

Dracula's Homepage: www.ucs.mun.ca – site hosted by internationally recognized Dracula expert, Elizabeth Miller.

Federal Vampire and Zombie Agency (FVZA): www.fvza.org – this site claims to represent a secret federal agency responsible for controlling the world's vampire and zombie populations while overseeing scientific research into the undead.

European vampire research website: www.shroudeater.com – this site is rich in historical vampire documents and case studies.

Nocturnus: www.nocturnusonline.net – website for "mortal" and immortal vampires.

Monstrous vampires: www.vampires.monstrous.com – this site contains information about the origins, habits, and powers of vampires.

The Sanguinarium: www.sanguinarium.net – a network, community, and resource for the vampyre subculture.

Sanguinarius: www.sanguinarius.org – a worldwide communication, information, and support network for all blood drinkers, psychic vampires, and those who choose to live the vampire lifestyle.

VampGirl: www.vampgirl.com – vampire website with women in mind.

Dracula's castle: www.draculascastle.com – website dedicated to Bran Castle where Vlad the Impaler murdered thousands of people.

"Count Dracula legend": www.romaniatourism.com – a website sponsored by the Romanian government with details about the life of Vlad the Impaler.

An Ebook of Stoker's classic novel is available from: www.literature.org.

The Vampire Library: www.vampirelibrary.com – a resource for readers of vampire fiction, literature, and non-fiction books.

Index

Apuleius **31**
Aquinas, Thomas 176, 309
Arabia
 afrit **9**
 algul 15, **257**
 amine **20**
 ghoul lore **257–8**
archetypes **31**, 326
 vampire 31, 43, 155, 326, 401,
  420, 438, 484, 489, 499, 566
Ardisson, Victor ("Vampire of
  Muy") xv, **32**, 244, 291
Argens, Marquis d' 454
Aristotle 629
Armenia **32**
 Dakhanavar 32, **167**
art **32–3**
asanbosam 8, **34**
asema **34**, 304
ash **34–5**, 29, 269, 336
Ashanti people 34, 431
ashes **35**
 of the caul 35, 370
 eating/drinking 35, 98, 99,
  282, 296, 333, 334, 370, 400,
  421, 477, 503, 509–10
 finding vampires 92, 238, 608
 of the heart 35, 98, 99, 219,
  285, 510, 584
 scattering 34, 63, 106, 178,
  201, 239, 258, 336, 393, 560,
  580, 609
 see also cremation
Ashkenaz, Hasidei 201
Ashton Smith, Clark 485
Asia 80, 126
 cannibalism x, 113, 401
 cat/vampire association 120
 demon vampires 176
 Drunken Boy **200**
 flying vampires 240
 ghosts 256
 vampire butterflies 30
 vampire gods 261
 vampire magicians 383
 vampire mythology 436
aspen **35**, 211, 325, 555
Assier, Adolphe d' **35**, 37
Assyria **36**
 demons 176
 ekimmu 36, **207–8**
 evil eye 216
 mermaids 394
 utukku 36, **597**
 vampire tradition origins 32,
  36, 210, 435
astral body 35, **36–7**, 123, 257,
  371
 Aboriginal beliefs 41
 Bebarlangs 61
 ka 331

poltergeist attack 466
 and premature burial 285
 and psychic vampirism 37,
  283, 290, 452–3, 480–1
astral vampires **37**, 142, 170,
  553, 603
 Bell Witch 66
aswang **37–9**, 71, 131, 240,
  451–2, 471
"Asylum" (Van Vogt) 439
Atlantis 438
attack **39–40**
Attila the Hun 583
Australia 32, **40–1**
 cannibalism x, 113
 shamans 538
 yara-ma-yha-who 40–1, **647**
Austria **41–2**, 583
 All Souls' Day 16
 alp **18–19**, 254
 habergeiss **274**
 soul cake 549
 vampire frenzy **255**
 see also Styria
*Authenticated History of the Bell
  Witch of Tennessee, An*
  (Ingram) 66
auto-vampirism xv, **42–3**, 123,
  142, 222
 Jungian perspective 326–7
Autonomous National
  University of Nicaragua 26
awakening **43**
Azande people 198
Aztecs **43**, 347, 576
 blood-drinking x
 civateteo 131, **141**
 deities **395–6**

Ba 206–7
Babylonia **47**
 demons 176
 ekimmu 47, **207–8**
 evil eye 216
 Lilith 359
 uttuku 47, **597**
 vampire tradition origins vii,
  36, 47, 126, 435
Bad Lord Soulis **47–8**, 500
bad signs/omens **48–9**, 71–2,
  105, 122, 154, 370, 543
baital/vetala **49–50**, 310,
  436, **619**
 King Vikram and the Vampire
  (Burton) 338
Baital Pachisi 50, 619
bajang **50**, 120
Balderson, John L. 554
Balkans 98, 116, 133, 182, 268,
  285, 314, 383, 453, 541
 Gypsies 485, 643

see also Albania; Macedonia;
  Montenegro; Serbia;
  Yugoslavia
Baltic 34, 336, 638
Banderas, Antonio 312
Banks, Leslie **51**
banshee **51–2**, 240, 274
Baobhan-sith **52–3**, 97, 227
Bara, Theda 601
Barbarella 6, 612
Barber, Paul **53**, 171, 172, 322,
  476
Baring-Gould, Sabine 233
Baron Blood **54**
Báthory, Elizabeth xv, 12, 33,
  54–7, 84, 142, 155, 192,
  222, 233, 286, **291**, 371,
  392, 584
 Countess Dracula 57, 235, 279,
  454
 lesbianism **356**
Batman 59, 147
bats 23, **58–9**, 89, 411, 622
 bhuta shape-shifting 69
 digestion 85
 pishtaco guise 454
 see also vampire bats; zotz
Bats: A Natural History (Hill
  and Smith) 652
Battyány-Waldstein family 231
Baudelaire, Charles **59–60**, 460
Bauhaus 264, 408
Bava, Mario 235–6
Bavaria **60–1**, 254, 415, 473
Beardsley, Aubrey 32
Bebarlangs **61**
Beckinsale, Kate 595
becoming a vampire **61–3**
 Bavarian lore 254
 Bulgarian lore 102
 Gypsy lore 268
 Romanian lore 508
Begbie, P. J. 449
beheading *see* decapitation
Belanger, Michelle 77, 213,
  481, 482
Belgium
 vampires of Farciennes
  230–1
Belgrade Vampire 64, 465
Bell Witch **64–6**
Bell Witch Haunting, The (film)
  64
Bellatoni, Nicholas 634
Belle Dame sans Merci, La
  (Keats) 334–5, 459
Belle Morte, La (Aiken) 460
bells 477
Benedict XIV, Pope 315
Bengal
 chordewa 120, **133–4**

Benson, E. F. 21, **66–7**, 362,
  433
Benzoni, Girolamo 58
Beowulf 361, 436
"Berenice" (Poe) 60, **67**, 457,
  473
Berg, Karl 343
Bergstrom, Elaine 57
Bertrand, Sergeant François
  67–8, 155, 244, 291, 347,
  419
Berwick Vampire **68**, 210
Bhagavat-purana 331
bhayankara 574
bhuta/bhut **68–9**, 241, 310,
  474
"Big Bang" 167
binding a corpse **69**, 116, 453,
  475
biology of vampires **70**
birds 23, **71**; *see also* cockerel;
  crows; fowl; kikik; owls;
  vultures
Birmingham Vampire **71**, 400
birth of a vampire **71–3**
bite **73**; *see also* kiss of the
  vampire
black **74**
Black, Jacob **75**, 587, 588
black and white **76**
black blood 62–3, **74**, 393, 531
black cats 49, 120, 162, 509
black cloaks and capes 143
Black Dagger Brotherhood
  series (Ward) **75**, 634–5
Black Death (bubonic plague)
  210, 315, 497
black dogs 23, 184, 269, 407
black horses 294, 649
black magic 69, **75–6**, 163, 177,
  288, 391, 527, 549, 560, 626
 Dracula's ability 187, 383
black magicians **76**, 304, 383
black mass **77**
"black riders" 175
Black Sabbath 236
black stallion **77**
Black Sunday 236
Black Veil, the **77**, 154, **213**,
  524
blackthorn **77**, 340, 350, 546,
  649
Blackwood, Algernon **78**, 362,
  387, 580
Blacula 9, **78**, 236
Blade (film trilogy) vi, 9, **79**,
  148, 149, 182, 236, 609
Blade (TV series) 79
Blade the Vampire Hunter
  78–9, 132
Blair Witch Project, The 64

and social control 437

exhumation xi, 63, 64, 68, 73, 81, 88, 95, 98–9, 120, 125, 134, 152, 173, 181, 186, **218–19**, 238, 251, 255, 258, 282, 287, 296, 333, 335–6, 349, 350, 369, 381, 382, 393, 397, 404, 407, 418, 419, 420, 448, 455, 462, 473, 493, 494, 504, 510, 512, 526–7, 544, 551, 560, 562, 569, 575, 609, 634, 648, 649–50

exorcism xii, 47, 81, 123, 130, 158, 176, 202, **219–20**, 256, 289, 385, 466, 470, 495, 544, 562, 628, 639

explanations of vampirism **220–2**

extraterrestrials **223**

eyebrows **223**

eyes **223**
  changes during transformation 531
  closing/covering **399**
  vampiristic 268
  see also blue eyes; red eyes

fairy/fairies 51, 52, 96, 159, 171, 223, **227–8**, 267, 275, 354, 409, 553
  leanhaum-shee 313, **351**

fallen angels **228–9**, 438

familiars 47, 50, 71, 119, 227, **229**, 497, 500, 519, 569

Family of the Vourdalak, The (Tolstoy) 514, 578

Famous Monsters of Filmland (magazine) 6, 147

fan clubs **229–30**

Fangland (Marks) 364

fangs xv, 30, 73, 86, 111, 138, 141, 180, **230**, 234, 261, 294, 304, 331, 401, 407, 426, 439, 531, 570, 581, 618, 635

Fantasy and Science Fiction (magazine) 353

Farciennes, vampires of **230–1**

Farrant, David 289

Fasti (Ovid) 441, 559

Fates 227

Father Christmas **136**

Fatinelli, Ludovico 62, 222

Fealaar, Vampire of **231**

Fearless Dracula Hunters (film) 252

Federal Vampire and Zombie Agency (FVZA) 11, 184, **231–2**, 307, 410, 449, 498, 547, 621

Feehan, Christine **232**, 363

Fellowship of the Ring, The (Tolkien) 175

female vampires **232–4**
  "made" through teaching 370
  mating with humans 502

Feng Shui 130

Fernandez, Florencio 156

Ferrell, Rod 156, **234**

Ferrera, Abel xvii, 7

feu-follet (fifolet) 9, **234**, 423

Féval, Paul 362

Fevre Dream (Martin) 364

fiction x–xii
  animal vampires **24–5**
  appearance of vampires 30–1
  characteristics of vampires 126–7
  creating a vampire 154
  destroying vampires **179–80**
  dhampirs **182**
  heightened senses **534–5**
  kiss of the vampire 338–9
  life of a vampire 358
  origins of vampires **439**
  staking 556
  vampire attack 39–40
  vampire hunters **609**
  vampire powers 472
  vampire sex and love **536–7**
  vampires and sunlight 358, 563
  victims 619, 620
  see also comics; literature; poetry

"fig hand" 217

films **234–7**
  animal vampires **24–5**
  appearance of vampires 29, 30–1
  destroying vampires **179–80**
  dhampirs **182**
  gay/lesbian vampires 252, 293, 355, 356
  good vampires 262
  science fiction 531
  Spain 551
  staking 556

finding vampires **238**
  see also detecting/detection of vampires

fingernails **238**

Finland **238**

fire 179, **238–9**, 477; *see also* burning

Fisher, Terence 277

fishing nets **239**, 254, 269, 477

Fitzgerald, James 116–17

Five Books on the Structure of the Vampire Body (Vesalius) 70, 531

fleas/flies **239**

Florescu, Radu 118–19, 194, 392, 625

Flowering of the Strange Orchid, The (Wells) 15, 387, 439, 530

Flowers of Evil (Baudelaire) 59–60

Flückinger, Johann **239–40**, 361, 445, 446–7

flying vampires **240**, 411, 471

Fodor, Nandor 466, 572–3

folklore vii, **240–1**
  characteristics of vampires 126, **240–1**
  female vampires **232–3**
  kiss of the vampire 338
  living vampires **370**
  psychic vampirism 481
  vampire children 132
  vampire immortality 306–7
  vampire sex and love **536**
  vampire sunlight tolerance 563
  victims 619, 620

Fonda, Jane 6, 612

food **241**, 475

Fool There Was, A (film) 601

"For the Blood is the Life" (Crawford) **242**

Forbes, Pat 572–3

Forever Knight (TV show) **241–2**

Fortis, Giovanni Battista "Alberto" 404

Fortune, Dion **242–3**, **479**, 481

forty days **243**, 542

"four hunters, the" (folktale) **53**

fowl **244**

Fowler Museum of Cultural History 53

Fox sisters 552

foxes x, 23; *see also* huli jing; kitsune

France 32, 112, 215, **244–5**, 251, 647
  Antoine Léger 143, 244, 291, **354–5**
  body-snatching 90
  Celtic druids 275
  Gabrielle de Launay **174**
  garlic tradition 250
  Gilles de Rais 84, **177**, 244, 291, 347
  Martin Dumollard 156
  Mercure Galant **394**
  Sergeant Bertrand **67–8**, 155, 244, 291, 347, 419
  spiritualism 452
  three Maries 331–2
  vampire plays 554

Victor Ardisson xv, **32**, 244, 291

Viscount de Morieve **244–5**, **403–4**

werewolf legends 638

Francisci, Erasmus 115

Frankenstein (Shelley) 499, 594

Frankenstein films 277

frankincense **245**

Frederick the Great of Prussia 520

Freemasonry 382

French Revolution 244–5, 403–4

Freud, Sigmund **246**, 324, 326, 393, 424, **483**

Fright Night (film) 236

Fuller, J. F. C. 160

funerals *see* burial customs; corpses

Fuseli, Henry 545

Gaddis, Vincent 316

Galen 86, 376

games, vampire **249–50**

Ganja and Hess (film) 9

garlic xi, 21, 22, 28, 34, 38, 54, 61, 69, 99, 105, 125, 130, 132, 178, 181, 202, 217, 241, **250–1**, 253, 254, 276, 288, 298, 337, 371, 386, 409, 411, 455, 474, 476, 478, 498, 507, 509, 510, 544, 560, 577, 578, 584, 612, 635, 640, 650
  aversion in porphyria 185, 468
  in *Dracula* 188, 190, 250–1, 511, 609, 616, 639
  sensitivity in rabies 493

Garmann, Christian Frederic 255

Gautier, Théophile **251**, 361, 460

gay culture **252**

gayal/geyel **251–2**

Geisserlin, Clara 252–3

Gelnhausen **252–3**

Genesis 82

Gentleman's Magazine 464

George, Feast of St./St George's Eve/St George's Eve, Feast 21, 250, 251, **253**, 477, 508–9, 612

George III 468

George IV 561

Gerard, Emily **253–4**, 285, 426, 527, 529–30, 582, 584

Gere, Richard 406

Germany **254–5**
  All Souls' Day 16
  alp **18–19**, 254

O'Bannon family 352
obayifo 8, **431**
obour **431**
Observations on the Revolution 97
obur **431**
O'Carroll, Tadhg 351–2
Occult Review 42, 208
occultism/occult theories 76, 265, 285, 401, 421, **431–2**, 520, 562, 626
causes of vampirism 123
Dracula's expertise 383
holy objects 293
living vampires 371
occult theories 37, 127, **283**, 290, 431, 452–3, **480–1**
psychic attack 478, 479, 480
psychic self-defense 482
shadow 538
thought forms **574**
vampire/Satanism link 527
vampire transformation 581
see also Blavatsky, Madame; Crowley, Aleister; Fortune, Dion; Hartmann, Fritz; necromancy
Odin 35
O'Donnell, Michelle 138
ogoljen **433**
ohyn **433**
oil **433**
Oil and Blood (Yeats) 460
oiwa 323
Ojibwa people 416
Olcott, Henry Steel 80, 480
Old Dracula/Vampira (film) 9
old hag **433–4**, 604, 619
old hag syndrome 433–4
see also hag attack
Old Testament 82, 149, 163, 202, 238, 417
Oldenburg **433**
Oldman, Gary 93
Oliphant, Laurence 480
Omega Man, The (film) 303
On the Nightmare (Jones) 434
On the Truths Contained in Popular Superstition (Mayo) 64, 391
oni 323
"Operation Vampire Killer 2000" 465
opji 333, **434**, 622
Order of the Golden Dawn, The 76, 382
Origin and History of Irish Names of Places (Joyce) 5–6
origins of vampires **434–9**, **604–5**

Orlok, Graf **439**
Orpheus 593
Osiris 206
Ossenfelder, Heinrich August 25, 361, **439–40**, 457
Otherworld 10, 124
Ottoman Turks 623, 624
out-of-body experiences 10
outsiders 49, **440**
Ovid 355, **440–1**, 476, 559
owenga 441
owls 23, 69, 280, **441**
Oxford English Dictionary 603

pacu pati **445**
p'ai 132
"Pale Faced Lady, The" (Dumas) **445**
palis **445**
palm hair **445**
Pamfile, Tudor 259
Panchatantra (folktales) 495
Paole, Arnold xii, 42, 84, 88, 183, 240, 255, 292, 298, 373, 424, 437, **445–8**, 464, 484, 535, 550, 604, 650
"Seen and Discovered" (*Visum et Repertum*) report 41–2, 446–8
Paquin, Anna 282, 586
Paracelsus 14, 402
paranoid schizophrenia 128
Parasite, The (Conan Doyle) 186
parastic/symbiotic entity 123
Parque de Juegos (film) 551
past-life recall 501
Patric, Jason 374
Pattinson, Robert 162
Pavlovic, Dom Marin 350
Pecos, Hugo 11, 19, 232, 307, 410–11, **449**, 498, 547–8, 621
pelesit 385, **449**, 465
penanggalan/hantu penenggalan x, **279–80**, **384**, **449–50**
Pentecostal "deliverance ministry" 220
Pentsch Vampire *see* Cuntius, Johannes
Periander of Corinth 418
Perkowksi, Jan **334**, 456, 461, 560
Persia 404
owl/death association 441
palis **445**
Peru 454
Sarah Ellen Roberts **506–7**
Pest, Thomas Preskett 617

Petronius **450**
Petrov, Radovan 527
Petrovici, Emil 561
Pettigrew, T. J. 616
Phantom, The (Boucicault) 93
phi 572
phi song nang 572
Philinnion 458, **450–1**
Philippines **451–2**
aswang **37–9**, 71, 131, 240, **451–2**, 471
Bebarlangs **61**
chupacabra 138
danag 167
garlic 250
ghouls 257
manananggal **386**
mandurugo **387**
Philip II of Macedon 451
philosopher's stone 13, 14
Philosophical Dictionary (Voltaire) 464
Philostratus 27, 209, 348
Phlegon of Tralles 450
Photobacterium fischeri 151
Physiologus 394
picks **452**
Picture of Dorian Gray, The (Wilde) 641
Piérart, Z.-J. 284, **452–3**
Pierce, Meredith Anne 363
piercing **453**
Piercing the Darkness (Ramsand) 481
pigs **453**
Pihsin, Dorothea 332
pijavica **453**
pisacha 310, **453**
pishtaco **454**
Pitt, Brad 312
Pitt, Ingrid 235, 278–9, 312, **454**
Placide's Wife (Mashburn) 485
plagues *see* Black Death; epidemics
Planck, Max 489
Planet of the Vampires 531
Pliny the Elder 35, 394, **454**, 473, 629
Plogojowitz, Peter xii, 84, 183, 241, 292, 298, 437, **454–6**, 484, 535, 640, 650
Pluto 58
Plymouth Brethren 160
Pniewo Vampire **456**
po **456**
Poblocki, Franz von 63, **282–3**, 511
Poe, Edgar Allen 60, 67, **457**, 473, 638
poetry **457–61**

lesbian vampires 355, 356
Pokrovsky, Captain 368–9
Poland xi, xii, 98, 205, **215**, 238, 267, **461–2**, 584
blood bread 462, 477
cholera/vampire link 133
drinking ashes 509
noon to midnight vampire activity 168, 563
ohyn **433**
prone burial 178
protective blood of vampires 87–8
Stanislav Modzieliewski 156
upior/upier **461–2**, 512, **595–6**, 603
upyr 215
see also Kashubs; Roslasin; Silesia
Polanski, Roman 236, 252
Polidori, John vii, xiii, xv, 190, 200, 233, 263, 361, 402, **462–3**, 514, 555, 613, 614–15
and Byron 107, 108, **463**
political vampires **464–5**, 613
Poliziano, Angelo 348
polong 385, **465**
pelesit pet 449
poltergeists **465–6**, 569
Bell Witch 65
kozlak **341**
Thornton Heath **572–3**
Polycrites (Philocrites) **466–7**
Polynesia **467**
pontianiak **467–8**
Pomerania **467**
pontianak 279, 310, 324, **384**, 441, **467–8**; *see also* langsuir
Pontianak (film) 468
poppy seeds xi, 27, 106, 152, 336, 420, 422, **468**, 475, 546, 560
porphyria xiv, 83–4, 122, **183**, 222, 435, **468–9**
dolphin hypothesis **185**
Porras, Tata 39
Portugal 99, 371, **469**
Possega vampire **469**
possession **469–70**, 218
dybbuk **202**
and exorcism **219**
sneezing 547
spirits 553
see also demonic possession
Posthumous Humanity (d'Assier) 35
potsherds **470**
pouka 116
Powel, Hulda 282
power of suggestion **479–80**

role-playing games **249**
Romania xii, 54, 91, 205,
 214–15, 238, 267, **508–10**
 ash drinking 35, 509–10
 bad signs 48, 122, 508
 bat/vampire link 59
 burial customs 69, 106, 475,
  541, 572, 641
 Castle Bran **118**
 Castle Poenari 289–90
 caul disposal 121
 Ceauşescu regime 464
 Children of Judas 103, **131**
 crossroad superstitions 159
 daylight vampires 423
 death's head moth beliefs 171
 descriptions of vampires 126
 destroying vampires **509–10**
 detection and prevention 509
 double-hearted vampires
  285, 546, 560
 Dracula banned 194, 585
 food at the gravesite 241,
  475
 fumigation by vampire
  smoke 503
 The Girl and the Vampire
  259–60
 Gypsy vampire curses 163
 hens jumping over corpses
  325
 horse vampire hunters 295
 incense use 308
 iron forks 314
 knot-cutting before burial
  340
 "made" living vampires 370
 mirror-covering 398–9
 modern vampires 400
 moroi **404**
 newly weds 422
 nosferatu 215, 426
 power-gathering vampires
  541
 pregnant women 473, 508,
  522
 protection 77, 113, 145, 250,
  251, 477
 red/vampire association 500
 seventh sons 536
 shadow beliefs 538
 Solomonari **530**
 St. Andrew's Eve/Feast **21**,
  276, 476–7
 St. George's Eve 253, 508–9
 staking 29, 105, 285
 strigoi vii, xi, 13, 69, 215,
  241, 437, 482, 508, **560–1**,
  584, 642
 Toma family 400, **578–9**
 vampire origins 604

vampire tourism 584–5
vampire witches 612
varcoloc 424, **616**, 633
Vlad the Impaler honored
 624, 625
weaknesses of vampires
 636–7
white wolf cemetery guards
 643
zmeu 650
see also Wallachia
"Romanian Folkloric Vampire,
 The" (Perkowski) 560
Romanticism 108, 594, 604
Rome, ancient xi, 209, **510**
 Caligula **111**
 coffin nail charms 314
 coins on corpses 145
 demons 176
 empusa 314
 festivals of the dead 27
 hawthorn charm 284
 lamia 314
 larvae **350**, 351, 355
 lemures 350, **355**
 poltergeists 465
 Saturnalia 292
 striges/strix xi, 126, 314,
  441, 450, 476, 510, 550–1,
  559, 642
 see also Classical mythology
Romero, George 651
"Room in the Tower, The"
 (Benson) 66–7, 433
ropes **511**
rosaries **511**
Rose, William G. 504
roses 341, **511**
Rosicrucians 382
Roslasin **511–12**
Ross, F. Clive 158
rowan **512**
Rowlands, Alison 336
Rowling, J. K. 175, 396, 588
Royal Society 14
Ruda, Manuela and Daniel xv,
 156–7
Rudiger, Joshua xv,
Rudorff, Raymond 189
rusalka **395**
Russia xi, 98, 238, 267, 336,
 512–14
 bad signs 122
 burial with whiskey (*rachia*)
  641
 carpet wrapping 116
 chupacabra 121, 137–8
 crossroad superstitions
  159
 daylight vampires 423
 erestun **210–11**, 512, 612

eretic/eretica **211**, 213, 286,
 512, 527
eretik/eretnik **211**, 596, 642
excommunication/vampirism
 link 286
eye of a corpse 223
fowl blood cure 244
heresy/vampirism link 527
insects escaping from
 vampire pyres 155, 239
Ivan the Terrible **316**
literature 262
Marusia **389–90**
need fires 419
noon to midnight vampire
 activity 563
obogie doma burial pits
 127–8
protective blood of vampires
 87–8
Rasputin **496–7**
rusalka **395**
stake lore 336, 555
trial by water 636
upir 389, 512, 545, **596**, 603
upyr 215, **596**, 603
vampire magicians 383
vampire origins 604
vampire tongue 570
vampire witches 612
vourdalak **627**
xloptuny **647**
Russian Folktales (Ralston) 512
Russian Orthodox Church 642
 inovercy **311**
Ruthven, Lord; *see* Lord
 Ruthven
Ryder, Winona 94
Rymer, James Malcolm 230,
 263, 402, **514–15**, 617
Rzaczynski, Gabriel 462

Sabbatarians 381, **519**, 528,
 608
sabbats 141
Sabella or Blood Stone (Lee)
 353
Saberhagen, Fred 362, **519**
Sade, Marquis de **519–20**
sadism xv, 55–6, 85, 123, 177,
 222, 519
Sadist, The (Berg) 343
sadomasochism 86, 246, 327
*Saga of Darren Shan,
 The/Cirque du Freak* (Shan)
 540
Saint-Germain, Comte de
 (real) **520**
Saint-Germain series (Yarbro)
 363, **520–1**, 647
Saint-Hillaire, Paul de 230,

 231
Salem's Lot (King) 337, **521–2**,
 609
Salem's Lot (TV movies) 522
Salic law (*Lex Salica*) **522**
salt 18–19, 38, 130, 220, 238,
 254, 288, 324, 372, 386,
 409, 445, 452, **522**, 608,
 637
Samhain 16, 275
sampiro (*liugat*) 13, **522–3**
sanguinarians 40, 43, 84, 86,
 142, 286, 370–1, 401, 498,
 523–4
 Black Veil **77**, **213**
 COVICA **154**
 ethics 212–13
 mortal inheritors 311
 Sanguinarium **524–5**, 540
 Sanguisuga **525–6**
Santorini 296, 505, **526**, 628,
 642
Sarandon, Susan 298
Sarbanovac Vampires **526–7**
Satan (Devil)/Satanism 48, 52,
 90, 159, 170, 176, 177, 215,
 253, 265, 288, 322, 360,
 376, 399, 423, **527–8**, 574,
 620
 night association 423
 pacts 77, 162, 372, 383, 432,
  549, 576
 reanimation/vampire
  creation 135, 499, 505
 and vampirism 16, 134, 161,
  386, **438–9**, 527–8
 and witchcraft 211, 229, 559,
  642
Satanic Rites of Dracula, The
 (film) 235, 278, 353
Saturday 269, 339, **528**, 589,
 597, 608, 628; *see also*
 Sabbatarians
Saturnalia 292
Satyricon 450
Saul, King 202, 417
Saxo Grammaticus **528**
Scandinavia 304, **528–9**, 638
 Celtic druids 275
 mara 274, **387–8**, 424, 434,
  529, 545, 604
scapegoats, vampires as
 436–7, 484–5
Scars of Dracula (film) 278
Schertz, Charles Ferdinand de
 88, 91, 381, **529**
schizophrenia 506
Scholomance 187, 527,
 529–30
schrattl **254**
Schreck, Max 426

The Element Encyclopedia of Vampires

The Element Encyclopedia of Vampires